NORTHERN FURY

H-HOUR

Bart Gauvin & Joel Radunzel

Northern Fury: H-Hour

ISBN 978-1-7338385-0-4 (paperback)
ISBN 978-1-7338385-2-8 (hardcover)
ISBN 978-1-7338385-1-1 (eBook)

Published by: Ursus Rising

CONTENTS

 **PREFACE**

"History doesn't repeat itself, but it does rhyme."
—quote ascribed to Mark Twain

ON 18 AUGUST, 1991, hardline members of the Communist Party of the Soviet Union (CPSU) placed the president of the USSR, Mikhail Gorbachev, under house arrest at his vacation *dacha* in Foros, Crimea. In the preceding years, the USSR had been experiencing a period of political and economic upheaval that was threatening the very integrity of the centralized Union holding the Soviet republics together. As president of that Union, Gorbachev advocated the New Union Treaty, which would have devolved much of the political power of the centralized Soviet State down to its subordinate republics. The hardliners, styling themselves the "State Committee on the State of Emergency," intended to seize control of the Soviet Union's government, prevent the passage of the New Union Treaty, and maintain the power of the CPSU over its tottering empire.

The Emergency Committee's coup attempt, what came to be known as the "August Coup" or "August Putsch," unfolded over three dramatic days in the streets of Moscow. It included notable acts of heroism by those opposed to the hardliners, as well as inexplicable blunders by the plotters. Those officials opposed to the Emergency Committee's takeover congregated at the Russian parliament building—known as the "White House"—in central Moscow, where they were quickly surrounded by Red Army tanks and paratroopers, which had been brought into the capital by the hardliners. A standoff ensued.

The coup plotters became increasingly hesitant to use military power to crush the growing popular influence of the dissenters inside the White House.

Then, in one of history's dramatic moments, the president of the Russian Republic, Boris Yeltsin, arrived at the scene of the stand-off. Brazenly climbing onto one of the encircling tanks, he grabbed a megaphone and delivered a stirring, defiant address to the crowds of Russians who were beginning to converge on the scene. Yeltsin's speech rallied popular support against the Emergency Committee's actions. Within hours, ordinary Muscovites were pouring into the city center. There, they used civilian vehicles and their own bodies to block the passage of a column of Red Army armored vehicles moving towards the White House. These vehicles were carrying units of elite Soviet commandos, whose mission was to launch a belated night assault on the dissenters within the parliament building.

With resistance coalescing around Yeltsin, and the Emergency Committee's best chance at military victory checked by the actions of ordinary citizens, the coup collapsed. Gorbachev, escaping from house arrest, returned to the Kremlin. Once there, he dismissed the plotters from government and charged them with treason. Within ten days the Communist Party of the Soviet Union was banned in the country it had ruled for seventy years. Within six months, that country had ceased to exist. The Union of Soviet Socialist Republics shattered into its constituent parts. And with that, the Cold War, which had threatened the world with nuclear annihilation for nearly half a century, came to a close, "Not with a bang but with a whimper."

More than a quarter century later, the failure of the August Coup, the collapse of the USSR, the end of the Cold War, all appear to have been inevitable, a culmination as it were of decades of economic and political mismanagement in the Soviet Union, of an inability to compete with the wealthier powers of the West, of an unforgiving geography. But were these events so inevitable? Did the coup *have* to fail? Did the USSR *have* to collapse? When one studies the actual events of those three rainy days in Moscow in 1991, the answers to these questions seem less and less obvious, the actual outcomes increasingly unlikely.

Indeed, the plotters of the Emergency Committee included a list of some of the most powerful men in the USSR, including the Soviet vice president, the defense minister, and the chairman of the KGB, among others. Couldn't this impressive collection of officials, had they acted with greater decision and displayed less timidity, have succeeded in wresting control of the government away from Gorbachev and holding their faltering empire together? What if the plotters had arrested Yeltsin before he could rally support for the opposition (as they nearly did)? What if they had launched an assault against the White House a day earlier, before crowds of ordinary Muscovites could intervene?

Of course, no one can know for sure the answers to these counterfactual questions, but many of the potential alternate histories that they suggest are fascinating, and troubling. The story of *Northern Fury* takes place in one of those troubling, alternate worlds that could have resulted had a strong, charismatic leader taken control in the early hours of the August Coup and pushed it forward to a successful conclusion. It describes the hot conflict between East and West that could have erupted had the Cold War continued into the mid-1990s, a conflict in which the armed camp that Europe had become since the end of the Second World War erupted into one of the most dangerous chapters of history that the world would ever see.

One should note that, as the book's title suggests, our story focuses only on the *northern front* of this potential global war (we hope to tell the stories of the other fronts in other books). Our intent with this book is *not* to issue a warning of impending doom to present-day policy-makers, or to pass judgement on the actions of past leaders, or to advocate for any particular political, military, or social policy going forward. Nor is our intent to simply take the reemerging antipathy between Russia and the West and project it back into the early 1990s, when the world was more heavily armed than it is today (though the reemergence of this centuries-old tension *is* a rather interesting rhyme of history). Rather, we wanted to tell the best, *human* story possible, against the backdrop of an alternate history that is both strange and familiar.

In telling this story, we realize we are walking in the footsteps of other authors who have used fiction to tell the "future history" of the very conflict we posit. These novels include General Sir John Hackett's *The Third World War*, Tom Clancy's epic *Red Storm Rising*, Harold Coyle's *Team Yankee*, Ralph Peters' *Red Army*, and Eric L. Harry's *Arc Light*, to name the more notable examples. We would be lying if we said that these particular novels did not fascinate us and influence the writing of our own story of World War III. *Northern Fury* certainly does share many characteristics with these other works, and this is where the apocryphal quote from Mark Twain comes into play.

Why *does* history seem to rhyme? Why do John Hackett's and Tom Clancy's and nearly every other work of Cold War-goes-hot fiction seem to fall into the same familiar patterns? Why do we still see these patterns reflected in the current geopolitical tensions in Europe, where a coalition of Western European nations face off against a monolithic, fearful Russia? The reason is that while you can "make history" (and in *Northern Fury*, we do), you have to "live with your geography." The map on which the great game is played does not change nearly as quickly as we think it does. Indeed, the problems of geography faced by Vladimir Putin's Russia today are essentially the same ones faced by Gorbachev's Soviet Union a quarter century ago, and by Peter the Great's Russian Empire two centuries earlier. It seems that whenever we humans begin to believe that we have escaped the bonds of our geography, as many westerners did after the end of the Cold War, it always comes roaring back with a vengeance to remind us of the tyranny of the map. So, readers of *Northern Fury* will certainly find some familiar themes at play if they have read any of these other works of World War III fiction.

But despite this, we think that readers will also find our story a new, unique, and fresh look at this potential conflict. Why? Because history *doesn't* repeat itself. It *only* rhymes. The way human beings act within their geography is unique in every age, and far less deterministic than it seems in hindsight. And nothing brings out the worst—and the best—in human beings like that activity we call "war." Perhaps this is why war has been such a compelling canvas for the stories we tell each other, from Homer's *Iliad* to the present day. In war stories, as in war, the decisions the characters make really matter. And the decisions they make, ultimately, are a reflection of who they are, or at least who they want to be.

In the end, *Northern Fury* is the story of the people, on both sides, who would have had to fight the war that we here imagine. We have been careful to remain true to the constraints of reality and the details of the military organizations that existed at the end of the Cold War (when ships sink, they will not reappear; when squadrons and regiments are decimated they must be reorganized; one cannot conjure divisions out of thin air), and we think that those "grognards" who care about such things will be pleased with the depth of our research and attention to technical, geographical, and historical accuracy. But the drama of the story comes from the characters, the people, and from their struggles against each other, against geography, and against themselves. And in this respect, we think we have an exciting story to tell.

A word is appropriate here about how this story even came to be. Both of the authors (Bart and Joel) are career soldiers who have served in the Canadian and American armies, respectively. While this gives us a good depth of knowledge in the arena of land warfare, we are both amateurs when it comes to the naval and air operations that comprise the setting for much of the *Northern Fury* story. Nevertheless, we have both felt ourselves drawn to study air and naval history, as well as modern air and naval operations. Perhaps the sea and air domains of warfare are just different enough from our day jobs that they are able to capture our interest as hobbies without seeming to be too much like work. That shared interest, coupled with the game, are what led us to collaborate and tell this story.

The alternate history story of *Northern Fury* originated with Bart not long after the end of the Cold War, and he has been telling the story ever since, largely through scenarios created for naval warfare simulations. The most recent of these simulations, a game called *Command: Modern Air and Naval Operations*, developed by Warfare Sims and published by Matrix Games, is the first that was powerful enough to encompass the depth and breadth of the World War III story he envisioned. With the *Command* platform at his fingertips, Bart was finally able to begin crafting the *Northern Fury* story in game form.

Command is a remarkable program. It models in minute detail the complexities of modern technological warfare. The program does this so well, in fact, that the US military has partnered with Warfare Sims to use their software to model and train for contemporary tactical problems. *Command* has also been a major commercial success, a testament to the hard work of the developers at Warfare Sims who have crafted a game that is not only militarily and professionally useful, but also very fun for amateurs like ourselves to play and learn something about post-World War II naval and air combat. Moreover, we would be remiss if we did not give credit where credit is due. This book would not have happened were it not for *Command*.

In 2015, Joel began playing Bart's *Command* scenarios, and was immediately hooked by the story that was unfolding on the map interface in front of him. The story was so exciting that Joel began writing up his experience playing the game in a series of fictionalized "after action reviews" online on the Matrix Games website. Bart liked what he saw of his story in Joel's writing. He proposed a collaboration, whereby the *Command* scenarios and this novel would tell the *Northern Fury* story in tandem. What this means is that nearly every engagement in this book is "playable" as one of Bart's scenarios in *Command*.

Now, in the interest of full disclosure, *Northern Fury* is *not* simply a recounting of Joel and Bart's playthroughs of *Command* scenarios. On the other hand, we found that the tandem acts of building and playing through these engagements provided many of the dramatic moments that occur in the written story. According to legend, Tom Clancy and Larry Bond's *Red Storm Rising* came to be through a similar process, utilizing Larry Bond's tabletop naval simulation *Harpoon*. We hope our own storytelling proves a worthy continuation of this intersection of gaming and fiction.

So then, whether you fancy enjoying our tale in written form, or by diving into the *Command* simulation to see if you can do better than the characters of our novel, we hope you are as gripped by our story in "hearing" it as we have been in telling it.

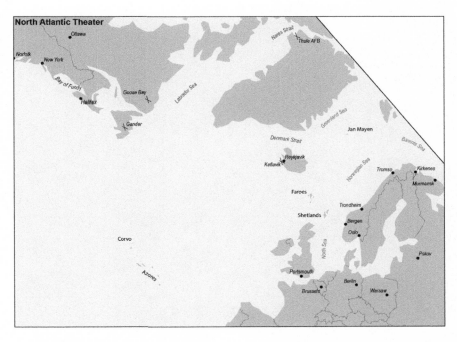

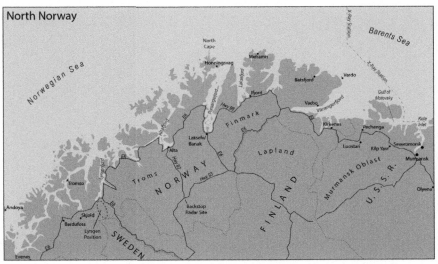

PART I: LINE OF DEPARTURE

"In the land of the blind, the one-eyed man is king."
—Erasmus

 **CHAPTER 1**

1525 MSK, Sunday 18 August 1991
1225 Zulu
Presidential Dacha, Foros, Crimea, Ukrainian Soviet Socialist Republic

PAVEL IVANOVICH MEDVEDEV felt the weight of the pistol holstered under his arm as he strode into the expansive, red-tile-roofed *dacha*. Cool sweat dampened the shirt beneath his gray suit as he passed out of the balmy Crimean heat and into the air-conditioned interior. His right eye adjusted from the bright outdoor sunlight. His left didn't, useless as always. The well-known Soviet hard-liner proceeded through the palatial residence's entryway and foyer. Recognizing his stocky, bear-like build and thick head of white hair, several uniformed and plain clothes KGB agents quickly stood aside. Bits of angry conversation echoed from deeper in the *dacha*'s interior as Medvedev strode into the depths of the building. Entering the foyer, he saw three of his co-conspirators sheepishly huddled together.

"What's going on here?" demanded Medvedev in the precise, educated Russian that betrayed his Moscow roots. Frustration hovered at the edge of his voice.

A thin, bookish looking man, Oleg Drugov, a junior member of the Politburo and Medvedev's one true friend here, spoke first, "The general is in there with him." Drugov inclined his head towards the open door of the president's salon. "He...he is not being cooperative."

As if to emphasize the point, Medvedev heard from the other room his country's president shout, "Damn you, you're going to do what you want! But report my opinion!"

The president is somehow still in control here, Medvedev realized. *Are we really going to dither and let him stall our entire plan?*

Seconds later the deputy defense minister, a general of the Red Army and the senior member of the committee that had flown to Foros to depose the USSR's president, burst out of the room, red-faced and agitated. Seeing Medvedev he said, "There is no reasoning with that man. He refuses to see the chaos that is engulfing our country."

Medvedev fixed the general in his gaze and asked, "Then why are we still talking?"

None of them sees what needs to be done. How can they be so weak? The weight of his pistol was nothing compared to the weight of responsibility that was settling upon his shoulders.

The general spread his arms in frustration as the nearly panicked words tumbled out of his mouth in rapid bursts, "He will not declare a state of emergency. He will not resign. He will not even agree to stay silent to let us do what needs to be done! The man is…is…," the general was breathing heavily now, raging against his impotence but, Medvedev noted, clearly ignorant of what to do about it.

Useless fop. Medvedev breathed heavily, allowing the smells of the sea from outside to calm him. He looked from the general to the room from which he had just emerged. "I will talk to him," Medvedev said and started towards the door.

"You?" the general asked. "You've been his loudest critic! What makes you think he will listen to you more than any of us?"

Turning his head to look into the man's wild eyes and seeing only fear behind the shattered veneer of strength, Medvedev said coldly, "Because I understand him better than you ever will. I will talk to him."

The general dropped his gaze and stood aside as Medvedev brushed past him to the doorway. *This is it,* he thought, *this is the great throw of the dice.* Pausing to look back over his shoulder, Medvedev saw another of the plotters, the Central Committee Secretary of the CPSU, speaking into a rotary telephone in one corner of the sitting room, presumably talking to the other conspirators in Moscow. Two plain-clothes KGB agents were whispering to each other in another corner, looking uncomfortable. Only Drugov was silent, watching him intently from across the room. Rejecting the quiet buzz of inactivity behind him, Medvedev turned back to the door. *There's no going back now. How can the others not see that? How can they not see what must be done? How can they not see what will happen if we fail?*

Silently, he entered the president's salon, unbuttoning his gray suit jacket as he went. The room contained a sitting area with an ornate couch and chairs, two low coffee tables, and a wall-sized colorful painting set against the dark wood paneling that evoked the waves of the Black Sea beating against the cliffs outside of the *dacha's* windows. Facing a couch with his back towards the newcomer, the President of the Union of Soviet Socialist Republics stood in his shirt sleeves, breathing heavily as he sipped water from a crystal tumbler. The top of the president's bald head was bowed, almost as if the man was praying. After a moment Medvedev cleared his throat and the president turned. Surprise obvious on his face at the identity of this latest visitor.

"What are *you* doing here?" demanded the president, the birthmark on his head blazing red as it always did when he was agitated. "You are part of this coup as well, are you? I should have known."

"*Tovarich* President," Medvedev began, ignoring the questions and quietly shutting the door behind him. "We desire your help, your *cooperation*, in averting the disaster that is engulfing our country—"

"You want me to get out of the way so those *idiots* out there can plunge Russia into violence for some pipe dream of a glorious socialist future?" interrupted the president. "Do you really think—"

"Do *you* really think," Medvedev broke in, exasperated, "that this 'Union Treaty' is anything less than a death sentence for our country, for our place in the world? Can you not see, that path only ends in our country's impotence and international chaos? If we continue, *tovarich* President, then this ground we are standing on won't even be Soviet a year from now!"

"You cannot know that," responded the president, calming himself and pushing his glasses back into place. "Our best hope of holding the Union together is through mutual respect, through reform of our government systems.

You of all people know how badly we've been mismanaged for the past seventy years."

"No, *tovarich* President, we are far beyond the point where talk will suffice to hold the republics to our will. You're already letting the Baltics go. You've abandoned our buffer against another invasion from the West. Who will be next? Georgia? Kazakhstan? Belarus? *Ukraine*? If we sign this treaty, if we do not take bold steps *right now* to quell the devolutionary forces within our borders…"

Medvedev's voice trailed off. His right hand, almost of its own will, wandered forward to the plush of an armchair next to him.

"And what would you have us do, eh? Send in the tanks like it's 1968? If we accept that you're right about the future—*and I don't*—," said the president, shaking his finger, "do you really think that holding this country together through bloodshed can ever solve our economic problems? Do you have any idea how the West will respond if we use violence to hold onto this empire? They can cripple us without ever firing a shot."

Medvedev sighed. This argument was going nowhere it hadn't already been dozens of times before. "How do you think the West will treat us when our nation is dismembered into twelve or more divided states instead of being a single powerful one?" he asked, his voice beginning to soften. "How do you think they will look on us when the United States is the only superpower in the world? When they are free to do whatever they want without us to counterbalance them? No, *tovarich* President, we must keep the republics with us by any means. Any other choice will lead our nation, and the world, into chaos."

Medvedev could see the wind blowing out of the president.

"We've been over this many times, Pavel Ivanovich," the president said wearily, turning away, "you and I cannot see eye to eye on these things. You and your friends in the other room are going to try this," he waved his hand, "this plot. You won't succeed. Even if you do, you will come to see that my way is the only one we can take."

"You are a great man, *tovarich* President," Medvedev said, his hand slipping from the velvet of the armchair into his coat. "I truly regret that we cannot agree on these things. I would gladly follow you, if I did not know with such certainty that the road down which you are leading us will end in disaster for Russia and the Soviet Union. I cannot allow that."

The president turned back to look Medvedev in the eye. The gunshot exploded in the enclosed space of the room and the man jerked upward violently, clawing at his shirt as if there was a stinging insect against his chest. Then he fell backwards and slumped onto the couch, looking up at Medvedev through thick-rimmed eyeglasses that were now askew, the shock on his face turning slowly to understanding as his mouth worked to draw in a last breath.

Arm outstretched, Medvedev looked down over the smoking pistol. "I am truly sorry, but there *is* another course for Russia." Lowering his arm and wiping the pistol on a corner of his coat, he continued, "This was the only way. You and I could not agree on how, but I promise you, I *will* preserve Russia's greatness. Take comfort in that."

Slowly, the light faded from the president's eyes, and then he was gone. Medvedev had aimed for his heart, rehearsing the shot in his mind over and over on the flight down from Moscow. His hand began to shake and he willed it to stop. As he returned the pistol to its shoulder holster, the door behind him crashed open. The other conspirators burst in, led by the general and followed by KGB officers with weapons drawn. They stopped and looked in shock at the scene: Medvedev, the slumped figure of their president behind him, the blood.

"What have you done Pavel Ivanovich?" gasped the general.

Medvedev looked the man full in the face and said, "*Tovarich* Minister, the president has suffered a heart attack. I do not believe he will recover."

The tall, broad-shouldered general stood in shock, his tousled wavy gray hair completing the image of a man completely out of his element. He stared past Medvedev at the former president seated on the couch, head rolled back in death.

Medvedev crossed the room in three great strides and grasped the general's shoulder with one hand to give him a gentle shake. Firmly but calmly he said, "Minister, we must now declare a state of emergency. The president is dead. Our country is in grave danger."

The general jerked a nod and turned to face the others. He opened his mouth, but closed it again. He swallowed, trying to speak, but no words came.

Must I really do all this myself? Medvedev thought. He stepped past the general and began issuing orders.

"You," he said, pointing at the senior KGB officer in the room, whose sidearm was pointed down at the floor. "Get a doctor. Someone you can trust. The president has died from a heart attack and his body must be cared for. Take your men and make arrangements while I talk with the officials here. The Soviet Union is in grave danger."

Unsure what to do, the officer looked to the others in the room for guidance. None contradicted the order, so the man withdrew in bewilderment with his subordinates.

Medvedev walked over to the door and closed it again, turning his attention to the CPSU Secretary, who was silently staring at the body.

"What measures have been taken to secure Moscow?" asked Medvedev.

The secretary shook out of his stupor and in a halting voice said, "Em…the Ministry of Defense will…will be moving troops into the city tomorrow. The defense minister is seeing to it. We have ordered a quarter million handcuffs and, em, three hundred thousand arrest forms to be delivered from Pskov. KGB has doubled the pay of all officers. It," the man had to stop and think, "these should be enough measures…" His voice trailed off.

Do they not have more of a plan than handcuffs? Medvedev wondered, growing more annoyed by the second.

He stepped back and looked at the four men in the room. The general represented the military. The CPSU Secretary represented the Party. Also present was the deceased president's personal secretary, who had provided insider intelligence on the president's intentions. Finally, there was Oleg Drugov, last to enter the presidential salon, a junior member of the Politburo and one of Medvedev's closest allies in his ongoing crusade to hold the Soviet Union together. Together, they represented a transitional body, the old, reformist government giving way to a new, hardline one, though killing the president had not been part of anyone's plan except Medvedev's. The four stood still, processing the shock that Medvedev's action had just inflicted upon them and the impact it would have on their futures.

"Listen to me, all of you." Medvedev said, snapping their attention back to the present. "The fate of our country rests on a fulcrum. I know none of you intended for matters to unfold this way," Medvedev gestured at the corpse behind him, "but if we are to succeed in pulling our Union back from the brink of dissolution we must now be absolutely firm in what we do. No one can be allowed to stand in our way. No one! There will be more unpleasantness in the coming days. Our countrymen will die, many perhaps. If you thought we could accomplish this civilly, you were gravely mistaken. We are executing a coup, whether you admit this to yourself or not, and it will only succeed if we strike hard and strike quickly before the enemies of our country understand what is going on."

Medvedev paused, then said, "*I* have committed us to this gamble. If you disagree with what I have done, you must arrest me now and go on by yourselves. But heed my warning: if you are not completely ruthless in this hour of peril then the tide of history will turn against each of you and against our country."

The others stood in silence, staring at him for several moments.

Then the CPSU secretary said in a quiet voice, "What would you have us do now, Pavel Ivanovich? You have committed us to this path, what is your plan?"

Medvedev had prepared himself for the other conspirators to order his arrest then and there. He was content that his actions gave them the best chance of success, even without him. *But if they are willing to follow my lead, if they are willing to allow me to do what is necessary…* When he spoke, his voice was one of authority and confidence. "We must move quickly to consolidate control over the central government. Where is the KGB chairman right now?"

"He is at Lubyanka Center, in Moscow," responded Oleg Drugov.

"Get him on the telephone, quickly," Medvedev ordered.

The short, precisely-dressed man opened the door and went back into the sitting room where a rotary telephone sat on an end table.

"My plan, what you—what *we* should do," Medvedev said to the others, "is to return to Moscow and eliminate anyone that still wishes to lead us down a path of liberalism and fragmentation. Then we must use what state power we still have to quell the counter-revolutionary elements in the republics. Once we have reasserted the central control of the Party over the outlying regions, we can concern ourselves with repairing the dysfunction in our economy and government. None of this is possible if we allow the Union to dissolve."

The others nodded, growing more composed behind Medvedev's firm leadership.

A call from the adjoining room announced, "Pavel Ivanovich, the KGB chairman is on the line here."

Pavel strode into the sitting area. He took the receiver from Drugov's hand, placed it to his ear and, "Hello, Vladimir Alexandrovich."

"Pavel Ivanovich," came the frosty reply, "I hear you have taken matters into your own hands down there. You should have consulted the rest of us in the Emergency Committee before taking such a drastic step."

"My friend, it was the only way," Medvedev said this slowly, carefully. "I think you know that. Regardless, what is done is done and there is no going back now. Are you prepared to maintain order in Moscow?"

"We are prepared to do so," responded the KGB chairman, "but if I am not to arrest you for murder I must know what you are thinking. What is your plan for restoring order to the country and for cleaning up this mess you've made?"

Even he doesn't know what to do, Medvedev thought, taken aback.

"*Tovarich* Chairman, where are our opponents? Where is the RSFSR president?" he used the acronym for the Russian Soviet Federative Socialist Republic within the USSR.

"At his *dacha* outside the city. He returned from Kazakhstan yesterday," answered the KGB chairman. "We've had him under surveillance for weeks. What do you propose?"

"He must not be allowed to return to the capital. It would be best," here Medvedev's tone became stony, "if he suffered some sort of natural death or accident in the next few days."

A pause followed.

"You are serious about this, Pavel Ivanovich?" the KGB chairman asked, surprise creeping into his voice.

"He is dangerous to us, very dangerous," Medvedev responded. "He has already done our country much harm. He must be removed if we are to reassert control over the Russian Republic and the rest of the Union."

There was silence at the other end of the phone for a few moments, then, "Who else do you intend to kill before this is over?"

"Anyone who threatens the security and cohesion of the USSR, *tovarich* Chairman," Medvedev responded without hesitation. "You must have lists of those who would oppose us. There must be hundreds, maybe thousands. Arrest them all. Whether we succeed or fail will depend on how well we can control the situation in the next few hours while we have the benefit of knowing what's going on, and they do not."

There was another long pause from the man in Moscow, then, "Very well, Pavel Ivanovich. I will do as you suggest. I had hoped to accomplish our objectives with as little turbulence to our citizens as possible, but it appears you have set events on a different course." Pavel heard papers shuffling through the earpiece, then, "I have an emergency plan to shut down the Metro here in Moscow tomorrow morning, to restrict air and rail travel, and to suspend the sale of petrol. These measures should allow us to do what we need to without the chaos of people in the streets."

"Yes. Do it," agreed Medvedev. "What about our media?"

"I have already arranged to take radio and television stations loyal to the republics off the air tomorrow," answered the chairman. "The only stations broadcasting will be the ones we control."

"We should wait as long as possible to make our own public statement," urged Medvedev. "The longer we can keep our opponents in the dark, the better. How long can you control the news?"

Preventing journalists from filing and broadcasting stories from the capital was still possible, but it would only be a matter of time before news started leaking out through the Western embassies' diplomatic channels. Once that happened, the news would start to filter back into the USSR through conduits such as Radio Free Europe and other liberal propaganda. In the hours before that happened Pavel hoped that he could keep the Soviet people ignorant of the goings on here and in Moscow.

"I agree, Pavel Ivanovich," said the KGB chairman. "We have the newspapers, television, and radio under our thumb. This can be held for perhaps seventy-two hours. But you and the others need to return here as quickly as possible. I predict things are going to be very interesting in the coming days. My men down there will handle the president's...the *former* president's affairs. I will see you soon." There was a brief pause in which the KGB chairman coughed uncomfortably. Then he concluded with, "Oh, and Pavel Ivanovich, please don't shoot anyone else without telling us first."

The line clicked off.

Medvedev let out a breath before returning the receiver to its cradle. *I might actually survive this*, he thought. He looked up to see Oleg Drugov staring at him. *All he needs is some training and he'll be really effective*, thought Medvedev, *and I have many tasks for him.*

Turning to the general, Medvedev said, "You must contact the Defense Ministry and ensure they are ready for unrest in Moscow. Tell them to begin planning for interventions elsewhere in the Union if that becomes necessary. What are the defense minister's plans?"

The general had recovered some of his composure. He responded, "We have thought this through. The *Tamanskaya* Guards and *Kantemirovskaya* Tank Division will move into the capital tomorrow morning to maintain order. *Alpha* and *Vympel* groups will be prepared to deal with resistance. The interior minister has several OMON teams ready." He referred to special police and counter-terrorism teams of the KGB and Interior Ministry. "We are bringing in a battalion of *desantniki* as well." These were the elite paratroops of the Red Army.

Will Misha be among them? wondered Pavel, thinking of his son. He put the question out of his mind. It was not the time to be distracted by family or pride for his two sons, the younger in the *desant* forces and the older serving as a naval officer. "What about *Voyska* PVO?" demanded Medvedev. "What about our air defenses? While the government is in flux over the coming days we are vulnerable to a surprise attack from the outside. Are there plans to mobilize reserves?"

"I do not know, we had not discussed it," answered the general.

Medvedev swore to himself. *They clearly have no guts. Do they lack brains as well?*

To the CPSU secretary, he ordered, "See to our flight back to Moscow. We must return as quickly as possible." Then he turned to Oleg Drugov and said, "Walk with me."

Medvedev turned and left the president's salon, Drugov following him closely. The two men squinted as they emerged into sunlight and onto a semicircular patio overlooking the sparkling Black Sea several dozen meters below. Medvedev's one working eye adjusted more quickly than his friend's two. They walked away from the palatial *dacha* and to the edge of the patio before either man spoke.

"You should have told us what you were going to do, Pasha," chided Drugov when they were beyond earshot of the house, using his friend's familiar name.

"And would any of you have agreed?" responded Medvedev.

Oleg smirked. "*Nyet.*"

"Committees are weak, Oleg," explained Medvedev. "That is where we are vulnerable. We are incapable of swift action because everyone is waiting for everyone *else* to assume the risk. If we continue like this our efforts to preserve our country will fail."

"But killing the president…" interjected Drugov.

"Highly regrettable. He was a great man, far better than those weaklings back there," Medvedev jerked his head towards the *dacha*. "That's why I had to do what I did. Had he lived, he could have rallied forces against us. On our side, we have too many who have grown used to the safety of bureaucracy, of shared responsibility. If we are to succeed we need swift, decisive, ruthless action, not half measures by this so-called 'State Committee on the State of Emergency.' The very name sounds like a product of bureaucratic negotiation." Pavel spat to show his disgust.

"And who do you propose should make these decisions, Pasha?" Oleg asked significantly, his piercing blue Slavic eyes looking into Medvedev's through his horn-rimmed glasses.

"Are you implying that I should make the decisions for us? That the others would let me?" Medvedev asked, surprised.

Drugov remained silent.

Medvedev shook his head in wonder. "I came here expecting to be arrested, even executed for what I just did. It seems the lethargy of the committee is working for me in this instance," he said wryly. "I've forced their hand by doing something none of them would have agreed to. I had hoped that the KGB chairman, at least, would be more decisive. He was bold to place the president under surveillance several weeks ago, but he seems to have lost his nerve. I thought I was too junior, too unknown to take charge of this coup, but…but you are right, my friend. I am beginning to think otherwise. If the others can be convinced to give me a free hand, I *know* I can hold our nation together. I am willing to do what is necessary. Much damage has been done, and it will take force to undo it, but I can see it undone!" He punched a meaty fist into a bear-like palm to emphasize his determination. Then he said more quietly, "The rest of them certainly don't seem to have a plan."

"I think they will defer to you, so long as you succeed," Drugov warned. "They are afraid right now. If you fail, they will abandon you to save themselves."

"We cannot fail, Oleg. Failure means chaos. Not just for our country, but for the world. This new Union Treaty will pave the way for the breakup of the USSR. If that happens, any attempt to repair our economy will fall apart as well. Can you imagine what the impact will be if we lose the shipyards of Ukraine? The oil of the Caucasus? The Central Asian republics? Minsk? Kiev?" Medvedev went on, "We won't control half the population or industry we have today if the country continues down the path we're on."

"I know Pasha, I know. That is why the Emergency Committee is doing this," said Drugov quietly.

"No, Oleg, they don't know. They don't *see*," Medvedev's annoyance was returning now. "None of you *see* that if Russia is relegated to the place of a third-rate power, even for a short time, that the doors will be opened for international chaos. The world *needs* us to counterbalance the United States, even if the world doesn't realize it."

"You really think the United States is such a threat to world peace?" asked Oleg.

"You know I admire that country, my friend," Medvedev answered, calming himself. "But they are a young country. They are idealistic like the leaders of our revolution were sixty-five years ago. They think that the constraints of history, of geography, don't apply to them. They think they are the pinnacle of human progress. One of their scholars even penned an essay titled 'The End of History!' Can you imagine the arrogance? As if their society is the culmination of all history and the rest of the world should bow to their inevitable supremacy."

Drugov shook his head in amusement. Medvedev continued.

"I can see it, Oleg Borisovich. Without us to restrain them, the well-meaning Americans will run rampant through the world, encouraging people to cast off the 'repressive' governments that have kept peace between rabid groups of fanatics for so long. After their adventure earlier this year in Iraq they will think that they can control the forces that they unleash without ever getting their hands dirty. By the time they realize their mistake it will be too late, and our detached republics, the Arab states, Africa, maybe even Asia will all be plunged into violence and chaos. Yes Oleg, as much as I like and admire the Americans, I do think that they are a threat to world stability. And the most dangerous thing? Once they have led the world into chaos they will blame *us* for everything and work tirelessly to keep us weak."

Medvedev was breathing hard now. He was unused to the heat and was becoming excited. "We cannot allow ourselves to become weak." Medvedev continued, "Right now, the Americans think they are invincible because they just destroyed a third-rate army of a crackpot Arab dictator in the desert. If they are allowed to think that *we* are so impotent, if they strip away our republics and co-opt our former allies, there is no telling how far they will push the frontiers of their alliances. Where will it stop? The Vistula? The Don?"

"You know I agree, Pasha," said Drugov quietly, "but can we undo the damage that has already been done?"

"We must try," said Medvedev through gritted teeth.

Both men turned as the CPSU Secretary called to them from the *dacha*'s entrance, "Comrades! Our aircraft is ready whenever we wish to depart."

Medvedev gave Drugov a knowing look.

"Let's go. The fate of our country is decided in Moscow."

 **CHAPTER 2**

1400 MSK, Monday 19 August 1991
1100 Zulu
**Outside the Supreme Soviet of Russia Building (the 'White
House'), Moscow, Russian Soviet Federative Socialist Republic**

WITH HIS ONE good eye Pavel Ivanovich Medvedev stared up in
frustration at his country's legislative building. Dubbed the "White
House," the fifteen-story white structure with its broad square base
and wide-faced central tower with rounded ends was a model of Soviet-era
architecture, lacking both the graceful lines of older Russian buildings and
the raw engineered strength of Western skyscrapers. It was a metaphor for
the dysfunction in his country, which could never seem to reach the same
accomplishments as its distrustful opponents in the world. The humid, gray,
summer overcast accentuated the milieu. Architectural dysfunction, however,
was not the object of Medvedev's frustration today; the current occupants of
the building, the resistance to his coup, held that glorious position.

*How could the KGB chairman have been so negligent, moved so slowly on
his promise to round up dissidents?* he raged, clenching his jaw in anger. *This
should never have been allowed to happen.* He calmed himself, forcing his fists
to unclench and his mind to work through the assets and liabilities. *At least
the Russian president is in custody. Better if he'd been eliminated. I'll need to see*

to that later. Our opponents know what is going on, but they have concentrated themselves in one place…I can make this work to Russia's advantage.

Several dozen liberal members of the RSFSR legislative body had arrived at the building in the early morning hours and were now actively barricading themselves inside while trying to summon popular support through word of mouth. How they had learned about the coup was another outrage. Vladimir Alexandrovich, against Medvedev's advice, had broadcast a statement by the Emergency Committee over state radio earlier in the morning. Now their opponents at least had an idea of what was occurring.

There was very real danger here. In front of Medvedev a cordon of low slung tanks surrounded the building, separating the dissidents from a group of civilians who were beginning to gather in the wide streets around the White House. Medvedev had exited his Zil limousine on the Novoarbatsky Bridge, which spanned the Moscow River, and looking north he could see soldiers and blue-uniformed *militzia* officers moving about aimlessly between the armored vehicles, unsure of what to do. *If the traitors inside are able to gather support from the people, all could be lost.*

Medvedev started walking briskly towards the nearest tank, surprising Oleg Drugov and the two plain-clothed KGB bodyguards who accompanied him. The others hurried to keep up with his determined pace as he passed through a thin crowd of milling civilians.

At least shutting down the Metro and trams has limited the numbers here, he thought.

He approached the nearest soldier, a young man who had forgotten to shave before duty this morning. Medvedev spoke in a firm but friendly voice, "Soldier, good day. Where is your commanding officer? I must speak with him."

The young man hadn't noticed Medvedev but quickly collected himself, looking relieved to be asked a question that he could answer. He pointed up the street towards the tank in front of the main entrance.

"The major is over there, *tovarich*. At the command tank."

Medvedev thanked him, gave the young soldier's shoulder a fatherly squeeze, and continued, the black metal perimeter fence on their right and the concrete embankment of the Moscow River on their left. As he drew closer Medvedev made out a major with black tanker epaulettes standing behind one of the hulking vehicles, conferring with a pair of younger officers. The man looked up as Medvedev approached, Oleg and the bodyguards trailing behind.

"*Tovarich* Major," Medvedev said in the same fatherly voice he had used with the soldier earlier, "may I ask what's going on here?"

The man looked unsure, unwilling to divulge his thoughts to this unknown newcomer. He decided on a safe response. "Sir, my orders are to isolate this building. I've arrayed my sub-units to accomplish this task."

"Good, good," responded Medvedev warmly, "I have just come from the Ministry of Defense, and I can tell you that this task is vital to the security of the state. I thank you. The marshal sent me over to assess the situation," he lied. "Do you know why you are here, young man?"

Now the officer looked uncomfortable. He glanced at his lieutenants before speaking. "Someone from in there," he indicated the White House, "came out a few minutes ago and told us that there is a coup underway."

Medvedev allowed his face to show weary sadness before responding.

"He was correct, my young patriotic friend. There is grave danger facing our nation," Medvedev said. Then leaning in conspiratorially and lowering his voice, he continued, "It is not public knowledge yet, but the president is dead."

A look of shock passed over the major's face.

Medvedev went on, "Counter-revolutionary elements are trying to take advantage of this tragic event to illegally seize power for themselves. Those in there," he looked to the legislative building, imposing behind its black fence, "are part of a plot to enrich themselves at the expense of the people. Fortunately, the State Emergency Committee sniffed out their plans before they could do great damage and ordered you here just in time."

The soldier looked unconvinced. Medvedev was impressed, the man was clearly more intelligent than he'd thought. *A professional. I'll have to try a different tactic. No more asking, time to command.* He looked back at the growing numbers of civilians gathering near the bridge and on the far side of the boulevard.

Medvedev changed his tone, speaking sharply now but still in a low voice, "Now pay attention. The President of the USSR is dead. The vice-president is in control at the Kremlin. Those people in there want to circumvent the lawful constitutional power of the government, a government elected by the people of the Soviet Union, and one you are sworn and ordered to protect."

Medvedev looked over and saw a staff truck parked in the street with a megaphone on the hood.

"I know you will do your duty, as any good Red Army soldier would," Medvedev said. "The enemies of the state have gathered inside the building here. You will keep them there and prevent them from receiving any more support from dissidents on the outside. Are my orders clear?"

The man nodded slowly.

Compliance, at least, Medvedev thought.

"Right now, I require your loud speaker to address the citizens gathering here. I promise it will only make your job easier," he assured the soldier and, without waiting for a reply, he walked over to the truck, retrieved the megaphone and then returned to the tank.

"With your permission," Medvedev addressed the tank officer, "I will address the people now." When the man didn't object, Medvedev continued, "I wish to stand on your tank so they may see me."

The man looked startled but again didn't protest.

Medvedev's frame suffered from the same thickening at the waist common to most Russians of his age, but he'd been athletic with the build of a shot-putter or heavy-weight wrestler in his youth. With Drugov's help he put his feet into one of the loops on the tank's armored skirt and pulled himself onto the front glacis, then stood and accepted the megaphone from his friend. Drugov and the two KGB guards scrambled up after him as Medvedev put a foot up on the tank's turret and reached down to offer a hand of greeting to the two surprised crewman. In his friendly, fatherly manner he shook their hands, asked them where they were from and thanked them for their service to the state.

Medvedev turned and looked out over the crowd stretching away from him up and down Krasnopresnenskaya Street. Some were looking up at him now. A television crew from the *Vremia* state broadcasting service pointed a camera up at him. Behind him was the mass of the Russian Soviet Republic's legislative building, occupied by men who would see this country dismantled. In front of him was the Moscow River, lifeblood of the Russian heartland, always under siege but never conquered. With his thick white hair tousled by the warm summer breeze, Medvedev raised the megaphone to his lips and began to address his countrymen in a deep, level voice, his words tumbling out at the rapid rhythm favored by Russians.

"Russians! Hear me, you have come here because you wish to know what is happening to our great country. I thank you for your concern. Allow me to inform you about the threat that has developed against our nation." The low mutterings from the crowd that had been rampant before settled slightly, he was gaining their interest.

Several people shouted queries up at him, while others attempted to quiet the throng with calls of "*Tischa*! Hush! Listen to the man, friends." Medvedev put his hands out, palms down, and waved them in a calming motion. With the noise quieted to a manageable level, Medvedev seized his moment. In a booming voice, aided by the megaphone he announced, "The President of the Soviet Union has died." Gasps exploded up from the crowd at this piece of news. *That'll get them to listen*, thought Medvedev, but without a pause he continued, "The people in the building behind me," he said, pointing at the White House, "are eager to exploit our great president's passing to enrich themselves and take power away from the government, from the leaders that *you* have elected!"

There were shouts of anger mingled with cries, but mostly the crowd waited for the man on the tank to continue.

"Those traitors in there think that if they break apart the Soviet Union they will be able to control the pieces, to carve out their own little capitalist kingdoms where they can reign as oligarchs," Medvedev accused, warming to his narrative. "The government is responding to their challenge. The brave soldiers in front of you are evidence of that. But we need your support so we may resolve this crisis without bloodshed, if those inside will allow us to do so," he added in a tone that indicated that he thought that outcome to be doubtful.

Medvedev was talking without notes, speaking from the heart and carefully balancing his passion with his willingness to bend the facts to his purposes. The *Vremia* camera crew was filming. He went on, feeling his rhythm, balancing his indignation at the dissidents inside the White House with respect and admiration for the crowds in front of him, juxtaposing the chaos of a disintegrating USSR with the order and prosperity that a rejuvenated Union would provide. He saw heads nodding in the crowd, though some skeptical looks remained. After several animated minutes Medvedev concluded his address with a delicate deception in which he artfully blended truths, half-truths, and lies: "Russians, the traitors in there are trying to destroy the reforms that have put more responsibility in the hands of you, the Soviet people. They would have you believe that *they* are the reformers, but they lie! They would have you believe that they are championing your rights, but they are only here for their own enrichment. They think that by overturning the government they will be able to control *you* better, but we know differently, do we not friends? You are not so easily manipulated."

Here he smiled inwardly at his own deception, then continued with a promise. "Do not support them! Allow the legitimate government to restore order and I swear to you, the Soviet people will keep their place at the forefront of human progress. The Soviet Union, supported by you, citizens, will be a model of strength, stability, and prosperity for the world to follow!"

Medvedev ended his speech with a flourish of his arm. Some of the people below shouted questions amid scattered applause as he climbed down from the tank, coming face to face again with the major.

"*Tovarich* Major," Medvedev ordered, "I leave things in your capable hands. Allow no contact between the traitors inside the building and those out here. I will return as soon as I can."

The man nodded. Medvedev could tell that he was still not completely convinced, but uncertain enough to comply. Medvedev made his way back to his car, the driver quickly opening his door. Drugov and the security detail were still in tow. They got in, as Medvedev hurriedly barked "Ministry of Defense!"

Armored vehicles and soldiers clogged Arbat Street on the way to the ministry building. Medvedev led his small entourage through a side entrance, navigating the massive bureaucratic building until they arrived at the office suite of the minister of defense. Medvedev announced himself to the secretary, who went in and conferred with the marshal before beckoning him in.

The marshal, thick framed like Medvedev, but older, was sitting at a massive desk, his olive drab uniform resplendent with row upon row of ribbons. The man looked worried, weary, unsure of what to do.

"Pavel Ivanovich, what brings you here?" The old soldier looked up.

"*Tovarich* Marshal," Medvedev said without salutation, "our endeavor to save this nation rests on a knife's edge. Our opponents are gathering at the White House. I was just there, and the situation is critical. The officer in charge is too junior and he is not clear about where his loyalties lie. You should replace him immediately."

The marshal rankled at this intrusion upon his prerogatives. "You wish to tell me how to do my job, Pavel Ivanovich?"

"No, *tovarich* Marshal," Pavel said, soothingly, "I only bring you a report from the critical front in the battle, and my own assessment of what must be done. We cannot allow personal loyalties to interfere with our duty to serve the state. I also wish to inform *you* first of what I will tell the Emergency Committee, because I know a soldier like you will see need for action more clearly than others. *You* are able to start the machinery in motion here for what must be done."

"What is your recommended course of action, then?" asked the marshal, placated a little by the deferential response.

"We must conduct an assault to recapture the White House as quickly as possible and eliminate the dissidents inside," Pavel said decisively. "We cannot allow popular support to build behind the traitors cowering there. Right now, the people are confused, but if they start to believe that the quislings are the champions of their rights, then our cause is doomed. Do we have forces that could do the job tonight? During darkness would be best, I think."

The marshal grunted, then responded, "The combined *Alpha/Vympel* team that seized the Russian president last night is here. They could be over at the White House in a few minutes. They are accountable to the interior minister, but it appears he is having a nervous breakdown. Coward."

Always trying to spread out the responsibility, aren't we? lamented Medvedev. "In that case, you must assume sole control over the security forces." He pressed, "No one else has your experience or authority. Will they be enough?"

"There is a *desant* battalion in the southern part of the city, a unit from the Tula division. I would trust them first to support an assault. Your son is with them, I believe," answered the marshal.

So, Misha is here. Aloud Medvedev said, "I urge you to order the assault, *tovarich* Marshal. I will go to the Kremlin and convince the others, but we must crush the resistance before it can coalesce. Will you order it?"

The man pondered Medvedev for what seemed a long time. Then he spoke. "You are a bold man, Pavel Ivanovich. I don't approve of what you did down in Foros, but you are right. Bold action is what is needed now to save our country. I will order the assault troops into position. Persuade the rest of the State Emergency Committee, and I will give the order for the attack."

— —

Pavel arrived back in front of the White House several hours later. The young major from earlier was gone, he noted, replaced by a loud, stocky colonel whose loyalty was less inhibited by intelligent questioning. The crowds had dissipated as night fell with no sign of action. That was good. Medvedev didn't want spectators to what was about to unfold.

After departing the Defense Ministry, Medvedev had arrived in the Kremlin to find the other members of the Emergency Committee once again indecisive about how to proceed. As he entered the conference room, a television set was playing a news broadcast of his speech from atop the tank. His stock soared with the other plotters, not least because his public actions had removed the onus from each of them to assume the dangerous role of leadership. He'd leveraged the emotional thrill of his new-found influence, convincing them to approve a nighttime assault on the legislative building. Now he was back to ensure it happened.

Before making the short drive from the Kremlin to the White House, Medvedev led the other plotters into the Kremlin's press room, where they confirmed Pavel's ascendance in front of the media by deferring to him and his forceful, logical arguments in front of the television cameras. Medvedev proved a persuasive voice in opposition to the dissidents while the other plotters largely looked on and nodded approval as he spoke. Now he was unquestionably the public face of what none of them would call a coup, at least publicly. Even the Soviet vice-president had remained passively silent, allowing Medvedev to dominate the media event with his unique mixture of Soviet populism, Russian nationalism, and firm hostility to the dissidents, who he repeatedly referred to as "traitors" and would-be oligarchs.

Medvedev walked through the gathering darkness with his entourage, turning off of Noviy Arbat Street and passing under a grove of trees. The special assault element, composed of commandos from the Soviet Union's two elite counter-terrorism teams, *Alpha* and *Vympel*, was assembling in a park one block east of the objective, shielded from view by a large office building.

Medvedev scanned the scene, trying to make sense of the formations of dark shapes moving to and fro on the yellow lit pavement. The counter-terrorism teams seemed to be gathered at the north end of the lot, looking dangerous in an odd, relaxed way, with their black weapons, body armor, and night vision devices. At the southern end of the lot stood the paratroopers, here and there a blue-and-white-striped undershirt catching the light beneath olive tunics and equipment harnesses. Between the two groups a knot of officers from the two elements congregated. Medvedev approached the group, incongruous in his gray business suit and tie, and heard the final few words from the KGB colonel coordinating the assault.

Medvedev approached the man as the group broke up, the officers returning to their units. "Good evening, *tovarich* Colonel. Can you tell me what the plan is here?"

The man immediately recognized Medvedev, who had risen to national and even international prominence in the past few hours.

"Of course," the colonel responded. "In," he looked at his watch, "thirty-five minutes we will cut all power to this part of the city. Special police units from the Interior Ministry are already blocking traffic from approaching the White House, and our main assault element," he indicated the commandos nearby, "will breach the rear of the complex, overcome any resistance and arrest the dissidents inside. The *desantniki* will, at the same time, breach the front fence with an armored infantry vehicle and seal off all exits from the front of the building, arresting anyone who tries to flee."

Medvedev nodded. Then he said, "I wish to speak to the officer in charge of the assault sub-unit."

"Of course, sir," the colonel said.

The KGB officer led Medvedev over to the commandos, then called to one of the dark shapes in the crowd, "Major Khitrov! Someone to see you."

Medvedev saw one of the men turn. The lit end of a cigarette dangling from the man's mouth flared as the dark shape appraised the newcomers through the semi-darkness. Medvedev felt the hair on his neck stand up the way it did when a wolf looked directly at him on one of his hunting trips in Siberia.

"Yes?" the man asked around his cigarette.

"Major, a word?" Medvedev said, and his hands itched for a cigarette of his own to banish the uncomfortable feeling.

"Certainly," the tall, athletic figure responded, the cigarette still held perilously between his lips.

"Walk with me," Medvedev commanded. The major complied, easily falling into step with the older man as the two moved away from the larger group of commandos.

When they were a sufficient distance away, Medvedev turned to the commando and asked, "Major...Khitrov, yes? Do you know what is at stake in this assault?"

"My skin?" came the irreverent response.

Anger flared within him at the flippancy of the younger man. He controlled his emotions before going on. "My young friend," he said coldly, "the future of our nation is at stake here. Many can see it, but none of them realize what must be done to preserve the Union. Half measures will not do. The people in there," he jerked his head towards the office building, beyond which stood the White House, "are more dangerous than they know. Even if your attack is completely successful, many of them could prove to be dangerous to us, to our country. Even as prisoners." He let the statement hang in the air for a second, then continued. "I'm sure you've seen the news reports. There are men in there with guns and masks who have sworn to resist you. What is the difference between those hooligans, the armed ones, and the ones they are protecting?"

Khitrov eyed the older man with narrowed, predator eyes as he took another long pull on his cigarette. The fiery glow glinted off his own dark eyes under his specialized helmet. Then he turned his head up and blew smoke into the darkness above them. "Sir," he said, still looking up, an air of amusement still in his voice, "what exactly is it that you want me and my men to do?"

"Only what is necessary to preserve the Soviet Union," Medvedev answered. "The deaths of a few traitors is sometimes necessary. Now is one of those times. The stakes are as high as they have been at any time since the Great Patriotic War."

Khitrov's eyes came back down, catching the light of the cigarette again as he looked directly at Medvedev. His face was classic Russian, with high cheek-bones and Slavic eyes, but Medvedev fleetingly realized that it lacked the deep, almost-hidden emotion of a true Russian. Khitrov remained quiet for a moment. He reached up and took the cigarette from his mouth, flicking it away nonchalantly. Then he spoke. "Very well, sir. I will kill who you need me to kill. I respect a man who can see what he wants to accomplish and won't let anything get in his way. But, allow me to offer you a warning. Violence sends many messages, and the one received is often not the same message that was sent."

"I will keep that in mind, Major," answered Medvedev, tamping down his annoyance at being lectured by this younger upstart. He held out his hand, and Khitrov took it. The men shook once. Khitrov turned and walked back to his men, calling his lieutenants to him.

Medvedev rejoined his entourage, then walked towards the groups of paratroopers gathered at the other end of the lot. *Maybe I can find Misha*, he hoped, then dismissed the idea. *Duty first. Let him accomplish his mission. I will find him afterwards.* Instead he moved among the dark shapes of armed men, observing their preparations, hearing low murmurs of conversation and smelling the damp nighttime smells of summer in Moscow: the sweet smells of lime and alder trees that lined the sidewalks and buildings mixing with the damp, musty odor of the nearby river and the smoke of dozens of cigarettes. He peered into various small circles of soldiers, many of whom were checking each other's equipment or just standing quietly, smoking as they waited for the coming assault. Within a few minutes a series of not-quite shouted commands prompted the dark milling shapes to spread out. The same was occurring with the *Alpha* group at the opposite end of the lot.

The soldiers shook out into loose formations at either end of the lot, then waited in heavy suspense. Minutes passed, then a shrill whistle blast pierced the air. The city around them went dark. Street lights, buildings, and the floodlights that usually illuminated the White House itself, which just before had been reflecting a glow onto the low clouds overhead, all extinguished. In the trees the engine of the BMD, an infantry vehicle on tracks, revved. Shouted commands penetrated the darkness, and the two assault groups flowed quietly but quickly out of the assembly area. The commandos moved past the northeast side of the office building, the *desantniki* around the southwest, amid the swishing sounds of uniforms and soft creaking of webbing.

Medvedev and those with him followed the KGB colonel coordinating the assault as he moved behind the paratroopers to the Svobodnoy Rossii plaza. From there they could watch, or rather listen, as the assault unfolded in the enforced darkness of the blackout.

The first tell-tale sound was a metallic crash as the BMD breached the heavy front gate, followed by the rush of paratroopers quickly securing the front of the building. A minute passed, then two, then there was a muffled explosion from the rear of the structure, followed by several bursts of automatic gunfire. More explosions, fainter now, sounded from within the building, along with more gunshots as the operation progressed deep into the massive structure. Gradually the sounds of combat from inside the building changed from bursts of automatic fire to single shots.

At this point the colonel, monitoring progress from a staff car, spoke a sharp demand into his radio handset. Medvedev watched the man's reaction closely. He couldn't hear either the question or the metallic response, but when the answer came through the colonel looked up with narrowed eyes and studied Medvedev. The shots continued, singly and in pairs, and now Medvedev could hear people fleeing the front of the building, some loudly begging the paratroopers outdoors to take them into custody, to protect them from the horrors inside.

Medvedev walked over to the colonel by the staff car and asked, "What is going on?"

The man was uncomfortable. He responded, "Major Khitrov reports he is mopping up resistance inside. He says the building will be secure shortly. No casualties to our force."

"Very good. I wish to enter the building, once the Major thinks he has things under control."

It only took half an hour. The colonel led Medvedev and his party to the front entrance. In the dark paratroopers held dozens of prisoners, kneeling in front of the legislature building, fingers intertwined behind their heads.

Flashlights shone into some of their faces as the soldiers processed them with the help of uniformed KGB troops.

Medvedev touched his guide's elbow and said, "Colonel, I want these prisoners at Lefortovo before sunrise. This whole scene must be cleaned up before first light. Maintaining order in the city depends on it."

The man nodded and called one of the KGB officers over to give the order.

"Father?" a familiar voice pierced the darkness from among a knot of paratroopers nearby.

Medvedev looked up. His heart swelled with pride as he saw a tall, athletic paratrooper wearing captain's insignia approaching. He couldn't make out the man's face in the darkness, but his gait was unmistakable.

"Misha!" Pavel called. The older man stepped forward and enveloped his son in a powerful embrace. Throughout this day Medvedev had put on one act after another, but there was nothing feigned about the love and pride he exuded as he leaned back to look at his youngest child. "How are you, my boy?" he asked warmly as he released his son. "I came here hoping to see you."

"*Normalna*, father," responded the young officer. Medvedev could hear concern in his son's voice as Misha continued in a hush, "What is going on in there? So many dead…the prisoners here are saying that the soldiers inside were killing everyone they saw!"

"I will look into it," Medvedev promised. "But these people," he indicated the prisoners kneeling on the concrete, "are dangerous. They wish to destroy our country."

Misha remained silent, unconvinced. *He has always been the intelligent one, the sensitive one*, Pavel reflected. Medvedev changed the subject to distract his son from the ugly business.

"It has been too long since you visited," Medvedev chided. "Once your duties here are complete, take some leave. I would love to spend time with you. Come over to the apartment."

Misha was non-committal. "I will need to ask my commander, father."

"I will speak to him." Pavel offered.

"No!" came the firm plea. "Please, father, don't. I will ask him; but allow me to complete my duties."

The answer only made Pavel prouder. He had been prevented by his blind eye from serving in his nation's armed services, something he'd always regretted. But the pride he would have felt in his own military service paled in comparison to what he felt for his two sons.

"Very well, son," Medvedev said warmly, "you are a grown man. Just remember, it does my old heart good to see you."

"I will, father." The young man's voice softened.

Out of the dark a voice called out. "Mikhail Pavlovich! Have your sub-unit start moving these prisoners to the trucks."

"I must go, father. It is good seeing you, but I have duties to perform," Misha said. Medvedev didn't notice, but the young man's eyes touched on the White House with concern.

"Of course, of course," Medvedev answered quickly. He embraced his boy again, and the young officer merged back into the confusion of shadowy shapes moving through the nearby darkness. *Best he be protected from the ugliness of what must occur here*, thought the father.

The KGB colonel had been waiting impatiently several paces away. Now he approached.

"Sir," he announced, "Major Khitrov says all is safe inside. We may enter when you are ready."

"By all means, lead on," said the older man.

They walked up the front steps and passed through a bank of glass doors, entering the dim foyer of the grand building. *Alpha* commandos, holding lights, provided the only illumination inside as they moved between dark shapes that lay crumpled on the floor. The colonel led Medvedev and his party through the room. The metallic smells of gunpowder and something else, something with a sickly-sweet flavor that Medvedev couldn't quite place, filled his nostrils. As Pavel passed one of the shapes he felt his shoe slip slightly on the smooth, faux marble floor. He looked down to see that he had stepped in a dark puddle, and then he knew what the smell was. *Blood*, he realized as he walked on, leaving dark footprints as he went.

They continued on to the rear of the foyer, where the shadowy shape of Khitrov leaned against a large reception booth. His helmet was off, revealing a bristly, shaved head. A cigarette dangled from his lips, its end glowing red. His body language communicated nonchalance, but the cigarette's glow glinted off hard eyes as he watched the party approach.

"Major Khitrov, your report," demanded the colonel.

The major made a show of slowly smashing out his unfiltered Russian cigarette onto the reception booth's counter before responding. Medvedev could see the colonel's frame tense in anger. *There is conflict between these two.*

"*Tovarich* colonel," he said easily, "all resistance in the building has been eliminated. My men suffered no losses. Some of the work was... messy. But," he spoke now to Medvedev, "nothing you won't be able to clean up, I think."

"Goddamn it, Khitrov!" exploded the colonel. "Look around you. None of these people are even armed!"

Medvedev's eyes were adjusting to the low light coming in from outside now, and he could see the bodies that dotted the floor of the broad room. One of the corpses was wearing a ski mask, with an AK-74 carbine on the ground nearby.

"Some of them were," responded the major, still nonchalant. "Not that it mattered."

"Not that it mattered?" raged the colonel. "These are Soviet citizens!"

"I do not say that it does not matter that they were unarmed and were killed," answered Khitrov coolly, "only that the ones that were armed did not matter. My men are too good to be bothered by such amateurs."

"These were traitors, Colonel," Medvedev interjected. "They were working against the state, protected by men bearing arms against the state. Their death helps ensure the survival of our country. Had they lived, they would have been a danger to the legitimate government. Keep these things in mind."

The colonel looked at Medvedev for a moment, then stalked off to inspect the carnage elsewhere in the building.

Khitrov lit up another cigarette, eyeing Medvedev the whole time. Finally, he spoke. "So, *tovarich*, what next, eh?" There was amusement in his voice that grated on the older man.

"What is next, major, is that we all do our duty to save our country," came the frosty response. "I thank you for doing yours."

He turned and walked between the sprawled bodies back to the front doors, picking his way awkwardly through the charnel house of his own creation by the faint light coming through the building's front bank of doors. A gentle rain was beginning to fall. The damp felt refreshing on his bare head. Looking down the broad steps he saw the familiar thin figure of Oleg Drugov, ascending towards him at the head of a plain-clothed security detail, several more than the two accompanying him earlier. Drugov had remained behind at the Kremlin when Pavel returned to the White House. There was the trace of a smile on his face.

"Oleg Borisovich," Pavel hailed, "what news?"

"Good and bad," the man said as he reached the top of the wide steps. Medvedev could see that his friend had much more to say.

"Well?" Medvedev prompted. "Out with it!"

"The Emergency Committee was meeting while the attack here was going forward," Oleg said. "When it succeeded they took a vote."

"On what?" Medvedev asked, on his guard now.

"On you, Pavel Ivanovich. They took a vote on you," Drugov answered.

"What about me?" Medvedev was starting to see where this was going.

"They voted to make you interim President of the Soviet Union, Pavel," Oleg announced, before going on quickly, "The vice-president said he wouldn't stand in the way, that he thought you were more qualified to lead us through this difficult time."

He's right, I am more qualified than that fool, Pavel thought. *Even so…*

"Do you accept, Pavel?" asked Drugov, somewhat anxiously.

Medvedev looked down, past the wrecked black metal gate and the BMD, and across the wide boulevard, flowed the wide Moscow River, ancient life-blood and protector of his country. *Of course, I accept*, Medvedev thought, *but some of those blind men on the Emergency Committee will not like it when they realize that I consider them part of the problem. They think they are getting a mouthpiece, someone they can control. Won't they be surprised?*

"Yes Oleg, I accept this responsibility," Pavel said quietly, looking across at the slowly flowing river. Then he turned. With a wry look he asked, "Was that the good news, or the bad?"

Drugov smiled. "The good news, of course, *tovarich* President."

"And the bad?" asked Pavel.

His friend grew serious. "Just a few minutes ago the Estonians declared independence. Several of the other republics are making similar noises."

President of the Soviet Union Pavel Ivanovich Medvedev gritted his teeth at the news. *Not while I still draw breath they don't.* He turned his good eye toward his friend.

"Come, Oleg Borisovich. There is much work to do."

 **CHAPTER 3**

0805 EST, Monday 2 November 1992
0305 Zulu
Times Tower, New York City, New York, USA

"YOU MOONLIGHTING FOR other employers now?" The almost-unfriendly challenge was offered in a nasally New York accent. Jack Young, rising star foreign affairs reporter for the *New York Times*, felt his pulse quicken. The advance copy of next month's *The Atlantic* had finally landed on his untidy desk, shoehorned at the margins of the buzzing, cubicle-filled newsroom floor. Seeing his name on the front cover of a publication always thrilled him. Jack looked up from the magazine to his pudgy, spectacled editor who was peering down at him with a mixture of amusement and annoyance.

"Not moonlighting, Bill, just practicing my craft," said Jack with his typically disarming grin. "Doing my part to make the *Times* look good."

"We'd rather you do that in the pages of the *Times*," retorted Bill half-heartedly.

"I know, I know," Jack said, raising his palms in mock surrender, "but the article was too long for even a Sunday edition, remember. You said so yourself."

Bill waved one hand dismissively. "Is that article on our president's relationship with the Russian president ready? I want to run it tomorrow."

"Trying to swing the election, are we?" teased Jack.

Bill scowled in return. The editor didn't have much of a sense of humor.

"It's right here. I'm just making my final edits and I'll walk it over." Jack tapped his screen.

"Make sure it's not late," Bill warned as he turned to walk back to his office. Then the older man paused. "And Jack?"

"Yeah Bill?"

"Good work on that *Atlantic* piece." Then the man stomped off, annoyed by the sliver of humanity he'd just shown.

"Thanks," Jack said to his back, surprised, but grinning again.

As the editor disappeared into his windowed office, Jack leaned back. He loved being a reporter, but sitting here at his desk Jack knew that he cut a far different figure from his colleagues around the newsroom. Instead of a cheap suit or blazer that seemed to be the uniform for his peers, Jack wore clothes more suited for a hike in the Catskills than a stroll through the concrete canyons of Manhattan. His Land's End collared shirt and blue jeans were distinctly out of place, and his tall, lanky frame, topped by an angular head with a severely receding hairline, made him easy to pick out even from across the newsroom.

His workspace set him apart, too. Around his desk and on the off-white wall behind his chair were taped clippings of stories and pictures he'd sent back from places like Saudi Arabia, Kuwait, Iraq, Yugoslavia, the Ukraine, and Poland; testimonies to his thirst for a meaty story and, if he was honest with himself, to a certain vanity in seeing his name in print. He had another trip planned for Poland. He wanted to get closer to the simmering unrest brewing there as it tried to shake off the influence of the newly resurgent Soviet Union.

The readership of the *Times* leaned towards the cosmopolitan, but Jack's interests lay squarely in the drama of human conflict in the earthier parts of the world. Indeed, that interest was what had prompted him to secure funding from the *Times* a few weeks ago for a circuit of Eastern Europe, which had borne the fruit of the article in the magazine now on his desk.

Jack looked down at the magazine. He touched his name on the glossy cover while savoring the satisfaction of the moment. Then he lifted it from his desk, flipped to the piece he had authored, and began to read:

BACK IN THE USSR?
Jack Young, reporter

As Washington prepares for a turbulent election night that will see US voters choose between "it's the economy, stupid" or "who's going to stand up to the Soviets?" now would seem a good time to take a step back. A review of the truly stunning reversals to the revolutions of 1989 that have taken place in the USSR and its sphere of influence over the past eighteen months is pertinent. A year-and-a-half ago the Soviets showed every sign of relinquishing their control over the states of the more or less defunct Warsaw Pact and withdrawing into their heartland to lick their economic and social wounds. Today, however, they are reasserting their dominance in ways more reminiscent of 1968 than the heady days of 1991.

Indeed, since the August 1991 coup and the untimely death of the previous Soviet president, the USSR's charismatic new leader, Pavel Medvedev, has presided over a stunning and unlikely re-emergence of Soviet geopolitical and military power. How has he accomplished this turnaround? What are its implications for European and global security in the near future? The man who takes over in the Oval Office next January would do well to consider these questions.

Jack noted with satisfaction that his photo of the stocky Russian leader reviewing this year's May Day Parade in Red Square headed the next section.

Pavel the Terrible

In the turmoil that followed the August Coup, the hard-line administration of Pavel Medvedev and his clique seemed ready to collapse under the weight of the same pressures which had prompted the now deposed Soviet government to institute Perestroika and Glasnost. The Soviet economy was sputtering, the military appeared demoralized and inept following the withdrawal from Afghanistan, and republics of the Union appeared ready to declare their independence from Moscow, indeed, some already had.

Medvedev moved quickly to quash these stirrings by renouncing the New Union Treaty and sending troops into the Baltic republics to assert Soviet control in a short, violent campaign. The nationalist movement in Ukraine, however, proved more difficult to defeat. Here the Soviet president was forced to bring in troops from as far away as Siberia, with the bloody results broadcast to the world from Kiev this spring.

A photo that Jack had taken during the violence in that Ukrainian city emphasized the point. It showed a tank on the bloody pavement of Kiev's October Revolution Square with a score of bodies lying in the background.

Independence movements in the Central Asian republics failed to coalesce after the grim resolve Moscow had shown in the west. Even so, separatists in the Transcaucasus region, particularly the Georgian Republic and its neighboring areas, are still a sore spot for the Soviet administration.

Within the Russian Republic, Medvedev has cracked down on political opposition with a skillful combination of soft and hard power, complementing the violent purges which followed hard on the heels of the August Coup. Medvedev has used the Soviet justice system to make spectacular examples of several opponents who were incautious enough to oppose him while engaging in real corruption elsewhere. Several prominent opposition politicians have ended up in the labor camps that form the bulk of the Soviet penal system, and one district governor was executed for misappropriating state funds. Perhaps most stunning of all was the fall of the KGB chairman and his replacement with Anton Laskin, a Medvedev loyalist. All in all, Medvedev seems to have pulled the USSR back from the brink of political dissolution and set it on a more stable social footing.

Military Reform

Part of the key to understanding Medvedev's success has been his complex relationship with the Russian military. Army support for the August Coup, we have learned, was in no way assured. We may never know how close the Red Army came to intervention on the side of the sitting government in those chaotic days. Nevertheless, Medvedev quickly won the support and then the loyalty of his generals and admirals by committing the Russian economy to modernizing and expanding Russia's conventional forces. Strengthening his hand with the military is the commitment of his two sons to a life in uniform, one in the navy and another in the elite parachute forces, the desantniki.

To illustrate this, Jack had included a stock photograph of the Russian president grasping the shoulders of his sons. The older wore the blue uniform of a naval officer, while the younger was dressed in the army uniform, striped undershirt, and blue beret of a Soviet paratrooper. The genuine pride on the face of the father told the story nicely, Jack thought.

Cutbacks to Soviet conventional forces under the previous Soviet president have been reversed, and an aggressive naval build-up has kept Soviet ship-yards busy, and workers employed, year-round. In return, the military has supported Medvedev's reform of its ranks. Corrupt or incompetent officers have been purged and even executed in some cases. The brutal practice of "dedovshchina," in which experienced conscripts ruthlessly hazed new induct-ees, has apparently been abolished. Beyond simply upgrading and purchasing new weapons, the Soviet defense establishment has put enormous efforts towards improving the living conditions, pay, and morale of its soldiers, and towards professionalizing some of the junior enlisted ranks. Outside defense observers have noted improvements in the morale and efficiency of a force that just last year appeared to be on the verge of impotence. Today, the Soviet military's support for Medvedev is unquestionable.

Now, Russia's conventional forces—ground, naval, and air—appear more powerful than at any time since the Brezhnev era. While President Medvedev's government appears to have honored all standing treaties regard-ing the reduction of nuclear weapons, its relationship with the Conventional Forces in Europe Treaty has been more contentious. Whether the Soviets can sustain this force structure for the long term remains to be seen.

It's the (Russian) Economy, Stupid!

A photo of drably-clothed civilians lined up to buy bread in Tallinn was inset into the following section.

One of Medvedev's greatest accomplishments has been to turn the anger of the Soviet people at their difficult economic conditions outward. Indeed, western leaders have played into Medvedev's hand by the punitively ham-handed ways in which they have imposed economic sanctions, punishing the USSR for the violence in Poland while ignoring the excesses of the pro-western faction in that country's internal turmoil. While one can never really tell in a society as secretive as that of the Soviet Union, all indications are that the Soviet people have wholeheartedly bought into Medvedev's vision of a rejuvenated USSR, as well as his antagonism towards 'NATO encirclement,' economic and otherwise.

The Soviet 'Near Abroad'

Here Jack had included a map with the states of Central Europe outlined in red.

From the perspective of western leaders, the most troubling aspects of Medvedev's foreign policy are the USSR's destabilizing influence in the ongoing chaos in Poland. There, the Solidarity government has apparently failed to solidify its role as a popular governing force. The unrest stems in part from Soviet interference in Poland's internal affairs. Solidarity's inability to bring some of the former communist regime's more notorious figures to trial, as well as the Red Army's de facto military occupation of the socially and ethnically fractured Czechoslovakia are also contributing considerations.

In Poland, the Soviets have practiced a sort of hybrid engagement, offering material support and even military "volunteers" to the pro-communist and pro-Moscow factions on the one hand while vociferously denying any involvement on the other and condemning the excesses of what they call "The regime in Warsaw." Every faction in the Polish quagmire has been guilty of excesses on some level, but it has been Russian influence that has kept it in simmering chaos for the past year. The Polish state may suffer political and cultural fracturing akin to what is occurring further south in Yugoslavia.

The Czechoslovak situation is much different. As chaos spread in Poland the Soviet Union negotiated the rights to withdraw their forces stationed in the former East Germany through Czechoslovakia, citing concerns that the conflict in Poland could jeopardize the Baltic and Polish routes. The Czechs were no doubt surprised when they realized that the Soviets understood the agreement as allowing them to withdraw their forces to their country rather than through it. By the time the Czechoslovak government understood what was happening they were essentially presented with a fait accompli by Medvedev: accept Soviet "protection" or be subject to whatever coercion thousands of Soviet troops already present could exert. Since then the Soviets have skillfully played upon social divisions between Czechs and Slovaks to forestall any meaningful resistance to their occupation. Today, Czechoslovakia is an armed camp, a Soviet dagger in the heart of Central Europe, containing almost all the forces that had been present in the former East Germany along with those that never left Czechoslovakia.

The rest of the Eastern Bloc nations have elected, more or less willingly, to remain in Moscow's orbit. Hungary has been the most unwilling. Bulgaria and Romania have managed to overcome political unrest within their own borders, reportedly with Soviet assistance, and repress, or at least counterbalance, their more progressive elements. The effect has been to provide Medvedev with badly needed allies as much of the rest of the European community has nominally turned against his country.

Wherefore art thou, NATO?

In the heady days after the near-dissolution of the Warsaw Pact and the seemingly impending implosion of the USSR, many pundits questioned whether there would be any need for NATO in a post-Cold War world.

Pavel Medvedev himself answered these doubts when he categorically denounced his predecessor's Helsinki Declaration that Moscow would not interfere in the affairs of eastern European nations and instead demanded the withdrawal of a reunited Germany from the Atlantic Alliance as a precondition of Soviet withdrawal from their erstwhile allies' territory.

The alliance certainly has renewed purpose; however, many of its sixteen long-standing member states have chosen to pursue "peace dividend" cuts to their militaries as if the Cold War had actually ended. Even the mighty United States, secure in its military superiority following the fireworks of the Persian Gulf War, has seen fit to slash its commitments in Europe and reduce the size of its ground forces there, though the US president has so far managed to forestall reductions to the Navy and Air Force budgets. France remains a vociferous element in NATO's political branch, but has so far continued in its status as a "non-military" member of the Alliance, though the French military has maintained much of its Cold War force structure. Other member states have made or are planning far deeper cuts to their conventional war-making capabilities, with the Norwegians being the one notable exception. These cuts, while they have freed up significant funds for social programs, have weakened NATO's hand against the Russian leader.

Germany, in particular, has been balancing their imperative to remain within the Alliance with their desire to placate Soviet fears and appease leftists who have demanded an end to collective security. Accordingly, the Bundeswehr has faced more severe cuts than any other NATO military. To date these cuts have failed to elicit any softening of Moscow's demands for a German withdrawal from NATO.

Here a colored graph showing reductions in the numbers of each NATO members' armed forces, broken down by troops, tanks, artillery, aircraft, and ships, highlighted Jack's point.

These cuts stand in stark contrast to the economic stick that Europe and America have been willing to wield to express their displeasure at the USSR's actions in its independence-minded republics and in Eastern

Europe. Sanctions have targeted many categories of Soviet exports and imports, and while they have surely hurt the USSR's economy, they have also prompted Russia to seek a closer trading relationship with China. These measures have certainly highlighted the economic vulnerability of the USSR's geography. It remains to be seen if western sanctions will be successful in forcing Medvedev to soften his stance against NATO and Eastern Europe. For now, they seem to have only strengthened his hand by giving him an antagonist to demonize before the Soviet people.

This leaves western leaders to ponder how to best handle a resurgent Soviet Union. The apparent end to the east-west antipathy two years ago followed by its dramatic and rapid return have left many in NATO countries with a distinct "Cold War weariness," hampering the efforts of those governments who would prefer a firmer military stance against Moscow. How has the balance of power shifted? Where will the pieces of the new Europe fall? How long can the Russian economy stand in opposition to and isolation from the west? Whoever occupies the Oval Office next January will need to consider carefully the answers to these questions. The future of Europe, and possibly the world, depends on it.

After finishing his readthrough, Jack leaned back and reflected on what he'd written. He'd mentioned that the about-to-be-inaugurated president should consider the goings on in Moscow. That was obvious. But would the general public in the west care? With the economy slowing down and the distractions of everyday life, did they even need to? Jack pushed the thought aside and leaned back into his work. He had deadlines to meet himself.

 **CHAPTER 4**

0845 EST, Friday 6 November 1992
1345 Zulu
Julian C. Smith Hall, Camp Lejeune, North Carolina, USA

COLONEL (SELECT) Robert Buckner, United States Marine Corps, set down his copy of *The Atlantic* on a cheap, government-issue desk. He pulled his woodland pattern uniform shirt off of the back of his swivel chair and put it on, hoping that he had finally stopped sweating from his morning physical training in the coastal North Carolina humidity. His sweaty olive drab workout uniform still hung from the door of a gray wall locker in the corner of the small office. As he buttoned the shirt, he processed the article he'd just read. *Who occupies the Oval Office indeed*, he thought.

The magazine sat next to today's edition of the *Washington Post*, where subdued headlines trumpeted the tenth day of confusion following one of the closest presidential elections in U.S. history. He picked up the newspaper and began to scan the front page. There was one column analyzing how the three-way presidential race had initially seemed to hinge on domestic issues, but the re-emergence of Soviet power had brought foreign affairs back to the forefront of the electorate's mind. Another article related how vote counts still remained in doubt in several key states.

He flipped the paper over. One of the below-the-fold headlines even included an article detailing a wry offer by the Soviet president to provide observers to ensure the unresolved contest was adjudicated fairly. Buckner snorted. *As if that guy cares about fair elections*, he thought.

In another column, a political commentator opined that regardless of which candidate eventually came out ahead, neither would have a mandate to pursue their agenda. Neither of the traditional parties had won even forty percent of the popular vote. That view was just fine with Buckner. *If they don't have the political capital to pursue a domestic agenda, they don't have the political capital to cut defense spending any further either. Job security!* he thought the last with a wry grin as he finished buttoning his battle dress uniform. *Not that I've got to worry about job security now,* he mused. He had received the news just a couple weeks earlier that he had made the list for promotion to full colonel. *Those shiny eagles will look good on the old collar*, he thought, now with a genuine smile. He just had to wait for news on when, or *if,* he reminded himself, the Corps would entrust one of its precious regiments to him to command.

The round wall clock in his office ticked past zero-nine-hundred hours, and Buckner set the two publications aside to concentrate on his work for the day. He sat down at the desk and began reviewing training plans submitted by two of those coveted regiments, the 2nd and the 6th Marines. Buckner's current job was the G7, training officer on the staff of the 2nd Marine Division, with its four regiments, three infantry and one artillery, and associated units based at Camp Lejeune.

His current job title made him wince slightly and his eyes were drawn to the story of his career as told by the guidons and plaques adorning the small area of his office walls. The guidons all represented units he'd commanded as he climbed the ranks as a career Marine officer. His current staff job was the penance he had to pay to earn his next command, a coveted Marine Regiment.

A lance corporal from his staff section walked in and lightly rapped his knuckles on the open door.

"What is it, Billings?" he asked, looking up from the reports.

"Call from the division commander's office, sir. Major General De Vries wants to see you," the young man said.

"Did they say what it was about?" Buckner asked, standing up and grabbing his notebook off the desk.

"No sir, just that the general himself wants to talk to you," answered the lance corporal.

Buckner felt his heart begin to pound. *This is it. This is when I find out if my slaving away for the past two years here pays off with a command.* He snatched his starched and blocked eight-pointed cover—his wife, Helen, always called it a "hat," like the rest of the world.

Colonel (Select) Robert Buckner left his office and walked rapidly as he navigated the long corridors to the central nexus of the sprawling red brick Julian C. Smith Hall. The building was named after a hero of his. Julian Smith was the Marine general who commanded the landings on Tarawa during World War II, and the headquarters of the 2nd Marine Division and II Marine Expeditionary Force was named in his honor. As he went, each step clicking smartly down the hall, Rob could hear in his mind the gentle chiding of his wife, Helen, as she reminded him that too much of his self-worth was tied up in getting this next command. *Commanding Marines is what I was made to do, it's who I am. I'm good at it,* came his internal retort. He ascended some broad steps and strode into the foyer of the general's office suite. The aide-de-camp, a captain, stood up from his desk and gave a greeting when he saw Buckner enter. The younger man guided Rob to the open door of the general's plush office.

"Sir," the captain said as he entered the division commander's office, "Lieutenant Colonel Buckner is here."

"Thanks Josh," Rob heard the gravelly voice from within the office, "send him in."

Buckner walked into the large office with its bank of windows overlooking the oval green of the building's front entrance. Major General Rick De Vries was sitting behind a large executive desk to one side of the room. Bald and barrel-chested, the two-star got up and walked around the desk as his visitor entered.

"Rob, come in," came the gruff command, "shut the door behind you."

Uh oh. Rob felt his heart sink. He slowly closed the wooden door and turned back to face his commander, now perched on the corner of his desk, arms crossed and chin down. Then De Vries looked up and Rob could see it in the man's face.

After a few awkward seconds he said, "Rob, there's no easy way to break this to you, so I'll just be direct. You didn't make the command select list. You won't be getting a regiment."

Buckner thought that he was prepared for this news, he'd rehearsed his response to this contingency in his mind for days, but hearing it become a reality staggered him. His head spun and his throat constricted. He looked down, opened his mouth to respond, but no words came. He didn't trust himself to speak.

"I know this isn't the news you wanted, Rob," the general's words were uncharacteristically gentle. "I can tell you that you were very competitive. Hell, I'd give you one of my regiments right now if it were up to me." The comment was empty and did nothing to alleviate the disappointment that was overwhelming Rob's senses.

"Why not?" Rob finally managed to croak, bitterly.

"Say again?" came the general's response, somewhat guarded now.

Buckner was starting to regain some of his composure, but his voice was still pinched. "Why am I not on the list, sir?" he asked.

"You know the board doesn't disclose how the selections are made," answered the general, still speaking softly.

"May I see the list?" Rob didn't even notice that he had omitted the obligatory "sir" from the end of his request.

De Vries paused, then uncrossed his arms and reached back to retrieve a memo from the center of his desk. He handed the sheet of paper to Buckner.

Rob scanned the document. It contained a short list of names, and the regiments to which they would be going. All the names had one thing in common. *Desert Storm. They all deployed to Desert Storm, while I sat back here at the War College.* He stopped reading and looked up.

"Sir, Tom Pile was selected ahead of me to lead 6th Marines?" Rob asked, indignation creeping into his voice.

"Yes," the two-star responded, taking the memo back, "what's your point, Rob?"

"He's...," Buckner was losing his cool, his dreams for higher command, maybe even a star, slipping away, "all he did in Saudi was...was get coffee at CENTCOM headquarters!"

"He's a good officer, Buckner." Gone was the general's soft tone. "The Corps only has so many regiments to hand out. You didn't get one. I understand you're disappointed. You wouldn't be worth your salt if you weren't. But lashing out at a brother officer like that is bad form. I expected better of you."

The younger Marine winced at the rebuke; it stung because it was warranted.

The general continued, softening his tone again, "Rob, you're a good Marine. You got your promotion to colonel. You'll pin on when? January? February? You've had a successful career." Buckner noticed that De Vries was already talking about his career in the past tense. "There are lots of roles for you to fill besides a regimental command. Take the weekend to sulk a little, think about it, and then I expect you back here Monday, ready to work, with a good attitude. Roger that?"

Buckner swallowed, then gave a half-hearted, "Roger that, sir."

De Vries stood up from leaning against the desk and patted Buckner on the shoulder. Rob, took the cue, mumbled his thanks and exited the office, quickly walking past the aide-de-camp, not wanting the junior officer to see his face. Rob made his way back to his office, not speaking to the Marines in his section as he passed through the shop, closing the door behind him.

Sitting, Rob allowed himself to rage against his circumstances. *It's not fair. My whole career I've done everything the Corps asked of me. It's not my fault I've never seen combat.*

Too young for Vietnam and at the War College during the Persian Gulf War, Buckner had also missed Grenada, Lebanon, and Panama, always being in the wrong unit at the wrong time. *Not that I didn't try,* he thought, *but when the Corps told me to shut up and do my job, I did. And this is the reward I get.*

Colonel (Select) Robert Buckner spent the rest of the work day distractedly reviewing the training plans of regiments he now knew he would never command. He left work early and on the way home stopped by the liquor store to pick up a bottle of Jack Daniels. He usually made a point of not drinking to excess, but tonight he wanted to deaden the pain of a career that was coming to a slow, unremarkable end.

— —

Two days later, Rob Buckner was standing in his usual pew at the base chapel, listening to Helen at his side sing the hymns picked out for the service. Rob was in slacks and a button-up shirt. Helen wore one of her Sunday dresses she knew he liked best, trying to cheer him up. He was still moping. They had talked late into last night about their future. Should he retire? The economy wasn't in the best place right now for someone who had been a Marine infantry officer his whole life. But serving out the rest of his career in one thankless staff position after another didn't appeal to him either, and with no prospects for further promotion he would have to retire sooner rather than later anyway.

Rob couldn't concentrate on the hymnal he and Helen were sharing, and when the music ended they sat down to listen to the chaplain's sermon. He didn't hear a word, so consumed was he by thoughts of what he could have done differently, what decisions he could have changed to avert this ignominious end to what he had thought until Friday to be a successful career. Before he knew it they were standing up for the closing hymn. Helen's beautiful voice again sang the verses, her comforting arm around his waist. The chaplain spoke a benediction, and everyone filed out of the chapel into the mild but sticky North Carolina fall weather.

Rob walked with Helen behind their two teenage kids down the chapel's front steps, but turned as he felt someone touch his elbow.

"Colonel Buckner?" came the calm salutation. "That was some sermon. I've always liked Chaplain Smith."

"Sir?" Rob said in surprise, looking into the fatherly face of Vice Admiral Arthur Falkner, who had been standing beside the chapel's entrance, inconspicuous in his slacks and sports coat.

"I was hoping to see you here," said the admiral easily, extending his hand.

Buckner took it, still caught off guard. He and Falkner had worked closely together before, when the two were both stationed in the Mediterranean about ten years ago, but not since.

"I wasn't expecting to see *you* here, sir," Rob responded. "Didn't you just take over 2nd Fleet up at Norfolk?"

"That I did, Rob. I'm down here for a conference with II MEF. Hello Helen!" Falkner greeted Rob's wife with a smile, which she returned.

"Hello, Admiral," she said with genuine warmth, "so good to run into you. How's Paige?"

"Fine, fine," he responded. "She's enjoying decorating the new quarters up at Norfolk. I know she'd love to catch up with you."

"Give her a 'hello' from me," Helen said easily. The admiral said he would, and Helen discretely guided the kids away to another knot of people on the chapel lawn.

"You said you were looking for me, sir?" Rob asked, somewhat warily.

"That I was, Rob," Falkner responded in his soft-spoken mid-western accent. "I have a job offer for you."

"Sir...," bitterness began to creep back into Buckner's voice as he looked down.

"I know you didn't make the command list, Rob," the older man said quickly. "The Corps is missing out on some serious talent, and I don't intend to make the same mistake. I'd like you to come work for me as my N3 for expeditionary warfare."

Buckner was taken aback.

"Sir," he responded, "that's...that's a one-star billet."

"I'm less concerned about the rank than the person, Rob," Falkner said. "I know you. I want you on my staff. What do you say?"

Rob paused. He felt humiliated here at Camp Lejeune, having failed for the first time in his life to achieve a career goal. Arthur Falkner was one of those once-in-a-generation leaders, someone that people would kill to work for. *I'd be doing a lot more than reviewing training plans, that's for sure.* Rob's mind got away from him. *I'd have my fingers in real operations up there, planning amphibious landings, training and deploying real Marine Expeditionary Units, working with other countries' forces. And after my behavior here in front of General De Vries on Friday...*

Rob had to shake himself, bringing his mind back to the churchyard with his family, and Falkner.

"Sir, can I talk it over with Helen?" Rob asked. "It would mean another move for the kids and…"

"Of course, Rob, of course. Take care of your family. Talk it over. I'm heading back up to Norfolk this afternoon. If you want the job, give my office a call." The admiral reached inside his sports coat and handed over a business card. Buckner took it and the admiral went on. "Keep this in mind, Rob. If we've learned anything over the past few years it is that the world can change on a dime. I'm building my team up at Norfolk right now. I intend to be ready the next time the world takes a turn for the worse and I want you on that team. Don't take too long making your decision."

Rob nodded. "I won't, sir."

 **CHAPTER 5**

0130 CET, Friday 13 November 1992
0030 Zulu
East of Ossówka village, Biała Podlaska Voivodeship, Poland

S ZYMON'S RUBBER BOOTS splattered through cold mud onto hard earth as he ran along the cow path. The muddy trail crossed the fields between the small farming village of Ossówka and the dark mass of forest to the east. The boy's *babcia* had shaken him awake, told him to run to the forest as fast as he could with a warning for the men.

"The guardsman is out looking for them," *babcia* had said. The guardsman was a communist sympathizer sent up from Biała Podlaska, the city just to the south. "He knows what they're planning, tell them to hurry!"

The cold rain was easing now, the low, broken clouds overhead moving rapidly east allowing moonlight to peek through. When the boy reached the tree-line he stopped, unwilling to charge headlong into the black wall of the forest. In the daytime he loved to play in these woods, but at night, especially this night, he was daunted by the long, spindly white birch branches, reaching out like ghostly arms. There were graves in these woods, said older boys from the village, ghosts as well. He caught his breath and tried to gather the courage to pass over from pasture to trees when he heard it.

The metallic, rhythmic *chunk* and *swish* of several shovels biting into the earth and tossing dirt, mingled with low murmurs ahead through the trees. The boy peered in and thought he saw the red glow of a cigarette. Taking a deep breath, he plunged forward, feeling the ground under his feet change from the muddy grasses of the fields to the softer moss-covered forest floor. Feeling his way towards the sounds, Szymon tripped over something, a root, and stumbled into a thick bush, shaking the bare limbs and cracking several twigs. The murmuring stopped, then a hiss as the digging sounds ceased as well. He extracted himself from the bush, scratching his hand in the process, and called out, "*Tata?*" *Father?*

The harsh white beam of a flashlight, switched on from ten meters in front of him, destroying what night vision his eyes had begun to afford him. Szymon shielded his face with the back of his hand, trying to see who was beyond the light. "*Tata?*" He called again, fear creeping into his voice.

"It's your son," came a low growl from behind the light. Another hissed command and the shovel sounds resumed.

"Get over here, boy!"

Even though the command was given in a low, harsh tone, the child was relieved to hear his father's voice. The light switched off. Szymon scrambled forward until he was standing in a small clearing. The dark shapes of grown men were around him now. He couldn't recognize any of them in the shadows. Moonlight glinted off the barrel of an old hunting rifle carried by one of them. He recognized the distinctive front sight post of a Kalashnikov slung over the shoulder of another.

A strong hand grabbed his upper arm and spun him around.

"What are you doing here?" The query was delivered in a low, harsh growl that came from the back of the throat.

"*Ba...Ba...Babcia* sent m...me, *tata*," the boy managed.

Father released his arm and squatted down so the two of them were at eye level. "What did she say, Szymon?" Softer now, the familiar sweet smell of currant *sok* on his breath.

Comforted by the closeness of his father, he spoke rapidly, "The guardsmen, they are looking for you...for all of you. *Babcia* said they know what you plan to do," he allowed the message to tumble out, not really sure he understood what it meant.

The boy heard a muffled curse from someone in the darkness, then more clearly, "Alright, that's all we have time for. Let's get this over with." His father stood up quickly and looked in the direction of the voices.

Soft moonlight came and went with the passing clouds as Szymon's eyes focused on the small clearing where they were gathered. At one end, farthest from him, four dark shadows were digging holes side-by-side. They were barely knee-deep in the shallow trenches. One of the diggers was sniffling and murmuring short, unintelligible words. Eight or more other shadows were there, but in the darkness they seemed more numerous. These, including his father, were carrying rifles, the boy realized. Some had their weapons pointed at the shovel-wielders.

"That's enough!" came an order from the gloom. "Drop those and come here." Little Szymon recognized the voice of a neighbor, a young man named Piotr.

The men converged on the four diggers as hands reached out to yank them out of the holes. The smallest pleaded as he was dragged, stumbling, in front of Piotr, and then they were lined up side by side and their hands were bound.

Another figure stepped forward, slightly stooped. He straightened as best he could and addressed the four in a clear, faltering voice of an old man: "This liberation court of the Polish people will come to order," the voice said. "You are each charged with crimes against the Polish people. Tonight, your guilt will be determined. How do you plead?"

The youngest's shoulders heaved in a great sob as he almost collapsed, but another of the accused spat loudly and looked up to stare defiantly at the speaker. Piotr lunged towards the defiant one, but a restraining arm from Szymon's father held him back. Mumbles of "not guilty" came from the other two.

The stooped old man began again in a formal tone, as if pleas had in fact been entered in a court of law. Starting at the end of the line he pointed and said, "You are charged with the crime of killing peaceful citizens of Poland as they marched for our freedom through the city of Lukow this October past. What is your defense?"

The boy heard one of the accused men clear his throat and swallow. His voice sounded dry and cracked when he spoke. "I was a soldier in our army, we…my unit…we were only following the orders of the officers. We—" his plea was cut short.

"'Just following orders is no defense!" hissed Piotr, enraged.

"The marchers weren't peaceful!" the defendant blurted out. "They attacked us with clubs! We were defending ourselves. We were afraid."

"Silence!" the stooped judge commanded coldly. "So, you admit you fired on the citizens in Lukow?"

"We didn't have a choice!" the man pleaded, panic in his voice. "They were going to kill us!"

"We've heard enough," the stooped man said, nodding to two others. They seized the defendant as the self-styled judge continued, "We, the liberation people's court of Poland will do the duty that the communists' lackeys in the Public Prosecutor's Office refused to do. We find you guilty of crimes against the Polish people. May God have mercy on your soul."

The man was dragged backwards, thrown into his hole and held there at gunpoint.

Next the stooped man turned to the sobbing boy, his size betraying his youth. Szymon could see the fuzz of a mustache on his upper lip in the moonlight.

"You," he said. "You are charged with being a member of the traitorous communist regime's ZOMO informers; of collaborating with the enemies of our people, and delivering patriots to be tortured and killed by the communist pigs. What is your defense?"

Slowly raising his bound hands as if in prayer, pleading with tears streaming down his face, he said between sobs, "I've told you, I was never in the ZOMO. I don't know what you're talking about. Why are you doing this to me?"

Some of the accusers began to falter. Then Piotr walked up to the self-appointed judge and hissed in his ear, "You *know* he is guilty! My wife *saw* him go into the City Guard station in Biała just two days before my brother disappeared. You *know* what Andrzej said those pigs did to him. Now they will not even let us have the body!"

The sobbing boy looked up. After a second he asked through tears and in a broken voice, "Am I not your brother, too, Piotr?"

Piotr turned to him and said, "You were, once," before turning his back and stalking off into the darkness.

The stooped man paused, before pronouncing "You are found guilty."

Men pulled him back to the freshly dug holes, his heels dragged in the wet moss, his pleas lost in the night. The result was no different for the third accused. He'd been discovered with a brand-new AK-74 assault rifle, packaged and labeled with Cyrillic letters, in his workshop. His defense that someone else must have left it there fell on deaf ears to those who saw a new Russian weapon as clear proof of collaboration with the Medvedev regime's agents.

"What you are doing here is *exactly* why there are people accepting help from the Soviets!" the man shouted as he was dragged backwards.

The fourth man, the one who had spat, would not go meekly either. When he was told to defend himself, Szymon was surprised to recognize the calm, defiant voice of his school teacher.

"Father!" Szymon whispered loudly, grasping his father's sleeve.

"Hush, boy," came the stern rebuke.

The teacher was saying, "…all we try to do is build a just society, to create economic equality. No wonder the SB spends so much effort to hunt you down! And this is how you plan to hand our country back to the Germans, eh? This is how the fascist collaborators did it back in 'thirty-nine too. You are fitting heirs to their—"

The butt of a Kalashnikov smashed into his face. He staggered to one knee, but slowly stood back up, spitting blood and teeth.

The sudden growl of engines approaching from the south broke the tension. Men reached for their weapons and looked toward the approaching danger. Piotr came scrambling back from the darkness, and with vengeance and anger on his voice snarled, "There's no time. Finish this!"

The judge nodded, and the fourth defendant was dragged back to his hole without a spoken verdict. The four condemned men waited in their shallow trenches, the teacher standing in defiance, blood dripping from his face, the boy whimpering, and the other two with heads bowed, looking at the ground that was about to receive them. The accusers gathered in a shallow crescent around them, weapons half raised.

Father grabbed Szymon's arm and in a tone that brooked no argument commanded, "Leave here son. Go home. Run!"

The boy ran, frightened and stumbling again. The trees reached out to grab him, to drag him back to those holes. He heard the first shot. Putting hands over his ears, Szymon ran faster, but he couldn't keep out the sounds of gunfire, the murder that was tearing his country apart.

— • —

City Guardsman Dabrowski, chief police officer for the Biała Podlaska Voivodeship, including the village of Ossówka, thought he heard gunfire. The engine noise of his little four vehicle convoy might be playing tricks on his ears, but as he entered the village, he heard it again. His head snapped right to look out the passenger-side window in the direction of the sound. The headlights of one of the GAZ jeeps behind him caught a small boy sprinting across the field between the village and the forest. The police officer watched as the boy climbed over a fence, disappearing somewhere into the one road village. *We are too late*, he thought.

The convoy stopped in the middle of the village. Dabrowski exited his car and watched his men disembark from the two GAZ jeeps and the light truck behind him. Of his many policemen, he'd only been able to muster four trustworthy officers for this call. He'd been forced to contact the local army commander for more men. That had taken time, and worse, he didn't know how far he could trust the soldiers jumping from the truck.

As Poland descended further into chaos, Dabrowski knew the army would fracture, with some units supporting the Solidarity government, others the communist-dominated Defense Ministry, and still others pursuing personal objectives. He and the commander of the army detachments in this area sympathized with the communist elements, though neither were diehards. *Let's hope everyone can keep their personal politics to themselves and just do their duty tonight*, he thought.

Dabrowski stepped away from his car and looked up the village street. Their arrival in the town had not been quiet. The villagers, most in night clothes, were standing in half-opened doors and windows, peering out at the spectacle. *Almost all women*, the police officer realized. *Where are the men?* He gritted his teeth; he already knew the answer.

The disappearance of a soldier who came from this village yesterday afternoon had had Dabrowski nervous; then he'd gotten a phone call from an informer, who had since disappeared. That was when he knew he had to mobilize and stop the dissidents here in Ossówka. The guardsman shook his head and heaved a resigned sigh. This area was collapsing into the same cycle of violence and revenge that had engulfed so many other communities across the country over the past months. Dabrowski gave the order for his men to round up the villagers for questioning.

He hated that it had to be this way. *The post-communist government had so many advantages, but they squandered them by antagonizing the Soviets*, he thought. Faced with unexpected pressure from the east, the new Solidarity régime in Warsaw had failed to re-establish trust in the country's law enforcement after the travesties of martial law in the eighties. As institutions fractured, officers followed the guidance of whoever happened to control the local department, or simply acted as individuals in whatever capacity they saw fit. *As I am doing*, he thought.

Dabrowski watched as two soldiers approached a young woman wearing a long nightgown standing in a doorway. As the men drew near, rather than withdrawing as many of the other citizens had, she stepped forward and began shouting accusation at them. The soldiers were soon shouting back.

As other villagers looked on, the woman berated the soldiers. With a speedy jerk she grabbed the barrel of the nearest soldier's assault rifle. The man reached to secure his weapon as the woman yanked and in doing so a finger slipped into the trigger guard. Before Dabrowski could shout a warning, the street was lit by muzzle flashes and filled with the distinctive crack of rifle fire. The woman spun and fell onto the dirt road.

Villagers screamed or slammed their doors and retreated. Dabrowski thought he heard a masculine voice utter an anguished cry from the fields beyond. He turned to look just as the fiery, flower-shaped muzzle flash of rifle fire winked in the pasture. A hammer blow knocked him back against his car. His last sensation was hearing gunfire erupt all around him. Then his world went black.

1330 CET, Friday 27 November 1992
1230 Zulu
Ossówka, Biała Podlaska Voivodeship, Poland

Three weeks later, Jack Young stood in the muddy track that passed for a road running through the ghost village of Ossówka. Despite the heavy mist beading on the reporter's coat, Jack's head was uncovered as a mark of respect for the tragedy that had unfolded here: a bare head in the Catholic tradition of this country. Looking around at the empty houses that lined the street, the dark, pane-less windows, the shattered doors hanging off their hinges, Jack couldn't help but feel a sense of foreboding about where this story would lead.

Crossing the street until he was standing under the eaves of an abandoned home, grasping for some shelter from the wet, a fleeting thought crossed his mind that the village must have been a nice place to live. Not wealthy, by any stretch of the imagination, but small and cozy in the way that rural, tight-knit communities could be. Fishing his notebook out from inside his jacket, he flipped it open and reviewed his notes for completeness. He didn't want to come back to this place of death if he didn't need to.

A little boy, Szymon had been Jack's main source for piecing together the events of that terrible night three weeks ago. He had sat with the boy and his grandmother. *Babcia, he'd called her*, Jack remembered. Their farmhouse was quiet as they recounted the massacre through an interpreter. They were two of a small group of survivors.

The census official back in Biała Podlaska, told Jack that the population of Ossówka was, *had been*, just under four hundred. Jack couldn't be sure, but the village didn't seem to contain more than a few dozen shell-shocked people now. *Would this town ever be that nondescript, cozy place it once was?* Jack wondered.

Babcia recounted what she remembered of the massacre, how the soldiers began shooting, how the chief police officer—Dabrowski had been his name—fell dead in the middle of the street, other soldiers and guardsmen falling around him. She described how soldiers broke into homes, shooting the terrified inhabitants in their rage and fear. Eventually, more soldiers arrived from Biała Podlaska, and then the real killing began. The situation devolved from a running gun battle into a full-fledged massacre as the soldiers sought revenge for their fallen comrades. The gray-haired old woman had described it all in grisly, bitter detail. Her anger, *hatred*, Jack thought, was plain to see.

Nonetheless, Jack sensed there was more to *Babcia's* story. When the old woman finally finished, he looked at Szymon. The boy's haunted eyes had barely blinked during the entire interview, and he'd remained silent as a ghost. But when Jack's enquiring look gave him the opportunity to speak, the words spilled out of his young lips almost too quickly for the interpreter to translate, despite several attempts by his *babcia* to shush him.

"They shot my teacher," Szymon had said at one point, his voice wavering. "Why did they do that? Why did father let them do that? And the brothers, why do they hate each other so much?"

Jack, a professional reporter, was usually good at distancing himself from emotional connection with his sources. This little boy, though, in this damp, dead place had been so wronged that Jack couldn't help but empathize with him. Szymon's account of what occurred in the woods confirmed what the police in Biała Podlaska had said about why Dabrowski and the soldiers had come to Ossówka in the first place. The villagers weren't entirely innocent, a fact confirmed by the muddy shallow graves he'd found on a short walk into the woods. On the walk back across the field he unconsciously paused to wipe mud from his hiking boots, an act which evoked a fleeting realization in his literary mind. *The western world has wiped the mire of Eastern Europe off of our collective consciousness for decades, even centuries.*

That's why this is so ugly, Jack thought. There were no good guys, only victims of the hatred and geopolitical gamesmanship engulfing Poland. Jack liked to report on conflict because, deep down, he'd never moved past his love of the comic book superheroes of his childhood. Battles between good and evil to protect the weak. He found that he was always looking for heroes in his stories, and the villains they would fight. Situations like this reminded him that the world wasn't a piece of fiction. There were no camps of good and evil.

Flipping his notebook closed, Jack walked towards the car where his interpreter waited to take him back to Warsaw. He'd come looking for a story that exemplified the violence starting to rip Poland apart. He'd found it here in Ossówka. As he walked, he started to compose the closing lines he would submit, a closing that reflected his own dark mood after seeing firsthand how that conflict was turning brother against brother. *The Second World War grew out of Poland more than fifty-three years ago. Now, with every circular act of violence and reprisal spreading bloody vigilantism in the country's muddy streets, the Third could be taking root.*

PART II: AREA OF INTEREST

"Their drills were bloodless battles, their battles bloody drills."
—Flavius Josephus

 **CHAPTER 6**

0755 CST, Sunday 13 December 1992
1355 Zulu
Petawawa National Forest, north of CFB Petawawa, Ontario, Canada

T HE TWO HELICOPTERS threw up a swirling white cloud of ice crystals in the pink rays of morning light as they flared and descended into the small clearing deep in the Petawawa Garrison's wooded training area. The craft were Canadian CH-135s, copies of the venerable UH-1N Twin Huey, their two-bladed rotors beating the frigid air with a distinctive *thwack-thwack.* In unison, the pilots pulled back slightly on their collectives and dropped carefully through the icy cloud. The skids sank softly into the layer of snow that hadn't been blown away by the rotors' downdraft. The doors on both sides of the olive drab-painted choppers slid open with a bang on touchdown as more snow cascaded from the branches of surrounding trees, adding to the snowy vortex.

Four men in parkas with white covers and woodland pattern camouflage pants jumped out of each helicopter. One man on each side ran out three paces hunched over beneath the spinning blades before dropping into a prone firing position and aiming his black carbine away from the aircraft. The others yanked rucksacks and bundled skis out of the cargo compartments and into the blowing snow. The last bundle hit the ground just as the helicopters' engines increased to a high-pitched roar. The craft lifted upward, gently at first as the pilots cleared the men on the ground, then more rapidly as the Hueys' noses tilted downward, accelerating the helicopters forward. Elapsed time on the ground for the birds had been about twenty-five seconds.

Sergeant David Strong pulled himself up to a kneeling firing position as the roar and violence of the downdraft gave way to the rhythmic *thwack-thwack* of receding rotors. He watched the aircraft clear the evergreens at the edge of the field and bank right. In moments they were out of sight, the sound quickly fading. After the noise, the silence of the forest was almost deafening, and the sergeant experienced the now-familiar loneliness of being left behind in remote places. He breathed it in as he took in the scene around him. The snowy clearing was enclosed in a palisade of dark trees. Above the treetops the southeast sky was glowing indigo with the sunrise, while the northern and western skies maintained the deep blue of night.

Strong twisted to look back over his shoulder. The other three members of his team were also up and kneeling, training their weapons towards the four points of the compass and stealing quick glances back at their leader. In the middle of their diamond was the equipment. Thirty meters away the other quartet knelt in their own diamond formation. The sergeant caught the eye of one of his team, the hulking Master Corporal Roy, and after a silent hand signal the man got up, moved to the center and retrieved his rucksack and skis before returning to his post in the small perimeter. The other two did the same, moving one at a time in their pre-rehearsed order to haul their equipment back to their posts. Finally, Strong moved back and grabbed his own pack.

Once each man had donned his rucksack and snowshoes, skis lashed vertically along the sides of their packs, Strong gave another hand signal. The team stood up in silent unison and began jogging, still in their loose diamond formation, towards the nearby tree line. To his right the sergeant could see the other team doing the same, cutting a parallel course towards the protection of the trees. They passed from the growing morning light of the clearing into the soft semidarkness of the forest, where, after several dozen meters, they linked up with the four men of the other group. After another hand signal the men dropped their rucks into the snow and knelt. Six of the soldiers formed a single oval perimeter while Strong and the other team leader moved to the center.

The two knelt and dropped their packs in the middle of the perimeter. The other man, Colour Sergeant Edwards of 22 Special Air Service Regiment, spoke the first words since they had exited the helicopters. "Well," he said in a deep voice, betraying faint traces of a Cockney accent, "shouldn't we be going?"

"Change our dress first, eh?" responded Sergeant Strong in his softer Canadian dialect. "We need to strip down for movement and adjust our camouflage."

"Adjust it 'ow?" asked the Brit.

"Woodland pattern on top, white pants," came David's quiet response.

"Why's that, mate?" asked Edwards. The British SAS men were conducting a week of cold weather familiarization with Strong's newly-forming Canadian Joint Task Force 2. The Canadian special operations unit would officially stand up next April, and a troop of the SAS Regiment's D Squadron was here for several weeks to assist with the activation. The Canadian sergeant was impressed by the British NCO's willingness to ask questions and learn, despite the brash front that the man put up to the world. Both groups of elite soldiers were learning.

"White on top, green on bottom was good for the low brush of the clearing," explained Strong, patiently, "but in the trees, we'll blend in better with it reversed. You'll see. We'll have to stop and change again for the leg of the route that goes along the lakeshore."

Edwards nodded. Uniform adjustments were a normal part of small unit infantry movements. He was on this training patrol to learn the nuances of his craft that were unique to cold, snowy environments. The two leaders went to their respective teams and quietly gave the order. One at a time each man retrieved and donned his white pants cover and stuffed the heavy parka into his ruck, then strapped the snowshoes on the back of their rucksack with bungee cords.

Several of the combined patrol were beginning to shiver. The ambient temperature was just a couple of degrees below freezing, but their worn clothing was light in anticipation of the movement ahead. A hand signal from Strong brought them to their feet. Each shouldered his pack and snapped on skis, then slung his weapon tight across his chest so it would not interfere with the poles but could still be brought up to a firing position at a moment's notice.

Corporal Tenny, demolition expert for the Canadian team, took point, and the eight men skied into a single file: Canadians in front, Brits behind, five meters between each soldier. They had nearly thirty kilometers ahead of them. Tenny shot a quick bearing with a compass lashed to his webbing, then started south at a moderate pace.

After several minutes Sergeant Strong skied up until he was following just behind Tenny, skiing in his subordinate's tracks. His patrol had only been together for a few days as JTF 2 slowly coalesced at their new Dwyer Hill facility northwest of Ottawa. Strong hadn't really gotten to know the three other men he would lead yet. *Several hours skiing through the woods should fix that*, he thought, looking forward to the chance to both converse with his men and observe their stamina. He engaged Tenny in quiet conversation as they glided through the evergreens, asking the other man about his family, interests, hobbies, the usual.

Tenny was the youngest member of the team, displaying the quick wits and cockiness of his youth. He was also single, but with a girlfriend back in Ottawa. He seemed to exhibit the pattern of one failed relationship after another, common to many elite soldiers. Strong got the impression that this latest relationship was already on the rocks. Professionally, Tenny was familiar with all manner of explosives and the various creative ways in which they could be employed to solve almost any problem, and he so far hadn't been shy to suggest such solutions in their patrol planning. *If all you have is a hammer,* Strong thought with a smirk.

Satisfied that he'd gotten some background on his youngest patrol member, David dropped back five meters until he was near to his radioman, Corporal Brown. Brown was a fast talker, and it didn't take much prodding for Strong to learn from the man's staccato prose about his conflicted identity. Brown was Inuit on his mother's side but his father was a hard-drinking miner in the Northwest Territories. He wasn't shy about which of his two estranged parents he loved more, and David learned after a few minutes of conversation that Brown liked to be called Clark as a nod to the Inuit name his mother had given him: Aclark. Issues of parenting seemed to be weighing heavily on the radioman, as David knew already that Brown was newly married with a kid on the way. Strong wasn't sure yet which event had come first: the marriage or the pregnancy. Brown continued from one subject to the next, not waiting for his sergeant to offer either questions or comment. *I hope he can be more concise on the radio*, Strong thought as he worked to extract himself from this conversation and drop back again to his last patrol member, the hulking, shave-headed team medic, Master Corporal Roy.

Felix Roy was a quiet giant. He'd spoken the least of any of them in the few hectic days they'd been together. The master corporal was a Québécois, *that* David had gleaned from the thick French-Canadian accent that seasoned Roy's few words. The bigger man responded to Strong's queries with mostly monosyllabic grunts as they skied one behind the other, but David learned that his team's medic was married to his high school sweetheart, that they had four children together, David had nearly choked at this revelation, and that he had done his previous service, unhappily, with the Canadian Airborne Regiment.

Despite the big man's thriftiness with words, David felt the most drawn to Roy among the three members of his patrol. The hulking, almost brooding quiet wasn't unfriendliness. Rather, the man was calm, self-assured, patient, highly competent, and obviously very happy with his home life. The sergeant left the conversation feeling comforted and surprisingly envious. He'd have to endeavor to turn that envy into respect. Instinctively David ended the conversation and skied to the front of the file to take point from Tenny.

David had always pushed himself harder than anyone else, seeking greater challenges after each new accomplishment. He hungered for acclaim. Maybe his parents, good people though they were, had failed through apathy or absent-mindedness to praise him growing up, or maybe it was just innate. Strong only knew that he lived for the accolades he earned in each new job, endorsements became all the more satisfying as his accomplishments became more impressive. This addiction to approval drove him ever onward. Trying out for JTF 2 had followed a very successful tour leading a reconnaissance section of the 3rd Battalion, Princess Patricia's Canadian Light Infantry out west in Calgary. He'd finished at the top of the grueling selection course to earn this new role in his country's most elite unit. Now his job was to pull himself and the three other members of his patrol together into a cohesive team. He skied harder.

They continued through the forest, eschewing the frequent fire breaks and dirt roads that crisscrossed the woods. As the sun rose higher in the southeastern sky the temperature crept above the freezing point. The snow began to stick to their skis, making their progress under eighty pounds of equipment punishing.

Kilometers passed, and the only sound in Sergeant Strong's ears was the gently rhythmic *swish-swish* of his skis. David looked over his shoulder as the patrol approached their first navigation checkpoint. Tenny and Brown both had grimaces on their sweaty faces, apparently unhappy with the pace set by their leader. Roy's face, further back, was impassive, harder to read. Behind him, the Brits' file was starting to stretch out some. *Not so used to skiing, eh?* thought David. He was sweating as well, around his belt and under his webbing, but he knew that he could march any of them into the ground.

They reached the navigation point and a hand signal sent the patrol silently gliding into a cigar-shaped perimeter where they unclipped their skis and knelt. As the men took turns taking pulls of water from their green plastic canteens, Strong met the SAS patrol leader, Edwards, at the center of the formation. The Brit's face was streaked with sweat and he too looked less than pleased. He confirmed the impression with his first words: "Mate, you're the expert in this sort o' thing, but all this sweat can be a problem, as cold as it is out 'ere, can't it?"

"Cold?" answered the Canadian with a smile. "It's not even below freezing today. We'll do this again in a couple months and it'll be thirty below."

"All the same," came Edwards' measured response, "this ain't selection any more, chum. For us, or for your blokes either. You need to watch your pace so you've got some juice left for the show. You can dehydrate in the cold, too, you know."

David knew the Brit was right. It took quite a bit of self-assurance for someone as competitive as Edwards to recommend a slower pace. *But he has years of experience in the world's most renowned special forces community*, thought David. *He's got nothing to prove to us.* If Strong was going to hone the sort of team that would confirm to his superiors, and more importantly to himself, that he was every bit as worthy to be in the same class as men like Edwards, then he needed to set the tone early and keep the pressure on. *Of course*, he admitted to himself, *working the men into a heavy sweat on the opening leg of a long cold weather march would be a major mistake on a real mission.*

"I take your meaning," David answered with a curt nod that ended with him looking down. "Brown will take point for the next leg. We don't need to change undershirts until we stop for a longer period. I'll check in with November Zero One," that was the exercise control center's radio call sign, "and we can be moving again in five minutes, eh?"

Edwards nodded and both leaders moved back to their teams. Brown made contact with the headquarters via the radio in his ruck, relaying the patrol's position and status. While Brown was speaking quietly into his handset, David pulled out his map and re-checked their position on the route. They had traveled about a third of the distance, making better time than they'd planned. David hated making mistakes and berated himself silently for pushing too fast.

Brown led the team along a lake full of dark water not yet frozen over. The patrol paused to again reverse their camouflage pattern to better blend in with the rocks and low vegetation near the shore. Over the next several hours, each member of the patrol, Canadian and British, took their turn at point, navigating the group through woods and around clearings and icy ponds. The combined British-Canadian team ended their march, skiing out of the forest and hand-railing a dirt road into one of CFB Petawawa's firing ranges.

Members of what would become the JTF 2 headquarters troop were standing by at the firing lanes with a diverse array of weapons laid out on sandbags, ready for use. Strong and Edwards had arranged during their planning session for the firearms to be pre-positioned here. They were mostly of Soviet origin and included various models of the AK rifle, RPK light and PKM general purpose machineguns, and even a heavy tripod-mounted DShK machinegun, called a *dushka* by westerners.

The patrol "went admin" as they entered the range area, dispensing with the tactical patrolling techniques they had been practicing up to this point. They skied up to an open-sided shed at the rear of the range and cached their rucksacks, skis and weapons in two neat rows, massaging their shoulder where the straps had been cutting in for the past several hours. Their legs wouldn't get a rest for a while yet.

The two leaders gathered their men around and explained the exercise. It was a simple weapons familiarization, made more difficult by their fatigue. The men would pair off, one Brit with one Canadian, and cycle through each station, disassembling, reassembling, and then engaging targets with the various weapons. The men went back to their rucks, changed their sweaty undershirts and added layers against the cold, then paired off and fanned out towards the firing line.

An olive drab painted VW Iltis jeep crunched up the gravel access road towards the firing lanes. Another player in this tactical exercise was not expected. Strong could see the lanky frame of the JTF 2 sergeant major in the driver's seat. Next to him was his counterpart, the sergeant major of the visiting SAS troop. *Excellent*, thought David, *a chance to show the leadership how well we've prepared.* The Iltis came to a halt near the shed and the two senior warrant officers swung themselves out of the doorless vehicle. Smiling and apparently joking with each other, they walked towards Strong and Edwards.

Sergeant Strong greeted his superiors, excited for the opportunity to show off his team, then turned and waved towards Brown and one of the SAS troopers. The two men were walking up to the big DShK, its bulbous flash suppressor capping the end of a meter-long barrel. Each man was trained with the weapon in front of him, but weapons familiarization was a highly perishable skill, particularly on a rarely seen heavy firearm like this one. Strong followed the two men over to the firing position, the other leaders in tow.

Brown dove right into his task, removing the machinegun from its tripod with his SAS companion's help and field stripping the weapon until its parts were all laid out on a poncho to one side of the firing post. David was gratified by Brown's performance, but he winced as the younger man progressed through the reassembly process. Strong saw him forget to re-insert a key pin as he fed the gas return back into the receiver. The British soldier, kneeling next to Brown, caught the mistake and pointed it out. The Canadian swore, embarrassed, and pulled the return back out, replaced the pin, then reinserted the tube.

Soon the two men had the machinegun up on its tall spider-like tripod and were loading the belt of huge linked 12.7-millimeter rounds from a green metal ammunition box. The incident with the pin had been a minor slip up, but Strong couldn't help feeling embarrassed at his team member's performance. *I should have scheduled some more hands-on time with these,* he berated himself, *Both sergeants major watching*! It was ridiculous to feel this way, and David knew it. Casual glances at the two sergeants major didn't reveal if they'd noticed Brown's mistake. Regardless, Strong made a mental note to schedule some more familiarization with the armory sergeant upon their return to Dwyer Hill.

Rounds exploded from weapons up and down the firing line, first the rapid single *cracks* of the AKs, then the staccato *bangs* of the lighter machineguns. Finally, Brown and his companion put the DShK into operation. The big rounds roared out of the barrel, sending tracers arcing downrange towards the targets more than a quarter mile distant. In seconds all the targets were down and each pair of commandos unloaded their weapon before rotating to the next station.

Strong walked over to Edwards and both of them moved to the AK-74 station together. As David picked up the rifle, a smaller caliber version of the venerable -47, Edwards spoke in his cockney that felt like it should be confrontational but came across as measured and calm. "You can't let it get to you, mate," he said softly enough that the two sergeants major a dozen meters away wouldn't hear.

"Can't let what get to me?" asked the Canadian in an equally quiet voice, seating a magazine in the Russian assault rifle. He hadn't thought his embarrassment had been visible to anyone, nor that the British colour sergeant could read him so easily.

"Ev'ry little thing that goes sideways," Edwards responded. "I've been watching you today. From one professional to another, if you let yourself dwell on every mistake, you'll never make it. You'll burn yourself out, and you'll burn your chaps out too."

David brought the rifle up to his shoulder, sighted down the barrel at a target about one hundred and fifty meters away, and squeezed off two rounds in quick succession. The target rotated down with at least one impact. David switched fire to another, more distant target, and dropped that one with two rounds as well, then worked his way through the other green silhouettes in a similarly efficient fashion. Finished, he safed the weapon and looked at Edwards.

"What if we'd been in a firefight, eh? Screwing up with a crew-served weapon could be the difference between winning and being overrun."

"I'm not talking about yer blokes, mate. Be 'ard on 'em. You need to be. But you need to be 'ard on 'em so they get better, not so you can feel fulla yerself because they're better. If yer using yer blokes to scratch some need for personal fulfillment," he shook his head. "They're smart. They'll cop to it right quick. Savvy?" Edwards had quickly cut through to David's heart of hearts. It *was* all for himself, not his men, and that had always troubled him. He looked back to see if the sergeants major had seen his marksmanship demonstration. To his disappointment they were moving off along the rest of the firing line, watching the others operate the foreign weapons.

David turned, brought the weapon back up, flicked off the safety catch again and emptied the remainder of the thirty-round magazine in a series of double shots, knocking the targets down as soon as they came back up. When the rifle's action clicked open, Edwards took the weapon from him, seated a fresh mag, and matched Strong's performance, knocking down one target after another. As the last round was fired, Edward's empty magazine locking the AK's action to the rear, the older Brit turned to David and went on. "Look, mate," he said in a friendly tone, "I saw some action last year in Iraq, y'know? I was with 2 Para in the Falklands too and I've done my bit in Northern Ireland. I've seen all manner of sergeants, and yer a good one. I see a lot of me in ya, and yer gonna do fine. But ye've got to understand that this job is about *them*," he cocked his head towards the other six men on the lanes, "and not about *you*."

David nodded, not quite agreeing. He knew the man was generally right, but there were different leadership styles and his had been effective and rewarding so far. He saw the two sergeants major walking back to their Iltis, apparently moving on to observe one of the other combined patrols. Strong felt he'd missed an opportunity to impress them, show them how competently he'd organized his team in some professional conversation. Not wanting to continue the conversation with Edwards, the Canadian nodded and changed the subject. "The demo range is just a couple clicks down the road from here. When we're done we can pick up and move there in less than thirty minutes. I hear your man can make C4 and det cord sing, eh?" he asked.

They would have the opportunity to play with explosives until darkness, practicing building all manner of charges to destroy doors, breach walls, and mangle equipment, before moving on to the day's closing exercise, setting a concealed patrol base for the night.

"He can at that," affirmed Edwards. "But see 'ere, what's this about some nippy weather coming in later tonight? We going to be uncomfortable?"

"Nippy?" responded Strong with a grin. "It's going to be downright cold! We've got a strong cold front coming through that's going to drop temps down to negative twenty or so. Snow too."

The Brit grimaced. "Bloody 'ell, mate. I've been in Norway for some exercises, but ain't never spent the night out in weather *that* cold."

Strong's grin grew bigger. "We do it all the time." *We've still got some things to show you Brits, too*, thought Strong, pleased. He liked Edwards, but having the SAS come in to show the Canadians how the special ops thing was done grated on his ego. It would feel good to watch them struggle through the frigid night alongside the more cold-hardened Canadians. *Wars aren't always fought in nice weather, after all.*

 **CHAPTER 7**

1335 MSK, Monday 4 January 1993
1035 Zulu
Central Committee Building, 4 Staraya Square, Moscow,
Russian Soviet Federative Socialist Republic

S NOW WAS FALLING gently on *Staraya Ploshad*, literally translated as "Old Square," the broad boulevard that stretched away in either direction beneath the thick window panes of the top-floor presidential office suite. President of the Soviet Union Pavel Ivanovich Medvedev sipped tea from a delicate glass tumbler set in a silver holder as he watched the citizens of Moscow stroll and play in the park below. The tea was brewed in the manner Russians liked it: from a traditional *samovar*, hot and strong. Pavel savored the contrast of the warm bittersweet liquid and the winter scene before him.

Below, Muscovites were carrying on as they had for decades, centuries, enjoying the winter weather as best they could. Lovers strolled arm-in-arm in their heavy coats and fur hats. Old *babushkas* stood here and there with their cloth shopping bags, watching and snapping at the children running about throwing snowballs and doing what children everywhere do in the snow. Men who recognized each other stopped to discuss the weather, or politics, or more likely, hockey. The snow was, ironically, able to crack the typically dour Russian public persona. The Soviet president felt comforted by the scene. *We*

Russians cannot be brought low by the long winter, he thought with pride, *we are brought together by it.*

Still, winter had been hard on the city this year. The economic chaos unleashed by his predecessor's reforms, Medvedev's own political changes, and most importantly, the sanctions imposed by the west over the Polish situation had translated into hardship for the Soviet people. Food shortages had troubled the capital this winter. Meat, eggs, and fresh vegetables had all been in shorter supply than was normal for the winter months. Pavel knew from reports that even staples like cheese and tea had been scarce. Ordinary Muscovites walked the streets with cloth bags tucked in their pockets so that they would be ready to join a queue for some prized food item should it form during their day. Just a few days ago, from his limousine driving out of the city down the broad *Profsoyuznaya Ulitsa*, he had looked out his window to see a man outside an apartment block pull a pig carcass out of the trunk of his decrepit Volga automobile, throw the thing onto the hood, and begin lopping off frozen chunks of meat, offering them to the highest passing bidder. *This is no way for citizens living in the capital of one of the world's two superpowers to live*, Medvedev had raged and the image still stung. He was only the second president of the Soviet Union, his deceased predecessor being the first. If the economic encirclement of his country worsened Medvedev could easily be the last.

The western governments were forcing these conditions on his beloved country out of fear. *They'll continue to attack us, and when we finally take measures to ensure the safety of our borders, borders these westerners have invaded again and again for centuries, they will use their fortuitous geography to strangle us.* Pavel realized he was gripping the metal handle of his teacup so hard that he was pressing into his knuckle. He relaxed the pressure, took another sip of tea, and calmed himself.

The Soviet president refocused himself on the problem. The USSR *could* resurrect itself economically, of that he was sure. Much to the chagrin of many of the original coup plotters, Medvedev had proved to be no hardline communist. He was not beholden to the disastrous ideologies and policies that had hampered his country for so long, but neither was he above using the structure and influence of the Communist Party, headquartered in this very building, to achieve his ends. He'd continued many of the common-sense reforms of his predecessor, while reining in much of the attendant chaos that was creeping in prior to his ascendance. His currency reforms were particularly successful, heading off massive inflation the previous autumn. *None of it means anything if the west will not trade with us, if they continue to cut us off from the resources, finances, and markets we need*, Medvedev knew.

It all goes back to Poland for them, he thought bitterly. *Can they not see? As long as a reunited Germany remains part of NATO, we cannot simply withdraw from Central Europe and allow them to roll up to our frontier unmolested once again. Do they not remember what the Germans and the rest of Europe did to us twice this century?* Poland, in the midst of tearing itself apart from within, was ripe for interference. Medvedev's administration had been offering support—moral, financial, and physical—to the elements in Poland who were friendly towards his regime in Moscow. Without this intrusion, Poland would no doubt be on a path to stability and even prosperity today, but also on a path towards alliance with the west, and that was something that Medvedev could not, and would not, tolerate.

For western powers the issue was Poland, but for Medvedev the crux was the re-united Germany. *Twenty million of our people dead, and they expect us to just sit back and trust that the Germans won't threaten us once again, this time from behind the Americans' nuclear shield?* Pavel's father had been a tanker in the Great Patriotic War, had fought under Zhukov as the commander of a T-34 tank company. He'd fought almost to the gates of Berlin before being killed assaulting the Seelow Heights in the closing days of battle. Pavel had been old enough to remember the tearful anguish with which his mother received the news. He had never forgotten nor forgiven his nation's enemies for what they had done to his country, his family. *Allowing Germany to reunite was the greatest mistake my predecessor made, especially after he announced that he would not demand they withdraw from NATO as a precondition.*

The tea was cooling now. Pavel felt his breathing come easier as he refocused his eye on the people strolling and playing in the park below. Snow was falling gently, little wisps that barely made it to ground. On the far side of the boulevard, Pavel noticed a family dressed in colorful western-looking winter clothing. *Americans.* They were becoming less common in the city after the chaotic days of the last few years. Businessmen, tourists, missionaries had all flooded into Moscow and taken up residence when it appeared the Soviet regime was tottering. A whole community of Protestant missionaries had settled down in the southern part of the city. The KGB had quietly looked into them to see if they could be American intelligence agents, but the conclusion was that they were no threat. The new KGB chairman reported, as far as his Bureau could determine, that the Americans had all but abandoned human spying in the USSR over the past year.

The president's reflections were interrupted by a soft rap on the wood-paneled door. He turned and set his tea on the corner of his desk, an executive sized monstrosity stained with a shiny dark lacquer. "Enter," he commanded.

The door cracked and his secretary, a thin, gray-haired woman in her fifties, announced, "Marshal Rosla is here to see you, sir."

"Excellent! Please send him in," said Medvedev, his mood brightening. *One more* Politburo *vote in my pocket.*

The secretary stepped back into the foyer and in her place Marshal Aleksandr Rosla, scourge of the wayward Baltic Republics and pacifier of the Ukraine, strode confidently through the door and into the president's office, peaked hat under his arm. The soldier walked directly up to within three paces of Medvedev's desk and halted, braced at attention.

Pavel took a moment to look at his new defense minister. In many ways the man was a younger image of himself. Barrel-chested under his olive drab tunic with its rows upon rows of ribbons, his waist was just beginning to tell the tale of too many unfiltered cigarettes and too much cheap vodka, the daily diet of the Russian "Everyman." His hair was jet black and swept back, his facial features almost Asiatic. Intense, dark eyes made him look like a man who had determined to put his head through a brick wall, and was about to do it. Satisfied, Medvedev walked around his desk and took the soldier's hand.

"Welcome, welcome, Marshal," Pavel said as he pumped Rosla's hand once in a distinctly Russian handshake. "I am very pleased to have you in the Politburo. Your accomplishments and abilities have preceded you."

"Thank you, *tovarich* President," responded the marshal, "that is kind of you to say."

"Nonsense!" responded Medvedev. "You have more than earned your place in the government. Your operation against the dissidents in the Baltic republics was masterful, and your handling of the Ukrainian mess demonstrated keen political acumen. I need men like you working for the security of Russia… excuse me…for the security of the Soviet Union. Please, please," Medvedev indicated a sitting area to one side of the room, "be seated. Let us talk."

The two men moved to a set of plush leather chairs arranged around a low coffee table and sat. Medvedev noted that Rosla maintained a ramrod posture even when seated. *A soldier's soldier.*

"Marshal," the president began, "I like to know the members of my government as people. Tell me about your military career before we sent you to save the Soviet Union from those counter-revolutionaries in the Baltics." Pavel knew much of the man's story already, but he wanted to see how Rosla told it himself.

"*Tovarich* President—"

"Please, Marshal," interrupted the older man, "in private let us dispense with this *tovarich* business. I have no time for that nonsense. Many of the old Party's ideas and policies have led us to near-ruin and we cannot be tied to them. Pavel Ivanovich will do."

"Very well…Pavel Ivanovich." The soldier looked somewhat uncomfortable using his president's name. "I've spent almost my entire time in the Red Army with the *desantniki*. I studied at Ryazan School for airborne troops in my youth and at Frunze after that. I have commanded troops at all levels. I saw action several times in Afghanistan and then in the Caucasus, and you know of my activities in the Baltics and the Ukraine. I've tried my best to serve the interests of my country at every level."

"Indeed," responded Pavel. *Understated with his exploits.* Medvedev knew for a fact that Rosla had done far more than just "see action" in Afghanistan. He had been one of the Soviet Union's most effective battalion, and then regimental, commanders early on in that long, sad conflict. He had been particularly known for his innovative tactics and bold, even reckless operations.

"Aleksandr Ivanovich," Medvedev changed the subject, "I must tell you that I harbored doubts about the effectiveness of your predecessor. The man meant well, but he was old, and I don't believe he had the stamina that your new job requires. I need clear analysis from the ministers in my government, and I believe you can provide this. So, tell me, Marshal, are our armed forces prepared to repel an attack from NATO?" *Best to ask the hard question now, instead of hearing the answer in front of the whole Politburo.*

Rosla sat back in his chair, thinking. After a pause he spoke: "That is not a simple question, Pavel Ivanovich," Rosla answered carefully. "What sort of attack? Under what circumstances? With what weapons? I do not wish to equivocate, but the western success in Iraq two years ago was very troubling. Their equipment and training are formidable."

"To answer one of your questions," Medvedev responded, a serious note creeping into his voice, "so that there is no misunderstanding between us, I am asking about an attack using what the westerners call 'conventional' weapons. As long as I am President of the Soviet Union, our country will not be the first to use special weapons, either atomic or chemical. Down *that* road lies only the destruction of our great country, an outcome I have dedicated my life to prevent. We will maintain our deterrent force to guard against a western attack of this kind, but I will not authorize special weapons use under any but the most catastrophic circumstances. Is my position clear to you?"

Rosla looked surprised, but recovered quickly and nodded.

"Good," Medvedev went on, "now, please, your assessment of our military position with regards to NATO."

Rosla nodded again, and began. "Your military reforms have done much to even the overall balance, Pavel Ivanovich. Two years ago, we had entire units digging for potatoes in the fields just so the soldiers could eat. Today we are in a vastly improved situation, and for that I thank you. But there is much work still to be done, and I thank you too for giving me the opportunity to do it."

Medvedev nodded, acknowledging the compliment.

Rosla went on, "Our army's position in Czechoslovakia is powerful, but tenuous. Our lines of supply are strained and vulnerable to attacks from bandits operating in Poland. If NATO gains control in that country, our position in Central Europe could become untenable. If that occurs, NATO will be beyond the Vistula, directly on our frontier, and free to prepare one of their dangerous, set-piece, multi-corps attacks if they so choose, as they did in Iraq. Repelling a well-prepared invasion of that scale on our homeland would be…difficult."

Difficult without the use of special weapons, the Soviet president noted Rosla's omission. Still, Medvedev was impressed. *A lesser man would try to establish his influence by emphasizing the strength of the ministry he leads.* Medvedev was pleased, and he let himself show it by nodding in agreement. He needed men that were not only effective, but honest.

"So," the president probed, "how does our nation prevent such an eventuality?"

Now the marshal leaned forward and spoke earnestly. "Pavel Ivanovich, I would hope that the answer to that question lies with the Foreign Ministry, not mine. But regardless, NATO *cannot* be allowed to establish themselves in Poland."

Medvedev nodded, then said, "Marshal, you will see in the Politburo meeting in a few minutes that you and I are of the same mind, that we are taking material steps to prevent just such an eventuality."

The president paused before broaching the next subject. "However, if the worst happens and war with the west becomes necessary, what are your thoughts on how it should be fought?"

A smile turned one side of the soldier's mouth upward. "My thoughts on that subject will no doubt dismay my colleagues in the tank and motorized rifle forces," Rosla said.

"How so?" asked Pavel, intrigued.

"My thinking is colored by my career in the *desant* troops," Rosla explained. "We traditionally work much more closely with our air and naval components. My view is that we have concentrated too much on the central front at the expense of the strategic flanks. I agree wholeheartedly with our historical conclusions that we must fight on the offensive whenever and wherever possible. If the worst were to happen and war with NATO became necessary, I have ideas about how the new geopolitical situation could allow us to economize our forces on the main front so that we could hit our enemies at their more vulnerable points."

"And where are those?" Medvedev queried. Though not a soldier himself, military strategy fascinated him. That the younger man was willing to think creatively excited him.

"When I say strategic flanks, I am speaking specifically of the areas around the Arctic and the Black Sea. The northern flank is the more difficult, but offers the greatest rewards."

"Go on," Medvedev encouraged.

Rosla did, outlining in broad terms how the altered situation in Europe offered intriguing possibilities in the event of hostilities with NATO.

"I can see how your brethren from our armored troops may take issue with your concepts, Aleksandr Ivanovich," Medvedev said, nodding in agreement, "but your thinking is sound, I think. Instruct *Stavka* to start making plans along these lines...just in case."

There was a rap at the door and Medvedev responded with a "*Da?*"

His gray-haired secretary opened the door and softly announced, "*Tovarich* President, the interior minister is here."

Pavel's face brightened. "Ah, yes," he said, "send him in."

Oleg Drugov breezed through the heavy double door and into the presidential office suite. Medvedev could see how easily people could overlook his friend's physical appearance, *Nevertheless, his small frame camouflages an impressive and ruthless intellect*, Medvedev thought. *The opposition members of the Politburo underestimate him at their peril.*

"*Dobre denh*, Pavel Ivanovich," Drugov greeted his president.

"Good day to you, Oleg Borisovich," Pavel returned the greeting before gesturing to Rosla and saying, "You have met the new member of my government?"

"Not officially, no," Drugov said, taking a step towards Rosla and offering his hand. The big soldier took it, and the two men eyed each other as they shook. *Each is trying to judge the measure of the other*, Pavel thought, noting that the handshake lasted just a beat longer than needed.

"I am pleased to meet you, *tovarich* Interior Minister," Rosla said after the barely perceptible pause. "The support of your ministry's OMON teams was most helpful in our campaign to crush the dissidents outside Kiev last summer."

Drugov nodded acknowledgement, then said, "Think nothing of it, *tovarich* Defense Minister. From what I hear, you and your forces did the real work."

Medvedev smiled. He thought he could see an alliance beginning to form between these two, one of whom he knew was eminently capable and loyal, and the other he believed to be as well. The sight pleased him.

The gray-haired secretary rapped at the door again.

"The Politburo is assembled in the meeting room, sir," she announced. "Five minutes until the conference is scheduled to start."

"Thank you, Irina," responded the president. Then he turned to his interior minister and his new defense minister. "Should we be going?"

The three men walked out of the presidential offices and down a hallway decorated with the heroic paintings of socialist workers and soldiers gazing ahead confidently at whatever challenges lay on the horizon. Two uniformed KGB officers standing outside the Central Committee conference room straightened to attention and one turned to open the heavy wooden doors as they approached. The Soviet president swept into the room; here he was also the Chairman of the Politburo, the true ruling council of the USSR. His gait and posture radiated assurance and authority as he surveyed the scene.

The principal members of the Politburo sat around a large conference table, while their various aides and staff members sat quietly in chairs behind them along the ornate walls of the large room. Oleg Drugov moved around the table to take his seat. The position of interior minister had become vacant after the previous minister suffered a mental breakdown and attempted suicide shortly after the coup. *Who better than Oleg to fill it?* Another close ally, Anton Laskin, took the helm of the KGB after the previous chairman, the original leader of the Emergency Committee, was caught dabbling in corrupt business dealings with the west to line his own pockets. Pavel offered the man a quiet retirement or a very public trial, and the chairman wisely chose the former. All in all, Medvedev now directly controlled more than two thirds of the votes in this room, and votes in this room were the only ones that really mattered.

Medvedev's allies on the Politburo were no mere sycophants, however. He'd hand-picked each one based on their proven accomplishments. Thanks to their abilities, the Soviet government was functioning more efficiently than it had in decades. They were younger, more energetic, more open to creative thinking than the old generation they replaced. Most importantly, they were loyal to Pavel and his vision for the USSR's place in the world.

Pavel's eye came to rest at the end of the table. Opposite his own seat sat the scowling face of one of the few remaining original members of Emergency Committee: Vice President of the Soviet Union. The man was a true believer in world socialism, so much so that Pavel had as of yet been unable to find a true weakness in him that could be exploited to force him out of office. *Well,*

I have marginalized him and those who think like he does. That will have to do for now, Pavel soothed himself.

Rosla, unprompted, walked around the side of the table to the defense minister's chair, about half-way down, and sat. Medvedev remained standing for the moment behind his seat at the head of the table.

"Welcome, gentlemen," he began. "Thank you for being here today. Allow me to introduce someone most of you have met and all of you have heard of, the newest member of our committee: Minister of Defense, Marshal of the Soviet Union Alexandr Ivanovich Rosla!"

Polite applause filled the chamber. Rosla acknowledged the welcome with a polite nod of his head.

Medvedev sat, opened the folder in front of him, and called the Politburo meeting to order. "*Tovarichi*," Medvedev began with a subtle inside joke, knowing that his allies in the room despised the socialist moniker almost as much as he, "our agenda for today's meeting will cover NATO's continued rejection of our demand that the united Germany withdraw from their alliance, the situation in Eastern Europe in general, and from Poland in particular. We will conclude with a decision and vote on how to proceed on the Polish question."

Heads nodded around the table.

"Foreign Minister?" Medvedev prompted, addressing his hand-picked chief diplomat, Georgy Vasilevich Garin. "Please, your report on the German issue."

The veteran diplomat looked down at his folio and began his remarks. "Germany and the NATO Council continue to rebuff our arguments that, with Germany united we should discuss dissolving both NATO and the Warsaw Pact, or at least that Germany should withdraw from the NATO alliance…" Garin continued for several minutes, detailing German attempts at conciliation, *Feigned, no doubt*, Medvedev thought. There were broader western claims that NATO was a *defensive* alliance, and thus not a threat to the Soviet Union. *We have heard that before*, Pavel thought, darkly.

"To conclude," continued Garin, "we have made no substantive progress in our efforts to mitigate the German threat, and have garnered significant opposition from the west, both diplomatic and economic, due to our perceived involvement in the Polish conflict."

Everyone around the table knew that Russian involvement was far more than "perceived," but appearances had to be maintained.

"Do none of them remember what the Germans did to us, to everyone in Europe, just fifty years ago?" Medvedev asked rhetorically, heat in his tone. "Twenty million Soviet citizens dead! The heartland of our country in ruins! And they have the temerity to try to punish us for protecting ourselves from another such catastrophe?"

The foreign minister remained silent, looking at his president.

"Thank you, Georgy Vasilevich," Medvedev said, more calmly. "Now, what of the situation in Poland?"

Garin went on, "The parties in Poland that are friendly to us are losing ground, despite our moral and material support." The man licked his lips before continuing, "The Pope's statement supporting Warsaw's Solidarity regime two weeks ago may prove decisive. NATO has not officially taken a position on the conflict but individual states, specifically Britain, France, and Belgium, have offered political and economic support to the Solidarity regime."

"What of the Germans?" asked Medvedev.

"So far nothing but statements in support of a peaceful resolution to the conflict," answered Garin, who managed to keep any emotion out of his voice.

Of course, thought Pavel, *a "peaceful resolution" to NATO would mean a regime hostile to us.*

"Defense Minister," Pavel addressed Rosla, sitting in his new seat, "are there signs of NATO military intervention in Poland?"

"Nothing *directly* related to Poland," Rosla answered. "But as you know, while the Germans have reduced the size of their armed forces, they have moved many of those forces east into the former German Democratic Republic, nearer to Poland. They could intervene very quickly, if they so choose. While the Americans and British have both marginally reduced their commitments on the continent, they still maintain powerful formations in Germany that could intervene as well."

The president nodded, then spoke to the entire assembled Politburo.

"Friends, you know the two pillars of our government's foreign policy," he held up one finger. "First, friendly relations with the west depend on a neutral Germany that cannot threaten the Soviet Union in the near future. Second," he raised another finger, "NATO and the Western European states must withdraw to their side of the Rhine to demonstrate that their alliance truly is defensive. I am happy to entertain ideas from our other allies in Eastern Europe, but the Solidarity regime in Warsaw has given us every indication that they intend to pursue a course of alliance with the western powers. This we cannot allow."

Medvedev rapped his knuckles on the table for emphasis and continued: "As such, the vote before us today is whether or not to begin giving decisive support to the elements in Poland who oppose the Solidarity regime's reckless course." Medvedev now motioned to KGB chairman Laskin. "Anton Andreevich," he ordered, "please briefly tell us how we would affect this strategy."

Laskin removed his eyeglasses and explained, in a soft, reasoned voice, how the KGB, already engaged in funneling funds and small arms to the Polish opposition, was laying the groundwork for opening the spigot to transfer heavy weapons and "volunteers" across the Belorussian Republic's border, while at the same time launching a propaganda campaign that would fan the flickering flames of violent opposition to Warsaw.

All in all, it was a masterful strategy, Medvedev thought. The Soviet Union would vociferously deny any and all involvement in the conflict, stalemating opposition in the UN, while ensuring that the Polish government's focus remained squarely on its internal problems. The move would forestall any possible moves to admit Poland into NATO.

When Laskin finished, Medvedev continued, "Now tell me, what is your assessment of the risks of our proposed strategy? Interior Minister?"

Oleg Drugov, a pained expression on his face, answered, "Pavel Ivanovich, the western sanctions over the Poland situation have already hit our economy hard, forestalling the recovery that our reforms should be bringing about. If they decide to strengthen those sanctions because of this, to further cut us off from world markets, I fear our economy could falter. If we have another harvest as bad as last year's, collapse is more imminent. We are just now beginning to tap the potential of our oil and natural gas reserves in Siberia. If we are not allowed to sell them, if the Americans won't sell us grain…"

Now the vice president, silent until this point, joined the conversation. "We have no need of their 'markets,'" he said with contempt. "Your 'reforms' are making us vulnerable to the forces of world capitalism, Pavel Ivanovich."

Idiot, thought Medvedev, *don't you see that our vulnerability is the result of such blind ideology as this, enforced by people like you for decades?*

"That is a debate for another time, *tovarich* Vice President," Pavel responded. "Let us deal with the situation at hand."

The vice president retreated into sullen silence.

Marshal Rosla cleared his throat.

"Yes, Defense Minister?" prompted Medvedev.

"Sir, with all respect to my KGB colleague," Rosla nodded across the table to Laskin, "I am dubious about the success of continued covert involvement in Poland," said Rosla.

"Did you have some other suggestion?" challenged Foreign Minister Garin. Open debate was encouraged in Medvedev's Politburo, and Rosla had not yet proven himself in this forum of ideas.

"Direct military intervention," came the decisive reply. "We have done it before, in Poland even. Also in Hungary, and in Czechoslovakia. Each time our actions were decisive."

Rosla had pointedly omitted any mention of the USSR's "direct intervention" in Afghanistan, Pavel noted.

"Such an action would surely bring heavy economic consequences from the west," countered Garin.

Rosla nodded, conceding the point.

"Nonetheless," said Medvedev, enjoying the lively exchange of ideas in this chamber that for too long had been a model of open conformism and covert backbiting, "direct intervention is something we must at least consider. How would you suggest we do it, Defense Minister?"

"Our forces would need time to prepare," Rosla answered, leaning back. "The threat of military interference from NATO would be much higher than in the previous examples I have cited. I would not feel comfortable intervening unless we were ready to counter that eventuality."

"How long?" asked the KGB chairman.

"Our air forces are currently in the best shape. Three months at most. I would want time to improve the readiness of our ground force reserves. That would take nearly six months at least. I am far less familiar with our naval forces…" here the marshal turned in his seat and beckoned a blue-uniformed naval aide to stand. "Captain First Rank Ivanenko, how long does the Navy require before they would be ready to repel aggression from NATO?"

The naval officer rose hesitantly from his seat against the wall, looking distinctly uncomfortable, but he spoke with confidence.

"*Tovarichi*," he began, "our fleet has suffered much from poor maintenance and faulty supplies of parts and weapons for a long time. We are correcting these deficiencies, thanks to the reforms enacted by this government, but these things take time. Our crews also need training before they will be of an acceptable level. I do not wish to speak for my superiors, but our internal assessments are that we require something in the order of twelve months to be fully ready."

The marshal nodded and the junior officer sat back down.

"A year!?" blurted the vice president, outraged. "What was your predecessor doing with all the resources we threw at him, Rosla?"

"I endorse Captain First Rate Ivanenko's statement," said the marshal, ignoring the vice president's outburst. "But allow me to suggest that this timeline, though seemingly long, offers some possibilities."

"Such as?" prodded Medvedev.

"Let us pursue our covert intervention in Poland," Rosla suggested. Turning to Drugov, he asked, "Interior Minister, if NATO and the west respond with the sanctions you expect, can our economy hold on for at least another year?"

Drugov thought for a minute, then nodded. "I believe we can, though it will be…unpleasant, for our citizens."

"If we can survive economically," Rosla continued quickly, "and our covert strategy proves to be ineffective, then we would be prepared to launch a direct intervention in Poland in just under a year. The people of Poland are very religious, as are our adversaries in the west. A surprise invasion during their Christmas holiday would likely catch them unawares and allow us to achieve our aims before NATO could gather themselves to respond effectively. With Poland firmly under control, we'll be able to negotiate a solution to our economic challenges from a position of strength."

Heads nodded around the table. Medvedev considered his new marshal. The plan was creative, economical, and it allowed some flexibility in its timeline. *A good choice*, Medvedev thought to himself.

"I would only note," offered Laskin, who, despite being a Medvedev ally, was clearly uncomfortable with the direction the meeting was going, "that direct intervention will create a situation in which military conflict with NATO would be very likely, even probable." No one moved to interrupt, so the foreign minister continued, "It is true that many of the NATO states care little for Poland, but the most powerful ones, the British, the Americans, and the Germans, will surely push for a response because they'll feel threatened. *And* if our actions are too aggressive we could even see France return to the military structure of the NATO alliance. Would our forces be prepared for such a war, against an aggressive NATO, in the timeframe you suggest, Defense Minister?" Laskin finished with the challenge directed right at Rosla.

"If we are not, the president will have my resignation a year from now," was Rosla's firm reply. Heads were nodding their agreement, or at least their willingness to follow Rosla's aggressive plan.

"Very well," Medvedev intervened, bringing the discussion to a head, "the proposal before us is that we immediately commence increased covert support for elements in Poland who are friendly to us and opposed to the Solidarity regime in Warsaw. Furthermore, I propose that we direct the defense minister to immediately commence preparations for direct intervention in that country, and to bring the armed forces to a state of readiness within a year's time. All in favor?"

The vote was unanimous. Even the vice president approved, though the scowl on his face showed what he thought of his assembled colleagues in Medvedev's camp.

"Very well," Medvedev concluded the meeting. "I thank you for attending, and I wish you all a belated *Dehn Roshdehnya*."

With the New Year's greeting delivered and accepted, the Politburo members rose from their seats and began gathering their aides to return to their various ministries around the city.

"Marshal Rosla," Medvedev beckoned.

"Yes sir?" answered the defense minister as he approached the head of the table.

"I have spent too much time here in Moscow in the past months, as did your predecessor. I gather that you will not be so desk-bound," said the president.

Rosla shook his head with a smile. He most certainly would not.

"Very good," Medvedev continued. "I would like to get out and see the training of our armed forces for myself as much as possible. Please arrange a circuit for me over the next several months so that I may learn the different elements of our military."

"Of course, Pavel Ivanovich," responded the defense minister. "This old *desantnik*," he said, patting his chest, "will be learning a thing or two as well. I assume you will also want to see your sons during this time?"

Pavel smiled as he accompanied Rosla out of the room, "Yes. Of course."

 **CHAPTER 8**

1025 EST, Thursday 11 March 1993
1525 Zulu
US 2nd Fleet Headquarters, Building W-5,
Naval Station Norfolk, Virginia, USA

"TO CONCLUDE, OUR analysis indicates that the Soviet Red Banner Northern Fleet is on track to achieve a peak level of efficiency, both in equipment readiness and training, sometime in the December to January timeframe. That is when they will have the most hulls, both refurbished and new construction, available to go to sea, and when their crews will be at their highest level of training. Sir, pending your questions, that concludes my brief." 2nd Fleet's N2, or chief intelligence officer, Ed Franklin, stood waiting for his chief's comment.

He's good, thought Colonel Rob Buckner looking around as the N2 wrapped up his weekly intelligence briefing to Vice Admiral Falkner and his staff. Franklin, a bespectacled navy captain, had just delivered another masterful performance, weaving disparate bits of data and information into a coherent narrative that communicated the most salient elements of the past week's developments around the North Atlantic. This was only Buckner's second briefing with the staff, but already he was growing to appreciate Franklin's skills as both an analyst and a presenter of intelligence.

"Thanks, Ed. Good job," responded Arthur Falkner in his mild accent and calm manner. "I want to go back to something you said a bit earlier. Do you see a connection between the Sov's naval buildup and what's been going on in Poland, or are those situations developing parallel to one another?"

Franklin was standing at the foot of the table, which was shoehorned into the cramped conference room of the headquarters building located just a few blocks from the piers where the might of the US Atlantic Fleet was moored. The table was barely large enough to fit the fleet's sizable number of principal staff officers, most wearing the tan khaki work uniforms of the US Navy. Franklin took a sip of water from a plastic bottle as he visibly composed his response. Buckner had noted over the course of his few interactions with the intelligence officer that the navy captain took the time to be precise with his words.

"Sir," Franklin said, "I'm trained not to believe in coincidences. The start of the Soviets' accelerated training regimen and increased procurement activities *did* coincide with the increased tempo in their interference in Poland. Unfortunately, with all the funding that's been cut from our human intelligence organizations over the past few years, all we really have is satellite and signal intelligence to go on. That, and what the Soviets choose to tell us themselves. Even the defector stream has dried up of late."

At the head of the table, Falkner nodded. The shift in priorities for the US intelligence community to rely on technical, in place of human, sources of information was so far failing to impress the customers.

Franklin went on, "Satellite imagery can tell us about *actions* but not *intentions*. Without someone in their government who knows and is willing to talk, we can't be sure what they're up to. But to answer your question, sir: Yes, I think their naval buildup is related to their involvement in Poland. My read is that they are trying to project strength globally ahead of a more open and decisive intervention in Eastern Europe, like before Hungary in fifty-six, or Czechoslovakia in sixty-eight."

That's ominous, thought Buckner. Recently, a *New York Times* reporter had gained notoriety for breaking the story about an ugly incident at the Polish village of Ossówka. The slaughter there had become emblematic of the violence and chaos that was now engulfing Poland. Violence in that country had increased dramatically alongside signs of Russian meddling, and the opinions of western governments had hardened against the Medvedev regime. *The world hasn't been this polarized since the seventies. And now the Soviets are sharpening their bayonets.*

"I read it the same way," said Falkner. "What do you make of the timing of it all, Ed?"

"It's tied to logistics, sir," Franklin offered, ticking off his reasoning. "So much time needed to refit a ship," one finger, "only so many dry-docks available," another finger, "only so much capacity in their naval and weapons industry," the third finger. "It all adds up to a long lead time to get their whole fleet ready at once."

Rob noticed Captain Hank Elliot, Falkner's somewhat portly N4, or fleet logistics officer, nod in agreement.

"On the other hand," Franklin went on, "they look to be on track for maximum readiness right around Christmas. They could be planning a Christmas Eve or Christmas Day operation, hoping our response will be delayed due to the holiday. They've done it before, in Afghanistan in seventy-nine. I don't like it, sir."

"Alright, let's talk logistics then," Falkner said, turning his attention to the fleet logistician. "Hank, where's the trade off? What vulnerabilities is Red Fleet leaving itself open to by readying so much of their fleet so quickly?"

Captain Elliot removed his black-framed standard-issue eyeglasses before responding in his thick Boston accent, "Admiral, they'ah going to run into the same problems we would. The tradeoff is that they'ah going to have to stand down a lahge numbah of their ships shortly after the timeframe we'ah discussing. They'ah going to be ready too quickly for themselves to manage."

Falkner nodded and turned back to his N2, but his next question was clearly directed at the entire staff. "So, assuming the Sovs are readying for some sort of open confrontation with Poland about nine months from now, what are the odds that they are planning something more ambitious to go along with it? Something to which we might need to respond?"

The feisty, diminutive Rear Admiral Walter Forrest, Falkner's chief of staff, answered first. "Sir," he said, "I'd still rate the probability as low. The correlation of forces, especially in our theater, is just too much in our favor. It might be a different story if Congress hadn't voted down those cuts to the naval budget last year. We've managed to retain a lot of ships that were looking to be scrapped, and keeping *Ranger* in the reserve fleet, *Forrestal* as a training deck, and *Saratoga* in commission gives the Navy some strategic flexibility," Forrest noted, listing off aircraft carriers that had been slated for retirement as part of the hoped-for "Peace Dividend" when all the pundits had been giddily declaring the Cold War to be over. "We've already switched *Sara* to the Pacific which allows us to keep *Carl Vinson* facing the Soviets in the Atlantic. As it stands, the Russians would have to achieve both strategic and operational surprise to have any chance of really hurting us, and I just don't foresee that happening."

That's why they call it a "surprise," Rob thought.

With the resurgence of Soviet power over the past two years, the Navy and Air Force had won some significant victories in Congress allowing them to keep their powerful force structure from the eighties largely intact. This included retaining older surface units and maintaining the production of the fantastic new *Seawolf*-class submarines. Despite this, the Navy's budget was strained to the breaking point keeping ships crewed and trained. The Army, on the other hand, well the Army had never been good at playing politics in the halls of Congress.

Now Falkner's N3, the fleet operations chief and Buckner's direct superior, Rear Admiral Xavier Johnson, spoke up in his deep southern drawl, "I agree with Walt. December is an awful time to fight a war up there in the Arctic. I have trouble believing that, given their druthers, the Soviets would actually plan an offensive up there during that time. It would severely limit the efficiency of their ships and aircraft."

Buckner frowned and leaned forward. *That's the opinion of someone who's served in warm climates his whole career,* he thought. Rear Admiral Johnson was from Mississippi and had spent his entire career to this point in the Med, the Persian Gulf, and the Indian Ocean. It seemed that, for him, cold weather was good reason to call off the party, whether that be a three-mile jog or a war. *Cold weather would limit* our *ships' efficiency too.*

"Rob, you disagree?"

Buckner looked up. Falkner was looking at him, and now the rest of the staff were as well. He hadn't realized his skepticism was so obvious. *Great.*

Second staff update brief and I'm already being called upon to publicly contradict my boss. I really need to get that demeanor under control.

Buckner cleared his throat and dove in, "Sir, I don't disagree that December would be a terrible time to fight a naval war in the Arctic," he responded. *Best to try to be as diplomatic as possible.* "However, the purpose of a navy is to influence operations on land, right? Winter in the far north actually offers some positive conditions for offensive *land* operations. For example, the tundra terrain up there is marshy and largely impassible in the spring and summer, but in the winter it's frozen and trafficable by vehicles. Don't we say that weather and terrain are neutral? Both sides have to operate in them. What's important is how you adapt to the conditions. The Russians could be banking on the assumption that they can adapt better than us. Also, Captain Franklin," he addressed the N2, "you were just saying that our human sources in the Soviet Union are drying up. Doesn't that make it more likely that the Russians could achieve at least *strategic* surprise?"

Rob chanced a sidelong glance at Admiral Johnson to gauge his reaction. The big man's dark, craggy face was impassive, impossible to read. *Great*, the Marine thought again, unhappily. Admiral Falkner liked to have the members of his table debate, disagree, and challenge one another. It led to better decisions. That was no guarantee that everyone *else* at the table would be as welcoming of opposing views among *their* underlings. *How's that for a first impression in the shop.*

"All good points, Rob," Falkner was saying. "I agree, we can't take for granted that the Soviets see the strategic balance or the operational conditions the same way we do. We have to take their buildup seriously."

Falkner paused, then addressed the whole staff. "Gentlemen, I want a proposal by next week on how we can arrange the fleet to maximize our available combat power for the North Atlantic and Europe this December. I also want to schedule some major training exercises around Iceland for that time to validate our winter operations proficiency and let the Sovs know that we're ready for any and all eventualities. Xavier, see if we can get the Brits to play in those."

The N3 nodded and made a note.

Falkner went on, "Give me some ideas. What are our options to maximize our carrier battle groups in the North Atlantic during that time?"

Hank Elliot shifted unhappily in his seat, making scratches with a pen on his yellow notepad and flipping through some printouts in front of him. After a moment the logistician said, "Well sir, we could staht by puttin' carrier refits on hold stahtin' this fall. That would need approval from the CNO—"

"I'll get it," interjected Falkner, who was friends with the chief of naval operations, the Navy's representative to the Joint Chiefs Staff in Washington. "What else?"

"We could spend some money to accelerate *Eisenhower*'s refit," Elliot went on, "get her back in the water by October and delay her departure for the Med by a few weeks. That, along with the *Carl Vinson* will give us at least two carrier groups to play with in December. I don't have the details in front of me on our surface and submarine forces, but I can brief you on those next week, sir."

Admiral Johnson stirred. "I should note, sir," he rumbled, "that the actions Captain Elliot is proposing would leave us with *no* carriers available for the North Atlantic in the January-February timeframe."

"I agree, it's a risk, Xavier," Falkner acceded. "Hank, what can we do to mitigate?"

Elliot responded, "Not much for January, sir. We can accelerate *Enterprise*'s overhaul. That would need to be approved by the CNO as well," a quick look to Falkner, who nodded, and Elliot continued, "but at best we could have 'Big E' doing her workups by mid-February. That still leaves us with a sizable gap in carrier availability."

"Ed," Falkner addressed his intelligence chief, "you said the Sovs will likely need to stand down their fleet for maintenance as well after December?"

"Yes sir," the N2 confirmed.

"Then I think we can assume some risk. Let's move forward with the assumption that we will execute as Hank just outlined. I'll get the okay from the CNO. He and I were baseball teammates at the Academy, so I think I can swing that," he added with a smile at the baseball pun, a few, including Buckner smiled too, knowing their chief's love of America's pastime. "Okay, let's move on with the brief. N3?"

Buckner watched as his boss the N3, and the N4 too, who normally would brief after him, looked down at notes detailing deployment and maintenance schedules that had just been left in smoking shambles by their admiral's characteristically decisive decision-making. Rob couldn't help feeling a twinge of guilt at the part he had played in their discomfiture, but he knew that Falkner's action plan was the right one. Rob was feeling increasingly pleased with his own decision to come work for the admiral.

Falkner also seemed to sense his staff officers' mood, because he said with a half-smile, "Okay, that was unfair. Based on these developments, why don't you all go back and update your estimates. I'll expect updated schedules by this meeting next week."

The rest of the staff nodded, relieved.

With the Fleet's business concluded, or at least deferred, Falkner ended the meeting with, "Alright, any other points? No? Then thanks team. Good job, and let's get back to work."

The officers crowded round the conference table rose in noisy unison, wooden chairs scraping across the hardwood floor, coming to attention and rendering the customary salute to their commander before gathering their notes and coffee cups, and filing towards the door.

Rob was gathering his files as well when he heard Falkner call to him from the head of the table, "Colonel Buckner, a word."

He began working against the crowd towards the head of the table, passing Admiral Johnson on the way who admonished him quietly to hurry back when the "old man" was done with him, as they had a lot of work to do given the outcome of the meeting.

Falkner was making some annotations on a sheet as Rob approached. The commander of the US 2nd Fleet, responsible for operations in the Atlantic Ocean and presumptive commander of NATO's powerful Strike Fleet Atlantic in the event of war with the Soviets, motioned for the Marine to sit as he finished up.

Rob contemplated his chief. The man was physically unremarkable. With thinning white hair, he would have fit in easily with the wiry local farmers of the admiral's hometown in rural southern Minnesota had he been wearing blue jeans instead of Navy khaki. His face was open, friendly, honest. The flint and intelligence behind those blue eyes belied the truth; this man was a leader. After a few seconds the admiral handed his notes to his flag lieutenant, who quietly departed, and then it was just Falkner and Buckner in the room.

Sitting back in his chair Falkner looked up and said "So, Rob, how are you settling in?"

"Well enough sir, thank you." Rob answered. "My apologies it took me so long to get up here. The people down at Lejeune were less than happy about letting me go early. I appreciate the opportunity to work here."

That was an understatement. General De Vries had been livid about Buckner's early departure from 2nd Marine Division.

"You getting along alright with Admiral Johnson?" Falkner asked next.

"No problems on my end, Admiral. I hope he doesn't hold what I said in the meeting against me, though," Buckner said.

"He's a good man. He won't hold it against you at all. He *will* be hard on you, but I think you'll find he's fair, too. How are Helen and the kids settling in?" Falkner asked without pause.

"They stayed down in North Carolina for a few months, sir. Wanted the kids to finish out the school year before we moved. Helen wasn't thrilled about it, but I think it's best," Rob answered.

"I think you're right," Falkner agreed. "My Ellie went to three different high schools in four years. This life is hard on kids, Rob. I appreciate your family making the sacrifice to come up here."

"Thank you, sir."

Falkner paused, then went on, "So to business." He let out a puff of air. "I wanted to take a minute to talk to you about how I'm going to use you on my staff."

Buckner's interest was piqued. Positions on a military staff were relatively well defined. He was in charge of planning amphibious operations, reporting to the N3. If Admiral Falkner had something else in mind for him, well, that was intriguing.

"Now I know you were looking forward to being chained to your desk over in the 'three' shop," the older man teased, "but I recruited you for more than coordinating amphibious training plans. I need someone I can use as my eyes and voice around the fleet and with the fleets of our allies. Someone I can trust to understand my orders and explain them in person if necessary, someone who understands my intent and can improvise in a pinch. I can't go sending my N3 off on courier missions, so I think you're my man. You up to it?"

"I think so, sir. I'm excited for the opportunity," Rob answered, feeling gratified at the trust that Falkner was showing in him.

"Good! I know you're disappointed about not getting your regiment, Rob," Falkner's summary of the Marine's feelings was understated in the extreme, "but I think you'll find your job here rewarding, and I'm glad to have you. We have a lot of Gulf War veterans around the fleet, and around the military, who seem to think we've proven to the world once and for all that no one can beat us. They may well be right, at least right now, but I imagine the Russians see things differently. I actually value the fact that you weren't over in the desert, Rob. If things ever go hot with the Soviets, I seriously doubt they are going to play into our hand like Saddam did."

Buckner nodded, gratified that at least one person in the world seemed to value his strengths and career's worth of experience.

"You are going to have a lot of influence on the fleet's operations, Rob," Falkner went on, building up his subordinate. "I'm going to work you hard, and you still work for Johnson too, so you're going to be pulling some double duty. Expect to travel a lot in your capacity as my liaison. May want to look into one of those new frequent flier programs," the admiral suggested with a smile.

"Yes sir," Buckner responded, returning the smile.

"Alright, for now head back to your shop," Falkner ordered. "I'm sure Xavier has plenty for you to do. He's aware of how I plan to use you, so don't worry about that. Get yourself settled in, and let me know when the family gets here."

Rob stood and departed. As he left the conference room the spark of excitement had returned, this was going to be more than another desk job, he was moving forward into unknown territories.

 # CHAPTER 9

1000 MSK, Tuesday 29 March 1993
0700 Zulu
Northeast of Pskov, Russian Soviet Federative Socialist Republic

G UARDS COLONEL ILYA Romanov stood in the open paratroop
door of his Ilyushin Il-76 jet transport looking down over the deep
green of the birch forest cover giving way to the lighter green of the
drop zone's rolling grassland. The slipstream whipped around him, tugging
at his camouflage uniform as well as the forty-kilogram load of parachutes,
rucksack, and weapon hanging from him like saddlebags on a mule. The
ribbed cloth padded helmet fastened under his chin hid his close-cropped
blond hair, framing an open, high-cheekboned Slavic face. His eyes, a deep
blue, hid nothing, though he sometimes wished they did. All he hoped was
that when his soldiers looked at him, they saw a confidence and strength that
he wished to inspire in them.

Using both hands to brace himself against the metal frame of the open
door, the *desantnik* officer leaned forward until his entire upper body was
protruded outside of the aircraft, almost into the one-hundred-fifty knot slipstream, rotating his head to look towards the rear of the aircraft. This part of
a jump never failed to thrill him; it was just him, hanging out of a jet aircraft,
suspended between earth and sky. He visually inspected the transport's skin

for any protrusions that could harm him or his men when they jumped in the coming seconds. All looked in order, and using his arms he levered himself back into the airplane.

Romanov turned and clapped the jumpmaster on the shoulder, indicating that all was in order. Looking down the dimly-lit cavernous interior of the transport, he could see his "chalk," the close-packed, swaying line of *desantniki* who would momentarily follow him out into the void. An identical chalk stood against the opposite side of the fuselage where Major Misha Medvedev was just completing his own door check. These and the rest of his command, the 234th Guards Airborne Regiment of the 76th Guards Airborne Division, were his men, and in such moments of shared danger he cherished the camaraderie with them.

Catching the eye of the next jumper in line, his Jewish *commissar*, Major Ivan Sviashenik, he smiled. The commander always jumps first, the same as every paratroop unit in the world, but most political officers that Romanov had known were reticent about participating in such training. A look of mutual respect passed between the two officers as their eyes locked briefly, both men swaying with the motion of the aircraft as they neared the drop zone.

The jumpmaster on Romanov's side of the aircraft clapped his colonel on the shoulder and shouted into his ear over the roar of the wind, "*Ten seconds!*"

Romanov turned to square up to the door, and waited for the indicator light to switch from red to green.

━ ▪ ━

The deep whine of the jet transports' turbofan engines increased to a scream as the vee of three Ilyushins flew low from right to left over the drop zone. Even inside the protection of the enclosed observation tower, Pavel Medvedev could feel the raw power of the engines that propelled each of the blue-, white-, and gray-painted transports. He watched the aircraft through an over-sized set of binoculars from the elevated perch of the climate-controlled tower sheltering him and the other dignitaries from the early spring of the Russian landscape. The large plate glass windows gave a panoramic view of the tree-lined rolling grassland before him. This field was one of the training drop zones for the 76th Guards Airborne Division, stationed south of the nearby medieval city of Pskov.

The president focused on the nearest aircraft. The big jet was moving so slowly it seemed to be floating. Behind the lead vee followed three more aircraft, and three more behind those. He could see the open cargo ramp in the rear and an open door just forward of the high-slung wing. The camouflage-clad silhouette of a man was visible filling the dark rectangle. Medvedev watched the figure intently, waiting for him to jump.

Instead, a large drogue chute billowed out the back of the wide-bodied transport. Pavel shifted his attention just in time to see it yank the dark, boxy, shape of a vehicle out of the aircraft and off the rear cargo ramp. The president's heart skipped a beat as the vehicle nosed down and plummeted towards the ground, but a huge parachute blossomed into a canopy, almost gently swinging the squat, olive colored vehicle until it was upright underneath the green dome. When it was within a few meters of the ground the straps between parachute and drop platform erupted in a flash, engulfing the vehicle in jets of thick, gray smoke. The entire package settled almost gently onto the damp, grassy clearing, the parachute drifting with the wind until it collapsed a little beyond the landing point. The entire descent had taken less than a minute.

Eight more vehicles had been dropped in a tight pattern by the lead trio of aircraft, a mix of armored BMDs, soft-skinned trucks, and tracked mortar carriers. They all landed in quick succession, wreathed momentarily in the smoke of their firing retro-rockets.

Next to the president, Marshal Rosla noted, "We drop the armored vehicles with their crewmen inside. This means they're able to move into battle very quickly and the rocket braking system protects them from the impact."

I would not wish to be one of those crewmen. Pavel imagined the cramped interior of one of the fighting vehicles as it swung through the air under its parachute and grimaced. He was gaining some new insight into why Russians venerated their *desantniki*, even assigning a national holiday, Airborne Forces Day, to honor those who had served in the elite airborne assault forces.

Medvedev shifted his attention upward where long lines of paratroopers swayed under drab, olive-colored parachutes. While these were still in the air the next trio of transports roared overhead, disgorging their own loads of paratroopers from their doors and the rear ramps. He focused through his binoculars on one man as he stepped from the nearest aircraft, gravity pulling him downward while momentum carried him forward with the vector of the plane. After only a moment, the falling figure's static line, still attached to the aircraft, yanked out the parachute, which caught the wind and blossomed rearward like smoke on a breezy day, arresting the *desantnik*'s forward momentum and slowing his descent.

Two more soldiers exited the same door in the time it had taken the first jumper's canopy to open, and more followed at the rate of one each half second from each of the aircraft's exits. Soon the entire drop zone lay under a blanket of descending parachutes. Medvedev continued to watch his jumper dangle below his canopy. The man held his legs together and assumed a half-sitting posture as he approached the ground. Pavel felt his own body tense just before the paratrooper landed and collapsed into a controlled roll and then disappeared into the tall grasses and gentle folds of the drop zone.

The roar of the transports turned to a departing moan as Pavel pulled back from his binoculars to take in the whole scene. *Desantniki* were landing all over the vast, drop zone. Medvedev was surprised at how empty the scene in front of him became even from his perch ten meters off the ground. Occasionally he caught sight of a soldier tramping this way or that under the weight of his equipment, or a parachute draped over a bush, but he was having increasing trouble making sense of the seemingly empty field in front of him. *Interesting*, he thought, *that so many soldiers can just disappear so quickly, even in such open terrain.*

"Pavel Ivanovich, if you look over there," Rosla said, indicating a small depression in the ground several hundred meters distant from their observation tower, "you can see an assembly area for one of the assault subunits. The *desantniki* will gather there and at other points around their commanders until they have assembled a large enough force, and then they will commence their attack on the objective. Speed and surprise are everything in these sorts of operations."

Medvedev focused his glasses on the indicated area, though his bad eye slowed the process. *There it is.* A figure was kneeling in the low area, the man had extended a flimsy telescopic pole with a ragged purple flag at the top, and several other figures were already gathered around him, kneeling and facing out with their weapons ready. Pavel located another assembly area, this one marked by a light blue flag. Turning his attention back to the first group, he saw first one and then a second of the armored vehicles drive slowly into the depression.

"And there is the regimental command group," Rosla continued, indicating a small knot of figures clustered at the top of a knoll. "Guards Colonel Romanov is commanding."

Through the binoculars, Pavel could see a figure, which he assumed was the man Rosla had mentioned, kneeling and pointing while balancing what looked to be a folded map on his knee. Next to him was another kneeling soldier with an antenna sprouting from the rucksack on his back. Pavel watched the first figure take a handset from the radioman and speak into it.

A tinny voice came through speakers at the rear of the enclosed observation tower.

"All stations, all stations," it said, "this is Stork Command. Send update on your assembly progress in sequence. End."

Marshal Rosla leaned over and softly explained, "That is the regiment's commander, Colonel Romanov. Now his subunit commanders will update him."

Medvedev nodded as he shifted his attention back to watch the soldiers assembling around the purple flag. He saw one of them lift a radio handset and heard, "Stork Command, this is *Orel* One-One-Zero. We are fifty percent assembled and preparing to move into our supporting position."

Rosla looked at his watch and grunted, "That is bloody fast for an assembly, even in daytime."

A second voice crackled through the radio speaker. "This is *Sova* One-One-Zero, we are thirty percent assembled. We will be ready to commence the assault in ten minutes."

"This is Stork Command. Hurry up, *Sova*," came the terse, tinny reply.

Two more similarly brief reports crackled and hissed across the radio net. Then, after several minutes of radio silence, Medvedev heard, "Stork Command, this is *Sova* One-One-Zero. We have assembled minimum force and are prepared to execute the assault."

"Acknowledged, *Sova*," came Stork's reply, then, "all subunits, this is Stork Command. Execute Phase Irina. Acknowledge in sequence. End."

The requisite replies, "*Orel*, executing," and so forth followed.

Rosla grunted again, looking at his watch. "That was a *very* fast assembly," he said.

The Soviet president looked sideways at his minister of defense and chided, "I thought I instructed you to show me no Potemkin villages, Aleksandr Ivanovich."

The marshal looked back, catching his president's eye, and said, "This is no Potemkin village, Pavel Ivanovich. This is a normal, large-scale training exercise. The soldiers participating did not even know you and I would be observing until just before they boarded the aircraft."

Medvedev nodded. Then a smile crept across Rosla's serious face and the marshal said, "Of course, I would be lying to you, sir, if I said I hadn't selected what I consider to be the finest regiment in the Red Army for your first exposure to our training."

Medvedev returned the smile, and both men brought their attention back to the panorama before them. After searching for a few moments and refocusing properly, he watched as a group of men followed behind two BMDs as the squat armored vehicles crawled up a slope. Reaching the crest, the men spread out into a skirmish line, vehicles in front and paratroopers going to ground. Soon puffs of smoke appeared, followed seconds later by the *pop-pop* reports of rifles firing what Medvedev knew were blank rounds.

Medvedev scanned beyond the firing line to the target, a village overgrown with stunted trees and bushes a couple hundred meters beyond them. The houses and buildings were clearly abandoned, the windows and door-frames empty, walls overgrown.

The radio speakers hissed to life, "Stork Command, this is *Orel* One-One-Zero. We have suppressed the objective."

"Understood, *Orel*. *Sova*, this is Stork Command, execute Phase Katya."

"Executing, Stork."

Motion to the left of the village caught Pavel's attention, and he swiveled his binoculars. Two columns of figures were jogging towards the village in the wake of two more of the turreted BMDs, some firing their weapons as they ran. The fire continued from *Orel's* firing line as *Sova's* assault element approached the village, the disconnect between the visual puffs and the *popping* sounds giving the scene a surreal quality. Then the radio crackled again, "*Orel*, Stork, cease fire."

"This is *Orel*, ceasing fire."

A red signal flare shot up from the advancing element and the firing from *Orel's* skirmish line slackened, then ceased. To the left the advancing BMDs halted several dozen meters from the village, both rocking forward slightly on their suspension as the paratroopers that followed, surged past and spread into the village.

"This is where the assault element enters and secures the objective," explained Rosla, watching through his binoculars.

Medvedev again lost sight of many of the figures as they moved in and among the buildings, but little scenes here and there showed that the mock assault was still ongoing. Down one alley he saw a camouflage-clad figure toss a small object through a window and then flatten himself against the wall, simulating a grenade attack. At the corner of another building he saw one soldier kneel and point his weapon, while four more moved swiftly past him and burst through the open door of a small house. After several minutes Pavel could discern no further movement. Then the radio speaker crackled again.

"Stork Command," the voice in the speaker said, "this is *Sova* One-One-Zero. The objective is secure. End."

"This is Stork, copy. All elements proceed to the objective. End," came the reply.

Events seemed to have slowed to a standstill from Medvedev's perspective, but now the fields around the village came alive with organized movement. At different points around the drop zone groups of figures stood, shouldered their packs, and began trudging towards the group of buildings that occupied the center of the vast clearing.

"The exercise is concluding," said Rosla. "I am very pleased with their level of training and proficiency. Would you like to meet the regiment's officers, Pavel Ivanovich?"

"Very much so," answered the president, setting down his binoculars.

The two men, followed by their aides and plain clothes security detail, exited the observation tower via a rear door and descended the three flights of grated metal stairs to the wet gravel below. Rosla and Medvedev wedged their big frames into an UAZ-469 jeep and with a command from the marshal the vehicle bounced along a dirt road, really just two muddy tire ruts, leading down the gentle slope. A small convoy followed.

As they drove, Medvedev watched as small groups of paratroopers trudged under the weight of their equipment toward the village. About a hundred meters ahead he saw a small truck, bogged down in a mud hole to the left of the trail, its rear wheels spinning and throwing up rooster tails of dark, wet earth. Several muddy figures were straining against the vehicle's rear frame, helping push the truck out of its predicament.

As the jeep approached the mired truck, Medvedev saw another group, one carrying a radio pack, jog up to the vehicle, drop their weapons and packs and put their backs into freeing the truck. Everyone was knee-deep in mud behind the rear tires, but the vehicle started rocking. Successive oscillating heaves, coupled with revs of the engine that covered the helpers with yet more wet earth, finally freed the truck, which climbed tentatively out of the hole before bouncing away.

Marshal Rosla ordered the driver to stop. As the jeep bounced to a halt, he stepped out into the mud. Surprised, Medvedev followed suit. His dress shoes, ill-suited to the wet conditions, slipped and slid, picking up large chunks of mud as he joined his defense minister in front of the vehicle.

Rosla walked confidently towards the milling knot of mud-splattered soldiers as they turned in surprise at the incongruous sight of the marshal, dressed in his olive tunic complete with shoulder boards and ribbons. Two members of the group stepped forward and stiffened to attention just as Rosla called out, "Colonel Romanov, I should have known I'd find you doing some labor below your rank," his tone was loud, good-natured.

"One cannot just walk past an important task and expect others to come along and do it, *tovarich* Marshal," came the equally good-natured reply. The speaker was a fit, well-built figure as far as Medvedev could tell through the mud and grime that coated the man's uniform.

Rosla marched up and shook Romanov's hand, then pulled him into a warm embrace. Stepping back, the marshal proclaimed, "It is good to see you, Ilya Georgiyevich. It has been too long." Turning back to the president, Rosla said, "Sir, allow me to introduce the commander of this operation, the Colonel of the 234th Guards Airborne Regiment, Guards Colonel Ilya Georgiyevich Romanov."

Medvedev stepped forward and took Romanov's hand. Romanov possessed handsome features, but not rakishly so. His eyes were blue, his hair hidden underneath the brown helmet. The entire effect of the man's open, angular demeanor inspired instinctive trust from Medvedev, as the president was sure it did for the colonel's soldiers. He was thinner than Medvedev and Rosla, athletic, of medium height and build, clearly in the prime of physical conditioning. "Greetings, Colonel. I offer you my compliments on the exercise. From what the defense minister explains, your soldiers performed very well."

"Thank you, sir," responded Romanov, "I am very proud of my men. They've worked hard in the past months. There are still many things we can improve, particularly the speed of our assault force assembly, but any faults are mine, not the men's."

"I judged that your forces assembled very fast, Ilya. You're too hard on yourself, as usual," chided Rosla.

"Perhaps, sir. We reduced the minimum force requirements for the assault unit, to improve how rapidly they could transition into the attack, but I would like to see them move a few minutes faster to maintain surprise and initiative," answered Romanov, respectfully.

Rosla nodded, conceding the point. He turned to face Medvedev, clapped a meaty paw on Romanov's shoulder, and said, "I knew this rascal when he was a young officer on his first tour in Afghanistan. He had some odd ideas about how we should interact with the locals, trying to understand them or allow them to preserve their backwards way of life or some such nonsense. We held on to him anyway." The last was delivered in a teasing tone of voice.

Romanov smiled and responded, "I don't deny it. I believe some of our methods in that war were," the man paused, and said, diplomatically, "heavy-handed. At times counterproductive. I wrote as much in an article published in *Military Thought* last year."

Medvedev's guard was immediately up. He possessed the typical Russian disdain for Asiatics, and he considered the Afghans to be worst of all after the past decade. *If this man has sympathies for those ragheads…*

"…and how are the new contracted soldiers working, Ilya?" Rosla was asking. Introducing limited volunteer service to the Red Army, soldiers who agreed to a longer term of service than the typical *srochniki*, or draftees, in exchange for better pay and other benefits, had been one of the more controversial of Medvedev's military reforms. *The vice president almost had a stroke when we agreed to that one*, Medvedev remembered with a smirk.

"Very well, sir," Romanov answered. "We have few of them to date, but those who have joined us are displaying a higher level of moral-psychological motivation. I just promoted one to junior sergeant last week. Send us more! We have benefited very much from a slower tempo of operations of late as well. Time to train rather than be policemen." The 76th Guards Airborne Division had been used and reused over the past several years to quash unrest in the Caucasus, the Baltics, and in Ukraine.

Foreign sympathies aside, Medvedev could not help liking Romanov. He exuded an openness, an honesty that Pavel found too rarely in the corridors of power. Over the colonel's shoulder the president noticed another officer, still braced at attention, but a slight smirk turning up one corner of his mouth. "And who is this officer?"

Romanov turned, then said warmly, "Ah sir, allow me to introduce my regiment's *zampolit*, Major Ivan Avramovich Sviashenik."

A Jew for a political officer? Medvedev thought, surprised, noting the man's patronym "Avramovich," which meant "son of Abraham." *That* is *unusual*. He reached out and shook the major's hand. "How do you like being in the *desantniki*, Major?" he asked.

"I fancy it very much, *tovarich* President," responded the *zampolit*. "I wished to join the airborne forces as a combat officer in my younger years, but there were *circumstances* that were in the way." The man said, slowly, "Then I discovered that most *zampoliti* do not volunteer for the VDV, and, well, I saw the opportunity to join these fine men in another capacity, *and* promote proper Marxist-Leninist ideology, of course," he added, almost as an afterthought.

Circumstances like your ethnicity, I am sure, reflected Medvedev, not buying the man's half-hearted endorsement of socialist thought. The president turned his attention back to the commander. "Colonel, I understand that my son is an officer in your regiment. I am sure he is not here now because he is avoiding me. He does not like to think that his name influences his success as a military officer."

Romanov smiled an easy smile, nodding, "You are correct, sir. Major Medvedev asked to be assigned to duties at the far end of the drop zone and I obliged." Romanov's face turned earnest, though still friendly. "Of course, your son need not worry, *tovarich* President. He is a good officer. I am pleased to have him on my staff."

Medvedev knew sycophancy when he saw it, and this compliment bore no mark of it. It was an honest comment from a professional to the father of one of his subordinates, and Medvedev accepted the praise at face value. His chest swelled with pride.

"Well, you keep that scallywag in line," Pavel said warmly, "and tell him I am still expecting him to come hunting with me on his leave in June."

"I will sir," answered Romanov.

"Tell the president what you are doing now," Rosla prompted, guiding the conversation back to military matters.

Romanov nodded again. "Of course, sir. We are making our way to the objective, the village up there. The regiment's officers are gathering and then we will conduct an after-action review. It is something the Americans do in their training, they get together and determine what went well and what needs improvement after an exercise. I find it to be a very intelligent procedure. I've tried to instill my officers with a sense of humility, a desire to learn and improve. We conduct one of these reviews after every exercise. Anyone can speak, and anyone can be criticized, even," he touched his chest with a smile, "the commander. We have seen great improvements come out of it."

Again, Medvedev was impressed. He tried to imagine a group of political *apparatchiks* similarly sitting around and honestly critiquing each other. He found it likely that such an exercise would end in shouting and blood within minutes.

"I would like to implement this method throughout the Red Army," Rosla agreed, "but I believe we must overcome some issues of culture before this is viable. Not every commander is a Colonel Romanov!"

"I thank you, sir," Romanov said, clearly embarrassed.

"Well," the marshal said, "*tovarich* President, we should allow the colonel and his officers to conduct their review. There are other things I would like to show you. The division commander has a briefing for us back at Pskov."

The men shook hands all around and parted ways, Medvedev and Rosla to their jeep, the *desantnik* officers re-shouldering their packs and weapons and trudging on towards the mock village.

Inside the jeep, as he was trying to scrape the mud from his shoes, Medvedev looked back at his defense minister and asked, "You mentioned the colonel's sympathy for the *Afghanistansi*. He seems very impressive, but is that not a sign of weakness?"

"Weakness?" Rosla's face showed shock. "Pavel Ivanovich, that man should have a Hero of the Soviet Union medal pinned on his chest!" Rosla shook his head, "Weakness. I was his commander in Afghanistan and let me tell you a story about a young *Captain* Romanov. We were conducting a helicopter insertion in a mountainous area to interdict a Mujahideen caravan route. The altitude was very high, over three thousand meters, so the helicopters could only hold half of the normal compliment of soldiers, and the landing zone was small due to the terrain, only large enough for one aircraft to land at a time. Well, the Mujahideen were waiting for us. I don't know how they knew where we would land, but they did. Romanov was on the first aircraft to land. The enemy allowed the first two choppers to unload, then they opened a heavy fire on the third and forced it to break off. Romanov was stranded on that mountainside with barely a dozen men, and now those Mujahideen were closing in, firing, trying to finish him off."

Rosla had Medvedev's full attention, the president leaning in, as the marshal excitedly recounted the war story. "But did he panic? Not Romanov. He grabbed a radio from his forward air controller, who *was* panicking, and called in the supporting gunships almost on top of his own position, really within fifteen meters. Then he led his men forward with bayonets, *bayonets*, Pavel Ivanovich, and drove those ragheads completely off the mountain. I was there, in the regimental command post. I heard the whole thing over command net. That man is the best we have in our army, maybe in any army. If his instincts say to go soft on the *Afghanistansi*, well, I trust him."

Medvedev nodded, impressed. What his son Misha had said about his commander had also been positive. Now Pavel was especially glad to have his son working under such a man. Satisfied, he changed the subject. "How is Plan *Boyar* coming along?"

The marshal let out a sigh. *Boyar* was the codename they had settled upon for the contingency plans for intervention in Poland and the actions taken to counter NATO interference in that country. "Not as well as we would wish," Rosla admitted. "We are gathering indications that NATO is making preparations of their own to improve their readiness by this December. They may be in a much better position to counter us in Poland than is acceptable."

"Regardless," Medvedev countered, "I wish to review the plan while I am in Siberia in June. Can you have it to me by then?"

"You will have it," Rosla acknowledged, "but I warn you that many things may change between now and December."

———

Several hundred meters farther up the road, Colonel Romanov and his staff were still trudging under their packs, covered in mud, towards the village for their review. The colonel was teasing his *zampolit*.

"'*And* promote Marxist-Leninist ideology, of course,'" Romanov mimicked his political officer. "Some priest of Marxism-Leninism you are!" The ribbing was good-natured, and it was nothing new. Major Sviashenik was anything but a good socialist, had worked and studied to become a *zampolit* solely to secure his place among the *desantniki* that his race had otherwise denied him. Romanov knew this, and he did not care. Sviashenik was a good officer, *zampolit* or not, and the colonel was glad to have him. The younger man was always volunteering to be the first jumper from an aircraft, to lead reconnaissance missions, to do all the things Ilya usually expected of a young, motivated combat officer.

"Well, *you* were not the model of political tact, either, my Colonel," countered the major with good humor, "telling the president that our policy towards the *Afghanistansi* was all wrong."

The whole staff chuckled as they walked. Romanov had worked hard to create an easygoing atmosphere among his officers, albeit one in which he was the undisputed, benevolent autocrat. "Perhaps we all need more political tutoring," said Romanov shaking his head in mock despair. "Say, Sviashenik, isn't that your job?" More chuckling.

"You have me there, Colonel. I suppose I will need to continue to study the works of Marx and Lenin to ensure that our regiment can obtain even greater heights of excellence." The riposte was delivered with a slight undertone of bitterness, and Romanov let off.

They continued in a jovial silence towards what future they did not yet know.

 **CHAPTER 10**

1100 EDT, Monday 14 June 1993
1600 Zulu
Aboard HMCS *Onondaga*, off Cape St. Charles, Labrador, Canada

" **U**P PERISCOPE."
The burnished metal tube hissed upwards in front of Lieutenant
Commander Eddie "Skip" Hughes, captain of one of the Royal
Canadian Navy's three British-built *Oberon*-class diesel-electric submarines,
the *Onondaga*. As the tube containing the boat's search periscope extended
to its full height, Hughes stepped forward, slapped down the handles, and
grasped them at a crouch to bring his face level with the optic's eye pieces.

Sergeant David Strong watched the process from a kneeling position in
the corridor. He was wedged between the small submarine's banks of silent
diesel generators in the compartment aft of the cramped control room.
Strong and the three other members of his special forces team, Tenny,
Brown, and Roy were out of their element aboard HMCS *Onondaga*. They
had conducted dozens of exercises in the preceding months, but this was the
first in which they would actually transfer from ship to shore. This exercise
represented a culmination of their rigorous training regimen and a chance
to validate themselves in the type of mission they would be called upon to
execute should war ever arise.

Indeed, this was the first time since World War II that a Canadian submarine would be used for such a purpose, but in wartime special forces would almost certainly deploy covertly from a boat like *Onondaga*, which was small, quiet, highly maneuverable—and expendable. Strong and his team were to become the designated experts in maritime deployment within their squadron, and this was their first chance to exercise under realistic conditions. Strong was fascinated, having only ever experienced this sort of thing in movies up until now.

The captain hurriedly crab-walked the periscope through a full circle. He paused twice, mashed a button with his thumb, and called out, "Northern headland, bearing three-three-zero. Southern headland, bearing two-four-three. Surface is clear." Then slapped the handles back up, stepped away, and ordered, "Down periscope."

As the tube slid downwards into its well, Strong saw the chief petty officer click a stopwatch and announce: "Eleven-point-three seconds, sir."

Hughes swore under his breath, grimaced, and stepped forward. He squeezed between the periscope tube and the chief petty officer to join the navigator at a small table no larger than the kind of fold-down tray one would find in the back of a typical airline seat. He used a compass and protractor to plot the boat's position.

"Five meters under the keel," the navigator said softly.

Strong shifted his weight to the other knee and looked over his shoulder. His team waited, lined up in the corridor behind him dressed in black dry-suits with hoods pulled up over their hair and ears. The hulking frame of Master Corporal Roy looked almost comical crammed as he was into the cramped corridor, the patrol's gear all around his feet. Strong turned forward in time to see the boat's executive officer cross the control room in one step and say to the captain, "Sir, should we get the swimmers top side?"

The *Onondaga's* hull was more akin to the submarines launched during the Second World War than the sleek cylindrical shapes of more recent designs. This didn't mean the *Oberon*-class boats were outdated or lacking in lethality, however, far from it. It *did* mean that the width of the sub's control room was limited to what one could expect from a city commuter bus, with a much lower ceiling. The *Oberons* were small, a mere ninety meters long and less than a tenth of that in width. The compartments available to the crew were nowhere more than four meters wide. The submarines' designers had knowingly sacrificed creature comforts at the altar of lethality and stealth. Even with all the noise-dampening features incorporated into the boat's design, or maybe because of it, Sergeant Strong could hear every word spoken in the control room.

"Not yet, XO," Hughes was saying. "We've got plenty of water under us, and every mile we move closer to the shore is one less our guests need to cover in an open boat."

Hughes was a short man, stocky from too many days living inside a steel hull and enjoying good navy cooking. In their three-day transit from Halifax to the southern end of Labrador, Strong had come to understand that the boat's captain was supremely confident in himself, even to the point of arrogance. Now he was showing that he was aggressive, too.

"Captain," the XO was saying in a low voice, "I feel obliged to note that the depth is going to decrease rapidly on our present course, and the charts of this area have been off before."

"Noted, XO." The response was dismissive, but not unfriendly. "I've been here before. Maintain current speed and heading."

The role of any good executive officer was to preserve the ship that he served, whereas the captain's job was to put the ship in harm's way to accomplish the mission. That tension was now at play in *Onondaga's* control room.

"Maintain current speed and heading, aye," acknowledged the boat's chief, his hand on the back of the helmsman's seat.

Strong and his men had become familiar with the sailors in front of them over the past few days. To describe the conditions in which *Onondaga's* sixty-nine crew lived as "crowded" would have been an understatement. The vessel didn't even possess enough bunks to accommodate its usual compliment and adding four landlubber passengers to the mix had done nothing to alleviate the strain. Even so, the navy men had been especially welcoming, making space for the commandos and their gear and taking time to familiarize them with the ship's systems and operating procedures. The passage from Halifax to Labrador had been educational.

Onondaga continued throbbing slowly into the bay south of Cape St. Charles. Despite the control room's air conditioning, Strong could see sweat beading on the temples of the navigator as he tracked the vessel's progress with grease pencil and compass. Strong could imagine that grounding one of his nation's precious few submarines might be a significant event in the career of the vessel's captain and his officers. His appreciation for Commander Hughes' guts, and his abilities, was growing by the minute.

Another moment and the navigator said in a taut voice, "Two meters under the keel."

Hughes did not react. Even Strong was starting to feel tense. The boat's XO was casting sideways glances at his captain through the gaps in the sensor mast housing wells, which bisected the control room.

Now the captain ordered "Up periscope" again and repeated his earlier crab walk performance. The scans were for navigation purposes, but also to simulate a wartime check for threats in the area. They also helped the small submarine to avoid icebergs, which were still present around the Labrador coast this time of year. This time Hughes was more satisfied, both with the bearings to the landmarks and the speed with which he conducted the triangulation.

"One meter under the keel, sir," the navigator's voice cracked slightly as he looked up from his chart and protractor.

Hughes finally said in a calm voice, "Engines all stop. Helm, keep us level. Starboard one-five, bring us to zero-nine-zero."

The XO's hand had been resting on the engine control dials. He quickly turned the knobs and announced, "All stop, aye," as the massive banks of batteries housed beneath their feet stopped providing power to the boat's two propeller shafts.

The captain turned and looked back at the four commandos kneeling in his generator room and asked, full of confidence and apparently oblivious to his XOs nerves, "Sergeant Strong, are your boys ready?"

Now came the part they had been rehearsing all morning. Strong felt the soft pulsing of the sub's electric propulsion cease as he stood and responded, "Ready, Captain."

Hughes nodded. Then he turned back and ordered, "Helm, five degrees up on the planes. Surface the boat."

"Five up. Surfacing, aye."

Strong felt the deck beneath him take on a slight incline. Then it began to roll slightly. A terse, "Let's go," had his team turning around in the cramped space, facing aft. A sailor in a heavy rain slick was at the rear of the corridor, hands on the lever of the access hatch leading up through the pressure hull to the rest of the world. The rocking increased as the sail and then the hull of the submarine broached the surface.

The captain barked an order from the control room and the sailor yanked the hatch open, pushing it up as saltwater dripped and daylight flooded into the boat. Now it was the JTF 2 team's turn to act. The sailor pulled down a ladder and Corporal Tenny scrambled up and out, followed by Brown. Once on deck, the two men turned and reached back to accept the gear being hefted up by Roy and Strong.

In seconds the two corporals hauled up the bundled inflatable raft, silenced outboard motor, and four plastic weapon cases lashed to four water-proofed rucksacks. They then reached in and helped pull first Roy and then Strong up and out into the bright sunlight. The sergeant, coming up through the hatch, took a mouthful of frigid saltwater as a wave broke over the deck, though his black dry-suit otherwise shed the water down into the submarine. Spitting out seawater, Strong squinted and assessed their deck-side situation. After three days sealed in a dimly lit submarine, his eyes hurt as he took in the blue sky, the rolling blue-green sea, and the submarine's knife-like black mast towering two and a half stories above them. He didn't have time to consider the waves breaking against the hull and over the deck. They each had work to do.

Roy attached an air hose, run up through the hatch, to the cylinder containing the raft and the vessel hissed, unfolding into shape. Brown was already attaching the outboard motor as Strong joined Tenny in tossing the rucks inside, securing them to handles on the raft wall using carabiners. Finally, the four men jumped into the raft, still perched on the submarine's deck. Sergeant Strong was in the rear of the raft, manning the outboard motor. Giving the motor a quick rev to ensure it was operational, he looked back at the sailor whose head was poking above the open hatch. Strong gave him a thumbs up, and the man disappeared below, slamming the hatch shut.

Moments later *Onondaga*'s ballast tanks blew and sent white mists of spray into the air on either side of the raft as the sub began to submerge by the bow, slipping beneath the waves and leaving the raft and its occupants to bob on the swell.

Strong depressed the outboard motor's throttle, accelerating past the submarine's submerging sail, heading northwest towards the gray-green shore. He took a moment to look forward over the backs of his men. Roy was at the bow with his body atop the gear, the other two with a leg each almost dangling into the water to either side. Looking towards the land, Strong took his bearings on a wrist-band compass. He looked back just in time to see the dark fin shape of *Onondaga*'s sail silently slip completely beneath the waves.

Strong had spent significant time studying the chart of their intended landing area, memorizing the ins and outs of the rugged shoreline in anticipation of this moment. Now was his first look at the real thing and he needed to judge exactly where he was. *There.* He saw the cove they had selected as their landing point, a small, sheltered area with what appeared now to be a cobble beach. *That Commander Hughes really put us right on top of the place*, Strong noted, pleased. He adjusted the outboard slightly and depressed the throttle, making for the cove.

As the small raft picked up speed and bucked over the rolling swells, water occasionally lapping and splashing over the inflatable sidewalls, Strong took a moment to absorb the scene around him. They were moving through a large inlet with low, rocky, treeless shorelines stretching away ahead and to both sides. To the east was open ocean. Above, the sky was a brilliant blue, and Strong relished the warmth of the June sun on his back as he steered.

The swell lessened as he steered into the sheltered cove. A hundred meters from the beach Brown, the team's radioman, and Tenny, the demolitions expert, reached into the center of the raft and unzipped their watertight weapons cases, removing their carbines and aiming them over the bow. Their leader slowed the throttle as the rocky bottom became visible through the pristine water, and then the raft gently scraped on the stones. Tenny and Brown splashed into the lapping waves on either side of the boat, keeping their weapons high and wading forward the last few meters to dry land. Roy stepped out of the bow and began dragging the raft up the beach while Strong tilted the motor into the boat and jumped out to help him.

With the raft on dry land and the two corporals kneeling nearby providing security, Strong and Roy unpacked their own weapons, then set them aside on the rocks and unloaded the rest of the gear. The hulking Québécois took

Brown's position in the patrol's small perimeter so the smaller man could assemble the team's radio, an academic exercise at this point as *Onondaga,* the only station that could hear them out here in the wilds of Labrador, was currently underwater. With that task accomplished, Strong gave a signal and the four men shouldered their loads and moved in a wedge formation up the rocky, mossy headland overlooking the cove.

After a couple hundred meters they reached the low crest of the headland. Here they transitioned out of their dry-suits, taking turns peeling off and stowing the rubbery clothes and putting on olive drab combat uniforms. When the change was complete, Sergeant Strong "called" the exercise. The other three relaxed visibly, speaking in normal tones once again and carrying their weapons more loosely as they walked back down to the beach. They could train tactical operations on land at Dwyer Hill whenever they wished. Time in boats, and especially with a real RCN submarine, was a novelty.

As the team trudged back down the slope, Brown and Tenny picked up with the light-hearted, mildly insulting banter that had become a mainstay of their increasingly close relationship.

"Hey Will," Brown said, "too bad your girlfriend couldn't see you in the dry-suit, eh? This one might actually stick with you if she did!"

Tenny had been through three girlfriends since the team had formed last fall, and Brown and his own young wife had been on double dates with all of them, if for nothing else but the story that was sure to come out of the experience.

"Be nice, Bear," Tenny responded in mock indignation, using his friend's nickname. Brown always introduced himself with the first name "Clark," but when Tenny had discovered that his friend's given name was actually "Aclark," the Inuit word for Brown Bear, the younger man had dubbed him "Bear" and proceeded to call him nothing but. Eventually Strong and Roy had joined in, and the nickname stuck. "You know," continued Tenny, "I'm the model of gentlemanly virtues around the ladies. They flock to my magnetic personality. My stunning good looks are just the gravy."

Strong and Roy, bringing up the rear, both snickered. Tenny was many things, but a "gentleman with the ladies" was not one of them. He had been known to keep more than one relationship going at a time, which helped explain why they never lasted very long.

"Oh yeah?" the half-Inuit corporal teased. "That must be why they always leave so happy, eh?" The young corporal had been at the center of some spectacular public dressings down from his erstwhile girlfriends, so much so that he already possessed a reputation around the task force.

"You know it, Bear!" was Tenny's answer.

The back and forth continued all the way to the raft. Strong enjoyed the camaraderie of it, but from a distance. He envied the easy, natural relationship the two men shared. He had always struggled to form friendships, and his role as the patrol's leader added another layer of awkwardness to his interactions, at least in *his* mind. Tenny and Brown had each other. The huge, silent, Felix Roy had his wife and kids. Strong, in moments like this, was painfully aware that he had only his profession to keep him company in his off hours.

During a real operation they would have deflated and stowed the raft in a hide site, along with a bottle of compressed air to re-inflate it for exfil. In this case however, they arrived back where they had simply left the raft tied up on the beach. The four began to strip off their combats and get ready to zip back into their dry-suits. All were shirtless and barefoot when suddenly Brown stopped, looked at Tenny and said, "Hey Will, you up for a swim?"

"Are you crazy? That water can't be warmer than two degrees!" responded Will.

"Warm enough, unless you're scared of a little cold, eh?" said Bear. Before anyone could respond he had stripped off his trousers in one smooth motion and was running barefoot across the rocks towards the water.

"You're crazy!" Tenny called after him as Brown entered the water with ungraceful splashing footsteps before performing a shallow swan dive so he was completely submerged. After a moment Bear resurfaced and stood up with a splash, gasping from the cold but remaining where he was, waist-deep in the gently rolling saltwater.

Between gasps he called back, "You coming in or what?"

Tenny looked over at his sergeant and said once more, "He's crazy!" just as a flesh-colored mountain of a blur flashed between them. Felix Roy repeated Brown's performance, running into the surf until the splashing water checked his momentum, then diving in head-first. He too jumped up, gasping and flapping his long, muscular arms like a bird.

Strong turned back to Tenny, who was looking at him with a bewildered, pleading look in his eyes. Strong smiled, stripped off his trousers, and sprinted towards the water as the corporal let out a four-letter expletive.

Strong dove in, gliding above the rocks in the shallow water. He didn't feel uncomfortable initially, but after a few seconds the cold hit him and literally took his breath away. He planted his feet and stood half out of the water, gasping like the other two before joining in with their laughter. After much teasing and encouragement, Tenny finally stripped down and entered the water. He didn't dive, instead comically trying to remain upright on the uneven, slippery rocks. After a few steps he fell in, flailing back up as the other three loudly enjoyed his clumsiness and discomfort. Then the four men waded back to the beach, naked as the day they were born.

They collapsed onto the ground and Strong savored the warmth radiating off the rocks in the sun. The transition from warm to bracing cold and back to comforting warmth brought on an invigorating high.

Strong looked out to sea, past the mouth of the cove, and the sight caused all his latent insecurities to come rushing back. There was *Onondaga* on the surface, the low, dark profile of her hull broken by the tall rectangle of her sail amidships and the bulbous protrusion of the large sonar dome at the bow.

Did they see us? He wondered, suddenly concerned. *What will the sergeant major think if he hears we were wasting training time goofing off, taking a swim?* The RSM likely would not care, but that didn't make it into Strong's thoughts. *I need to get this back under control.*

He stood up, grabbed his dry suit, and said, "Get dressed," in a voice that was too demanding for the circumstances.

Tenny and Brown looked up at him, surprised by his change in tone. Brown looked ready to respond, but then Roy stood also and said in his deep French-Canadian accent, "You heard the sergeant. Let's get to it!"

PART III: DECISION POINT

"War is always a matter of doing evil in the hope that good may come of it."
—Sir Basil H. Liddel-Hart

 **CHAPTER 11**

2200 KRAT, Tuesday 15 June 1993
1500 Zulu
Eastern Sayan Mountains, Tuva Autonomous
Soviet Socialist Republic, Siberia

P AVEL MEDVEDEV LEANED back from the wooden table and pinched
the bridge of his nose in an attempt to fight off the onset of a headache.
Can I not escape my country's woes, even here in the depths of Siberia? He
was having trouble seeing the future, seeing how to move his country past its
present troubles and back into its rightful place as a secure global superpower.
In front of him on the remote *dacha's* rough dining room table he fixed his
eye on an open folder containing the voluminous Plan *Boyar.* Included in the
folder were assessments from KGB and GRU, both of which communicated
the grim appraisal that *Boyar* possessed only the slightest chance of success if
NATO decided to counter the Soviet strike on Poland.

Those assessments, along with a troubling brief on the state of the Soviet
economy from Drugov's Interior Ministry and another unflattering report
from the Foreign Ministry, had been delivered by Senior Captain Ivanenko,
Marshal Rosla's naval aide. The navy man had departed several hours previously, driving back down the narrow, wooded mountain paths that passed as
roads in this part of Russia's deep interior. With luck, he would make it back

to the dusty crossroads town of Kyzyl before sunrise. There he would board a military transport for the several-hours return flight to Moscow.

Medvedev smirked as he remembered the look of fear on Ivanenko's face following the president's teasing admonition. *Keep alert for wolves on your journey*, Pavel had said, *they are as big as mastiffs from feeding on reindeer in these mountains, and they travel in packs. Oh yes, and they like to hunt at night.* Of course, Medvedev knew Ivanenko would be perfectly safe. The same could not be said for the plan now in front of him.

Not that *Boyar* was unsatisfactory, Medvedev reflected sourly. It was excellent, brilliant even. Medvedev marveled at how Rosla had combined grand simplicity with elegant misdirection, the way it played to NATO's preconceptions of how a war in Europe would unfold while directing the Soviet military's blows against politically decisive weak points. Rosla, as he had hinted in their first meeting, proposed to shift much of the USSR's efforts to the strategic flanks in a way that stood a good chance of decisively altering the calculus on the vital central front and even overturning the current world order in the USSR's favor.

Unfortunately, *Boyar* possessed one glaring weakness. *Surprise. Surprise must be complete if we are to have any chance of success.* Given that *Boyar* was, like all Soviet war plans, predicated on an initial NATO act of aggression, in this case an interference in the goings on in Poland, strategic surprise was all but impossible.

It had been such a good week up until this point, the president mused, leaning back. He looked across the table, out the western windows of the expansive log construction *dacha*. The retreat was set on a ridgeline, giving views of other low, uninhabited, wooded ridges rippling away to the horizon. All these were dark now, the fading light of a long summer day wreathing the last summit in an orange halo.

Misha, his son, had accompanied him on this, his first vacation since ascending to the leadership of the faltering USSR. The young man brought along a friend, though not one of the female variety as his father would have liked. The other man was a *Spetsnaz* officer assigned to the group at Pskov. When the two boarded Medevedev's aircraft, Pavel had the distinct impression that he'd met the man before. He experienced the electric feeling of being too near a wolf during a hunt. But even the man's name, Ivan Ivanovich Khitrov, hadn't sparked Pavel's normally sharp memory, so he let the moment pass.

Upon arrival they linked up with their local Mongolian guides to prepare for the main event of their getaway, the wolf hunt. Pavel was the most experienced hunter in the group, at least as far as wolves were concerned. He'd taken up the sport as a young Party official helping to oversee the construction of the Baikal-Amur Mainline Railroad northeast of this presidential getaway in the 1970s. The future president kept the hobby to himself, not wanting to admit to such a bourgeois pastime, even in the less restrictive socialism of the post-Brezhnev era. Still, Pavel slipped away as often as he could to hone his skills against Siberia's endemic predators during his yearly two weeks of paid vacation. *And that Khitrov showed me up in just one morning*, Medvedev thought, the memory souring his mood further.

The men had risen long before dawn on their first morning at the *dacha*. The guides led them, rifles in hand, along a winding footpath to a low ridge overlooking a long, sloping meadow surrounded by thick forest. There they waited for their predators-turned-prey in the chill, damp, pre-dawn darkness. As the eastern horizon started to brighten, the moaning howls of a dozen or more wolves rose from among the trees far up the valley. The Mongolian guide stood, cupped his hands to his mouth, and let out his own piercing howl, imitating the wolves. Medvedev, who had practiced his own wolf call over numerous hunting expeditions, stood up next to him, adding his own howl to their faux wolfpack. Misha, a veteran of several hunting trips with his father, also joined in, though his calls lacked the skill of the older men.

The three of them stood there on the ridge, howling into the dawn, the wolves up the valley answering them and drawing closer as the sky brightened. Pavel remembered having looked back at his son's friend. Khitrov had admitted the previous night to never hunting wolves before, and now he watched the others' wolfish antics with a bemused smirk. His predatory eyes briefly met Pavel's good one, and then Khitrov turned and let out a howl so authentic that it nearly startled the others into silence. The hairs on the back of the president's neck stood up as if there was a wolf right there among them.

The calls worked, and before long they were catching glimpses of gray pelts moving between the trees below, trotting up the valley. One huge, beautiful wolf, the best specimen that Pavel had ever seen, paused on a flat rock in the clearing just downslope from the party's perch, a perfect shot. Medvedev, both as president and elder of their group, by default was granted the honor of the first shot. Sitting in the *dacha* now, Pavel cringed with the memory of what followed.

He had sighted down the scope of his hunting rifle. This was the point where he always struggled with his eye during a hunt; judging distance was difficult. He knew the shot would miss in the last millisecond before the firing pin struck the cartridge. It ricocheted off the rock. The report of the rifle startled the huge wolf and sent him fleeing as Pavel swore at his own clumsiness. Then, the supposedly novice hunter in their group, Khitrov, stood and with one smooth, efficient motion, brought his rifle up to his shoulder, sighted down his scope, and dropped the running wolf with a single, perfect shot, tumbling the animal end over end in mid-stride.

The gray pelt, even bigger up close than they'd realized, was now drying on a rack outside the *dacha* alongside the smaller ones taken during the following days by Pavel and Misha. *A good week*, Pavel thought again. They dined on reindeer venison, on huge pike fished from the nearby mountain lakes, on berries gathered for them by the families of their local guides. Medvedev allowed a smile to pass across his face as he reflected. *A man could really disappear in these mountains, live off the land, not be troubled by the goings-on in the outside world.*

The president's eyes snapped open and he sat up with a start. Turning, he saw Khitrov standing just inside the doorway, looking at his president with that annoyingly bemused smirk.

"Is there something you need, Ivan Ivanovich," Pavel asked gruffly, trying to mask his discomfort.

"No, thank you, *tovarich* President. I was simply coming in to find my smokes," the other man said.

Khitrov walked over to a side table and picked up a pack, pulling out an unfiltered cigarette and resting it between his lips, allowing the paper cylinder to hang precariously. The younger man looked around and patted himself, then turned to Pavel and asked, "You wouldn't happen to have a light, would you, my President?"

Medvedev fished uncomfortably in his pocket before pulling out a silver lighter. Khitrov leaned over the table and Pavel obliged him. The younger man leaned back, taking a long drag on his cigarette before contentedly blowing a stream of smoke at the ceiling in a way that was oddly familiar. Medvedev, still seated, watched him.

"Was there something else, Ivan Ivanovich?" Medvedev asked impatiently. "I am very busy tonight."

Khitrov looked down at the president, through the smoke, and seemed to ignore the pointed question. After a moment he spoke. "You don't remember me, do you, sir?"

"Should I?" Pavel asked, on guard now. This man *was* familiar, and he apparently knew something Pavel did not.

Khitrov took another drag, then spoke again, the cigarette dangling precariously from his lips. "Perhaps. Perhaps not. I am no one of importance, but then again, maybe I am not so unimportant after all."

"What is your meaning, Ivan Ivanovich?" Medvedev asked, trying to keep his anger at the impertinence in check.

After a moment, Khitrov answered bemusedly, "I may be the reason that you are president today." He paused, then asked, "You really don't remember? I lost my dream job on the Alpha team for helping you."

Medvedev looked closer, becoming increasingly annoyed. Then, suddenly, the memory came flooding back. *The high-cheeked Slavic face, the wolfish eyes, the dangling cigarette, the brash attitude. This is the Alpha team leader who led the assault on the White House two years ago!*

Pavel's blood chilled. Misha was sleeping off several vodkas in the other room. His bodyguard, Igor, was lounging in the front of the *dacha*, and the rest of his reduced security detail was otherwise engaged. Pavel was here with Khitrov, alone. *Why is he here? What does he want?*

Khitrov saw his president tense, and chuckled. Quickly raising his hands, palms forward in mock surrender, the *Spetsnaz* man said, "My President, you have nothing to fear from me. I am your man. I became your man when I killed all those people for you in Moscow." He dropped his hands, pulled out a chair without asking permission, and sat. "Indeed, I admire you. You are someone who knows how to use violence. This is something I have studied for a long time. Not many people have the *khrabrost* to do it."

"What is it you want, Ivan Ivanovich?" Medvedev repeated, but his tone was more even now. He realized that earlier, as Misha had been drinking vodka and Pavel had been sipping the same, Khitrov had not touched his own glass. *What's he playing at?* Medvedev wondered.

Khitrov's smile managed to convey very little warmth. He responded, "Only the opportunity to use my talents more effectively. My superiors in Alpha were...*displeased*...after I followed your orders at the White House. They relieved me, banished me to Pskov, that backwater. I am an educated man, my President. I have graduate degrees in psychology and political theory. I need an outlet for my education, my *talents*. My service to you left me hungry for more," a pause as he drew on his cigarette, "more influential pursuits."

"And what *are* your talents?" Medvedev asked warily.

"Political violence, of course." Khitrov answered point blank. "I have studied this my whole life. My research at Leningrad State University was focused on this, and," he raised a finger for emphasis, "I have some practical experience, in Afghanistan and in Moscow, as you know." Khitrov smirked at his own little joke and took another pull of his cigarette. The tip flared.

"Ivan Ivanovich," Medvedev said slowly, "while I appreciate the service that you did for me and for Russia in Moscow two years ago, I am not sure I understand where you think your talents would be useful." Pavel was regaining his composure, trying to wrest back control of the conversation after his initial shock.

Khitrov leaned forward and indicated the folder in front of Medvedev with his chin. "What are these?" he asked.

"*These*," Pavel responded coldly, putting his palm on the folio, "are marked *Most Secret.*"

"No matter," said Khitrov, leaning back, feigning disinterest. "I know what they contain, more or less." The man was confident, poised. "I can help you."

"You know what these folders contain?" Medvedev responded, dangerously. "Were you listening in on my aide's briefing, Ivan Ivanovich?"

"Of course not, my President," answered Khitrov, as if the very idea were absurd. "Your security men hustled me out of the *dacha*, and did a good job of it too. No, I know what is in those folders because I know you, or at least of you. I have studied the world situation from your perspective."

"Go on," Pavel said. *This should be good.*

Khitrov took one last pull from his dying cigarette, then said, "You plan to invade Poland. You are worried that NATO will try to stop you. This worries you because if they do intervene, we may lose." He blew out a thick cloud of smoke. "Am I close?"

Pavel was growing more annoyed by this man, but intrigued as well. "Perhaps," he answered, "what else do you think you know?"

"I know that you have a plan to deal with NATO. Why else would a naval officer come all the way out here to brief you? I know from your mood right now that *you* know the plan will fail. And I know why." The younger man was obviously enjoying this.

"Why will it fail, my young soldier?" asked Medvedev, keeping his tone as light as he could, humoring the young wolf.

"Because it is a *military* plan, my President, not a *political* one," explained Khitrov. "We soldiers are very conventional, predictable. We think in terms of destroying the enemy's equipment and formations, and we often forget about the political will that a nation must possess to actually prosecute a war to its conclusion."

Medvedev decided to indulge the younger man a little further, if only because he was exhausted from poring through the reports before him and needed the distraction, and perhaps, *This young man is getting at something interesting.*

"Take me through your thinking," the president ordered.

Khitrov nodded, then stood and retrieved a half-empty bottle of *Russkaya Standard* vodka from a side table along with two crystal tumblers. He returned, sat, and poured, making sure that Pavel's tumbler was fuller than his own. Then he quashed his cigarette in an ashtray and began.

"*Tovarich* President, despite what the western media says about you, you are a man of your word, are you not?" he asked, but didn't wait for a reply. "When you say you will not stand by while a united Germany remains a part of the NATO Alliance, you are serious. Yet, the western governments, the Americans, the British, the Germans, do not take you seriously. They posture and offer symbols of conciliation, but refuse to relent on this issue, even though our own Warsaw Treaty alliance is a skeleton of what it used to be. So, you keep our army in Czechoslovakia, and you support the dissidents in Poland."

Pavel nodded.

Khitrov went on, "Well, how does the west respond? With ever more crippling economic attacks. They refuse to buy our goods, even the oil and gas that your interior minister is pulling out of the ground in Central Asia and Siberia as fast as the holes can be drilled. We possess perhaps the greatest energy reserves in the world, but without customers..." the young officer let the thought linger, like the remnants of smoke still wafting from his cigarette butt.

The *Spetsnaz* man was right. Petrochemical supplies in the Persian Gulf were now secure, and the energy being pumped out of the North Sea's muddy depths, added to the reserves in Canada, left the United States and Europe feeling secure in snubbing the alternative Soviet supplies. Their intransigence was threatening to derail all of Drugov's herculean efforts to make the Soviet Union a major energy exporter. *One of those American senators even had the gall to suggest, on the floor of their senate chamber, that NATO close the Baltic approaches and Bosporus to all of our shipping until we withdrew unilaterally from Poland*, Medvedev fumed silently.

Khitrov continued, "So, my President, you plan to invade Poland. If I am not mistaken, you plan to do so when they are celebrating their Catholic Christmas this December, no? Crafty of you and the marshal, but perhaps too crafty."

Medvedev's blood chilled and his anger flared at the same time. *How has this man worked all this out on his own? Who does this major think he is, criticizing the defense minister?* Khitrov continued to speak, clearly enjoying the conversation, so the president held his tongue, for the moment.

"The problem with this hypothetical plan of the marshal's," Khitrov spoke the word "hypothetical" with a raising of his eyebrows, overtly indicating that he knew the plan was anything but, "is that it misjudges NATO politically, and this dooms the plan militarily. If I am not mistaken, once we have established a government friendly to us in Poland, you intend to offer the west an exchange: withdrawal of our forces from Poland and Czechoslovakia for German withdrawal from NATO, assuming of course that this gambit does not result in broader war. Am I correct?"

Pavel said nothing.

Khitrov continued as if the older man had agreed, "My President, I am sure your foreign minister has hinted at the obvious. The United States and the other NATO governments will never assent to this exchange. Why should they? You intend to offer them two potentially neutral states for one that is already firmly in their camp. This is not an equal trade. What is more, no matter how sincere you may actually be for peace, my President, the western leaders do not trust you. They don't trust the USSR. They will not believe that you are offering a true deal."

At this point Khitrov fished out another cigarette and placed it in his mouth without lighting it, speaking from the back of his throat around the unlit smoke in the manner that so annoyed Medvedev.

"What is more, I am sure your intelligence officials are telling you that the NATO militaries are becoming wise to your timing, yes?" Khitrov asked with a raised eyebrow. "Their Christmas holiday is too obvious. You cannot conceal the preparation of forces as large as ours, and if NATO is prepared for our move they will be far more likely to intervene"

In fact, Medvedev recalled, *the foreign minister rated the chances of just such an outcome at fifty percent or greater.* Captain Ivanenko had even mentioned how a source in the American dockyards had revealed that the US 2nd Fleet was altering the maintenance schedule for its carriers so as to have as many ships as possible available in December for operations in the Atlantic.

"Any competent officer must know that we cannot hope to decisively defeat NATO under these circumstances, without *complete* surprise," Khitrov was saying, "not if the westerners are allowed to commence hostilities when they are fully ready. At least, not without resorting to atomic weapons…"

Medvedev cut the young officer off forcefully, "I will never assent to starting an atomic war. Do you understand?"

Khitrov leaned back, his hands up again in mock surrender. "Of course, of course, my President," he said around his cigarette, "I of course agree. The game loses its fun when the explosions become too big."

You view all this as a game? Medvedev thought as he contemplated his son's friend. *Still, this young wolf has just told me all the high points of the critiques that the KGB, GRU, and Foreign Ministry have offered of Boyar.*

"Assuming you are correct in all of this," Pavel waved his hand in the air, "*speculation*," he said acidly, "what do you believe we should do about it? Any fool can poke holes in a plan, *tovarich* Major. Much more difficult is patching them up. You said you could help. What path do you advocate?"

"War, *tovarich* President," Khitrov said simply, spreading his hands as if the answer were obvious. "Surprise, pre-emptive war against NATO to achieve our aims and reshape the strategic balance of the world in our favor. Escalate to de-escalate. The defense minister is an intelligent man. I am sure his military plans are good, but they require surprise to succeed. The circumstances of the world situation in the coming year offers a favorable opportunity to achieve this surprise. If we escalate the situation quickly enough, and in a way that frightens NATO leaders and their people enough, then the west will be more inclined to give us what we demand, if only to pull themselves back from the brink of destruction."

"Go on," Medvedev said, unconsciously leaning forward as he grew more intrigued.

"First, sir, some principles for political violence," Khitrov explained. "Do you remember the advice I gave you that night in Moscow? No? I told you that people are prone to learn lessons from violence different from those you wish them to learn. The message sent is rarely the same as the message received. Therefore, each act of violence must be aimed at a material target as well as a political one. Destroying material resources forces people to act in the way you wish, and if they are forced to act, then they are more likely to learn the lesson you intend."

Medvedev nodded. *This is logical.*

"If one can make an opposing country's population learn the proper lessons through violence," Khitrov continued, "one can very quickly sap their will to continue the struggle. This is one of the weaknesses of our opponents' 'democratic' societies. Even if we cannot force the western governments to demand peace, properly applied violence can tie down large enemy forces in tasks that do nothing more than make the people *feel* safe. Do you know how many resources the Americans expended securing their west coast from phantom fleets and phantom air armies during their war with Japan? All because local officials demanded that they be protected from non-existent threats."

ᴐv was becoming animated now, clearly excited by the opportunity to present his thoughts to such an elevated figure, to try to influence the course of world events. He took his cigarette between two fingers and asked politely, "Another light, my President?"

Medvedev admitted to himself that he was starting to enjoy listening to this brash young man's thoughts. He fished his lighter from his pocket again and produced a flame, allowing the major to puff his smoke to life.

After a long pull, Khitrov began again. "As I said, my President, I have given this problem much thought. Your Christmas invasion will not work, for the reasons I have given you. But there is another opportunity, *if* you are willing to make war on NATO from the start. Here is what I propose…"

For several minutes Khitrov outlined his thoughts. Very quickly Medvedev began to marvel at the grandeur of this junior officer's vision, the way it attacked their opponents on so many levels, hitting them militarily, politically, economically. Before long the president was nodding in agreement as each individual attack was described with clear material and political objectives. Soon Pavel pulled a world map out of the folio and the two men stood around it as Khitrov pointed and gestured at one key point after another. Medvedev was taken aback when Khitrov revealed his timing for the proposed war, but after the other man explained his reasoning, Medvedev found himself in full agreement. *Why has no one else thought of this?*

The two men talked into the early hours of the morning, polishing off the remainder of the bottle of vodka and Khitrov's pack of cigarettes between them. Finally, Pavel sat back in his chair, exhausted but mentally energized.

He looked up and said, "Major Khitrov, I thank you for this. Before you came in here, I could not see a way forward out of the trap that our opponents are laying. Now my vision is restored. Do you believe in this plan?"

Khitrov sensed an opportunity, and he seized it. He looked Medvedev in the eye and said, "With all my heart, my President."

"Good!" Medvedev answered. "Then prepare yourself. When we leave here you will come with me to Moscow and brief the defense minister on your ideas. I do not know how you have done it, but your thinking on this matter will nicely compliment the plan he and STAVKA have devised."

Khitrov nodded, not the slightest hint of trepidation creeping into his expression.

"We are calling it Plan *Boyar*," Pavel went on, feeling relaxed from the vodka, "and I want you in charge of integrating and implementing these schemes into it. You can expect a promotion and a transfer to Moscow to go along with this responsibility. No more languishing with the bumpkins around Pskov, *da?*"

Medvedev leaned forward in his seat and clapped the younger man on the shoulder.

"So," Khitrov ventured after a moment, "What will the Politburo say?"

"I haven't agreed just yet," Medvedev answered in a jovial tone, "but I am intrigued. This plan has great risks, but perhaps you are correct, that we should 'escalate to de-escalate' the situation, as you say. I like the concept. I came to power on a roll of the dice, a roll that you helped turn in my favor. Perhaps just such a gamble is necessary in this dilemma as well. But, either way, do not concern yourself with the Politburo. I can handle them."

Khitrov flashed his predatory smile, showing his teeth. The image no longer made Medvedev uncomfortable. *This man is a wolf, but he's my wolf.* The major raised his tumbler towards the president in salute, the last swallow of vodka sloshing around the bottom of the glass. He downed the drink in one fluid motion.

Pavel Medvedev's headache was gone. He could see Russia's way forward. The path was dangerous, and he had not decided to take it yet, but in his heart he knew he would, soon.

 **CHAPTER 12**

1128 MSK, Sunday 5 July 1993
0828 Zulu
Trinity Cathedral, Pskov, Russian Soviet Federative Socialist Republic

T HE PRIEST FINISHED chanting the scriptural litany with a long, low, *"Amen,"* sung over his chest-length gray beard. As the sound echoed in the vaulted ceiling, the red-robed clergyman blessed the congregation, making the sign of the cross using three extended fingers in the Russian Orthodox fashion.

Guards Colonel Ilya Romanov, standing among the other congregants, crossed himself and repeated the amen. Beside him, his wife Elena and their two teenage children did the same. The priest was adorned in striking embroidered vestments, worn today to commemorate Saint Elizabeth Romanov and her attendant nurse Barbara, who were martyred by the Bolsheviks in 1918. He retrieved his incense censer from the altar and progressed down the cathedral's aisle, swinging the smoking orb as he went. As he exited the cathedral, the congregation filed up to the altar and crossed themselves before the crucifix beyond. Ilya, his family in tow, did the same.

Romanov always felt calmed by the solemn reverence of the Orthodox service, happy to share his faith with his family and others of their community. He put his hand lightly in the small of Elena's back as they walked back towards the cathedral's entrance, their son Petya and daughter Irina walked ahead. They emerged from the cool, white interior of the church into the brilliant blue sky and bright, warm sunshine of a beautiful Pskov summer day. Father Yevgeny was greeting his flock with single-pump handshakes as they departed.

Ilya regarded the priest warmly as they waited in the queue to exchange Sunday greetings. Persecution of the church had been the on-again, off-again pastime of the Communist government since 1918, and not all Orthodox priests were so well-respected, but Father Yevgeny was a shepherd in the best clerical sense of the word. The Orthodox faith in the Soviet Union had survived and even thrived due to people like him. He was slow to judge those around him, quick with a word of grace during confession. Perhaps his most impressive trait was his ability to show deference to the laws of the nominally atheist State in which he ministered while not compromising the core tenets of his religion.

In turn Petya, Irina, and Elena filed past to greet the clergyman. Finally, Ilya stepped forward and took the priest's hand, saying, "Thank you for your sermon today, Father. I had not considered the example of the Savior washing his disciples' feet as an example for leadership. I believe your message is relevant in my own profession. I would like my officers to follow this example."

"Thank you, Colonel Romanov," responded the priest with a smile, "I am pleased the message touched you. It was also the Savior who said, 'greater love has no man than this, that he lay down his life for a friend.' Quite an example of leadership for a soldier, *da*? Ah, speaking of laying down one's life, do you claim any relation to the saint we honor today?"

Romanov shook his head. "No father, as far as I know there is no link to the old royal family. Romanov is not so uncommon a name," he answered.

"I suppose not. Yet the name is noble. Fitting for a noble man such as yourself. Please, enjoy this lovely weather. Go with God's blessing," Father Yevgeny said.

Ilya caught up with his family on the lawn next to the church. Pskov's Trinity Cathedral dominated the center of the medieval *Krom*, the fortress at the confluence of the Pskova and Velikaya Rivers. The church's four black and one golden onion domes towered over the *Krom's* squat, ancient walls, overshadowing the Romanov family as they crossed the peaceful green inside

the castle and exited the fortress through the south gate into the bustling Karl
Marx Square, where trolleybuses and trucks rumbled past.

Not quite as bustling as it was two years ago, Ilya recalled, remembering the
heady days before the coup in 1991. Then the USSR had appeared to be on
the brink of collapse and western goods were flooding the informal markets
in every Russian city. Petya, his son, had taken a liking to blue jeans and
American rock music. Now, with increasingly harsh sanctions imposed by the
west, no such luxuries were evident in the kiosks scattered around the square.

The Romanovs maintained a tradition of taking a family walk around
downtown Pskov each Sunday after church regardless of the season, if the
colonel's duties permitted of course. Both Ilya and Elena were from Moscow,
but in the last two years they'd fallen in love with this smaller, older city
on the western margin of their country. The pace of life here was slower,
the architecture less dominated by Brezhnev-era concrete slab apartment
buildings. This was a city that was proud of "their" *desantniki* from the
76th Guards Airborne Division, garrisoned at the airbase on the southeast
edge of the city.

The family walked south along the tree-lined sidewalks flanking Leona
Pozemskogo street, looking at the sparse merchandise being offered by the
street merchants on the way. After a few dozen meters, Petya was hailed by
some school friends on their way to play football at a nearby field. Ilya let his
boy join them. *Boy?* Ilya thought, *He's seventeen, nearly a man himself.* Irina,
two-years-younger, went as well. That left Ilya and his bride of nearly two
decades on their Sunday walk. Elena strolled ahead, admiring a kiosk offering
the season's first apples, probably trucked in from the mountains around Almaty.

As she turned, Romanov caught sight of the slight bulge beneath her
Sunday dress. She was a vision, thin and willowy with golden hair, more
beautiful than the day they had married, and his heart swelled with love. The
new baby had come as a shock to both of them. Both had considered her too
old for another pregnancy.

The vision took Ilya back to the early days of their marriage, when Elena
carried Petya in her womb. The two of them would walk through markets
like this and admire the produce. Fresh food had been scarce in those days
under the mismanagement of the socialist government, and Romanov's pay as

a junior officer did not allow him to spend much outside the state-managed *Universam* food stores. Mostly they just admired the colorful produce at a distance. On some days, especially as the pregnancy progressed, Ilya would splurge to buy his bride an apple or a pear, thinking all the time about the health of their child.

Romanov understood at the time that his country was capable of so much more, that the brand of socialism forced on them by the Party was holding the Soviet Union back from its true potential. The USSR produced more apples than any country on earth, and yet the fruit that Elena touched, then as now, was clearly of inferior quality, small and in many cases worm-eaten. At the time Ilya had not failed to make the direct connection between communist mismanagement and the health of his unborn child. This fact did much to explain why he had never become a Party member. *Well, that and the fact that the Party never accepts the openly faithful,* Ilya thought wryly, not for the first time.

The food scarcity this summer was different. The reason was obvious; in fact, Romanov could see it from where he strolled. It was trumpeted by the headline of yesterday's *Izvestia* in a newspaper rack at the street corner: *Soviet president demands end to Imperialist encirclement, insists that sanctions against USSR are illegal.* President Medvedev was continuing and even expanding the economic reforms of his predecessor, practically throwing the USSR's doors open to foreign trade. The problem was that none of the world's most important economies were interested. The Americans, in conjunction with the European Economic Community, soon to become the European Union, refused to conduct business and pressured others to forsake the Soviet markets as well. The Soviet economy was forced to rely heavily on internal resources, hobbling the president's reforms and causing hardships for ordinary citizens.

Of course, it's not all bad, Romanov thought, as ahead he spotted a towering green and yellow pyramid across the street from Lenin Square. *Some of what we produce is actually quite good.*

"Ilya, look," Elena said, happily tugging his arm, "melon season is here!"

They hurried to where the mountain of melons was piled four meters high. Every summer trucks from the southern reaches of the USSR brought millions and millions of melons to cities across the Soviet Union. Swarthy-skinned southerners from Ukraine, the Caucasus, and the Central Asian Republics piled the fruit on seemingly every street corner and then lived beside their produce until it had all been sold off to eager city-dwellers. Elena loved the oblong yellow-skinned melons that Russians called "torpedoes," similar to western cantaloupes, but sweeter, while Ilya preferred the traditional red-fleshed ones with green rinds.

As they approached, Romanov saw that the vendor was negotiating price with a familiar character.

"...and you call these ripe? They don't even sound hollow when you tap them," Major Ivan Sviashenik was saying incredulously, bending over and rapping his knuckles on a melon as he did so. "Your prices are outrageous!"

Romanov walked up and clapped his regimental *zampolit* on the back. "Expounding on the virtues of socialism, eh Major?" Ilya asked in a teasing tone.

The younger man turned and smiled, slightly embarrassed upon meeting his colonel in public. "Good day, Colonel. This man and I were just discussing the concepts of supply and demand. Yes, demand for his melons may be high," he indicated the mountain of fruit with his hand, "but so is his supply. As one of his first customers, I should receive, what do they say in the west, a discount, *da?* Especially for fruit that is not even ripe."

The vendor waved his hand dismissively.

Ilya made a show of examining the produce himself while Elena said, "Good day, Ivan," to Sviashenik with the warm, motherly tone she reserved for officers in her husband's unit.

Rapping his own knuckles on a pair of melons and hefting them to judge their weight, the colonel rendered his judgment. "These are excellent melons!" he addressed the olive-skinned southerner, "What's your price?"

"For someone like yourself who is a good judge of fruit, two hundred for the green ones, three hundred of the torpedoes," answered the smiling salesman.

"Wait!" cried Sviashenik, incredulously, "that is half the price you told me!"

The vendor shrugged his shoulders and said, "He asked nicely."

Before the political officer could go on, Romanov said, "One of each if you please, and one for my friend here."

"Of course, *tovarich*," the man said, turning to select the fruit from the mound.

"You see, Ivan Avramovich," said Ilya with a playful smile, "not all is capitalism versus socialism. Sometimes you just need to see people as people." He accepted the two melons from the vendor with thanks, and handed the yellow one to Elena to carry.

Sviashenik gave the melon-monger a dirty look as the man handed him a specimen that was significantly smaller than the first two, but held his tongue.

"Thank you, Colonel," Sviashenik muttered as they walked away. "I will be sure to repay you at the base."

"Nonsense!" Ilya assured him. "Consider it a gift. You've earned it. Are you heading to the trolley stop?"

"Thank you again, sir," the major said, and then in answer, "Yes, I'm taking the trolley back to base."

"Good," announced Romanov. "We'll walk with you as far as Rizhsky *Prospekt*." He then immediately dove into talking shop, "We are getting more contract soldiers, up to twenty percent of the levy coming this September. That along with those already in the regiment will mean that nearly a quarter of the men are contracted. Tell me, Ivan Avramovich, what do you make of them?"

The political officer considered his response, then said, "I am perhaps not qualified to comment on their technical training. From a political standpoint, they are no great socialists—"

"Neither are you," Romanov cut in, with a sidelong smile.

Sviashenik smirked. "Neither is our president, or our young Major Medvedev," he said. "Do not tell the Politburo I said that." Pausing, he went on, "Whoever we get, I think they had better start learning Polish."

"Why do you say that?" asked Romanov.

"It is clear to see," Sviashenik went on. "Things are coming to a head in Poland. I would not be surprised if we intervene there before the end of the year. President Medvedev's statements are becoming increasingly firm on the matter. Last week he announced again that he would not allow the Germans to establish themselves on the border of the Soviet Union. His rhetoric is growing more belligerent each week."

Ilya nodded. He had observed the same in the state-controlled newspapers. Then he asked, "What of NATO? If we intervene directly do you think they will use force to stop us?"

Sviashenik shrugged. "Who knows? They went to war over Poland once before. They have been willing to use their economic advantages so far to try to pound us into submission. Why not military advantage as well?"

"That would mean war," Elena said, concerned. "Why must we concern ourselves with the chaos in that country? Can we not just live in peace? Why must we continually wrestle with the Americans over this country or that?"

"If only the world were so simple," Romanov agreed. "Right now, we *are* like two wrestlers. Our opponent thinks he has us nearly pinned and is applying pressure to finish us. Our president does not strike me as the kind of man who will submit to this." He gave Elena's hand a knowing squeeze, silently reassuring her that he was only coaxing the political officer out of his shell with such talk, trying to get to know the man better.

The major shook his head. "We will have a good indication of what President Medvedev intends soon, I think. If the old bear intends to start something, he will not let our grandfathers go on schedule in September."

Ilya nodded. He hadn't considered that. The Red Army received new levies of two-year draftees, "*srochniki*," twice a year. If the "grandfathers," the men whose service was supposed to be complete this fall didn't depart then, Ilya thought, *we'd better prepare ourselves.* He would have to start taking measures so the barracks do not become overcrowded, for one thing.

They reached the trolley stop and the colonel said, "Thank you for your thoughts, Major, and blessings on this Lord's Day. No. Forgive me, Saturday is your holy day, is it not?"

"It is Colonel, but I am not devout. Thank you for the melon. I will enjoy it for lunch today," said the *zampolit.*

They parted ways, Sviashenik waiting to catch the trolley back to the base while Ilya and Elena turned and walked the short block down to the Velikaya River bank before turning back north. The political talk with the *zampolit* troubled both of them. Ilya's tours in Afghanistan had been hard on Elena, and she prayed daily that he would not be sent off to another war. For Ilya, the issue was more complicated. He did not want to see his country as the aggressor in another conflict, but, *If what the president says is true and the west is truly trying to strangle us and force us to accept NATO—German—influence and armies in Poland, then they are also directly harming the health of my family, my unborn child, for political gain, and they do it intentionally. This must be opposed somehow. Our president will surely act.*

Walking north along the riverbank, the colonel took in the familiar scenery. Small, quaint monasteries and churches dotted both sides of the river, their onion domes making the scene distinctly Russian. Ahead again was the *Krom*, that Russian fortress that had seen so many invaders over the years. Like any good Red Army officer, Romanov knew his country's military history well. It was a history of struggle to turn back one invader after another. The Mongols who had driven the original *Rus* out of Kiev and then north, into the forests. The Tatars. The Teutons, who had been driven out of this very city by the great Prince Alexander Nevsky. The Swedes. Napoleon. The Germans. Hitler.

Why do they hate us? Fear us so? wondered Ilya. *Why do they regard us as such barbarians?* Walking up the bank with Elena, surrounded by the beautiful symbols of his country's culture, with the imposing walls of the *Krom* before them to remind him of his duty, Ilya knew that if his country called, he would proudly answer again, like generations of Russian soldiers before him.

 **CHAPTER 13**

2230 EST, Friday 30 July 1993
0330 Zulu (31 July)
Aboard USS *Mount Whitney*, off Cape Henry, Virginia, USA

ROB BUCKNER STEPPED through the hatchway leading out of USS *Mount Whitney*'s dimly lit central island superstructure and into the warm, breezy, starlit night that reigned over the ship's expansive deck. He walked the dozen meters to the railing on the port side of the ship and stopped. The dark line on the horizon, set against the dark blue of the sea below and the starry night sky above, denoted the southern headland at the entrance of Chesapeake Bay. A light winked rhythmically from that line. *The Cape Henry lighthouse, most likely*, Rob thought. Beneath him the gentle *swish* of the ship's hull sliced through the sea. Ahead he could just make out the string of lights adorning the Chesapeake Bay Bridge-Tunnel, stretching across the ship's course. The *Mount Whitney* would pass over one of the two tunnels on her way back into Norfolk tonight.

The Marine colonel pulled a cylindrical plastic case out of his trouser pocket, unscrewed one end, and tapped a cigar out of it. *Helen would be pissed if she could see me right now*, Rob mused, as he always did when he engaged in this vice. He had picked up cigar smoking from his platoon sergeant as a second lieutenant fresh out of Quantico. Helen hated the smell, and he only indulged when in the field, which still earned him a withering look whenever he returned home. *Now "in the field" means a comfortable bunk on this pleasure bucket*, Rob thought, contemplating the flagship of the US 2nd Fleet beneath his feet. *Not even the stench of sweat and dirt to cover up the cigar smoke. You've come a long way from sleeping in the rain and the mud with only your woobie for comfort.*

Buckner took a Zippo lighter out of his other pocket and lit the cigar. He kept one hand cupped to protect the flame from the breeze and flicked the lighter several times, sucking in until the comforting aroma of smoldering tobacco filled his senses. He put the lighter away and inhaled deeply, savoring the warm, earthy taste. Exhaling, he watched the wisps of smoke blow back towards the ship's stern. Beyond the dissipating smoke he could see the green and red running lights of USS *Carl Vinson*, the massive *Nimitz*-class aircraft carrier with whom *Mount Whitney* and the embarked 2nd Fleet staff had been training for the past several days. Rob took another pull from his cigar as he contemplated the exercise they'd just concluded.

Admiral Falkner insisted on realistic training, not only for his operational forces, but for his staff as well. Hence, Rob was on the flagship, bunking in a closet-sized cabin with a Navy captain, across the passageway from the slightly more spacious quarters of two rear admirals. Some staff grumbled about the inconvenience of going to sea just to do their normal work, causing Buckner to smirk, as he remembered training exercises with the Marines where he had formulated and issued orders under a poncho in the pouring rain with only his red-lensed L-shaped flashlight to illuminate his map. *Some of these swabbies are a little soft*, he thought.

The new commanding officer of the *Vinson*, Captain Ben Stevenson, had taken the exercise as an opportunity to show off his aggressiveness. Over the course of four days he'd pushed his carrier's air group hard, launching one simulated "alpha strike" after another while still maintaining a heavy combat air patrol day and night. Even Buckner, who was only passingly familiar with carrier operations, was impressed with the tempo, the rumbling sound of jet engines overhead at all hours of the day and night. Admiral Falkner was pleased as well, and he let Stevenson know earlier this afternoon. Four days of heavy air operations was about the limit of what a lone carrier could sustain before magazines began to run empty and crews began to drop from exhaustion, but Stevenson had managed the drill with such precision that Falkner's staff estimated that "Battle Star," as many sailors colloquially referred to the supercarrier, had at least another day of fight left in both ship and crew.

Rob turned his head as a dark figure exited the hatchway behind him. The dark shape materialized into Vice Admiral Falkner, who joined Buckner at the rail. Rob stiffened as his chief approached.

"'Evening, Rob," said the admiral, waving his hand dismissively at his subordinate's rigid posture. "Relax, son. I thought I'd find you out here. Most of the staff is packing up their sea bags so they can get down the gangplank as quick as possible when we put in. I figured an infantryman like yourself packs light, am I right?"

Rob smiled and nodded in acknowledgment. He prided himself on keeping his bags ready to go at a moment's notice, something his instructors at Quantico had pounded into him.

"Beautiful night for a smoke," the admiral went on. "Mind if I join you?"

"Of course not, Admiral," said Rob.

"Good, good." Falkner pulled a pipe from his pocket and went through the motions of packing the bowl with loose tobacco from a small pouch in his breast pocket. As he did so he asked, "How's morale on the staff?"

"I would say it's good sir," Rob answered. "There's the usual griping about being here while there are everyday fires to put out back at Norfolk, but overall I think everyone appreciates the value of coming out here and doing it like we would in wartime."

"Not everyone," said the admiral. "I know several of the staff don't believe in coming out to sea. They think we could, and should, run a war from the headquarters in Norfolk." Falkner shook his head. "They're wrong, Rob. The proper place for a fighting admiral and his staff is at sea, not stuck in an immobile concrete building waiting for the next *Russki* cruise missile or nuke to obliterate the place." Falkner's tone was not defensive, but rather instructive. He retrieved a small matchbook from his breast pocket and struck one of the flimsy matches. The flame immediately flickered out in the warm breeze. The admiral tried again, this time shielding the match against his body, but the result was the same. "You would think," the older man chuckled, "that after thirty years I would have learned to do this by now."

Rob fished out his Zippo and handed it over. Falkner thanked him and sparked the flame into the pipe's bowl, finally lighting it. After a few seconds he let out a satisfied puff, watching the smoke dissipate astern. Then he turned to the Marine and asked, "What do you think, Rob? Honest opinion. Is it worth it, taking the whole staff out like this on a regular basis?"

"Well, sir, to be honest, I rather enjoy it. Pretty comfortable digs for a Marine."

"They are that," agreed Falkner in a low voice, thick with smoke. "*Mount Whitney*, and *Blue Ridge* over in the Pacific, are probably the most advanced communication platforms ever created. They were designed from keel up as command ships. Even better comms than *Vinson* back there." The admiral motioned with his pipe astern, towards the distant behemoth. "Did you know they were designed to act as alternate national command posts in the event of nuclear war? God forbid, of course."

"I didn't, sir," answered Rob after a moment. *God forbid indeed*, he agreed silently, briefly imagining riding out a nuclear war on this tin can while families and cities were incinerated ashore. *Though I could have guessed, based on the antennae that sprout from every surface on this can.* "Admiral, I'm no expert, but some of the staff say we're more vulnerable at sea if the balloon goes up. I mean, one lucky Russian sub captain and 2nd Fleet loses its whole primary staff."

"It's a risk, I admit," Falkner acknowledged. "In fact, if I were the Russians and decided to go nuclear, this ship is one of the first things I would target," Falkner nodded as if concedeing before continuing, "If I could find it, and there's the rub. When we're mobile, we're hard to find. At Norfolk they always know where we are. When we're at sea, they have to find us before they can hit us."

Buckner nodded, conceding the point and taking a deep pull on his cigar.

"Anyway, Rob," the admiral said, changing the subject, "I've read your reports but haven't had a chance to ask you about your world tour. How was Hawaii and Japan? How was England?"

Falkner had sent him on a feeling-out expedition to 2nd Fleet's counterpart headquarters at San Diego, Pearl Harbor, Yokosuka, the Persian Gulf, and

Naples, and then on to Portsmouth in the United Kingdom. Buckner was acting as Falkner's eyes, to see if they were seeing the same troubling signs of a Soviet Christmas gambit as 2nd Fleet.

"Well, sir, I didn't have much time to work on my tan in Hawaii, if that's what you're getting at," Buckner said wryly. Falkner had a good sense of humor and rewarded Rob with a chuckle. "Pacific Fleet agrees with our assessment of what the Russians are doing, as does 7th Fleet at Yokosuka. They see the same ramp up in readiness for the Soviet Pacific fleet that we do here, and they're adjusting their overhaul schedules accordingly. They won't have as big of a gap in coverage as we will after the New Year, but they have more ocean to cover."

Falkner grunted as he took another puff from his pipe. "I'm concerned about that gap in our carrier readiness. Right now, the Russians have us reacting to their schedules. I don't like it."

Rob was surprised. The admiral was receptive to criticism from others, but Buckner had never actually heard the man express doubt about a decision already made.

"But sir," Rob said, "I thought the idea was that they'd have to stand down after the New Year as well. At least, that's what Ed Franklin's been briefing."

"Ed's not wrong, but he's handicapped because we don't know the Russians' intentions, if they even know themselves." Falkner tapped his fingers on the ship's railing and went on, "They could conceivably delay yard work for several weeks or even months, if need be. We, on the other hand, are committed to our new maintenance schedule. The chief of naval operations had some trouble getting the money from Congress to speed up *Enterprise*'s refueling, and he had to cut back on weapons procurement to balance the books. That means we're not buying nearly as many of those new AMRAAMs as quickly as I would like." Falkner referred to the new fire-and-forget AIM-120 air-to-air missiles now being fielded by the fleet to replace the older and far less capable AIM-7 Sparrow missiles.

"Truth be told," the admiral continued, "I'd rather we retire some of our older ships if it meant we could train more and build up some ordnance reserves, but, congress has their own priorities, I suppose." The older man shrugged and took another puff from his pipe, "Maybe they're right. More ready hulls will be better if it comes to shooting. Hard to believe the Soviets would really try something in this day and age though." The US Navy had been holding steady at just under the peak goal of six hundred warships set by the Reagan build-up of the eighties. The maintenance on all those hulls was becoming increasingly difficult as a divided Congress tried to find ways of cutting corners and balancing the budget.

The admiral paused before saying, "I wonder if we're not pushing the Soviets too hard with these sanctions. From what you read in the news, things are getting pretty hairy over there. I'm inclined to take Medvedev at his word when he says he won't stand for it much longer."

"Congress and the president seem to think that's a good thing, that it's only a matter of time until the economic screws make ordinary Soviet citizens start to question Medvedev's leadership," responded Buckner.

"Maybe, maybe not," said the admiral, and Buckner found himself zeroing in on the admiral's every word. Geopolitics was not his game, but it was certainly an interest. "I'm inclined to take a man at his word until he proves me wrong." The admiral continued, "So far that old bear in the Kremlin has done everything he said he would. Franklin Roosevelt thought the same thing about our sanctions against Japan back in forty-one, and how did that turn out for Pearl Harbor?" Falkner let that thought linger.

"Anyway, how was England? Did my old friend Pete Reeves show you a good time?" The admiral continued in a more upbeat tone.

Rear Admiral Peter Reeves, Royal Navy, had done more than show the visiting American Marine a "good time." Rob hadn't felt a hangover like that in years, and his sides still hurt when he remembered about how hard and long he had laughed at the gregarious British sailor's off-color sea stories.

"Sir, the admiral sends his regards," Buckner answered. "He asked me to convey that the Royal Navy is on board for a combined exercise in mid-December. He says he will have *Invincible* and a task force ready to play red team for us. My report on that trip is on your desk back at Norfolk. Admiral Reeves also meant to send along a bottle of scotch, but…I think we drank it."

"He would, the scoundrel," Falkner laughed through his pipe. "Great news. Always love working with the Brits. The Royal Navy may not be what it used to be, but by God they have a sense of their history over on that side of the pond. You ever read about Horatio Nelson?" Falkner was always recommending books to his subordinates. "What a leader that man was! Great book. *Decision at Trafalgar* by, it was Dudley Pope, I think. Well worth a read. A jarhead like you would really appreciate him, even if he *was* a navy man. Excellent study in leadership."

"I'll check it out, sir," said Rob. He would. The colonel had learned early on that Falkner only recommended excellent reads.

Falkner shifted gears again, forcing Buckner to keep up, though he was starting to learn the admiral's subtler body language. Softening his tone, Falkner said, "How are you doing, Rob? You've had a few months to get your feet planted. You're meeting all the lofty expectations I have, but how are you getting on?"

Buckner took a pull on his cigar while he gathered his thoughts. The admiral always remembered to ask after his officers' welfare, but Rob hadn't been prepared for the question because the answer was complicated. *Do I tell him?*

"Sir, working for you has been a great experience, and I'm grateful for the opportunity."

"But?" the older man prompted.

"Well, sir, this job is also the end of the line for me, and I know that. No command means I'll never get a star, and I've been putting thought towards retirement. Helen and I have our eye on a piece of land up in Wisconsin. Nice place where the kids could finish out school and have a solid home-base to come back to when they go off to college."

Falkner nodded. "Can't say I'm surprised, Rob," he said softly. "You've been doing good work here, but I sympathize with where you are right now. What sort of timeline are you thinking about?"

"Sir, if nothing comes of this threat from the Soviets in December, I'll probably drop my retirement papers after the New Year. I could be out by next summer."

"We'll be disappointed to lose you," responded Falkner. "I'm sorry the Corps doesn't see the same potential in you that I do, Rob. Have you thought about what you plan to do once you're out?"

Buckner flushed in the darkness. *That's the real question, isn't it? I've been doing this for so long that I don't know how to do anything else. Not that I really want to do anything else.* "Not much, sir," he admitted aloud. "I imagine I'd try to find something in the Twin Cities, back near my hometown, but I haven't given it much thought yet."

Both men lapsed into silence, enjoying the warm land breeze and the stars overhead as the engines of *Mount Whitney* thrummed beneath their feet.

The admiral broke the silence first, "Well Rob, don't rush out of here without a plan. Your job is yours as long as you want it. No pressure from this end for you to leave." Falkner took the pipe out of his mouth and continued, "Ah. Looks like my tobacco's done. Thanks for the company on deck. Not often do I get to shoot the breeze with a shipmate."

"Thank you, sir," Rob responded. Falkner walked back to the superstructure and disappeared through the hatchway.

Buckner took the last few puffs of his cigar, savoring the solitude and reflecting on Falkner's advice. The lights of the Chesapeake Bay Bridge-Tunnel were closer now. The Cape Henry lighthouse still blinked to port. If only he had such signposts for his own life. *I can't see myself sitting behind a desk for the rest of my working life. All I know is being a Marine.* He flicked the stub of his spent cigar overboard into the darkness and thought bitterly about his peer, Colonel Tom Pile, even now taking over as commanding officer of 6th Marines. *That regiment should be mine.* Instead, he was plotting the quiet demise of his twenty-two-year career.

 **CHAPTER 14**

1450 MSK, Monday 16 August 1993
1150 Zulu
Central Committee Building, 4 Staraya Square, Moscow,
Russian Soviet Federative Socialist Republic

A SUMMER RAIN WAS falling on Moscow. *The same kind of weather as during the coup two years ago,* thought Pavel Medvedev, seated at the head of the heavy table surveying the Politburo's conference room through the haze of stale cigarette smoke. The space was far less crowded than most Politburo meetings. For this special gathering, only the principal members could be present. The room was oddly silent as each man around the table contemplated the momentous vote they had just taken. *They all understand that this was the most important decision they will make in their lifetimes, perhaps the most important decision in the history of Russia.*

Pavel was satisfied that this meeting, and especially this vote, had gone well. Laying the groundwork since his return from holiday in June, he was once again clear-eyed about the course his country must take. *Of course, the NATO governments and their allies played into my hand nicely in that regard,* the Soviet president reflected. Their escalating involvement in the violently fractured former Yugoslavia had caused stirrings of pan-Slavic nationalism in the beleaguered Soviet populace. Moreover, Pavel knew from KGB sources that the American president had just deployed special troops under the name "Task Force Ranger" to Somalia. This fact had helped Medvedev tip a couple of votes in his favor in recent days. He had highlighted the action as evidence of global meddling by America, which would only grow worse if left unchecked.

The Soviet vice president had openly expressed agreement with the plan, apparently impressed by its sweeping ambition. The small opposition clique voted unanimously in favor of Medvedev's proposal. *Though not without the old fool making a ridiculous harangue about the inevitable global victory of world socialism*, Pavel noted to himself with disgust.

The overall vote was decisive but not unanimous. To Pavel's surprise, his longtime friend and interior minister, Oleg Drugov, had abstained, as had Foreign Minister Garin. Even Marshal Rosla, seated to the president's right for this meeting, had hesitated briefly before casting his affirmative vote. That was only a small matter; each of those men could be counted on in the coming trial. *They understand that for this throw of the dice to work, we must put every ounce of our nation's power into the effort.*

President Medvedev waited for the pregnant silence to linger a few more heartbeats, allowing the gravity of their situation to oppress the men around the table a little longer. Then he spoke: "So, we are agreed then. We will postpone, for a time, our direct involvement in the Polish mess. We delay until the more opportune time and then we will escalate the world tensions for the purpose of eventually de-escalating them to our advantage. We will go to war, *cut* cancerous Germany out of NATO, *fracture* that alliance, and *ensure* that the west can never again threaten our nation's commerce and well-being. By doing this, we will force the Americans to once again acknowledge us as equals, thus ensuring a lasting peace and saving the world from a future of chaos."

Escalate to de-escalate, Medvedev recalled Khitrov's words. *Brilliant.*

Heads nodded around the table. Medvedev went on, shifting his good eye from man to man as he spoke. "Make no mistake, *tovarichi*, we have committed to a hard path, but it is a journey we *can* finish. A journey we *must* finish. I have complete faith in all of you to do your duty," he concluded, not in total honesty as his eye settled on the vice president, who stared back at him coldly.

The Soviet vice president held Medvedev's gaze for a moment, then spoke. "*Tovarich* President," he said, his voice dripping with false admiration, "I commend you for this momentous decision, for leading our country with courage in this dark hour. You and I have not always agreed in the past, I admit, but today and onward you will have my complete support."

Medvedev nodded, "*Spasibo, Tovarich*," he said. *Thank you, Comrade.*

His thick gray hair tousled after the long meeting they had just completed, the vice president continued, "To that end, allow me to suggest an adjustment to this 'Plan *Boyar.*' You said earlier that you will work tirelessly to prevent the use of atomic and other special weapons. I ask: Why? From my understanding, all of our traditional war plans call for these weapons to be used on the battlefield. Why remove the most powerful weapons from our brave soldiers' hands just when they need it the most? The western countries do not have the political will to—"

"Stop." The command from the Soviet president was abrupt. He fixed the vice president with an icy gaze, then said slowly, "I have made clear that I *will not* authorize the first use of atomic weapons." Pavel's knuckles rapped the table for emphasis. "You know this, *Vice* President. Down that road lies the destruction of our country, and the world." Pavel paused again, bringing his emotions under control. Then he went on, "We will maintain our atomic and special weapons arsenal as a deterrent to the western powers. I have already told you of our plans to ensure from the beginning that our enemies understand that *we* will not use such weapons if *they* will not. That is all I intend to say on this matter."

The vice president's look smoldered from the rebuke. For a long moment Pavel thought he was about to continue the argument, but after what seemed like an eternity the other man dropped his eyes and nodded, slowly.

Pavel looked away and continued to address the rest of the Politburo. "From this point forward, the Ministry of Defense's mission will be the primary effort for our nation. We are at war from this moment onwards, though our enemies do not, and *cannot,* know this. Marshal Rosla will oversee the preparations, and I expect each of you to support his every request."

The marshal's head nodded solemnly, as did the others around the table, some more reluctantly than others.

"Marshal, you are authorized to begin concrete preparations for Plan *Boyar* immediately, with the adjustments we have discussed," Medvedev informed his defense minister.

"Yes, *tovarich* President," Rosla acknowledged.

"Anton Anreevich," Medvedev turned to KGB Chairman Laskin, "many of your operatives will be taking orders from my man in the Ministry of Defense, Colonel Khitrov. I trust his judgment completely on this matter, and I rely on you to ensure your directorate carries out his instructions, in accordance with Marshal Rosla's general plan. The colonel will share his plans with you in full, but *he* will choose who else in your bureau knows what."

Laskin nodded, with just a hint of hesitation.

Pavel paused for effect, then issued a stern warning. "I must stress again that secrecy is of the utmost importance. Let me be clear to all of you. If word of this plan leaks to our enemies, we are finished. Our country will collapse. NATO and the Germans will once again be at our doorstep. The world will descend into chaos under American mismanagement. Understanding the seriousness of our potential failure, I make you a promise: if secrecy from this meeting is breached, I will discover who the culprit is, and that man will face the full weight of Soviet justice. That man's end will not be pleasant. You all know I am capable of this. Each of you will tell only the people in your ministries who absolutely need to know, and none of them must be given the whole picture. Do you understand?"

Heads nodded soberly around the table, even the vice president's.

"Foreign Minister." Garin looked up at his president. "You have much groundwork to complete and little time to do it. You understand that we must present our enemies with so many problems around the world that they cannot deal with the main one. When the time comes, they must not be allowed to concentrate on the decisive front. Above all, you must keep those damned Chinese neutral. You are authorized to offer anything, threaten anything, to achieve the necessary conditions for our success, so long as you do not compromise the secrecy of our plans."

Garin nodded jerkily, then licked his lips and asked, "May I—," the man halted to think before continuing, "May I threaten the Chinese with atomic weapons to keep them from interfering? I do not ask for their *use*," he added quickly, "only that I may *threaten* their use."

Pavel sat back. He had not considered this. With the west, the threat of annihilation for the Russian people was very real. With the Chinese and their pathetic strategic arsenal just the mention of atomic weapons might be enough to stave them off.

"I submit it to a vote," the president said after a moment. "What are your thoughts?" He swept his eye around the table. Many heads nodded. *A majority, or at least what looks like one.*

"Very well, Georgy Vasilevich," Medvedev concluded. "You may threaten the Chinese with special weapons. I only ask that you do so judiciously."

The man nodded, then said, "Pavel Ivanovich, the timing for the start of hostilities, it will be condemned by many around the world—"

"The hostilities will be condemned by our enemies no matter when we start them," Medvedev broke in. "Their outrage is disingenuous. *They* have forced us to this point of desperation. *They* have dragged us to the brink. We have made every effort to warn them about their actions and our own, but they haven't listened. When we strike, we will do so with every advantage we can muster, and timing is everything, Foreign Minister. You know better than anyone the sensibilities of the west. Outrage is acceptable, as long as it serves a purpose."

Garin relented, sinking back into his chair. His task was herculean. Organizing a world coalition in which the members would not know they were a team of marionettes would be difficult, but Medvedev knew his foreign minister to be a brilliant emissary. If anyone could pull off the necessary diplomatic gymnastics before February, it was him.

Finally, Pavel turned to his old friend. "Oleg Borisovich," Medvedev said, "can you keep our economy together for a few months longer? Can you carry us until we secure for you the resources and freedom our industry and our people need?"

A vision of the interior minister like a circus performer keeping plates spinning on thin canes came briefly to Medvedev's mind. Drugov had been working miracles in Medvedev's streamlined government, maintaining the Soviet ruble, shifting scarce resources around the vastness of the USSR, and forging ahead with developing energy resources in Siberia, even dipping into the vast diamond reserves.

Drugov looked Medvedev hard in the eye for a long moment, then nodded. "My President, our armed forces will have everything they need when the time comes. You have my word."

Medvedev nodded back. With Drugov, he knew, it was not an empty promise. Pavel trusted his friend to tell him if he could not deliver. With that, the Soviet president stood, signaling the end of their momentous meeting. He looked around the room one last time.

"My friends, I commend your courage," said the president. "This is a great day for Russia and for the USSR. We have been on the brink of disaster for years now. The plan we have agreed upon will re-balance the world order; it will ensure world peace for the generations to come. I thank you for your support. Go! There is much work to be done."

The Politburo members stood with a scraping of heavy wooden chairs across marble floor. Two years ago, Medvedev had changed the course of history with his clear vision for the future of the Soviet Union. Now, he would change it again.

PART IV: APPROACH MARCH

"Everything in war is simple, but the simplest thing is difficult."
—Carl von Clausewitz

 **CHAPTER 15**

1615 MSK, Tuesday 12 October 1993
1315 Zulu
Main Ministry of Defense Building, Arbatskaya Square,
Moscow, Russian Soviet Federative Socialist Republic

C OLONEL IVAN IVANOVICH Khitrov took one last long pull
from the stub of a cigarette held between his thumb and forefinger.
As he blew out between his teeth, adding more smoke to the stale haze
that perpetually filled his small top-floor office, he scanned the documents
spread out before him on the cluttered desk. While many saw only a mess,
to Khitrov this was an orderly system imposed on the hundreds of folders,
papers, and maps strewn around the room, right down to the small chess set
he always kept on the corner of his desk. Of course, the system was known
only to him, and he wasn't about to share the secret with visitors, particularly
the type who were annoyed by the mess. He mashed the cigarette butt into
an ashtray set among a pile of KGB papers detailing the comings and goings
of the Norwegian royal family, leaving the smoldering pulp to burn itself out
in the ash of its forebears.

Not in his wildest dreams had Khitrov ever expected to wield so much
power. The full weight of the KGB's First Chief Directorate, the organ of the
spy service responsible for foreign operations, was his to command, as was its

counterpart in the military's GRU service and some of the more *interesting* units of the Soviet armed forces.

His new rank was a perk as well, especially with the higher pay that was accompanying the president's military reforms. Khitrov had vaulted upwards two grades in rank by presidential decree since returning to Moscow. His ascent had angered some, but he cared little about them or their opinions.

He could call any department in this building, and even any directorate across the city at KGB headquarters at Dzerzhinsky Square, and within hours a report or record would arrive at his door. So far though, he'd been disappointed. *So much power, so much potential, and their plans are so unimaginative. So* conventional. *What a waste!*

Khitrov felt for another cigarette in his breast pocket. Finding only an empty pack, he swore under his breath and shifted his attention back to the current problem. He would not be able to work long without a steady flow of nicotine, but his concentration would be ruined if he left to walk down to the small commissary. He picked up a map of the southwestern United States, the location of each border crossing site was marked by a small X. He had another for the Americans' northern border, and yet more indicating ports and airports both important and obscure. *These Americans make this so easy! Do they have no concept of border security?* thought Khitrov, remembering the heavily fortified frontiers in Europe that had been a hallmark of east-west frontiers for half a century.

Khitrov refocused: how to send a message to the Americans, more specifically to the American president, to convince him that the United States could not wield its nuclear stick without inviting its own swift obliteration. He picked a bishop piece off the chess set and twirled it between his fingers. Khitrov had outlined his plan to accomplish this to President Medvedev several weeks before. The old bear had grasped at the concept, taking it to the Politburo to convince them to go to war. Now it was up to Khitrov to work out the details. He knew the effect he wanted to achieve, knew how to achieve it, but the devil was in the details. *Targeting*, he thought, replacing the bishop. *How do we find the targets on the day of the attacks?*

He swiveled around and rifled through details of the satellite communication systems used by naval bombers and submarines to set up their missile attacks. *If I could have Tu-95 reconnaissance bombers off each coast of the United States when hostilities begin,* his thoughts trailed, *but no, that would be suicide.* It wasn't that Khitrov cared about the lives of the crewmen he sent into harm's way, but he understood that men going into battle needed at least the illusion that they might survive. Besides, using the big four-engine bombers was too obvious, too *conventional.* Khitrov's lips twisted into a smirk. *We will not win this war by doing things the* conventional *way,* he reminded himself.

His eyes passed over a sheet detailing the performance of the small Antonov An-2 transport aircraft, so useful for putting special purpose troops down in remote areas. He paused as he looked at the black and white photo that accompanied the data sheet.

The distinctive high-top wing of the Soviet biplane triggered a memory, reminding him of something. The angle of the photo, the single engine, the aircraft's ability to land just about anywhere. He snapped up the paper, *The German boy!* The complete thought finally formed in his mind. Five years ago the newspapers had been filled with the story of an idiot German youth, *What was his name?* Khitrov wracked his brain. *Rust?* The boy had flown his rented Cessna airplane from Helsinki straight through what was supposedly the most sophisticated air defense network on earth, and landed right in Red Square, literally in the shadow of the Kremlin, Khitrov remembered with amusement. *Unconventional indeed.*

He picked up the receiver of a green telephone on his desk and dialed a number from memory. *If Marshal Rosla is so keen on that new jump jet of his, perhaps I should profit from its technology as well,* he thought through the static of the special-secure line connecting to Dzerzhinsky Square. The call rang through and buzzed just once before a woman's voice answered, "First Chief Directorate."

"*Da,*" he said without salutation, "this is Khitrov. I need information."

He heard shuffling as the person at the other end of the line grabbed pen and paper. These requests had become routine between him and KGB headquarters. The clerk at the other end of the line knew the drill by now.

"Please proceed," the woman's voice said.

"Flight regulations in the west," he went on for several seconds, detailing the information he wanted.

When he was finished the voice said, "Yes, Colonel. Will there be anything else?"

"I will call you with further requests when I have them," Khitrov said and hung up.

He picked the receiver up again and dialed a second number, this one to a line here in the ministry building. A male voice answered, "Naval aviation."

"This is Khitrov. I need some information on that new Yak-141 fighter of yours. The one that can take off vertically? Yes. I need to know about its sensor capabilities." He explained for a moment. He hung up when he was sure the young naval officer on the other end of the line understood.

Khitrov was most of the way towards solving this problem, one of hundreds he had wrestled with over the past few weeks. Every team infiltrating countries in the west, whether it be the United States, Norway, Australia, Japan, or Spain, needed to employ an ingress method different from every other team as part of the colonel's plan for maintaining secrecy. In most cases the agents wouldn't know what their mission was until they arrived at their destinations and linked up with their equipment, which itself would have arrive via a unique, roundabout route. Some of the Soviet covert teams were literally circumnavigating the globe, changing papers and identities at every stop, essential to avoid detection by western intelligence services. Every problem required a bespoke and innovative solution, and Khitrov thrived on the all-absorbing work. He jealously guarded his responsibilities from would-be interlopers who he knew would do their best to muck it all up. Every piece of his intricate puzzle was elegantly simple, like the single stroke of a brush, but together they would come together into a masterpiece.

The colonel stood, meaning to make his way to the first floor for another pack of smokes, when he heard a knock at his door. He stopped, annoyed, and answered, "*Da?*"

The door opened, and Marshal Rosla's naval aide, Ivanenko, entered the cramped office and shut the door behind him. From the look on the other man's face, Khitrov knew that this was not a friendly visit. *Not this man again*, his mind groaned. They had been butting heads ever since Khitrov began to appropriate naval resources for his operations. Beginning to feel tense as the nicotine of his last cigarette wore off, he asked, "What is it, Ivanenko? I am busy."

"I am sure you are," the naval officer said. "You are doing an excellent job of unraveling our strategy for countering American naval power and protecting the *Rodina*."

This argument again, thought Khitrov, his impatience growing. He decided to play coy. "How am I endangering the motherland today, Captain?"

"You know what I am speaking of, Khitrov," said Ivanenko angrily. "This plan of yours for our submarines."

"Which submarines? You have so many," answered Khitrov, egging Ivanenko on.

"You know very well which submarines! The ones we need to sink the American aircraft carriers. You are frittering them away with this scheme of yours!"

"Frittering?" Khitrov asked, feigning surprise. "Please, Captain, elaborate."

"We have discussed this before, Colonel," said Ivanenko, voice rising. "You know that our doctrine for dealing with the American carrier battle groups relies on careful coordination between our surface fleet, our naval aviation, *and* our—"

"—submarines. Yes, yes, yes," Khitrov interrupted, waving his hand dismissively. "So why are you here now?"

Ivanenko paused, visibly calming himself, resolving to rely on reason with this infuriating man. He began to explain, "The defenses of the American carrier groups are very strong. To overcome them will require close coordination to mass our missiles against them, and even then, we will require luck to be successful."

"Why?" Khitrov delivered the question with the faintest hint of a smile on his lips.

Ivanenko was taken aback. "Why what?"

"Why must you sink an American aircraft carrier?" The question was delivered in a mildly disinterested tone.

The captain looked dumbfoundedly at Khitrov, his mouth slightly agape, as if he could not comprehend how someone could ask such a bizarre question. After a moment he stammered, "Why? Because, well, it is self-evident isn't it? Everyone understands. The carriers are how the Americans can bring attack aircraft within range of our country, threaten our fleet bases, attack the *Rodina*."

Ivanenko was gaining steam on this track, "If the American carrier groups are allowed a free hand, they will hunt down our strategic missile submarines!"

"You mean the submarines that carry the atomic weapons that our president has pledged repeatedly not to use?" Khitrov prodded.

"That is not the point, and you know it, Khitrov!" Ivanenko almost shouted. "You are putting our strategic deterrent at risk! This scheme of yours could lose us the war!"

The smirk on Khitrov's face remained unchanged, but the small step he took towards the naval officer communicated menace, stopping the other man's rant in its tracks. The two were face to face now, Ivanenko surprised that he was suddenly short of breath, staring into the wolfish face of a killer. The smirk grew slightly at Ivanenko's obvious discomfort.

After a moment, the former *Spetsnaz* officer spoke. "You are mistaken, Ivanenko." He glanced down at the navy man's shirt, spying something desirable in the other man's breast pocket. He reached out and delicately plucked a cigarette from the pack in Ivanenko's uniform shirt, putting the smoke in his mouth while he continued to talk around it, enjoying how easily he could intimidate this small-minded man. "Yes, mistaken," Khitrov said again. "I have looked at the navy's analysis. Even your most optimistic projections say that you will be able to destroy, what? Two? Three, American carriers? They have twelve more! What will it accomplish?"

"The aircraft carriers are great symbols of American power," Ivanenko replied more calmly, choosing to ignore the minor theft just committed by his adversary. "If we can destroy one or two, their people will lose the will to fight. Look at how they are already responding to this silly mess in Somalia last week? They lose a mere eighteen soldiers in a battle and you'd think they'd lost a war! How will they respond when we sink a ship carrying five thousand?"

"You have much to learn about violence and psychology, my friend," responded Khitrov, patting the other man on the shoulder with false warmth. "Their people are upset at those minor losses because they do not see the reason for them. They *will* see a reason to sacrifice in the coming war with us. That is why we cannot attack *symbols*. We must attack things that force their people to act in the way we want them to act, to change how they live their lives, to understand the things we want them to understand."

Ivanenko tried again. "If we can sink the first carriers that come north, we will have opened up our ability to interrupt the Americans' lines of communication across the sea to the central front during the critical early days of the war."

"Your thinking is too conventional, Ivanenko," Khitrov lectured, as if speaking to a particularly dull pupil. "Why do you insist on attacking the enemy's ships when they are the most heavily defended, clustered in convoys and guarded by warships?" Khitrov shook his head, like the schoolmaster. "*My* plan will accomplish your objective before the Americans even know that the ships need guarding. Besides," he turned and walked away from the other man, "I thought that one of the points of delaying the beginning of hostilities was that the American carriers will not even be present at the outset. Correct?"

"But the cruise missiles!" Ivanenko spluttered, "The submarines' missiles will have all been used up by the time the carriers arrive! They can only be reloaded in port," the navy man asserted, trying to regain composure.

"Then I suggest," responded Khitrov, slowly, lowering himself into his seat and snatching a pawn off of his chessboard, "that you begin planning how and where to reload them in the most expeditious manner possible." He retrieved a lighter from the clutter to one side of his desk and lit the stolen cigarette, blowing the first puff of smoke in Ivanenko's direction through fingers that held both the pawn and the smoke.

"You are wrong, Khitrov. You are dangerously diluting the strength of our fleet at the critical hour." Ivanenko said it like it was a proclamation.

Why must I deal with such imbeciles, thought Khitrov, his lip curling with disgust. "Very well, Captain," he said coolly, the smirk gone from his face. "If you feel so strongly about this, perhaps you and I should go see Marshal Rosla and ask his opinion?"

"Marshal Rosla is not a navy man! He does not understand the complexities of naval warfare."

"Excuse me, Ivanenko," Khitrov interrupted as he placed the pawn into an impossible position on the board, "but did I hear you impugn the defense minister's intelligence?"

The naval officer blanched. "No, of course not, I simply meant—"

"You simply meant that he, and the president as well, are foolish to entrust such planning to me, a mere *Spetsnaz* officer, *da*? Let us go to them and see if they will realize the error of their ways." Khitrov moved for the door as if he meant to walk to the marshal's office down the hall right now.

"No, Khitrov," the man said, biting off what he really wanted to say. "You win."

The colonel stopped and turned. *That's better.* "Then I suggest," Khitrov said with ice in his voice, "that you get back to work implementing this plan of mine to win us the war and stop wasting my time with your dead-end doctrines!"

Ivanenko glared into Khitrov's wolfish face, brave for just a moment, then spun on his heel and walked out of the room, slamming the door behind him.

Glad to be done with the distraction, Khitrov went back to work, savoring his stolen cigarette. He knew Ivanenko wasn't completely wrong. The Soviet Navy would have to deal with the American big deck carriers in the North Atlantic eventually. That was the brilliance of Marshal Rosla's Plan *Boyar*. It allowed the Soviets to alter the terrain, the strategic geometry of the engagement, before the Red Banner Northern Fleet came to grips with the American battle groups. If all went as planned, *And nothing ever does*, Khitrov reminded himself, they would be able to deal with the American task forces one at a time as they raced north, rather than as a single, massive fleet as the US Navy would prefer.

To create such a serendipitous situation required imagination, imagination that people like Ivanenko lacked. *Medvedev has it*, the colonel reflected. *I saw it in him two years ago at the White House. Rosla does as well, though not to the same degree. They have the ability to see things differently, to judge how others will respond.* The marshal's war plan was certainly creative, but they needed *him*, Khitrov, to drive it through to success.

He drew out the last tendrils of smoke from the cigarette and shifted his attention to another problem, a map of Iceland, tacked up on the back wall. *This one will be fun*, he thought.

 **CHAPTER 16**

1600 MSK, Wednesday 24 November 1993
1100 Zulu
Severomorsk Naval Base, Murmansk Oblast,
Russian Soviet Federative Socialist Republic

P RESIDENT PAVEL MEDVEDEV braced himself against the icy wind
sweeping down the fjord from the north as he strode along the worn
concrete pier, trailing his older son by a half step. The breeze—*It would
have been called a windstorm down in Moscow*, reflected the older man—cut
through his fur-lined coat and cylindrical fur *shapka* cap that covered his thick
white hair. The cold did not seem to faze Sergei, who hurried out along the
pier with uncharacteristic haste. *The boy has never been this excited*, thought
Pavel with a smile as he lengthened his stride to keep up.

Sergei Pavlovich Medvedev was no longer a boy and had not been one in
many years, but his demeanor right now was a good approximation of how one
would have looked on Christmas morning. He stopped two thirds of the way
down the long, empty pier and turned to look his father full in the face, his
expression beaming with pride. "Here he is!" Pavel's oldest son swept his arm
expansively towards one of the dark gray-painted ships tied up alongside the pier.

Pavel looked at the vessel his son was indicating. In truth, he could not
tell the difference between this boat and the half dozen others that occupied

berths along the many piers here in the harbor of the Red Banner Northern Fleet's main base. This ship was important to the young man, though, and Pavel knew why.

"This is your boat?" the president asked.

"*Ship*, father, we call him a *ship*," Sergei said with a smile as he turned to take in the sight. Pavel continued to look at his son. *He truly is a younger copy of me*, thought the president. Only the boy's jet-black hair, hidden under his equally black uniform *shapka*, adorned with the insignia of an officer of the Soviet Navy, set the younger man apart. Whereas Misha, the younger son, favored their mother's slighter frame, Sergei was thick-chested and, like his father, thickening at the waist. *Too many sedentary days at sea*, thought Pavel. Also, like his father, Sergei had been a wrestler in his youth, displaying his inherited ruthlessness and determination in his knack for finding an opponent's weakness and exploiting it with a fury that rarely failed to produce a victory. Sergei's face possessed the same bear-like quality that made Pavel so striking on television and in photographs. Pavel's chest swelled with pride as he took in his son's black uniform jacket with its rows of colorful ribbons and brand-new shoulder boards displaying the four stripes and five-pointed star of a captain (second rank) in the Soviet Navy. *He is the right person for this command*, decided Medvedev, satisfied that the strings he'd pulled with Rosla to secure the captaincy for his son would not be wasted effort.

"His name?" asked the president. Captain Ivanenko, Marshal Rosla's naval aide, had briefed him on the ship, but Pavel did not want to take this moment away from his son.

"The *Admiral Chabanenko*," Sergei said, as if announcing the name of a firstborn son. "He is a Project 1151.1 anti-submarine destroyer. The best in the fleet. We call this a *Fregat*-class ship. The Americans call him an *Udaloy*, but they are in for a surprise if things ever get hot. This ship is far more capable than our older Project 1151s, and he's mine!" That Christmas morning look returned to Sergei's face.

The older Medvedev turned and really looked for the first time at the ship his son would command. The president admitted to himself that he knew next to nothing about naval affairs, something that had been driven home to him in an uncomfortable conversation with Captain Ivanenko on their flight to

Murmansk. Even to his untrained eye the Russian president could tell that the *Admiral Chabanenko* was a lethal ship of war. It looked the part. *He*, Pavel reminded himself, remembering that such traditions as personifying a warship correctly were important to naval men.

The second of two ships alongside this pier, his son's new destroyer possessed a long bow that sloped backwards with a grace that exuded both speed and strength. Two long side-by-side gun barrels protruded from a single globe-like turret, squatting just in front of the ship's superstructure. The gun turret was flanked on either side by two long rectangular boxes, each pointed forward and canted slightly upwards at the front. Medvedev correctly took these to be missile launchers, each box holding four large weapons. The destroyer's bridge sat low, the wings hanging over the armaments. *Like a rifleman pulling his weapon into his shoulder*, Pavel thought. Behind the superstructure, two squat smokestacks gave way to a hangar and helicopter landing pad at the ship's stern. Altogether the ship's appearance communicated lethality, and Pavel knew from the briefing that he could not even see the ship's most lethal feature: the sixty-four vertical launch missile cells built into the destroyer's deck.

"I congratulate you, my son," the Soviet president said warmly. "He's a handsome ship. Even I can see that. Your command of him is well-earned." Pavel was proud of his son's service and accomplishments, but he was also honest enough with himself to know that it was his name that had earned Sergei this ship.

"Thank you, father," responded Sergei. "I know I would not have achieved this without your help. Rest assured, I will command him in a way that makes you proud."

Pavel was surprised at his son's acknowledgement of the subtle hints the president had used with his military staff to goad them into this action. Usually such things went unsaid in their family. Though Pavel knew his son to be a hard-working and competent officer, a good choice for this post, he also knew that the Soviet Navy would not have entrusted one of its newest and most advanced warships to just any newly promoted junior captain. Whereas Misha went to great lengths to distance himself from his father's influence, Sergei had always used his family name to get anything from better cuts of meat at the *Universam* food stores to dates with girls who would never have looked his way otherwise and, now, the command of a prized ship in the rapidly expanding Soviet fleet. *This command is truly important to him, an end finally, not just a means,* Pavel realized, turning and looking at his oldest with a new measure of respect.

"I am already proud of you, my boy," the president said as another icy gust swept down the pier. "I always have been." *Those westerners think our system of patronage is corrupt,* reasoned Pavel. *They are blind to the flaws of their own supposedly pure meritocracy. They cannot see that our culture allows one who has already been successful to elevate others in whom he sees the same talent. Those in the west fail to understand that only idiots do favors to elevate other idiots.*

"When is your assumption of command ceremony?" Pavel asked.

"Next week," responded Sergei. "On Friday. The shipyard workers are aboard right now, finishing their work on our sensor and command systems. You should see them, father! With this ship I will finally be able to track those quiet, slinking submarines that the Americans and British send up here. Much of the crew is already aboard, helping with the work. I want them to know their sensors and weapons better than any crew in the fleet."

"Can we go aboard and see them right now?" Pavel asked.

Sergei looked down, slightly uncomfortable. "I would love to give you a tour, father, but," he paused, "if we go aboard now, the workers will stop as soon as they see you. I need them working every minute if I am to take my ship to sea after the ceremony. *Kuznetsov,*" he spoke of the Russian fleet's first real, big-deck aircraft carrier, which *Admiral Chabanenko* was assigned to defend, "and the rest of my squadron are already out there, training," he tilted his head north. "I need to train my crew to operate with the flagship. Nothing can be allowed to delay our sailing. You understand?"

"Of course, of course," responded Pavel. In truth, the ship itself was of little interest to him, and visiting his son and his son's new command was only a portion of the tour. Rosla had arranged for the president to inspect not only this vital port on the USSR's Arctic coast, but a cross section of the Red Banner Northern Fleet's combat power, including surface ships here at Severomorsk, submarines based farther up the rugged fjord at Polyarny, and bomber regiments at air bases scattered around the dirty, isolated naval city of Murmansk.

"Perhaps we could come back at eighteen hours, after the workers have left?" suggested Sergei.

"Unfortunately, no. I have a schedule to keep myself, you know," answered Pavel, looking back to where the pier met the access road, seeing Captain Ivanenko and the other aides who had accompanied him stomping their feet to ward off the cold. Pavel was growing chilled as well, but he desired some information from his son before departing. He wanted some assurance that the encouraging reports coming to him from the Ministry of Defense were actually true.

"Tell me, Sergei," he began, "how are things here, in the fleet? How is the spirit of the sailors and officers? Is the fleet ready for any emergency?" Pavel had not told his son about the Politburo's decision to resolve their differences with NATO by force of arms and he had no intention of doing so.

Sergei looked his father full in the face. "Father, two years ago, before you took over the government, our navy was disintegrating. Ships were lying idle at their berths because we had no fuel to sail, no crews to train, no weapons to fire. Our ships were literally rusting away before our eyes because of the old regime's neglect. All that has changed now. Ships that we were going to write off as too expensive to maintain have been modernized. We are fielding powerful new weapons and launching wonderful new ships like mine here." He waved at the *Admiral Chabanenko*, "That says nothing of the morale! The higher pay certainly has something to do with it, but so does the fact that we are actually training now, improving every day. In my years in the fleet I have never seen such a high level of proficiency and happiness."

Pavel nodded. His son's opinion agreed with the reports Rosla had been forwarding to him about the overall improvements in the Soviet military establishment since he had made its reform a priority. Medvedev trusted Rosla, but he was gratified nonetheless to see the marshal's optimism confirmed.

The president decided to ask his son one more question, prompted by the discussion that Ivanenko had been bold enough to start with him during their flight. "What are officers in the fleet saying about the order to remove atomic weapons from our surface ships and hunter submarines?"

The young captain paused to consider for a moment, then responded, "There is certainly some discomfort. Many believe that atomic weapons give us our best chance to destroy the American fleet if it threatens the *Rodina*.

There is another, more aggressive group who says that removing these weapons, which we cannot use without permission anyway, will allow more freedom. It'll allow us to throw heavier salvos of missiles, allow our submarines to remain at sea longer and sink more ships. If we are not going to use the weapons, then they are merely ballast, in truth."

"Who do you agree with?" Medvedev asked his son.

Sergei smiled. "Father, give me the standard weapons. I do not wish to have to call back to Moscow and have a chat with you just to fire one of my missiles or torpedoes!"

Pavel smiled and nodded. He had not been anywhere close to reconsidering his order to divest the fleet of many of its atomic weapons, but Ivanenko's passion for the issue had at least given him pause. Medvedev could not agree with the man's position, but he knew the naval officer's motivation was for the defense of the *Rodina*. Ivanenko was chafing in his position at the ministry, and Rosla intended to duly reward his services with a command in the very near future. The Soviet president looked back at the *Admiral Chabanenko*, feeling concern creep into his mind as another icy blast blew off the water. In just a few weeks his boy would be taking this ship into battle. He never allowed himself to imagine what the worst outcome of that fact might be, what the outcome had been for his own father in 1945. Pavel chose to focus on the pride, and not the fear. His sons were serving their country and they were both competent and happy in that duty.

"He is a handsome ship," Pavel repeated, "I am sure you and your crew will serve your country well in him." He turned and began walking back towards the knot of aides at the end of the pier, Sergei followed.

As they walked, his son asked a question of his own. "Tell me father, all this training we are doing, all this emphasis on having the whole fleet ready by next month...are we building to something?"

Pavel stopped and looked at his son, "Why do you ask?"

"Officers are talking, father. Having the whole fleet ready like this is, well, exciting to say the least, but," his son paused, "there is speculation as to what it all means. We will have to stand many of our ships down for maintenance after the new year. Many think that we will confront NATO or the Americans before then, when our strength is at its greatest."

He wanted desperately to tell his son the truth, to allow him to prepare himself for the trial ahead, for the war of his generation. Honesty to himself kept him from divulging the truth to his son. *Sergei's character has flaws.* The boy might be tempted to use the information as power, to advance his career further or for his gain, whatever it may be. Pavel knew of other moral flaws in his son as well, that his marriage was less than happy, due no doubt to his enjoyment of entertaining any attractive woman who happened to look his way. *What if the NATO intelligence services have spies up here that we don't know about? What would I do to one of my ministers if I discovered that he had told one of his sons? No, I cannot tell him.*

Pavel chose evasion, not wanting to lie outright. "Sergei, we will not be confronting NATO this December." *It will be later than that*, Medvedev finished to himself. "We simply wish them to see that we are powerful once again, that they cannot push us around anymore as they've been trying to do. Then you and your comrades will return to port to refit." Pavel did not doubt that the enemy's ships would also be recouping.

Sergei looked only partially convinced, but he nodded all the same. The two men turned and resumed their walk back down the pier, past the other, smaller warship tied up alongside. Another frigid gust enveloped them, ruffling Pavel's heavy coat and penetrating to his skin as if he wore only summer clothes. Snow began to fall as they rejoined the presidential entourage. The leader of the USSR took leave of his son and climbed into his limousine for the drive back to the airport where a helicopter was waiting to fly them up to Polyarny.

As his driver pulled away, Pavel looked over his shoulder to see his oldest son striding back up the pier. Had he been religious, he would have said a prayer for Sergei's safety. Instead he lost himself in mental checklists, trying to ensure that every action he could take to bring about a quick victory over his country's enemies had been taken. Outside the vehicle, thick white snow-flakes fell, sticking to the windows. The winter up here in the far north was promising to be a cold one indeed.

 **CHAPTER 17**

1645 AZOT, Tuesday 21 December 1993
1745 Zulu
USS *Mount Whitney*, north of Corvo Island, Atlantic Ocean

L IEUTENANT ABBY SAVAGE eased down on the collective control of her SH-3G Sea King, decreasing power to the aircraft's two turboshaft engines. Peering down over her left knee through the plexiglass of her blunt-nosed cockpit, she shifted the stick and began lowering the helicopter towards the slowly pitching deck on the fantail of the ungainly gray ship below.

"Thirty feet," announced the thick Texas twang of her co-pilot, Buck Hennessy.

Abby's gentle touch on the collective kept the helicopter descending slowly, just a few feet per second. She could see the white lines of the flight deck's markings growing larger. They also oscillated like a seesaw as the flagship rocked with the motion of the waves.

"Twenty feet," Buck said.

Sloshing water from the pooled rain sprayed outward from the flight deck of the *Mount Whitney* under the pounding of the Sea King's downdraft. Abby concentrated on maintaining the forward and downward motion of her aircraft through a stiff wind blowing out of the northeast.

"Ten feet."

Abby felt slight pressure against her hand through her joystick-like cyclic control as the wind shifted. A strong gust blew from starboard, but someone watching the helicopter would never have known, as she subtly adjusted to the new conditions. With five feet beneath the helicopter's boat-like underside, Abby shoved the collective lever down to the floor, nearly idling the engines. The Sea King's landing gear settled onto the deck as gently as a sleeping baby laid to rest by its mother, at the exact geometric center of the landing pad.

"And we're down," said Buck. "Another good landing, Abbs, not that you need me to tell you that, I reckon."

"Securing the engines," Abby replied as she cut the power plant back to idle. Then, keying her radio, she called the ship, "November Oscar, this is Angel Lead, we're secure and ready for a hot refuel, over."

"Roger, Angel Lead, we'll run the hose," came the response.

"Thanks, November Oscar. Angel out," Abby said. Then she keyed the intercom and said to her crew chief in the back of the aircraft, "Okay, let our passenger know it's safe to get out."

Abby heard the Sea King's side door slide open with a bang. A second later the Marine Corps colonel who'd been their sole passenger appeared out the side of her cockpit window, scuttling over beneath the spinning rotor blades towards the edge of the flight deck.

"Who d'you s'pose that feller was?" asked Hennessy through the intercom, even though the two pilots were side-by-side in the cockpit.

"I don't know, Buck," said Abby, "but he's getting some awfully special treatment, even for a colonel."

Abby and Buck, pilots in the US Navy's air rescue helicopter squadron HC-2, the "Fleet Angels," were used to playing chauffeur for Navy bigwigs up and down the US east coast when they weren't performing their primary role, but Abby had hoped this cruise would offer something a bit more exciting. She and Buck, along with their crew chief and the crew of a second Fleet Angels Sea King, had deployed aboard the carrier *Carl Vinson* as part of Admiral Falkner's efforts to "get everything that floats and everything that flies out into the Atlantic to show the Reds we mean business," as her squadron commander had reported, third-hand, the 2nd Fleet commander's words.

"I mean," Buck was saying, "I can't figure what's so important about this feller that we had to fly all the way from *Vinson* to that there Corvo Island to pick him up and then bring him all the way back here, and in bad weather, no less."

"I can't figure it out either," Abby said. Buck always talked too much. The six-foot five-inch Texan couldn't seem to help himself. Sometimes Abby, whose petite five-foot-four frame looked almost comical next to her lanky copilot, found his volume and his drawl a bit much, but right now he was giving voice to her own frustrations. *Is playing glorified bus driver all the Navy thinks I'm good for?* she thought. *I'm out here with the fleet, flying from an aircraft carrier, finally, and still all they can find for a woman pilot to do is ferry around mid-level officers like I'm some New York cab service?*

"Anyway," Abby said, refocusing on their mission, as demeaning as it might feel right now, "let's get fueled up and back to *Vinson*. Maybe they need us to pick up a loaf of bread and some coffee creamer along the way."

Hennessy snorted at the quip as they began their pre-flight checklist once more. The *Mount Whitney* deck crew were snaking a fuel line out to the Sea King, and Abby put her bitterness aside as she caught sight of the Marine colonel disappearing into the ship's superstructure. *If they want me to be a bus driver, then I'm going to be the best goddamn bus driver they ever saw,* she promised herself for the thousandth time.

— • —

Colonel Rob Buckner passed from the damp wind and noise of the flight deck into the relatively quiet passageways of *Mount Whitney's* interior. Having just completed the last leg of another whirlwind tour, he was decidedly tired but alert. This time he'd been in the Mediterranean, liaising with Falkner's counterpart in the US 6th Fleet. If it ever came to war with the Soviets, the two fleet commands would be passing ships between each other through the Straits of Gibraltar as the situation dictated, and Falkner wanted to ensure a good working relationship with the other HQ.

The deck pitched beneath Rob's feet as he made his way towards the conference room. Rob was no stranger to helicopter flights, and he'd been impressed by the smooth flight from Corvo Island, as they'd been flying through the remnants of a storm that'd been lashing the fleet for the past several days. He caught a faint whiff of vomit, evidence that some of the command ship's sailors were still suffering the effects of the passing storm. After a while even the Dramamine, which Buckner knew the ship's corpsmen dispensed like candy in rough weather, wasn't enough to keep down the contents of some stomachs.

Rear Admiral Forest, the chief of staff, kept 2nd Fleet's staff on a disciplined schedule, and Buckner knew that he was in time to pop into the daily commander's update brief, or CUB. Navigating to the conference room within the bowels of the ship, he arrived at an open door, where he could see the daily briefing about to start. He slipped in, looking around at the attendees as he did so.

The conference room was emptier than usual, only principal members of Vice Admiral Falkner's staff occupied the seats around the conference table. Rob Buckner took his seat behind his nominal boss, Rear Admiral Johnson, who he greeted with a quick nod. Rob wasn't feeling seasick himself, but neither were the smells of dinner being prepared in the ship's galley particularly appealing to him with the current motion of the ship. The Marine officer was ready to be done with his tour, done with this exercise, and to be off this ship, a sentiment he shared with the rest of the staff. *Especially if we aren't going to have a war*, he thought.

Admiral Falkner, seated at the head of the table, the 2nd Fleet's crest affixed to the bulkhead behind him, nodded, indicating that the briefing should commence.

The short, wiry chief of staff stood and steadied himself against a roll of the deck. He began, nodding to his commander and the other officers present, "Sir, gentlemen, as mentioned this morning, we're replacing the standard CUB with a decision brief to the commander," he nodded again to Falkner, "as to whether recent changes in the Soviet force posture permit us to return the fleet to port in time to allow many of our crews to celebrate the Christmas holiday with their families. As you know sir, if we wish our ships to arrive home by Christmas Eve, we must make the call in the next few hours. Principal and other key staff members are assembled here, and the commanders of the *Carl Vinson* and *Eisenhower* carrier battle groups are joining us via conference call, as is Rear Admiral Reeves aboard *Invincible*. Gentlemen," Forest addressed the speakerphone in the center of the table, "can you confirm that you are receiving?"

Metallic, static-distorted responses emanated from the speaker.

"Roger."

"Loud and clear."

"Jolly good."

The chief of staff nodded, then concluded, "Very well, I'll be followed by the N2, who will detail what the Soviets have apparently been up to in the past few days."

Forest resumed his seat heavily, just as the ship bottomed into the trough of a wave. 2nd Fleet's chief intelligence officer, Captain Ed Franklin, stood and removed the glasses from his thin, bookish face. He nodded to a junior officer, who clicked on a projector that shone a map of northern Europe and the North Atlantic onto a screen on the port bulkhead. The map was annotated with red symbols and markings clustered north of the Kola peninsula and, more menacingly, all around the strife-riddled country of Poland. The intel officer walked over to the projection and began to speak.

"Sir, as you know, Soviet naval forces have brought themselves to an unprecedented level of readiness over the past two months. In the first two weeks of December we've seen the Red Banner Northern Fleet conduct exercises," he tapped the red markings north of the Kola with a pen, "in the Barents and Norwegian Seas involving more ships and complex operations than in many years. This included carrier flight operations in coordination with surface action groups that have shown far more capability for offensive, expeditionary operations than we have seen to this point. Our counterparts over in Pacific Fleet are reporting Soviet exercises out there on a similar scale."

Now Franklin moved the pen to Poland. "More troubling," he continued, "is that the Soviets simultaneously launched snap exercises of unprecedented size involving a significant portion of their forces in Czechoslovakia. These exercises were apparently coordinated with other forces in the western USSR. During these operations we've seen significant logistical elements move from the interior of the USSR to forward staging areas in a way that indicated a Soviet intention to initiate a direct intervention in Poland. These actions drew statements of concern from many in the international community and prompted the US president to implement many of the discretionary sanctions against the Soviet Union authorized in the most recent Congressional bill.

Even so, a week ago, all signs pointed towards imminent Soviet military action to intervene in Poland, regardless of the international consequences."

Buckner looked at the map. The scale of the Soviet exercises, at sea, in the air, and on land, had been impressive. *A year ago they wouldn't have been able to put on a show nearly half as big*, he thought. *Fortunately, it looks like that's all it was, a show.*

Franklin paused and stepped away from the projection. He deftly shifted his weight through a deep roll of the deck before continuing, agreeing with Rob's unspoken assessment. "All of that has apparently changed in the past seventy-two hours. War, or at least an invasion of Poland by the Red Army, seemed inevitable, but our first indications that the Soviets were standing down came from submarines trailing their major surface units in the Barents Sea. They reported that the Soviet fleet appeared to be returning to port. These reports were later confirmed by our units on X-Ray Station and by satellite imagery which now shows nearly every Russian surface unit, and a very large number of their submarines, back in port with cooling reactors and power plants, as you can see from this imagery, taken about six hours ago when the satellite had clear skies over the Kola."

Now Franklin's assistant distributed folders marked with red and white striped tape and emblazoned with the words "Top Secret" to the principal staff members around the table. Over Admiral Johnson's shoulder Buckner could see that his superior's folder contained high quality faxes of overhead imagery showing the familiar landscape of the Soviet base at Severomorsk. As Johnson flipped through the contents, Buckner saw that one true color picture showed the base's piers jammed full of warships, some of the smaller vessels rafted up two and even three deep alongside each other.

The next image gave the same perspective, but was clearly produced by a thermal sensor. The black and white images showed the engine spaces of the ships in different shades of darkness, with the ones that had been berthed the longest emitting the least heat. *They'll need some time to get the engines going again if they want to send those ships back out*, Rob realized.

"Then, two days ago," Franklin went on, "the Red Army began shutting down its training exercise in Europe, returning troops to their barracks, even shipping some reinforcing units back to their bases in the interior. It appears what we are seeing is a nearly global stand down of Soviet military forces."

At this point Falkner broke in, asking, "Any indication as to why, Ed? Why go to all the effort of putting yourself on a war footing and then shutting it all down?"

"My read, sir," answered Franklin, who had anticipated the question, "and my contacts at State and NSA agree, is that this was a play on Medvedev's part to break the diplomatic logjam with NATO regarding the Polish situation, and perhaps drive a wedge between Germany and NATO at the same time. The Soviets probably thought if they amped up the pressure enough that we would back down over their interference in Poland. I think they were also trying to encourage the elements of the German government that were making noise about no longer needing 'collective security' to start asking themselves if they really want to fight a war with the USSR over Poland. The question was, how far was Medvedev willing to take this? Was he willing to actually invade Poland? Their stand down indicates that the answer was, *or is,* 'no.' This surge of readiness and exercises was a huge bluff, and one that has apparently failed."

"It's not surprising, really," rumbled Admiral Johnson. "Even with all the resources they've put into their military in the past couple years, the balance of power is still heavily in our favor, especially since they can't lean as deeply into their remaining Warsaw Pact allies any more. Frankly, their economy is on the rocks."

There was a pause that Falkner filled with a: "Hmm…" Non-committal, Buckner noticed. *He's not convinced yet.* The admiral nodded for Franklin to continue.

"Sir," the intel officer went on, an uncharacteristically hopeful note creeping into his voice, "what this means for us is that the Russians won't be able to put their fleet back out to sea in any sort of strength for at least a week or two, and we'll likely have several days' advance warning if they try. The same is true for their forces in Europe." Franklin stepped back behind his chair, grasping the backing as the deck pitched again, and finished with, "Sir, that concludes my brief, pending your questions."

"Thank you, Ed," Falkner nodded. Then he turned to Johnson and asked, "Xavier, give us a recap of how our forces are arrayed right now."

The N3 straightened in his chair and said, "Task Groups 20.1 and 20.2, *Eisenhower* and *Vinson* and their escorts, have been operating together southwest of Iceland for the past week. *Invincible*'s task group, west of the Faroes, has been playing red force to our blue force, supported by the 57th Fighter Squadron out of Keflavik, and doing a mighty fine job of it too, if I do say so myself." The rear admiral had raised his voice into the speaker for the last part.

"We do what we can, old boy," came the very proper response from Admiral Reeves through the speakerphone.

"Who knew a baby carrier could pack such a punch?" said Captain Ben Stevenson's teasing voice through the speakerphone from aboard the *Carl Vinson*.

"We do have some experience fighting a real war from this ship," reminded Reeves, referencing *Invincible*'s vital role in the 1982 Falkland Islands War.

"The Gulf War doesn't count, I guess?" asked the captain of the *Eisenhower* good-naturedly through the phone.

"Given our deployments, sir," Johnson refocused the group and addressed his chief, "we are well postured to counter any Soviet movement into the Atlantic, be it air, sea, or submarine. The Soviet withdrawal back to their ports has increased the lead time we have if things go hot. This gives us some operational flexibility. We now have the option of engaging the Soviets north of Iceland if the balloon goes up, if we so choose. Overall, sir, I feel very confident with the force we have assembled right now."

Falkner nodded once more, then turned to his logistics chief, Captain Hank Elliot, and said, "Hank, how are we on sustainment?"

The portly N4 looked up from his notes and responded, "We're as ready as we'll evah be, sir. All carriers have full tanks of aviation fuel, all magazines have complete war loads configured for anti-air and anti-surface wahfare. Fleet trains ah standing by to the south to replenish our stocks if and when necessary."

Falkner grunted, then said half-jokingly, "Too bad it's not the real deal. We're as ready as I've seen us in years. That's probably why the Sovs aren't going to try us, I suppose. Walter," he addressed the chief of staff to his right, "what's the impact if we decide to stand down our own forces?"

Admiral Forest was ready for the question. "Sir, really very little. *Eisenhower*'s not going back to port anyway since she's headed for the Med, so we can keep her on station a few more days. More than just getting our boys and girls home for Christmas, *Vinson* needs some work in port. Captain Stevenson has been running his carrier hard for the past few months."

"It's what the taxpayers pay me for," quipped Stevenson from the speaker.

"The sooner we get *Vinson* into port, the sooner we can do the necessary work and get her back out," added Captain Elliot.

"Hank, what's the status on *Enterprise*'s accelerated refit? When can we expect her ready for operations?" asked Falkner, switching gears somewhat.

"Sir, she floated out of dry dock last week," answered the N4, indicating that the most expensive and complicated part of the carrier's refueling and overhaul was complete. "We're on track to get her back to the fleet in mid-January. I believe Admiral Johnson has a workup scheduled for her in the Caribbean for mid-February?"

The N3 nodded that Elliot was indeed correct.

"Later than I would like," lamented Falkner, "but I suppose the yard dogs have done their best." His tone communicated that he was not sure they had.

2nd Fleet's commander steepled his fingers to consider the question at hand: whether to cut his available combat strength by more than half by sending *Carl Vinson* and *Invincible* back to port in time for their crews to enjoy the holidays with friends and family. The admiral had built his reputation in the Navy as a firm but fair operator, someone who truly cared about the people under him but didn't let that care deter him from the mission at hand. *If he lets us go home*, Buckner thought, watching Falkner, a man he'd come to know fairly well over the past year, weigh his options, *it means he really believes this scare of the past two weeks is over.* The whole staff held their breaths, waiting to hear whether they'd be making a joyful homecoming on Christmas Eve, or eating sliced galley turkey and instant potatoes here aboard ship for the holiday.

The deck rolled slowly one way in the swell, then the other. After a few more moments Falkner dropped his hands and announced, "Xavier, give the order; *Vinson* and *Invincible* and their groups can head for the barn. *Eisenhower* will stay on station just in case the Russkis decide to try some sort of bolt from the blue. I'm not convinced this," he waved his hand in a circle, "whatever it was they were doing was actually just a bluff. Just doesn't feel right to me, but we can't stay on station forever, and it seems they've given us some breathing room. I'm still uneasy until we get *Enterprise* back, but there's nothing we can do about it now. We made our bed and we've got to lie in it."

Buckner watched as everyone in the room seemed to visibly relax, everyone already imagining being free of this pitching ship. That is until Admiral Forest said, "What about the flagship, sir?" Buckner realized that Falkner had said nothing about whether or not *Mount Whitney* could return home.

A smile crept across Falkner's face at the tension that had so quickly left and then re-entered the room. He let the question hang in the air for just a moment before saying, "Well, what say you, Walter, has the staff earned a Christmas leave?"

Forest smirked mischievously back at his chief and said, "Well sir, we could use the time for a little more work on our concepts for operations north of Iceland," The mental groan from the rest of the staff was no less anguished for its silence. Rob's thoughts flashed to his son Joshua. This would be his last Christmas at home before heading off to the University of Wisconsin on an NROTC scholarship. "I suppose it wouldn't hurt to give them the time off," concluded the chief of staff with a smile that grew into genuine warmth.

Admiral Falkner's grin also grew wider. "Very well, Walter, give the flag captain the order. We're heading home." Then as smiles broke out around the conference table, the admiral said loudly in his best imitation of Charles Dickens' Scrooge: "Be here all the earlier the next day! Merry Christmas."

CHAPTER 18

1745 CET, Friday 24 December 1993
1645 Zulu
Ministry of Foreign Affairs, Victoria Terrasse, Oslo, Norway

"HAVE YOU FOUND a man down there, then?" said the speakerphone.

"*Mother!*" Kristen Hagen said as her hand shot across the desk to snatch the phone's receiver from its cradle, taking the device off speaker. She could feel her cheeks burning as she swiveled her tall frame toward the open door of the bland Foreign Ministry office to see if anyone had been passing near enough to hear the embarrassing question, realizing in the same instant that her fear was unfounded. *Everyone's gone home for Christmas.*

Over the receiver, Kristen could hear her father chuckling from the living room of their modest family home in Kirkenes. The small town was nestled in the northernmost fylker, or county, of Norway.

"*No,* I have *not* found a man," said Kristen, trying to make her voice sound exasperated. She smoothed a wisp of blond hair back over her ear in annoyance. *Why do these phone calls home always go this way?* She tried to change the subject. "I'm spending my time learning how to be the chief of staff for a new foreign minister."

Her mother's tone changed with the mention of the new foreign minister. "Yes, we were so sorry to hear about Mr. Holst's stroke."

"Had to read about it in the papers up here," Kristen heard her father say in the background, the unspoken part of his message Kristen understood: *You should call us more often.*

Until recently, the Norwegian Ministry of Foreign Affairs had operated efficiently under the able leadership of the brilliant Johan Jørgen Holst, who had thrown his heart and soul into trying to broker peace between Israel and the Palestine Liberation Organization. His efforts had come so very close to producing a meaningful agreement, but some unhelpful meddling from the Soviet foreign ministry had scuttled the talks before they'd even convened in Washington last September. Kristen more than suspected that some illicit arms shipments to the PLO from the USSR via Syria were involved.

The disappointment, or perhaps the effort he'd expended in the failed attempt, had been too much for the elderly statesman, and he collapsed from a stroke in early December.

"I'm afraid the doctors are less and less positive about his recovery," Kristen said, sad about her erstwhile chief's failing health but relieved to be discussing something other than her love life.

"Yes, I know you really enjoyed working for him," Kristen's mother was saying, "but doesn't the new minister like you as well? He made you his chief of staff, after all."

"Well, he's not exactly the new minister yet," Kristen said, "not while Minister Holst is still with us anyway." Kristen suddenly felt uncomfortable talking about her career while the man whose poor health had propelled her to the next rung of her ministry's administration clung precariously to life just a few kilometers away. She loved working here, and she was ambitious to one day, perhaps, run for a seat in the *Storting* so that she might have the chance to *be* the minister, not just serve on his staff. "I would much rather he recover than take the promotion."

"Of course, Kristen, of course," her mother said. "How have things been at the ministry otherwise?"

"Oh my goodness, busy!" Kristen said picking up her tone, thankful once again for the change of subject. "We've been working like mad to finalize preparations for Lillehammer. I never knew a sporting event like this could take up so much of the ministry's attention. We barely have time to focus on anything else."

"What takes up so much time?" asked her mother, showing a genuine interest in her oldest daughter's work. "We're really looking forward to watching."

"Visas for the athletes," Kristen answered. "The USSR team is giving us some real headaches. They've been switching out athletes like crazy over the past few weeks, and every time they do it creates more paperwork."

"That's that devil Medvedev's doing I'm sure," Kristen heard her father say. "He's probably worried about some Ukrainian figure skater defecting while they're here." Having lived his whole life in Kirkenes, less than ten kilometers from the Soviet border, Kristen's father had never warmed to their Slavic neighbors. Sometimes, after dinner, over glasses of aquavit, her father would recount with bitterness his childhood memories of how the Soviet liberation of Northern Norway in 1945 had left so many of the small communities in ruins.

"Yes, well," Kristen said, "I don't think they're doing their team any favors, anyway."

"Well, we're of course very proud of you and we're looking forward to watching your handiwork," her mother said.

"Thanks, *mamma*," said Kristen into the phone. "Is Anna there? I feel like I haven't talked to her in ages."

"Sorry, no. She's out with some friends enjoying the Christmas cheer this evening," mother said. "I think one of them might even be a boy," she teased.

Time to go before they try to set me up with one of the boys back home, Kristen thought.

"Well, it's wonderful to hear your voice, *mamma* and *pappa*, but I need to go back to the apartment and make my own Christmas cheer."

"Don't be lonely, Kristen," *mamma* said. "You know we always love it when you come home for the holiday."

"I know, *mamma*, but with the Games this year and the minister's health it was just too much. Maybe I can make a quick flight home in the spring, after it's all over."

"We'll look forward to it, Kristen. Happy Christmas."

"Happy Christmas, *mamma*."

 **CHAPTER 19**

2030 EST, Friday 24 December 1993
0130 Zulu (Saturday 25 December)
Dwyer Hill, Ontario Canada

S NOW WAS FALLING softly outside the cozy Roy house, nestled into the small family housing area just up the road from Joint Task Force 2's unassuming rural base west of Ottawa. Sergeant David Strong sat, sleepy from the delicious meal and happier than he'd felt in months. Indeed, he'd been at ease ever since arriving at the home of his team's medic for Christmas Eve supper. The single-story dwelling was tastefully decorated with just a couple of strands of colorful lights, along with a wreath at the front door and candles in the windows. The scene reminded him of some of the happier moments of his childhood.

Felix Roy welcomed him, his massive frame making the cramped entry-way feel even smaller as David removed his boots and coat, snow dusting the foyer. That was when pandemonium enveloped them. Before David knew what was happening the four Roy children clustered around his ankles, pulling at his discarded outer garments and arguing in a bewildering mix of youthful French and English with each other over the right to ask their guest his drink preferences. A firm word from Marie, Felix's wife, dispersed them, or rather displaced them to another room of the house where the noise continued unabated. Then she greeted David warmly in her lyrical Québécois-accented English with an embrace and a kiss on each cheek.

She was a beautiful woman, as petite as her husband was huge. She moved with a graceful confidence that seemed to create an aura of peace in the small household. David's appreciation of her was bittersweet. She and Felix reminded him of the domestic tranquility he hadn't found in his own life.

Marie, before returning to the kitchen and keeping the children in line with periodic forays to the back of the house, ushered David and Felix into the small living room. "Bear" and his wife sat on the couch good-naturedly teasing Will "Crash" Tenny about the spectacular termination of his latest relationship. The Browns' toddler played on the floor at their feet. David and Felix didn't contribute much to the joshing conversation but laughed at the jokes and enjoyed the company all the same. The group had developed a good work dynamic over the past year, but David was always awkward in a non-military setting.

Before too long Marie's voice summoned them to the dining room where every spare chair in the house was crammed around a table set with a feast consisting of *tourtière*, a sort of meat pie, a meatball and gravy stew that Marie called *ragoût de boulettes*, fried potatoes, pea soup, with maple syrup pie and a yule log cake for dessert. The smells had been tempting the guests since they arrived and now the hour of their deliverance was at hand.

At one end of the table, Felix bowed his head. Everyone else followed suit, and he blessed the food according to his Catholic tradition. Then he produced a bottle of red wine for the meal, a sore point for David. According to regulations and JTF 2's own internal policies, members of the unit were forbidden from consuming alcohol while on recall status, as they were now. David opened his mouth to object to this breach of discipline but thought better of it when he saw his medic pour a small glass for the oldest of the children, giving her the honor of taking the first sip this Christmas Eve. *They're French Canadian*, he rationalized. *Wine with a meal isn't really alcohol to them, I suppose.* This supposition was confirmed when Felix circumnavigated the cramped table, filling everyone's glass in turn.

David realized that the other two members of his team were looking at him out of the corner of their eyes, waiting to see if he would drink the wine. Corporals Brown and Tenny clearly wanted to imbibe but were wary of their sergeant's reaction. Part of Strong's reputation, his identity even, was as a stickler for upholding rules and regulations. Doing otherwise made him uncomfortable. Once again, Felix forced his hand, raising his glass from the head of the table and wishing everyone a *"Joyeux Noel!"*

Almost in reflex, David raised the glass to his lips, tasting the wine. That was all the other two needed. They each drank as well, and Strong thought he saw the hint of a smile at his expense on Tenny's face. Regardless, the tension was broken. David wasn't particularly happy about it, but then, he wasn't particularly unhappy either. They all sat down and began passing the food. Each person's knees bumped those of their neighbor, but no one minded in the festive, communal atmosphere the Roys had created.

The meal was Felix and Marie's idea. The four men of Joint Task Force 2 had been on alert since the beginning of December when the Soviets began conducting their global readiness exercises. That meant none of the Canadian commandos were allowed to travel more than an hour from the base. Even then, everyone was required to sign out at their squadron's staff duty desk, detailing where they would be and how they could be reached in an emergency. Strong and the other team leaders were even issued some of the new pagers that the task force had purchased to speed their recall. David was at least thankful that his team was being held in readiness at Dwyer Hill, rather than spending the time cooped up at the Halifax naval base from whence they were likely to deploy in wartime. With no one allowed to travel home over the holidays, the Roys decided to provide the family atmosphere most people craved this time of year.

Now, two hours later, Strong patted his full belly as he sat alone in the Roy's living room. Felix and Marie were putting their excited children to bed with remonstrations that Santa would come more quickly if they went right to sleep. The Browns had departed after dinner, their toddler nearly asleep in Bear's arms, and Tenny followed them out a few minutes later saying that he needed to call his mother in Vancouver. David wasn't ready for the evening to end quite yet. Now, as he heard the Roys lulling the youngest of their children to sleep, he suddenly realized he was intruding. *It's Christmas Eve! They don't want me here.*

The sergeant stood up to leave but realized the children had carried his coat somewhere into the house and he didn't know where it was. He awkwardly sat back down on the couch. After a few more minutes in which Strong berated himself quietly for his lack of social tact, he heard Felix's heavy footfalls coming from the rear of the small house. He stood as the big man appeared in the living room, carrying another bottle of red wine. Strong opened his mouth to make his excuses, but before he could speak the medic rumbled, "Would you share a glass with me, Sergeant?"

Strong paused. Dinner was one thing. *A drink by itself.* "Better not, Felix. We're on recall," he reminded his master corporal.

"Yes," acknowledged Roy in his Québécois accent, "but it's Christmas Eve, *non*? Besides, I was at the aid station this morning and the commander was there. I overheard him tell the surgeon that we will stand down if the Russians don't pull anything by tomorrow. We can take our chances." His tone was relaxed as he stepped over to a china cabinet wedged into a corner of the small room and retrieved three wine glasses. The big man paused and David saw him also pull out what looked like a bottle of whiskey. Roy apparently thought better of it, however, and David thought he saw the ghost of a smile on his face as he replaced the whiskey bottle in the cabinet. Instead, Felix deftly uncorked the wine bottle and poured himself and David a small glass each.

Accepting the proffered drink with reluctance, David tried to be at ease. He *should* be at ease. This was an opportunity to try and build a friendship, something he craved.

Their four-man team, now honed to a fine edge could anticipate each other's' moves and idiosyncrasies in the field, but here in the living room of a cozy family home Strong felt like a bit of a stranger, even to himself.

Roy, taking a seat across from Strong, was the rock of the team.

Strong sighed and took a sip of the wine.

Roy smiled. "See? Not so hard."

"What?" David asked, but he knew.

"To live a little. Be a rebel now and then. Not concern yourself with what the next evaluation report says," said Felix, leaning over and giving Strong a soft punch on the shoulder.

"It's that obvious, eh?" David asked sheepishly, flushing.

Felix looked down, still smiling. "Maybe a little," he said. Then he went on, "You know you don't have to work so hard to impress us. We all have great respect for you. You've built a good team. A *great* team. I've heard the commander say so. He respects you too. Do you ever plan to lighten up on yourself?" *And on the rest of us*, Roy didn't say, but Strong could sense it.

"I don't know how," the sergeant admitted in a moment of honesty. "I've never been able to before. I've just always been trying to get to the next achievement, I guess. Did the commander really say that?"

Roy chuckled a little and nodded.

Strong paused for a moment, then asked, "How do you do it, Felix? How are you so confident in yourself all the time, so natural around everyone? The way you talk to your kids is the same as the way you talk to the colonel."

Felix cocked his head towards the kitchen, saying nothing for a moment. David could hear the sounds of Marie starting to clean up from the meal, dishes clinking and water running in the sink.

"My reason is in there," said Felix, indicating the kitchen. "I doubt myself every day. We all do. We're men. It's what we do." The big man paused, then went on, "But then I get to come home to a wife every night who makes me feel like I'm her knight in shining armor, and four kids who seem to think that the highlight of their day is when I walk through the front door. It does wonders for the self-confidence, let me tell you," he said with a grin.

David took another sip of the wine. "Well, I haven't got a wife," he said lamely. "Haven't even had a girlfriend since I was just out of high school."

"Why not?" asked Felix, genuinely surprised. "Trust me. You're not going to find a girl by spending all your hours at work. You need to get out. Go dancing! Show the girls out there who David Strong really is." Roy raised his glass towards his sergeant and took a swallow of wine by way of demonstration.

David was suddenly distracted by a mental image of Felix's huge frame doing moves at some Montreal discotheque. He raised his wineglass to his lips to hide a creeping smile.

Felix turned serious, though still maintaining a warm tone. "Look, David, you don't need to impress anyone. You," he pointed a finger at David's chest, "are an amazing team leader, the best sergeant I've worked with. You have so much to be proud of."

Strong considered what Roy was saying. "I don't know how to let up, Felix," he said. "I've been doing this for so long, it's just become who I am."

Felix looked his team leader in the eye and said, "Who you are, Sergeant David Strong, is a fine soldier. I think you may be the only one who doesn't fully grasp that. Don't fret about being chummy with the rest of us. You're not our friend really, not in the usual sense anyway. That doesn't mean we don't like you or you don't like us. Quite the opposite, really. What it boils down to is this: you need to be able to put us into danger when the time comes. It's your job to balance our lives against the mission. You can't be worried about what we'll think when you're making a decision to finish the job." Felix sipped his wine and then leaned forward, locking eyes with his team leader. "On the other hand," Felix's eyes twinkled, "we don't want you worrying about what the commander or anyone else will think when you have to make the call to pull us out before the mission's done, eh?"

David smiled as the bigger man patted him on the shoulder. He appreciated the encouragement, particularly because he saw the ways that the master corporal supported him at work, keeping the other two team members in line when they could have begun complaining.

"Thanks Felix," the sergeant said, before throwing back the last of his wine. Then, "I really appreciate you. I don't know that I could hold the team together without you."

"You would do just fine," assured Felix.

"Maybe," David allowed. *It wouldn't be as painless.* Then he stood. "I'd better be going. I imagine you have better Christmas Eve plans than listening to me mope."

Roy stood too. "You don't think I opened this bottle just for you, eh? I have a date with my wife to put the gifts under the tree. And, if I'm good, and the wine does its usual tricks on my woman, I should have a nice Christmas Eve too," he said with a wink.

"*Felix!*" came the indignant cry from the kitchen.

"Yes, well, you best be going," the big medic said quickly, retrieving David's coat from the hallway where the children had stowed it away inside a bench.

David stepped out the door, then turned and offered the master corporal his hand. "Merry Christmas, Felix," he said. Then seeing Marie over Felix's shoulder, he called, "and thank you Marie for a wonderful meal."

"Merry Christmas, David," they both said in near unison.

David turned to walk to his car as the door closed lightly behind him. He took a moment to savor the lightly falling snow and the crisp cold. It had been a wonderful evening. That talk with Felix hadn't been what he'd expected, but was encouraging nonetheless. He'd enjoyed the wine, his first sip of alcohol in several weeks, but there was a small twinge of fear for the reprimand he expected if his superiors found out about his breach of discipline.

Then Strong smiled to himself, remembering Roy's admonition to worry less about what others, superiors or otherwise, thought of him. *The recall will be over tomorrow, anyway,* he thought. *It's not as if the Russians are going to* do *anything.* The packed snow on the walkway squeaked under his feet.

 **CHAPTER 20**

1705 EST, Wednesday 5 January 1994
2205 Zulu
Times Tower, New York City, New York, USA

E VIDENCE OF THE 1994 New Year's celebration still hung between the desks in the *New York Times* buzzing newsroom as Jack Young worked to meet the deadline for the morning edition. The reporter needed just a few more minutes for a final read-through before he handed in his copy. As he looked up, he could see the assistant editor making the rounds to crack the whip on delinquents like him. Jack hated to hand in a product that actually needed editing. The routine foreign policy piece would probably be buried somewhere on page A4 where readers would see it only after digesting all of the stories detailing city politics, NFL playoff news, probably the Dear Abby column, and the domestic political drama consuming the president and congress in the aftermath of the midterm elections. *Who knew the contested end to the election two years ago would have such a lasting impact*, Jack reflected.

The article before him was one he'd been ruminating over since returning from the former Yugoslavia in November. The collapse of the peace process was turning that country into another Poland. He wanted to write something that connected all the dots across Europe, that tried to make sense of the tense situation in which the continent found itself. He looked back down at the text on the small screen of his Xerox word processor and began reading from the beginning:

EUROPE STEPS BACK FROM CRISIS AS WORLD UNREST GROWS

Jack Young, reporter

President Pavel Medvedev has ordered a worldwide stand down of Soviet military forces following last month's major exercises, which showed a surprising level of capability and readiness. The Soviet Defense Minister, Marshal Aleksandr Rosla, declared the drills a success, saying that they had demonstrated the USSR's "reinvigorated ability to deter aggression from any quarter, but especially from the west," where the Soviets continue to view NATO with a wary eye, questioning the alliance's defensive purpose after the reunification of Germany three years ago.

Despite the marshal's stated mistrust, President Medvedev and his government have significantly softened their rhetoric since the middle of last month. US State Department officials have noted that the Soviet president apparently dropped one of his staple demands: That a united Germany withdraw from NATO as a precondition for normalized relations. This softened stance has led some experts to speculate that last month's worrying build-up of military activity might have been the last gasp of a Soviet administration that is belatedly learning the lesson its predecessors already knew: the USSR can no longer compete with the west in any sphere save the military one, and the dramatic conclusion to the Persian Gulf War three years ago brings even that assumption into question.

Lending credence to this interpretation is President Medvedev's call for talks with the US to re-negotiate the treaty limiting conventional forces in Europe. One administration official stated that the US would be amenable to such an agreement, provided the Soviets cease their interference in the internal affairs of Poland and the states of the former Yugoslavia, where UN peacekeepers are struggling to contain growing violence. Many pundits note that the US military, increasingly challenged to respond to contingencies all over the world, would likely welcome such an outcome.

So far, the Kremlin has given no firm indication of any shift in Soviet policy concerning these two flashpoints, maintaining instead the official story that "the Soviet Union is not interfering in the affairs of any state, but supports in spirit the rights of those in Eastern Europe who are resisting the fascist tendencies of their governments. Even so, many European and some American diplomats are quick to interpret the relaxed Soviet tone, accompanied by the military stand down, as a major step towards lasting peace in Europe.

Jack looked up. The assistant editor was standing at his desk. "Bill wants to know where your story is, Jack," she said in her nasally New York accent. "You're ten minutes late."

Jack decided to deflect with charm. He smiled at her and pointed to the screen of his word processor. "It's right here Jane, just giving it the final look-over now. Tell Bill he won't even need to look this one over."

"I won't be telling him that," Jane said. She wasn't known for her sense of humor, especially when up against the daily deadline.

"Five minutes," Jack assured her. "I'll have a hard copy, and one on disk, if you want it."

"Just get me the hard copy," she responded, walking away. He watched her plod heavily on to another reporter across the newsroom who, Jack saw, was furiously pecking on an old typewriter. He turned his attention back to the second part of his article.

Despite the dramatic lowering of tensions in Europe, some Defense Department officials have noted that Soviet involvement around the globe has seen a dramatic uptick in the past several months. Renewed arms shipments to Nicaragua and Cuba drew sharp criticism from the White House just before the November midterms. Defense officials say that the USSR has made dramatic diplomatic and economic inroads into many other parts of the world in recent months, including Libya, India, Vietnam, and Africa, re-establishing a global Soviet presence that had all but disappeared two years ago. The Soviets appear to be pursuing a covert strategy of destabilization reminiscent of the darkest days of the Brezhnev era. Perhaps this is an attempt to replicate the frozen conflicts now embroiling Poland and Yugoslavia as a way to counter American influence. The Soviet government officially denies any connection to leftist uprisings cropping up in the Third World of late, saying only that they respect the rights of people who seek to throw off the yoke of authoritarian governments supported by the US and Europe.

The consensus appears to be that the Soviet exercises last month were a bluff, and that destabilizing activities around the world are a sign of weakness, a desperate and unsustainable attempt at remaining globally relevant. Many in Washington expect that major concessions on Poland might be forthcoming over the coming months as the Soviets attempt to get out from under the weight of economic sanctions. For now, Europe and the world appear to have avoided a war that seemed very possible just last month.

It could use more artistry, Jack thought, as he waited for the word processor to noisily print his copy. It was the sort of mundane page filler that took up much of the space in any daily paper, despite his own paper's claim to contain "all the news that's fit to print." What he needed was to get back out in the field, someplace where he could be reporting *real* news again, rather than providing variations on months-old stories. Jack enjoyed the drama of investigation, the pull of real stories with real import. The printer stopped and Jack stood and grabbed the sheet, walking towards Bill's office.

As he neared the frosted glass enclosure that demarcated the editor's domain, Jack saw his friend Jonathan Blackwell exiting the office. Jonathan worked at the sports desk, and he wore a grin on his face that made Jack stop to see what good fortune had just befallen the sportswriter.

"What's up Jon?" asked Jack. "You look like you think the Giants have a snowball's chance in hell of getting past the 'Niners this year." Jack was a Jets fan himself, and never missed an opportunity to razz the cross-town team.

"Oh yeah?" said Blackwell, "well we might at that. I guarantee we'll beat the Vikings in the first round, and hey," his grin grew broader, "at least we made the playoffs. How'd your Jets make out this year?"

Jack made a show of cringing. "Be nice, my friend. I'll remember that when you're singing a different tune in February. You look to lose Phil Simms and Lawrence Taylor in the off season."

"True enough," said Blackwell, "but that's Future Jon's problem. I'm focused on the here and now, *that*, buddy, is the first round of the playoffs against Minnesota this weekend."

"Seriously," Jack probed, "what's going on? You don't usually walk out of Bill's office looking like you won the lottery."

"Well," the sports writer said, "this time I did. Win the lottery, so to speak. Bill's putting up the money to send me to cover the Winter Olympics next month. I'm headed to Lillehammer!"

"Norway!" Jack exclaimed. "Gonna be cold this time of year, or so they tell me. Have fun brother! Great opportunity."

"Thanks, Jack," Blackwell said, walking away.

Jack walked into Bill's office and delivered his article. He was saved from the usual scolding by another reporter who rushed in just behind him with a piece that Jack could tell right off the bat was going to need some major revising. Jack took advantage of the diversion to make his escape.

As he walked back to his desk he thought about Blackwell heading to Norway in a few weeks. Jack enjoyed the excitement of covering the drama of human conflict in the world's hotspots, but part of him yearned for an assignment where he could cover the best of humanity rather than the worst, someplace where nothing bad ever seemed to happen.

PART V: MOVEMENT TO CONTACT

"There are only two stories: a man goes on a journey, or a stranger comes to town."
—Leo Tolstoy

 **CHAPTER 21**

1615 EST, Sunday 9 January 1994
2115 Zulu
Brighton Beach Avenue, Brooklyn, New York City, New York, USA

THE STRANGER STEPPED off the heated subway and into a cold wind on the open-air elevated platform. The sign on the station's siding read "Brighton Beach" in white letters upon a black background. *Odd*, thought the man, *elevating the metro line above the street like this.* Cars and busses were passing noisily on the boulevard below, pedestrian traffic bustled on the sidewalk.

Overall, the man was rather unimpressed with his experience of the New York City subway system. These Americans apparently took no pride in their public transportation. Certainly not as much pride as his country put into its own city trains. Where he came from every Metro stop was a unique work of art, almost a cathedral. Here the metro was crowded, dirty, ugly, and certainly inefficient. At one connecting station he had been forced to wait fifteen minutes for a train. This had made the last leg of his long journey, crossing from Newark to Manhattan and then to Brooklyn, very frustrating.

Shouldering a small backpack, the athletic, upper-middle-aged foreigner took the stairs and descended to street level. Glancing left and right, he checked to see if anyone was paying him any untoward attention. No one was. The sights at ground level, in contrast to the elevated subway platform, were jarring in their familiarity, given all the places he had visited on his trek so far. Damascus, Johannesburg, Paris, Singapore, Los Angeles, Minneapolis, Newark. Each place had smelled, looked, and tasted very different, but none reminded him so much of his point of origin as this place did now. Looking up and down the boulevard he saw more signs in Cyrillic lettering than he did in English. *No wonder they call this place "Little Odessa,"* he thought, before remembering that the area was beginning to earn a new nickname: "Little Russia."

The Brighton Beach neighborhood of Brooklyn had decades ago become a destination for Ukrainian Jews fleeing *pogroms* in the Soviet Union. They congregated here, forming an ethnic community, just as so many other immigrant groups coming to the United States had done. Such communities provided familiarity to the first-generation immigrants while allowing access to the broader culture of the great city to the new arrival's children. It was this second generation who would inevitably identify more with their new home than with the old country. When the Soviet Union was teetering in the late '80s and early '90s, a new surge of immigrants flooded into the neighborhood, this time it was mostly ethnic Russians rather than Ukrainian Jews. With the rise of Medvedev after the August 1991 coup, another, smaller surge had arrived, mostly political outcasts no longer welcome in the resurgent USSR, along with a few others. It was one of these "few others" that he sought now.

He'd memorized the name of his destination before departing, wanting no written proof that might compromise him if some security official became suspicious. His precautions had been unnecessary. The US Customs official at Los Angeles International Airport, which Mr. Taylor made sure he referred to as "LAX," had barely looked at him before she stamped his passport, smiled, and said, "Welcome to America, Mr. Taylor. Always fun to see Australians come through here." Of course, Taylor was not his name, nor was he Australian, but she would never know that. Once past that pathetic obstacle, internal border security had been non-existent, in stark contrast to the Soviet Union where citizens needed a pass just to travel from one city to another. He was a veteran traveler to America, but he still marveled at the anarchic idea that any person could cross any state boundary in this country, even board an airplane, without *any* sort of papers.

Spying a sign in the distance that indicated his destination, he walked towards it. The modest restaurant was decorated tastelessly with politically-themed *Matrioshka* stacking dolls and imitation *Samovars*. Draping his coat over a chair, he sat at a flimsy table and picked up a menu. No one else was in the establishment at present. After a few moments a middle-aged man with a day's growth of beard and a dirty apron covering a protruding gut came out and asked brusquely for his order.

Mr. Taylor spoke the memorized phrase slowly in Russian, enunciating every word, "How is the *Borscht* today? Your uncle Vladimir tells me that no one but he makes it better."

The man's eyes narrowed, but without missing a beat he responded with equally clear enunciation, "Sadly we are all out of the *Borscht*. Perhaps you would enjoy the *Pirozhki* instead? They are my Uncle Vladimir's favorite."

"Yes, that sounds nice," responded Taylor, completing the challenge and response, "with tea, please."

The cook relaxed visibly and sat down across the table before leaning in conspiratorially.

"Are we secure here?" Taylor, whose real name was Vasily Volkhov, asked calmly in Russian.

The aproned man nodded his head. "*Da*, I swept the whole place just last night. No listening devices, no visitors. I am sure their security forces don't suspect me. We're safe."

The man in the apron had been living here, managing this pathetic excuse for a restaurant, for over a year now. *If he is compromised*, the Volkhov thought, *then the whole operation is blown.*

"The others?" he asked.

"They are all here. I've moved them to safe houses in the neighborhoods specified in my instruction. So many! Can you tell me what is going on?" asked the cook in wonderment.

Taylor, or rather Volkhov, *did* know what was going on. He was actually the only person in this city, in the world in fact, other than the man who had personally selected him for this mission, who knew in full what he and those who had preceded him were here to do. His response was deadpan. "I would prefer you did not ask such questions."

"Of course, of course," the aproned man nodded jerkily. "It is just, well, there are so many! I can't imagine—"

"Then don't." his tone was icy as he cut the restauranteur off. He let the silence hang for a few moments to be sure that this expatriate understood that no further questions would be entertained. "There will be several shipments arriving over the coming days. I'll be relying on you for secure places to store them. I will also require several vehicles when the time comes. Trucks. You received the funds?"

The cook nodded that he had.

"Good." Taylor's tone softened. "You will have the details of exactly what we require when you need to know. In the meantime, a visit to each of the safe houses is in order, I have briefings to deliver to the teams. There are also several points around the city to see in the coming days. Do you have a room for me?"

"Of course," the aproned man responded.

Mr. Taylor paused. Travels ended, he was beginning to feel the effects of the journey. His mind told him he needed to sleep, but his body was telling him that it was, *what? Morning? Afternoon?*

"The ocean is near, is it not?" he asked.

"Yes of course, just that way," the man answered, pointing behind him.

"Let's take a walk."

Both men retrieved their jackets and, after the owner called to someone in the back to tend the place, they exited the front of the restaurant. Walking down Brighton 4th Street towards the beach, they passed between low-income apartments that reminded the man masquerading as Taylor of the buildings in his own city. They emerged onto the boardwalk, lined with benches that were presently covered with dirty snow. Beyond the benches he could see the water, small waves lapping up onto a sandy beach, an icy breeze blowing off the sound. *Not as cold as back home*, he thought turning up his collar, *but cold enough*. To his right, down the Strand was Coney Island, the amusement park's rides and Ferris wheel idle for the winter season. It looked almost post-apocalyptic in the stillness of winter, bright colors dulled by the gray sky.

Looking back out to sea, across what the Americans called the Lower Bay, he could make out the low shape of the Sandy Hook peninsula. There, on that sand spit, at the mouth of the expansive New York harbor, was an American

Coast Guard station built on the site of an old coastal defense artillery fort. *Fort Hancock*, the Russian remembered after a moment. The layout of the facility had been much more important to him than its name.

The Russian shifted his gaze to take in the whole Lower Bay. *It is all going to begin right here*, he thought. Of course, his mission briefing had not said so explicitly, but he was an intelligent man, and it did not take a genius to figure out the import of the missions he was to oversee here. Volkhov knew nothing of other such missions elsewhere in the world, or even elsewhere in this country, but could not imagine that his was the only one. *That can only mean one thing. The war will start with a dagger thrust to the heart of this powerful country.* The thought pleased him. He turned abruptly on his heel and began walking back to the restaurant, the restaurant owner scrambling to catch up. There was work to do, but first, rest. *The "go" order must come soon. All the pieces are coming together.*

 **CHAPTER 22**

0855 EST, Monday 31 January 1994
1355 Zulu
US 2nd Fleet Headquarters, Building W-5,
Naval Station Norfolk, Virginia, USA

C OLONEL ROB BUCKNER walked through the front door of the 2nd Fleet headquarters building five minutes before the start of work. He was nursing a hangover, compliments of the big game the night before. *Or maybe it was because I finally do*␣*d my i's and crossed my t's on the retirement paperwork*, he reflected, patting the tactical knapsack he used as his daily briefcase. Regardless, Super Bowl XXVIII or not, retirement or not, Buckner prided himself on his timeliness and the quality of his work. *That won't change once I drop this paperwork off with the personnel section*, he promised himself.

Rob passed by the Marine guard just inside the doorway, flashing his identification card as he did so, then navigated his way through the narrow corridors until he arrived at the operations staff section's bank of offices and cubicles. As he passed by the open door of the N3's office he heard Admiral Johnson rumble, "Rob, how 'bout that game last night?"

Buckner stopped, stuck his head through the door and said, "Wasn't much of game in the second half, sir. Those Bills can't seem to catch a break."

Love of American football was something he and the N3 shared, to the benefit of their working relationship.

"Definitely not against my 'boys,'" crowed Johnson in his deep Mississippi drawl. "That running back Emmitt Smith was magnificent." The 2nd Fleet N3 was a fan of the now back-to-back NFL champion Dallas Cowboys.

"Don't remind me," said Rob in mock disgust. The Cowboys had defeated his beloved Green Bay Packers in the second round of the playoffs this year on their way to the title.

"Why the long face, Colonel?" teased the admiral. "There's always next year."

"There is at that sir," Rob said, still fighting back the dull pain in his head but enjoying the light banter with his boss. "That new quarterback of ours, Favre, he's our ticket to the big game. Give him a couple years and we'll be there."

Johnson pointed at Rob and winked. "Mississippi boy, he is," the admiral reminded the Wisconsin-born Marine.

Rob nodded good-naturedly, letting his chief bask in his team's big win for a moment. Then he asked, "Any priorities for me this week, sir?"

Johnson leaned back in his chair and said, "Just *Enterprise* sailing at the end of the week. She'll be getting back in tomorrow from a three-day cruise. Then it's a quick turnaround and out again for ten days off Puerto Rico. After that we'll bring her back in, get her outfitted, and send her on up north for a few weeks."

"Any amphib business you need me to handle, sir?" asked Buckner.

"Not this time, Rob. Things are pretty quiet," answered Johnson. "There hasn't been a peep from the Russians in weeks. You just keep working on setting up that joint exercise with those paratroopers from Ft. Bragg."

"Roger, sir," Buckner said as he headed to his cubicle in the cramped office suite to begin his last several weeks in the service of his country, massaging his temples as he tried to dispel the dull thumping in his forehead.

 **CHAPTER 23**

1005 EST, Friday 4 February 1994
1505 Zulu
USS *Enterprise*, one hundred miles east of
Cape Hatteras, North Carolina

S
UNDOWNER ONE-ONE, THREE *quarters of a mile, on and on, call*
the ball, Captain Russel Armstrong recited in his head, mimicking the
commands he would be receiving from the Landing Signal Officer if
this was nighttime. Being that Armstrong was landing in clear weather, both
pilot and signaler were operating "zip lip." No radio calls. He could see the
ship sliding into view through his heads-up display as he banked to line up
on the landing area. The gray bulk of the carrier USS *Enterprise,* which just
seconds before had looked so tiny and alone on the vast blue ocean, was looming
rapidly larger. Its white wake trailed back towards him like an enormous tail.
Leveling his wings, Armstrong fixed his gaze on the yellow light of the ship's
optical landing system, the "meatball" that would guide him down to a safe
landing. As he rolled out on approach he was sharing his time between the
meatball, lineup, and angle of attack coaxing his Tomcat onto the right line.

Sundowner One-One, Tomcat ball, Armstrong acknowledged to himself.
At night or in poor weather he would have spoken the acknowledgement
into his radio, confirming his callsign, aircraft type, and that he could see

the light. For now, the silent drill kept him sharp. Armstrong was the kind of pilot who left nothing to chance, never missed an opportunity to drill the procedures of professional flying into his mind and, more importantly, into the minds of the pilots he led.

He felt a buffet of wind through his stick as that carrier's stern grew ever larger. Slight, practiced pressure from hands that were working the throttle and stick, kept the ball exactly where it belonged and the big jet on lineup as Armstrong continued his perfect glide path.

His peripheral vision noted the grey deck rushing up at him at what, to an amateur, would be a terrifying speed. To Armstrong, after twenty-four years of carrier flying, it was just the day to day, exhilarating even. Almost clinically, he noted an uptick in his pulse and breathed a little deeper to slow it. Then the ship was all around him and he felt twenty-five tons of airplane slam onto the deck, turbofans screaming as he jammed the throttles forward to full power. He grunted with satisfaction as his tail hook caught the number three arrester wire, shoving him and his RIO, the radio intercept officer in the plane's back seat, forward into their harnesses. As soon as the yellow shirt gave him the throttle back visual signal, Armstrong cut power to his engines. The big jet rolled back as tension came off the wire. They were down. *Perfect landing*, Armstrong thought with satisfaction. It wasn't a boast, just an observation.

Once unhooked, Armstrong followed the directions of the deck crew as they guided him towards his parking place on the nearly empty deck. In minutes the Tomcat's canopy was lifting and he was climbing down a ladder, glancing at the stenciled "CAPT Russel Armstrong 'Longhorn'" beneath the cockpit that announced him as the fighter's pilot along with his callsign. His RIO followed him down. Both made their way aft along the deck to the carrier's island as another Tomcat, its tailfin showing the red and white rising sun emblem of the squadron VF-111, the "Sundowners," slammed down amid the ear-splitting shriek of its engines. That one only caught the number one wire, Armstrong noted, filing the fact away in his subconscious, always evaluating the pilots under his command. As the CAG, commander of the *Enterprise's* air wing, the 'G' in the name being a historical reference to air groups, Armstrong's judgements could make or break the career of any pilot aboard the ship.

They entered the island's hatchway and there Armstrong was greeted by a familiar figure, the skipper of the *Enterprise*, Captain John Newton.

"Longhorn!" Newton said, grasping the pilot's shoulder, "Welcome to Big E! Glad to have you aboard. Decided to get the cruise off to a good start, showing all your young pilots how carrier landings are done, huh?"

Armstrong let the corner of his stoic Cherokee mouth turn up slightly. He wasn't known for his jovial sense of humor, though his exceedingly dry wit made its appearance from time to time. The "Longhorn" moniker had been bestowed at flight school, when his classmates had been amused to observe the usually reserved Armstrong's loud support for the football team of his *alma mater*, the Oklahoma Sooners. Being the cruel aviators that they were, his classmates decided his callsign would be the mascot of the school's Red River rival, the Texas Longhorns. The nickname stuck, which was why his white helmet now bore the orange silhouette of a longhorn. Armstrong, unwilling to surrender completely, had added the flourish of a crimson lasso capturing the bovine's prongs. "Hiya Newt," he said in a deep, slow voice that hinted at his ancestry. "Gotta see the young bucks come in, y'know?"

Their exchange paused as another Tomcat roared onto the deck. When the noise subsided, Newton said, "Come on. I'll show you to your quarters so you can drop your gear."

The CAG shook his head. "I'd rather head straight to PriFly, Newt. Want to see every landing."

Newton shrugged. "Suit yourself. This way."

Armstrong looked over at his backseater and said in a loud voice over the flight deck noise, "Willie, fill out the yellow sheet, then you can go and get yourself cleaned up. I'll have a briefing with all the air crews an hour after everyone's on board to put out the training schedule." The other man threw a half salute and disappeared into the bowels of the ship.

Newton and Armstrong ascended the seven flights of stairs up to the flight control deck, the carrier's primary flight control bridge, high in the island superstructure. Two more jets slammed onto the deck outside with a roar that reverberated through the bulkhead as they climbed. In the lull between the scream of jet engines Newton, a fellow naval aviator asked, "How was the flight in, Rus?"

"Fine, clear skies all the way," answered Armstrong. "The deck crews need some work, though. That aircraft director who parked me would have put me over the side."

"That's why we're out here, Rus," Newton said, and Armstrong picked up on a slightly defensive tone. "I had to pull a lot of this crew together from scratch after the CNO accelerated our refueling and overhaul by six months." Newton continues, "We're still short some key personnel, and we didn't get a chance to really work flight ops during our day cruises last month, not like we normally would if we'd stuck to the normal timeline." He paused as another fighter screamed onto the deck. "These next ten days will get the boys into fighting shape, though."

Longhorn nodded his agreement. The Navy had found the funds to speed up Big E's overhaul, along with the complicated refueling of the ship's eight nuclear reactors, but the process of gathering the five thousand members of her crew six months early had been a logistical headache, to say the least. Even so, Armstrong was pleased to be aboard the ship with the most storied name in the US Navy. *Enterprise* was the successor to the famous carrier that had fought through nearly every campaign of the Pacific War and survived multiple hits by Japanese bombs and *kamikazes*. That ship had undeniably been a "lucky ship." Armstrong wasn't even a little bit superstitious, but he couldn't help feeling that some of the luck had rubbed off onto this new *Enterprise*, along with the name. *We'll come together*, thought Armstrong, *it'll be a bit rough, but we'll do it.*

Today, this latest *Enterprise* was southbound out of Norfolk, steaming for the warm waters off Puerto Rico to work up the ship, its crew, and the air wing, forming the new team that would give the carrier its punch. Armstrong reasoned that ten days of continuous flight operations and maneuvering should be enough to get them all into a reasonable degree of proficiency.

Another VF-111 Tomcat, its red-and-white-painted vertical stabilizers standing out brightly against the blue sky and ocean, slammed down, catching the number two cable in an adequate landing performance.

"It would have been better," Newton continued while Armstrong kept his eyes on the incoming jets, "to just keep us on our original overhaul timeline. I'm not sure what the old man was thinking the Russians were going to try to pull this winter. They had their fun in December, and it apparently broke them pretty good. Barely a ship has sortied from Murmansk in six weeks!"

Longhorn jerked a nod and added in his slow drawl, "Yeah, I had to truncate Air Wing Fallon training. Still need to qualify a few pilots on air-to-ground work, but we're all up to date on air-to-air quals."

Newton looked down at the stern of the ship as yet another jet, this time a Tomcat bearing the black-and-red tail markings of squadron VF-51, the "Screaming Eagles," roared onto the deck. He lifted his gaze to take in the aircraft stacked overhead at intervals. Once all the Tomcats were aboard, they would begin recovering Longhorn's two squadrons of F/A-18 Hornets and one of A-6E Intruders, followed finally by the support aircraft, including *Enterprise*'s compliment of EA-6B Prowler electronic warfare birds, E-2C Hawkeye aerial radar aircraft, S-3B Viking sub hunters, and ES-3A Shadow electronic snoopers. Big E's helicopter contingent was already aboard, two of them keeping pace with the ship to port in case one of the jet jockeys decided to take a swim with his airplane.

"I'm not so sure, Newt," Armstrong said, in his usual slow, measured tone. "The Sovs sure are talking a good game right now, with their calls for disarmament and reconciliation, but they've never stopped messing around in Poland and the Balkans. I read one news report said they're playing around in the Caribbean again too. Falkner just wants some assurance that he can respond if the shit hits the fan."

Armstrong hadn't risen to the near top of naval aviation profession by bad-mouthing his superiors, he knew how to play the game and navigate navy politics. He also knew that his reputation as a steady, firm leader with little tolerance for mediocrity and nonsense had landed him the command of *Enterprise*'s air wing. *And the Tailhook Scandal thinning the competition a couple years ago didn't hurt my chances of command either*, he thought, cringing inside at the embarrassment *that* scandal had caused the service. That Armstrong had managed to stay aloof from the more raucous side of the naval aviator community his entire career had saved him from being stained in any way by that ignominy.

Another Tomcat screamed down onto *Enterprise*. *This is beginning to look like a real battle-ready carrier, not an oversized barge*, thought Armstrong as he surveyed the growing number of warplanes parked below. Crew were moving some of the jets to the elevators for the short trip to the hangar beneath the flight deck. Longhorn followed Newt's gaze to take in Big E's three escorts, spread out in an arc to starboard. The *Ticonderoga*-class Aegis cruiser USS *Cowpens* was near aboard, while the two *Spruance*-class destroyers *O'Bannon* and *Thorne* were steaming farther afield, closer to the horizon. Armstrong noted a Sea King helicopter ascending from the fantail of the *O'Bannon*. The screening vessels would also benefit from the opportunity to train together for an extended period of time as well.

"There's value in being prepared for the worst." Armstrong said, breaking the silence.

"Yeah, well, we'll see," said Newton, sounding unconvinced. "I still say the Soviet Union is toast within the decade. Hell, I thought they were toast before the coup two years ago."

If Armstrong was honest with himself, he would admit that he agreed with his fellow aviator. But he'd always seen the value of being prepared for the worst, which was the whole point of getting Big E out of drydock half a year early. *Besides,* he thought, *the tropical climate down there in the Caribbean will be a nice break from the dreary Virginia winter.* Being from Oklahoma, Armstrong was less than fond of the damp, and he detested the cold.

— —

Two miles away, a helicopter was lifting off from USS *O'Bannon.*

"Clear of the superstructure," came the crackle in Abby Savage's earphones as she applied pressure with her feet to the control pedals, rotating her Sea King to avoid the hangar and antenna mast.

"Roger, Buck," Abby acknowledged as she pushed her cyclic joystick forward while simultaneously pressing down the collective lever to dip the helicopter's nose towards the sea and increase power to the engines. The forward and upward acceleration pulled the Sea King away from the destroyer.

"Whew," whistled Buck. "Look at that landing stack above the Big E. Flight deck looks busy as a one-legged man in an ass-kicking contest."

Abby looked over at the long, flat silhouette of *Enterprise*, where a fighter was just touching down on the carrier's stern. Other big jets were taxiing to their parking spots on the forward part of the ship, or else to the elevators on its flanks. She could make out the dark shapes of more jets stacked up above the carrier, like bees over a hive. Helicopters kept pace with the big ship's forward progress. Far ahead of the task group, Abby could just make out one of the carrier's other helicopters dipping its sonar reel into the swell of the Atlantic, the crew probably calibrating their hydrophones for the upcoming exercise. *All the pieces of a real battle group coming together, and here we are, playing ambulance for a nineteen-year-old kid with appendicitis*, she thought, bitterness creeping in.

Abby and Buck had been spun up this morning to fly out to *O'Bannon* from Norfolk to evacuate a young crewmember who'd taken ill the previous evening. Normally *O'Bannon*'s own helicopter would have handled the task but—and this really stuck in her craw—the destroyer's assigned helicopter crew had been decertified a week prior due to some childish antics, and so the ship had sailed without an embarked aircraft. *Apparently* no *helicopter onboard is better than one piloted by a woman*, she thought.

The task group had called Norfolk saying that all of their other helicopters were tied up either helping to recover *Enterprise*'s air wing or preparing for the upcoming work-ups off Puerto Rico, and could Fleet please send out someone to evacuate the sick kid? So, here they were, tantalizingly close once more to being a true part of the Fleet, like Abby had always dreamed, and yet still as far away as ever.

"Okay, Buck," Abby said, refocusing on her task, as demeaning as it might seem right now. "Let's get our boy to the hospital." She dipped the nose of the Sea King further towards the swell below, accelerating away towards the beach.

 **CHAPTER 24**

2200 MSK, Friday 4 February 1994
1900 Zulu
Presidential Dacha, Foros, Crimea, Ukrainian Soviet Socialist Republic

P AVEL MEDVEDEV SIPPED his vodka in the expansive sitting room
of the presidential retreat. He had not returned here since that fateful
day over two and a half years ago when he shot his predecessor and set
his country onto a new, more perilous course. Sitting comfortably, basking
in the isolation and luxury, the current Soviet president understood why the
other man had liked this place. The fantastic views of the Black Sea out the
window and the sound of waves on the beach below was soothing for a man
with the weight of the world on his shoulders. And the shores of the Black Sea
were far from the dreary skies and snowy streets of Moscow.

Medvedev looked over at his guest. Marshal Rosla was perched on another
of the chairs, his olive drab uniform in sharp contrast to the gold and red
furnishings of the room despite his many rows of colorful ribbons. The man's
jaw was set. He was determined to see this gamble through.

"You have no objections then?" the Soviet president asked his
defense minister.

The marshal shook his head, then paused and asked, "So you will not
consult with the rest of the Politburo?"

"And give them a chance to get cold feet?" Medvedev asked wryly. "No, Marshal. They all made their decision months ago. It was the right decision then and I won't allow them the opportunity to reconsider now. Once the pieces are moving it will be impossible for anyone to turn back. You are familiar with the story of the Spaniard Cortez when he arrived in the New World, are you not?"

Rosla nodded and smiled. "So, this is why you have isolated yourself down here for the past two weeks? So when the time comes to burn your ships there would be no one around to stop you?"

The president allowed himself to smile as well, but just for a moment. Then his face turned deadly serious. "Issue the orders, Marshal, on my authority. War operations will commence as planned."

 **CHAPTER 25**

1930 EET, Sunday 6 February 1994
1630 Zulu
CompuCafe, Annankatu 27, Helsinki, Finland

I VAN KHITROV WALKED through the door, passing from the dark, cold Helsinki street into the warm, new, chic cafe that was doing its best to make waves around this Nordic city, and indeed the world. He removed his hat and overcoat, handing them to a hostess, and quickly surveyed the space around him with a trained eye. The room contained a small bar serving warm drinks and light snacks, the smell of coffee and chocolate wafted toward the Russian's nostrils. He wasn't in Helsinki for the cuisine. What interested him was what made this newly-opened cafe unique: dozens of new, off-white computers, their boxy monitors perched atop rectangular CPUs, lined the perimeter of the cafe.

Khitrov thanked the hostess and walked to a terminal. As he settled into the plush, modern office chair, playing and looking the part of a visiting businessman, he considered the wonder of the technology he was about to employ. *Electronic mail. I type a message, click a button, and instantaneously my note arrives all over the world. Amazing!* he marveled.

CompuCafe, the establishment that Khitrov was currently patronizing, was the first of its kind in Europe, so far as he could tell. The cafe allowed customers to use a computer to "surf" the world's newest domain of information flow, the World Wide Web. The elegant simplicity of the whole idea appealed to Khitrov. One computer terminal and a telephone line allowed him to connect to an ever-expanding realm of people and information. Even better, the whole system, had grown out of US military efforts to provide reliable networked communication to its nuclear forces. *The same system they designed to safeguard their strategic weapons now allows me to coordinate a complex attack against them from thousands of kilometers away.*

The colonel smiled to himself as he considered the irony. He used the mouse to banish the monitor's screen saver of bizarrely dancing and rotating geometric shapes, and then double-clicked to open the internet browser. Khitrov waited through the screeches and warbles as the modem connected to the phone line, and then navigated to the email server he had selected for this purpose. His smirk disappeared as the obnoxious "You've got mail" voice alerted him to a message from his team in Iceland waiting in his digital inbox. While he believed this form of communication was obscure enough to be secure from enemy counterintelligence, his instructions had been clear: *Keep communication to an absolute minimum and await my orders.*

This place had been chosen to issue his final "go" order for several reasons. The position of Finland in the brave new world of a resurgent Soviet Union was awkward in the extreme. The Finns wished to look west, to integrate with the coalescing European Economic Community and the other Nordic states, but their country shared a long border and a contentious history with its massive eastern neighbor. Additionally, the Medvedev regime had been less than subtle in communicating to the Finns that the USSR would not look favorably upon any moves drawing them closer to NATO. Then the United States government had played into the Soviets' hands, canceling a planned sale of F/A-18 Hornet fighter jets for fear the technology might find its way to the Russians. The move left the Finns with little alternative than to turn to Russia to upgrade their aging air force, and the Soviets were all too happy to oblige, for a price.

Khitrov's smile returned as he considered how unsuspecting this country was of the part they were about to play in the coming conflagration. The USSR was sorely short of allies these days and one of Khitrov's more challenging tasks had been to manufacture new ones. He had done so, though few of the Soviet Union's new "friends" quite knew it yet.

Turning his attention back to the screen, he ignored the message from the Iceland team for the moment and began a new email. In a few moments he'd typed out the brief message, in Finnish, of course, meant to resemble an order from a local restaurant for bulk gourmet coffee. He then added the addresses of the message's recipients from memory. To a careful observer, the address list might look suspicious. It included ten recipients scattered around the globe, in locations as diverse at New York City and Sharm-el-Sheikh, each the senior operator in their particular area. He surmised however, that the message's origin, would protect it from any such undue scrutiny.

Khitrov re-read the email twice, ensuring that no single letter was out of place. Once sent, the message would initiate a chain reaction. Upon receipt, the "go" order would be dispatched to corresponding networks by other varied means, instructing the teams to open sealed envelopes containing only the specified date and time for the operations they were to conduct. All other preparations had been completed over the past weeks and months.

Khitrov clicked the "send" button on the screen without hesitating. He then leaned back in his seat to savor the feeling of power, the anticipation of the storm he had just unleashed with the slightest of pressure from his finger. All the other pieces that would begin moving in the coming days—the armies, bombers, ships, and submarines—these could all be recalled at the last minute. Not so his part of the plan. Once begun, there was no turning back for the men he had sent around the world for this sole purpose: to make war on the west.

The message disappeared into what people were calling "cyberspace" with a pleasant *ding* that struck the colonel as anticlimactic. Khitrov rocked in his seat, still savoring the excitement of what he'd just done, the culmination of months of work. The task was not finished, he knew, but up until this point his greatest fear was that all his labors would come to naught, that peace would break out before he could execute his plans. That danger was now past.

The Russian read and responded to the email from his Iceland team, clearing up a question about targeting details for the American airbase at Keflavik, then closed out his browser, stood up, and walked to the cafe's entrance. He retrieved his coat and hat from the hostess, smiled at her in a very un-stereotypically Russian manner as he donned them, and then strode out into the biting-cold winter night.

 **CHAPTER 26**

0330 EST, Thursday 10 February 1994
0830 Zulu
Naval Station Norfolk, Virginia, USA

THE CORDLESS TELEPHONE'S loud warbling pulled Rob Buckner slowly from the warm comfort of a deep slumber. He rolled towards the sound, momentary confusion befuddling his response. He managed not to fumble the phone as he swung his feet out of bed and onto the carpeted floor. Blinking through bleary eyes, the Marine saw 03:31 glowing red on his bedside alarm clock. *What now?* he wondered grumpily as the phone continued to ring.

Buckner mashed the connect button, ending the obnoxious noise, and put the cordless to his ear. "Buckner," he grunted.

"Sir," came the businesslike voice on the other end of the line, "this is Lieutenant Walters, 2nd Fleet duty officer."

Rob straightened. "Yes?" he asked, trying to sound more awake than he felt.

"Sir," the officer went on, "Admiral Falkner has initiated a limited recall of the staff principals and select others. He directed that I contact you by name, sir."

Recall? Rob thought. "Roger, Lieutenant. I'm en route. Did he say why?"

"There's a developing situation over in Europe, sir. The admiral wants the staff in here to start talking contingencies."

That was unusual. *Falkner doesn't spook easily. He's got to be* really *concerned to pull the staff out of bed three hours early, in port*, thought Buckner.

"Thanks, Lieutenant," Rob said, feeling himself becoming more awake by the second. "Anything else?"

"No sir, that's all," the officer responded.

"Roger. Buckner out," said Rob, ending the call.

He returned the phone to its cradle and stood up, hearing Helen stir and utter a "Hmmm?" from the other side of the bed as he walked to the bathroom. "What's going on, sweetie?" she asked groggily.

"Just need to head into work early," Rob answered softly. "Go back to sleep, dear."

He shut the door behind him in the bathroom hoping not to disturb Helen any further as he scraped a razor across his stubble. In two minutes, abolitions complete, he tiptoed back into the bedroom to don his khaki service uniform that Helen had laid out for him the night before. Rob paused long enough to brush a soft kiss across his wife's cheek. She let out a content "Hmmm" as he made his way to the door.

Downstairs Rob started the coffee. A recall was a timed event, requiring the officers and staff to arrive at the headquarters as soon as possible and within sixty minutes after the alert went out. Rob took the recalls seriously, but he lived within a short drive of the headquarters building. Helen always reminded him, usually after he'd mis-buttoned a shirt or mumbled something incoherent, that he wasn't much good to anyone this early in the morning without some caffeine.

As the percolator bubbled and steamed, filling the kitchen with the comforting aroma of brewing hot coffee, Rob stepped into the living room and turned on the TV, flipping through the channels until he found CNN. Immediately, things started to make sense.

The anchor on the television screen was holding a speakerphone conversation with someone the on-screen text identified as one of the network's foreign correspondents for Eastern Europe. A simplistic map was inset at the top right of the screen, appearing to hang over the grim-faced anchor's shoulder. The map showed the outline of Poland with a large dot denoting Warsaw. The scroll at the bottom of the screen read, "Coup in Warsaw; gunfire heard at the *Sejm*."

The anchor was saying, in his well-rehearsed and deeply serious voice, "Lily, can you tell us any more about these reports we're hearing of Soviet troops in the east of the country?"

"Yes Bill," a distorted and slightly garbled female voice said as a still picture of the reporter appeared on the TV, showing the face of an attractive middle-aged woman, "Just a few minutes ago our source called to say that forces of the USSR crossed the eastern frontier of Poland early this morning. Apparently, there was some limited fighting with the Polish border guards, but the situation here is very confused. No one really knows what's going on right now. A few moments ago, we saw a pair of helicopters fly over us here in Warsaw. We could see red stars painted on them. I can hear military jets overhead, but we can't see them through the clouds and...just a minute...yes, yes...okay. Bill?"

"Yes Lily?" the anchor said, showing just the right amount of concern for the viewers.

"They're telling us we need to leave. There are soldiers downstairs and—"

There was a loud *bang* on the audio followed by some shouts and a startled scream. Rob strained to listen as violent, but more distant voices filled the live feed. The last sound was a clear "*Ruki vverkh!*" before the line went dead. *Russian for "hands up,"* Rob realized.

The on-camera anchor looked stunned for a moment, then recovered himself. "Lily?" he said, "Lily, can you hear us?" Then to the camera he said, "We seem to be experiencing some technical difficulties with our feed from Warsaw. Er, we'll get back to them just as soon as we can. For now, yes, uh, for now let's recap what we know."

The TV man looked down at the paper notes on his desk, as if reading. After a moment he said, "In the early morning hours of today, Warsaw time, unknown elements took control of government buildings around Warsaw. Television and radio stations appear to be off the air, though one station did report that factions seeking rapprochement with Moscow had seized the Polish prime minister for unspecified 'crimes against the people and against world peace.' A couple of hours ago, fighting broke out around the *Sejm*, the Polish legislature building. Putting the pieces together, there seems to be some sort of coup ongoing in Warsaw. Just minutes ago we began to receive reports that Soviet troops are crossing the border into Poland and..." the anchor trailed off and put his hand to his ear, "Yes, we'll take a break now and be right back with the latest."

Rob's thoughts were mixed as the program cut to commercial. He felt some passing concern for the fate of the reporter, but he was far more interested in the events she had been reporting on. On the one hand he felt apprehension about an unfolding crisis that was clearly not in the interests of his country or its allies. On the other hand, the development was exciting. *Why is it so easy to get excited about watching the world change in front of you?* Rob wondered. He knew the answer. Military types were like elite athletes who never got to compete after training hard for the big game. Despite knowing intellectually that the test would be an awful experience, Rob longed for the chance to prove himself in the greatest arena imaginable.

Pouring the coffee into a travel mug, he exited through the garage and sat down into the seat of his Jeep Cherokee, started it up, and backed out into the street. A short drive later he walked past the bleary-eyed Marine guard, travel mug in hand, flashed his ID, and made his way directly to his office. To his surprise, Admiral Falkner was already in the N3 area, waiting for him.

"Morning, Rob," said the admiral. Buckner had worked with Falkner long enough to know when his chief was tense, despite Falkner's ever-calm demeanor. "Thanks for coming in," the admiral said, as if there was a choice in the matter. Being courteous was Falkner's way. "The rest of the staff is on their way. We've got a long day ahead of us. *You've* got an even longer one ahead of you."

"No problem sir," Rob answered, intrigued. "I saw the news about Poland, anything we need to be concerned about?"

"Too early to tell," said Falkner. "We've been picking up some increased activity in the last few days. A break in the weather over the Kola gave one of our satellites a peek at some of their northern fleet's smaller combatants warming up their boilers, and we've gotten some SIGINT hits indicating internal troop movements, that sort of thing. But nothing that can't be explained by this business in Poland."

"You don't think a coup in Warsaw is all there is to it, sir?" Buckner probed.

"It might be. Then again, it might not. Regardless, you know I always like to be prepared. In this case though, our hands are being tied," said Falkner.

"How so, sir?" asked Rob.

"I just took a call from the chief of naval operations," the admiral started and then paused. "Our instructions are to 'not make any provocative moves' that might 'escalate the situation.'" Falkner's tone of voice made clear what he thought of the CNO's restrictions. "The State Department wants to see how things develop before we start moving any assets. They want to use those movements to send a message to the Sovs when they think the time is right. The CNO says we're going to try to handle things through the UN for now, but the Soviets have a veto on the Security Council, it'll just be a sham."

Falkner shook his head at the situation, then went on, "Not that we have anything to move right now anyway. Our bullpen is pretty thin, what with *Kennedy* down in the Caribbean keeping an eye on the Nicaraguans, and *Vinson* and *Roosevelt* in refit, *America* just back from the Med and now in dry-dock. The only piece we really have that could move right off the bat is *Enterprise*, and her crew and air group have had precious little time to train up. For now, we're not even allowed to move Big E north."

Buckner nodded. Falkner wasn't in the habit of unloading his concerns upon subordinates. *Something else is going on here.*

Falkner saw the inquisitive look on the Marine's face and said, "I suppose you're wondering why I'm confiding all this to my resident jarhead. Well, here's why: if I can't move *my* ships to the right place, maybe someone else can move theirs. I'm at least going to get my people to where they can do the most good if the balloon goes up. The folks in Washington may not think this is a crisis yet, but they don't pay us to be complacent. You've got your sea bag ready?"

"Uh, yes sir," answered Rob, surprised. Standard operating procedure for 2nd Fleet staff officers was to be prepared to go to sea at once, their bags packed and ready at all times.

"Well, Rob, you'd best go get it. Time for you to do what I brought you here to do. I'm sending you to the UK to be my eyes over there. If things really get hot, the only real asset we have to throw in the Russians' way right now is the Royal Navy and that tiny flat top of theirs. I want you over there as my liaison to Admiral Reeves. Go see the adjutant. He's got the details. Your flight leaves in four hours."

"Yes sir," Rob said, surprised. *Four hours? Do I have time to run home and tell Helen?* He looked at his watch and did some quick math. *Probably not. I'll have to call.*

Rob was having trouble wrapping his mind around the idea that this whole situation was any more serious than previous Soviet invasions in their sphere of influence, *It's like the Baltics two years ago. The Russians wouldn't actually try something more serious. Would they?* A look into his admiral's face left Rob more unsure than he'd been a moment before.

 **CHAPTER 27**

0400 CET, Saturday 12 Feb 1994
0300 Zulu
Athletes Village, Lillehammer Olympic Park, Norway

T HE SIX ATHLETES, moving with purpose through the yellow-lit darkness, carried the heavy duffels across the cold, windswept parking lot towards the open back doors of an idling Ford transit van. Each man carried two heavy bags bearing the logo of the Soviet Union's Olympics Biathlon team, and the ease with which they moved was evidence of their superb conditioning. Indeed, these men *were* true Olympians, some of the most elite winter athletes in the world, ostensibly here to compete in the Games scheduled to begin less than twenty-four hours from now.

Unfortunately, thought the team's captain, who loved competition in this context as well as in his true profession, *we will have to wait for another time and place to test ourselves against the rest of the world's elite athletes.*

The men arrived at the van and loaded the bags, a rehearsed maneuver made to look natural. Three of the team members were not truly ones who would have been selected to compete in the Olympic biathlon event, but then again, that consideration was irrelevant. Each of them had been training hard for this day, though their training regimen had looked decidedly different from that of other nations' athletes. Sportscasters in the west had been commenting on the numerous new faces on the Soviet team, and the absence of others, on what was the largest Soviet Olympic roster to date. Many speculated that these were the new generation of Soviet athletes, part of Medvedev's effort to renew the image of Soviet vitality in all spheres.

As the last man heaved his duffel into the van and slammed the door shut behind it, the team captain saw some movement across the parking lot. *There, right on schedule.* More than two dozen men performing a similar activity under the streetlights, loading baggage into a small cargo truck and then climbing into three passenger vans. The team captain recognized the broad shoulders and shaved head of his counterpart on the Soviet Union's Olympic Hockey team.

Noting the other team's departure, the captain pulled himself into the van. Then, without looking at the driver, he ordered, *"Davai."* Go.

They rolled out onto the sleepy streets of Lillehammer, proceeded west several blocks, and then merged onto the E6 highway. Here they accelerated, keeping Lake Mjøsa on their left. They were going north.

 **CHAPTER 28**

1100 MSK, Saturday 12 Feb 1994
0800 Zulu
**USS *Connecticut* (SSN 22), X-Ray Station, northeast of
Murmansk, Russian Soviet Federative Socialist Republic**

T HE SLEEK, COLD cylindrical hull of USS *Connecticut*, the second
of the United States' new and lethal class of *Seawolf* nuclear attack
submarines, glided through the dark, icy waters of the Barents Sea like
some prehistoric shark, silent and listening. Inside the boat's pressure hull,
Commander Ethan Rogers tensely monitored his bridge crew. They went
about their duties in a hushed and businesslike manner, as if the Russians at
the Red Banner Northern Fleet's main naval bases just a few dozen nautical
miles to the south and west might hear them if they spoke too loudly. The
maneuver they were about to perform, coming shallow to establish brief
communications with COMSUBLANT—Commander, Submarine Forces
Atlantic—via an E-6 Mercury communications aircraft was routine enough.
Of course, you can't take anything as routine up here in the Soviets' back yard,
Rogers reminded himself.

"Con, sonar," came the hushed call from the boat's sonar room, just
forward of control.

"Con, aye," responded Rogers immediately.

"Sir, my scope is clear. No contacts on either array," reported the sonarman.

Rogers nodded, forgetting for the thousandth time that the sonar technicians could not actually see him. Their report was the last bit of assurance the captain needed before taking his boat to communication depth.

Connecticut was one of several submarines currently lurking off the north coast of the Soviet Union's Kola Peninsula, patrolling on what NATO submariners had been calling "X-Ray Station" for the past thirty years. During those three decades at least one, and usually several, American and British submarines had constantly been on station in this cold, shallow patch of water that covered the exits from Murmansk, the Kola Inlet, and the White Sea, monitoring the comings and goings of Russian warships. This was Commander Rogers' fifth patrol on X-Ray Station in his twenty-three years of Navy service. All told, Ethan Rogers had spent over six months of his life up here in these waters, *Which is longer than my first wife stayed with me,* he thought wryly. The sea was a cruel mistress, especially for the men of the Silent Service.

"COB," Rogers said, addressing the chief of the boat, standing behind the two nineteen-year-old sailors at the controls of the three-billion-dollar submarine, "where's the top of the layer?" He referred to the thermocline layer, a stratum of water in the ocean with a significantly different temperature than the sea above and below. This layer impeded sound from passing through it, allowing submarines to use the thermocline as terrain in which to hide.

"Layer tops out at one hundred thirty feet, sir," answered the chief.

The captain nodded, then said, "Alright. Con, all ahead slow, up five degrees on the planes, make your depth one hundred thirty feet."

"Aye aye, sir, all ahead slow, making my depth one hundred thirty feet," answered the sailor on the dive controls.

"Sparks," Rogers said, signifying by institutional nickname the communications officer standing next to the captain's chair, "stand by to release the buoy. Chief, ready on the stopwatch."

Both men responded "Aye" in unison.

Rogers felt the deck tilt gently upward as the boat ascended from the depths. Command of *Connecticut* more than made up for the hardships Rogers had put up with to get here, he thought, still pondering his first wife. Three years ago, he had despaired of ever seeing the inside of one of the *Seawolf*s, let alone command one. With the supposed end of the Cold War imminent, the whole class was in danger of cancellation, part of the "Peace Dividend" the politicians talked about. *That bastard Medvedev sure fixed* that *in a hurry though*, reflected the captain. Rogers couldn't believe his good fortune when his name had shown up on the list for command of *Connecticut*, the second of what would eventually be twenty-nine of the big, lethal subs. Except he *could* believe it. *I've got a wake of failed relationships that proves I'd sacrifice anything for this job*, he thought soberly.

"Skipper, depth is one hundred thirty feet and hovering," reported the sailor at the helm.

"Scope clear, Skipper, no contacts," called Sonar over the intercom.

"Release the buoy!" ordered Rogers.

"Time, start," announced the chief, clicking the button on his stopwatch.

"Buoy away!" said Sparks.

Outside the hull, a winch began to unreel a long metal cable, on the end of which was a buoy that floated an antenna. This allowed the submarine to remain submerged while sending and receiving burst VHF radio messages via the E-6, which was turning racetracks near the North Pole. The submariners used this method on a daily basis to send routine situation reports back to their headquarters, Task Force 42, in Norfolk, and to receive whatever updates the shore-weenies back there deemed important enough to send them. In an emergency, COMSUBLANT could send *Connecticut* messages while she was running deep via ELF—extremely low frequency—radio waves that could pass through some depth of water, but ELF was slow. Only a few letters could be sent at a time. Consequently, it was only used for the most urgent of communications, like the start of a shooting war.

"Layer relatively weak," the head sonarman was reading from his instruments. "Low salinity, water temp is two degrees C, won't get much bounce on the CZ, Skipper." The CZ, or convergence zone, was a sound phenomenon in the water connected to the thermocline layer. In effect, sound transmitted in the water would bounce off the layer at predictable distances, creating bands, called convergence zones, within which another ship could be heard more readily than if it were closer but outside of the CZ band.

"Buoy on the surface," announced Sparks. "Transmitting."

Now the boat's ECM—electronic countermeasures—officer spoke up. "Skipper, we're getting faint radar hits on the buoy." A pause, "It looks like routine ASW stuff." *Anti-submarine warfare*, Rogers translated in his head automatically.

"SITREP transmitted," said Sparks, "receiving now."

"Thirty seconds," announced the COB, urgency creeping into his voice. The longer *Connecticut* remained shallow, the greater the chance she would be detected by some lucky Russian.

"Con, sonar," came the chief sonarman's voice, "I'm picking up high speed turns at one three five degrees relative, twin screws, twenty-plus knots, heading our way, distance unknown. Designate Contact Sierra One-Seven."

Rogers tensed. There was a ship out there, a fast one. Most likely a Russian frigate. *Did they intercept our burst transmissions? Unlikely.* No telling how close the contact was in so little time. The captain bit back the urge to hurry his men just as the chief announced, "Forty seconds."

"All messages received," reported Sparks.

"Secure buoy," ordered Rogers. "Chief, where's the bottom of the layer and the floor?"

"Layer bottoms out at two-thirty, the floor's at four-fifty," answered the COB, just before growling, "Fifty seconds!"

"Buoy secured, sir," announced Sparks, deflated.

"Con," said the captain, "make your depth three-five-zero, right full rudder, come to heading zero-nine-zero. Once we pass two-fifty bring her up to eight knots. Chief, time?"

"Fifty-seven seconds, Skipper," reported the wiry older man as the deck tilted forward beneath them. The COB was eyeing the young communications officer with something that approached disapproval. "Nine seconds slower than yesterday."

"Con, Sierra One-Seven contact is fading, probable *Grisha*-class, but I can't be sure," interjected sonar. *So, it* was *a Soviet frigate*, thought the captain. *Bad luck we came up so close to her.* Of course, the chances that the Russian had gotten a hit on *Connecticut* was nearly nil. *Still, it's a bit too close for comfort.*

"Skipper," called the ECM officer, who was at his console reading the intercepts from the buoy's electronic eavesdropping sensors, "looks like a lot of aerial activity up there. We got radar hits from at least two Be-12 Mail flying boats, one Il-38 May, and two others I can't classify."

That *was* a lot of birds in the air, thought Rogers. Still, none had been anywhere close enough to have a chance of detecting his stealthy sub. *In the end, just another day on X-Ray Station*, mused the captain. The most dangerous part of today now over.

"Alright," said Rogers, "secure from general quarters. XO, you have the con. Sparks, once you get the transcripts bring them to my cabin and have your petty officer report to the COB for debriefing."

Rogers stood up and walked the few steps aft to his cabin. Entering, he shut the door and sat down at his small desk to continue his ongoing work of reviewing efficiency reports for his officers. Part of the joy of commanding an elite *Seawolf* was that the boats came with picked crews. The officers and sailors aboard *Connecticut* were the best that the submarine service could provide, and they had rallied around their aggressive captain in the best traditions of the Navy. The skipper had even heard some of the petty officers referring to the boat's crew as "Roger's Jollies," a mildly profane acknowledgment of the nearly piratical mission assigned to submariners in both peace and war. Of course, the high quality of his crew presented the captain with a problem in writing evaluations. *How do I rate the officers on the boat against each other when each one is a top performer in his own right, and would probably be a superstar on any other boat?*

A polite knock at the cabin door pulled Rogers from his reflections on the problem. "Enter," he said.

Sparks, also known as Lieutenant (junior grade) José Santamaria, slipped tentatively through the door and handed the captain a printout of the messages they had received.

"Anything interesting?" asked Rogers, glancing at the paper.

"Uh, yes sir," said the young man, who, the skipper knew by now, grew nervous when addressing senior officers. "Yes, sir, Norfolk reports that HMS *Churchill* picked up a boomer yesterday and tracked her north towards the icepack. The rest is just routine. *Baltimore* is still on track to arrive on station tomorrow to replace *Philadelphia*."

Two boomers in a week? wondered the captain. *That's unusual.* The Soviets didn't typically like to keep as many of their nuclear ballistic missile submarines—boomers— at sea like the NATO navies. *We haven't detected any return of the ones that are already out there,* thought Rogers. *Is there more to this?*

The NATO submarine presence on X-Ray Station was rather strong at the moment, the captain knew, consisting of the American *Los Angeles*-class boats *Boise* and *New York City*, the British HMS *Trafalgar* patrolling far to the north, and *Connecticut* here off the inlet. Rogers was glad to see *Baltimore* arriving as a replacement. The *Philadelphia*, another American submarine assigned to X-Ray Station, had detected and followed a Soviet *Delta III*-class boomer days previous. Now the *Churchill* was off chasing another one, weakening the screen that was acting as a hedge against the temporary absence of big carriers in the north Atlantic. Each boat off station meant more chances that a Russian warship could slip out undetected.

"Any word on a replacement for *Churchill?*" the skipper asked.

The young officer shook his head. "Nothing yet, Skipper."

Rogers nodded. "Okay, Sparks, carry on. I've got some reading to do."

Santamaria nodded and backed out of the small cabin, clearly relieved that the daily one-on-one interview with his captain was over.

Rogers smiled to himself. *That boy's going to need to grow a pair quick, or the chief will eat him alive.* The COB had a reputation for riding young ensigns and junior lieutenants hard, sometimes, perhaps a bit too hard.

The captain returned his attention to the officer evaluations, back to routine.

1200 MSK, Saturday 12 Feb 1994
0900 Zulu
TAKR *Baku*, Kola Inlet, Murmansk Oblast, Russian
Soviet Federative Socialist Republic

Contra-Admiral Ilya Petrovich Ivanenko looked out from the flag bridge of the *Baku*, final ship of the *Kiev* class, the USSR's first and oldest true aircraft carrier. Rugged, treeless hills flanked the Kola inlet and rose to either side of him, white snow covering black rocks. *Baku*, technically considered a "heavy aviation cruiser" by the Soviets due to the missile and gun armament on her bow, plowed through the cold gray seas of the inlet connecting the Russians' northern fleet bases to the Barents Sea. Stretching fore and aft of the carrier in a long column was the most powerful escort with which Ivanenko had ever sailed, consisting of a cruiser, three destroyers, including two of the powerful *Fregat*-class, and three smaller frigates. Farther ahead, on the gray northern horizon, Ivanenko could just make out the antenna masts of four frigates, denoting the position of an ASW group, one of three that had left the inlet ahead of his own force.

Ivanenko was relieved to be going to sea, thrilled at the part he was about to play in what he knew would be the great event of his generation. Of all the men on the warships around him, he was the only one who knew the storm about to break upon the North Atlantic, and the world. The rest possessed no real inkling of why they'd been recalled to their ships on such short notice and then put to sea after many weeks of dockside maintenance and drills. Indeed, until three weeks ago, Ivanenko himself had been chafing in his Moscow office advising Marshal Rosla.

He was also glad to be free of that insufferable Khitrov. It wasn't that the *Spetsnaz* officer's ideas for dealing with the Americans were all bad. They weren't. *Some were even brilliant*, Ivanenko had to admit. The problem was that the man gambled with the fate of the fleet like a drunk at a craps game, never being satisfied with the doctrine the Soviet Fleets had developed over decades of shadowing the American navy. Now the newly promoted *Contra-Admiral*, who still stole glances at the star on his shoulder boards, was in a position to see that at least one of the Red Banner Northern Fleet's task forces operated according to correct doctrine in the coming fight.

Ivanenko was grateful for the new rank, and even more so for the command of the *Baku* task force. Marshal Rosla was nothing if not loyal to those who served him, and the old paratrooper had interceded to ensure that his erstwhile aide received this plum assignment. *Baku* and her consorts would gain the mouth of the inlet in less than thirty minutes. At that point his task was to coordinate the efforts of his force with the three ASW frigate groups, as well as dozens of maritime patrol aircraft operating from bases all along the Soviet Union's northwest periphery. These operations were all oriented towards the attainment of one end: find the blasted NATO submarines that were always lurking, smug and silent, off his country's coast, and destroy them.

Looking down and to the left at the flight deck, the admiral could see that his carrier was loaded to capacity with helicopters and jump jets. *Beyond capacity*, he reminded himself. The dozen stubby-winged Yak-38M fighters were lashed down on the margins of the deck to allow ASW helicopters to fly off during their initial passage through the Barents Sea. Newer, more formidable airframes occupied the ship's cramped hangar deck.

The *Contra-Admiral* was eager to get on to his primary mission, the one where his air group would be given the opportunity to truly shine. For now, he focused his thoughts on the task at hand. *Today we find them*, he thought. *Tomorrow we sink them.*

CHAPTER 29

Olenya Airbase, Murmansk Oblast, Russian
Soviet Federative Socialist Republic

THE GUTTURAL, MANLY roar of nearly seven thousand voices shouting an enthusiastic *"Hurraaah"* resounded in the frigid arctic night. Marshal Aleksandr Rosla, speaking to the officers and men of the assembled 76th Guards Airborne Division, nodded in satisfaction. The stirring culmination of rhetoric in this address had been particularly successful, Guards Colonel Ilya Romanov thought. He watched with mixed feelings as the marshal, who was dressed identically to the thousands of *desantniki* around him, whipped the assembled paratroopers into a frenzy of patriotic fervor. The formations of the division's three infantry regiments crowded to the front, left, and right, around the low platform from which Rosla was speaking, while the members of the division's artillery and specialty units stood behind him. Romanov stood at the head of his 234th Guards Airborne Regiment, which, along with the rest of the division, was assembled amid Olenya Airbase's offices, machine shops, and storage sheds to listen to their chief. The structures protected the expansive concrete pad on which they were all assembled from the biting Arctic winds, but only just. The whole scene was lit by the white beams of floodlights from the tops of the surrounding single-story structures. These pierced the polar darkness, but did nothing to push back the cold.

"Those westerners, the Americans and their German and British lackeys, think that we," he paused for just a moment, "Think that *you* are weak, *tovari-chi!*" the barrel-chested marshal was shouting, the faintly Asiatic features of his face lending intensity to his address. "They have forgotten their history!" he went on. "Who was it that smashed the *fascisti* before the gates of Moscow?" The cheering from the assembled *desantniki* began again. "Who destroyed them on the streets of Stalingrad?" The shouts grew louder. "Who routed their vaunted armies and drove all the way to Berlin, planting our red banner on the *Reichstag?*" The *hurrahs* now reached a crescendo as Rosla asked, "The Americans? The British? No!"

Ilya Romanov felt the stirrings of intense pride as his chief recounted the glories of Soviet arms. *The old* desantnik *knows where to strike to get at the hearts of these men*, he thought, remembering the time not too long ago when Rosla had commanded this very division. He stole a glance over his shoulder at the massed files of young men behind him, their layered uniforms of white smocks over mottled green overcoats made each appear larger than he was. Despite the frigid temperature, which was rapidly falling below minus fifteen degrees C, each man kept his outer garments open in a vee below his neck, revealing the blue and white striped undershirts that were the hallmark of their elite community. Each had also removed his gray fur *shapka* hat for the marshal's speech, donning instead the sky-blue berets of the *desantniki*, despite the cold that nipped at exposed ears.

Ilya turned back as the defense minister continued in a more subdued tone. "No, my children, it was not the westerners who defeated the *Nemtsy* in the Great Patriotic War. It was young men, just like you. Young *Russian* men. Young *Soviet* men. Those people out there," he gestured emphatically to the west, "know *nothing* of the sacrifices we Soviets made to save the world from fascism. They know *nothing* of the toughness of the Soviet soldier! *That* will be their downfall!"

Ilya saw that the defense minister's tone had now softened. The marshal looked down and said, "Children, I do not try to tell you that the coming fight will be easy. No, no, quite the opposite. The Americans are wily opponents.

Their technology is powerful, and they use it well. They will be difficult to defeat. We do not underestimate them." Now the old soldier looked up again, and his tone hardened. "No, it is *they* who underestimate *you*! They think that because they kicked around that little shit in Iraq three years ago, that now the whole world must bow and acknowledge their greatness! They think that they can surround us, cut off the life of our country, destroy *your* families' livelihoods. They think we will do nothing because they think we are so *awed* by them. Well, I have a message for them. *They have not yet met the fighting 76th!*" He concluded, shouting the division's motto, "*We are everywhere, where victory awaits!*"

The formations all around exploded into more guttural cheers as the marshal stepped forward and jumped from the low platform as if parachuting from a transport. He landed spryly, directly in front of Major General Egorov, the division's commander, and grasped the other man's forearm in a powerful two-handed handshake.

Looking back over his shoulder again, Ilya could see the enthusiasm and pride in the faces of his men as they cheered. There, in the front row, young Major Medvedev's face was beaming with anticipation. Even the normally cynical regimental *zampolit*, Major Sviashenik, was grinning and clapping his gloved hands. Ilya felt pride as well after what had been a truly rousing speech. *Am I the only one here with reservations?* he wondered, looking at the beaming faces of the soldiers. *War with NATO? How did this all come about so quickly?*

Three days previous in Pskov, the division had received recall orders without so much as a warning or explanation. Romanov assumed they were being readied to move west, towards the unfolding intervention in Poland. The division's *desantniki* rapidly loaded their vehicles, guns, and equipment aboard trains, then boarded the crowded passenger cars. Ilya had barely been able to steal time away from his regiment to hurry back to his quarters, where he had kissed Elena and their new baby goodbye and charged seventeen-year-old Petya to look after his mother and younger siblings. This was not the first time Ilya had been forced by the needs of the service to leave his family under confusing circumstances, but it *was* the most unexpected, *and the most serious*, he thought. Ilya's surprise multiplied when, only a few miles into the journey, he realized that the train was carrying them not west, but north. The transition from peace, to intervention in Poland, to war with NATO, had been a bewildering one.

Rosla had started his speech explaining how KGB intelligence now knew that Germany, supported by the United States and the NATO Alliance, had been preparing to invade the socialist Polish republic at the behest of traitorous elements in that violent and chaotic country. If allowed to commit this travesty, where would they stop? Rosla asked. Lithuania? Ukraine? Would they ever be satisfied unless the USSR was dismembered and impotent before them? Romanov was unsure if he could buy the whole story, but, *Rosla has never lied to us before, has he?* A massive pre-emptive offensive against the NATO armies was part of nearly every Soviet war plan, but he honestly believed these scenarios would never come to pass. Now that they had, he hoped that the justification for his country's offensive was as solid as his chief had just contended minutes before.

Romanov could hear the marshal saying warmly to General Egorov, "Timofey Petrovich, your men have much work to do and don't need to keep listening to an old blowhard like me. Send them back to their tasks, then join me in your command post with your officers and their *zampoliti*."

The division commander turned and summoned his colonels with a barked order. Romanov and the other commanders came running.

"Gentlemen," Egorov said, his thin mouth, nearly hidden beneath a thick, gray mustache, "get the soldiers back to the railhead and have them finish moving the guns and vehicles." He stomped his foot. The 76th's *desantniki* had spent the better part of the day down-loading their equipment—BMD assault vehicles, mortar carriers, self-propelled assault guns, artillery—off the trains at the small rail terminus half a kilometer south of this remote airbase, deep in the frozen forests and marshes of the Kola peninsula. Meanwhile, division officers were busy securing lodging for the men in the concrete slab apartment blocks of the nearby garrison town of Vysoky, many of whose residents had already been forcibly removed to Murmansk, ninety kilometers to the north.

The senior officers gave the proper orders to their subordinates, who began marching the formations of *desantniki* out of the enclosed vehicle park, switching out their blue berets for the warmer gray *shapka*s as they went. As the division dispersed, the regimental and division officers followed their marshal into a drafty hanger that had been converted into a planning bay. Maps lined the walls, though these were currently covered with white bedsheets. Ilya savored the warmth of the heaters in the room as he passed through the door, removing his headgear as he did. His exposed ears had been starting to burn from the cold.

When the officers were inside, Rosla removed a flask from his uniform jacket and retrieved a stack of battered aluminum shot glasses from an aide. Most of the officers were familiar with this ritual. As this division's commander, the marshal performed it before each major jump and before the unit deployed to combat. The big man handed one of the small shot glasses to each of the officers, then poured a small amount of clear vodka into them, giving each man in the room a quiet and friendly word of encouragement as he did so.

When the flask arrived at Romanov, Rosla paused, then said "Ah yes, Ilya Georgiyevich. You don't drink, yes? Well you must, this once. Bad luck, otherwise."

Ilya smiled sheepishly as the marshal poured a splash of the liquor into his glass and moved on. When each of the cheap glasses was charged, Rosla raised his own, with a loud, *"Dlya Rodiny!" For the Motherland.*

The assembled officers repeated the toast with gusto, then altogether threw back their heads as they tossed the burning, cheap liquor down their throats. Romanov only sipped his, tasting for the first time in years the obsession that had nearly ruined both his military career and marriage. That had been a different life, long ago.

With the ritual complete, the marshal turned to business. "Men," he said, "I know the question that is in each of your minds: where will your country employ the finest division in the Red Army, eh? Well, wonder no more."

With a sweep of the defense minister's arm, aides yanked down the sheets covering the wall maps around the room. On the largest one, Romanov could see the familiar, jagged shape of the island he had feared would be their objective.

"Iceland!" Rosla boomed over the exciting murmuring that had filled the room. "The 76th has the honor of executing the decisive piece of our effort to defend the *Rodina* from the American fleet. I would have it no other way. You will have a couple days to prepare before the first drop. Your comrades in the 36th Air Landing Brigade will have their turn tomorrow, launching from Kilp Yavr into Norway. It is a difficult mission I have assigned you, but I know you are up to the task. General Egorov has the mission order and will brief you after I depart." He paused to let the news sink in. "For now, are there questions? Remember, brothers, you are among friends here. There are no secrets among *desantniki*."

Romanov was not sure that was true. He had many questions. *If this war is a response to NATO aggression in Poland, why such a deep thrust into the North Atlantic? How can we be expected to seize an objective so vital as Iceland, directly in the teeth of the American fleet? How will this all end?*

Major Sviashenik surprised Ilya by speaking first, asking a question that was at the back of everyone's mind. "*Tovarich* Marshal, I thank you for your confidence in us, but might Iceland not be an island too far?" No one interrupted so Sviashenik continued, "What I mean is, how will we be supported so far from the strength of our naval and air bases?"

Ilya knew the real question that his regimental political officer was asking: *Are we being sacrificed?*

Many in the room sucked in a collective breath as Rosla soberly contemplated the *zampolit's* bold challenge. Romanov braced for the marshal's response. To Ilya's surprise, Rosla's words were measured, even sad.

"Major–," Rosla thought for a moment, "–Sviashenik, isn't it?" asked the marshal. "I am glad you have asked this question. I will answer it." Looking around, the big defense minister addressed the entire group. "Men, I have always spoken honestly with you, yes? So I will be plain with you. Even as we speak, measures are being taken to ensure that your seizure of Iceland will succeed. I cannot tell you what they are, but I ask you to trust me, as you have in the past. As to Iceland being an 'island too far,' as you say, well," the marshal paused. "You may be correct. The mission we have assigned you is an impossible one, just to look at it, even I admit that. I will make no promises to you that we will win the war before the Americans and their marines counterattack against you." He paused and looked each of the men in turn. Romanov met his gaze. "I'm not asking you to die needlessly. You will be our flank guard, the honored right wing of our entire strategic offensive. Some of you will die, yes. All I ask of you is that you resist as long as your units are capable of resisting. If the war lasts too long, then yes," Rosla nodded and then answered the unspoken question, "you may very well have been sacrificed." He paused again, letting the truth settle. "We are giving you every tool we can to allow you to prolong your resistance, but I do not pretend to tell you that you can hold forever. I will make every effort to end this war in victory before that time comes, but I doubt that it will be so quick. General Erogov has my instructions about what to do if and when that difficult time comes."

Ilya was stunned. *The division being sacrificed? What will become of Elena? What of my children?*

"I know this is hard for many of you to hear," Rosla was saying, "but you must understand, your role is to buy the *Rodina* time to win the war. Our plan is a good one, but we must keep the Americans as far away as possible for as long as possible. I trust your commander to decide how far you can resist before the end. Know that we value your lives."

The officers nodded soberly, the excitement of their mission giving way to the seriousness of the task they had been assigned and its consequences. Quietly processing through these revelations, Ilya Romanov appreciated at least the honesty of their chief, and the trust he so clearly placed in them to do their duty regardless. *The* Rodina *must be in severe danger for them to place us in such a dangerous position*, he realized. *If Elena, Petya, Irina, and baby Sasha are in danger, I must do everything in my power to protect them.*

Seeing that there were no further questions from the subdued officers, Rosla said, "Very well. Know that I have the utmost faith in you and your men. Take these days you have and plan your operation well. I have arranged for several of you to accompany the aircraft carrying the 36th into battle tomorrow. A helicopter will be here to collect you in a few hours. Observe and learn, so that your *desant* may be even more successful. That is all."

The officers around the room straightened to attention and saluted. Rosla returned the salute, then swept out of the room and into the floodlit vehicle park beyond. He had many other tasks to complete this night, the night before the vast armed forces at his command initiated a world war that was nearly as much a surprise to them as it would be to their enemies.

As the officers in the room relaxed and began to talk among themselves, Ilya overheard General Egorov say quietly to the division *zampolit*, Sviashenik's direct superior, "Get that Jew of yours in Romanov's regiment under control, will you?" Romanov winced. Sviashenik was a good man, would have made an excellent company or battalion officer. He just needed to learn when to keep his mouth shut. *But then, they have bigger things to worry about now.*

 **CHAPTER 30**

1900 CET, Saturday 12 Feb 1994
1800 Zulu
Lysgårdsbakkene Ski Jumping Arena,
Lillehammer Olympic Park, Norway

THE VOLUNTEER ORGANIZER was in a panic as she scrambled to find the coordinator for the Parade of Nations. Her responsibility was to place the Soviet national team in its proper place in the procession, but there was a problem. A big problem.

Short cropped blond hair was starting to stick to her forehead as she ran past the milling and joking athletes from around the world. As she rushed around, she shielded her eyes from the blinding white lights. Meant to illuminate the opening ceremony for a global television audience, the lights reflected off the towering ski jump and surrounding mountains, making them blindingly bright and giving the whole place a surreal quality. Finally, the young woman spied her supervisor, a tall man making annotations on a clipboard. She ran up to him and said breathlessly, "They're not here!"

Her supervisor turned sharply towards her and reactively said, "Who? Who's not here?"

"The whole Soviet team!" the volunteer blurted out. "There are only forty of them here for the parade, and they're all as bewildered as I am! Just a few figure-skaters and members of the women's team." The girl couldn't catch her breath, "There should be over one hundred and seventy!" She was clearly feeling the pressure of the embarrassment that would ensue if the Olympic opening ceremony featured chaos and confusion.

The coordinator dropped his clipboard to his side. "I was afraid of this," he said.

"Afraid of what?" the young woman asked, perplexed that her supervisor was not more surprised, even angry, by her report.

"The Bulgarian and Romanian teams," he explained, "they are very thin too. Someone must call Oslo."

2100 CET, Saturday 12 February 1994
2000 Zulu
Ministry of Foreign Affairs, Victoria Terrasse, Oslo, Norway

"Yes sir, I understand," the foreign minister said into the phone. From the other side of the minister's executive desk, Kristen Hagen watched him finish his conversation with the prime minister. After another moment he said again, "Yes, sir. We'll take care of it. Thank you, Prime Minister...Yes, good bye." The foreign minister returned the phone lightly to its cradle, then looked up at Kristen through thick glasses that made his eyes appear unnaturally small.

The man looked overwhelmed, she thought. He was dealing with a crisis that was so unanticipated, so sudden, so bizarre, that Kristen worried he was being harried into inaction.

"What did the prime minister say?" she prompted.

The minister paused, then responded, "He agreed with your recommendation that we suspend the Games until we can determine the whereabouts of the Soviet athletes." The man sounded beaten down. *Defeated already?* Thought Kristen with chagrin.

Kristen nodded, as much to shake off her despair as to encourage the minister, her blond ponytail following suit. It seemed the only logical thing to do after the very public and very awkward opening ceremonies less than two hours before. The parade of nations had begun late, throwing off the entire program of Norwegian cultural demonstrations and prompting surprised comments from the international array of sportscasters covering the Games. The scene only become more bizarre when bewildered and pitifully small contingents of athletes from first Bulgaria, then Romania, and finally the USSR, entered the ski-jumping arena, prompting yet more exclamations of surprise and speculation from the television hosts.

Kristen immediately understood that a security crisis was at hand. To her surprise, the minister had been harder to convince. He still couldn't grasp that this event, combined as it was with the crisis in Poland to their south and now the ever-increasing signs of Soviet military mobilization, spelled danger for Norway.

"I will inform the Olympic Committee and start arranging phone calls with the foreign offices of some of the more sensitive countries who sent teams. Some are here to witness the Games and will want a face to face meeting with you or the prime minister," Kristen said without missing a beat as she took notes. "They will be asking for an explanation. Do you have any guidance on what we should tell them, sir?"

The foreign minister shook his head, still looking disoriented. Then he said, "This should have been a time of joy for our country. Why must the Soviets ruin the Games with such antics? As if the travesty in Poland wasn't enough. Now they must steal the spotlight from us. Now it is *we* who will be blamed for reversing the Olympic Committee's decision yesterday." The International Olympic Committee, pressured by several of the non-aligned member nations of the UN General Assembly, including some who had not even sent athletes to the Winter Games, had elected yesterday to move forward with the competition despite the unfolding turmoil in Poland.

He doesn't understand how serious this situation truly is, Kristen realized. *He is still viewing this as some public relations dance.* Out loud she said, "Yes, sir." Then, in an effort to refocus her chief on the real issue, "But given what was said at the emergency NAC meeting yesterday," she referred to the North Atlantic Council, the political leadership of the NATO Alliance, "don't you think we should focus our efforts on addressing more *immediate* concerns?"

"What was said at the council yesterday," the minister said testily, "is that we should do nothing to provoke the Soviets. We have no UN backing for any action—"

"That's because the Soviets hold the veto on the Security Council." Kristen interrupted.

"—and many of the alliance members are of the opinion that our economic sanctions against the USSR are what is making them edgy in the first place. The Germans certainly don't want to do anything that would seem to confirm the Soviet's accusations that *they* are at fault in Poland," the foreign minister finished, ignoring her.

Kristen's blue Nordic eyes flashed with irritation. She had spent the previous two days crafting and faxing a position paper for Norway's representative to the NAC, only to see her minister decide that they should do nothing that would endanger the upcoming Olympics. The meeting in Brussels had ended with a decision to defer any action until the next day to allow the situation in Poland to develop. The chief of staff was opening her mouth to respond when the desk phone rang again.

The foreign minister picked up the receiver, clearly thankful for the reprieve from having to answer the tough questions posed by his senior staffer. "Foreign Minister," he said, "yes, hello Jörgen." *The defense minister*, Kristen knew.

Kristen could not hear the other end of the conversation, but watched as her boss tensed almost immediately. Kristen knew that the Defense Ministry *was* taking things seriously. Her counterpart had called Kristen a few minutes ago from the Akershus Fortress to assure her that the King and Crown Prince, who had both been present in Lillehammer to open the Games, were safely under escort of the army's *Hans Majestet Kongens Garde*, the Royal Guard. They were returning the King to the palace here in Oslo, and the Crown Prince to his post with 21 Missile Torpedo Boat Squadron in Bergen, where he was serving as a newly commissioned ensign.

"No. No," the minister was shaking his head as though the receiver could communicate that for him. "I will not," he continued testily.

Kristen barely listened to the minister's one-sided conversation, her thoughts drifted. She realized that Norway, along with Turkey, were the only NATO countries that shared a direct border with the Soviet Union.

"Thank you Jörgen, goodbye." The minister returned the phone to its cradle with a click that brought Kristen back to the situation, now, in this room.

"That was Defense," the foreign minister told Kristen. "He wanted me to convince the prime minister to allow him to begin a full mobilization. Can you imagine how that would look in the news tomorrow? We cancel our country's first Olympics and then the next day call up the Home Guard?" He was shaking his head.

"Well," Kristen countered wearily, "I suppose it would be less embarrassing than having our army caught unprepared for an invasion. Where are the Soviet athletes? We know many of them are military officers, and there are more than a hundred of them unaccounted for in our country right now while the Soviets mobilize their own forces."

The minister leaned back in his seat and shook his head angrily, saying, "Miss Hagen, you speak as if there is going to be a war. I understand your concern, but in my judgment, such an event is out of the question. President Medvedev is simply flexing his muscles in Poland to try and distract his people from their wretched economic conditions, nothing more."

"What if you're wrong, sir?" Kristen asked.

Her chief smiled, tiring now. "I am not." Then after a pause, "You have been working long hours these past few days, Miss Hagen. Get me the number for the IOC so I can call and inform them of our decision. Then go home. Get some sleep. We can deal with the rest tomorrow. I wish I could say 'enjoy the Games' but…"

Kristen suddenly realized that she *was* tired. She nodded and even feigned a half-hearted smile at the minister's attempt at humor. She gathered her notes, handed over the card of the IOC president, and left. *Maybe fatigue is affecting my judgment, making me tense and more fearful.* She shook her head, *Still, it's all very concerning.* As Kristen walked down the hall and collected her coat and hat, she couldn't help remembering that her mother, father, and sister lived far to the north, just a few kilometers from the Soviet border. She was not particularly well-versed in military affairs, but couldn't imagine that her hometown would *not* be a target for any potential Soviet invasion. She left the historic nineteenth century Victoria Terrasse to catch a trolley for her apartment, and she tried to put the thoughts out of her mind.

# CHAPTER 31

2200 CET, Saturday 12 Feb 1994
2100 Zulu
2nd Mechanized Battalion, Skjold, Troms, Norway

R*ITTMESTER* ERIK JOHANSEN strode out the door of his spartan office into organized chaos in the warm open bay that housed his command. *Rittmester*, meaning "master of the horse," was a unique captain-equivalent rank in the Norwegian Army, held by officers who commanded a formation of cavalry. In this case, Johansen's command constituted the reconnaissance cavalry squadron of the 2nd Mechanized Infantry Battalion of the Norwegian Army's Brigade *Nord*, the regular formation tasked with the defense of Northern Norway. The *rittmester* title was a bit of a misnomer in this modern age. The cavalry soldiers' mounts were M113 armored personnel carriers and Mercedes G-Wagons rather than horses. Even so, Johansen savored the dash and history of his position. His short, powerful frame, thick but short-cropped blond hair, and dashing good looks would have looked impressive on a cavalry horse a century ago. Pausing, the *rittmester* surveyed the busy scene before him in his squadron's work bay.

Soldiers stood in a long file in front of the weapons cage, where the arms room sergeant dispensed personal weapons with his usual reticence under the watchful eyes of one of the squadron's *løytnant* troop leaders.

Each soldier, or *dragon* in the Norwegian cavalry, accepted his gun-metal gray G3 rifle, a Minimi light machine gun or MG3 medium machine gun, and then moved over to another cage where a corporal handed over boxes of ammunition, belts of machine gun cartridges, and grenades. The *dragons* filed past the ammunition issue and over to tables where another corporal supervised them loading the shining brass rounds into magazines, ensuring they loaded a tracer as the third to last round to alert the shooter that it was almost time to reload.

Elsewhere, crews were assembling their venerable M2 Browning heavy machine guns, screwing the meter-long barrels into receivers and using their specialized gauges to check the weapon's headspace and timing. Nearer to Johansen, other sergeants were moving among the rows of packs, skis, and snowshoes, meticulously pulling and prodding at the rucksacks lined up in the middle of the floodlit bay, ensuring each was packed according to unit standards. All except the newest draftees had practiced such alerts before, some several times. Even so, a no-notice deployment like this, in the dead of winter, when the soldiers had been expecting to sit back over the weekend watching the Olympics, seemed spiteful. Johansen felt a cold wind blow in as the bay's door opened, allowing a detail of *dragons* to carry several bundled tents out to the squadron's waiting vehicles.

The *rittmester* turned as his tall executive officer, *Løytnant* Sigurd Berg, approached with a clipboard and a bemused look on his face.

"So, sir, Brigade was so upset about the opening ceremonies being messed up that they called a full alert, eh?" he asked with a wry grin.

"Something like that," Johansen responded, less amused than his subordinate. He liked Berg, liked that he was more jovial than the typical Norwegian. The young officer was popular with the men, and competent to boot, all a commander could ask for in a company lieutenant. *He just needs to learn when to keep that humor in check.* "We're headed up to Banak."

"Banak?" the *løytnant* asked, surprised. "What for?"

Although not always practiced, Banak was the normal place for the squadron to assemble in such a situation. In the event of a war with the Soviets, the overall strategy called for Brigade *Nord* to conduct a delaying action in Finnmark, giving time for NATO reinforcements to establish a strong defense in the mountainous Lyngen position, where the Lyngen fjord and the Swedish border forced an invader to attack on a narrow, difficult front.

"Somebody up at Brigade is worried that the Russians may try something, and they want us up there to make them think twice. That, and we will be there to screen if the rest of the Brigade moves forward, just like we've rehearsed."

Johansen knew what Berg was thinking by the look on the younger man's face: *What on earth does command think the Russians are going to try this time of year?* Like the rest of Norway, the *løytnant* had probably been looking forward to an easy Sunday watching the Games, hoping that this alert would be over by morning. *So much for that*, thought Johansen.

"It's the wrong time of year for a war, isn't it?" Berg said, impertinent as usual.

"Your guess is as good as mine," responded the squadron commander without a hint of humor, "but regardless, we're going. There's a Hercules waiting at Bardufoss to fly most of us up to Banak. I'll be on that plane with the troop leaders and most of the men. You will road march the vehicles up the E6 and meet us there tomorrow." Now it was Johansen's turn to grin as Berg sighed. *A road move, the bane of any XO's existence.*

"Don't look so down, Sigurd. It will be a beautiful drive along the fjords, so long as you can keep the tracks on the road." teased the commander. Then he turned serious and said, "We're on a short timeline. The Hercules leaves from Bardufoss in four hours. The sergeant major is arranging the busses to get the men there. I'll be flying to Bardufoss in a helicopter in thirty minutes to get a full briefing from brigade. You'll need to depart here with the vehicles by twenty-three hundred so you can meet us at Banak. If the weather holds, and there aren't too many break-downs, you should make it to Banak by noon tomorrow. We've done this before, several times. You know the way. Gather up the officers and troop sergeants in the ready room. I want to give the warning order brief in five minutes."

"Yes sir," Berg saluted, turning on his heel.

— —

Thirty minutes later, Johansen was bracing himself against the arctic night and the downdraft thrown by the descending Lynx helicopter. The bird's green and red landing lights were approaching out of the darkness onto the Skjöld garrison's parade field fifty meters away. Despite his light-hearted tone with Berg earlier, the twenty-nine-year-old *rittmester* was concerned. The chaos down at the Olympics, his squadron's no-notice deployment to Banak, and now the uneasy tone coming down from the 2nd Battalion's commander and staff gave the young officer a sense of foreboding. *This can't be the real thing, can it?* he thought.

Standing next to Johansen was Major Laub, the 2nd Battalion's operations officer, who would be accompanying him on the flight to Brigade *Nord*'s headquarters in Bardufoss. As both men turned away from the flying ice crystals thrown by the downdraft, Johansen saw the same look of concern on the major's face. Laub had come to the squadron's bay just as Johansen was finishing his orders brief. The major informed Erik that 2nd Battalion was attaching a battery of Bofors anti-aircraft guns to their road party, as well as an anti-tank section and a section of pioneers.

Johansen had watched as Berg tallied up the new vehicles and concluded that the size of his convoy had just ballooned from a dozen vehicles to nearly twice that number. *Making it on schedule is going to be difficult with all these hangers-on*, thought Johansen.

Berg, a relatively big man even for a Norwegian, was clearly thinking the same thing as he let out a forlorn sigh before reining in his emotions. Straight line distance to Banak was 250 kilometers, but the road distance was more than twice that, and there was no guarantee that the roads would be free of snow this time of year.

Brigade was flying people from the service battalion to petrol stations along the route to provide refueling support to the squadron, but Johansen didn't envy his executive officer the trip, especially now that it was complicated by vehicles from three other companies. On the other hand, the attachments significantly increased the firepower of Johansen's reconnaissance squadron. As he and Laub left the bay for the parade field, Berg walked out right behind them with the squadron's vehicle crews. He was en route to the vehicle park to link up with the rest of his expanded column.

A gray-painted Coast Guard helicopter from 337 Squadron, the "Lynxes," settled onto the flat, snowy parade ground amidst a cloud of ice crystals. The crew inside slid the passenger doors open as Johansen and Laub ran forward, bent low beneath the still spinning rotors. They climbed into the aircraft and settled into mesh seats. The crew chief scrambled back to help buckle the two officers' five-point harnesses while another crewman slid the doors closed against the frigid swirling air. Johansen, wearing his white parka and snow pants, fumbled with his harness as he tried to help the crew chief. This normally would have drawn a sour comment from the taciturn Laub, but tonight the major was looking straight ahead, obviously concerned.

The crew chief finished buckling Johansen in, then leaned forward into the cockpit with a thumbs-up. Immediately the helicopter lifted off and tilted forward. As the pilot banked to the left to fly back down the glacial valley that led from Skjöld to Bardufoss, Johansen caught a glimpse out the side window of his soldiers in the blue darkness. They filed out the yellow-lit door of the squadron bay and onto a pair of waiting busses. For them it would be an hour drive in the dark over icy roads to get to Bardufoss. Most of the soldiers would sleep for the entire trip, he knew. For Johansen, the journey was a ten-minute flight, with most of his planning and work still ahead of him at the airfield. The young commander sat back in his seat as the helicopter settled into a westward course down the valley, with dark mountains rising high above the aircraft to either side. It was going to be a long night.

CHAPTER 32

1643 EST, Saturday 12 Feb 1994
2143 Zulu
2nd Fleet Headquarters, Building W-5, Norfolk
Naval Station, Virginia, USA

IT TOOK ONLY half a ring before the receiver was snatched up: "Admiral Falkner," the US 2nd Fleet's commander answered into the secure telephone on his desk.

"Art?" the admiral heard through the slight static of the secure connection, "this is SACLANT." Falkner was surprised that the commander of the US Atlantic Fleet was using his official NATO title. *That can only mean trouble.*

"Sir," Falkner said to his old Academy classmate, "what can I do for you this afternoon?" The admiral had spent a long Saturday at the headquarters, watching increasingly troubling reports of Soviet military activity trickle in through his intelligence staff. He had already drawn his own conclusions about what it all meant. Given his deductions, Falkner had been anticipating, even hoping for this call.

"We're going to DEFCON Four," SACLANT announced curtly.

Falkner paused, gathering himself before responding, "Only DEFCON Four, sir?" He had been hoping for a higher level of alert given how fast the situation was developing.

"Look, Art," Falkner's superior explained, "the State Department wants time to pursue diplomacy before we start throwing our military weight around. They've convinced the president that anything more drastic could be viewed as a provocation by the Soviets right now."

"Provocation?" Falkner said, keeping his tone in check but pressing his point, "Frank, if this ends up being the 'bolt from the blue' Soviet offensive it's beginning to look like, we need to get moving as fast as we can to counter it. Our assets are completely out of position, just like I warned you they would be."

"I don't like it any more than you do," his boss agreed, "but—" There was a pause from the other end of the line as Falkner heard the muffled sound of someone speaking in the background. Then the man's voice was back. "Art, lots going on up here at the Pentagon right now. We'll be pushing out the official DEFCON Four warning in the next few minutes, but I'm telling you now, get the word out to your command, fast."

"Roger, sir," Falkner acknowledged, then added, "thanks, Frank."

"Thank *you*, Art. I'll keep you updated." The line clicked off.

Immediately Falkner rose from behind his desk and walked out into his office's foyer. His flag lieutenant was there, faithfully working behind his own smaller desk.

"Ben," he addressed the young officer, "tell Admiral Forrest to get a message out. All hands. We're adopting DEFCON Four. I want every ship and station to take whatever measures they deem necessary to strengthen the security of their commands. And I want them reporting anything, *anything* they can give us on Soviet naval movements. Clear?"

"Aye, sir," the lieutenant said, rising from behind his desk. He quickly added, "Is there going to be a war, sir?"

"God, I hope not, Ben," Falkner said wearily. Then his fatherly tone hardened into something more menacing, though his voice remained soft, "If there is, we're going to kick those red bastards all the way back to Moscow before we're done."

 **CHAPTER 33**

2300 CET, Saturday 12 Feb 1994
2200 Zulu
Headquarters, Brigade *Nord*, Bardufoss, Troms, Norway

R*ITTMESTER* JOHANSEN, ACCOMPANIED by Laub, was taken aback by the number of high-ranking officers present around the conference table in the Bardufoss Air Base's headquarters building. He recognized Brigade *Nord*'s G3, the lieutenant colonel responsible for the Brigade's operations, as well as the Brigade's chief intelligence officer, the chief of artillery operations, and the chief of staff. He also noticed several blue air force uniforms sitting and standing around the cheap conference table. The young officer felt out of place with his white coveralls, combat rig, and helmet under his arm, and he was already starting to sweat in the overheated room. He began looking for a place to take off his parka when he felt someone slap his back in a friendly greeting.

"Erik!" he heard his assailant almost shout in a familiar voice. Johansen spun around until he was looking into the familiar face of a young air force captain.

"Jan Olsen!" Erik Johansen exclaimed as he shook his boyhood friend's hand in a warm greeting. "So, the air force is sending their delinquents over to the army to get some education in soldiering now?"

"Hardly," responded the flight-suited captain good-humoredly, "they say you ground pounders can't do anything without us giving you top cover. I'm taking a flight of F-16s up to Banak to set up a patrol over the Cape."

"Banak?" Johansen asked as he unzipped his parka. "I'm headed up there with my squadron tonight."

"Then we'll be there together," responded Olsen. The two men had grown up together in Trondheim but had lost touch over the years. "I just got the orders a few minutes ago. They pulled me out of bed to let me know. I'm taking six jets up there in a couple of hours."

"What's this all about, anyway?" Erik asked, lowering his voice as he set his parka and helmet aside. As boys Jan and Erik had shared many secrets, from where their grandfathers kept the aquavit, to which girls in their small class were fancying them at the moment. "Are the Russians up to something? We don't usually get air support on our exercises."

"Damned if I know. I think that's what this briefing is about."

The young officers heard a throat clearing and looked over to see Major Laub's disapproving glare. A few others in the room had noticed the pair's noisy reunion as well, but Laub had a reputation for being short with company grade officers. Just then Brigade *Nord*'s commander, a full colonel, walked into the room. The Brigade's sergeant major called the assembled officers to attention, silencing the murmuring conversations that had been providing background noise. A wave of the colonel's hand sent them all converging on the table at the center of the briefing room. Laub jerked his head towards the table, directing Johansen to move closer. In seconds, everyone had found a seat.

Brigade *Nord*'s G2, or chief of intelligence, stood up, removed his glasses, and looked around at the assembled group. Johansen could read the worried look on the uncharacteristically short Nordic man's face as he straightened the papers on the table in front of him. "Gentlemen," he began, "as many of you know, our government made the unprecedented decision just a couple of hours ago to cancel the Olympic Winter Games. What they haven't told the media, at least not yet, is the reason for this decision, though I think the cause is apparent." The major paused to ensure he had the attention of everyone in the room. "This evening, officials in Lillehammer discovered that most of the Soviet, Bulgarian, and Romanian Olympic teams have disappeared from the

Olympic Village. As you know, many of their athletes are drawn from their militaries, as are ours. We have no record of them departing Norway, so we must assume that they are at large within our borders."

The intelligence officer paused to allow the murmuring in the room to die down. Then he continued, "Approximately two hours ago, we began detecting a large number of small ships departing the Soviets' Kola ports, along with increased activity at the major Soviet air bases there." The tall, thin officer took a breath and then continued, "NATO has reported similar activity from Soviet forces in Czechoslovakia, but this can be more reasonably explained by their ongoing intervention in Poland. AF South has also reported activity in the Black Sea and the Mediterranean. Given all this, the minister of defense has decided to move to a higher level of alert and to begin forward deployment of some units to forestall any further Soviet adventurism."

At this point the brigade chief of staff stood and walked over to a map of Northern Norway and the Kola Peninsula hanging on the wall. He turned and looked directly at Johansen and Olsen, two of the more junior officers in the room.

"Gentlemen," he said, "you are the units being pushed forward, along with a few Home Guard platoons we are activating at," he indicated on the map, "Kirkenes, Vardø, Vasdo, Mehamn, and Bats fjord, essentially everywhere east of Banak, near the Soviet frontier. The prime minister is not yet ready to approve a full mobilization for fear it will antagonize the Russians. If the situation continues to develop however, I believe we can expect this sometime tomorrow or the next day." The chief of staff surveyed the map for a moment, letting the room do the same before the G2 took over the briefing once again.

"While a ground invasion by the Soviets would be very difficult this time of year," the bespectacled short man began meaningfully, "they have significant assets to mount air and seaborne assaults against us. In the event of an invasion, we can expect to face the Russians' 26th Corps comprised of their 69th Motorized Rifle and 77th Guards Motorized Rifle Divisions. These will almost certainly be joined by the 76th Guards Airborne Division from Pskov, the 36th Independent Landing-Assault Brigade from Leningrad, and the 61st and possibly the 175th Naval Infantry Brigades. In short, as you already know, they have a lot of combat power to throw at us. Nearly five divisions, and that's before they mobilize reserves. About the only piece of good news is that, given how suddenly this has all developed, the Soviets *should* require several days to get themselves organized before commencing major offensive operations."

Erik thought the man seemed rather unconvinced by this logic. *It may be sudden to us,* thought Johansen, *but the Russians have probably been plotting for a while.*

"Despite the season, the weather is supposed to be calm, cold, and relatively clear for the next several days," the G2 continued, "so if they want a war, this would be a good time from their perspective to start one. I will be followed by the G3."

Brigade *Nord*'s operations officer, a stocky major named Pettersen, rose and looked around the room. "Gentlemen," he began, "this is not a proper orders brief. We are not at this point executing our full mobilization and deployment plan, but we *are* operating under the assumption that all the 2nd Mechanized Battalion will deploy forward tomorrow, and we'll be flying elements of the Telemark Battalion to key points in the hinterland. As such, the battalion's cavalry squadron, under *Rittmester* Johansen," he nodded towards Erik, "will move to Banak tonight to screen the deployment and secure the airfield. A flight of six F-16s, led by *Kaptein* Olsen," this time he nodded at Jan, "will also deploy to Banak to conduct defensive counter-air patrols in case the Russians try to test our airspace. The G4 is out coordinating the fuel for your movements right now. We are short on facts at the moment, but we have rehearsed this before. What are your questions?"

Johansen looked around, making quick eye contact with Jan and wondering at how, despite the very different paths they had taken since childhood, they were now together again when their country was in danger. He asked, "Sir, with *Kaptein* Olsen's detachment at Banak, can I assume we will have fighter ground attack from the F-16s on call while we are there?"

"No," Pettersen responded, "the Air Force is there solely to shield our airspace from enemy incursions. They do not have an air-to-ground mission."

"Sir," Erik pressed, "my squadron is configured for reconnaissance. We don't have much firepower ourselves. With no air support, we will be very exposed until the rest of the battalion moves up."

"We all know the capabilities of your squadron, *Rittmester*," noted Major Laub testily.

"Yes, sir," responded Erik, standing his ground, "but normally the whole battalion would be deploying together and I could call on our artillery for support. In this case we are going to be far forward of any artillery."

Laub was opening his mouth to respond when Major Pettersen said, "*Rittmester*, you raise a valid point." Turning to the brigade's artillery operations officer, another *kaptein* seated across the table, and asked, "have we any response on our request to Porsangermoen?"

The artilleryman stirred, then nodded, saying, "Sir, yes. We're moving a battery of 105-millimeter howitzers up to Banak from the training area at Porsangermoen. They should be there before your vehicles arrive."

This wasn't as good as the heavy self-propelled guns from Brigade *Nord* that Erik was used to calling on, but the addition made him feel somewhat more comfortable.

The artillery *kaptein* continued, "We are also sending along two forward observers from the Brigade artillery battalion. I believe you have trained with them before? They'll link up with you after the briefing. The air force is sending along some RBS-70 teams as well."

This last addition pleased Johansen. The RBS-70 was an effective, man-portable air defense missile, especially when it was used against low-flying targets like helicopters. He still felt uncomfortable being sent so far ahead of his battalion with such limited support. *Is anything really likely to happen anyway? All this is going to just end up being another exercise.*

The briefing moved on to some logistical considerations and after a few minutes the chief of staff dismissed Olsen and Johansen to see to their units while the staff continued to prepare the deployment order for the Brigade. Erik grabbed his parka and helmet and walked out of the room with Olsen. They exited the headquarters building into the frigid night air, then across a small parking lot and into an expansive hangar where ground crew were preparing a C-130 Hercules transport for flight. When they stopped, Olsen touched his army friend's elbow.

"Erik," the pilot said, "it's really good to see you. Don't worry about the air support business. If things go hot, we'll make sure to keep the Sovs off your back. You should see the things we can do in our Falcons! Wonderfully nimble jets. We can take on anything the Russians send at us. Don't worry yourself."

Johansen smiled weakly at his friend's assurances. "Thanks Jan. Maybe when this all turns out to be a false alarm we can catch up with each other at Banak before coming home. I want to hear about what you've been doing with your life. How did things work out between you and Eva anyway?"

"Eva," Olsen laughed, "that was ages ago! We've certainly got some catching up to do. Maybe we'll get a game of cards going during my 'crew rest.'"

The two men shook hands. Then the fighter pilot's face turned serious as he looked his friend full in the face. "I mean it Erik," he said, "if things get serious, we'll keep the Russians off your back. I won't let you down. You can count on me and my pilots."

Johansen nodded. Olsen released his hand and walked towards the door as the two promised forward observers approached. These soldiers were experts at coordinating artillery support and had accompanied the *rittmester*'s squadron before on training deployments. Erik respected their abilities and was glad to have them. Johansen shook the men's hands before moving deeper into the hangar.

At the back of the hangar Erik could see the air force RBS-70 teams with their launchers and missile reloads, some sitting on their packs, others sprawled out on the concrete, using their rucksacks as pillows to catch a few minutes of sleep. He was just thinking of doing the same when he heard the hissing and squealing of air brakes. The busses carrying his command had arrived outside. Erik smiled as he heard the familiar sounds of his sergeants barking at the sleeping soldiers, herding them off the busses. The men filed into the warm hangar, fell into troop formation, then on command dropped their packs.

Johansen's squadron *stab-sergeant* approached with his commander's pack and weapon. Erik accepted them and asked, "How was the drive, sergeant?"

"Easy, sir. The roads were clear, no ice. Probably too cold for that. Most of the men got some rest the whole way from Skjöld."

Johansen drew a deep breath and said, "They're going to need it."

 **CHAPTER 34**

0540 MSK, Sunday 13 Feb 1994
0240 Zulu
**USS *Connecticut* (SSN 22), X-Ray Station, northeast of
Murmansk, Russian Soviet Federative Socialist Republic**

COMMANDER ROGERS AWOKE to the duty officer gently shaking his shoulder.

"Skipper?" the young man was saying softly. "Skipper?"

Rogers sat up in his bunk. The captain tried to wipe the sleep from his eyes with both palms as he croaked, "What is it?"

"Skipper, you're needed on the bridge. The XO has the con and an ELF message just came in," the man reported.

The captain nodded wearily and grunted, "Alright, give me a minute."

The officer withdrew as Rogers moved to his small sink to splash water on his face and run his hand across the stubble he had neglected to shave before lying down. Glancing at the ship's clock above the small mirror he saw: 02:41. The submarine operated on Zulu, or Greenwich Mean Time, while on patrol. *So much for a good night's sleep.*

The skipper slipped on his shoes and walked the few paces from his cabin, barking, "Coffee!" as he entered the control room.

The executive officer, anticipating his commander's foul mood, wordlessly and rapidly relinquished the captain's chair to its rightful occupant.

Settling into the seat, Rogers asked his second-in-command gruffly, "What's up, XO?" as a seaman appeared at his elbow handing him a steaming mug of dark brew. Rogers took a tentative sip and allowed the taste of the bitter coffee that came out of *Connecticut*'s galley to bring him fully awake.

"Sir, ELF just came in," the XO, reported, "DEFCON Four. We've got a lot of surface activity in the channel to our east, but we need to go shallow within the next hour to receive a message from COMSUBLANT. Doesn't seem to be much wiggle room in the order either, Skipper," he finished, handing over the message printout.

Rogers snapped the message out of the XO's hand and read it. He looked up at the tactical display, noting that the number of surface contacts on the screen had indeed multiplied since he'd turned in less than three hours before. *This is going to be fun*, he thought, his mood darkening further. Then shaking his head, he ordered, "General quarters!"

The crew of the *Connecticut* went through the well-practiced drill of bringing their boat up to communications depth. During the ascent, the sonar room continued to report on the contacts to their east, "Lots of pinging at something, Skipper. Multiple active sonar sources between bearings zero-five-five and zero-seven-zero."

That's odd, thought Rogers, *there shouldn't be any other boats nearby except us. No chance of finding us if we can hear them from twenty miles away.* He took a long draught from the steaming mug, but he was already wide awake. *It's almost as if the Sovs want to be absolutely sure that there's no one else in the channel.*

The drill of retrieving the burst satellite message lasted only thirty-eight seconds this time, since their antennae received only one short message and sent none. Even so, the captain was wincing by the time the communications crew reeled the buoy back down.

"Sir," the ECM petty officer was reporting, "lots more activity up there than last time. It's going to take me a while to sort it all out and classify. I can't guarantee they didn't get a radar hit on us."

Rogers swore under his breath. That would mean he would need to maneuver the boat to a completely new spot to preclude any nosy frigates finding him, and the shallow waters here at the mouth of the Kola Inlet didn't offer an abundance of good hiding places for a deep-water nuke-boat like his. *This is going to take hours*, Rogers thought. *That message better be worth it.*

"Sparks," the nervous communications officer, Lieutenant Santamaria, approached with the print out and handed it over, then backed away in anticipation of the outburst he expected from his skipper. Rogers looked down, seeing that the message was just three measly lines, and read:

FROM: COMSUBLANT
TO: CMDR, USS CONNECTICUT SSN22

ADOPT DEFCON 4 RPT ADOPT DEFCON 4. ADOPT INCREASED INTELLIGENCE GATHERING POSTURE AND STRENGTHEN SECURITY MEASURES. EXPECT INCREASED REDFLT ACTIVITY IN NEXT 72 HRS. END.

"God*dammit!*" he raged, throwing the message on the deck in frustration and slopping hot coffee over his hand.

After a moment, the XO ventured, "What is it, Skipper?"

Rogers calmed himself down and shook his hand so that splatters of coffee flew all around the control room. He leaned over and picked up the message and handed it over to the XO. The second-in-command scanned it, muttering, "…increased intel gathering and security…"

"No shit, Sherlock," Rogers said, venting his frustration, "that's what DEFCON Four means! They didn't need to call us to comms depth to tell us that, *and* we already know the Russians are getting ready to sortie. We can hear it for ourselves." He gestured vaguely to the east. "Probably some pansy-assed staff puke trying to be a little too helpful, putting us all at risk so he can look busy."

His outburst done, the captain took another slug of the coffee and settled deeper into his chair. There wasn't time to spare on tantrums. *Let's get this done.* "Alright," he said wearily, starting again, "let's start the evasion drill. Con, make your depth…"

CHAPTER 35

0400 CET, Sunday 13 Feb 1994
0300 Zulu
Sørstraumen Bru, along the E6 eight kilometers
south of Bufjord, Troms, Norway

L *ØYTNANT* SIGRUD BERG, Executive Officer of 2nd Mechanized
Battalion's cavalry squadron, stood at the front of a long line of military vehicles, staring in frustration at the scene in front of him. He
and his motley collection of M113s, G-Wagens, and trucks pulling 40mm
Bofors guns had been on the road for nearly five hours, creeping through the
night along Norway's rugged Arctic coast at between twenty-five and forty
kilometers-per-hour. In the darkness to his left was the black expanse of the
open-water Kvænangen fjord. Behind him rose snowy-white, glacier-carved
mountains. The E6, the only major highway leading into Norway's far north,
was just a narrow two-lane road at this point. In short, he could take in at
a glance all of the terrain factors that made military operations in Northern
Norway so difficult, especially in winter.

Occupying his thoughts at this particular moment was not the physical
landscape but rather the jumbled wreck of an overturned flatbed truck, its cargo
of large pipes strewn all over the two-hundred-fifty-meter-long Sørstraumen

Bru. The bridge was the only way across the Kvænangen fjord, and right now it was impassable.

Berg could see rotating blue lights on the other side of the wreckage, about halfway across the span. *The local* Politi *must have just gotten here too*, he thought. Ahead in the darkness he could see an officer in a fluorescent yellow vest picking his way through the pipes towards the military convoy. The *løytnant* walked forward and met the man.

"Hello there," the local greeted him. "What the hell happened here?"

"I was hoping *you* could tell *us*," answered Berg.

"No idea, I just got here myself," the police officer gestured back to his car across the wreckage. The man was far too up-beat, his friendly manner grating on Berg's impatient nerves. "Have you talked to the driver?"

"There was no one here when we arrived," answered Berg, trying with what he thought was admirable success to keep his frustration out of his voice.

"Odd," muttered the local, "when I saw you, I expected that there had been an accident with one of your tanks. Have you checked the cab?" The truck itself was still upright, though the cab was lodged awkwardly on the guardrail. Only the trailer was on its side.

"We did. No one there," responded Berg. "The cab is locked."

"No one called us about an accident," the police officer went on, puzzled. "I came down here from Bufjord when another trucker said there was an accident on the bridge. We really need to find the poor chap. It's a cold one tonight. Have you looked around the shoulder?"

Now Berg was getting impatient. He unclenched his teeth long enough to say, "Look, we are on a mission and we need to cross this bridge as soon as possible. When can you get it cleared?"

"Cleared? That will take hours with a mess like this. We'll have to bring a crane in from Alta. And we can't do anything until we know where the driver is and if he's safe," said the *Politi*, still far too upbeat for the circumstances.

"Look," Berg repeated the word, like it was grounding him and his growing exasperation, "this is a matter of national defense. We don't have hours to wait around while you drag some construction worker out of bed. I need to get these vehicles," he swept his hand at the column stretching back from the west side of the bridge, "to Banak," and he drew his arm back around to point east as emphatically as he could.

"Calm down, calm down," the *Politi* man said, raising his gloved palms at Berg. "Let me see what I can do." He turned and started picking his way back over the jumbled pipes blocking the highway.

Berg swore under his breath. The squadron's march had started off well enough. He'd gotten all the crews and vehicles lined up in the squadron vehicle park and for once there hadn't been any problems getting the encrypted radios from three different companies to talk to each other. They'd actually departed early.

Then, a hundred kilometers out from Skjöld one of the M113s had sputtered to a halt. The crew had gotten the track running again after some quick tinkering, but the delay had annulled their early departure and the young officer wasn't confident about that particular vehicle's ability to make it the rest of the way to Banak. Now, on top of the mess on the bridge, one of the trucks towing a Bofors gun was also acting up. The *løytnant* turned stiffly and started trudging back toward his vehicles.

As he approached his G-Wagen, a sergeant with a satchel over his shoulder walked up from the rear of the column. Berg didn't recognize the man, but the NCO strode right up to him and said confidently, "Excuse me sir, I may have a solution." In the dark, Berg heard more than saw the smirk on the man's face.

Now Berg remembered; the sergeant was in charge of the Pioneer section that had joined the squadron back at Skjöld.

"Pedersen, isn't it?" Berg queried. The sergeant nodded. "Okay, what's your solution, Sergeant?"

"Well sir, I've got enough C4 in this satchel and back at our track to drop the whole bridge if we wanted to. I've got plenty to make this," he gestured towards the wreckage on the bridge, "go away."

Now it was Berg's turn to smirk. *Pioneers. They just love to remind you how much they play with explosives. Although…it's not actually a half-bad idea.*

Berg shook his head, amused, saying, "I don't think the *Politi* will take too kindly to us blowing vehicles off the E6."

"Suit yourself, sir. I'll be here when you need me," the sergeant responded light-heartedly as he spun about and walked back towards his own track.

What's gotten into everyone that they're so cheerful tonight, wondered the big XO.

Berg turned to his driver. "Get the troop sergeants. I want both winch tracks up to the front. We're not waiting for the locals to clear this road. We're going to do it ourselves."

 **CHAPTER 36**

0500 CET, Sunday 13 Feb 1994
0400 Zulu
Banak Air Station, Lakselv, Troms, Norway

R ITTMESTER JOHANSEN STARTED awake as the C-130 Hercules bounced down onto the icy runway at Banak. Around him in the cramped transport, his *dragons* also stirred in their fold-down mesh seats. He'd come to appreciate this part of a deployment, the time in transit, as it offered a reprieve between the responsibilities of planning at the origin and those of execution at the destination. The young *rittmester* felt the weight of command descend on his shoulders once again as the aircraft taxied.

The Hercules rolled to the southern end of the airfield's single runway and then to a hangar housing two Westland Sea King rescue helicopters of 330 "Viking" Squadron. The Vikings were the only permanent military force at Banak Air Station, situated on a wooded peninsula at the head of the Porsangerfjord and just north of the town of Lakselv. Johansen stood up from his seat as the aircraft jerked to a stop. He was at the rear of the bird, and behind him rifles, helmets, and equipment clattered together and swished against tight-packed white parkas as the forty-five troopers of his command readied themselves to disembark. The ramp at the rear of the plane held a pallet stacked high with rucksacks and the RBS-70 launchers and missiles, all secured under a mesh of cargo netting. An icy predawn breeze assaulted the warm interior of the transport as the rear ramp lowered with a whine. Once the motion stopped Johansen led his command in file off the airplane, walking down the ramp, past the baggage pallet, and across the floodlit tarmac to the relative warmth of the nearby hanger, passing another Hercules being unloaded by the air force ground crews there to service the inbound F-16s. An officer in a coast guard flight suit was inside to meet them.

The naval man walked up to Johansen and said, "Are you the commander of this group? I got a call from Bardufoss a couple hours ago telling me to expect you."

"Yes, I'm *Rittmester* Johansen. We're here to secure the air station until the rest of Brigade *Nord* moves up."

"When will that be?" asked the other man.

"I don't know right now," he paused, reminding himself that it was now Sunday, despite the dark pre-dawn sky outside, "Possibly today, if they deploy at all. Regardless, we are here to get things ready for them. I'll need some transport to recon our defensive positions."

The Coast Guard officer nodded, "I've got several vehicles from the air station parked for you outside, and some snowmobiles as well. I was told to expect some soldiers from Porsangermoen, but they haven't arrived yet."

Johansen nodded his thanks. Behind him his sergeants were supervising the squadron's *dragon*s as they unloaded equipment from the ramp of the Hercules and deposited it in troop formations on the hangar floor. As Eric pulled a topographic map from his hip pocket, his two troop *løytnantar* joined him, G3 rifles slung over their shoulders.

"Andreas, Nils," he addressed the two young *løytnantar*, stabbing the folded chart with his finger, "you know the plan. Our host," he indicated the Coastie, "has provided us with transport. I need you to take our forward observers and recon your troop positions. Andreas, you'll take the eastern approaches to the town. Nils, I want you to leave a section here at the air-field and put the remainder south covering the highway. Remember, we have an artillery battery coming up from Porsanger. Call me on the radio if you link up with them. I'll be around shortly to inspect your positions and then we can start moving the men forward. For now I'll be posting our air force attachments around the airfield. Our vehicles should be here by noon. Get to it."

"Sir," both white-clad *løytnantar* responded in unison, then moved away towards the milling soldiers to collect their radio operators and artillery observers before exiting the rear of the hangar.

Johansen walked over to the air force sergeant, who was inspecting the last of his missiles unloaded from the Hercules, and said, "Sergeant, I'd like you to post your teams in the outbuildings around the airfield so they have some shelter. I may move a team or two forward later, but for now let's keep them close. Come with me and we can designate their posts."

Johansen had been to Banak before on drills, several times in fact, but he'd never been accompanied by air force missileers. *One more indication that this may be serious,* he thought as he collected his rifle and led his radioman and the sergeant out to a waiting four-by-four. Johansen opened the driver's door and got in, starting the engine with keys handed over by the Coast Guard officer. They drove around the forested perimeter of the air strip, using the blue landing lights of the runway for navigation in the pre-dawn darkness. At the suggestion of the sergeant, Johansen pulled over to designate the first RBS-70 position.

Stepping from the vehicle, the *rittmester* heard a screaming roar grow louder overhead. He looked up to see green and red navigation lights attached to the dark shadow of a landing F-16. Erik watched as the fighter swooped in and landed amid an incandescent swirl of ice crystals. He could see the lights of three more of the nimble jets stacked up and descending from the north. A deep rumble overhead belied the presence of two more. *We'll keep the Russians off your back,* his pilot friend Olsen had assured him. He took comfort in the thought as he got back into the four-by-four and continued his circuit.

——

Several thousand feet overhead, *Kaptein* Jan Olsen was also thinking about the pledge he'd made to his friend. As fighter pilots went, he was as cocky as most, but he was also a professional, and was painfully aware of how many dozens of combat aircraft the Russians could throw at him if it came to aerial combat. He would need good flying and creative tactics to win against their potential enemy's numbers. Along those lines he had worked out a hypothetical battle plan with his fellow pilots that would, he hoped, take advantage of the peculiarities of the rugged terrain here in Northern Norway. He wanted to make sure they could offer up a few surprises. Other pilots from his 332 "Eagle" Squadron were even now dispersing to several other airfields further west in order to prevent the valuable jets from being caught on the ground in an attack. Now that they were up here, he just hoped that wouldn't have to execute these contingencies.

 **CHAPTER 37**

0710 CET, Sunday 13 Feb 1994
0610 Zulu
Passenger terminal, Kirkenes Lufthavn, Finnmark, Norway

T HE NORWEGIAN MINING town of Kirkenes sat nestled in Arctic pre-dawn darkness along the Bøkfjorden, an arm of the much larger Varangerfjorden that emptied into the Barents Sea off Norway's far north coast. The town's three thousand residents existing about four hundred kilometers north of the Arctic Circle and had the dubious distinction of being the most proximate of all Norwegian communities to the Soviet border.

Given the rapidly escalating security situation, the army's Varanger battalion, garrisoned adjacent to the town airport, had deployed during the night to pre-selected battle positions, overseeing the one bridge across the Bøkfjorden that connected the two countries. A mere section of twelve soldiers remained in the garrison to secure the single icy runway that connected Kirkenes to the outside world.

The airport clerk had arrived for work exactly on time, ten minutes ago. Kirkenes Lufthavn wasn't a particular busy airport, but it was a key station for responding to emergencies and supporting the mining industry here in the far north, and thus the desk needed to be tended at all times. She was just pulling out a sheaf of the ever-present forms when she noticed the men. *That's odd*, was her first thought.

Several men, all young and fit, had just entered the terminal and were milling about the small passenger waiting area. The clerk checked her schedule. *Just as I thought, no flights for another eight hours.* Of course, milling about the heated waiting area wasn't exactly a crime. *Even so, it's a little…odd.* The clerk's thoughts repeated the only word that came to mind so early in the morning.

She stepped out from behind her work area and walked out to the waiting room. There were even more people here than she'd realized, at least ten. Maybe a dozen? Several were outside, smoking.

"Can I help you?" one of the men asked in accented Norwegian, stealing the line right from her lips. His smile looked forced.

"Yes," the clerk responded, "are you waiting for a flight? We don't normally see so many people so early on a Sunday. The next flight isn't until the afternoon. Can I call you a taxi? The Rica Hotel in town has a good breakfast. I could call ahead for you and have them get the coffee started if you want."

There were a couple of sidelong glances between the other men in the room. The one who'd addressed her merely shrugged. "We just completed a survey of a mining site down south. We would rather just wait here. Do you mind?" the man asked with a chilling smile. He produced a ticket and handed it over. It was for the next flight leaving in several hours.

The explanation was not convincing, but, considering how many of them there were, she decided not to press the issue. Instead, she nodded, handed the ticket back, and retreated to her work station. She made a pretense of resuming her paperwork and then put her pen down and walked the few steps to the Lufthavn's office, shutting the door behind her. The woman picked up the phone on the office's cheap desk and dialed the number for the airport's security officer, a retired police officer from the town.

After three rings, a woman's voice answered, "Hello?"

"Yes, Annette, this is Anna Hagen. Is Nils there please?"

"No," came the elderly woman's response, "he's out skiing this morning. May I take a message for him?"

"That won't be necessary," Anna answered. "Thank you." She placed the receiver back in its cradle.

She scolded herself for being so easily intimidated. *What are you doing? What is making you so paranoid today? Just go back out there and do your work.*

So that's what Anna Hagen did. The men milled about the waiting area as she emerged from the office and returned to her work station. She busied herself with the paperwork, doing her best to avoid the nagging feeling of danger she just couldn't seem to shake. If Nils, the local *politi*, wasn't available, then the only other place to call for help was the army garrison south of town. A few suspicious characters hanging around this little airport certainly didn't warrant alerting the army.

 **CHAPTER 38**

0755 CET, Sunday 13 Feb 1994
0655 Zulu
Along the Goahtemuorjohka River, along the
E6 northeast of Alta, Troms, Norway

LØYTNANT SIGURD BERG stood on the hood of his G-Wagen, munching on a cold sausage sandwich from his vehicle's grub box, his convoy stretching out on the road behind him, stationary once again. The crews were milling about outside their vehicles, relieving themselves and eating their rations. The weak Arctic sun was just beginning to brighten the gray southeast sky above the snowy forested mountains to his right. To his left, the shoulder of the E6 highway dropped off precipitously into a dark narrow gorge filled by a fast-flowing stream with thick ice on its steep banks. Berg took another large bite of his sandwich as he pondered the new obstacle blocking his path.

The accident back at the Sørstraumen bridge *could* have been a coincidence. It had been very odd, with no driver anywhere to be found, but there were conceivable explanations for that. *This*, however. There was no way *this* could be an accident. Berg was looking at a thirty-meter-long well-formed *abatis*, composed of twenty large Norwegian Spruce carefully dropped in an interlocking pattern across the road, creating an impassable barrier. There was a cold feeling in the pit of his stomach as he thought about what this meant. *Someone is deliberately trying to keep us from getting to Banak.* The implications of that conclusion were not palatable.

Broader implications aside, he still needed to get his ungainly convoy to Banak, especially if something big was afoot. *There must be something going on.* Berg dreaded the idea of having his column strung out on the narrow E6 at the start of a shooting war. He needed a way to get past the *abatis*, and this time he knew exactly what to do.

Setting his sandwich down on the roof of his vehicle, Berg turned to face back down his line of vehicles. He cupped his mittened hands to his mouth and at the top of his lungs yelled, "Sergeant Pedersen!"

A few moments passed before, "Sir?" The pioneer sergeant was looking up at him with a grin on his five-o-clock shadowed face.

"Pedersen," called the *løytnant*, "I think we need some of your 'solution.'"

The NCO's grin became a maniacal smile. He threw a half salute and began trotting back towards his M113.

"And get those winches up here!" Berg shouted to the rest of his troopers.

 **CHAPTER 39**

0800 CET, Sunday 13 Feb 1994
0700 Zulu
SCT Surjøya Container Terminal, Port of Oslo, south of Oslo city

S VEN SORENSEN STEPPED out of his battered Volkswagen Apollo
onto the icy pavement. He shivered and pulled the knit cap down over
his ears as an icy wind gusted off the dark gray waters of Oslofjord and
across the concrete quay of the shipping terminal. Sorensen's thermometer
had registered minus thirteen degrees Celsius when he'd walked out of his
working-class apartment building into the predawn darkness.

I'm getting too old for these early winter mornings, he told himself, wishing
he had a coffee to warm his insides. He pulled a manila envelope out of his
jacket and began trudging towards the line of trucks parked against the nondescript warehouse at the port's main dry goods terminal.

He was scanning for the license plate indicated in the instructions.
Normally he was dispatched directly from the trucking company office, but
this morning's job wasn't ordinary. His manager had called him at home the
night before and told him that a customer had requested him by name to
make a special delivery the next day. His manager hadn't known where or why,
but the customer promised double the normal fee for a rare Sunday delivery,
and he would get Monday off as compensation. Sorensen couldn't complain.

Spotting the license plate, he walked towards the two-ton box truck emblazoned on its sides with inviting pictures of pastries, teas, and coffees. The typed instructions stated that the cargo was intended for a catered event this afternoon at the *Storting*, Norway's parliament building. As he walked around to the driver's side he noticed that the truck was riding very low on its rear axle. *That must be some load of pastries*, he thought. He settled onto the cold padded bench seat and started the engine, cranking up the heat as he blew into his cold fists.

As the cab warmed, Sorensen pulled his instructions from the envelope and read. He knew how to get to the capital district, but his parking directions were specific. *Well*, he thought, *that makes sense, maybe the prime minister will be at the event. Maybe even the King!* The thought made him proud. The monarchy was extremely popular in Norway. The current King's grandfather had earned the everlasting love of his people by the dignified defiance he'd shown to the Germans during the Second World War. This love had been transferred easily to his heirs. Sorensen was pleased by the possibility of serving his monarch directly in some small way.

He shifted the truck easily into gear and pulled away from the warehouse, then turned and motored across the parking lot and onto the E18 northbound. As he did so he fiddled with the radio knobs until he tuned into his favorite morning news station. In the gray dawn he didn't notice the nondescript sedan pulling onto the highway several dozen meters behind him.

The news on the radio dismayed the old driver. The hosts were excitedly discussing the stunning cancellation of the Olympic Winter Games. Sorensen had planned to watch the opening ceremony last night, but turned the television off after much confused commentary by the sports anchors as to why the lighting of the torch and the parade of nations had both been delayed. He wasn't particularly interested in the pageantry, anyway. He was old enough to remember when Norway was the poorest country in Europe, and he was proud of how far his nation had come. Like most *Norge*s he was anticipating a strong showing in the winter sports competitions. *We'd dominate biathlon whether or not our team marched around in some silly circle*, he thought, *but cancel the Games? What idiot made that decision?* The radio hosts were speculating that it had something to do with the chaos going on in Poland. *That country has been in chaos for the last five years. So what?*

The eastern heights were casting a gloomy shadow across the fjord as the delivery truck exited the highway onto Kong Hakon's Gate towards the city center. Sorensen glanced to his left and idly noted that over on the far side of the harbor nearly every window in the Ministry of Defense building at the Akershus Fortress was ablaze with light. In fact, the whole complex was lit up like a Christmas festival. *Those buggers are working early…or late, and on a Sunday too. Probably earning double overtime pay in those cushy government jobs.*

Sorensen easily navigated his ungainly vehicle through the empty early morning streets of the capital district. The *Storting*, was now in view at the end of the Nedre Vollgate. He drove right up to the south face of the yellow brick and granite structure and looked out the passenger side window. Sorensen was mildly surprised to see that the arrangements promised in his instructions had all been carried out. The traffic bollards that normally blocked access to Wessels Plass, the compact pedestrian park on the south side of the *Storting*, had been removed and the snow banks had been cleared all the way up to the yellow brick wall of the building.

The delivery man turned slowly onto Wessels Plass and, following his specific instructions, inched the vehicle up to the side of the building to just beyond where the bollards had been, centering the truck on the south wall of the nineteenth century structure just short of the large, wooden side door. He had parked so close that after he killed the engine, engaged the parking brake, and turned off the headlights, he was compelled to slide across the bench seat and exit out the passenger side door. As he did so, a dark colored sedan drove slowly by on Akersgata Street and disappeared behind the eastern back wall of the parliament building.

Following his neatly typed instructions, Sorensen locked the cab of the truck and ensured the cargo area in the back was also secure. With that final check complete he walked across the Wessels Plass plaza, dropped the truck keys into a pre-addressed envelope, sealed it and, at the far end of the plaza, found a mailbox where he deposited the envelope. Job done.

Well, almost. I still need to get paid, he thought as he started towards the pre-arranged rendezvous with the job's client, the nearest McDonald's restaurant located a little over half a kilometer away on Storgata Street.

Since he had some time to spare, Sorensen walked around the front of the *Storting*, taking some time to admire his country's legislature building before turning right to walk down Karl Johans Gate, quickening his pace as the cold, gloomy dawn brightened slightly into a cold, gloomy day. He continued several blocks down the mostly deserted boulevard, passing the seventeenth-century Oslo Cathedral with its spare stone walls, imposing belfry, and sculptures warning sinners passing by of the fate that awaited them. Sorensen had never been particularly religious, but this part of the capital's architecture always struck him as darkly ominous. He hurried on to the left around the cathedral and turned up Storgata Street.

The McDonald's was located in the corner of one of the nineteenth century row buildings that typified downtown Oslo and most other northern European cities, and the delivery man reveled in the warm sanctuary it provided. He looked to the counter with its brightly colored menu, but before he could step forward a man in a dark coat tapped him on the shoulder.

"Mr. Sorensen?" the man asked in English. Like most Norwegians, Sorensen spoke fluent English, but he couldn't place this man's accent. He wasn't Norwegian.

The delivery man turned until he was looking down into the smiling angular face of a short but athletic middle-aged man with a receding hairline, the effect of the man's pinched smile mimicking a badger, or a weasel. He was holding a brown paper bag in one hand and an insulated paper cup in the other.

"Yes?" answered the Norwegian.

"You made the delivery as agreed?" asked the man. When Sorensen nodded, the short man continued, "I took the liberty of buying you a cup of coffee and some breakfast. You must be chilled after a morning like this. Consider it some small thanks for your help in our enterprise." He handed over the items and motioned to one of the tables as another customer entered.

As they sat, Sorensen thanked him for the meal, but the hot coffee was what he really wanted. He *was* chilled, and the warm cup felt heavenly against his aching hands. He lifted the paper vessel to his lips and savored the bitter taste of the dark liquid. There was an odd flavor to the drink, but then, it *was* McDonald's coffee, after all. He didn't usually go for fast food and wondered what was inside the paper bag.

When he looked up, he noticed the other man watching him intently, making him slightly uncomfortable. "Do you have the payment?" he asked, more brusquely than he'd intended.

"Of course, of course," the weasel-faced man burst out as if he'd completely forgotten. He reached into his coat and pulled out a white letter envelope, then handed it over. Sorensen peeked inside just enough to note that the proper number of paper *Kroner* appeared to be present. "It's all there," the man assured him in a jovial voice, again with that odd accent.

Feeling sheepish, Sorensen took another sip of coffee before looking into the paper bag. As he pulled out a wrapped sandwich, he tried to soften his earlier outburst with some small talk. "What was this delivery for, anyway?" He noticed a corner of the man's smile turn down at this inquiry.

"Oh, nothing important," the he said with a dismissive wave, "there is to be a reception later in the day, catered by our company. We simply need our food and equipment properly positioned. We couldn't get any of our normal catering drivers to make the delivery so early in the morning," he added quickly. It seemed a reasonable explanation, even if it didn't explain why the instructions were so exacting. Looking the man over, Sorensen noted that he was meticulously dressed, with each layer of his suit in perfect order, just like the instructions.

"Thank you again for the meal," Sorensen said as he bit into the sandwich. "Can I ask your name?"

"Kinnunen," the man answered quickly. He seemed uncomfortable now. "I'm Finnish."

Sorensen's coffee was now cool enough that he could take a more satisfying drink. He saw his Finnish companion's expression relax as he washed the sandwich down with several sips. As he finished the meal, Sorensen realized that he was starting to feel a headache coming on. *The coffee should help that*, he thought, as he took another sip.

The other man, Kinnunen, was watching him closely again. "Is there something wrong?" Sorensen asked.

"You don't look well."

Suddenly I don't feel well. The delivery man was starting to become short of breath.

"Do you have a history of heart attacks in your family?" Kinnunen asked softly as the Norwegian opened his jacket and loosened his shirt, trying to draw in a full breath.

"No…" Sorensen answered between increasingly rapid breaths. "I…I think…I may need a…a doctor," he said in a voice that weakened by the second. His face was turning bright red as well.

"Yes, my friend," Kinnunen answered, "let me go get someone." The other man stood and gingerly took the envelope of *Kroner* from the tabletop in front of Sorensen.

KGB agent Anatoli Skorniak, alias Kinnunen, walked past the struggling truck driver and over to the front counter where he mentioned to the girl taking orders that the man at the table back there seemed to be in some difficulty. She looked and saw that he appeared to be having trouble breathing. When she looked back, Skorniak was already out the door and getting into a dark sedan. That was when Sorensen lost consciousness, slipped off his chair and fell heavily to the floor. His heart had already stopped, forever.

It would take hours for Sorensen's employer to be notified about his death. Even then, no one would be able to trace his steps back to his delivery, parked flush against the south wall of the *Storting*.

CHAPTER 40

1120 MSK, Sunday 13 Feb 1994
0820 Zulu
HMS *Trafalgar* (S107), northern edge of X-Ray
Station, 300 miles northwest of Murmansk

OMMANDER EDWARD DAVIES, captain of Her Majesty's Ship *Trafalgar*, sipped his third cup of black tea. The mornings on X-Ray Station were colder than he could have imagined, even in the climate-controlled compartment of a submarine. His command, the lead ship of her class, had been on station here in the frigid far north for more than three weeks now, meaning that the supply of shelf-stable milk for his morning brew had run out days ago, leaving the captain "a bit peeved," as he liked to say with typical English understatement. At this moment, however, his thoughts were distant from the deficiencies of the steaming liquid. Rather, his thoughts were thirty-five miles to the north, to be exact.

"Con, this is sonar," the young officer in the nearby sonar room reported in very proper Queen's English, "I am not yet able to distinguish the various contacts in the group at bearing zero-three-zero. There are certainly more than a dozen, warships and amphibious transports. They are in the first convergence zone, thirty-five miles from us, the center of mass of the formation is a very tight group. They appear to be following a similar course to the one that Sov surface action group followed a few hours ago."

Davies nodded. His sleep had been interrupted in the early hours of the morning when a surface action group consisting of a Soviet *Kresta*-class cruiser, accompanied by three destroyers, had transited north of his boat at a rapid twenty knots. That had been unusual enough to pull him out of bed, where he'd only spent a short amount of time since the NATO Alert State 2 warning had arrived earlier in the night. *But this*, he thought, *this is truly irregular.*

"Very well," he ordered with his usual politeness, "helmsman, bring your course to three-three-zero, speed five knots. We'll see if we can't let our towed array sort them out over the next few minutes, shall we?" The towed sonar array was a system of hydrophones attached to a long cable stretching from the rear of *Trafalgar*. The array allowed the submarine's crew to monitor sonar contacts at a greater distance and with more accuracy than more constrained hull-mounted sensors.

A few minutes later the sonar room reported again.

"Con, sonar," came the young officer's voice, "we are starting to get a better picture. Seems one of the heavies is an *Ivan Rogov*-class amphibious landing ship. We can also make out at least two *Alligator*-class landing ships, and perhaps four," a pause, "No, six of their newer, smaller *Ropucha*-class. Possibly a freighter or two as well, sir."

"Bloody hell," muttered the boat's executive officer, standing next to Davies as he thumbed through the control room's red ship identification binder, "the only *Ivan Rogov* in the Northern Fleet is the *Mitrofan Moskalenko*. She can carry about a battalion of naval infantry, fifty to sixty armored vehicles, four helicopters. With all those other landing ships up there we're looking at enough lift for an entire Soviet naval infantry brigade, at least!"

"As far as the escorts, sir," the sonar officer was continuing, "I'm still having trouble classifying some of them, but it appears to be a rather large contingent. At least one *Kresta*-class, and I believe we can hear an *Udaloy* and a *Kashin*. We're losing the sound of several others on the far side of the landing ships. The whole lot are moving along at a rather good clip, sir. Sixteen knots, at least."

What the devil is an entire Soviet naval infantry brigade doing transiting the wastes of the central Barents Sea in the dead of winter? wondered *Trafalgar*'s skipper. *Is this related to that warning from the Yanks earlier?* Without delay he berated himself, *Of course it is, you fool! There's only one real explanation, isn't there?* Davies did not like the conclusion he came to, did not like it in the least. *First things first*, he reminded himself. *Observe and report.*

"XO," the captain said, addressing his second-in-command, "we will come shallow and send a report on these contacts back to Fleet, then I want to reel in the towed array, go deep, and spend a few hours sprinting ahead of this group at," he did some quick mental math while looking at the chart before him, "twenty-two knots. We'll get ahead of them to have a closer look. I have a feeling those Russian landing ships may be intending to make a, shall we say, *unscheduled* port call somewhere warmer than here, and I don't doubt the admiralty will want us to determine where that might be."

The XO looked stunned for a moment as he processed what his commander had just said. There was going to be a war, and the troops in those transports to their north were troubling proof.

"Seriously, Captain? Are you having a laugh?" the officer asked, a note of incredulity slipping into his voice.

"Deadly serious, Tom," Davies said. "Though I hope to God I'm wrong."

# CHAPTER 41

1228 MSK, Sunday 13 Feb 1994
0928 Zulu
TAKR *Baku*, Barents Sea

C ONTRA-ADMIRAL IVANENKO SURVEYED the gray, windy surface of the Barents Sea through a large set of binoculars. From his perch on the flag bridge, he could see the dark gray, knife-like shapes of his task group's escorting warships arrayed in a broad circle around the flagship. Beyond the ships, Ivanenko could just make out the flitting shapes of a screen of ASW helicopters, their over-under coaxial rotors and squat, bulbous fuselages making them look for all the world like enormous bumblebees. These extended the reach of his search as the *contra-admiral* prosecuted his mission of locating the lurking American submarines. The crew of one these helicopters had just given Ivanenko's task force its first break in the twenty-four hours they had been at sea.

Ivanenko was beginning to wonder if the enemy submarines were really there when the report from the southern margin of the *Baku* group's perimeter arrived, stating that he had lowered his dipping sonar almost directly atop what sounded like an American *Los Angeles*-class submarine. Two other helicopters quickly converged on the location and a third took off from the carrier deck below, and they hammered the enemy submarine with active sonar pings, giving a precise if fleeting position on the American boat.

Ivanenko turned his attention to the nautical chart at the center of *Baku*'s flag bridge. Grease pencil marks on the Plexiglas-covered map showed the progress of the search operation. *It is truly amazing that we haven't found any American submarines until now*, he thought bitterly. Black grease marks indicated the long lines of sonobuoy sensors that now crisscrossed the southern Barents like a net. Ivanenko had never seen an effort like this, with literally dozens of maritime patrol aircraft and helicopters combing the waters off the Kola Peninsula with every sensor they could bring to bear. *Just as I planned.*

A crewman was finally adding a blue X to mark the contact. *The first of many*, Ivanenko told himself as he scanned the rest of the chart, refreshing his understanding of the evolving situation. A red mark to the chart's northwest indicated the position of *Baku*'s sister ship, the carrier *Kiev*, which, with her escorts, had transited his patrol area at high speed several hours before. That group had been unable to locate any enemy during their passage, but, *Kiev*'s objectives lay farther to the west and north. Elsewhere on the chart were the locations of Ivanenko's three hunter groups, slowly trawling through the sanitation area in an attempt to ambush any lurking NATO submarine.

Before the contact, Ivanenko was beginning to have doubts about his concept. The quiet American *Los Angeles*- and British *Trafalgar*-class submarines were notoriously difficult to detect, let alone track, but such a massive effort should have turned up *something*. *Contra-Admiral* Ivanenko did not even wish to consider how difficult detecting one of the newer American *Seawolf*s would be. Even randomly-placed depth charges had not spooked any lurking submarines into revealing their positions.

"Tell the screen commander," Ivanenko ordered his communications officer, standing on the far side of the map, "that I expect him to maintain a firm contact with this American." In the past, American submarines had proven dishearteningly adept at eluding their pursuers. The *contra-admiral* did not intend to allow this one to slip through his fingers before he had the opportunity to engage it. Ivanenko looked at his watch. The wait was growing interminable. *Should we have started shooting earlier?* he fretted. *Would it have been worth warning the Americans about what is coming?*

As Ivanenko's order was being transmitted another report came in.

"*Contra-Admiral!*" the young communications officer announced, "Hunter Group *V* just reported that they've detected another American submarine near the coast, another *Los Angeles*, sir!"

Good, thought Ivanenko, growing more confident by the minute, *very good. This plan is starting to bear fruit.* He doubted that these were the only two American submarines in these waters, but if he could bag both of them then he would have done much to clear the way for the rest of the fleet, now putting to sea from its bases along the Kola Inlet.

 **CHAPTER 42**

1500 MSK, Sunday 13 Feb 1994
1000 Zulu
Severomorsk Naval Base, Murmansk Oblast,
Russian Soviet Federative Socialist Republic

S AILORS CARRYING ALL manner of baggage and supplies scrambled up the gangplank onto the brick-colored deck of *Admiral Chabanenko* before quickly disappearing into the destroyer's interior. Captain (2nd Rank) Sergei Medvedev watched as his crew arrived for the surprise recall. Sergei had just received the news himself less than two hours ago. He was sipping a cup of tea from the ship's mess, strong and sweet, to deal with the hangover.

Medvedev was not in a good mood, having not expected this recall. *Of course*, he reflected darkly, *you did not expect a lot of things, did you?* Not the recall last night, not the fight with his mistress at the party, and certainly not his wife showing up and meeting the mistress. He hadn't even expected to get drunk last night, but that at least had been a predictable result of the wife and mistress fiasco. *Perhaps its better that I am going to sea right now,* he thought with a smirk, *let the sea swallow the troubles for me.*

The several months since Medvedev had taken over as captain of the *Admiral Chabanenko* had been a resounding disappointment. He'd taken his ship to sea exactly once. Much of his ship's work-up training had to be

296

conducted quay-side, and even that had been truncated by the need to fix numerous maintenance problems inherited from delinquent shipyard workers.

One positive of the quay-side time was the opportunity to upload full stocks of ammunition, less the nuclear-tipped ones his father had restricted. He should have been excited about this recall, the chance to finally take his ship back out to sea, but he was not confident in his crew or his ship's readiness. Thus, combined with the hangover and last night's feminine fireworks, his mood was dark to say the least. Crew members, picking up on their captain's cues, were discretely avoiding him.

Looking around the harbor, Medvedev could see the entire fleet was stirring. Across the harbor, the berths for *Kiev*, *Baku*, and their escorts were empty. *That* was something. Rarely did both helicopter carriers sortie at once. Something was clearly on the horizon.

Captain Medvedev watched as a junior officer, clearly a courier, pushed his way up the gangplank and through the hatch directly below the bridge. A few seconds later the man was handing over a packet of papers. Orders. Sergei accepted them and scanned their contents. *Interesting. I am assigned as lead anti-submarine ship for carrier* Admiral Kuznetsov. *"Strong escort,"* was how the orders put it. *This looks like*, the realization was slow through his headache, *a war order!* The vodka-induced mind fog began to fade. *Is that what's going on? War?*

Medvedev scanned further, then swore under his breath. He turned and barked at one of the enlisted men, "Go tell the chief of the ship to ensure the flag-bridge and quarters are prepared! The group captain and his staff will be embarking with us shortly." *Of all the lousy luck, I get stuck with that man*, Sergei thought, his blood pressure rising. He despised Group Captain Gordinya, the officer in charge of his destroyer squadron. The man thought he knew everything, listened to no one, and, in Sergei's opinion, had the intelligence of a particularly dull king crab. Gordinya, just like that invasive species, would soon be boarding *Admiral Chabanenko* whether he was wanted or not. *How long will we be out?* Medvedev thought, scanning the logistical portion of the order. The list of provisions that his *matrosi* were hauling on board was long, too long for a short cruise. *Can this be the real thing?* He wondered. *Probably not, but there was no telling what those warmongering Americans were up to these days.*

Over the opposite side of the pier, Medvedev could see the mighty battlecruiser *Kirov* preparing to get underway. That ship would also be part of *Kuznetsov*'s battle group. *If this* is *the real thing, it will be good to have that monster along.* A *Kirov* displaced more than a World War I dreadnought and was armed to the teeth with missiles. It was a formidable addition to any formation.

The captain looked back down at his own ship's quay to see Gordinya and his staff arriving. *At least I won't have to deal with the ladies,* he thought with a sigh, as he turned back to his quarters. War with the Americans seemed like a more welcoming prospect right now than facing his irate wife or mistress.

 **CHAPTER 43**

1105 CET, Sunday 13 February 1994
1005 Zulu
Ministry of Foreign Affairs, Victoria Terrasse, Oslo, Norway

K RISTEN HAGEN WAS spending her Sunday trying to smooth over
what had become a foreign relations disaster: the canceled winter Games.
Three hours of phone calls, faxes, and diplomatic notes to the participating nations explaining Norway's actions had been just the beginning.
The continuing drumbeat of news from the north, from central Europe, and
elsewhere around the world was leading Kristen to believe that she would be
composing notes of greater import for her minister soon. *Is this really what I
think it is? Are we on the brink of war, and just sitting here waiting for a superpower, the Russians or the Americans, to act?*

The foreign minister popped his head into Kristen's office and said with his
usual politeness, "Ms. Hagen, I've been reading the troubling news coming in
this morning and I am concerned our allies may be unnecessarily provoking
the Soviet Union at a very delicate time."

Of course, that's *what would concern him.* Kristen thought, growing ever
more frustrated with the man's deference to the people who were clearly
trying to pressure her country and its allies. Her previous chief, dead from a
stroke, had always managed to balance diplomacy with real backbone. The

new minister didn't seem as well-balanced. Firmness was what her country needed now, and her foreign minister, despite all his diplomatic skill, did not seem the man to provide it. *Fortunately, the prime minister and defense minister are made of sterner stuff.*

"I do not wish for Norway to be party to such provocations," said the minister. "I want you to go to the Akershus fortress and make sure the generals over there aren't going beyond what the prime minister has allowed."

"You want me to go and ensure they aren't mobilizing beyond what the prime minister wishes?" Kristen confirmed. She knew that the leader of Norway's government was even now sitting with the King, informing him that he intended to order a full mobilization to counter the Soviet threat. The foreign minister had resisted that decision, again with his usual politeness, continuing to argue for more time to allow diplomacy to diffuse the situation. Kristen was glad for the opportunity to go somewhere where people were actually *acting* as opposed to delaying. She stood, grabbed her jacket, and said, "I'm on my way."

Again, her chief seemed to waffle. "Perhaps not," he said. "Such an intrusion into the defense minister's prerogative at a time like this might be impolitic. Wait for now and perhaps you can go when we have greater clarity."

Kristen slumped back into her chair, still gripping her coat. She was trying to keep the exasperation out of her voice when she answered, "As you wish, Foreign Minister." *This man doesn't grasp the danger we are in.* Kristen turned back to her writing, her delay tactics and apologetic statements, *It's all meaningless.* She realized this with a sinking feeling as she started typing.

 **CHAPTER 44**

1400 MSK, Sunday 13 February 1994
1100 Zulu
Around Koskama Mount, four kilometers from the Norwegian border,
Murmansk Oblast, Russian Soviet Federative Socialist Republic

THE LAUNCH SITES had been carefully surveyed weeks before, six small clearings within sight of road P10, paralleling the Soviet-Norwegian frontier. Two days previous, groups of *gulag* prisoners had been trucked out to this cold, marshy slice of the Kola to walk back and forth over the deep snow in the clearings, packing it down sufficiently to allow the missile TELs—transporter erector launchers—to turn off the icy two-lane road and ride their eight huge wheels to the six very exactly marked points on the earth's surface.

The TELs had arrived yesterday, the launch crews erecting tents and firing up oil heaters against the long night ahead, remaining a safe distance away from their large, volatile weapons. Today their hour had come. At the six widely spaced locations, crews initiated the launch sequence. Hydraulic systems whined as they elevated the improved R-300 Elbrus missiles, known as the SS-1e "Scud-D" in the west, until they sat in the vertical launch position. In minutes this initial task was done, all six of the large missiles fueled, elevated, and inclined ever so slightly westward. The crews sat back in their nearby launch control vehicles and watched as their clock ticked down toward the designated time.

1205 CET, Sunday 13 Feb 1994
1105 Zulu
Banak Air Station, Lakselv, Troms, Norway

Rittmester Johansen watched Berg's column crunch and squeal onto the access road leading to the airfield's Coast Guard compound. He'd placed his squadron headquarters in the expansive Coast Guard hangar after making a circuit of his troop leaders' proposed positions around the wooded, mitten-shaped peninsula that housed Banak Air Station. As the lead truck slowed to a halt, the *rittmester* recognized his hulking executive officer in the passenger's seat. Berg yawned, fighting off the effects of the long drive from Skjöld. Behind Berg's G-Wagen an M113 rumbled past towing a second of the boxy personnel carriers. Johansen gawked as further back in the column another M113 turned onto the service road towing a truck which was itself still towing a Bofors gun. His amusement was cut short however when he saw the look on Berg's face. Then, the tall *løytnant* stepped from his vehicle and said, "Sir, there's going to be a war."

Back in the hangar Johansen handed a mug of bitter cocoa to Berg as the younger officer related the sabotage along the E6. Outside, the vehicle crews linked up with their dismounts and guides led the tracks and trucks away to their troop positions at the airfield and on the margins of Lakselv. Johansen had been feeling more confident before this troubling news arrived. He'd just returned from observing the emplacement of the 105-millimeter artillery battery, which had also been delayed on the road from the Porsangermoen. The battery commander, a fellow *kaptein*, and his troops were assigned to the training center at Porsangermoen, with the practical effect being that they emplaced and fired their guns far more frequently than the average battery and were at peak efficiency. All of that was not a substitute for the comfort that the rest of his battalion could provide.

"I need to call Bardufoss," said Johansen, turning and striding towards the office rooms housing the Coast Guard's tiny command center.

As he approached, his radioman stuck his head out of the door and called, "Sir, Battalion is on the line for you. They say it's urgent."

Erik increased his pace and took the handset of the civilian telephone from the young soldier. The high frequency radios that the squadron was supposed to use to talk back to Bardufoss were spotty at best over this range. The civilian telephone system was much more reliable, if less secure. "Johansen here."

"Johansen, this is Laub," said the major with his usual brusqueness. "What's your status up there?"

"Sir, my vehicles just arrived. They encountered obstacles along their way here that my *løytnant* described as sabotage. There was a vehicle wreck blocking the Sørstraumen Bru and a full-on abatis further east."

"Sabotage? Why is this the first we're hearing of it?" snapped the operations officer, an edge in his voice.

"Sir, we're operating hundreds of kilometers apart. The HF radios have been very unreliable since we left, and besides, *Løytnant* Berg was observing radio silence, per your instructions," responded Johansen, sticking up for his subordinate. He had opposed the radio blackout restriction, and didn't want his XO to suffer one of Major Laub's tongue lashings for no reason. "He used his wreckers to clear the bridge and explosives to get through the abatis."

Laub grunted. "We're seeing some troubling signs elsewhere too," the major relented. "The situation has deteriorated over the past couple of hours. The prime minister just approved full mobilization and the forward deployment of 2nd Battalion, followed by all of Brigade *Nord*." That would put the brigade on the road in the next couple of hours, Johansen knew.

"I'm headed back up to Skjöld soon to move with the headquarters. What are your deployments up there?" Laub asked.

"We're very thin. I have a troop east of the town, a section each at the airfield and screening south of the town, and I'm keeping the anti-tank section and the pioneers in reserve. The battery from Porsangermoen is set up west of the airfield. All as we rehearsed on the last alert."

Laub grunted again. "Well, the battalion should be there after midnight. If the war holds off for another day, we'll be ready. There aren't any flights available for an advance party so we'll default to the standard deployment areas. Keep Brigade informed of any other developments. Laub out."

The line clicked off abruptly. Johansen stood for a moment holding the handset. Conversations with the major were usually unpleasant, one-sided affairs. He would have appreciated a little more insight into the "troubling signs" Laub had mentioned. If the Russians really were coming, he would need every advantage he could get.

 **CHAPTER 45**

0625 EST, Sunday 13 February 1994
1125 Zulu
Brighton Beach Avenue, Brooklyn, New York City, New York, USA

VOLKHOV, ABANDONING THE Mr. Taylor identity earlier that morning, swore, vehemently and repeatedly. Losing his temper so openly was out of character; he was a professional. At least he'd remembered to utter his oaths in English, rather than Russian. The *Spetsnaz* officer slammed his fist into the side of the object of his rage, the rental van that was to carry him and his team to their target. Looking down the alley towards the beach from where he stood, Volkhov could see his objective across the wide, gray waters of New York Harbor.

We should be over there right now, waiting outside the station gates! Volkhov raged to himself. As far as he knew, every other team was already in position around the city, ready to execute their parts in the plan hatched months before. *And here we sit! Why did we not position ourselves in New Jersey yesterday?* The hindsight was almost too much to take.

Shaking the pain out of his hand he noticed that he had left an indent in the van's exterior. *Good! Piece of trash,* he cursed again at the silent vehicle. The six men had departed the safe house before dawn, carrying their heavy duffels, and loaded themselves into the rental. Not until they were all comfortably ensconced in their seats had the driver turned the ignition and nothing happened. Several more turns of the key and an inspection under the hood had brought the realization that the problem was the battery, or rather the fact that there was no battery under the hood any more.

It hadn't taken long to realize that some hooligan had decided to lift their van's battery for his own uses, whatever those were. If Volkhov could have found the man now he would not have hesitated to kill him with his bare hands.

Instead, he was forced to stand by while the deep-cover restaurant owner worked to acquire a new battery. That process had eaten up minutes, then hours. Now, here they sat, scant time before they were to execute their operation, within tantalizing sight of their objective. As was expected of *Spetsnaz* leaders, Volkhov had assigned his own team the most difficult objective. *It will be much more difficult if they are alert and waiting for us.*

0630 EST, Sunday 13 February 1994
1130 Zulu
US Coast Guard Sandy Hook Station, Ft. Hancock, New Jersey

The six members of the incoming US Coast Guard watch shift sat beside their counterparts on the outgoing shift. The night watch officer updated everyone on the situation in their area of responsibility, the busy and expansive harbor and ports of New York and New Jersey. The twelve men were all familiar with each other after years of service together, and low murmuring about the debacle enveloping the Winter Games in Norway and the Soviet invasion of Poland had filled the smallish watch room until the briefing officer cleared his throat.

"We've got a chilly morning out there, twenty-eight degrees with moderate winds from the northwest. Heavy cloud cover, sea state three, with a chance of isolated snow and sleet over the water."

Transitioning away from the weather he went on, "The cutter *Dallas* is outbound for a four-day fisheries patrol and will be out of our area in about four hours. We have *Tahoma* inbound from Kittery, Maine. She'll be tying up at Governor's Island for some maintenance later today. Patrol boat *Adak* has duty off Staten Island this morning. For air support, we have…" The officer went through the drill, listing each resource at the Coast Guard's disposal in and around the New York Harbor area. The incoming shift, and their leader, USCG Commander Jim Ingalls, listened with the boredom that comes with routine until—

"Wait a minute," Ingalls interrupted, "say that again? The Air Force is doing what?"

The briefer paused and looked back down at his clipboard. "Oh yeah," he said, "I forgot to mention this at the beginning. We got word a few hours ago that we're at DEFCON Four. No real change for us, just keep our eyes and ears open more than normal. The Air Force has an AWACS bird up patrolling south of Long Island and the Air National Guard has some fighters up as well."

"DEFCON Four?" Ingalls asked, surprised, "that's a big deal, Hank. Any instructions come with it on what we're supposed to do?"

"Nope," answered Hank, eager to finish up his shift and get home, "just 'assume DEFCON Four,' that's what it says, Jim."

"Okay," Ingalls said, not completely satisfied.

"For surface traffic," Hank went on, "today we have six outbound, four transiting, and nine inbound. The biggest inbound is the cruise ship SS *Queen Elizabeth 2*, finishing up a trans-Atlantic crossing. She's southeast of Long Island right now. The most concerning outbound is that Bulgarian deep-sea trawler, the," Hank checked his clipboard, "the *Trogg*, that's been dragging her feet in port for repairs the last few days. Oh, and there's one of those Soviet intelligence-gathering ships, the *Kursagraf*, making its way up the Jersey Shore, staying just outside our twelve-mile territorial waters. Standard snooping stuff. She's under Algerian registry and flying the Finnish flag, but we know she's Soviet."

Ingalls nodded. "Nothing we can do about that," he said. "*Dallas* is keeping an eye on her?"

Hank nodded the affirmative.

Ingalls went on, "Can we have the Port Authority board that trawler, the *Trogg* you said? Check for contraband or something?"

"I don't see why not," Hank smirked, and nodded to one of the other watch officers, who made the radio call while the briefing continued. Then Hank went on, "Other than that, normal small boat traffic expected during the day, normal Sunday air traffic out of JFK, La Guardia, and Newark, and we can expect the pleasure seekers and flying schools to have their small planes airborne in the next couple of hours. Questions?"

Ingalls had lots of questions, especially about this DEFCON Four business, but it was clear Hank didn't have the answers, or the patience to answer. He shook his head. "No. Head on home, Hank. We've got the Sunday shift. Should be quiet as usual. I hope."

0640 EST, Sunday 13 February 1994
1140 Zulu
Near Asbury Park, New Jersey, USA

The farmer sat in his beat-up Chevy pickup. His breath was white in the cold of the pre-dawn light, the truck's idling engine loud in the damp, icy air. Sipping a mug of coffee to fend off the cold he was feeling in his bones, the old man watched the first of three small planes bump down to the end of the long-abandoned grass runway to start its takeoff run. The three aircraft—two single-engine Piper Cherokees and a twin-engine Beechcraft—had been occupying the abandoned airfield's lone dilapidated hangar, which had been used as a barn until recently. This morning was the first time that the farmer had seen all three pilots arrive at the same time.

This small, rural plot of land in eastern New Jersey had once been known as the Asbury Park Neptune Air Terminal. It had been a popular hub for skydivers, novice fliers, and vintage aircraft enthusiasts before high taxes had forced its closure more than two decades before. The farmer had bought the land in the hopes of turning some of the old grass runways and taxiways towards crops, but rains often flooded the low-lying areas, including the runway, and in the end he'd been saddled with the same tax burden that had doomed the air terminal, without much agricultural production to show for it. Even his secondary reason for buying the airstrip, a desire to fly his own Cessna 172 aircraft on occasion without needing to pay the airport fees, had failed when his eyesight had begun to go.

Thus, when the strange man with a foreign accent had approached him three weeks ago and offered to rent the old hangar for a handsome sum, the farmer jumped at the opportunity. The money had duly been deposited in the farmer's nearly empty bank account, and a couple days later the planes had arrived, bouncing down onto the old runway that now ran through a low canyon of new growth trees. Not until last night had the farmer considered that the FAA or someone else in the government might be interested in planes taking off from his farmland, and he'd come down here this morning to see if he could clear up the issue with the pilots.

Unfortunately, he was too late for conversation. The three planes' engines were already coughing to life, propellers spinning in the early morning light, when he pulled up in his trusty pickup. *Well*, the farmer considered, *as long as nobody asks any questions…what people don't know can't hurt 'em.* He sat back to watch the takeoff not realizing how wrong he was.

The old man reached down to turn on his radio, tuning in to one of the few country music stations in this decidedly *un*-country part of the US as the Beechcraft's engines howled to max. The plane started its takeoff roll, gaining speed as it traveled down the runway. When it passed in front of the farmer's truck, a loud burst of static came through his radio speakers, drowning out the crooning sounds of his country music. *That's odd*, he thought, turning the volume down and then back up as static receded.

The first plane was just winging into the air as the second began to roll. The static blaring inside the truck each time one of the two Piper Cherokees took off. *Must be some sort of transponder*, thought the farmer. As the third aircraft rolled past him, he noted the tail number: 216R. He watched this plane as it climbed into the air and then banked left before settling into an easterly course, flying into the gray light of the winter dawn.

The three aircraft each took a different course, all flying generally east, until they crossed the Jersey Shore and went "feet wet" over the cold, gray waters outside the broad, natural entrance of New York Harbor.

 **CHAPTER 46**

1448 MSK, Sunday 13 February 1994
1148 Zulu
**USS *New York City* (SSN 696), western edge of X-Ray Station,
eighty miles west of USS *Connecticut*, Barents Sea**

G OD HELP US, thought Captain Alan Jones.
The half-prayer sprung from his half-remembered childhood,
enduring long, cold services in his family's drafty Catholic parish
in Cape Cod.

"Con, sonar," came the latest call from the sonar room, "new contact near
aboard, active sonobuoy bearing zero-seven-seven! Designate this contact as
Alpha Two-Two."

Jones, USS *New York City*'s shave-headed skipper, winced. He and his boat
were in a bad spot, and he knew it. The waters of the Barents Sea were already
claustrophobically shallow for big nuke-boats like his *Los Angeles*-class submarine, and his proximity to the Soviet coast of the Kola made it even more so.

"XO," Jones said, tension creeping into his voice as he walked over to his
executive officer standing at the map table, "what's the plot look like?"

"Not good, Captain," was the response. "That makes four active buoys
in the last half hour," the officer moved his finger to the map, indicating
locations, "this latest contact makes two to the east, one directly north, and

the fourth is to our south. Along with that dipping sonar that's been working to the west, we're pretty well boxed in."

"What about surface contacts?" asked the captain.

The XO traced his finger across the chart to the southeast of the line marking the sub's course. "Sir, we're tracking four skunks right now, bearing is about zero-eight-zero. They're in a group, diamond formation. One is a *Grisha*-class frigate for sure, one may be a *Pauk*, but no ID on the other two yet. They're closing on our location at twenty-two knots." That was an ASW hunter-killer group if he'd ever seen one, thought the captain. *Looks like they know where we are.*

"What about that *Victor* we got a sniff of a few minutes ago?" prompted Jones, asking after a faint submarine contact the sonar room had reported to their east.

The XO shook his head, saying, "We lost him. He was closing in our direction, doing about twelve knots. Assuming no change in course or speed, he should be right here." The XO pointed to a spot very close to theirs.

Aircraft, surface ships, and a submarine all hunting us, Jones considered. *How am I going to get us out of this one?* The skipper wiped his brow. He'd been in some tense spots before, but he'd never been boxed in and hunted like this, never seen the Russians put so many resources into such a small space. *They can't be doing this everywhere, can they? Did we stumble into some sort of major exercise?* The DEFCON Four warning, however, indicated that they should expect some trouble. *Regardless,* he thought, settling on a course of action, *this is too much trouble already. We need to get out of this fix.*

"We'll bring her up into the layer." he announced. "Helm, make your depth one-five-zero feet, speed six knots, course three-two-zero. We'll try and squeeze between that northern buoy and the dipping sonar, see if we can get out of the way of that ASW group."

1553 MSK, Sunday 13 February 1994
1253 Zulu
TAKR *Baku*, Barents Sea, forty miles northwest of USS *New York City*

"*Contra-Admiral!*" the communications officer called to Ivanenko over the low thrum of the carrier's engines as Ivanenko's task force accelerated west through gray seas under a canopy of mottled white clouds and ice-blue sky. "*Hunter Group V* reports that Submarine Contact Two has changed course to the north. They are shifting a helicopter to try to close the perimeter, but the group captain worries he may lose the contact if the submarine shoots the gap."

Ivanenko looked at his watch and fretted. *So close! Don't lose them now!* "What of Submarine Contact One?" Ivanenko asked tensely. He referred to the submarine their helicopter had detected to the north.

The staff officer responsible for ASW spoke up, "Our helicopters are maintaining faint contact, *tovarich* Admiral, but we have lost him several times. These American submarines are very difficult to detect, let alone track." It was the wrong thing to say, and the staff officer knew it, before the words were even out of his mouth.

Ivanenko fixed the man with his gaze and said icily, "I know that, you fool. Why do you think we have every seaworthy patrol craft in the fleet out here looking for them? Why do you think we have every airworthy patrol aircraft up hunting them?"

The man wilted under Ivanenko's stress-induced assault.

The *contra-admiral* looked at his watch again and came to a decision. *Attacking a few minutes early won't matter now, and it may prevent us from losing the prey*, he reasoned. He had the authority to do so straight from Marshal Rosla. Looking back up at the staff officer he ordered, "Tell our ASW screen and Hunter Group *V* to engage the contacts."

The officer blinked, "Sir?"

"Tell the group captain," Ivanenko said slowly, enunciating every word, "to destroy those two American submarines. We are at war, *tovarich*, though you may have been too slow to realize it until now."

 **CHAPTER 47**

1555 MSK, Sunday 13 February 1994
1155 Zulu
Crane Flight, Over the Gulf of Motovsky, Norway-USSR Border

MAJOR SASHA MITROSHENKO of the Soviet Air Force, called the *VVS*, or *Voenno-Vozdushnye Sily* in Russian, concentrated on keeping his light-gray twin-engine Sukhoi Su-27 air superiority fighter level. He was flying three hundred meters above the choppy, gray waves of the Barents Sea, and the wind fought him for every knot. He had just led his tight formation of eight fighters, callsign "Crane," in a gentle, low altitude turn to the west after taking off from their base at Kilp Yavr on the Kola Peninsula a few minutes ago. The pilot's concentration, however, did not prevent him from savoring the raw power of the engines pushing his sleek fighter forward at over five hundred knots.

Mitroshenko was intensely proud of his bird, and of his elite position within the *VVS*. Being selected to fly one of the Su-27s, codenamed "Flanker" by westerners, was a mark of the service's regard for his skill as a fighter pilot. The advanced Sukhoi fighter had been designed to challenge the American F-15 Eagle, supposedly the best air superiority fighter in the world, for control of the sky. *We will have to test that theory soon enough, won't we?* he thought with grim excitement.

Not yet, though. Right now, the advanced Soviet fighters and their pilots would be opposed by a small number of piddly single-engine Norwegian F-16s. Ten to twelve at most was the estimate in the mission briefing. *Those Norwegians jets are out of date and out of time*, he thought, feeling ever more the predator. His flight, and a second flight of eight more Su-27s crossing the frontier further south near the Finnish border, would swat the F-16s from the sky. Their real mission, however, was blinding the NATO defenders in the critical opening moments of the offensive by shooting down the AWACS airborne radar aircraft that was now circling off the northwest coast of Norway.

Pulling back on his stick slightly, he gained elevation as he and his seven compatriots flashed over the barren, white Rybachy Peninsula, their last terrain checkpoint before they were committed. They were paralleling the north coast of the Kola on a heading that would take them over the east-facing Varangerfjord, a course that would allow the aircraft to penetrate deep into Norway over nominally international waters before finally violating Norwegian airspace. Mitroshenko was banking on the rocky walls of the fjord to hide his low-flying jets from NATO radars until the last possible moment.

The snowy western coast of the Rybachy Peninsula flashed by underneath, yielding once again to the dark waters of the Barents Sea. Mitroshenko's pulse quickened as he keyed his radio and said, "Crane, this is Crane Lead, final checkpoint. Three minutes."

1257 CET, Sunday 13 Feb 1994
1157 Zulu
Viper Two-One, over Banak Air Station, Lakselv, Finnmark, Norway

"Viper Two-One, this is Magic," Jan Olsen heard the controller on the AWACS call through his helmet speakers, "you have multiple bandits heading your way. Bearing one-one-two degrees true from your location, range eight-five miles, speed five hundred-plus, angels one. You are clear to engage if they cross the border. Over." The E-3 Sentry's large, rotating radar had detected multiple unidentified contacts to the east of Olsen's position. "Angels one" signifying that the contacts were at approximately one thousand feet of altitude. The disturbing message was delivered in the emotionless monotone practiced by crewmen of control aircraft, meant to calm nerves in stressful situations. *Situations like this*, Jan thought.

"Roger, Magic," he responded, "turning to intercept." Olsen then keyed his radio again, calling his wingman, whose jet he could see several dozen meters off his wing outside his bubble canopy, and saying, "Viper Two-Two, hard-right zero-nine-zero, dropping to angels ten. Switches hot," this referred to the arming switches for six AIM-9L Sidewinder heat-seeking missiles attached to his wings, "on my mark…Execute!"

My God, this might be the real thing, Olsen thought, as he banked his nimble F-16 "Falcon" to the east and dove, settling onto a reciprocal course to the oncoming Russian jets.

"Bjorn," Olsen said, calling his wingman again, "it looks like they're coming up the Varangerfjord. We'll do it like we talked about this morning. Follow me down." He heard two clicks over the radio as Bjorn acknowledged without speaking. Jan's right hand applied slight forward pressure to the video-game-like sidestick to put his jet into a shallow dive. He watched the cockpit dials spin downward with the altitude while also scanning the sky ahead through the glass of his heads-up display and canopy.

As the two Norwegian F-16s closed with the approaching bandits, Olsen heard the AWACS controllers ordering, "Viper Base, Viper Bases Two, Three, and Four, this is Magic, scramble ready flights," instructing all the ready F-16s sitting on the tarmac, dispersed to fields around Northern Norway, into the air. The controller continued, giving orders to the other pairs of F-16s west of Olsen, "Viper One-One, vector zero-four-five, angels thirty. Viper Two-Three, support Viper Two-One…"

This is *the real thing!* Olsen realized, as the controllers in the E-3 calmly began to maneuver the Norwegian jets into position to parry the coming blow. Viper Two-Three, the flight of two F-16s patrolling over the North Cape to the north of Banak, would come south to support Olsen's flight, while the two Falcons of Viper One-One moved to intercept a southern group of bandits that had just appeared on the Sentry crew's radar scopes.

Across Northern Norway, pairs of F-16s converged on the two groups of bandits hurtling towards the frontier. The Norwegian pilots, excepting Olsen and Bjorn, kept their fighters at high altitude, while the Russians hugged the wavetops of the Barents Sea and the rugged arctic snowscape of the Kola. In the north, Viper Two-Three was replacing Olsen's flight over Banak, directly in the path of the first group of bandits, while Olsen and Bjorn went into a steep dive for the deck, heading east.

"Magic, this is Viper Two-One," Olsen said, tension giving his voice an edge as he bottomed out his dive, two hundred feet above the tundra, "range to those bandits?" They were speaking in English, standard practice when dealing with the multinational crews aboard the NATO AWACS.

"Five-zero miles, Viper Two-One," replied Magic. "Count is eight bandits headed your way." At a closing speed of over a thousand miles per hour the two groups of sleek, modern warbirds would cover that distance in less than three minutes.

"Magic, this is Tasman," Olsen heard over his radio. "Tasman" was the callsign of the Norwegian electronic countermeasures aircraft that was aloft to support the AWACS and the patrolling fighters. "We're detecting multiple emissions. We have good tracks on at least five Su-27 fire control radars from the group east of Banak, four more from the group one-two-five miles to the south, over."

Flankers, thought Olsen, *this is going to be tough.* The Sukhoi was a formidable aircraft, not quite as nimble as his own smaller F-16, but capable of carrying more missiles, including the radar-homing AA-10 "Alamo" that far out-ranged his own heat-seeking Sidewinders.

Olsen edged his stick slightly to the left, taking his aircraft just to the north of the Varangerfjord, down which the approaching Soviet jets were hurtling at near-wavetop level. In moments he was over the broken, low shrublands and snowfields of the Varangerhalvøya National Park, a low string of hills masking his two Falcons from the Russians over the fjord southeast to their right.

"Magic, range!" Olsen demanded.

"One-five miles to your south-south-west, Two-One," was the immediate, monotone reply.

The plan they had worked out called for the two F-16s of Viper Two-Three's flight to remain over Banak, drawing the attention of the Russian pilots, while Olsen and Bjorn used the rough terrain of the park to swing around to the north and get onto the tail of the intruders. It was a good plan, but they hadn't really anticipated four-to-one odds against Su-27s in this opening engagement.

Engagement! The realization hit Olsen again as he came to grips with the incredible changes turning his world upside down. Time seemed to slow down into a long, silent pause, but he was ripped out of the moment by the reality of his situation. *There won't be time for pausing this day*, he thought as he settled into the mindset he knew he'd need to survive. The Norwegian was suddenly and intensely aware of the frigid air rushing past his jet, of Bjorn to the right and slightly behind his own fighter, the brown scrub and white tundra below, and the Soviet fighters out of sight beyond the hills to his right. Just two days ago he had been preparing to take the weekend off and enjoy the national celebration that the Olympics provided. That he was about to launch missiles at Soviet fighters invading his country was surreal.

Olsen brought himself back into action. The pilot now reacted on instinct, allowing his training to take over, speaking in rapid-fire commands. "Viper Two-Two," Olsen called to Bjorn, "hard right and level. Now!"

Both fighters stood on their right wingtips in unison and rocketed through a gap in the low hills to their south, flashing over the coast mere meters above the small fishing village of Vadsø, then out over the dark, choppy waters of the fjord, continuing to bank until they had completely reversed their course and were flying east, in the same direction and behind the Russian fighters.

Now Olsen began scanning the sky above and to his front. *There!* He could see the dark spots of…*Four? There should be eight. Where are the others?*

"Eight miles, directly ahead of you, Viper Two-One," called Magic, a note of tension starting to creep into the normally unflappable controller's voice. "One is gaining altitude!"

"Bjorn, afterburners. Now!" Olsen ordered. Both men pushed their throttles all the way forward, accelerating their aircraft through Mach 1 to close the range on the tails of the Soviet interceptors.

In seconds, the Norwegians had pulled within missile range of the larger Flankers. Olsen could see the glow of the Sukhois' powerful, widely-spaced engines as he and Bjorn edged up, below and behind the bigger jets. Then he heard it.

"All Viper flights, this is Magic. Bandits have crossed the international border in force. Clear to engage. I repeat you are clear to engage. Good hunting and God be with you."

Jan Olsen took in a sharp breath of the oxygen flowing through his mask as he flipped the safety off the trigger on his joystick and completed the arming of his Sidewinder missiles. He swallowed, then called, "Bjorn, you take the right two, I'll take the left two. Engage on my mark."

Two clicks in his headset signaled Bjorn's acknowledgment.

Olsen looked through his heads-up display as the box indicating his first missile's infrared seeker settled onto the center-left Flanker, which was growing larger in his field of view by the second. The growl in his ears told him the missile was locked on. The Norwegian took another breath, whispered a brief prayer, and squeezed the trigger on his joystick, while at the same time announcing, "Fox Two!"

PART VI: H-HOUR

"Let your plans be dark and impenetrable as night,
and when you move, fall like a thunderbolt."
—Sun Tzu

CHAPTER 48

1300 CET, Sunday 13 February 1994
1200 Zulu
Over Varangerfjord, Norway-USSR Border

T HE SIDEWINDER LEAPT off its rail under Olsen's right wing and shot forward like a dart, leaving only the barest trace of a smoke trail for the Norwegian to mark the missile's course. At nearly the same instant, he heard Bjorn call "Fox Two!" as well, and another dart shot forward to his right. The Norwegians had been nearly within gun range when they launched, and Olsen fought the urge to watch his missile all the way into the Russian's tail pipes. Instead, he started to lock the seeker head of his next missile onto the leftmost Flanker just as the first Sidewinder exploded, sending clouds of shrapnel into the Su-27's engines. *One*, Olsen thought. Bjorn's missile exploded in the next instant as a jet of yellow flame shot out the back of his target. *Two.*

Olsen issued his "Splash one!" call over the radio just before Bjorn followed up with "Splash two!"

Olsen felt time speed up. The two stricken Flankers began to break up and fall from the sky in powered dives towards the snowy hills below. Olsen saw the brief burn of a rocket engine as one of the enemy pilots ejected. The F-16 jockey then had to jerk his small side-stick right, banking his fighter sharply to avoid a piece of Russian tailfin that had separated from its airframe. The maneuver threw off the Norwegian's aim, slowing his effort to get a good lock with his next Sidewinder. He reset his sights on the next twin-tailed Soviet jet and watched as the target box on his heads-up display wobbled, then settled around the profile of the Flanker.

Another growl in his headset told Olsen that is was time to launch his second missile of the war, but just as his finger tightened around the side-stick's trigger, the Su-27 in front of him pulled up and to the right in a nearly impossible 9G turn, releasing a string of brightly burning magnesium flares as it did so. Olsen pulled his stick back and to the right and worked his rudder pedals to stay on the Russian's tail while announcing "Fox Two!" once again. Another AIM-9L rocketed off its launch rail. Olsen knew it was a bad shot almost before the missile had cleared his wing. The Russian's turn had placed the flares into the crosshairs of the Sidewinder's infrared seeker instead of the Flanker's hot engine exhaust, and the weapon shot skyward, missing the Sukhoi's up-turned left wing by dozens of meters as both aircraft made their afterburner-fueled climbing turn to the north.

Olsen grunted as the high Gs of the maneuver pressed him into his seat. Both jets slowed as they executed their tight climbing turn, trading speed for altitude. *He's almost turning inside of me,* Olsen realized, the hairs rising on the back of his neck. The more powerful thrust from the Flanker's two big, afterburning engines was allowing it to pull away from the single-engine Norwegian F-16 in the climb, creating distance between the two aircraft. Olsen tried to bring the nose of his Falcon up a little more to give the seeker-head of his next Sidewinder a look at the Flanker.

There! The Russian eased up on his turn ever so slightly, bringing his aircraft into the Norwegian's frontal arc. Both fighters had reversed their course and were now flying east. Olsen heard once again the growl in his headset and squeezed the trigger, calling another "Fox Two!" as he did so.

The Sidewinder shot forward before curving up and to the right in an almost impossibly tight turn. Jan felt his heart thump once in his chest as he watched the weapon close with its prey, then disappear in a flash as the warhead detonated into an expanding cone of shrapnel. The Flanker shuddered visibly as its pilot nosed over and dove. Olsen tried to follow to make sure of the kill, but in that moment his ears were assaulted by the alarm of his

RWR, radar warning receiver, telling him that an enemy fire control radar had locked onto his aircraft.

Olsen snapped his stick over and dove back towards the fjord below, trying to break the enemy radar lock in the rugged terrain of the rocky coastline. *Where is it coming from?* He craned his neck around his canopy to try to catch a glimpse of his attacker, while calling to Bjorn, "Two-Two, jammers on!" He reached with his left hand to switch on his own fighter's DECM, or defensive electronic countermeasures.

Next, Olsen called the controlling AWACS, "Magic, Viper Two-One, I've got a fire control radar locked onto me. Where is he coming from?"

Instead of Magic, the crew on the nearby electronic warfare aircraft answered, "Two-One, Tasman, we're making noise at him, over."

Powerful radio waves, traveling at the speed of light, traversed the dozens of miles from Tasman's jammers to the two AA-10 Alamo missiles streaking towards Olsen's F-16, degrading their ability to react to the Su-27's control radar.

At the same time, Magic called, "Two-One, he's to your ten o'clock relative, angels four and closing. His targeting radar is on! Evade!" The warning was unnecessary; Jan's on-board RWR was already screaming at him that the Soviet fighter's radar was locked onto his aircraft.

Olsen pulled his stick even more to the right, trying to fly at a right angle to the incoming missiles. His eyes snapped to his left to try to pick them out of the sky.

There! Two dark dots at the head of thin contrails. He pulled the stick left, banking the aircraft to create an increasingly acute turn for the incoming missiles to navigate while keeping just above the wavetops. Pulling up slightly as he went "feet dry" over the northern coast of the fjord, Olsen reached down with his left hand and triggered chaff, packets of radar-reflective foil that exploded behind his aircraft in clouds to further confuse the missiles' seekers. Now the Norwegian could only hold his turn and watch the two contrails grow rapidly larger to his left rear. After what seemed an eternity but, in reality, was less than two heartbeats, the two missiles flashed behind his fighter's tailfin and exploded into the chaff, missing the F-16 by several hundred meters. Olsen felt his jet buffet from the explosions as he leveled out above the familiar, stark snow and rocks of Norway's far north.

Relieved, the Norwegian thought, *Thanks for the help, Tasman, they missed.*

A moment later, Olsen heard, "Two-One this is Magic, you've got two on your tail, eight o'clock, over."

The pilot felt his insides tighten as he craned his helmeted head, scanning through his visor for the two Flankers that were diving on him. In his maneuvers to evade the missiles, Olsen had allowed the Russians to get behind him. *I'm in trouble now,* he realized.

"Bjorn!" he called, fear giving his voice an urgency that had been lacking just minutes before, "where are you?"

"Hang on, Jan!" Bjorn called.

Olsen spied the two approaching jets as they dropped to scrub-top level directly behind him. Now on the north side of a ridgeline and flying east, their radars were unaffected by Tasman's powerful electronic rays. Jan looked back again just as his RWR started blaring once more, in time to see two flashes from beneath the wings of the righthand Sukhoi.

"Missiles inbound!" called Olsen, more loudly than he intended.

In the same instant he heard Bjorn call, "Two-One, break right!"

Jan clicked his microphone twice as he threw his stick to the right while at the same time pulling upward to gain altitude and launching chaff with his other hand. Bjorn said something, but Jan didn't register. He was too focused on his immediate threat, his RWR screaming at him, and the ground rushing by just a few dozen meters below. He looked back again, now out the rear-right of his canopy, trying in vain to catch a glimpse of missiles flying towards him at incredible speed. *I'm not going to make it,* he realized.

In that moment Olsen saw both Russian jets violently bank to their left and upwards. The RWR alarm in his headset fell silent, and both missiles shot past his left wingtip as the guidance they had been receiving from the launching aircraft's radar disappeared. Olsen craned to look out the rear-left of his canopy, keeping the Flankers in his sight, just in time to see a thin smoke trail intersect with one of them as an AIM-9L ploughed into its right engine nacelle, sending the graceful jet tumbling wing-over-wing into the rocks and snow below.

"Splash four!" called Bjorn triumphantly. *Four?* thought Olsen.

"Going after the other one," Bjorn was saying as he dove to pursue the surviving Flanker, which was fleeing east.

Magic interjected, "Negative, Viper Two-Two. Come to heading two-seven-zero, angels fifteen, and withdraw. We are picking up multiple bandits, approximate count two-zero and climbing, approaching from the east. Two bandits to your west headed our way at high speed. Viper Two-Three is vectoring to intercept. You come back and help, over."

Twenty more bogeys headed our way, thought Olsen as he brought his fighter back around to a westerly heading and began to climb. Bjorn joined him in formation on his wing. *How are we supposed to fight against numbers like that?* He took quick stock of the situation: three missiles left on his craft, two on Bjorn's. *Two Flankers ahead, two dozen bad guys behind.* He'd escaped two attacks by the Soviets' premier fighter and, together with his wingman, had downed *Four? Five? Three minutes into the war and I'm already losing track of what's going on.*

———

Major Mitroshenko swore into his oxygen mask. *Four aircraft lost in the first minutes of war. Proklyatye!* The Soviet pilot swore again. Crane Six had just called to report that he was pulling back across the border. Crane Eight was limping home on one engine and a shredded wing. That left only Mitroshenko, Crane Lead, and his wingman to face the NATO fighters aloft and complete their mission against the AWACS.

The *VVS* major clenched his jaw to put his rage aside, forcing himself to stop replaying the mistakes that had made a hash of his squadron over the past few minutes. He shoved the throttles forward to their stops, accelerating towards the lumbering radar plane now just sixty-five kilometers to his front.

"Lead, this is Two," the Soviet pilot heard his wingman call, "I see two contacts approaching from the northwest on my radar, ten-thousand meters altitude."

"You take them, Two," ordered Mitroshenko. "I'm going on to the radar control plane."

Crane Two's aircraft veered off the major's wing, vectoring northwest. After several moments, the other pilot volleyed off two of his Vympel R-27 missiles, called AA-10 by their western enemies, at the nearer of the two approaching

F-16s. Mitroshenko continued his climb towards the AWACS, which was now turning west and diving in an attempt to escape.

The oncoming Falcons broke left and right to avoid the R-27s, but the geometry of the Norwegians' approach vector conspired to ensure that Tasman's powerful jammers couldn't intervene to degrade the Soviet missiles' performance. The weapons streaked toward the lead F-16, which was desperately turning to evade. One of the missiles detonated just meters from the Falcon's cockpit, sending jagged shrapnel through aircraft and pilot. The Norwegian jet dropped from the sky, spinning towards the scattered clouds below.

The second Norwegian pilot, however, managed to evade and would soon be on Mitroshenko's tail. Crane Two, who had needed to keep his radar pointed at the lead F-16 for the entire length of his missiles' flight, was only now turning to intervene in favor of his leader.

Damn, thought the Soviet major, judging the range to the NATO AWACS, *not as close as I would like. Still, I'm in range…*

"Lead, he's closing on you!" called Mitroshenko's wingman.

That did it. Mitroshenko reached down and activated the two special weapons he had carried into battle for just this target. The R-27P missiles possessed a passive, as opposed to active, radar-homing seeker, designed to zero in on the radar emissions of another aircraft, rather than be guided to its target by the launching aircraft's own radar beams. Its improved seventy-five kilometer range made it a perfect weapon for engaging distant targets emitting powerful radar signals, targets like the E-3 Sentry AWACS ahead of him.

Mitroshenko craned his neck to look behind, trying to close the range by every kilometer possible before launching the R-27Ps and turning to deal with the fighter chasing him. He could see the smaller enemy jet, about four miles distant and turning into his six. Crane Two was maneuvering behind him for a shot, but Mitroshenko's wingman would not be able to engage in time. *No bother*, Mitroshenko thought grimly, *I've got something for you*, Norge.

Crane Lead twisted back around so he was looking forward and allowed his two special missiles' seekers to lock onto the diving AWACS. When both gave the same positive signal, he squeezed his joystick trigger twice. The two big missiles leapt off their rails, arcing upwards into the stratosphere on a ballistic course for the NATO control plane, fifty kilometers to Mitroshenko's front.

— -

Aboard Magic, a controller watching his scope suddenly called "Shit! Sir, I have separation on two small objects coming from that Flanker, closing with us!"

The tactical director on the AWACS, a US Air Force lieutenant colonel named McCall, responded through his intercom. "Has he locked onto us?"

"No sir, he's not even emitting," answered the airman.

That's strange, thought the light colonel, feeling uneasy. Then the memory hit him, *Passive homing missiles. They're tracking in on our own signal!*

"Shut down the radar!" McCall ordered into the headset of everyone in the converted Boeing 707's long fuselage, where more than thirty crew members were working to control the fight over this frontier with the Soviet foe, "Shut it down, NOW!" He switched the intercom to the plane's cockpit and called, "Missile! We have incoming, bearing zero-eight-zero. I'm shutting down the dome."

Over their heads, the thirty-foot diameter radar dome, which did its best to imitate a flying saucer trying to land on the back of the 707, ceased its six revolutions per minute as the crew cut power to the sensor. It wasn't that simple, McCall knew. The radar would take several dangerous minutes to power down completely. Until it did so, the Soviet missiles would have a signal to guide on. McCall felt the aircraft's deck pitch down even more sharply under his feet as the pilot dove to gain speed and distance on the incoming missiles. With nothing else to do, and a lot to worry about, he fixed his attention upon the overall air picture at his console to review the situation in the chaotic skies over Northern Norway and the seas off the northern coast.

McCall had to concede that Viper Two-One's ambush of the northern group of Flankers had been brilliant, despite the leakers who just launched at the colonel's own aircraft. To the south, however, Viper One-One flight had confronted another eight Su-27s under far less favorable conditions. The lead F-16 pilot from the flight had eaten a missile head on. His wingman was now fleeing west on afterburner, dodging missiles as he went, all eight Sukhois in hot pursuit. Farther to the east, the AWACS' radar had just begun to pick up the returns of dozens of contacts approaching from the Soviet side of the international border. Tasman was reporting multiple Mig-23 and Mig-29 fire control radars. More F-16 pilots were even now pushing their throttles forward climbing desperately from their dispersal fields at Banak, Tromsø, Evenes, and Bardufoss, but they would find a sky swarming with Soviet fighters by the time they reached altitude. Finally, seconds before powering down, McCall's ballistic radar operator had detected what could only be a rocket rising from just beyond the Soviet border. *Overall, not good. All hell is breaking loose.*

Offshore, the Norwegian coastal radar network and a P-3 Maritime Patrol plane were tracking multiple groups of Soviet ships moving west. A squadron of Russian *Osa*-class missile craft was sweeping towards the North Cape, having stayed just outside Norway's twelve-mile territorial sea boundary throughout the morning. Farther north, two surface groups of Soviet patrol frigates were ploughing westward through the gray, choppy waters of the Barents Sea.

Several other motley groups of Soviet ships were operating further east. The smallest were rusty World War II-era landing craft, now entering the wide mouth of the Varangerfjord on a course for the small port of Vardø. The largest was a group of merchantmen led by an icebreaker trailing the dangerous *Osa* missile boats westward along the coast. Perhaps more troubling was a pair of huge *Zubr*-class hovercraft racing across the water far out to sea at the incredible speed of sixty knots. Each of these impressive craft could carry up to a company of troops and armored vehicles.

McCall could feel the tension building in the cabin around him as the E-3 continued its dive away from the oncoming missiles. One controller nearby wiped sweat from her brow, despite the air conditioning meant to keep the AWACS's banks of computers humming at peak efficiency. Others looked up and around, as if trying to spot the incoming threats through the jet's fuselage. The tactical director decided to direct at least one crew member's mind away from the threat. "Lieutenant Visser," he called to the Dutch officer responsible for tracking naval movements, "what was the status of friendly naval forces before we shut down?"

"Eh," the man stuttered, caught off guard with his mind elsewhere. Then he gathered himself and reported, "Sir, the Royal Norwegian Navy has," he paused to double check, "nine missile boats staged around the North Cape. They are all at sea, divided into three groups. Well, four if you count the single boat returning from maintenance at Tromsø as a separate group. One group is west of the Cape, one is sheltering in the Laksefjord east of the Cape. The third just left Batsfjord on the Varanger peninsula, they just called to report that they are executing an attack on that group of *Osas* to their north."

The Dutchman went on, appreciating the chance to push the fear from his mind as he did so, "The *Norge*s have two submarines in the area. *Utstein* is on patrol somewhere off the Cape, and the older *Kobben* sortied several hours ago; she's sweeping up the coast past Tromsø right now."

"Major surface units?" McCall queried, hoping to continue busying the minds of his team with something that might prove useful if they survived.

The junior officer shook his head. "Nothing close," he said. "The *Norge* frigates *Bergen* and *Oslo* sortied from Tromsø two hours ago, but they won't be in play until after midnight. Other than that, the coast guard cutter *Nordkapp* left Banak an hour ago carrying a couple hundred evacuees from Lakselv but, by my judgement she won't clear the mouth of the Porsangerfjord before the Soviets get there."

McCall nodded, it was hard to really listen. He didn't know if he was going to make it through the next few seconds, and after that, the war. The drama of the small naval craft about to collide off the jagged coast of Northern Norway was only peripheral to the most important issue: keeping information flowing for the NATO forces.

Outside the E-3, the two R-27P missiles arced downward towards the piece of sky that the AWACS had occupied just before the aircraft's massive radar shut down. With a rapidly weakening signal to guide on, the first missile flew through this empty patch of atmosphere and continued downward, eventually smashing into the snowy forest far below without detonating, never registering that it had failed to hit its target. The second missile's seeker had picked up the last few electrons being emitted by the E-3's huge radar as it finally powered down completely. The R-27's warhead detonated twenty meters from the AWACS, spewing hot metal into the big jet's left wing, destroying the inboard engine on that side and igniting a fire that streaked back from the wing like the tail of a comet.

McCall felt the aircraft shudder as the pilot worked desperately to keep his wounded bird airborne while at the same time putting out the fire that threatened to engulf the entire aircraft. McCall felt his ears pop as the 707 dove. Others of the crew were cringing, clearly wondering if their lives were about to end inside this aluminum tube. Soon the E-3 began to run out of altitude, and McCall felt himself pressed downward as the pilot pulled back on the stick, easing the Boeing into level flight. He heard one of the flight crew announce that the flames were extinguished just as the AWACS crossed over the rugged fjords of the coast. Snowy rock and forest beneath gave way to black water as the wounded bird clung desperately to the air.

Rattled by the explosion, McCall worked to transfer the AWACS surveillance and control responsibilities to the network of ground radar stations that dotted the northernmost parts of Norway. "Call the *Norge* pilots," McCall told his controllers. "Tell them they'll need to rely on the ground stations until we can get a replacement for us up from Orland."

The ripping sound from the left side of the aircraft brought them all back to reality. The aircraft was coming apart around them.

Then the Scuds began to impact.

 **CHAPTER 49**

1302 CET, Sunday 13 February 1994
1202 Zulu
Over Finnmark, Northern Norway

T HE SCUD-DS FIRED by the battalion at Koskama Mount differed from earlier versions of the ubiquitous ballistic missiles, made infamous by Saddam Hussein's use of them during the Persian Gulf War three years earlier. This new iteration possessed a terminal guidance system, allowing the warheads to adjust their aim as they streaked back to earth, rather than relying solely on the perfection of the weapon's ballistic arc. The modification improved the Scud's accuracy so that it was now able to reliably hit precise point targets. Targets like the NATO ground radar stations that dotted the terrain across Northern Norway.

The first warhead streaked downward and crashed through the white plexiglass globe protecting the coastal surveillance radar at the northern tip of the Varanger peninsula. Its nine hundred and eighty-five kilograms of high explosives detonated inside the dome, blowing the protective white panels outward like a popping balloon and demolishing the fragile equipment within. Of the six Scuds fired, four scored direct hits on their targets with similar results. A fifth warhead struck close enough to the radar at the North Cape to shut it down for some time while the crew rushed to repair it.

Only in one instance did a Scud-D miss its intended target. The air search radar responsible for the skies over southern Finnmark, codenamed "Backstop," survived when the warhead failed to separate from the missile body, sending both warhead and pieces of the rocket tumbling downward to the boreal forests below. This radar immediately became vital to NATO's air controllers for maintaining situational awareness over the battle front, and they began vectoring precious F-16s in to protect it.

━ ━

Mitroshenko grunted as the high-G turn pressed him into the seat of his fighter. He didn't know if his missiles had struck the AWACS or not. He suspected not, since the emissions from the control aircraft had ceased shortly after he had loosed his weapons. Regardless, his attack had produced the desired effect: to deprive the NATO fighters over Northern Norway of aerial radar support at the same time that the Scuds demolished their ground radar network. This left the Norwegian pilots essentially blind in this modern age of electronic sensors and homing missiles, forcing them to activate their onboard radars and reveal their positions to the Russian assailants.

The Soviet pilot needed no help, however, in locating the F-16 that was close on his tail, staying with him through his tight, diving turn. Mitroshenko had just dodged one Sidewinder. His wingman was scissoring with Mitroshenko and the Norwegian, trying to get a shot at the assailant. The Norwegian had closed tight up on Crane Lead's tail, preventing the other Russian from taking a shot without endangering his flight leader. However, the NATO pilot's proximity also prevented *him* from employing his missiles, forcing the Norwegian to rely instead upon his aircraft's gun.

Mitroshenko intended to gain a measure of revenge against this pesky Nordic pilot; all he needed was to create the right conditions. To do this, Mitroshenko continued to bleed off speed via his Sukhoi's high-G turn, reducing his throttles to gain more maneuverability, the F-16 turning with him all the way. The Russian watched his airspeed indicator drop until—

He threw his stick over and pulled back, bringing his Su-27 to level flight. The Falcon driver behind him matched this gambit, but in the next split second Mitroshenko executed a maneuver for which the Norwegian was not prepared and which he could not match. The Soviet pilot pulled back hard on his stick, bringing the nose of his fighter up to near vertical. At the same time, he shoved his throttles forward, increasing power to his engines. The effect was a maneuver called the "Cobra," in which the Russian's airplane continued forward in level flight despite its nose pointing straight upwards, rapidly bleeding speed as the engines roared to maintain the fighter's altitude.

Grunting through the Gs of the challenging maneuver, he was vaguely aware of the white streaks of twenty-millimeter tracer rounds flashing by his canopy. Looking down over his shoulder to see the gray shape of the F-16 flash by underneath, close enough for him see the roundels on the other aircraft's wings and the visored face of the Norwegian looking up at him.

Mitroshenko now shoved his stick forward, bringing his nose back down until it was pointed directly at the F-16's tail, suddenly reversing the situation. The Russian did not intend to give his opponent the chance to turn the tables again. As the Norwegian aircraft gained separation from the Flanker, he locked the seeker heads of two of his short-ranged R-73 infrared homing missiles onto the Falcon's hot engine exhaust and fired. The white-painted darts shot forward, covering the distance between the two aircraft in seconds.

The *Norge* didn't even have time to trigger his defensive flares. The two missiles exploded within milliseconds of each other, riddling the Falcon with shrapnel. Mitroshenko watched the aircraft begin to tumble towards the clouds below, seeing if the other man would eject. *There.* A flash of fire as the Norwegian activated his ejection seat, the Falcon's canopy exploding outward as the pilot exited the cockpit atop a small rocket.

"Well done Lead!" Mitroshenko heard his wingman call over the radio net. The flight leader looked over to see the other Sukhoi forming up on his wing. He nodded to his comrade, realizing suddenly that he was soaked with sweat.

Over the radio, the controller on the A-50, the Soviet equivalent of the E-3, ordered "Crane Lead, this is Control 2. Turn southeast and withdraw towards the border. You have two enemy contacts approaching you from the east, low, and two more rising from your north. Let the second wave handle them. End."

"*Da,*" he acknowledged, then called to Crane Two, "left turn on me."

The two Russians settled onto a southeasterly course, heading away from the converging pairs of NATO fighters. Then Mitroshenko paused as a realization hit him: *Those two contacts coming up from the east are the same ones who ambushed us over the fjord!*

"Two, this is Lead," he called, "we're going after the two coming from the east. How many missiles do you have left?"

"Two longs, four shorts," reported Two, indicating that he still carried two R-27s and his full complement of the shorter-ranged heat seeking R-73s. *Two shorts and four longs for me,* tallied Mitroshenko. *Plenty.*

"Very well, Two," he called, "turning left and descending. Follow me."

"*Da*, Lead."

— • —

Olsen's elation at his and Bjorn's victories over the fjord had faded while he listened over the radio to the destruction of Viper Two-Three. Then Two-Four's frantic report that he was ejecting. Those Falcons had been flown by two of the six pilots who had come north with Olsen to Banak last night. They were all squadron mates, friends, and Jan already felt the loss acutely.

As Olsen and Bjorn climbed westward, they activated their radars to compensate for the loss of the AWACS' directions. Two blips appeared on the Norwegian scopes, approaching from the southwest. Jan's grip tightened around his sidestick.

"Two-Two," he called to Bjorn, "I've got two bogeys inbound, eleven o'clock, angels twenty, negative IFF", he referred to the "identification, friend or foe" systems installed on aircraft that sent out an encoded signal to identify them to friendly sensors, "let's head back to the deck and try to come up underneath them."

Attacking from above would have been ideal in most circumstances, but Olsen judged he wouldn't be able to gain an altitude advantage against the oncoming Soviets, and a low altitude approach would help neutralize the advantage of the Russians' long-range radar homing missiles.

As the two Falcons nosed downward, Olsen heard his missile warning system blare at him once again.

"Missiles!" Jan called to Bjorn as the Russian fire control radar locked onto his aircraft, missiles inbound. "Let's get down into the trees!"

Olsen willed his nimble fighter to dive faster as his guts tightened for the third time with the anticipation of the weapons rocketing his way. His altimeter spun downwards as he passed through a layer of broken clouds, emerging on the other side above the rugged arctic hills west of the town of Lakselv and its airbase at Banak. Olsen banked his aircraft northward in the dive, making for a steep-sided valley in the rocky, snow-covered hills. It seemed his RWR had been blaring at him for an eternity. *Where are those missiles?* He didn't have time right now to look, either they would survive, or they wouldn't.

Come on! Almost there, Olsen urged his Falcon forward, *almost...*

White and gray streaked by both sides of Olsen's canopy as his jet shot into the valley's mouth. The RWR abruptly stopped warbling in Olsen's ears as the two missiles flew blindly into the tundra below.

Damn! Mitroshenko swore to himself. All four of their missiles had failed to connect with the wily Norwegian jets, now snaking up a narrow valley perpendicular to his course.

"Follow me down, Two," he called to his wingman, intending to dive on the two NATO jets and finish them off with his short-ranged R-73s.

"*Nyet*, Crane," he heard Control 2 call over his radio. "You have two contacts coming up behind you. I repeat, leave them for the second wave. There is no need to engage at a disadvantage."

The major swore again. He desperately wanted revenge, but couldn't disobey another direct order without the risk of being grounded. He looked at his fuel gauge, which was showing the effects from his long climb towards the AWACS and subsequent maneuvering in afterburner. They were now low on both fuel and missiles, and locally outnumbered as well. Reluctantly, he vectored his aircraft to the southeast, climbing away as he did so with Crane Two on his wing.

Olsen wasn't sure what would await him and Bjorn as their jets emerged from the valley over the rugged Sværholt Peninsula. They switched off their radars while following the valley floor, but Jan held little faith that this tactic would conceal him from the Russians for long.

Then the Norwegian pilot finally heard directions from the surviving ground radar in central Finnmark: "Viper Two-One, this is Backstop. We've got you northwest of Banak. Come to heading two-six-zero and angels thirty. Two bandits to your south are withdrawing, but Tasman is reporting multiple new groups headed your way. Link up with Two-Five and One-Three south of Alta. We'll give you further directions from there."

Over Alta? Olsen thought. *That's seventy kilometers west of Banak! Have we been pushed back so far in just,* he looked down at the console clock and reality struck him, *five minutes, had it taken only five minutes?* His mind worked to reconstruct what had just transpired. *Three Falcons for five. Six? Flankers,* he tallied. As he flew his subconscious took over his thoughts, he registered that this was not a sustainable loss ratio for his small air force. *Fifty percent losses for both sides engaged so far.* Then he registered the fact that he was now receiving direction from callsign Backstop, rather than Magic, and he heard the ground controllers warning him that formations of MiG-23s and MiG-29s were boring westward to replace the dangerous Su-27s, the Soviets apparently now substituting quantity for quality. Then his mind remembered his promise to Johansen, back on the ground at Banak. *We'll keep them off your back.* He was beginning to doubt his ability to do so.

 **CHAPTER 50**

1503 MSK, Sunday 13 February 1994
1203 Zulu
Over the Barents Sea

A HUNDRED AND FIFTY miles to the east of the aerial melee over Norway, off the north coast of the Kola Peninsula, the pilot of a lone MiG-31 interceptor pulled back on his control stick, lifting the big, twin-tailed jet's nose upward towards the deep blue of the polar sky. He pushed his throttles forward to their stops to lite the afterburners of his huge turbofan engines, which gobbled up the thin atmosphere through large, boxy air intakes on either side of the cockpit. The fighter, call sign Icarus, accelerated upwards, pushing the pilot and his weapons officer into their seats. Already at ten-thousand meters altitude when the maneuver began, the MiG-31, called the "Foxhound" by NATO, passed the twelve-thousand-meter mark, then fifteen-thousand.

The Foxhound was a development of the older MiG-25 "Foxbat." With its powerful *Zaslon* radar and long-range R-33 missiles, the MiG-31 was designed and built to protect the USSR's long northern coast from incursions by nuclear-capable American bombers. It was not a dogfighter, being too clumsy to turn with more nimble aircraft like the Norwegian F-16s, but its top speed of nearly Mach 3 at high altitude, powerful radar, and long-range air-to-air missiles compensated nicely for this deficiency.

The crew of this particular Foxhound, however, were hunting neither Norwegian fighters nor American bombers. The armament slung under the center of their aircraft's fuselage consisted of a single, heavily modified and experimental R-37 missile. The prey for this missile: USA-34.

The satellite, just now rising over the dark, polar horizon, had been launched into low earth orbit by the Space Shuttle Atlantis six years earlier. As part of the United States' National Reconnaissance Office "Lacrosse" program of surveillance satellites, USA-34 carried a synthetic aperture radar that beamed energy down to earth's surface to detect large, moving objects like ships on the ocean surface. The satellite had passed over northern Alaska several minutes earlier at an altitude of four-hundred and forty kilometers. Its fourteen-thousand mile-per-hour velocity would carry USA-34 across the North Pole, bringing it over the Barents Sea within the next few minutes, where its wide-ranging radar would be able to see the dozens of Soviet ships, large and small, that had sortied from their Kola bases, seeing through the layer of broken clouds that blanketed the area. From there it would continue south, passing over Leningrad, Belarus, Ukraine, the Crimea, the Black Sea, and eventually the Eastern Mediterranean, all of which were places that the Soviet high command did not want the American satellite's sensors to see on this very busy day, or on any other hereafter.

As the MiG-31 climbed through eighteen-thousand meters, its crew received direction from technicians at the early warning *Dnestr-M* radar located in the snowy forests just west of the Soviet mining town of Olenogorsk, south of Murmansk. The radar tracked USA-34 as it hurtled along its predictable journey. While the MiG-31's speed was one of the aircraft's most impressive features, neither it nor any weapon it could carry could hope to come anywhere close to matching the satellite's velocity. If Icarus was to successfully complete its mission, they would need to be precisely positioned in time and space to hurl their anti-satellite missile, or ASAT, towards its rendezvous with USA-34.

The Soviet pilot saw his altimeter pass through twenty-thousand meters. They were now over the central Barents Sea, directly in the path of the target. He was having to work carefully now to keep his laboring engines from flaming out in the thin atmosphere. A few seconds more and they would be beyond the height at which their air-breathing jet interceptor could function.

Then the deadpan command came from the controller at the Olenogorsk site: "Icarus, this is Space Control. Launch in three...two...one..."

The ASAT missile separated silently from belly of the MiG-31. Both objects continued their upward trajectory for a few moments more, the distance between them growing as the pilot began to nudge his aircraft over on its back to begin the long, gliding descent back to their base outside Murmansk. Then the weapons' rocket booster fired, propelling the missile upwards into the deep blue stratosphere atop a column of white, billowing smoke.

USA-34's surface-surveillance radar was just beginning to come within range to detect the groups of Soviet warships in the central Barents when the Soviet missile, guided in its terminal phase by its own onboard homing radar, slammed into its fragile structure. The enormous combined velocities of the two objects made for an impressive release of energy as they both attempted to occupy the same exact space, at the same exact time.

A brief pulse of light in the polar sky announced the demise of USA-34, and with it NATO's ability to see from space for the next several hours. The only other Lacrosse radar satellite currently in orbit, USA-69, would not pass over this part of the globe for another five hours. Before that happened, it too was scheduled for a meeting with an ASAT-armed MiG-31, this time flying from a base in the Soviet Far East. Until the United States could launch replacement satellites into orbit, NATO would have to find their Soviet adversaries the hard way.

# CHAPTER 51

1507 MSK, Sunday 13 February 1994
1207 Zulu
TAKR *Baku*, Barents Sea

C ONTRA-ADMIRAL IVANENKO SLAMMED his fist triumphantly
onto the chart table with something approaching glee. His order to
begin the engagement early had paid off. The northern American
submarine had evaded two air-dropped torpedoes but had finally succumbed
to a third and was now a wreck on the bottom of the western Barents. The
submarine to the south, near the coast, had been somewhat more complicated.
In fact, one of the Soviet patrol aircraft prosecuting the southern contact had
very nearly dropped a torpedo on a Project 877 submarine, called a *Kilo* by
the NATO naming convention, instead of on the American. The crew of the
Be-12 patrol plane had only called off their attack at the last minute when
one of their passive buoys had detected the contact launching four torpedoes
of definitively Russian manufacture.

The near-disaster of the would-be friendly fire incident had given way to a
triumph, however. The Be-12's buoys had tracked the Project 877's torpedoes all
through the short run to the American submarine, which had barely enough time
to accelerate, much less evade the fish. Ivanenko had not known the friendly submarine was there. It was not supposed to be there. But, in the opening minutes of

a massive global war that was as much a surprise to many of the Soviet combatants as it was to their NATO enemies, such mix-ups were inevitable.

Contra-Admiral Ivanenko exulted in these opening triumphs for Russia. The American submarines had arrogantly trawled his country's coast for decades. Now two of them were dead. Ivanenko did not know how many NATO submarines were actually in these waters, but after this double victory he could not imagine any evading the incredibly intensive operation he had planned, organized, and eventually led, to clear the exits from the Kola bases ahead of the rest of the fleet. That fleet was now beginning to sortie from its bases along the length of the Inlet. *Initial task complete,* he told himself, checking the NATO submarine pickets off his mental tally of enemy forces. *On to the real task at hand.*

"Communications officer!" Ivanenko called.

"*Da, Contra-Admiral,*" the staff officer responded from his position across the flag bridge.

"Take down a message for the task force," Ivanenko ordered. He clasped his hands behind his back and paced while he made the pronouncement, loudly and proudly: "Well done! We have cleared the imperialist aggressors from our shores. Now we will proceed west at our best speed. We're taking the fight into the enemy's own waters. The might of our fleet is behind us. You are the vanguard of forces that will free our country from the encirclement of the Americans and their European puppets. We go forward to Soviet victory!"

As the staff officer jotted down the message, Ivanenko's mind looked ahead to his next objectives along the Norwegian coast. He already took for granted that, with the death of the two American submarines, his rear areas were for now clear of enemy threats.

0808 EST, Sunday 13 February 1994
1208 Zulu
US 2nd Fleet Headquarters, Building W-8,
Naval Station Norfolk, Virginia, USA

US 2nd Fleet's staff had been at work since the previous night's DEFCON Four warning. Increasingly tense reports out of the North Atlantic and the

Barents Sea were giving clear evidence of Soviet mobilization. Troubling reports continued to arrive from Europe, where the massive, coiled Soviet ground force that had been occupying Czechoslovakia for the past three years was also stirring. There were reports that Russian tanks, moving west from Belorussia, had reached Warsaw in the early hours of this morning. Vice Admiral Falkner hoped that the mobilization was just another dramatic instance of saber-rattling to cover the Soviets' interference in Poland. For brief moments Falkner had thought that the powerful Soviet force in Czechoslovakia would stay there, or that it would simply move north into Poland to support the thrust from the Soviet Union. But deep down, he'd known better. At this moment his worst fears were being confirmed.

"Sir!" one of the communications officers in the cramped operations room called, too loudly.

Falkner stood from his desk overlooking the staff area and walked over, his N3, Rear Admiral Johnson, at his heels. "What is it?" Falkner asked.

The junior officer licked his lips, then reported, "Sir, COMSUBLANT reports they just had two rescue beacons activate...both from boats on X-Ray Station."

It's started then, thought Falkner.

"Which boats?" Johnson asked.

The young man checked his notes. "*Boise* and," another check, "*New York City*, sir."

Two of the X-Ray boats gone, Falkner tallied quickly. *That leaves just...* Baltimore, Trafalgar, *and* Connecticut *to watch the Kola bases.*

"Get a message out to the fleet, every ship, every station, on every channel," Falkner said quickly. "We're at war."

 **CHAPTER 52**

1509 MSK, Sunday 13 February 1994
1209 Zulu
USS *Connecticut* (SSN 22), mouth of the Kola Inlet, Barents Sea

C OMMANDER ROGERS WAS sweating. The *Conneticut*, a big submarine by most standards, transited from the western to the eastern
side of the shallow channel that marked the mouth of the Kola Inlet.
*We should be out in deep water where we can take advantage of our speed, not
here, jammed up against the coast*, he fretted. *Connecticut* was in the middle of
a very sensitive maneuver, repositioning to put distance between themselves
and the Soviet patrol frigate they had detected when they'd come shallow to
receive the DEFCON Four message.

Rogers considered his boat's situation as he sat in his command chair,
sipping another cup of coffee. *Connecticut* was creeping towards the center of
the channel at three knots, barely enough to maintain steerage through the
dark, frigid water. So far, their passage had been uneventful. The sounds of the
patrol frigate were gently fading away behind the American submarine's slowly
turning screw. They'd heard nothing from Norfolk since the DEFCON Four
alert that had so thrown off his boat's routine. He'd begun to relax slightly
when the situation began to become more eventful again.

"Con, sonar," called the chief sonarman, "I'm starting to pick up a lot of noise coming from the inlet. Too intermixed to give any firm count or ID at this time. Multiple contacts, definitely."

"Got it sonar, keep us updated," said Rogers. *Great*, he thought bitterly, *we're in the middle of the channel with nowhere to hide. Just our luck.*

Minutes passed. Then the sonar room called again, "Con, we're picking up at least two destroyers I'm calling *Sovremennys*, designate these as Skunks Eight and Nine," a pause, "and there's another I can't put my finger on right now. Calling this one Skunk Ten. Others coming out behind them. They're doing turns for twenty-five knots and accelerating, they're really moving sir! They're going to close the distance on us pretty quick."

Rogers knew he had to act fast; *They'll be on top of us in minutes.* He couldn't increase his own speed for fear of being detected, but if he stayed here, they were almost certain to detect him anyway. *What to do?* An unorthodox plan began to formulate. *I've seen crazier shit done up here,* he thought with a grim smile.

"XO, what's the bottom material of the channel here? Right below us?"

"Uh…" his second-in-command had been unprepared for this question, but he recovered quickly, beginning to divine his skipper's intentions. He bent down and studied the chart table for a moment before saying, "Looks like fine silt from the yearly melt runoff sir. Should be nice and soft."

Rogers nodded, giving his number two a half smile. *The man's quick*, he thought. *He'll be ready for his own boat after this patrol.*

Turning to the chief of the boat, the captain said, "COB, we're going to put her down on the floor, shut everything down, go nice and quiet, and let them just pass right over us."

The wiry, crusty old COB turned from his position behind the helmsman and raised an eyebrow, "Sir?"

Rogers nodded again. He didn't mind being questioned, certainly not by his senior chief. The man had more time up on X-Ray Station than many of the junior officers aboard had in the service, and, truth be told, what the skipper was planning bore significant risk. Yes, the *Seawolfs* were exceedingly quiet, but they were also powered by a nuclear reactor, which required constant cooling, which meant constant pump noises even when the boat was sitting perfectly still. If it made noise, it could be detected, especially at this proximity.

"Make it so, COB," Rogers confirmed.

The chief nodded, turned back, and gave the necessary instructions. Then he turned again and quietly said to the XO, "Sir, we'd better warn the crew."

The XO nodded, reaching for the 1MC, "All hands, secure any loose gear, brace for impact."

"All stop," ordered Rogers.

"All stop, aye," came the response.

The large, highly advanced propeller of the *Conneticut* slowed; its curved, scythe-like blades coming to a stop amid the gently swirling sediment of the channel floor, the large attack submarine settling softly and anti-climactically into the prehistoric ooze of the channel floor. Rogers felt the deck take on a list as his command came to rest on a slight slope. *Now we wait*, he thought.

"Sonar, Con." the skipper called, "status on those contacts?"

"We've got at least seven vessels coming out at high speed, sir. Those two *Sovremennys*, I'm calling Skunk Ten an *Udaloy*, and, uh, Captain, can you come in here?"

Rogers was up, out of his seat, and across the few feet to the sonar room in seconds. "What is it?" he asked.

The chief petty officer in charge of the sonar section was tracing his finger along a distinctive set of lines on the "waterfall display," the computer screen showing the graphical representation of what the boat's acoustic sensors were hearing.

"Sir," the chief said, "take a look at this." He was indicating with the pointer and pinky fingers of his left hand at two lines "falling" down the screen from top to bottom. The green glow of the display was casting an eerie light onto the operators' faces.

"What is it, Chief?" the captain asked, not appreciating being made to wait for what looked to be vital information.

"Sir," the man said, "this is big. This contact here," he indicated the left-hand line, "Skunk Eleven, this one's a *Kirov*." Rogers stood up straight and let out a low whistle at the revelation. One of the Soviet navy's huge battlecruisers putting to sea *was* big news.

"Sir, that's not the half of it," the chief was saying. "Skunk Twelve, this one here," he indicated the right-hand line on the display, "that's the *Kuznetsov*. I'd bet a month's pay on it."

Rogers felt his blood run cold. The TAKR *Kuznetsov* was the Soviet Union's first, and only, so far as Rogers knew, big deck aircraft carrier, capable of carrying over three dozen fighters along with a large complement of helicopters. Moreover, it was the flagship of the entire Red Banner Northern Fleet. If one of the Northern Fleet's two *Kirovs* putting to sea by itself was big news, seeing both of the capital ships departing together at the center of a strong escort was almost unheard of. Something big was happening, and Rogers didn't like any of the explanations he was coming up with.

Lieutenant Santamaria was at the door of the cramped sonar room.

"What is it, Sparks?" asked the skipper.

"ELF message, sir. Fleet wants us to come to communication depth," the junior officer said quickly.

"*Now?*" blurted the skipper, still feeling the sting of annoyance at the lack of information the shore weenies had sent in the morning's transmission. The timing for this couldn't have been worse, with a ridiculously powerful Soviet task force about to pass directly overhead. The captain worked to get his anger under control, he had to weigh the odds. *Chewing out Santamaria for doing his job won't help anyone.*

"It's going to be a bit, Sparks," Rogers said after a moment, biting off another snide comment about the shore weenies back at Norfolk. "We're about to have the whole Red Banner Northern Fleet sail over the top of us."

Then the captain paused. *An ELF just as the entire Red Fleet sorties? What do you think that message is going to say, Ethan?* he asked himself. He turned to the communications officer and said, "Not your fault, Sparks. We'll go shallow just as soon as we can. For now, go get a contact report ready to send. We need to let Fleet know that the Soviets' big boys are putting to sea."

Sparks nodded and withdrew.

"Sir," the head sonarman said next, "there's one more thing." He pointed to another line on the waterfall display. "This contact here, Skunk Thirteen, it's new, not in the library yet. It sounds like an *Udaloy* but it's not like one we've heard before. It may be that new *Udaloy II* we've been hearing about."

Rogers grunted unhappily. The new iteration of the *Udaloy*-class was purported to be a far more dangerous version of the already dangerous class of ASW destroyer fielded by the Soviet Navy. Rogers hadn't counted on one of these passing just a few hundred feet over his head. *Damn, this is going to be close.* He retreated to his command chair to brood and wait.

The tension in the submarine's quiet command room was palpable as the Soviet task force approached the *Connecticut*. The boat had been rigged for silent running for days now, so no special orders were necessary to suppress unnecessary noise, but petty officers throughout the ship nonetheless watched the younger sailors like hawks, ready to pounce on any perceived threat to noise discipline. Nearly everyone sweated, despite the air conditioning, imagining that they could actually hear the thrumming noise from the thrashing propellers of the approaching Soviet task force growing louder as the warships approached.

"Con, Sonar," called the chief sonarman, "the carrier's escorts are spreading out as they clear the inlet. The lead ship is just about to pass right over us. It's probably the new *Udaloy II*, sir."

1511 MSK, Sunday 13 February 1994
1211 Zulu
BPK *Admiral Chabanenko*, Kola Inlet, two miles south of USS *Connecticut*

Sergei Medvedev was beginning to put his hangover and the drama of his home life behind him after three cups of strong tea brought up to the bridge from the galley. The tea and a brusque meeting with Group Captain Gordinya had gotten young Medvedev's blood pumping. He'd thought he was ready for anything but found himself still stunned by the developments of the past few minutes. The task group commander had called on the task group radio net to announce that German and American forces had attacked Soviet forces in Poland, and that war with NATO in defense of the *Rodina* had commenced. The announcement caught nearly everyone off guard, but the quick report from the task force commander aboard *Admiral Kuznetsov*, stating that ASW patrol forces had already sunk two American submarines, worked to steady everyone's nerves. *Still*, the Soviet officer thought, *there are certainly more enemy boats out there. If the Americans launched a surprise attack against us in Europe, then they will also almost certainly have boats to ambush us as we leave port up here as well. Fortunately,* Medvedev thought with a smile, *I have just the ship for the job of clearing inlet exits.*

The captain looked out over the bow of his ship as it crossed from the relatively calm waters of the inlet into the ocean swell of the gray Barents Sea. They sailed under a deep blue sky mottled by a layer of cotton ball clouds. Ahead and to the right, an Il-38 maritime patrol aircraft was approaching from the opposite direction, hugging the undersides of the clouds as it flew south to its base near Murmansk. Sergei watched the gray-painted aircraft pass to starboard, close enough that he could make out the red star on its tailfin and the spinning red circles of its four propellers.

From the patrol plane, his eyes drifted down to a dark shape on the horizon: another ship to starboard, the *Sovremenny*-class air defense destroyer EM *Besstrashnyy*, his name meaning "Fearless" in Russian. To his left, out the other window of *Chabanenko's* bridge, Medvedev could see *Besstrashnyy's* twin, *Gremyashchiy*, nicknamed "Thunderous" pulling away to port. Behind the trio of destroyers, the other ships of the task group were spreading out into a formation a dozen kilometers across, with the three largest ships at the center. Sergei could not see backwards from the bridge of his ship, but he knew from the chart before him that the aviation cruiser *Admiral Kuznetsov*, the battlecruiser *Kalinin*, and the air defense cruiser *Slava* were maintaining station several kilometers behind his own command. Bringing up the rear of the formation was the older *Udaloy*-class destroyer *Admiral Zakharov*.

Admiral Chabanenko was the lead ASW warship of the task force. In this role Medvedev's command had taken onboard the screening force's group captain, Aleksandre Mikhailovich Gordinya, who was a man so full of himself that not even the fact that Sergey's father was the President of the USSR seemed to make any difference. He would coordinate all of the ASW efforts of the task force. Despite this unwelcome addition, Sergei was pleased and impressed by the power of the force heading to sea in the company of his ship. Two air defense destroyers and two anti-submarine destroyers, including his own, escorted the formation's three powerful capital ships. *Kuznetsov's* dangerous Su-33 fighters, the navalized version of the Su-27, provided the task group's air cover. Massive *Kalinin* provided the formation with its anti-ship punch and was no slouch at air defense either. The cruiser *Slava* was the task group's most potent air defense asset, maybe the best air defense ship afloat. *Well*, Sergei corrected himself grudgingly, *maybe the American AEGIS ships are as good.*

"*Tovarich* Captain," the young officer spoke in a loud clear voice so that Medvedev wasn't sure if the man was repeating himself. The captain indicated that he was listening, "Our sonar officer reports a very weak contact directly to our front. He says it goes in and out, sir."

"Tell him I will be there in a moment," Sergei said as he left the bridge, descending a ladder and taking a passageway forward to his destroyer's sonar room. *A contact directly in our path?* He wondered. *Could this be an American ambush?*

Entering the compartment, the captain commanded, "Tell me of this contact, Sonar Officer."

"I," the junior officer licked his lips, "I cannot definitively call it a *contact*, Captain. It is so faint, and it comes and goes. I thought I was tracking movement, but now it's still."

"Show me," ordered the captain.

The young officer pointed to his display, indicating a series of very faint, seemingly unconnected dots amid the green noise of the computer display. Sergei strained to see a pattern amid all the lines of sound slowly falling down the screen.

After a moment, Sergei asked, "Can we deploy our variable depth array?"

The other officer shook his head, his eyes wide, as if he was afraid to disappoint his captain. "No, sir. It is still too shallow here for the VDS."

Medvedev nodded again, silently cursing himself for this misstep in front of his subordinates. "Very well, we will slow to see if we can give the bow sonar a better listen on the potential contact. It may be nothing, but we cannot gamble with the safety of the flagship."

Sergei grabbed an intercom from the sonarman's work station and called the bridge, giving the order to slow the ship to ten knots. As he returned the handset to its cradle, the sonar officer's screen flickered, then went black.

"What just happened?" asked the captain. "Where is the display?"

The junior officer, who was desperately punching keys, responded, "I don't know, Captain, the feed is just gone," the young sonar officer turned to one of his enlisted men and asked, "how is the display on your console?"

"*Nyet, tovarich* Lieutenant, and I am hearing nothing through the headsets. There must be a problem with the connection to the main array!"

Not now! thought Medvedev. His crew had experienced all the usual problems with breaking in a new ship in the one short cruise they'd taken since *Admiral Chabanenko*'s commissioning, but they had not spent nearly enough time at sea to work out all the kinks that new warships inherit from shipyards. *A failure of the sonar system? Now? Of all the rotten luck!*

"Fix it, Lieutenant," Sergei blurted, nearly shouting at his sonar officer.

The man swallowed as he nodded, then said, "Captain, with your permission, I will take a man and check the connections from the array to our computers. I think I may know where the problem lies, but—"

"How long?" demanded Medvedev.

"Ten minutes. Fifteen if we have to solder," the man said quickly.

Sergei worked to rein in his frustration. *The most advanced anti-submarine vessel in the fleet, rendered useless by bloody poor workmanship at the start of the war.* He took a deep breath and nodded. He had to trust this man, whom he knew to be competent and hard working. *If it can be fixed quickly, he will do it.*

The captain nodded. "Very well," he said, "I will return to the bridge. Call me as soon as the problem is resolved."

The lieutenant nodded jerkily, then grabbed one of the enlisted men in the room and hurried out.

Medvedev climbed the ladder back to the bridge, arriving just in time to see his executive officer, somewhat white-faced, return an intercom receiver back to its cradle.

"What is it, Number One?" Sergei asked, feeling the strain of the possible contact just ahead and not wanting more unwelcome news just yet.

"Sir," his second-in-command answered, "the group captain was calling. He wishes to know why we've slowed. He says we are interfering with the formation of the entire task group."

Damn that man, cursed Sergei. *Does he not care that there may be something out there that could ruin our war before it even starts?* He walked over, snatched the handset, and called the flag bridge a few compartments away.

"This is the captain," he said brusquely to the staff officer on the other end of the line, "let me speak to the group captain."

A moment later Group Captain Gordinya's voice came over the line, peremptorily saying, "What is going on up there, Medvedev? You are throwing the entire task group into confusion with your antics."

Antics? raged Sergei. *What do you expect the ASW screen you command to be doing, you idiot?* He didn't say it though, biting his tongue.

"Sir," Medvedev, said, trying to keep his voice even and temper cool, "we think we have a faint contact directly ahead."

"*Think* you have?" Gordinya interrupted. "Do you or do you not? What are your people doing up there, Captain?"

"It is very faint," responded Sergei, keeping his cool, "but we were just beginning to develop a track when our system malfunctioned and—"

"Malfunctioned?" the group captain snapped. "What sort of a ship are you running, Sergei Pavlovich?" The superior used Medvedev's patronymic, showing that he didn't care in this circumstance who his subordinate's father was. "You are saying you *think* you have a contact, but you cannot show me this supposed contact because of the poor maintenance aboard your command? For this you throw off the entire formation around the flagship? No! Ring up the ordered speed and let us clear this channel! Speed and deep water are our best protection."

Medvedev began to protest. "Sir—"

"No arguments, Captain! You are under my orders, and you will obey them. Get this vessel back up to your assigned speed, NOW!"

1515 MSK, Sunday 13 February 1994
1215 Zulu
USS *Connecticut* (SSN 22), mouth of the Kola Inlet, Barents Sea

The sound of screws churning the water over their heads was no longer imagined. Everyone onboard could hear the rhythmic *thrum* of powerful propellers turning rapidly a few hundred feet above *Connecticut*'s sail, even through the high-pressure steel of the submarine's hull. Rogers was back in his command chair trying to affect an air of nonchalance, but behind his eyes his mind raced. Sonar had just reported that in addition to the battlecruiser, now positively identified from their computer's signature library as the *Kalinin*, and the carrier, there was also one of the dangerous *Slava*-class cruisers in the formation. A sortie of all of these ships together could mean only one thing. *But*, wondered Rogers, *what can we do about it?*

The lead ship of the Soviet task group, almost certainly a new *Udaloy II*, Rogers now knew, had slowed briefly as it approached the patch of water directly over the *Connecticut*. Everyone onboard had held their breath for a moment, wondering if they'd been detected, but then the destroyer accelerated again and passed overhead without incident. Now the three capital ships were drawing near, and the American skipper had a decision to make.

Do I engage, even though I haven't received official word that a war has started? He wondered. *Do I dare?* There was that ELF message in Sparks' hands, but all it said was to come to communications depth. *What if the message Norfolk wants to give us is to avoid provoking the Russians at all cost? What if, instead of laying low, I put a spread of torpedoes into the guts of the Red Banner Northern Fleet and start World War Three?* He just couldn't take that chance.

Besides, Rogers reasoned, *engaging now, in these restricted waters, with a whole enemy task group around me is suicide.* Then he paused. *Or is it...?*

The skipper ran through the math. The *Seawolf* possessed a whopping *eight* torpedo tubes for their Mk48 ADCAP torpedoes, so they could engage multiple targets at once. He put it all together: three at the carrier, three at *Kalinin*, two at the *Slava*. *Then*, thought Rogers, *all we'd have to do is slip away in the confusion of burning and sinking ships.* It would be a submarine story for the ages, but it might also be suicide. Rogers reminded himself, *We don't even know if we're at war.*

Rogers made up his mind. He would stay put, wait for the formation to pass, clear the channel, and then report in.

As the sound of the Soviet propellers faded away above and to the north of them, Commander Ethan Rogers hoped he'd made the right call, though he couldn't shake a nagging feeling that he had not.

 **CHAPTER 53**

0816 EST, Sunday 13 February 1994
1216 Zulu
Off Breezy Point, Entrance to Outer New York Harbor

T HE ALUMINUM HULL of the sixteen-meter-long Port Authority pilot boat *Wanderer* bounced across the gray waters of New York Harbor's Outer Bay into a cold, damp wind that blew under a solid sheet of leaden clouds. A quarter mile directly ahead was the rust-stained and obviously well-used fishing trawler SS *Trogg* slowly churning on its course out of the harbor.

Protected from the wind and waves inside the pilot boat's enclosed wheelhouse, the senior pilot checked his logbook for information about the *Trogg*. She was Bulgarian flagged, and her being this far from home was reason enough for the Port Authority to be curious. That, and the fact that Eastern European fishing vessels in these waters were getting a little extra attention from the local authorities ever since the Cod fisheries had collapsed a couple of years ago. Russian factory trawlers had contributed enormously to that ecological disaster off the eastern seaboard of the United States and Canada, and locals were more than willing to extend the blame to the Soviets' allies.

Today though, the *Wanderer* was simply acting on a request from the Sandy Hook Coast Guard Station, whose watch staff was curious about what had kept the *Trogg* tied up so long in New York without obvious reason. The pilot looked up from the logbook as the ugly Bulgarian vessel loomed larger through the plate glass of his own boat's wheelhouse. The *Trogg* was nearly midway between the spits of Breezy Point and Sandy Hook, which formed the broad entrance to the expansive harbor, and *Wanderer* was closing in.

Taking the radio mic from in front of his helmsman, the pilot depressed the talk button and called over the harbor control frequency, "Fishing vessel *Trogg*, fishing vessel *Trogg*, this is the Port Authority pilot boat *Wanderer*, conducting a normal cargo inspection. Please come about and prepare to receive an official, over."

The senior pilot waited for a response as they pulled closer to the trawler's starboard beam. *Nothing.* He called again, "*Trogg*, *Trogg*, this is the Port Authority pilot *Wanderer*. Come about and prepare to be boarded, over." The radio speaker remained silent.

The pilot raised his binoculars and scanned the rusty fishing trawler, starting at the vessel's bow. She was a decent-sized ocean-going boat, perhaps a hundred feet long, with the wheelhouse in front and cranes aft. The official scanned up to the boxy wheelhouse where his eyes stopped. *That's strange*, he thought, *where's the captain? The wheelhouse shouldn't be empty when they're transiting the middle of the channel.*

A continued scan leftwards to the aft of the ship revealed that the vessel itself was rocking in the wind-driven swell. The pilot's eyes caught movement as three men appeared to be working at the rear of the trawler, doing their best to heave some heavy object that was hidden behind the gunwales. *That's odd too*, thought the pilot.

That's when the pilot saw out of the corner of his eye a dark object roll off the back of the trawler and splash into the choppy gray water. His immediate reaction was anger. *Dump in my harbor, will you? Right under my nose? Oh no, you don't.*

The senior pilot snatched the loudspeaker hand-mic for the hailer from its spot above his head. The megaphone boomed, "SS *Trogg*! This is the Port Authority of New York and New Jersey. Cease your activity at once and prepare to receive an official. You are engaged in illegal dumping. I say again, cease all activity and prepare to be boarded!"

At the sound of the megaphone, all three men at the stern of the trawler looked up, surprised. The pilot could see them exchanging rapid words, one clearly giving orders. A second man darted forward to amidships of the vessel and bent down. The pilot watched this man as he came back up from behind the gunwale. For a moment the official didn't register the distinctively shaped object the fisherman was holding until—

"Gun!" the pilot shouted as the AK-47 winked at them from a hundred yards away. He grabbed his helmsman, dragging the other man down as the plate glass of the pilothouse window spider-webbed and they heard the *thunk thunk thunk* that sounded like hard-thrown baseballs hitting the bulkhead. The pilot reached up and pulled the wheel all the way over to the right, then shoved the pilot boat's throttles to their stops. The metallic *thunks* now worked their way along *Wanderer*'s port side as the boat veered away from the *Trogg*, accelerating. Now the pilot could hear the cracking reports as the assault rifle continued to fire.

After a few seconds the firing stopped, and the two occupants of *Wanderer*'s wheelhouse tentatively pulled themselves off the deck and peeked back portside at the hostile fishing trawler. About two hundred yards away, the gunman watched them warily. The pilot reached for his radio hand mic while at the same time another barrel-shaped object rolled off the trawler's stern, entering the water in a splash of white foam.

Peering over the bottom lip of his shattered wheelhouse window, he called breathlessly, "Sandy Hook, this is *Wanderer*, over." The man with the rifle aboard *Trogg* was still watching them, the weapon at his shoulder now pointed down at the water. The other two continued to labor at the rear of the trawler, and were soon joined by a fourth man.

"*Wanderer*, this is Sandy Hook, over," came the response.

"Sandy Hook," the pilot said, trying to keep his voice under control as his own vessel opened the distance from the *Trogg*, "we just approached Bulgarian flagged trawler SS *Trogg* and observed them depositing several large objects into the water. They were unresponsive to radio hails and when we hailed them audibly one of the crew picked up a rifle and started shooting at us, over!"

There was a pause on the Sandy Hook end of the net.

Then, "Say again your last, *Wanderer*?" crackled the obviously surprised response from the Coast Guard Station.

Wanderer's helmsman, who was now up and peering back at the trawler as well, said quietly, "They just dumped another one of those things into the water. If I didn't know any better, I would say those were mines."

Mines? thought the pilot. *Naval mines? In the channel? Why would Bulgarian fisherman be doing that?*

"Are you sure?" he asked the helmsman.

"I was Navy ordnance disposal before I got out," explained the crewman, "and—there! There goes another one!" Yet another barrel-like object rolled off of *Trogg*'s stern and into the water. "They're mines for sure."

The pilot depressed the talk button on his mic again, his voice now slightly shaky. "Sandy Hook, *Wanderer*. I say again, we approached SS *Trogg*, and its crew fired at us with a rifle." he said by way of explanation. "My helmsman says they're dumping naval mines into the channel! He's former Navy and says he's sure about that. We've seen about ten of them go into the water." The pilot watched as another barrel rolled off the trawler, "and there's no oil slick or trash that we can see. Drug dumping is unlikely here, over."

There was a pause on the other end of the radio net as the watch crew at the Coast Guard Station processed *Wanderer*'s report. The pilot could see the crewman with the rifle on the trawler watching them from three hundred yards away, his weapon at the ready.

0817 EST, Sunday 13 February 1994
1217 Zulu
US Coast Guard Sandy Hook Station, Ft. Hancock, New Jersey

"Roger, *Wanderer*. Remain as close as you can and observe. We've got help coming your way, over," Commander Ingalls spoke into his radio mic.

Confusion was growing among the members of the Coast Guard watch staff. Commander Ingalls had not expected any trouble from the *Trogg*, so the report of shots fired was a complete surprise, *What the hell was that last call? Naval mines?* the Coast Guard officer wondered, bemused. *An overactive imagination over on the pilot boat or something to do with this DEFCON 4?* Ingalls wondered. The Coast Guard patrol ship *Adak* would be en route to the scene any minute from her station off Staten Island. That old Bulgarian rust bucket of a trawler couldn't make it far before an armed vessel got there. This lazy Sunday morning had certainly gotten interesting in a hurry.

The watch office telephone rang, Ingalls answered "Sandy Hook Station."

The call was from Coast Guard Headquarters in Washington. Ingalls listened for a moment to the voice at the other end, then his hand tightened around the phone involuntarily. *Interesting indeed.*

"You're serious?" Ingalls asked, "DEFCON One?" Other heads in the watch office turned in his direction at this phrase. "What does that mean for *us?*" He listened a little longer, then concluded unhappily with, "Understood."

The watch commander hung up the phone, stunned. *War?*

Commander Ingalls raised his voice and addressed the other men in the room. "Gentlemen, uh," He couldn't believe he was about to say this. "That was Coast Guard HQ and...we've been ordered to assume DEFCON One. Apparently, the Russians have—" Suddenly it all came together for Ingalls. The trawler. The gunplay. The dumping. *Naval mines!*

"Call *Adak!*" he almost shouted. "Tell them they need to stop that trawler, now!"

As the surface ops officer grabbed a radio to call *Adak*, Ingalls asked the room, "What vessels do we have transiting the channel in the next hour?"

The other man looked at his computerized radar display for a moment, then said, "Sir, the dry bulk carrier *Jiffy Blue* just cleared the narrows ahead of *Trogg*. Coming behind is the tanker *Delta Pioneer*, three miles out, and behind her the car carrier *Cape Lambert*, all outbound. Nothing inbound over the next hour."

"Get on the horn to *Delta Pioneer* and *Cape Lambert*," ordered Ingalls. "Tell them to halt immediately! Then call the NYPD and tell them we need help from their patrol boats to make sure no one wanders into the channel. The harbor is closed until further notice."

—◆—

Several miles away, inside the Outer Harbor, the crew of the small cutter USCGC *Adak*, on patrol off Staten Island, brought their ship about and pushed the throttles forward, bringing the vessel up to its full thirty knots of speed. With the report of shots fired arriving from *Wanderer* via the Sandy Hook watch staff, the dark-skinned, dark-haired, Brooklyn-born captain of the *Adak*, Lieutenant Jackson, ordered his small crew to man the ship's weapons, which consisted of a Mk38 twenty-five-millimeter cannon, a derivative of the weapon carried by the US Army's Bradley Fighting Vehicle, along with several .50 caliber machine guns and a Mk19 automatic grenade launcher. Below decks, the chief of the boat was issuing small arms to a seven-man boarding team, who would soon move topside and begin readying the ship's boat.

Jackson looked out over the gray, choppy waters of the Outer Bay to where the rusty hull of the hostile *Trogg* continued to churn southward in the broad channel. *Wanderer* was keeping a respectful distance about a quarter mile to starboard. Briefly, the officer's mind registered a sharp sound from behind him in the city, something that sounded at this distance like the slamming of a dumpster lid. He ignored it, focusing instead on the Bulgarian ship.

 CHAPTER 54

0818 EST, Sunday 13 February 1994
1218 Zulu
Brooklyn Bridge, New York City, USA

JACK YOUNG'S SUBARU Outback idled amid the other cars stalled on the ascent ramp to the Brooklyn Bridge. As was customary here in New York City, many of the stationary motorists with whom Jack was waiting took turns laying on their horns to express displeasure at the delay. It was an action the *New York Times* reporter, who hailed from the rural Lake Huron shore of Michigan, had never understood. *As if blaring horns are suddenly going to remind the drivers up ahead to step on the gas and clear the way*, he thought, half annoyed by the sound but also half amused. He kept his own hands safely away from his vehicle's horn.

Not that he didn't sympathize with the plight of his fellow motorists. *Traffic like this is unusual for a Sunday. If this doesn't clear up soon I'm going to have to cut the hike short.* Jack was on his way up to the Harriman State Park in the Hudson Highlands for some easy hiking, just a quick day trip up the Palisades to get out of the city and see something other than gray concrete and dirty snow.

Looking over the hood of his station wagon, Jack could see the Gothic arches supporting the span over which he and the others around him were waiting to cross. Traffic was definitely still moving. He could see cars jockeying into a single open lane on the right side of the bridge. An NYPD police cruiser had just worked its way forward on the shoulder past the idling cars, and Jack could see the blue flash of the cruiser's lights where the rest of the traffic flow should have been moving.

Jack settled back into his seat. *This might take a while*, he thought. Reaching down to his center console, he twisted the dial to turn on his radio, hoping that the NYPD would be quick about clearing whatever it was that was slowly destroying his Sunday leisure plans.

— —

The traffic around Manhattan this cold Sunday morning shouldn't have been as bad as it was, the officer thought as he stepped out of his patrol car and onto the bridge's asphalt surface. Traffic on Sunday mornings was usually steady but light; today, however, the calls had started to come in over the traffic net of backups at key choke points all over the city, including the Lincoln Tunnel, George Washington Bridge, and the bridges here on the East Side.

Here on the Brooklyn Bridge the officer could see the problem was a stalled box truck in the left-hand lane on the Manhattan-bound side of the bridge, the lane closest to the pedestrian walkway at the bridge's center. Looking through the span's scaffolding and out to his right, the officer could see the blue and red flashing lights of a fellow traffic police officer's patrol car over a quarter of a mile away, on the nearby Manhattan Bridge, both bridges crossing the East River. The other officer appeared to be dealing with a similar issue on that double-decked span.

What are the odds? The officer thought in passing as he started to walk forward to the truck, *another stalled delivery truck on the Manhattan Bridge.* Stalled vehicles weren't unusual impediments to traffic in this or any city, but two of them on two of the usually-congested bridges at the same time was terrible luck for anyone trying to get around this Sunday morning.

Walking along the truck's driver side, between the vehicle and the barrier, the officer arrived at the truck's cab and pulled himself up to window level and peered inside. *Where's the driver?* He wondered. Next the officer tried the door. *Locked.*

The police officer was walking around to try the passenger-side door when a huge white flash to his front, five hundred yards away on the Manhattan Bridge, suddenly filled the space that a millisecond before had been occupied by the stalled truck on the other bridge. He barely registered what had just occurred before the silent white flash of the explosion turned into gray smoke and dust within an expanding hemisphere of flying vehicles, bodies, and jagged chunks of the suspension bridge's support structure. After a moment the blast wave reached the police officer, compressed atmosphere tugging at his blue uniform as the thunderous *CRACK* of the explosion washed over him. Only then did the officer's brain send the belated signal to his body to flinch, and he did so, staggering backwards.

Bomb, he realized almost immediately. *Truck bomb.*

The officer continued to watch as the dirty gray smoke a quarter mile away begin to dissipate. He didn't even realize that traffic on his own bridge had stopped, commuters stepping out of their cars to peer at the wreckage being revealed up-river. The police officer could see jagged pieces of what had been steel support beams hanging down from beneath the long span, while several of the bridge's massive suspender cables either hung loose or twisted grotesquely outward from the blast site.

He was still collecting himself when a low rumble began to force itself into his racing consciousness. Looking across the water at the twisted metal, the officer saw an approaching subway train, a B-Line. It hurtled onto the span's lower deck at the eastern end of the bridge, its conductor realizing his peril too late. The train's breaks sent cascades of squealing sparks out into the air. The police officer watched the catastrophe unfold in slow motion, unable to tear his eyes away.

The train reached the area where the explosion had left a jagged, gaping hole in the lower deck. The front wheels of the lead car jumped off the twisted ends of the damaged track, the car tilting downward briefly before the momentum of the rest of the train began to jackknife the following cars in all directions in a bedlam of screaming metal and crashing glass that drowned out the terrified cries of the passengers within. A railcar exploded out the side of the double-decked bridge, taking with it several more support beams before tumbling the hundred feet to the river below. A second followed.

This last event sounded the death knell of the enormous, proud structure that had stood connecting the two boroughs of the great city for nearly a century. The police officer on the Brooklyn Bridge, along with a growing crowd of motorists, now unconcerned with getting to their respective destinations, watched in horror as the center of the Manhattan Bridge's nearly seven-thousand-foot span began to sag. As if in slow motion, and amid the popping of snapped suspension cables and the low groan of bending steel, the central span of the bridge broke in half, the two newly-created ends gaining speed as they rotated downward until they struck the roiling waters of the East River, one-hundred and thirty-five feet below, sending up a tremendous dirty white splash. Train cars, automobiles, and debris all spilled into the cold waters, creating a cascade of water that made the river appear from a distance as if it was boiling.

Belatedly, the officer recovered his senses enough to bolt for his patrol car. There was a radio there, and someone needed to report this, and fast! People were milling about among the idling vehicles around the officer, gasping and letting out anguished cries at the horror unfolding before them. The police officer arrived at his vehicle in a moment and reached in through an open window for his radio's hand mic. As he did so he looked up over the hood of the patrol car and realized: *White truck. Stalled. Center of the bridge. No driver,* his thoughts raced. The officer opened his mouth to warn the people around him, but the shout was still forming in his throat when the white flash and rapidly expanding blast wave of the ten-thousand pounds of high explosive in the rear of the white truck blew him and everyone around him, into eternity.

——

Jack flinched, his hands tightening on the steering wheel as the second, much louder *CRACK* washed over his car. The honking from the other motorists had stopped at the sound of the first explosion. Jack was surprised to register that it *was* an explosion, he knew because he'd heard them before just not in New York City. The sound rolled over them from their front right, like an angry god ordering them to be silent. Jack had been fiddling with the knob on his radio, trying to find his favorite local news station for a traffic update. Everyone's heads turned to look in the direction of the Manhattan Bridge, past a conglomeration of square, gray office buildings. Jack couldn't see the other bridge, but the god-awful metallic screeching and grinding sounds were enough to tell the veteran reporter that something terrible had happened. His reporter's mind instantly knew what it had been: *bomb.*

Now the gothic arches of Brooklyn Bridge directly ahead had vanished in a dirty yellow flash that almost instantaneously morphed into an ugly gray cloud of expanding dust and debris, cars, asphalt, and people cartwheeling outward like matchsticks tossed into a stiff breeze. The pressure struck with an overwhelming *BOOM.* Jack felt it in his chest more than he heard it, and his station wagon rocked on its suspension, the cab filling almost instantly with the smell of spent high explosives. *Two bombs,* Jack thought, almost subconsciously. *Two bombs on two bridges.* In that instant, Jack knew that this wasn't just a run-of-the-mill terrorist attack. This was something bigger. Bridges were strange targets for terrorists.

Small bits of debris rained down like hail on the stationary cars around Jack. He saw a nick appear in his windshield as rubble clattered off glass and metal. A second nick appeared after a particularly large piece of asphalt struck the windshield with a startling *bang.* Then eerie, oppressive silence settled upon a world enveloped in gray smoke and dust.

The silence didn't last long, however. Terrified motorists were opening their doors and scrambling out, running, stumbling back down the incline, away from the dissipating gray cloud. "Oh gahd, oh gahd, oh gahd," Jack heard a middle-aged woman wail as she sprinted past his driver's side window. It was so absurd he almost laughed until he saw a man dragging a teenage girl by the wrist, a gash in her head bleeding down over her wildly panicked eyes.

Reaching over the passenger seat, Jack opened his glove compartment and pulled out the first aid kit he always kept in his vehicle. Then he leaned back, opened his door, and stepped out right in front of the pair.

"Stop!" Jack called as the man tried to slither around him. "I can help, I've got a—"

"Out of my way!" the man shrieked, shoving his shoulder into Jack's car door and nearly pinning the reporter against the vehicle. Jack had been in a lot of bad places in his career, but never during the catastrophe, or war. It was always *after* the tragedy, *after* people had begun processing the violence that was upending their lives. Now, in the moment, in the unfolding brutality around him, the sheer animal fear of the man pushing past him, dragging the bleeding girl, frightened Jack more than whatever carnage lay ahead. All around, more people were abandoning their trapped cars, streaming rearward.

Standing there between the half-open door and his still-running Subaru holding the tiny first aid kit, Jack suddenly felt silly. *What do you think you're going to do for these people, Jack?* He asked himself. *Everyone who can run is running, and you're not qualified to help anyone who can't.*

He looked forward into the churning gray smoke and knew what he needed to do. Whatever had just happened here, it was important. Jack had no idea what was going on in the world beyond the bubble of his own rattled senses, but something told him that the bombs he'd just witnessed were part of something much bigger. It was a momentous story that would need to be told.

Instead of running, Jack ducked back into the car, tossed the first aid kit onto the passenger seat, and reached into the center console to retrieve the notebook and pencil he kept there. Straightening up, he looked forward onto the bridge, where he could see the yellow flickering of vehicle fires starting to illuminate the thick dust.

The story's up there, he told himself, and started walking towards the carnage.

 **CHAPTER 55**

1319 CET, Sunday 13 February 1994
1219 Zulu
Passenger terminal, Kirkenes Lufthavn, Finnmark, Norway

ANNA HAD ALMOST forgotten the strange group of men in the waiting area, having lost herself in the mundane mid-month reports required of Kirkenes' small airport, when the ringing of her desk phone pulled her attention up from the forms on her desk. She lifted the receiver and answered, "Kirkenes Lufthavn, may I help you?"

The voice at the other end of the line was rushed. "Kirkenes! This is the Ministry of Transportation and Communication in Oslo, Department of Civil Aviation. The prime minister has declared an emergency. It appears the Russians are attacking our forces in the North. We are initiating an evacuation of civilians from communities in Finnmark by air and other means. We need to know: what aircraft do you have on the ground there right now that can carry people south?"

Anna felt something tighten in the pit of her stomach. She had heard something this morning about tension with Russia, but evacuations? Attacks? She sat stock still. After a moment, she remembered that she needed to respond.

Pulling herself together, Anna said, "I'm sorry, can you please explain to me what's going on?" The Russian border was only a few kilometers to the east, she needed to know details.

There was a sigh at the other end of the line, then a weary, "Kirkenes, listen, there is no time. The Russians are…"

The speaker by her ear went silent at the same time that the window panes of Anna's office rattled once with a sharp *CRACK* from outside. Anna jumped at the sound, but held the receiver to her ear for a few seconds more before she realized that the line was dead. She set the telephone down and stood up, walking to her office window to investigate the noise outside.

Anna couldn't see anything out of the ordinary through swirls of blowing snow traversing the tarmac. Then she noticed, *What are the snow plows doing out there? The plowman cleared the pavement this morning.* She watched as the airport's two yellow plow vehicles drove at high speed from the taxiway onto the runway, one turning left and the other right. The vehicles stopped a third of the way up the runway in either direction. Anna saw a man jump out of each and start trotting back towards the terminal. *The men in the terminal,* everything was just too strange not to be connected somehow.

Anna's blood ran cold as her mind raced through all of the unknowns. She needed answers. She headed back out to the ticketing area to see what the few other staff members there could tell her. Anna opened the door to the office part way and stopped immediately. Something wasn't right, it was too quiet. Then she saw it. The legs of the Scandinavian Airlines ticket agent, a friend of hers, were sprawled across her field of view, framed by the rectangle of the end of the corridor. One of the legs was convulsing, bending at the knee and then straightening over and over. Anna's hand flew to her mouth as she stood frozen, unable to move.

At that moment one of the men she'd seen earlier in the lobby backed into the frame near the end of the hallway. He had a short machine gun slung over his shoulder, but what caused her heart to nearly stop was the knife in his right hand. He was wiping it clean, leaving bloody streaks on his trousers as he looked down at his handiwork. Then, to Anna's horror, he looked her way.

She reacted on instinct, slamming the office door closed as she caught a glimpse of the man starting towards her yelling, "*Stoi!*" The door was a heavy one, since the office was where the airlines kept their on-hand cash. She frantically turned the deadbolt, then looked around in a panic for something to barricade the door. She didn't need to look far. On one side of the doorframe stood a heavy gray filing cabinet. Anna stepped to her right and pushed against the top of the metal cabinet. It rocked once as the clerk heard the man's shoulder slam into the other side of the door.

Instinct told Anna that she was fighting for her life as the cabinet settled back onto its base with a *bang*. She stepped back, giving herself a better angle to push against the metal tower, then she set her feet and gave a strong shove, toppling her desk light onto the floor in the process. The three-drawer filing cabinet teetered on its edge for what seemed an eternity, then crashed downward across the doorway just as the man outside smashed his shoulder into it again.

Now Anna looked for something, *anything*, to reinforce her barricade. A third attempt to force the door, followed by an angry shout on the other side of the barrier, added urgency to her search. She ran to her desk and crouched behind it, pushing it so that it scraped across the floor. The young woman continued pushing until it slammed into the filing cabinet. Then she yanked it over to wedge the desk between the first part of her barrier and a corner of the wall formed by the utility closet that occupied a corner of her office.

Anna stepped back and took a breath. The man outside the door was talking to her now in rapid phrases of what she knew to be Russian but couldn't even begin to understand in her current frame of mind. She stood there breathing heavily, then jumped violently as a burst of gunfire shattered the door knob and bolt. The shots were followed closely by another attempt to force the door, which failed due to the tightly wedged cabinet and desk.

Anna Hagen was trapped. Her world, the whole world, had been turned upside down in the past few seconds. She didn't have the time or the where-withal to even consider what was going on beyond her current life or death situation. She only knew she had a few moments before the armed man outside the room found another way in, or shot or battered the heavy door into pieces. *I have to get out of here.*

She ran back to the window, which lead out to the airport grounds. She unlatched it and slid the framed pane upwards. Anna was planning to climb out, but motion to the left stopped her. She looked that way just in time to see four men, each armed with the same stubby weapon, kick in the door leading to the airport's three-story control tower and storm in. Their entry was followed by a small explosion and gunfire from within the other building.

No good. So where? she thought, feeling ever more like a cornered rat. Then it hit her: *Cleaning closet.*

Anna was desperate now as the attacker continued to batter at the door. She ran to the closet, snatching her winter coat off the back of the chair as she entered. Pushing past mops and brooms, she closed the door and climbed onto the lip of the large cast-iron laundry sink.

Having worked in the Lufthavn's old terminal for the past five years, Anna knew the building inside and out. Right now, the only pertinent piece of information in all of that knowledge was the access to the insulating crawl space offered through the ceiling of the closet. She pulled herself completely onto the sink, balancing on the rim, and reached up to yank the lanyard for the hideaway ladder to the crawlspace. It pulled down easily, and Anna climbed up until she was on her hands and knees in the cold, cramped space. As the office door finally collapsed under the violent assault, she retracted the ladder, sealing the crawlspace entrance.

Anna held her breath and listened to the man clamber over her makeshift barrier and stomp into the room. She dared not make even the slightest sound, but she was sure her heartbeat, pounding in her ears, was audible even outside the building. After what seemed like an eternity, she heard the man shout something out the window, belatedly realizing she had left it open. She heard his heavy footfalls move quickly back towards the door before returning once again to the window. *Is he looking for my footprints?* Anna wondered in a sudden panic, trying to remember if the concrete beneath her window had been cleared of snow or not. Then a scraping sound announced the man was crawling out the window, after which Anna heard him shout a question in Russian to some unseen comrade. Then footfalls on the tarmac receded into silence.

Letting out a long breath, she began to shiver, both from the shock and fear of her situation and from the drafty crawl space. Anna struggled into her coat, and crawled towards a vent on the runway side of the building that leaked daylight and cold air into the drafty space. She looked out through the slats to see the two yellow plows sitting in the middle of the runway. For now, no one else was in sight, and she took a moment to collect herself.

Anna considered her options. Stay here: *For how long? Can I give myself up?* Her shaking returned as she thought about her colleague in the lobby.

Was he dead? *Of course he's dead*, she told herself. *Why kill him?* she raged in sorrow. They were Russians, of course. War had come to her country. Would she survive today? Was this how her life would end, here, at the hands of some bloodthirsty Soviet spy? She let out a breath and considered her alternative: Leave: *How? Where would she go? How many men might be outside? Even if she did make it out, how would she survive the cold?*

Then she heard it. Anna listened for a moment before she realized that the low, repetitive, thunder-clap-like sounds she was hearing to the east, was actually gunfire, artillery from the direction of the border. *What now?*

 **CHAPTER 56**

1521 MSK, Sunday 13 February 1994
1221 Zulu
Luostari Airbase, Murmansk Oblast, Russian
Soviet Federative Socialist Republic

G
UARDS COLONEL ILYA Romanov ducked under the still spinning blades as he jogged away from the Mi-8 helicopter at this small,
icy airfield a mere thirty-five kilometers from the Soviet Union's
Norwegian frontier. The tarmac was crowded with dozens of helicopters,
Mi-8 transports, Mi-24 gunships, even some huge Mi-6 and Mi-26 heavy
lift birds, the latter being the largest helicopters in the world, vied for space
on and near the Luostari airbase taxiway. In between the helicopters, some of
whose rotors were just beginning to rotate amid the whine of engines, hundreds
of *desantniki* from the Red Army's 36th Independent Air Landing Brigade
were trudging in small files towards their assigned aircraft. Each paratrooper
carrying his weapon and heavy rucksack wore a white camouflage smock and
their distinctively broad-brimmed steel helmets.

Despite himself, Romanov was amazed at the scale of the operation unfolding before him. He had taken part in some large exercises, particularly in the
past two years, but nothing close to the magnitude of assaults that were about
to launch from this frigid strip above the Arctic Circle. Even in Afghanistan,

heliborne assaults had usually been conducted by relays of a few helicopters delivering only part of the assaulting unit to the landing zone at a time. Here, amid the snow skittering across Luostari's rugged and frost-cracked tarmac, was sufficient aircraft to deliver an entire airborne battalion in a single lift, nearly sixty helicopters in all. That was precisely the plan.

But he didn't head for one of the helicopters. Instead he trotted towards an Ilyushin Il-22 command plane at one end of the runway. The plane's four turboprops were just coughing to life under the aircraft's low-slung wings when Ilya arrived. Standing by the rear stairs leading up to the plane's passenger entrance, Ilya saw the helmetless, white-garbed figure of a *desantnik* officer watching him approach. As he drew close Ilya recognized the handsome Slavic face and thick head of black hair of his friend, Guards Colonel Roman Sokolov.

"Ilya Georgiyevich!" the other officer called out in greeting as Romanov drew near. "Welcome to my war!" He spread his arms to indicate the activity bustling in the cold around them.

"Roman Vasilevich!" responded Ilya warmly as he grasped the other colonel's gloved hand in his own. "Quite the show you're putting on here. We never saw anything like this in Afghanistan."

"We weren't crossing swords with NATO in Afghanistan either, my friend," said Sokolov as he slapped Ilya on the back and guided him into the aircraft. "Those decadent Westerners are never going to know what hit them when my brigade gets into the game! We'll finally have a real stand-up fight, instead of trying to hunt those skulking Mujahideen, *da*?"

Ilya smiled at his friend's bravado. Sokolov had always possessed a penchant for vigorously parroting the party line, even though Romanov knew him to be a serious-minded soldier whose sense of tactics was unclouded by ideology or sentiment. Sokolov's act was intended to inspire those around him with aggression towards their enemies, and it was usually effective, though not Ilya's preferred method for motivating his men. He gave the comment an upward twitch of his mouth and got down to business.

"Your battalion going into Kirkenes is loading up now?" Ilya asked.

"*Da*," Sokolov affirmed. The 36th Brigade's commander guided Romanov to a seat near one of the Il-22's windows next to a bank of radios. "The first battalion takes off in a few minutes. Strap in," he instructed Ilya, "We will be taking off shortly."

Romanov looked around the interior of the Il-22's cabin. Officers and technicians sat at banks of radios up and down the fuselage, while others moved markers around a map of northern Norway and the Kola. The aircraft was built to serve as a flying command post. Sokolov was using it today because his brigade would be conducting assaults against several points in Norway's far north. The nearest of these would be the Kirkenes Lufthavn, which the planners had assured Sokolov would already be in *Spetsnaz* hands by the time his *desantniki* arrived. The last would take place at Banak, two hundred and fifty kilometers to the west.

The 36th AirLanding Brigade's commander would be airborne throughout the day to provide command and control for the widely spaced operations. And Ilya, whose regiment wasn't scheduled to fly until the next day, and whose command would be operating over an even greater geographic extent over the coming days, would be riding along to observe.

"Thank you for letting me burden you with my presence today, Roman," Ilya said as they both buckled into their seats. In the competitive world of Soviet *desantnik* officers, such help between peers was not necessarily a given, and Sokolov was one of the more competitive of the lot. But Ilya Romanov had built a reputation in this sometimes-cutthroat community for tactical competence and for being a good peer. Sokolov and most other *desantnik* officers in the Soviet paratrooper world knew Romanov to be a man who would not betray his peers to advance his own career, and one that would always help his brother officers and their units if his help could advance the common mission. In return, he received both respect and help in kind when he asked for it, as he had in this instance.

"*Nichevo,*" the other officer said with a hand wave as the noise of the engines increased. *It's nothing.* If Ilya could learn anything today that would help him keep his own *desantniki* alive in the coming days, then this outing would be a success.

The Il-22's engines roared to full power and the aircraft bumped down the Luostari runway. In moments they were airborne and Romanov could see the white landscape of the Kola receding beneath the aircraft. As the Ilyushin banked, Romanov caught a view of the full extent of Luostari airbase. Dozens of helicopter rotors whirled like wheels above the drab olive- and brown-painted aircraft as lines of soldiers in white marched like ants beneath them. The first wave of Mi-8s transports, escorted by Mi-24 gunships, began lifting off in white swirls of ice crystals. Then the aircraft banked to the northwest, and Romanov's view changed to the icy blues and whites of the Arctic sky.

Leveling out, the Il-22 proceeded north, allowing Romanov to look to the west, across the frontier and towards Kirkenes. The Norwegian border town was a mere fifty kilometers from the Luostari airfield, a distance covered in less than fifteen minutes. The pilot kept the aircraft below the patchy clouds, which spread out like a blanket at three thousand meters altitude.

They began to circle over the Storskog–Boris Gleb border crossing station, giving both guards colonels a magnificent view of the border region and into Norway all the way to the town of Kirkenes and its airport just to the west. Beneath him the rugged tundra stretched away under its blanket of white, here and there patches of dark, windswept rock breaking through the ground cover. To the south, the boreal pine forests of Finland stretched away as far as his eyes could see, and to the north the white and gray landscape ended at the jagged coastline where snow and ice gave way to black, cold water. Amid this wilderness Ilya could see here and there the dirty ribbon of a road, or the colorful smudges of the settlements that populated this high latitude theater of the newborn global war.

Sokolov directed Ilya's attention downward as they flew over the wedge of snowy frozen lakes and forest where the course of the Pasvikelva River caused Soviet territory to jut northwestwards like a knife towards Kirkenes. From three thousand meters up, Romanov could see dozens of guns and rocket launchers pouring fire towards the northwest, each artillery piece easy to spot, surrounded as they were by halos of ice crystals and smoke thrown out by rapid firing in the frigid atmosphere. Dozens of rockets streamed in their terrible rainbow paths from one side of the frontier to the other, while the invisible one-hundred-twenty-two-millimeter shells of the guns exploded in tight patterns upon the positions of the unfortunate Sør-Varanger Garrison of the Norwegian Army. Romanov did not envy his enemy's position.

Below, most of the artillery of the Soviet 69th Motor Rifle Division, the spearhead of the Soviet thrust into Norway, was engaging. The Norwegians were only supposed to delay, but the weight of today's assault would almost certainly annihilate them before they could escape by land or sea. *Escape was always a forlorn hope for those Norwegians,* the colonel thought, considering the situation from the perspective of his adversaries, *but even doomed men need something to hope for. Better a forlorn hope like that than fleeing into the mountains to hunt us like they did the Germans.* Lifting his gaze to the west, Ilya could see the yellow flashes and dirty puffs of yet more shell strikes on what presumably was the Norwegian defensive positions nearer to Kirkenes.

He tapped Sokolov on the shoulder and spoke into the intercom over the noise of the engines, "How are you directing the artillery for your assault on the airfield?" Romanov could see flashes and smoke rising near the runway, ten kilometers beyond the border.

Sokolov nodded and answered in a loud voice, "*Spetsnaz* seized the airfield ten minutes ago. They are directing the deep fires. For the closer ones, the KGB border troops have kept good records on where the *Norges'* positions are." Romanov nodded. The Soviet special mission soldiers would be playing a similar role in his own regiment's assault tomorrow.

As Ilya was looking out of his window, trying to discern the pattern of the artillery strikes, several fast-moving objects flashed by a thousand meters beneath him. He made out the twin-tailed profiles of four Mig-29 fighters flying west. He then discerned a second westbound flight of four more fighters further south, and another flight of three jets, these ones single-tailed Mig-23s, returning in the opposite direction. The sky seemed suddenly full of military aircraft either flying towards or returning from Norway.

 **CHAPTER 57**

1330 CET, Sunday 13 February 1994
1230 Zulu
Banak Airbase, Lakselv, Troms, Norway

R*ITTMESTER* JOHANSEN STOOD back from the small crowd of milling civilians standing around the chief of the Banak Coast Guard station as the man belted out instructions. His message was punctuated by another sonic boom overhead and what was certainly an explosion not too far away. Low murmurs filled the air among the group of worried people waiting for evacuation in this small passenger terminal, confusion was mounting. The people had been called out from their homes by the local *Politi*, assisted by a squad of Johansen's *dragons*, after the belated evacuation order had come from Oslo.

"Again," the Coast Guard officer was saying loudly, "we have room for children under ten years of age, their mothers, and the elderly aboard the evacuation flights. We have only two aircraft and—"

"Is the government sending more?" shouted someone in the crowd.

The officer shook his head. "I don't know. I'm sure they will. For now, though, this is the priority: children, mothers, and elderly. We have space aboard the two aircraft for one-hundred and twenty-four passengers. Now we'll line up here, and as you pass by please give me your name," the man continued talking. *If he stops, the news would likely sink in and chaos would erupt*, Johansen thought. He knew that the town of Lakselv, just south of the airfield, contained more than two thousand residents, and that less than a tenth of these would fit on the two Fokker 50 commuter turboprop aircraft warming up on the tarmac outside for the flight south. A couple of hundred others were now leaving aboard the Coast Guard frigate *Nordcapp* up the fjord from the town. He could see and hear women and children begin to cry as they nonetheless followed instructions from the officer to form a queue. Families were being ripped apart before his eyes, nursing mothers, babies, and toddlers forced to leave behind fathers and older siblings. Some women began to say that they would not go but were quickly calmed by husbands, sons, and friends.

An elderly couple caught the *rittmester's* attention among the pandemonium of staff trying to gain control and direct the civilians, and tearful goodbyes. An old man was supporting a woman who Johansen supposed was his wife, speaking softly to her in the chaos. As they approached the airman with the clipboard the old man bent down, kissed the woman on the cheek in a very un-Norwegian display of open affection, and began walking towards the exit at the back of the small terminal.

Johansen started forward, intercepting the old man before he exited the building. "Where are you going, *Bestefar?*" he called, using the generic Norwegian term for grandfather.

The man turned. There were tears in his eyes.

"You should get on the plane," it was more of a question than a statement, Johansen realized.

The man was, like nearly all Norwegians, clearly athletic. Bundled against the cold in well-worn layers, he faced Johansen, drawing himself up to his full height, and said, "I was here the last time invaders came to our country, my boy. I am going—" his voice broke, and the *rittmester* could see that the old man was looking beyond himself, back towards the queue where the old woman was ambling towards the commuter plane, helped on the arm of a young Coast Guard air crewman. The man swallowed, composing himself, then continued, "I am going to do what I did in the last war. I am going home to get my rifle and fight the Russians, just like the Germans. This time my wife will be safe." The old man put his hand on Johansen's shoulder and looked into the *rittmester*'s eyes, asking, "Can you promise me she will be safe in the south, *Kaptein*? I will fight with you here."

Now it was Johansen's turn to swallow his emotion. He paused for a long moment, the old fighter's hand on his shoulder. Then he nodded and said, "We will do all that we can, *Bestefar*, I promise you that."

The old man nodded, and his hand dropped to his side. Then he was gone, out the door in a swirl of icy wind and blowing snow, to once more face his nation's enemies.

Looking over his shoulder, Johansen could see that the loading of the aircraft was continuing. They were fortunate that the two SAS Fokker commuter planes had been at Banak in the first place, though many people would still remain in the town. Nothing more here required his attention, so Johansen turned and walked towards his makeshift headquarters in the Coast Guard hangar.

Arriving in the small office, he turned to the man trying to contact battalion on the high frequency radio with a curt, "Situation report?" The phone line had gone dead hours ago.

"Sir," the man said, "we're getting a lot of interference. Hard to hear anything, but a broken transmission from Major Laub a few minutes ago said that the entire battalion was getting on the road, en route to Banak."

Johansen nodded. The electronic jamming of the radio communications was to be expected but, *Twelve hours!* he thought. *It will take 2nd Battalion twelve hours to get here. That's how long we have to hold Banak on our own. Can the Russians even get here by then?*

Johansen remembered the old man in the passenger terminal as his eyes caught sight of a framed piece of paper on the wall. The document was so familiar that he'd not even noticed it when they first arrived, but now, with his country under attack and his countrymen taking up arms of their own accord to defend each other, the famous "poster on the wall" took on new and vital meaning for Johansen. He began to re-read the lines of the ubiquitous document.

The "Directives for Military Officers and Ministry Officials upon an Attack of Norway" was colloquially known as the "poster on the wall" because of the unwritten tradition that it be displayed in every Norwegian military office. The document's origin was in World War II, when confusion in the Defense Ministry during the Nazi invasion of 1940, along with the traitorous radio broadcasts of the hated Vidkun Quisling, had so hampered the Norwegian military's mobilization that the country had succumbed to occupation in just two months. The Directive was a measure to ensure that history did not repeat itself.

Johansen's eyes scanned down the large piece of paper, lingering on the phrases that had become immortal to Norway's defenders since Royal Decree had published the regulation in 1949. *Commit all available forces to the defense as soon as possible,* he read. *Continue to resist even if the situation is hopeless... even if the King and government are captured or incapacitated...even if the enemy threatens reprisals against civilians...even if alone and isolated.*

Alone and isolated. The words stuck in Erik's mind. *That is what we are now.* His thoughts returned to the old man in the terminal. According to the Norwegian constitution, every citizen of the country bore the responsibility to defend it from aggression. Even so, he was humbled by the old partisan's commitment to this principle, his willingness to take up arms now in what would probably be called the third world war. *I will not fail him,* Johansen determined. Then, thinking of all the other civilians not fortunate enough to gain a seat on the evacuation flight he thought, *I will not fail any of them.*

Johansen stood suddenly and said to his radio operator, "Nils, come. We're going out to inspect the squadron's positions." He would make sure that his *dragons* had taken every measure possible to secure their country, this town, and its airbase from attack.

As the two men strode from the stuffy warmth of the office out into the cold of the February day, Johansen could hear the two Fokker 50 evacuation aircraft revving their engines as the first one taxied towards the runway. Overhead, the rumble of jets intruded on his consciousness like the nagging of a squeaky wheel.

 **CHAPTER 58**

1334 CET, Sunday 13 February 1994
1234 Zulu
Over Vadsø, Finnmark, Norway

"PILOT," ILYA HEARD Sokolov speak curtly into the aircraft's intercom, "my assault into Vadsø is scheduled to land soon. When will we arrive over the town?"

"Three minutes, *tovarich* Colonel," responded the pilot.

Ilya heard the drone of the Il-22's engines as they continued north. Their track took them across the Varanger fjord, where the first air battles of the war had occurred less than an hour before. The small town of Vadsø sat forty kilometers from Kirkenes. The aircraft settled into a lazy orbit three thousand meters above the small fishing community just as the transports and gunships of Sokolov's assault company arrived from the east.

Ilya watched with professional dispassion as the assault went in. Two groups of Mi-8 helicopters delivered the assault company to snowy landing zones around the sleepy fishing town. Splitting off, a group of four transports circled around the town while the other four landed a platoon on the flat eastern end of Vadsøya Island. There, a clearing around the archaic airship mast from which the famed arctic explorer Roald Amudnsen had launched his airship *Norge* to overfly the North Pole in 1926 provided a convenient landing zone.

A larger group of nine aircraft, including a huge Mi-26 carrying two small BMD armored vehicles, settled down around the thousand-meter-long runway of the small Vadsø airport, three kilometers east of the town. Romanov could also see four gunships, the big helicopters' stubby, down-turned wings laden with rockets and missiles, their pilots and co-pilot-gunners waiting inside their bulbous canopies to swoop in on any enemy who dared show himself.

They didn't have long to wait. The platoon on Vadsøya moved rapidly to seize the short causeway connecting the island to the rest of the town. Once across, they encountered the first resistance.

Romanov guessed that the Norwegian reservists had been deployed to defend the town's small harbor from a seaborne attack. The rapid advance from Vadsøya caught them repositioning to meet the new threat. A Soviet forward air controller, or FAC, was soon radioing directions and the lead gunship dove.

Romanov observed approvingly as the pilots executed a classic "form a circle" attack, which he'd often seen in Afghanistan. In this maneuver, the gunships dove one at a time, firing their rockets and chin-mounted cannon in a high-speed run at the target. Then the pilot increased power and pulled out of the dive, banking the helicopter sharply in one direction or the other. The evasive maneuver cleared the airspace for the next gunship to attack, while the first helicopter wagon-wheeled back around to rejoin the queue. The key advantage of this tactic was that it minimized the amount of time each helicopter was vulnerable to ground fire and that, if they received any, the following gunship could rapidly adjust to engage its source.

No ground fire rose to meet them today. Cannon shells spit out from the helicopter's chin gun while rockets rippled out of pods beneath stubby wings and streaked downward, exploding in sparks and gray smoke among the scrambling figures of the Home Guardsmen who had been foolish enough to be caught in the open in the confines of the snowy street. The first helicopter surged upwards and to the right while the second Mi-24, was just nosing over to begin its run above Vadsø's harbor-front.

Over the next several minutes the gunships methodically worked over the buildings and streets around the harbor area. Rockets and anti-tank missiles crashed into the warehouses and offices along the waterfront. Cannon shells riddled roofs and walls before exploding inside, terrorizing reservists and civilians alike. Despite himself, Romanov regretted the wanton destruction being dealt to the small fishing town. The effect was decisive however, as the gunships' fire provided cover for the *desantniki* to dash across the causeway and into the town.

Once the first soldiers were ensconced in a warehouse on the mainland side, they laid down a base of fire for the rest to advance deeper into the town, clearing buildings with grenades and bursts of rifle fire as they went. The Norwegians, still stunned by the speed and violence of the attack, either died or fell back to make a desperate stand north of the harbor area.

Firing from windows in the town hall, or *Rådhus*, a group of defenders caught an advancing Soviet squad in the open. Romanov saw three *desantniki* drop in quick succession in the open ground outside the house. Moments later he heard the platoon's forward air controller direct the circling Hinds to engage the structure. In seconds, rockets and missiles smashed into the *Rådhus'* heavy masonry walls.

The helicopters' gun runs suppressed the defenders sufficiently to allow a squad of *desantniki* to stream across the road into the fortified building. Circling overhead, Romanov could see the paratroopers disappear into the front entrance. He'd been in this sort of fight before, clearing from room to room, throwing grenades wherever they encountered resistance and finishing the defenders off with bursts from their AK-74s. The fighting would be close, violent, bloody, and quick.

After several minutes the radio crackled, "*Yastreb* One-Zero-Zero, this is Two-One-One. We have secured the harbor area and are encountering no more resistance north of our positions. I have casualties. The local clinic has been occupied to treat them. There is a Norwegian doctor here who has agreed to help. I will wait here for the rest of the company to arrive from the airfield. End."

Romanov nodded, satisfied with the way the action had played out. The platoon had done about as much as they could do against resistance in a built-up area, and the commander was wise to pause after overcoming the enemy around the harbor. The rest of the company was racing from the airfield, three kilometers east of town, advancing on foot but supported by the two tracked BMDs, with several commandeered civilian vehicles in tow.

Sokolov responded, "Acknowledged, Two-One-One. Treat your wounded, then be prepared to push on to your second objective. Have your company commander report to me when you have achieved linkup. End."

Romanov stood up and stepped across the Il-22's cabin to examine a situation map that showed the brigade's objectives. Grease pencil marks on plexiglass showed anticipated Norwegian positions in blue and planned Soviet assaults in red. Ilya saw that the company now taking control of Vadsø would leave a platoon to secure the town and airfield while the remainder of the assault company raced sixty kilometers west along undefended roads to seize the bridge over the Tana River. This was the next major choke point along the route from Kirkenes to the interior of Norway.

His eyes wandered to symbols indicating a seaborne assault on the ports of Batsfjord and Vardø, sixty kilometers to the north and northeast of Vadsø. Both towns, like Vadsø, were on the Varanger Peninsula, which bulged far into the Barents Sea towards the Soviet Union. Another attack looked to be aimed at the village of Ifjord, situated where the E6 met the head of the expansive Laksefjord. These ports, and more importantly their adjacent airfields, would enable Soviet forces to control the Northern Norway shoreline, allowing them to leapfrog seaward around Norwegian defensive positions. Romanov saw that the force going ashore at Ifjord consisted of two full companies of naval infantry, aimed at controlling the twenty-five kilometers of the E6 that traced the jagged head of the Laksefjord, the last major obstacle on the road to Banak.

Banak: the ultimate objective of this first day's offensive in the north. Ilya's pulse quickened as he took in what Sokolov had planned there.

Roman Sokolov tapped Ilya on the shoulder. He hadn't heard the other man come over to the map, being momentarily absorbed in contemplating the Red Army's strategy for the far north. In typical Soviet fashion, Ilya had only been privy to the plans for his own division's employment. Seeing the full picture gave him a sense of both the magnitude and the difficulties of his country's offensive here.

Sokolov indicated Vardø with his finger. "That's where we're going next," he said into the intercom. "We'll see what those naval infantry boys can do!"

 **CHAPTER 59**

1338 CET, Sunday 13 February 1994
1238 Zulu
Viper Two-One, over Alta, Finnmark, Norway

"VIPER TWO-ONE, BACKSTOP," the ground radar controller called. Olsen and Bjorn circled in their F-16s over Alta, seventy kilometers west of Banak.

"Go ahead, Backstop," Jan answered.

After ambushing the Flankers in the opening seconds of the war, he and Bjorn had been kept in reserve as other flights of F-16s surged forward to parry Soviet raids all over Northern Norway. Ten minutes earlier, Backstop had ordered another pair from Olsen's Eagle Squadron eastward to escort an evacuation flight out of Vardø, a coastal village in the far northeast. Jan clenched his jaw in anticipation, they would be called on next as their comrades either ran out of fuel, missiles, or were shot down or damaged in combat. *I'm ready*, he told himself

"Two-One, we have two evacuation aircraft lifting off from Banak," Backstop said. "Vector zero-nine-zero and fly top cover for them until they're clear. Right now we show nothing inbound to that location, but plenty of action to the south. The Soviets are violating Finnish airspace and moving across Lapland, over."

Olsen didn't like that last bit. If the Soviets didn't respect Finnish neutrality, it meant they could launch aerial attacks from a much broader front than Norway's own narrow frontier.

"Roger, Backstop," he acknowledged.

Once settled on an easterly course, he and Bjorn pushed their throttles forward and shot back toward the airfield from which they'd launched less than an hour ago. In under five minutes they watched the first blue- and white-painted Scandinavian Airlines Fokker 50 lift off the runway. Olsen looked down from ten thousand feet through scattered clouds to see the Fokker fly out over the fjord. Its propellers clawed the air under the aircraft's high-slung wings as it gained speed, then banked left, setting a southwesterly course for Swedish airspace. *Surely the Soviets aren't bold enough to pick a fight with the Swedes as well,* Jan thought. He and Bjorn banked their jets to circle the airfield as the second Fokker took off.

As they turned, Backstop called, "Two-One, continue east. The Vardø escort ran into some trouble and diverted to engage bandits to the southeast. Standby for immediate divert task but pick up the Vardø escort job, then remain over Banak. There is some major action developing to your south, but nothing from the east right now."

"Backstop, what about Kirkenes? Anything coming out of there?" Jan asked. Covering an evacuation out of there would be hairy, to say the least. He wanted as much information as possible to prepare.

"Negative, Two-One. Kirkenes tower went off the air a few minutes ago."

Olsen allowed that news to sink in for a moment. It was all happening so fast! He had already lost two of his pilots, one third of his Banak dispersal group in just half an hour of combat. People were fleeing the far north, and now Kirkenes had, what, *Fallen already?* Jan's hand tightened around his sidestick in growing anger and his breathing quickened. He pushed the emotion aside as best he could. *It doesn't matter right now. Get the evacuation flights to safety.*

They met the Vardø flight over the port town of Batsfjord on the north coast. As Olsen and Jan accompanied the passenger flight the short distance to Banak, the pilot called Olsen and told him they'd seen Soviet landing craft approaching Vardø from the east. Jan passed the information to Backstop as he and Bjorn finished their brief escort and turned back east.

While the civilian airliners fled to safety, they listened over the net as a major raid developed to their south. The Backstop radar station was the new target. *Bombers to finish the job that the Scuds started earlier,* Jan surmised, clenching his teeth. *Backstop is all we have now.* He threw up a silent prayer that his forces could, at the least, stall the Soviets. Until a replacement AWACS arrived, Backstop was vital for coordinating the defense of the Far North. Jan listened as four F-16s were vectored in to ambush a flight of MiG-27 fighter-bombers and their MiG-23MLD escorts. His comrades from 331 Squadron downed several of the raiders in two high-speed passes, forcing the remainder to break off and jettison their bombs into the snowy taiga below. Jan continued to listen as the NATO pilots, their mission accomplished, dove and streaked westward, away from the surviving Soviet escorts. Then it was Olsen and Bjorn's turn.

"Viper Two-One, Backstop. We have a raid developing to your northeast. I have eight. No. Make that ten bandits bearing zero-six-zero relative, heading northwest. Six at angels two, four more behind them at angels ten. Looks like the same composition as the raid we just broke up around our location. Expect MiG-27s escorted by -23s. Vector zero-two-five to intercept, over," the controller ordered.

Olsen's pulse quickened as he turned his nose to the northeast and readied himself for combat once again. They were growing short on fuel after the high-speed maneuvering earlier, and each of the Falcons only had half its missiles remaining, but he was confident. He and Bjorn had held their own against the best aircraft the Soviets could throw at them just a half hour before. The MiGs they were intercepting now were much older, no match for the sleek fighter he was flying. Both the MiG-23 air superiority fighters and MiG-27 fighter-bombers carried the NATO codename "Flogger" since they were based on the same single-tail, swing-wing airframe, which might have been cutting edge fifteen years before, but not now. *Still, there are ten of them against two of us.* Jan's jaw was beginning to ache with the tension.

"Bjorn," Olsen called his wingman, "we'll come in low from behind and break up the bombers before they know we're there. Then we'll do a climbing right turn and take on the escorts before they dive on us. Got it?"

Bjorn clicked his microphone twice in response. The two fighters rocketed north on their intercept course, descending through the broken clouds that separated them from the snowy landscape below. Backstop continued to give them course corrections as they approached the Russian jets from the left-rear until: "Two-One," the radar controller called, "those four escorts are turning towards you. Radars are coming on. Tasman IDs them as MiG-23MLDs." Static started to interfere with the radio control net as Russian electronic jammers turned their attention towards this part of the battlefield.

What the hell? wondered Olsen, *no way those Russians should have been able to know we were inbound yet. Unless—*

Backstop beat him to the punch, calling to inform him through waves of electronic noise, "Tasman is reporting…Mainstays radiating now…probably have you…MiGs your way…climb to engage, over." Olsen pieced together from the fragmented message that the Soviets apparently had their own AWACS, a Beriev A-50, NATO codename "Mainstay," up and directing the pilots of the escorting MiG-23s towards him and Bjorn. *Bad news coupled with more bad news,* Jan thought as he increased power to climb. The MLD version was the most modern Flogger, this had just become a much less favorable engagement.

Within a few seconds the Norwegians' radar warning receivers were blaring in their helmets, a clear indicator that missiles were inbound. *This situation is becoming a little too familiar,* thought Olsen as he scanned the sky ahead for tell-tale vapor trails.

"Two-Two," he called to Bjorn, you evade left. I'll break right. Once we shake the missiles, we'll scissor up into them. Ready and, NOW!"

The nimble Falcons rolled in opposite directions and diverged until they were flying away from each other and perpendicular to the oncoming missiles. Olsen continued scanning to his left until he caught sight of the thin white trail of the missile bending towards him. He waited for a long second, then punched his chaff dispenser twice, not noticing that nothing happened after the first chaff packet exploded out the back of his aircraft. Then he rolled left and pulled up, grunting through the high-G turn. He could still see the missile tracking him. The screech of the RWR continued to scream. Finally, Jan's tight turn forced the pursuing missile to turn so acutely that its seeker lost the return from its parent aircraft's radar, and it streaked harmlessly past his tail.

Olsen's maneuver had worked perfectly, and not just as an evasive tactic. Having shaken the missile, the nose of his own aircraft and the seekers heads for his three remaining Sidewinder missiles were pointed squarely at two oncoming MiGs. Now *they* were in range, and *he* had the advantage as he closed from their low front.

The MiGs were closing with Jan at a combined speed of a thousand miles per hour as he put the silhouette of the first one into his heads-up display, lining up a missile, and heard the warm purr in his helmet as the Sidewinder locked on: "Fox Two!"

In the same instant Jan saw a flash beneath the MiG's wings as the Russian pilot launched his own infrared-guided missile. Olsen threw his sidestick to the right to evade and punched the release for his hot-burning magnesium flare decoys. The Norwegian missile exploded into the left air intake of the Soviet jet, while a split second later the Russian missile's infrared seeker, struggling to maintain lock on the relatively cool front of Olsen's oncoming fighter, exploded uselessly into one of the flares trailing behind.

"Splash one!" Jan called in triumph, seeing the broken airframe of his victim spinning downward towards the ground. Then he threw his stick back to the left, executing a climbing turn to get onto the tail of the second MiG, while the Soviet turned his own ungainly fighter to try to do the same to Jan, the Flogger's swing wings fully extended to increase maneuverability. It was a losing proposition, Jan's nimble F-16 hopelessly outmatched the bigger Mig-23 in a close dogfight. In moments Jan was stitching twenty-millimeter cannon shells into the Soviet jet's tail from less than three hundred meters range. Yellow flame shot from rear of the MiG as the big bullets ripped through its fuel tanks, and Olsen saw the Soviet pilot's ejection seat shoot skyward.

Olsen had splashed two assailants, but while he did so the six fighter-bombers had continued towards the North Cape coastal radar station. Jan had lost track of Bjorn and couldn't raise him on the radio. He continued calling to Backstop, even though communications were nearly unintelligible due to the powerful jamming. Tasman had called earlier to inform all pilots that the jamming was emanating from a Soviet "Cub-D.". The Cub's four "Siren" electronic countermeasures pods were jamming whatever targets of opportunity the Norwegians showed them, in this case the radio frequency that Backstop site was using to communicate with Olsen's flight.

Jan decided to energize his radar in an attempt to find the MiG-27s. *There!* Six green dots on the screen, range twenty-four miles. A quick look at the LCD told Olsen that the MiGs were three hundred meters above the Porsangerfjord, heading due north, accelerating towards the Cape. He didn't think he'd be able to get to them before they reached the coastal radar north of Honningsvåg, but he intended to try with his last reserves of fuel. *If only I had more missiles*, Jan thought, his bitterness growing. By now he knew he wouldn't be returning to Banak for fuel or arms.

Pushing his throttles forward to their stops he dipped his nose to trade what little altitude he had for speed. Twenty miles ahead of him the Floggers screamed past the Norwegian Coast Guard Cutter *Norkapp*, whose crew was desperately making for the mouth of the fjord before they could turn south for safety. Going "feet dry" over the oil terminal at Honningsvåg on the southeastern coast of the North Cape's island of Magerøya, the MiGs pulled up to clear the rugged, ice-covered cliffs. Jan continued to close on the tails of the Russian jets, but, *I'm not fast enough*, he raged.

The Soviets' covered the distance from Honningsvåg to the radar station in less than ninety seconds. They released their bombs in unison, and twelve dark objects arced down towards the large white dome protecting the radar from the arctic elements as the swing-wing fighter bombers pulled up to gain separation from the coming explosions. The first blast was several hundred meters from the dome, the rest walked toward the structure in split-second thunderclap intervals. The last two bombs crashed through the already dis-integrating plastic dome and detonated in a massive cloud of gray smoke, dark rock, and dirty snow, abruptly terminating the radar emissions from the sensor. *Shit*, thought Jan.

The MiG-27s, turned east after obliterating the coastal radar, heading home. He wanted to exact some small revenge, maybe splash one of the bandits as they withdrew, but the intervention of the two surviving MiG-23s diving on him from behind had forced him to fire one of his remaining Sidewinders at extreme range and then turn south to save himself. His missile, fired too far behind its target in a tail chase, had fallen harmlessly into the choppy waters at the broad mouth of the Porsangerfjord.

Fortunately for Jan, the Russians had opted not to pursue, instead they turned to escort the fighter-bombers home. Continuing his evasive turn southward all the same, he pointed his jet's nose towards the Cape. He tried calling Backstop once more, "Backstop," Jan called, "give me a vector to Two-Two, over." He needed to form back up with Bjorn. To his surprise he received a clear reply. Apparently, the Soviet jammers now had other fish to fry.

"Two-One, Two-Two is gone," came Backstop's somber response. "Last plotted just south of your current position, no beacon."

Jan swallowed a dry mouth, *It can't be. Bjorn is too good a friend, too good a pilot to be gone just like that!*

Then his own eyes confirmed his wingman's death. As he pulled up and went feet dry over the Cape, he couldn't fail to see the pyre of black smoke rising from an orange fire on the snowscape to his front. As Olsen flew over the crash site, he looked down to see the broken piece of a wing lying in among the snow-covered rocks and other debris. The wing still showed the blue and red roundel marking of the Royal Norwegian Air Force. Backstop said no beacon, so he hadn't ejected either.

Jan blinked away tears as he continued southwest, realizing one of his closest friends was truly gone. A call from Backstop yanked his consciousness back into the present. "Two-One, come to bearing two-six-zero. Major raid developing against Banak. Clear the airspace so Three-Three can intercept. Vector for Tromsø to rearm and refuel."

And which wingman will I lose on that one, Olsen wondered bitterly. Now *three* of the five pilots who'd flown north with him were gone. Rage began to overtake the heavy sadness in his chest. The Russian invaders were stripping him of his friends one by one. They *had* to be stopped. Then he realized: *Raid. Banak. I promised to protect Erik!*

 **CHAPTER 60**

1340 CET, Sunday 13 February 1994
1240 Zulu
HNoMS *Terne*, off the North Cape

S IX MILES TO the west, between the rocky, icy cliff walls of the inlet called Tufjorden on the Atlantic side of the Cape, the Norwegian *Hauk*-class missile boat HNoMS *Tern* and her two older missile-torpedo boat compatriots, *Rapp* and *Storm*, were accelerating towards the mouth of the inlet when the radar station went silent. The small flotilla was one of three such groups that put to sea earlier in the day, when the world was still at peace, to lie in wait along Norway's craggy north coast as insurance against a Soviet naval offensive. Norway's numerous and dangerous fleet of small craft was an integral part of the defense plan in the event of war. That investment was about to be tested.

The technicians manning the North Cape radar, after surviving the Scud attack and repairing their equipment, had been providing the captain of the *Tern*, a tall, hollow-cheeked officer named Egil Møller, with position reports on a group of four Soviet *Nanuchka*-class corvettes passing through the gray waters twenty-two miles due north. As the three Norwegian craft crossed from the relatively calm waters of the fjord out to the chop of the wintry Barents Sea the reports ended mid-sentence.

Møller's group was en route to ambush the Soviet corvettes before they could turn southwest into the Norwegian Sea and make for the port of Tromsø. Møller was counting on the radar to provide targeting data so he could launch his Penguin II anti-ship missiles at their maximum twenty-mile range without having to turn on his own radar to provide a vector. The shorter range of the older Penguin I missiles on the other two boats would force his comrades on *Rapp* and *Storm* to close a further five miles to make their own attacks. The loss of the coastal radar severely limited the group's options.

The Norwegian tactic was to rely upon the rugged coastline behind them to mask their craft from the *Nanuchkas'* radar, and thus from the six radar-guided SS-N-9 "Siren" anti-ship missiles carried by each of the Soviet ships. This was important. The Soviet weapons out-ranged the Norwegians' infrared-guided Penguins by a factor of three, hampering a proper radar fix was essential for survival. Moreover, the Norwegians needed an accurate update on the Soviets' position in order to get the Penguins' short-range infrared seekers close enough to acquire the enemy ships. With the coastal radar now a smoking ruin, the only alternative was to find the enemy themselves by leaving the safety of the rocky cliffs and using their onboard radar, thus turning on an electronic search light that the Soviets could hardly miss. The small flotilla accelerated north out of the fjord to engage.

Møller ordered his command to their maximum speed of thirty-two knots. The *Tern* would need four minutes to close on the Russians, as long as they didn't change from their last reported course and speed. The older boats would need twelve.

— —

Aboard the lead *Nanuchka*, the MRK *Priboy*, the senior Soviet captain listened as his radar room reported tracks coming out of the fjord mouth to the west of the Cape. "Definite contacts, *tovarich* Captain," the technician was saying, "but I cannot pick them out individually against the cliffs. Too much clutter."

The captain nodded with a knowing grin. His intuition had been right. The strategy from the beginning had been to trawl along the coast, tempting the dangerous Norwegian boats out into open water where they could be destroyed by his longer-ranged weapons. He reached for his radio and ordered his flotilla into a prearranged turn to the north, away from the emerging Norwegians. He would force the enemy boats to chase him to where his sensors could track them sufficiently and guarantee hits with his missiles.

Three miles north of the Soviet corvettes, the modern Norwegian diesel submarine *Utstein* hovered at communication depth twenty-five miles off the Cape. Her captain smiled to himself as his small sonar room reported the course change for the Soviet ships. The *Nanuchkas* possessed far too much speed for his submarine to stalk them effectively, so he'd been hoping for *something*, probably the missile boats he knew were lurking in the area, to force the Russians ships north into the engagement envelope of his torpedoes. Now something had. Patience had paid off.

"Torpedo room," the captain called, "how is our firing solution to the contacts?"

"Captain, we have good solutions for all four. I assess that the lead two, contacts One and Three, won't be able to evade based on their new course," the *Utstein*'s weapons officer responded

The captain nodded, then ordered, "Very well. Prepare to fire one weapon each at One and Three. Stand by for the same at Contacts Two and Four on my order"

"Captain, high-speed screws to our front! Torpedoes in the water dead ahead! I estimate two thousand meters, captain!" screamed the sonar officer onboard the *Priboy*.

The Russian captain was stunned. He knew in that moment that his ship would not survive this attack. Even his nimble craft could not realistically hope to evade what almost certainly were homing torpedoes fired at point blank range. Despite this, he decided to do what he could in the two minutes or less that his command had left.

"Hard turn to starboard!" he ordered. "Weapons officer, I want a missile targeted at each of those contacts now!"

"But captain!" the weapons officer responded, "Contacts are still very weak, and our firing solutions are too poor!"

"We have no time," the captain responded as he felt the deck pitch beneath his feet, his ship heeling to starboard, "we must counterattack now while we're afloat!"

Seconds later the *Priboy* and its consorts had reversed their courses and were churning south as three missiles exploded out of the large tube launchers mounted to either side and beneath each corvette's bridge. Twelve fiery tails of gray smoke as they streaked south towards the oncoming Norwegian missile boats.

—— • ——

Aboard *Terne*, Møller judged that the enemy was finally within range of his Penguin II missiles and ordered their launch. The four weapons rippled out of the box launcher on the fantail of his ship. As his boat turned hard to port to make for the safety of the cliffs and inlets to the south, he ordered his radar turned on. Møller puffed out his sunken cheeks in a sigh, feeling craven breaking contact while *Rapp* and *Storm* continued on. At least he could help by reestablishing radar contact so that the other two boats could launch at their maximum range. Just as *Terne* settled into her southward course, Møller heard one of his lookouts shout, "Vampire!"

The missile warning would not have done *Terne* any good had the Soviet weapons been better aimed, but as it was the captain only caught sight of the gray-painted projectile as it shot past his ship, its active radar seeker homing in on the return it was receiving from the cliffs beyond. A second later he saw the corkscrewing gray smoke trail of a Mistral surface-to-air missile leave its pedestal mount aboard *Rapp*, still surging northward through the choppy seas. He tracked the defensive weapon as it feathered north, its smoke trail disappearing as the rocket motor burned out. Then there was a small puff in the distance followed by a bigger flash as the Mistral found the incoming Soviet weapon, exploding it half a mile away.

The captain pumped his fist in triumph, but his celebration was cut short a moment later when *Storm* disappeared, enveloped within a thunderous flash. The watery explosion morphed into a dirty gray cloud that obscured his view of the boat. When the cloud cleared, all that remained of the *Storm* and her nineteen crewmen were pieces of jagged debris bobbing in the swell.

———

"Captain, missile warning south!" the commander aboard *Priboy* heard his radar officer call. The threat would have concerned him more if he were not so certain that his command was already doomed by the homing torpedoes closing on his ship's stern. Now he only hoped that his ship could attract enough missiles to give the others in his flotilla a chance at survival.

"Defensive weapons released. Fire at will," he ordered in a soft, dream-like voice.

Forward of the bridge, the *Priboy*'s AK-630 close-in weapons system rotated slightly as the six-barreled rotary cannon in the small turret cued towards the radar returns from an incoming Penguin missile. The computerized brain of the system assessed the target's course and speed for a moment, then the gun let loose a strobing tongue of fire with an ear-splitting *BRRRRP* that sent a string of thirty-millimeter projectiles arcing forward. One of the large bullets connected, smashing the Penguin into pieces that careened violently into the water just a few meters away.

The other three *Nanuchkas'* defensive fire joined that of *Priboy*'s, sending streams of automatic fire southward to knock down three of the four incoming Norwegian missiles. The fourth evaded the Russian fire by performing an evasive bob and weave maneuver just before it dove through the plate glass of the *Priboy*'s bridge windows and detonated its warhead, killing the Soviet captain and his entire bridge crew. Seconds later the torpedo fired by the *Utstein* completed the corvette's destruction, along with one of her sister ships, in two massive watery explosions.

Minutes later, four more Penguin missiles, these ones fired by *Rapp*, swept in among the two surviving Russian ships. Two fell to gunfire, but two more dove into the rearmost *Nanuchka* and exploded. This ship's crew had just managed to evade their pursuing torpedoes, but now the small craft was left on fire and listing heavily.

Two Russian corvettes had been sunk and another crippled. Tallied against this was the loss of the Norwegian missile-torpedo boat, *Storm*, which in a stroke of luck or bad radar conditions was the only victim of the twelve missiles the Russians had launched, leaving Møller wondering how long he would last in this violent, confused high-tech form of war.

 **CHAPTER 61**

1342 CET, Sunday 13 February 1994
1242 Zulu
Northwest of Vardø, Finnmark, Norway

WHILE THE IL-22 Command aircraft flew the sixty kilometers northwest from Vadsø to Vardø, a second engagement between Norwegian and Soviet warships unfolded north of the town of Batsfjord. Ilya listened over the radio to catch snippets of the engagement. A pair of Norwegian missile boats sallied out from the jagged coast northwest of Vardø and engaged a line of Soviet *Osa*-class missile craft that were sweeping westward, sinking two before missiles from a lurking group of Soviet *Tarantul*-class corvettes annihilated the Norwegians.

Ilya Romanov let out a breath as the naval combat resolved. When the engagement began, he and Sokolov had looked out their windows to the north, straining their eyes to try to observe the action. The flashes on the horizon announced the sinking of the small warships, both NATO and Soviet. *Death*, thought Ilya, *those are just some of the many deaths taking place today.* A deep resignation, sadness even, was settling over his features as violence claimed lives all around him. The same sadness had gripped him during all of his combat duty in Afghanistan. From that experience, Ilya knew the feeling would soon metamorphize into a grim determination to end the conflict as quickly as possible, through swift victory.

Now Sokolov was explaining the engagement: "—was an ambush. The coastal naval forces commander used his own missile craft as bait to draw out the *Norges* where his larger ships further out could smash them. It seems to have worked. Their purpose was to clear the way for our landing at Ifjord."

Romanov nodded. *Still, two missile boats and their crews seem an expensive bait*, he thought, picturing the young men on both sides who had just perished in fire amid the icy waters. Even so, he had to admit that the ambush seemed to have achieved its purpose of destroying the Norwegian naval defense.

Next to Ilya, Sokolov grabbed a radio operator by the sleeve and ordered, "Get the navy on the line. I want to know what other losses they've taken and if they can still guarantee the safety of our assault convoy going to Ifjord. Go!"

The soldier nodded and made the call. A moment later, the radioman said, "*Tovarich* Colonel, the naval officer would like to speak to you directly."

Sokolov grabbed the hand mic away and spoke into it, "This is *Yatreb* Lead."

Romanov only caught one-sided snippets of the heated conversation which followed. "Can you secure those transports?" Pause. "Yes, we are *all* taking losses, what did you expect?" Then Sokolov snorted, "No. We do not have time for you to form another sweep. Can you not move forward with what you have left?"

Sokolov was growing visibly frustrated with the conversation. Finally, he threw the hand-mic down and walked back to the map. Ilya followed him and watched as his friend contemplated his options.

After a moment, Sokolov beckoned a radioman over and directed, "Contact those transports bound for Ifjord." The vessels carrying the landing force consisted of two huge *Zubr*-class assault hovercraft, which could skim across the wavetops at better than fifty knots and carried a full company of armored vehicles in their expansive holds. They relied upon their speed to evade attacks, but in the narrow confines of the fjord they would be vulnerable. Moreover, given their capabilities, the *Zubr*-class ships were not an asset that could be risked against unsure odds this early in the war.

"Tell them," Sokolov said through gritted teeth, "the navy cannot promise their safety from those blasted missile boats all the way to the objective. Order them to put in at their alternate landing site," he stopped to study the map again for a moment, "at Mehamn."

Romanov looked at the chart. Mehamn was one of the northernmost settlements in Norway, situated at the northern end of the Nordkinn Peninsula. It was tenuously connected to Ifjord in the south by the ribbon of pavement known as County Road 888. Ilya shivered as he imagined the conditions the naval infantry would encounter on their advance south from the town along a narrow, snow-swept road through the tundra.

"Won't those marines struggle to get to their objectives from Mehamn?" asked Ilya.

Sokolov looked over at him. "Those naval infantry think they're so elite, perhaps they should prove it! What do they have all those armored vehicles for, if not a situation like this?" He dismissed the concern with a wave of his hand.

Ilya wasn't so sure. He doubted those roads would be kept clear of snow through the long, dark winter. On the other hand, the eight-wheeled BTRs would be good vehicles to make the trip, and Romanov was impressed with his colleague's flexibility in ordering the change of objective. This flexibility also spoke well of the planning his staff had done to prepare this operation, the same kind of planning Ilya's staff was now conducting back at Olenya.

Pushing the thought from his mind, Ilya returned to his seat and directed his attention downward, looking at Vardø's harbor area. Below, a flotilla of small, antiquated landing craft carrying a company of Soviet naval infantry was passing unopposed through the harbor's breakwater, white wakes becoming visible as they entered the calmer waters. The vessels had departed the small Soviet Naval base at Linhammar north of Pechenga several hours earlier. Ilya continued to watch as the five-landing craft rumbled up to the snowy shoreline and dropped their ramps.

Eight-wheeled BTR-70 armored troop transport vehicles drove down the ramps and into the lapping surf, then up and onto the icy beach with white-clad marines trotting behind them. Romanov watched the infantry advance across the beach and the mere hundred meters south before reaching the Vardø tunnel, which connected the mainland and the town two and a half kilometers away on Vardøya Island. Another hundred meters, and the BTRs were rolling across the thousand-meter-long runway of the airport. From the island the town's Norwegian defenders, reservists all, could do nothing but watch as the Soviet troops took control of the harbor and runway.

Ilya looked on, contemplating the one-two punches of the airborne and marine descent across Northern Norway. These assaults would clear the way for the motor rifle troops in the Kola to sprint deep into Norway with their tanks and artillery, despite the restrictive terrain up here in the Arctic. *I can only pray for such smooth execution in my own operations,* thought Romanov.

Sokolov leaned across to Ilya and slapped him on the back, saying into the intercom, "We're heading from here down to Kirkenes to watch the assault there. After that, we fly west to Banak. My pathfinders are scheduled to go into the drop zones there in an hour."

Romanov nodded his understanding. Then, looking out the window, he could see their Il-22 had picked up an escort of twin-tailed MiG-29s, bringing the import of Sokolov's statement home to Ilya. They were heading back south, into contested airspace for the first time today. He hoped the *VVS* was doing as well clearing the skies over Norway as the marines and Sokolov's airborne troops were at seizing the ground.

 **CHAPTER 62**

1644 MSK, Sunday 13 February 1994
1244 Zulu
USS *Connecticut* (SSN 22), mouth of the Kola Inlet, Barents Sea

COMMANDER ETHAN ROGERS clenched and unclenched his balled left fist in frustration as he sat, waiting, in *Connecticut*'s control room. An old high school injury to his right hand had cut short a promising career as a quarterback, and his left hand always became more active when he felt stressed. He sported a five o'clock shadow, having not torn himself away from the control room long enough to walk the few meters to his cabin to splash water on his face and shave. His boat was out of immediate danger after its close brush with the *Kuznetsov* battle group half an hour before, but still very close to the enemy's sensors. After the formation passed overhead, the captain ordered his submarine off the bottom and proceeded towards the eastern side of the Kola Inlet's mouth. That's where they were waiting now, barely maintaining steerage-way in the shallow waters.

Satisfied that the worst was over, Rogers was about to order the boat to periscope depth to extend their electronic surveillance mast, checking for any lingering snoopers. There was also the need to receive the urgent message from Norfolk and send the burst contact report that Lieutenant Santamaria was keeping queued up in the communication room. That, after all, was the whole point of this patrol: to report on the activities of the Red Banner Northern Fleet.

"Con, Sonar." The call cut off the captain's thoughts, "More noise from the inlet sir. It sounds like we have another formation coming out. Multiple contacts. No classification yet, sir," the sonar chief concluded apologetically. The whole crew had picked up on the skipper's foul mood.

Rogers' fist clenched more tightly. The longer he delayed transmitting, the greater the opportunity for the Soviets to hide their carrier in the dark vastness of the Arctic Ocean.

"Very well," the skipper said tightly. "Let me know when you have something."

Minutes passed as this new group of Soviet ships emerged from the channel into the more open waters of the Barents Sea. When the chief in charge of the sonar room called again, his voice was far more unsure than it had sounded before. "Captain, I need you to take a look at this again."

Rogers was out of his seat and inside the sonar room in a heartbeat. The chief's face was inches away from the green "waterfall" display, studying the slowly descending lines of one of the new contacts.

"What is it, Chief?" the captain asked, impatience plain in his voice.

The sonarman seemed to ignore him for a moment. Rogers was about to repeat his question more sharply when the man leaned back into his seat, touched a finger towards the lines he had been studying, and said in confusion, "It's another carrier, sir."

Rogers was non-plussed for a moment. He knew that the Red Banner Northern Fleet's two helicopter carriers, *Baku* and *Kiev*, were both at sea already, and they had just listened to *Kuznetsov*, the Soviets' only full-sized carrier, depart the inlet half an hour before.

"What do you mean, 'another carrier,' Chief?" Rogers asked, his voice dangerously quiet. "We have all their carriers accounted for already."

The chief looked back at his captain and said in a level, steady voice, "I mean sir, that this new contact sounds…it sounds almost exactly like the *Kuznetsov*, sir. It's." The man paused for a moment to think, "It doesn't have that same rattle *Kuznetsov* gives off from her outermost port screw, but besides that this contact sounds *exactly* the same, screw noises, propulsion plant, the works."

Now the captain was puzzled. *Another carrier? It couldn't be, could it? How would the Soviets' have pulled that off without us knowing about it?*

"Chief, you're sure it's not the second *Kirov* that we haven't detected yet?" he asked. Was it possible they were mistaking one of the Soviet fleet's large battlecruisers for a second aircraft carrier?

"Negative, sir," responded the chief quickly, looking a bit miffed at his captain's doubt. "The *Kirovs* only have two screws. If you look here," he indicated the waterfall display with a finger, "you can clearly see this contact has four. The only ship in Red Fleet with four shafts is the *Kuznetsov*, and we already ID'd her half an hour ago."

Rogers nodded. *Need more coffee*, he thought. *This day isn't getting any shorter. If this really is a second* Kuznetsov-*class boat, then, well then damn the whole day to hell.* The captain decided to give voice to his conclusion. "The Soviets must have finished work on the *Varyag* without us realizing," he said quietly.

The lingering doubt he had felt about whether or not the world was at war vanished. There could only be one explanation for why the Soviets would rush their second big-deck carrier into operation and send it to sea right behind their first.

The TAKR *Varyag*, sister-ship of the *Admiral Kuznetsov*, had been under construction in the Ukraine when the USSR entered its turbulent times in the early '90s. For a while, it looked like it might be cancelled entirely due to lack of funds. By the time of Medvedev's ascension to power, the ship was rusting away down in the Black Sea. The military revitalization program had changed that. Ukrainian shipyards completed construction of the hull and propulsion systems, but then construction stalled again. The Soviet Navy moved the ship to its main base in the Kola last year, where the hulk had continued to sit in apparent neglect. Now, it seemed, that neglect had been more apparent than real. Rogers was seriously beginning to question his own decision not to attack the *Kuznetsov* earlier. *If the Soviets have two big-deck carriers to deploy into the Arctic seas then—*

"That seriously changes the balance of power up here," Rogers muttered.

The chief nodded in agreement. He'd been thinking the same thing.

"Okay," Rogers said. "Let's assume that it's the *Varyag*. What's her escort look like?"

The chief turned back to his console and grabbed his yellow notepad. Looking down he reported, "Escort looks to be like the *Kuznetsov* group, sir. So far we've got good tracks on two *Udaloy* class ships, and two of the *Sovremenny*—"

One of the other sonar operators in the room who had been staring at his own waterfall display as he listened intently to his headphones sat back and tapped the chief on the elbow with the back of his hand. The older sailor turned and asked, "What?" his voice betrayed his annoyance at being interrupted. Tensions onboard were high for everyone right now. They'd trained for this, but being in it was something totally surreal.

The younger sonarman removed his headphones and said, "There's the two cruisers, Chief." He indicated his display. "Following right behind the carrier, just like with the first group. No firm ID yet, but dollars to donuts that's another *Slava* and the *Kirov*."

Both the chief and the captain nodded at the younger man's conclusion. It was all starting to fit together. The Soviets were putting two powerful carrier groups to sea, each supported by a *Kirov*-class battlecruiser and *Slava*-class air defense cruiser. Even worse, one of them was built around a flattop that NATO didn't even know was in play yet.

Rogers clenched his fist in frustration once more. *This could be huge, the kind of thing that loses wars.* Rogers drained his coffee. *This needs to get to Norfolk right now.* Yet he knew that he couldn't risk it with such a powerful Soviet force so close.

Rogers briefly considered trying to sneak into the formation and attack this second carrier, but just as quickly dismissed the idea. With the *Kuznetsov* earlier, the Soviet ships had come to him. Now if he tried an attack on the *Varyag*, he would have to work his way into the formation, which was accelerating out of the inlet, already making fifteen knots in the choppy seas overhead. Even the ultra-quiet *Connecticut* would struggle to remain undetected while trying to catch up to a formation moving at that speed. *No*, Rogers reasoned, *observe and report. That's your mission.* He would wait, and send his contact report as soon as it was safe. *It'll have to be good enough.*

 # CHAPTER 63

1548 MSK, Sunday 13 Feb 1994
1248 Zulu
HMS *Trafalgar* (S107), northwestern edge
of X-Ray Station, Barents Sea

C OMMANDER EDWARD DAVIES was well-rested for a change, as was much of his crew after standing down from general quarters for the past four hours' deep speed run. He'd gone to bed himself in anticipation of a long day of playing cat and mouse with the group of Soviet amphibious transports they'd detected hours earlier. Davies shaved and took the time to make himself presentable before stepping out of his cabin just a few minutes before the ascent to communication depth.

Davies poured freshly boiled water into his teacup, and then spoke calmly in his precise accent: "Sonar, this is the captain. A contact report from you as soon as we pass through the thermocline, if you please."

"Aye, sir," was the immediate response.

Trafalgar ascended from the depths of the Barents Sea until the dark cylinder of her hull pierced the invisible horizontal boundary between the very cold and relatively-less-cold layers of water that stratified the ocean in this part of the globe.

After a minute, Davies heard, "Sir, we're getting unusually good salinity readings." That meant that sonar conditions would be better than normal for the British—and Soviet—sailors listening to their acoustic sensors in this patch of the sea. Low salinity in Arctic waters usually limited the performance of sonar relative to the excellent conditions present further south, but it appeared they had stumbled upon a bit of good luck.

"Sir?" came the tentative call from the chief sonarman.

"What is it, Sonar?" asked Davies.

"Captain, we have multiple contacts." A pause, like the sonarman couldn't believe it himself, "Multiple contacts in the first convergence zone, bearing two-six-zero, sir."

Contacts to the west? wondered Davies. *Thirty-five miles west of here is far too much distance for those rusty old amphibs to have steamed while we were running deep and rapid.*

"Is it our amphibious group, sonar?" Davies asked anyway.

"Getting classifications now sir," came the response. A moment later the mildly cockney accent continued, "No, sir, I don't believe it's the same group. It's just four of them." A pause, "Older. Sounds like a *Kresta*-class cruiser, a *Kashin*-class destroyer with maybe another one in tow, and a fourth ship we can't make out yet. Headed away from us, stern on. I estimate range at thirty-seven miles. We'll lose them soon sir as they pass out of the CZ."

Davies nodded, relieved that he had not miscalculated badly. What he really wanted to know was where the amphibs were. Four warships led by an older Soviet cruiser composed a formidable force, known as a surface action group, or "SAG." A single SAG was not of the same strategic import that the group of transports they had detected earlier.

The sub's communications officer entered the control room bearing a message flimsy, walked directly up the captain, and handed it to him. *Trafalgar* was now shallow enough to receive messages that had accumulated over the past several hours of deep running.

"Sir," the man said, "FLASH priority message from Fleet." The communication lieutenant's face was pale, and Davies saw the younger man's hand tremble slightly as he handed the message to his commander.

Davies kept his face and body impassive so as to impart confidence to the crewmen watching him out of the corners of their eyes. Everyone had been expecting this message, but all still wanted confirmation.

After a moment, Davies looked up, then stood, unclipped the microphone from its place overhead, depressed the transmit key and said, "Do you hear there, this is your captain speaking. The message we've all been waiting for, or dreading, I suppose. Well, there's nothing more to do but just say it: The Reds have decided to have a go at us. World War Three and all that. Don't fret about your families just yet, it's all nice and conventional. Started less than an hour ago."

The captain's aristocratic manner could come off as flippant to outsiders, but his crew knew him as an eminently capable submariner, and someone who remained calm under every circumstance they'd ever seen. This situation was no exception. Davies went on, "Now let me tell you what we're going to do. We're going to continue doing things just as we have been, just as we've trained for over these past months. I won't give you a whole lot of the sort of rubbish you see in the cinema, 'England expects' and all that. No, *I* expect each and every one of you to continue to do what you do so well: your job, and I will do mine. We will start by finding that group of transports we've been looking for and sending our report back to Fleet so they can do something about it. That is all. Carry on."

He clipped the microphone back up and resumed his seat. Davies noted with satisfaction that the sailors around the control room had turned back to their stations and were no longer peeking his way. They were a good crew, as good a crew as he could hope to take to war. *Which is fortunate*, he thought, a little grimly, *since that's exactly what I have to do.*

A few moments later the sonar room was calling again. "Captain, Sonar. Contacts entering the first CZ, bearing one-one-zero. Many contacts. Sounds like our amphibious friends, sir. Classifications coming."

East-southeast from us, considered the captain. *They've veered slightly south.* Was that important? Davies stood and walked forward to the chart table. If there really was a brigade of Soviet naval infantry aboard those transports, they could be bound for any number of destinations. He traced lines on the map with his index finger, first the west and then to the southwest. From

Trafalgar's current position, great circle routes offered nearly equidistant travel to Iceland, southern Norway, and even Scotland.

Despite his outward demeanor, Davies was still wrapping his mind around the idea of a World War with the resurgent USSR. He knew enough about the naval situation to realize that the Americans and their carriers were badly out of position. With the naval might of NATO far to the south, excepting the Norwegian fleet of missile boats and frigates and the surface combatants of STANAVFORLANT, the Alliance's Standing Naval Force Atlantic, steaming in the North Sea, those amphibious transports could get rather far before they encountered any serious opposition. Particularly if the Soviets sent their big-deck carrier out in support. Could they possibly try for Scotland?

Classifications for the eastern group were starting to come in from the sonar room. The escort appeared to be very strong, just as they'd detected earlier in the day. Several destroyers and at least one *Kresta*-class cruiser were shepherding the noisy transports. Davies briefly considered getting his command in position to conduct an ambush of the Soviet group, but dismissed the idea just as quickly. The Tigerfish torpedoes in his tubes were truly wretched weapons, with a maximum speed of less than thirty-two knots, slower than many of the ships at which they would potentially be fired. *If, on the other hand, I had a few of those wonderful new Spearfish weapons, but alas.* No, his mission was to observe and report. He had just told his crew to do their jobs, nothing more. That is what he would do as well.

"Communications, this is the captain," he called via the intercom. "Make a message ready for Fleet: 'Soviet amphibious group detected…'"

 **CHAPTER 64**

0851 EST, Sunday 13 February 1994
1251 Zulu
USCGC *Adak*, off Breezy Point, Entrance to Outer New York Harbor

" TRAWLER *TROGG*, THIS is the United States Coast Guard," blared the hailer across the choppy gray water. "Come about and prepare to be boarded."

Adak's skipper, Lieutenant Jackson, peered out from his wheelhouse at the rusty Bulgarian fishing trawler, continuing to bob forward in the swell two hundred yards ahead. There was no response to the hail, nor had there been one to the previous three. In front of Jackson, on the bow of his ship, three Coast Guards in orange life preservers and navy blue coveralls trained the cutter's big twenty-five millimeter Mk38 cannon towards the other boat. On either side of the wheelhouse, two more crewman did the same with M2 Browning .50 caliber machineguns, mounted on pintles on the *Adak*'s catwalk. Jackson, in charge of this small cutter as his first real command, was taking no chances with the hostile crew aboard the *Trogg*. Looking behind him, the lieutenant could see the Port Authority pilot boat *Wanderer* keeping its distance, it's shattered wheelhouse windows a clear testament to the danger of their current situation.

On *Adak*'s stern, Chief Everfield, an experienced old hand, was supervising the boarding party as they loaded into the cutter's launch, a rigid hull inflatable boat, or RHIB. Jackson was unhappy about sending his Coast Guards over to a ship potentially filled with armed enemies, but under the circumstances he didn't see an alternative. He'd watched the barrel-shaped objects continue to roll off the back of the trawler with maddening regularity as *Adak* approached from across the harbor. By now, everyone on board had heard the news that the objects were likely mines. He simply didn't have the time to wait for backup while whoever was on the *Trogg* continued to lay a minefield at the entrance of the most important harbor in the world.

As the Coast Guard ship approached to within a hundred yards, Jackson was lifting the hailer's hand-mic to give the *Trogg* one last warning when a figure appeared over the trawler's gunwale. The man lifted a rifle and fired a short burst in *Adak*'s direction. Jackson flinched as he heard rounds *ping* off his ship's bow.

"Gunner!" the lieutenant shouted to alert his crew manning the deck cannon, his Brooklyn accent showing through. He was angry now. "Tell 'em to cut that crap out. Give 'em a warning burst!"

The twenty-five-millimeter automatic cannon let out a deafeningly rapid-fire *thump-thump-thump*, and Jackson watched as three small puffs of foam appeared just in front of the still-moving *Trogg*. *Shoot at my ship, will you*, he thought. *I've got the bigger guns, dirtbags!*

Another mine splashed off the back of the converted fishing vessel, but this time it didn't seem to roll cleanly, instead entering the water end-first. Scanning more closely, Jackson saw that one of the trawler's two cranes was now swinging violently back and forth with the motion of the boat.

The mining ceased after that. Jackson could no longer see anyone on deck through his binoculars. He was seriously considering just lighting up the other ship with *Adak*'s cannon and machineguns, but a radio call from Sandy Hook informing him that something "was going on back in the City" and the NYPD wanted the crew and boat intact, put an end to that idea. Truth be told, the thirty-year-old lieutenant was still struggling to adjust to the idea that he was at war, and that the war was going on right here in New York Harbor. If trading shots with shadowy characters aboard a trawler dropping mines in the channel was any indication for how the rest of the war would go, Jackson feared the worst.

Now *Adak* was close, within fifty yards, and beginning to pull across the *Trogg*'s starboard bow. Motion beyond the rusty trawler caught Jackson's attention. He raised his binoculars and adjusted the focus, hearing before he saw: the throaty roar of an outboard motor cut through the sound of *Adak*'s own engines. A small, blue-painted RHIB appeared on the other side of the *Trogg*, skipping across the waves on a course away from the larger vessels and towards Breezy Point to the northeast.

Holding the binos to his eyes with one hand, he snatched his radio hand mic with the other and called, "Sandy Hook, *Adak*. We've got leakers from the *Trogg*! One small boat with outboard motor and what looks like…four, maybe five individuals, making for Breezy Point. I'm dispatching my boarding party to the *Trogg* and then I will pursue. Can we get some police backup on the beach, over?"

"Wait one, *Adak*," was the response. Jackson stepped out of his wheelhouse and called back to Chief Everfield, ordering him and his party across to the trawler. The RHIB roared away from *Adak*'s stern, heeling over as the chief maneuvered the boat expertly, pushing the powerful outboard motor to twenty-five knots in seconds. In front of the old petty officer, half a dozen Coast Guardsmen knelt in their orange life vests, blue uniforms, and baseball caps, training their M-14 rifles and Vietnam-era shotguns towards the deck of the *Trogg*.

Sandy Hook was calling as Jackson stepped back into his wheelhouse. "*Adak*, NYPD is pretty busy right now. Some confusing reports coming in from all over the City, but they've got some squad cars headed to Breezy Point. Keep those leakers in sight, over."

"Copy, Sandy Hook," Jackson said into his hand-mic. He ordered his cutter to full speed, directing the helmsman standing next to him to steer around *Trogg*'s bow. *Adak* surged forward in pursuit of the fleeing RHIB just as the chief maneuvered his own small boat up against the starboard side of the trawler's stern.

— ‑

From the RHIB, Chief Everfield directed one of his men up the rust-stained side of the *Trogg*, while the rest trained their rifles upwards. The first man slung his M-14 over his shoulder and scrambled the half-dozen feet up an access ladder, then swung himself over the gunwale and out of sight.

A second Coast Guardsman was already scrambling up the ladder in support when Everfield heard the first man call, "Uh, Chief?"

Something in the man's voice made Everfield push forward from his position next to the RHIB's outboard motor and climb the ladder himself. He swung his legs over the gunwale just as the second man up the ladder started retching, emptying his breakfast back over the side and into the sea.

The chief scanned the messy deck. It was covered in heavy chains and winches, some of which were still attached to the boat's wildly swinging crane, giving the trawler the eerie feeling of a ghost ship. In the center of the deck, positioned on tracks so as to roll off the rear of the boat, sat what looked like five fifty-five-gallon oil drums. One of the drums had clearly jumped off the rails, popping its lid off, which gave the chief a view of what was inside. The drum was filled with some sort of hard foam substance for flotation, he was sure, wrapped like a donut around what could only be a cylindrical explosive core. Attached to detonators in the explosives were what looked like six floating wires. Three led to a fuse at one end of the mine, while three more appeared to be attached to the still-sealed other end.

The chief's experienced eye quickly worked out the system that had been at play here. The mines sat on a pair of jerry-rigged rails, secured by chains attached to the crane. When the crew had been ready to release one of the weapons, they would use the crane to create slack in the restraints, allowing another barrel to roll forward to a sort of cradle, where a crewman would then need to reach across the rails to attach and arm the two fuses. It was a terrible system, Everfield thought, and one clearly executed by people with little seamanship. His eyes brought him to why the Guardsman was retching.

Streaks of red near the overturned barrel and the cradle were too bright to be rust. At the end of one of the streaks, laying among the chains and winches that covered the deck, was a severed forearm, still in its tattered sleeve. *He must have slipped and caught his arm just right to sever it like that,* the chief thought, clinical in his assessment, *otherwise he would still be pinned there. Sure lost a lot of blood too.*

Following their well-rehearsed drill, the other six members of the boarding party were pairing off, spreading out to search the trawler. One pair scrambled up into the wheelhouse, forward of the deck area. Another team disappeared below deck.

The chief decided to call in the carnage on deck to Jackson.

"*Adak, Adak*, this is Away Team," he said into his handheld radio, looking over the opposite gunwale and watching as the *Adak* pursued the fleeing RHIB across the gray harbor.

"Go ahead boarding party," crackled Jackson's voice.

"Sir," the chief began, "we have some interesting developments here. You can expect an injured man in that boat you're chasing."

"Injured how?" Jackson's voice crackled over the radio.

"Missing an arm, for starters," the chief said into his radio.

A pause followed, then the lieutenant came back with, "Say again, Chief?"

Just then a seaman reappeared from below decks and called, "Chief, you need to see this!"

"Wait one, *Adak*," Everfield said into the radio as he followed the Guardsman through the hatch, down a ladder and forward to the musty sleeping quarters in the bow. There the second team member was crouching over what looked, at first glance, to be a large stash of cocaine divided into dozens of rectangular white bricks. He stood up when the chief pushed his way forward between the rows of bunks that converged inward towards the bow. "What is it, boys?" the chief asked.

"Don't know, Chief," the other man said, "could be drugs, but, well, what do you think these wires are?"

Then Everfield saw it and froze. Several colored wires snaked into the white bricks. They led back to a pair of small green boxes taped to the side of the hull, *Is it a bomb? No.* Everfield realized what it was, *Scuttling charge.* The veteran Coast Guardsman felt a cold sweat break out on his forehead and an unpleasant ticklish sensation in his lower gut as he comprehended the danger he and his party were in. *Those bastards left a scuttling charge to kill us!*

"Back! Back!" the chief ordered the others firmly. "Get back on deck and move as far aft as you can."

"What is it, Chief?" the man who'd been crouched over the bomb said, not understanding, but sensing the fear in the old petty officer.

"It's a bomb. Now do as I say and get aft!" the chief answered.

The others needed no more encouragement. Next the chief grabbed his radio and called *Adak*. "*Adak*, Away Team. We have a situation here."

—●—

"...scuttling charge in the bow. Looks like it's rigged to blow, over," crackled through radio speaker in Sandy Hook Coast Guard Station watch center.

Ingalls' head shot up. *What now?* In the last few minutes it seemed all hell had broken loose. The DEFCON One call started the cascade of events, followed closely by the report from *Wanderer* that *Trogg* was mining the channel. Then a few minutes later, while Ingalls was discussing the closure of the harbor over the phone with the Port Authority, the man stopped mid-sentence and said, "Uh, gotta go. We've got a bridge down in the East River up here."

The line clicked off. Ingalls hung up and dialed NYPD headquarters, trying to come to grips with the disaster unfolding across his city. *No way one of the bridges could have actually* collapsed *into the river*, he thought.

A harried voice answered the line at NYPD headquarters.

"Which bridge?" the police officer answered testily. "We're responding to explosions all over Manhattan right now. It's like—" The man's voice was replaced by a series of muffled *bangs* coming through the speaker. Ingalls thought he heard someone in the background yell "*Gun! Gun!*" before the police officer on the phone said quickly, "Got a situation here." The line clicked off. Ingalls stared at the mute phone, dumbfounded. *Where are we, Gotham City?*

One of the watch center officers switched on the television hanging in a corner of the room and turned up the volume, drawing Ingalls' attention as he hung up the receiver. In seconds the entire room was transfixed by the images on the screen.

"—are saying that it was a truck bomb, but we're still waiting for confirmation," a reporter was saying into the camera, one hand pressed to her ear beneath a stylish cut of brown hair to block out the blaring sirens audible through her microphone. Behind her, the square base and distinctive glass-and-steel of the World Trade Center buildings were clearly recognizable, gray smoke swirling about.

"Looks like the 'Blind Sheikh' attack from last year," someone in the watch center muttered.

The officer with the remote impulsively switched the channel, conjuring up the local NBC anchor who was saying, "Just to reassure everyone, casualties in this attack *should* be low, we can hope, given that it's a Sunday. Still, our reporter on the scene says that damage to the front of the Stock Exchange is extensive and—"

The video feed displaying over the anchor's shoulder showed the narrow, winding, marble and granite corridor of Wall Street filled with emergency vehicles, their lights flashing and reflecting off the surrounding walls and windows.

Then the channel flipped again, this time to the most dramatic images yet. A reporter was speaking into the camera, the ticker below her showing the ABC logo and giving her location at Pier 35 on the East River side of Manhattan. She was speaking earnestly into the camera, but everyone in the watch center was so transfixed by the images behind the young woman that none even registered what she was saying. In the foreground of the shot, the long central span of the huge Manhattan Bridge sagged down into the East River like some enormous gray ribbon. The places where the span connected to the two suspension towers showed the jagged protrusions of steel beams and wires where the proud bridge's structure had pulled apart. Huge suspension cables hung limply from either tower, snaking from their high anchor points down until they disappeared into the water in confused coils that looked for all the world like tangles of knotted gray hair among the FDNY and NYPD watercraft that were plying the agitated waters around the disaster. *Looking for survivors*, Ingalls realized, belatedly.

Beyond the wreckage of the downed Manhattan Bridge, the still-standing Brooklyn Bridge showed signs of damage as well. The bridge itself was too distant to make out details in the grainy TV footage, but everyone could see the wisps of black smoke and occasional flashes of flame rising from burning vehicles on the center of the older bridge.

The reporter was saying something about a train derailment on the nearer Manhattan Bridge when Ingalls realized in a flash of horror that some of the jagged shapes protruding above the water in the middle of the river were New York City subway cars. That caused Ingalls to pay closer attention to what the smartly-dressed reporter was saying.

"—and the blasts here were not the only attacks either, Brian," the woman was saying as the camera panned back to her. "One officer manning a police rescue boat told us just a few minutes ago that the Holland Tunnel on the other side of the island is closed and that there is smoke coming out of the tunnel entrance. He also said that the NYPD may have prevented a similar attack on the George Washington Bridge, but so far we have no confirmation of that."

"Jessica," broke in Brian, the local anchor, in his gravelly-voiced concerned-journalist persona, "what of the reports of gunfire outside of several NYPD precinct headquarters? Do you have any information about that?"

That statement drew Ingall's attention away from images of the bridge, flashing his thoughts back to his futile call to the NYPD.

The woman on camera allowed a look of surprised concern to pass across her face before responding, "Uh, no Brian, I had *not* heard that, but that would certainly," she paused, "That would certainly fuel the theory about some sort of coordinated terrorist attack going on."

They don't know that all hell is breaking loose right here in the harbor too, Ingalls realized.

Immediately Commander Jim Ingalls was back to the problem at hand. He tore his eyes away from the television, forcing his fears about what the apparent attacks all over the city, all over the world, might portend. *Focus on what* you *can affect*, he told himself. *Mines in the harbor. Hostiles heading for Breezy Point. Men aboard that damned trawler that could blow at any second.*

A phone rang and one of the junior officers answered with a professional, "Sandy Hook Coast Guard Station." She listened for a moment, nodded, then said, "Wait one." Looking over at her commander while placing her hand over the telephone receiver's speaker, the younger woman said, "Sir, it's the FBI. They say with the terrorist attacks around the city and everything else going on that they're claiming jurisdiction over the trawler. They want us to bring it to the NYPD pier at the Brooklyn Army Terminal as soon as we have it secured."

"Did you tell him it's rigged to blow?" Ingalls asked, antagonism in his voice. He didn't want a bureaucratic turf fight right now. There was too much going on and too much at stake.

The younger officer opened her mouth, then looked at the receiver clearly perplexed.

Not her fault, thought Ingalls, *I wouldn't know what to do in her position either. The FBI's order makes sense under normal circumstances. We want to know for sure who's responsible for this.* The commander was trying not to show it, but he was reeling like everyone else from the rapid-fire blows of the surprise that they were at war, the mining of the harbor, and now the terrorist attacks across the city. *The whole world has gone mad.*

"Tell him we'll get the trawler there as soon as we can," Ingalls allowed after a moment, *Assuming it doesn't blow up.* Then he turned his attention back to more pressing matters. He focused on the situation map, mounted on the front wall of the watch center. The chart showed in blue the greater New York Harbor along with the patch of Atlantic Ocean south of Long Island and Rhode Island and east of the Jersey Shore. Numerous inbound and outbound ships were denoted by magnets on the map, which was mounted on a metallic backing. The markers that concerned him right now were the ones representing the two cutters servicing the harbor; *Adak* was at the entrance to the channel and chasing the fleeing—*Bulgarians? Terrorists? Russians? Could Russia be responsible for all this?*—towards Breezy Point, on the eastern side of the channel. South of the harbor mouth and just over twelve miles east of the Jersey Shore, the larger cutter USCGC *Dallas* was drawing near to that Finnish-flagged Soviet intelligence trawler, the *Kursagraf.*

Ingalls looked over at his surface operations officer and said, "Get on the horn to *Adak's* boarding party and tell them to disarm that scuttling charge if they can. Tell them I don't want them taking any chances and if they have any doubts about it, they need to get in the RHIB and get away. Tell them the FBI needs the boat for evidence, but it's not worth their lives." It was a bit cowardly, he knew, to put the responsibility for choosing to abandon the trawler on the shoulders of the chief, but Everfield was the man on the scene and Ingalls was confident that he would make a smart decision.

The surface ops officer made the radio call. A moment later the speaker crackled, "Sandy Hook, this is pilot boat *Wanderer*. We copied your last transmission and we may be able to help. My boatswain is former Navy, explosive ordnance disposal. Says he may be able to disarm your bomb. We're coming alongside the trawler now."

Finally, a bit of good news, Ingalls thought.

"Thanks, *Wanderer*. Be careful," the surface ops officer was saying when the man with the remote asked in a loud voice, "What's happening to the TV?"

Everyone looked again at the television in the corner. The screen had gone fuzzy with interference, but the picture and sound remained clear enough to see and understand. Two TV anchors, a smartly-dressed man and woman, sat behind what looked like the local news desk, but they weren't the regular ABC anchors who'd just been speaking. ABC was Ingalls' regular news channel, and the two on-screen anchors were not among the regular faces he knew from the station. Then the ticker at the bottom of the screen caught his attention. It read in bold letters: AMERICAN AND GERMAN FORCES INVADE POLAND AND CZECHOSLOVAKIA.

The officer with the remote turned the volume up. The image on screen shifted to footage of boxy tanks churning across a soggy field. *Looks like it could be somewhere in Europe*, Ingalls thought absently. Then the scene shifted to columns of armored vehicles transiting the narrow streets of a town whose houses showed white stucco walls and red tile roofs under wet, iron-gray skies.

The unfamiliar female anchor was saying in a serious and matter-of-fact tone, "The Pentagon reports that forces of the *Bundeswehr*, supported by American troops stationed in Germany, have begun cross-border operations to achieve NATO objectives in Poland. They say that the operational plan requires limited incursions into Czechoslovakia as well to prevent Soviet forces there from interfering in the operation."

The male anchor interrupted with a stilted phrase of his own, "Yes, Mary, such a surprise attack is typical of declared NATO doctrine. The Alliance leaders clearly felt threatened by the Soviet intervention to resolve the chaos in Poland. They apparently have decided to act pre-emptively to forestall Soviet intentions there."

Something was off, Ingalls knew right away. The Coast Guard officer couldn't put his finger on all of it, but alarm bells were going off in his head as he listened to the clearly-rehearsed commentary accompanying the fuzzy video of the two journalists. *No doctrine I've ever heard has* us *launching* pre-emptive *attacks against Soviet troops*, he thought. *Who are these people? Since when does NATO launch pre-emptive wars against the USSR?*

The picture on the television faded, becoming even more snowy. Ingalls could see the usual Sunday anchors again, the ones who had been on the television moments earlier, through the interference. They looked like specters in front of the newcomers. For an instant he could hear both sets of anchors speaking simultaneously through the static. *What's going on here?* He walked over and grabbed the remote from the man holding it, switching the channel back to NBC, then CBS. The same fuzzy video of the unfamiliar anchors appeared on each of the network channels.

"—NATO offensive into Eastern Europe appears to be absolutely massive," the male anchor was saying. "One *Bundeswehr* commander we spoke to compared the attack to the 'left hook' of the Gulf War three years ago, and—"

Ingalls' air operations officer, faithfully monitoring his own radio, interrupted, "Sir, that AWACS south of Long Island is calling. They say they're picking up some powerful emissions from that Finnish—" he broke off and seemed to have a moment of clarity, "—sorry, *Soviet*, intel ship, the *Kursagraf*. They say it's broadcasting on numerous commercial TV and radio frequencies!"

The surface operation officer's radio now crackled to life with, "Sandy Hook, *Adak*. These leakers are getting close to the beach at Breezy Point. We're going in close to pursue. I see flashing lights, looks like the NYPD is here. Any word on our boarding party and that scuttling charge, over?"

Ingalls head was reeling. He grabbed his radio, "Boarding party..."

 **CHAPTER 65**

0853 EST, Sunday 13 February 1994
1253 Zulu
Piper Cherokee 213R, over the Atlantic Ocean,
twenty miles east of Asbury Park, New Jersey

"YURI, IT'S TIME," the pilot called back amidst the noise of the small aircraft's single engine and propeller. "Are you ready to transmit the contacts?"

"One moment, one moment," said Yuri, in the rear of the four-person cabin. *Do you think I want to spend any more time wedged into this cold, cramped coffin than I absolutely have to?* he thought, annoyed. The short, slight-framed Yuri was seated sideways, hunched over a large, boxy piece of equipment that occupied the other rear passenger seat. He was peering into the green glow of an LCD display that showed several blips on a dark background. Each of the blips represented the position of a ship approaching or leaving New York Harbor. The ruggedized keyboard he was using to meticulously type the coordinates, course, and size, of the various contacts displayed the Cyrillic alphabet rather than the English one, which was perhaps less than surprising given that both men were conversing in Russian. It was attached to the larger display box by a thick, jerry-rigged cable, and both pieces of equipment were painted in the same olive drab hue common in the Soviet military.

"Well, *bistro*, quickly, Yuri. Others are waiting on us," the pilot urged as he turned back to maintain their lazy north-south racetrack pattern twenty miles off the Jersey Shore.

If I were back in my Tu-95, Yuri thought sourly as he continued to tap the keyboard, *I could just push a button, and all this information would transfer nice and neat to the uplink.* The system they were using was painfully jerry-rigged, especially when compared to those on the huge "Bear" long-range naval bomber. On board one of those huge four-engine aircraft, Yuri could stretch his legs, even walk around a bit when he needed a break from his radar operator duties. Now, confined in this little Piper Cherokee, it was an entirely different matter. Yuri's legs were cramping and he was feeling the mental strain of the mission. Sweat was beading on his forehead, despite the cold temperature of the cabin.

The radar sensor he was peering at wasn't nearly as good as the one on the Tu-95, either. Of course, their little Piper Cherokee would never have gotten off the ground with a sensor *that* big and heavy in its cabin. No, they were fortunate to have gotten one of the new small radars designed for the Yak-141 fighter jet. It was fortunate that the smaller radar even fit. They had needed to remove the seat, string the antenna along inside of the fuselage, and jam the receiver box into the cabin. It was very rough, but it worked. The sensor was now emitting electromagnetic waves out the left side of the aircraft, and these were bouncing off the metal hulls of ships moving up and down the coast. He counted more than a half-dozen blips, two of which, at the far northern edge of his radar's range, had been drawing closer together over the past few minutes.

Yuri had volunteered for this mission, not knowing what it would entail. His commander had recommended him as the best radarman his elite reconnaissance bomber regiment had. He'd been sent to meet a *Spetsnaz* colonel, and now here he was. It all seemed an exciting diversion from the normal drudgery of patrolling the Barents Sea, and so it had been, training with the *Spetsnaz* teams, drinking with them, womanizing with them.

Then the day came when he realized that his little escapade was more than a nice break from his Murmansk day job. That day had been when he and the five other members of his special mission team departed on their very indirect travel from Moscow to New York, via Damascus, Lagos, Buenos Aires, Rio, and Miami. They spent the last week in the US Northeast connecting with other agents in country, acquiring their aircraft, and moving them to the abandoned farm-field airstrip in New Jersey. Along the way Yuri experienced some of the comforts of America, the most amazing of which to him was the grocery stores. They were just so full and colorful, even in the dead of winter! Yuri never could have imagined a similar cornucopia in the USSR, even in the subsidized stores he had access to in Murmansk due to his privileged position as a naval aviator. It was enough to make him begin to question the weekly political education he'd received since being drafted into the Soviet fleet.

Yuri sighed. That was all in the past now. He had a job to do, and the faster he finished it the sooner they could land, and the sooner he could pry himself out of this rickety, flying deathtrap. Yuri finished transferring the last coordinate and contact report into the digital radio, the same kind he used in his bomber to transmit contact reports to the Soviet constellation of communication satellites, as well as to submarines down below. He had no idea who would be on the receiving end of *this* report. He could only imagine why they might need the positions of random ships outside one of the busiest harbors in the world, but that need not keep him from filling his role in whatever this little escapade really was.

Yuri called forward to the pilot through the drone of the engine, "Ready to transmit."

The pilot nodded and said, "*Da*, transmit."

0855 EST, Sunday 13 February 1994
1255 Zulu
Aboard K266 *Severodvinsk*, one hundred miles southwest of Long Island

"Final contact report arriving now, *tovarich* Captain," announced the communication officer from his station on the port side of the submarine's control room.

"About time." muttered Senior Captain Grigory Orlov, commander of the Soviet fleet's newest and most advanced cruise-missile carrying nuclear-powered submarine, an "SSGN" in naval jargon. His project 949A *Antey*-class boat, called an *Oscar II* by the Americans, had been at communication depth for over eight minutes now. Which was about seven minutes too long for Orlov's taste, especially as they were so painfully close to the coastline of his country's most dangerous enemy in the opening hours of war.

"Weapons officer," he growled, "how long until we can launch."

"Two minutes, *tovarich* Captain," said the weapons officer, not taking his eyes from the blue screens on which a pair of *starshini*—senior enlisted Soviet sailors—were typing in their final coordinates. Over the shoulders of the two sailors, the weapons officer watched to ensure that the targeting coordinates were loaded properly into the inertial guidance systems for each of the twenty-four huge P-700 "*Granit*" cruise missiles in canted launch tubes lining the flanks of the submarine's pressure hull.

Two more minutes, thought the captain, trying to calm his nerves, *only two more minutes, then we can do the deed and be gone from these waters.*

They'd been at sea for seven weeks now. *Severodvinsk* had departed the Kola Inlet on December 25th of the previous year, accompanied by the older and unimaginatively named *Charlie II*-class SSGN *K503*, and their escorting *Akula*-class SSN, or nuclear-powered attack submarine, the K157 *Vepr*. The three boats had slowly and quietly churned northward until they reached the acoustic camouflage provided by the grating, grinding arctic pack ice. The small flotilla continued under the icecap, passing east of Svalbard before turning west and making for the Nares Strait, the narrow passage between northern Greenland and Canada, which led from the Arctic Ocean into Baffin Bay.

Outside the Nares Strait, the group rendezvoused with the ancient November-class SSN *K115*. They transited the narrow waterway in the company of this prodigious noisemaker in the hope that whatever sensors NATO had in the channel would zero in on the noisiest of the company. The *K115* had turned back, leaving the three original boats to continue their journey southward, hopefully undetected.

After over a month at sea they emerged from under the winter ice pack into the Labrador Sea. There they waited, tucked against the rugged southwest coast of Greenland until it was time to transit to the edge of the North American continental shelf, a mere hundred miles south of Long Island.

The long passage across the top of the world had taken its toll on both boat and crew. Supplies of fresh food had begun to run out several days ago, and the submarine's passageways reeked with the odd smell combination of old cabbage, body odor, and lubricating oil. *At least there's still plenty of tea*, Orlov thought. He didn't even want to consider what conditions were like on the older, and far more cramped *K503*, or even worse, the relatively tiny *Vepr*. The upside, however, was that they were now all but certain that none of the stealthy American hunter submarines could be following them.

The final confirmation had arrived five minutes ago. *So, we're really doing this, then?* Orlov thought, still only half believing it, and not entirely happy. *Expending all our missiles on whatever random shipping passes our way?*

The two *starshini* were prioritizing the targets based on size alone. The largest contacts warranted four missiles, medium-sized ones: two, and the smaller targets would receive attention from only one. The commander of the *Severodvinsk* shuddered to think of the risks being taken by whoever it was that was flying around up there to provide the three separate contact reports he'd just received. Several dozen kilometers to the east, *K503* would be receiving the same reports. Both submarines' orders instructed them to expend their entire complement of missiles at whatever contacts the mysterious fliers above them reported. It was an odd mission, to say the least, but Orlov had to admit he could see the logic behind the tactic. *Better to sink these ships now, while they are alone and vulnerable, instead of later when they are escorted in convoys by warships.*

The Project 949A submarines, of which *Severodvinsk* was the newest unit, had been designed from the keel up to sink mighty American aircraft carriers with huge salvoes of supersonic cruise missiles, in concert, of course, with missile-carrying bombers and surface ships. Given the need to carry twenty-four of the ten-meter-long P-700 weapons, appropriately called "Shipwrecks" by NATO, the boats of this class were big, three-quarters the size of one of the *Kirov*-class battlecruisers. In fact, the Americans had even given his boat the nickname "Mongo" in recognition of the submarine's huge displacement and hitting power.

Sinking civilian and commercial vessels was not what Severodvinsk was made for. Orlov longed to hunt American aircraft carriers, but that would have to wait until they rearmed and re-provisioned at Reykjavik. His orders assured him that the Icelandic port would be under Soviet control by the time he arrived there. Orlov would believe *that* little detail when he saw it.

"*Tovarich* Captain!" the weapons officer called over from the missile station, the blue light from the control screens giving his face a deathly pallor, "all missiles are ready. At your command!"

Finally, Orlov thought, looking at his watch. *Ten minutes at communications depth already!* He stood and walked to the weapons officer's console, removing the missile launch key from around his neck as he did so.

"We will fire all missiles, alternating sides," the captain confirmed as he fitted the key into its slot next to the weapons officer's key. The other man nodded. Then they turned their keys in unison in their well-rehearsed launch drill.

The *Severodvinsk's* commander turned and strode back to his command chair as the other officer depressed the launch button for the first of twenty-four missiles they would fire that morning, "Firing One!"

The sixteen-thousand-ton submarine shuddered as compressed air and rocket propellant ejected the first missile from its launch tube, pushing it the two-dozen meters to the surface. The weapon roared out of the choppy seas atop a column of white smoke and seawater before arcing back downward on a northwesterly course. By the time the first missile was settling onto its wavetop-level flight pattern, the weapons officer was already announcing "Firing Two!" as the huge submarine shuddered again.

With relentless regularity one missile after another broke the surface of the Atlantic Ocean, nosed over, dropped to low-level flight, and accelerated to one-and-a-half times the speed of sound.

 **CHAPTER 66**

1559 MSK, Sunday, 13 February 1994
1259 Zulu
Main Ministry of Defense Building, Arbatskaya Square,
Moscow, Russian Soviet Federative Socialist Republic

VLADIMIR KHITROV LEANED back in a cheap office chair. His cramped workplace was filled with hazy smoke, a heaping ashtray sat next to the chessboard on his cluttered desk. He pulled a long, last drag from the stub of his cigarette. He'd been practically living here for the past several days, seeing to all the minute details that would put the finishing touches on his masterpiece, the symphony now unfolding on the television screen in front of him. Khitrov had pulled many strings with the KGB to have a television with access to US network and cable news channels installed so he could watch as the fruits of his labor unfolded before a global audience, gage the reactions of people around the world, and evaluate the impact on his enemies' psyche.

Minutes before, CNN had begun to broadcast images of the infrastructure attacks across North America. The American media was unwittingly executing their role in his plan, just as he knew they would. He counted on it. They even re-broadcasted the false, pre-recorded news reports transmitted across the American television networks. Khitrov was particularly proud of that little detail of his *maskirovka*. He cared not that the lifespan of those intelligence trawlers sailing off the great American metropolitan conurbations of New York and Los Angeles would be measured in mere minutes after the Yankees realized what was happening. Sowing confusion in the American press about who'd actually started the war, even if only temporarily, was worth the sacrifice in Khitrov's arithmetic.

The fact that CNN, in their typical desire to be the first with a "scoop," had rebroadcast to a global audience his little stage drama, recorded here in Moscow and starring two English language specialists from Moscow State University, was simply icing on the cake. Perhaps other news services, *The BBC, perhaps?* Khitrov wondered with a smirk, would also pick up the footage in their desperation to give their viewers some sort of information about the storm breaking around the world.

The CNN footage was covering the destruction wrought by Khitrov's agents on the great bridges and tunnels connecting Manhattan to Long Island and New Jersey, in San Francisco and even in Canada. A reporter across from the wreckage of the Manhattan Bridge had been talking about the series of ambushes that several of his teams had executed outside of various NYPD precinct headquarters. *That should slow their response*, Khitrov thought. *Give the teams time to break contact and prepare for their follow-on missions.* Nearly every Soviet *Spetsnaz* soldier, GRU operative, and KGB agent on earth was engaged in some way with the global onslaught Khitrov's plan had unleashed. He was willing to spend their lives, but also understood that they were resources not to be wasted unnecessarily. If the American police were worried about fighting off ambushes everywhere they went, then they would have fewer resources to devote to hunting down his teams.

Of course, the attacks Khitrov had coordinated were targeting far more than the police. He was bringing the war to the doorsteps of every American, forcing them to react not just physically, but psychologically. Hence the attacks on the bridges. He was restricting the lifeblood of New York City, forcing the huge quantities of food and commodities required to feed the great city to come across a few vulnerable ribbons of asphalt or railroad track, and that didn't even take into account the attacks on the City's water supply which should be occurring even now. Khitrov's mouth curled into a truly wicked smile. With any luck the average New Yorker would wake up tomorrow to find their city short of food, water, and all the other most basic supplies that made metropolitan life possible.

The plan was grander than just New York City, however. As if on cue, the feed changed to a report from San Francisco, where a grainy camera image showed the outline of the Golden Gate Bridge against the predawn sky, the center of its span engulfed in yellow-orange flames. Khitrov could not quite tell from the picture, but it seemed to him that the famous span was sagging. At the same time, the news ticker began to announce attacks in Canada, including an explosion at the Welland Canal locks, which controlled access to the Great Lakes, and at the MacDonald rail tunnel through the Rockies.

Khitrov nodded at the screen, pleased. News from the rest of the world would be much slower to reach him. Other places did not possess the same drama and spotlight of New York and the broader North American media market, but he was confident of his plan. He pulled a bottle of vodka out of his desk and poured himself a celebratory shot. He was actually enjoying himself, watching his tour de force unfold on television. In truth, Khitrov knew that all he could do was improve the odds of his country winning against the west, but he still thought of himself as the director of some great stage drama, and only *he* knew how all the intricate acts fit together.

The first act was coming to a close. Khitrov sat back, sipping the sweet, fiery vodka, and watched the continuing coverage. Absently picking up the bishop piece from his chessboard, he looked at his watch. It was just about time for act two to begin.

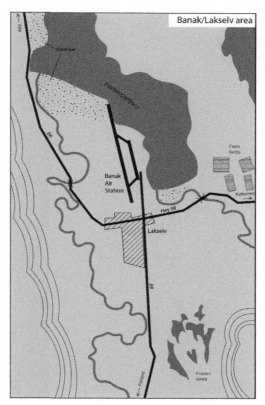

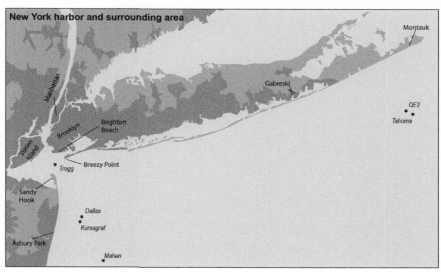

PART VII: DAGGER TO THE HEART

"There is never a convenient place to fight a war when the other man starts it."
—Arleigh Burke

 **CHAPTER 67**

0900 EST, Sunday 13 February 1994
1300 Zulu
E-3 AWACS "Darkstar," over the Atlantic Ocean,
twenty miles south of Long Island

"HOLY CRAP," MUTTERED the radar operator. Three small, low-flying contacts had just appeared on the scope of her console. "Hey Sarge!" she called into her headset to her supervisor sitting two consoles away in the Boeing AWACS aircraft monitoring the airspace along this stretch of the United States' Atlantic coast, "You gotta see this!"

Master Sergeant Troy Funk shifted his two-hundred-and-sixty-pound frame in his seat and switched his console to his subordinate's feed. "What is it?"

"Sarge, I've got three, no, there's another one! Four contacts that just appeared in my sector, bearing is one-nine-zero relative, range nine zero miles, altitude under a hundred feet, speed is—whoa, speed is over a thousand knots!"

Funk felt a cold knot take hold in the lower reaches of his gut as he watched a fifth contact appear on the scope. The only thing that could just appear out of nowhere and accelerate to Mach one-point-five like this was a missile. *That's not good,* was the only thought the master sergeant could muster as he ran a hand through his bristly salt and pepper crew cut.

The five, no, six, supersonic contacts all seemed to originate from the same patch of empty ocean about a hundred miles south of Long Island, and were fanning away from that point to the north and northwest. *Oh my God*, Funk thought, *is this really happening? Is this it?*

"Sergeant!" called another airman from two consoles down, "Vampire! I have multiple supersonic contacts on my scope as well. Bearing is one-two-zero, range one-five-five, wavetop altitude!"

That did it for Master Sergeant Funk. He said to the lieutenant colonel in charge of this flying command post, "Sir! Get on the horn to NORAD! We have multiple cruise missile contacts inbound towards the New York area from multiple sources"

Yet another officer was shouting, "Vampire! Vampire!" over the air defense frequency radio.

The warning from Darkstar traveled at light speed into space where it was received by a US Air Force communication satellite, which relayed it back down to the NORAD's Combat Operations Center nestled deep inside Cheyenne Mountain, just south of Colorado Springs. There it joined similar messages that were arriving from all around the periphery of the United States' maritime boundaries.

Moments later a radio call came in from "Looking Glass," the Strategic Command's airborne command post, which had been up and orbiting over the Midwest, waiting for doomsday, since DEFCON Four had been declared hours earlier.

"Darkstar," came the deadpan call over the SATCOM link, "this is Looking Glass. Please confirm what we're seeing over your data-link. It looks like we have a major cruise missile attack developing against the New York area. Is your data accurate, over?"

"Roger," Funk heard the officer in charge of the AWACS' controllers respond at the other end of the 707's brightly-lit crew compartment, "what you're seeing is accurate. We have more than a dozen vampires in the air, there are now three points of origin, over."

When the American president had ordered US conventional forces to DEFCON One at the commencement of hostilities an hour before, he also ordered the country's nuclear forces to assume DEFCON Two, a level of readiness not seen since the Cuban Missile Crisis. As a result, dozens of bombers were staging on airbase runways all over the United States, with thermonuclear weapons in their bomb bays and crews waiting for the word from NORAD that the world was, indeed, coming to an end. Now, it seemed, that moment might have arrived.

Funk knew that with the report of supersonic cruise missiles approaching the American coast, the commander of NORAD, a four-star general, would have to pick up his direct line to the US Strategic Command, or STRATCOM, headquarters at Offut Air Force Base in Nebraska. *The bombers are probably thundering down the runways right now*, thought Funk. *The ICBMs are probably in pre-launch countdown procedure.* Funk was sweating bullets and feeling nauseous. *This is Armageddon.*

There were now eighteen missiles inbound from at least three source points. Elsewhere in the cabin, Funk heard the announcement that the dreaded TACAMO—"take charge and move out"—message had been sent, alerting all of the Navy's ballistic missile submarines on deterrence patrol in the vastness of the world's oceans to be prepared to execute a retaliatory strike on only a few moments' notice. The Looking Glass system was now active, designed to keep the National Command Authority, military speak for the US president or his successor, in continuous contact with the country's nuclear assets.

A moment later, Funk heard a call from NORAD announce, "All stations, be advised, the BMEWS system reports *no*, I repeat *no* ICBM launches from the Soviet Union or anywhere else at this time." BMEWS was the Ballistic Missile Early Warning System, a network of sensors that watched the Soviet Union and the likely patrol areas of Soviet ballistic missile submarines for signs of missile launches. The fact that these sensors currently showed no signs of an attack was at least some small measure of good news. *If the Soviets were keeping their ICBMs in their silos, maybe it won't be Armageddon after all*, thought Funk, *just a war. Just a slower way to end the world.*

The next message from NORAD smashed whatever optimism the first message had garnered. "Be advised, cruise missile attacks are in progress all along both coasts. We currently have reports of missiles in the air off New York, Charleston, Savannah, Miami, Los Angeles, and Seattle."

Darkstar was partnered this morning with a pair of New York Air National Guard F-16A fighters, callsigns Jackpot Two-One and Two-Two, flying from Francis Gabreski Air National Guard Base in eastern Long Island. Funk quickly directed two more F-16s on the ground at Gabreski into the air and vectored the airborne Jackpot flight towards the most clustered groups of missiles. The fighters would never be able to get them all, Funk realized, despair creeping back in. If the missiles were nuclear, even one leaker would be catastrophic beyond imagination.

— ◆ —

The pilots of Jackpot Flight were tired. They'd been roused from their beds at zero-two-thirty that morning and summoned to their home base at Hancock Field in Syracuse. Between getting to the airfield, sitting through their DEFCON Four mission briefing, flying down to Gabreski, and then flying what had been, until this moment, a boring dawn patrol over the Atlantic Ocean, the two pilots had been doing well just to stay awake in their cockpits. The DEFCON One warning a few minutes ago caused them to perk up, but neither man really believed that anything was going to happen. Not here. All the action was in Europe.

Now those illusions lay shattered, and neither pilot was having any trouble staying awake. The two F-16s dove on afterburner in opposite directions to intercept missiles streaking towards the coast. Each fighter carried two medium-range AIM-7 Sparrow radar-guided missiles as well as two short-range AIM-9 heat-seekers, which in theory gave each fighter the ability to down at least four of the incoming vampires though neither pilot would have enough time to accomplish this. All they could do was thin out the enemy weapons as much as possible.

Jackpot Two-One fired first. He locked his radar onto the first of two missiles. Announcing, "Fox One!" as he squeezed the trigger on his sidestick, he loosed a Sparrow missile at a ninety-degree angle from the target, a dozen miles distant. The AIM-7 shot away, and the pilot watched its thin smoke trail curve to the right as it homed in on the larger Russian missile skimming the gray-blue wavetops ahead. Thirty seconds later, the pilot felt some satisfaction when he saw the small detonation of his missile followed a millisecond later by the much larger explosion of the Russian weapon.

"Splash one!" The pilot was already locking his radar onto the second missile, but here was where the disadvantages of the semi-active radar homing—SARH—seeker of the Sparrow began to tell. The missile required the launching aircraft to "paint" the target with its own radar to provide the missile's seeker a return to home in on. Thus, he could only engage one target at a time, as he could only get a radar "lock" on one object at a time. So even though his current targets didn't maneuver or shoot back, Jackpot Two-One still required time to destroy each missile in succession, and time was something the supersonic vampires would not provide the American fliers. Two-One launched his second Sparrow, this time at a much closer range, and watched his missile streak seven miles and then explode, sending shards of shrapnel into a second Shipwreck missile.

Only one more missile remained within easy range. Two-One dove towards it, trying to get his shorter ranged, heat-seeking Sidewinder to lock onto the target when suddenly the Russian missile intersected with a medium sized cargo ship that seemed to rise up ahead out of nowhere. The pilot in his single-minded focus hadn't even noticed it. For a split second the ship seemed to absorb the aptly-named Shipwreck. Then the freighter's deck heaved as smoke and fire shot out from every opening in the ship's center.

Jackpot Two-One pulled up on his stick and flashed over the stricken cargo ship now sitting in the center of a halo of white, heaving water. *These missiles aren't aimed at the City,* he realized, only a little relieved. *They're targeting the shipping around the harbor!*

"Darkstar, this is Jackpot Two-One," he called quickly, "I just saw one of the vampires blow away a ship. I say again, the vampire I was engaging just struck a ship, over."

The technicians on Darkstar watched as the missiles merged with slow-moving, ship-sized blips, resulting in momentary pulses on their radar screen. Two-One's report provided confirmation.

"Call NORAD," said the lieutenant colonel. "Let them know that the attack does not, repeat, *does not*, appear to be nuclear. Make sure they understand that it looks like the targets are ships."

Funk's thoughts turned to the burning and sinking ships beginning to multiply around the rectangular patch of Atlantic Ocean south of Long Island and east of New Jersey. "Get a warning out on all maritime frequencies about those missiles! Get Coast Guard on the horn they've a long day ahead of them."

 **CHAPTER 68**

0903 EST, Sunday 13 February 1994
1303 Zulu
Aboard USCGC *Dallas* (WHEC 716), New York Bight,
forty-five miles east of Monmouth, New Jersey

T HE OCEAN-GOING *HAMILTON*-CLASS cutter *Dallas* was
just drawing parallel to the Finnish-flagged, Algerian-registered,
Soviet-operated trawler SSV *Kursagraf.* The cutter's helicopter had
already been up circling the trawler for half an hour, though the intelligence
ship hadn't yet responded to any calls. The *Dallas*, her sleek lines resplendent
in the white and red Coast Guard paint scheme, provided a striking contrast
to the squat, ungainly-looking *Kursagraf,* which did a better job of imitating
a porcupine than an ocean-going vessel, what with the forest of antennae that
sprouted from bow to stern. With direction from Sandy Hook to use "whatever
force necessary" to halt the *Kursagraf,* the crew of the *Dallas* had just put a
shot from their deck gun across the trawler's bow and were now training the
gun, as well as several machineguns, on its bridge. A boarding party were
pulling away from the cutter when the missile warning from Darkstar arrived.

"What did he just say?" asked the cutter's skipper.

"I think he just said we have missiles inbound, sir," answered a watch
officer, the bewilderment in his voice matching the look on his captain's face.

"Radar!" called the captain, his volume rising with urgency, "what have you got on the scope?"

"Just starting to pick something up now, Skipper," responded the chief in charge of the cutter's radars. "Two contacts I think. Hard to tell in the chop. They're real low. Approaching from bearing nine-five-zero relative. Range is eight miles and closing fast!"

The captain snatched up the hand-mic for his ship's public address circuit, the 1MC, and announced, "All hands, battle stations air! Threat to the east! Warm up the Phalanx!" Then to his helmsman he ordered, "hard to starboard, all ahead flank. Try to put us on the west side of that trawler." *We might have just enough time*, he thought. *Dallas* surged forward on the propulsion of her two powerful engines, the cutter's bow angling from left to right across the trawler's stern.

"Range on the vampires now four miles, sir," called the radar officer.

"Battery release on the Phalanx!" ordered the skipper.

The Phalanx, what the skipper had always thought of as an oversized R2D2 ever since he'd see the Star Wars films due to its radar housing, sitting above a black rotary cannon, homed in on the incoming Shipwreck missiles. In seconds the range to the missiles dropped to three miles, then two. The Phalanx's fire control computer, working autonomously to help its twenty-millimeter shells occupy the same moment of space and time as the incoming missiles, judged the time right to let loose a ripping seventy-five round-per-second burst.

The cutter was just passing behind *Kursagraf* as the Phalanx fired. In that moment the radar picked up the antennae forest atop the intelligence trawler, causing the targeting computer to mistake the unexpected interference for a more proximate target. The cutter's skipper saw the cannon slew wildly as it continued to fire. He watched the stream of white tracers and shells rake into the *Kursagraf*, in the process devouring many of the antennae occupying the rear of the trawler.

What the skipper didn't know was that with the destruction of the antennae, the fuzzy news broadcast occupying the screen of hundreds of thousands of television sets around coastal New York, New Jersey, and Connecticut suddenly disappeared. Unfortunately, this was the only positive result of the mis-targeted Phalanx system, which never managed to re-engage the oncoming missiles. Only two slugs ever connected with the lead missile, and these failed to destroy it. The two Shipwrecks struck with enormous violence.

The missiles had been fired blindly and now struck blindly. The lead Shipwreck plowed into the *Kursagraf*, the huge missile crashing through bulkhead after bulkhead, ripping the small ship apart as it did so. Of small consolation for the crew was the fact that their countrymen's missile malfunctioned, failing to detonate its huge warhead due to the damage caused by the Phalanx's rounds. Instead of obliterating the small ship, the skipper from the *Dallas,* watched as the ten-meter-long lance of a missile continued clean through the *Kursagraf*, exiting into the sea on the trawler's far side, leaving the small ship on fire and rapidly taking on water through jagged holes in both of its flanks.

Dallas was less fortunate. In a flash the second weapon struck the fantail, burrowing into the cutter's stern before detonating its warhead. The rear third of the *Dallas* blew apart under the force of over three quarters of a ton of high explosive. The blast wave washed over the bridge, shattering every one of the plate windows and knocking the captain and crew flat.

After the roaring in the skipper's ears began to die away he opened his eyes to see the deck in front of his face covered with broken glass and blood. Disoriented he grasped the ship's wheel and shakily pulled himself up. Others were stirring, some groaning, others feeling with bloody hands at wounds.

The captain grabbed at his dangling hand-mic, succeeding on his second try. He depressed the speak button and rasped, "Damage control. Report." There was no response. After a second call yielded a similar result, the captain staggered out of the bridge and looked rearwards where he saw mangled wreckage engulfed in orange flames and black smoke. Worse, though, was what he felt beneath his feet. *Dallas* was settling rapidly by the stern. The captain made a snap decision, knowing then that his command wouldn't remain afloat much longer.

Staggering back into the shattered bridge, he ordered his stunned crew, "Give the order, all hands abandon ship!" He let that hang and then with the same immediacy said, "See if we can get a radio working to let Sandy Hook know what's happened."

 **CHAPTER 69**

0907 EST, Sunday 13 February 1994
1307 Zulu

US Coast Guard Sandy Hook Station, Ft. Hancock, New Jersey

"MAYDAY, MAYDAY, MAYDAY!" blared the radio in the watch center. "This is the *African Ruby*, we've had an explosion—"

The radio distress calls from panicked civilian crewmembers echoed around the Sandy Hook watch center like repeating hammer blows.

"Mayday, mayday! This is the *Valley Road*. We're declaring an emergency!"

"Mayday, mayday, mayday! This is *Nasico Navigator!*"

The number of burning and sinking ships now stood at nine, each with its own tale of woe. *We have thirteen souls on board...I don't know where three of my people are...We are abandoning ship...Casualties...casualties...casualties...*

Commander Ingalls knew that the first mission of the Coast Guard was search and rescue, but this! *How am I supposed to handle all of this?* It was just so far beyond anything they had ever anticipated. Then: "Sandy Hook, Sandy Hook, this is Coast Guard Six-Five-Four-Three, over," squawked the speaker. That was the callsign for the *Dallas'* helicopter.

"Go ahead, Four-Three," the rescue officer answered, his tone was tense but wary. He wasn't ready for any more bad news but, as a realist, he braced himself.

"Sandy Hook, I am airborne and surveying by sight," called the helicopter crew, "*Dallas* just took a missile and is going down fast by the stern. Rafts deployed, RHIBs conducting immediate rescue, boats in the water. That Russki intel trawler looks like it got hit too, not as bad, but it's also sinking. Appears to be about fifteen crew, no lifeboat apparent. They are abandoning ship. Several of the people on deck are, well," a pause and a cough, "I think they're trying to surrender to me. Request instructions, over."

Stunned, Ingalls called out, "How many people aboard *Dallas*?"

"Log says one-hundred-sixty-two," someone answered.

Ingalls paused. A maritime disaster of epic proportion was unfolding, and he had just lost the larger and more capable of the two cutters that could respond to the emergency. The rescuers would need rescuing. He reached over and grabbed the radio microphone on his desk and called to the helicopter, "Four-Three, what's your fuel status? Are you armed, over?"

"Unarmed. I can give forty-eight minutes on station," answered the helo pilot. "I'll plan to refuel at the Port Authority. Also, I have no rescue swimmer onboard. We left in a hurry, over." The helicopter crew clearly had no intention of rescuing anyone but their shipmates.

The watch commander took a moment to steady himself. All hell was breaking loose around the city, between the terrorist attacks, those weird television broadcasts, and now this massive missile strike on shipping outside the harbor. This was the start of World War Three. He needed to get control of what he could get control of and start doing what he could to save those people, some of them *his* people, out in the waters of the Atlantic on this frigid February morning.

"Okay," Ingalls' raised voice commanding silence in the watch center. Once he had it, mostly, he said, "We're starting this rescue operation right now. All hell is breaking loose back in the City and out there in the harbor, and *this* watch center," he pointed an emphatic finger at the floor for emphasis, "is going to be the command post that puts thing back together." Ingalls started issuing rapid-fire orders to his subordinates in turn. "Ops, start prioritizing wrecks by number of souls and proximity to rescue assets. Air, get on the horn to Gabreski. We need our birds in the air ten minutes ago!" A pair of Coast Guard C-130 Hercules rescue aircraft along with a pair of rescue helicopters were stationed at the Long Island air base. "The Hercs can drop bundles to the more distant wrecks. Tell them I want one to do a flyover of the *Dallas*…"

— ·—

The pilot of Jackpot Two-Two was vectoring onto a group of six missiles heading toward Providence, Rhode Island, with the lead two vampires on a slightly different vector than the other four.

Deciding to split his fire between the two groups and engage at maximum range with his Sparrow missiles, he managed to kill the lead target in each group. He then started a turning dive onto the surviving Shipwrecks, but misjudged his speed and only managed to bring his nose onto the very last missile as it flashed by beneath him. A snapshot with a Sidewinder caught and exploded this trail weapon, but now he was flying too slowly to have any hope of catching the surviving three. Jackpot Two-Two's fourth air-to-air missile hung uselessly on his left wingtip.

Pulling slightly back on his sidestick to gain some altitude, he looked out over the gray water to see what these particular missiles were aiming for, and looking beyond the missile he saw in the distance the silhouettes of two ships. One of them looked to him like it bore the distinctive white and red paint scheme of a Coast Guard vessel. The other ship was huge. *Black hull, white superstructure, red smoke stack, oh my God.*

Dead ahead was the Cunard Line ocean liner RMS *Queen Elizabeth 2*, sailing twenty miles southeast of Montauk and inbound to New York City after a leisurely and luxurious Atlantic crossing. The small US Coast Guard cutter was keeping pace half a mile behind. Jackpot Two-Two screamed over the unfolding disaster, craning his neck to look down in horror as the first missile obliterated the Coast Guard cutter, which vanished in the center of an ugly dark gray cloud with an expanding ball of red-orange flame at its core. Tearing his eyes away from the patch of ocean where the cutter had been and turning his attention back to the massive cruise liner, the pilot watched helplessly as the next Shipwreck missile flew into the hull of the proud ship, exploding a millisecond later.

Then his horror redoubled as second weapon ploughed into the cruise liner's stern. Exploding one after another, the two eruptions wreathed the ocean liner in an ugly cloud of black smoke, white heaving water, and wisps of steam.

The pilot circled back at an altitude of three thousand feet. Realizing that the missile chase on afterburner had eaten into his fuel reserves, he related what he was seeing to Darkstar as he turned for home. Coming around to the west he could see the broad sweep of New York Bay. The entire gray patch of ocean was dotted with pyres of oily black smoke.

———

Ingalls was beginning to feel that they were making a start in rationalizing the unfolding disaster, making it at least feel manageable. Then the floor fell out.

The air officer interrupted, "Sir, call from Darkstar." The man was pale. "I think we lost another cutter, sir."

"What?" Ingalls nearly shouted, "Where?"

"The Air Force is saying they saw a cutter eat a missile southeast of Montauk just a minute ago. The only ship we have out there is *Tahoma*, inbound this morning from Kittery, Maine. They say," the Air officer licked his lips, "they say there's nothing left. It's gone, sir."

"My God," muttered Ingalls. *Two cutters and crew gone in as many minutes.* "How many aboard *Tahoma*?"

"Ninety-eight, sir," was the somber response.

"Sir, that's not the worst of it," the air officer was saying.

"Not the worst of it?" Ingalls asked, incredulous and practically shouting. *What could be worse than losing two cutters and nine other ships in a single morning?*

"No sir." Air was shaking his head. "Darkstar also reports their pilot saw the *QE 2* take two missiles. They say she's burning." The silence that followed was heavy, interrupted by radio chatter.

Then the tinny call came through on the rescue frequency, a British accent: "Mayday, mayday, mayday! This is the *Queen Elizabeth 2*, we have suffered an explosion," a pause in the relay, "Belay that, two explosions. Missiles, I think. We're taking on water, we're on fire, and sinking by the stern." To the Brit's credit he didn't sound as shaken and shocked as he probably was, "I'm ordering everyone into the lifeboats, but many were destroyed in the blast. We have two-thousand three-hundred fifteen souls aboard." A pause and then repeat: "Mayday, mayday."

 **CHAPTER 70**

0920 EST, Sunday 13 February 1994
1320 Zulu
USCGC *Adak*, off Breezy Point, Entrance to Outer New York Harbor

"WANDERER IS PULLING up to the trawler now to assist your boarding party, *Adak*." Sandy Hook was relaying instructions to Jackson. "Stay on those leakers. The FBI will want them, over."

All in all, Jackson thought, the watch center was doing a pretty good job of playing quarterback to the growing chaos around the harbor. The commander on the other end of the radio was clearly tense but taking the unfolding disaster in stride. The Coast Guard lieutenant looked out the starboard window of his cutter's wheelhouse and assessed the small boat, about a hundred and fifty yards ahead. Frantic distress calls coming over the radio filled the background with buzzing, distracting noise. The only thing he knew that he *could* do for sure was catch the escapees from the *Trogg*, now motoring towards the shore in a small boat.

The eastern side of the channel leading into the Harbor ended in a triangle of scrub and marsh grasses. Breezy Point was a very apt name; the weather-beaten spit of sandy beach was defined by a rocky seawall and was otherwise barren. The fleeing RHIB, passed north around the seawall into the calmer waters of Coney Island Channel and turned to cut across *Adak*'s bow towards Brighton Beach, but seeing the flashing lights of NYPD squad cars waiting for them they veered sharply south towards the back side of Breezy Point instead. Jackson watched as the RHIB motored up onto the sand and shuddered to a stop.

Several dark-clad figures piled out into the lapping waves, two of them dragging the limp figure of another up the slope before dropping him behind a bush. A hundred yards beyond, two NYPD patrol cars were bouncing down the beach from the Breezy Point Surf Club, sirens blaring out over the water, blue and red lights flashing. *Adak*'s captain shifted his binoculars and watched as one of the patrol cars bounced to a stop, its front wheels stuck in the soft beach sand. Sweeping his glasses back to the figures on the beach, Jackson watched as another man retrieved something from the boat. *It's a gun!* he realized quickly.

Before Jackson could lift his radio to call a warning, he heard the staccato burst of an automatic rifle crack across the breaking surf. The gunman, standing next to the small boat, was aiming and firing at the lead patrol car, which slid to a halt as bullet holes spider-webbed its windshield. An NYPD officer leaned behind the open door of his stuck patrol car and returned fire with a pistol, but the match was hopelessly uneven, especially as three other boatmen retrieved rifles and sprinted the few yards to the brush. As they started to maneuver against the police officers, they looked more like soldiers than seamen.

Looking through his binos, Jackson knew what he had to do. *We're at war, ships are sinking outside the harbor mouth, and* Dallas *and* Tahoma *are gone. I'll be damned if I'm going to let a bunch of terrorists... No. Enemy soldiers kill more people,* my *people, in front of me.*

Calling to the Coast Guards manning the M2 machineguns on either side of the wheelhouse, Jackson shouted, "Gunners, engage those hostiles! Weapons release!"

The starboard .50 caliber machinegun roared out with the steady rhythm of a jackhammer. Jackson watched the tracers of the first burst reach out towards the RHIB and stitch a row of white puffs into the surf. The police officer from the second squad car was now out as well, having slid across his passenger seat. He was clearly wounded, one of his arms hanging limp, but the other hand rested a pistol in the vee between the car body and the open passenger-side door. Jackson saw the pistol buck once just as the machinegun next to him let loose a second burst. This one connected with a shooter standing ankle-deep in water next to the RHIB, a thumb-sized round catching him between the shoulder blades and slamming him face-first into the lapping waves. *Where are the other three?* Jackson continued to scan.

Several loud *pings* against *Adak*'s hull announced that at least one of the enemy gunmen was returning fire against the cutter. Jackson finally fixed the man in his glasses. The Coast Guard lieutenant flinched as a round *pinged* off the wheelhouse.

"Gunner!" he shouted, "Gunman, halfway up the beach, firing towards us. Two more running away behind him!"

Then the .50 cal let go with another of its jackhammer bursts. Tracers reached out towards the enemy gunman. Watching, Jackson was sure the man would be hit, but the bullets only kicked up puffs of wet sand all around him. The man flinched and began backing towards the vegetation.

Jackson shifted his attention to the two other gunmen. They were moving, crouched over, through the high beach grass, clearly trying to gain an angle on the police officers. The Coast Guard lieutenant maneuvered his cutter to unmask the second machinegun, then shouted to his port M2 gunner to engage. As he did so he saw the two men pause and crouch. One reached down into a cargo pocket and retrieved an object. He manipulated it with both hands for a moment, then his right hand stretched back behind him in a classic thrower's profile. *Grenade!* Jackson realized in a flash, *he's going to throw a grenade at that nearest squad car!*

The gunman's arm began to move forward in a throw, but in that instant the port-side gunner pressed his thumbs into his machinegun's butterfly trigger, letting loose a long burst towards the shoreline. Jackson saw tracers lance into the grenade thrower, and the man collapsed straight downwards as if he was a puppet whose strings had suddenly been cut by some invisible scissors.

The second gunman flattened himself into the beach grass as soon as the .50 caliber bullets began to kick up earth around him. Now Jackson saw him spring upwards as if he had landed on a beehive just before the earth around him erupted into an inverted cone of flying sand and brush. The grenade's explosion threw the man backwards, and Jackson saw the body arc through the air. Only then did his ears register that sharp *crack* of the detonation as it swept across the water.

Jackson was stunned at the damage his crew was inflicting on the gunmen ashore, then realized that this was point blank range for the .50 cal. *Well, don't take a knife to a gunfight, take a bigger gun*, he thought with a grim, clench-jawed smile. He saw the fourth and final enemy fighter take a round fired by one of the police officers. The man staggered, then turned towards the squad cars and tried to bring his assault rifle up to his shoulder. A final burst from the starboard M2 knocked him down for good before he could fire another shot. Then the beach was quiet except for the receding echoes of the gunfire resonating in his ears. The entire battle had lasted less than two minutes.

A moment passed, then Jackson grabbed the hand mic with one hand, reaching with his other to switch the radio's frequency to the universal police band as he did so.

"Officers on Breezy Point, officers on Breezy Point," he called, "this is the Coast Guard cutter *Adak* just offshore. Do you read me, over?"

He saw the officer in the passenger side of the nearest squad car, the one whose arm appeared to be limp, set his pistol on the seat and reach inside for his own hand mic. A moment later Jackson heard, "Coast Guard," the man was breathing heavily, "Coast Guard, this is Car Three-One. Thanks for the assist, over."

The other officer was now advancing towards the bodies in the sand and scrub, hatless and with his pistol held out in front of him. Jackson watched him approach the spot where the grenade had exploded, then stop and turn away. The man retched twice, then moved quickly past the grisly scene towards the surf, where the bodies of the other two gunmen lay motionless. Before he got there, however, something caused him to turn to the side and examine a small clump of low brush. The patrolman keyed the radio on his shoulder, and heard, "Uh, Sergeant, we've got a guy ovah heah. He's, uh, he's missing an ahm." Jackson registered the voice's thick New York accent. It brought him back to all the NYPD cops who had walked beats in his Brooklyn neighborhood growing up.

"Missing an arm?" the other officer called over the net. "Is he alive?" More sirens were approaching from the direction of the Breezy Point Surf Club.

"Yeah," responded the other police officer, "he's breathing. Tourniquet on the ahm. Looks real professional."

That's the owner of the arm the chief found on the Trogg, Jackson knew.

He keyed his own radio and said, "Car Three-One, we've got the arm to match your guy. The FBI is looking for these yahoos. Maybe we can piece things together for them."

———— ————

Back aboard *Trogg,* Chief Everfield was on deck, the rest of his boarding party now watching him from their RHIB, a safe fifty yards across the water. He saw *Wanderer* come alongside. Before the chief knew what was happening, a stocky man from the pilot boat scrambled aboard and strode purposefully up to him.

"What the hell are you doing here?" challenged the chief, indignant that a civilian would dare enter his domain without permission.

"Can it, Chief," the newcomer shot back, unfazed. "I'm ex-Navy, EOD. I'm here to disarm that bomb of yours. Where is it?"

The chief was taken aback. He shook his head and started saying, "No. I can't let you—"

"Chief," the other man cut in, his voice rising with annoyance, "are you going to show me where that scuttling charge is, or do I have to find it myself?"

Everfield nodded, recognizing another professional in the way the man carried himself, assured but not cocky. He led the *Wanderer* crewman down into the bow of the trawler. Seconds ticked by, then a minute. Then the two men emerged on deck. The stocky ex-Navy man was carrying a large package in his arms, like someone would a beer cooler. He seemed relaxed, even cheerful.

0925 EST, Sunday 13 February 1994
1325 Zulu
US Coast Guard Sandy Hook Station, Ft. Hancock, New Jersey

At Sandy Hook, Ingalls noted with satisfaction the report from *Adak* that the leakers from *Trogg* had been dealt with. Amid the chaos of desperate radio calls from sinking ships, this was a small victory.

"Get on the horn to *Adak*," Ingalls ordered his surface ops officer. "Tell them we've got a tug en route to bring the *Trogg* in. I want them to rendezvous with it and make sure they don't stumble across any of those mines, got it?"

The harried operations officer nodded and made the call.

At Breezy Point, Lieutenant Jackson was reporting police and EMTs swarming over the carnage. The one-armed man had been loaded into an ambulance with two NYPD officers and whisked off to the nearest hospital. The other four gunmen needed no hospital, only a coroner. More interesting than their corpses, though, was the equipment they'd been carrying: Soviet-made AK-type assault rifles, Soviet-made hand grenades, and, in the RHIB, Soviet-made blocks of military-grade explosives. The FBI was now present to relieve the Coast Guard and the NYPD of jurisdiction, and Ingalls was happy to let them sort through the mess. He had his own problems to deal with.

After the loss of *Dallas* and *Tahoma*, *Adak*, smallest of the three by far, was the only asset in New York harbor and was needed to rescue the hundreds of people that were in the water. *No. Thousands*, Ingalls reminded himself. First *Adak* would hand the trawler over to the FBI and then mark the extent of the minefield. *We're going to have to deal with those mines sooner rather than later*, thought Ingalls sourly. Clearing a harbor channel full of mines was *not* a scenario he felt prepared to deal with on his own.

"Riley," he called over to his air operation officer, "Call around to the military bases, see if any of them have anybody with mine-clearing experience. I'm going to call up to District One HQ in Boston to see what resources they can push us to start clearing the channel. If World War Three really just kicked off in Europe, we're going to need this harbor open *stat*, no matter who's on the offensive."

He reached for his desk phone, but before he could grasp the receiver it began to ring. He snatched it up and answered, the conversation was quick and he hung up with a, "Roger."

"Okay everyone, listen up. In case anybody had any doubts after three dozen missiles just tore the guts the of our shipping around here. We are at war, right here in our own backyard." He let that sink in for only a moment. "The sector commander and station chief are on their way in. More importantly, we now fall under the command of CINCLANT, along with the rest of First, Fifth, and Seventh Districts, effective immediately." He pronounced the abbreviation "CINCLANT," commander-in-chief, Atlantic, as "Sink-lant." The three Coast Guard Districts on the US eastern seaboard now fell under the command of the US Navy.

 **CHAPTER 71**

1427 CET, Sunday 13 February 1994
1327 Zulu
Tromsø Lufthavn, Tromsø, Norway

K*APTEIN* JAN OLSEN'S F-16 touched down on the icy runway north of Tromsø, causing eddies to swirl in the clouds of snow that skittered low across the tarmac. He'd never been so aware of the absence of other jets. Jan deployed the drag chutes to slow his fighter, then rolled onto a turn-off mid-way down the runway. He robotically followed the directions of a ground crewman who guided him into one of the small airport's civilian hangars, where an ad-hoc crew was waiting to refuel and re-arm his Falcon. Olsen pulled his canopy release as he entered the hangar, an icy blast of wind was a reminder that he was in Norway, north of the Arctic Circle. The wind died as the F-16 rocked to a stop and the hangar doors closed. Then he ripped off his oxygen mask in a sudden burst of anger and powered down his jet's systems.

As the sounds in the cockpit died away, Jan let out a long, ragged breath. Then he looked at his watch. *Thirteen thirty. The war is only ninety minutes old*, he realized. The weight of what had unfolded in that time hit him like a hammer blow. True, he had shot down three Soviet fighters and damaged another, but the losses were hard to take. He'd heard of two other downed Norwegian jets, and three of the six pilots who had flown up to Banak with him the previous night also gone. *Five pilots in less than two hours! We've got less than twenty-five in the whole squadron!* Jan raged. Those five included Bjorn, his closest friend in the squadron. He and Bjorn had been flying together since flight school.

To make matters worse, he had just landed at Tromsø, about two hundred and fifty kilometers *west* of Banak, where he'd started this fateful day. Where he was supposed to be. Despite the losses he and his fellow pilots were inflicting on the Soviets, they had still lost control of the airspace in the far north.

Olsen pounded his fist onto his thigh in rage and frustration. Then he did it again, and again, though in his anger he was still careful not to strike any of the instruments around him. The faces of his friends flashed before him, as if the heads-up display in front of him were a movie screen. It was hard to pinpoint what he was angrier at: The Russians, the war engulfing his country, or his friends and comrades who would never come home again. Or maybe he was just frustrated with his own government for not giving them more planes, better planes. His anger and frustration dwindled slowly, leaving him a sad ragged shell. A ground crewman leaned into the cockpit without a word and unbuckled Jan from his seat, allowing the pilot to climb out onto a ladder, now hanging from the aircraft. On the ground, Olsen barely acknowledged the crew. He located what he was searching for and headed for a small office on one side of the hangar.

Tromsø Lufthavn, like most of the airfields in Northern Norway, was not a true military airfield. Rather, it was a dispersal field to which jets could fly in wartime so that minimal numbers of aircraft were on the ground at the larger bases like Bardufoss and Orland. Large concentrations of parked aircraft were inviting targets, vulnerable to destruction in a surprise attack or, worse, a nuclear strike. The Royal Norwegian Air Force stored limited stocks of weapons and ammunition at these dispersal fields, but the facilities were primitive at best. Olsen strode into the small office, where an air force lieutenant was manning the HF radio and a telephone.

"I need orders for my next mission," Olsen told the man, without introduction.

The lieutenant looked up, saw Olsen in his flight suit and carrying his helmet, and nodded, "We're re-arming your aircraft now. Your squadron CO left a message a few minutes ago for you to call Bardufoss on arrival."

Olsen nodded back. "Any idea what about?" he asked.

The other man shook his head. Then he said, "The Russians have been hitting us hard and pushing us back." The man broke off, scanning Jan's face. "I'm sorry, you know that better than I. The other squadrons are on their way up from the south, and the Americans are sending some F-15s from England."

That must be the 493rd from Lakenheath, thought Jan. *Good pilots. Good jets.* The 493rd Fighter Squadron, the "Grim Reapers," was the American F-15C Eagle squadron based northeast of London.

"If we can hold on for a few more hours," the lieutenant was saying, "I think the generals are hoping we can stop the Soviets around Banak."

A few more hours? Jan thought. *We've already lost almost a quarter of our strength.* He thanked the younger officer and picked up the phone. *Will there be anyone left by the time help arrives?* he wondered.

"Jan," Olsen heard his squadron commanding officer's voice, "good to hear from you. Sorry about Bjorn. He was a good man and a good pilot." It was a poor eulogy for a man that Olsen had spent more hours with than perhaps anyone besides his parents, but, *This is war,* Jan thought. *This must be what war is like: loss.*

"We've got a major op coming together," the CO was saying. "I want you to stand down for the next couple of hours," that was *not* what Jan wanted to hear, "I need you fresh to lead a flight of four jets in a massed sweep to see if we can stop this Soviet attack in its tracks." *That* sounded better.

"We should have support from some Grim Reapers out of Lakenheath," the CO explained. "They'll start arriving within the hour. We'll have bits from at least three other squadrons: The Lions," he referred to the Norwegian 331 Squadron, "are working out of Evenes." Olsen nodded. His own 332 Squadron, the Eagles, worked together with the Lions often. The CO continued: "334 Squadron is backstopping here over Bardufoss, and Tiger Squadron," here he referred to the Royal Norwegian Air Force's 338 Squadron, "is on their way north with four of the new MLU Falcons."

That was excellent news, Jan knew. The MLU, or "Mid-Life Upgrade" F-16s were capable of carrying the amazing new AMRAAM missile, just like the American F-15 Eagle. Those weapons would give the NATO side a huge advantage once they arrived. His spirits were beginning to lift. *Maybe we can beat them back.*

His body registered that he could use some rest, get something to eat, then get back in the air to cut a swathe through the Soviet hordes and begin exacting some revenge for Bjorn and the others.

"The Dutch 322nd Fighter Squadron is flying up as well, but they won't arrive until tonight," the CO was saying. *The "Poly Parrots,"* Olsen smirked, remembering the Dutch Squadron's mascot. *I wonder if they're bringing the bird?*

"We've got a big fight, brewing, Jan," the commander concluded. "We're going to stop these Reds and start pushing them back so the army can secure the north. I need you to be ready, understood?"

"Yes sir," he said. "I'll be ready."

"I know you will, Jan," the man on the other end of the line said. Then, "One of the other ships you'll lead is up there at Tromsø already. The other two should be there in half an hour, they're just returning from beating back an attack on the Backstop site in Finnmark. I want you ready to launch at fifteen-thirty, so get some rest. You're going to need it." The line clicked off.

As he set the receiver down, Jan's thoughts turned back to Erik in Banak. He and his unit were isolated, they needed support, and Jan had promised to deliver. As if the controllers at the Backstop radar site had read his mind, the HF radio in the small room crackled to life: "All callsigns, be advised, major enemy strike going into Banak. Does anyone have enough missiles to intervene?"

The airwaves remained silent in response to this query.

He listened as the Backstop controllers began to describe the situation in the skies to the north and to direct the fighters defending the airspace. This fight was considerably harder than in training, especially considering the effective Soviet jamming emanating from aircraft just over the frontier. There would be precious little help for Johansen's cavalry squadron at Banak.

Hold on Erik! Jan urged silently, feeling the heat of frustrated rage return.

 **CHAPTER 72**

1429 CET, Sunday 13 February 1994
1329 Zulu
Banak Airbase, Lakselv, Troms, Norway

T
HE SUN SHINING through the patchy clouds overhead offered no warmth to the soldiers moving about below. The icy wind blowing off the fjord didn't help either. *Rittmester* Erik Johansen and his signaler waited outside of his G-Wagen just south of the airfield, tucked into the tree line among the stunted evergreens, boughs heavy with snow, the driver remained sitting behind the wheel. The sparse little crossroads town of Lakselv, their whole reason for being here, was off to their right front. On their way to inspect the troop positions guarding the southern approaches to the town, the HF radio call came in through the jamming static, warning that a raid was inbound to their position.

Johansen, deciding that being the one moving vehicle in sight might not be the best idea, halted at the edge of town. Immediately he called on his radio back to the airfield, just a few hundred meters north, and ordered the last two F-16s off the ground. The pilots from Olsen's flight had been waiting for the skies overhead to clear of Soviet aircraft long enough to make their vulnerable takeoff rolls; now they had no choice but to risk it.

As they waited, Johansen pulled out his map, flattened it on the hood of the truck, and visualized his reconnaissance squadron's positions. Two sections from 2nd Troop were guarding the eastern approaches, focusing their defenses on the bridge across the Brennelvo, with the third section back at the airfield with Sergeant Pedersen's pioneers and the two TOW missile-carrying M113s. The anti-air missile teams, now joined by the four Bofors gun crews, were scattered around the perimeter of the runway. Johansen's ace in the hole, the artillerymen from the Porsanger battery, were even now spreading white camouflage netting over their six one-hundred-five-millimeter howitzers in the woods northwest of the airfield. Finally, Johansen's 1st Troop was in positions on the southern edge of the town of Lakselv to protect against an attack from that direction.

Lakselv occupied a strategic position, sitting at the head of the hundred-and-twenty kilometer-long Porsangerfjord, which cut deeper than any other into Norway's rugged arctic coast. Banak and Lakselv, at the head of the fjord, were nestled into the valley that extended south from the water, bounded to the west by the Stabbursdalen highlands, whose sheer cliff faces overshadowed the town, and to the east by the Halkvarre Mountains, rising in some places to almost a thousand meters of glacier-smoothed altitude. The rugged highlands forced any attacker into one of two avenues of approach, either along the coast from the east on Highway 98, or up the valley from the south along the E6. Lakselv sat where these roads converged.

If Johansen and his men could deny this spot to the Soviets long enough for the battalion to arrive, then the Soviet offensive would stall up here in the ice and snow of the far north. If not...*I don't want to think about "if not."* He would not feel secure until the reinforcements arrived tonight with its company of Leopard tanks, two companies of mechanized infantry, another artillery battery—this one with heavy hundred-fifty-five-millimeter M109 mobile howitzers—and all the other trappings of a modern armored force. Once in position at this choke point, the Soviets were going to find it very hard indeed to dislodge such a force. *The issue is holding out until then.*

The scream of jet engines from the south tore the *rittmester*'s attention away from the map. The arrow-straight E6 highway gave him a clear vista between the colorful buildings of Lakselv on the right and the stunted tundra vegetation, brown sticks poking out of soft mounds of white snow, to the left. His eyes took a moment to focus. The low rumble of high-altitude jet engines overhead had been constant for the past hour, along with the sharper *crack* of explosions and the occasional deep sonic *boom*. This sound was different, though. It didn't come from above, Johansen thought. Instead it was reverberating off the rocky hills to the east and west.

Then he saw them. Two flitting objects to the south, barely at treetop level, turning north to come down the valley. His eyes played tricks with him as he lost the jets against the gray and white of the hillsides before reacquiring them as they leveled out. The roar of the two airplanes' engines grew louder. It felt like the jets were flying directly at him, with the round circle of the fuselages framed by the thin lines of wings and stabilizers giving only a small cross-section to observe.

The *rittmester* clapped his signalman on the back. The man, who was also looking to the south from their shelter in the low trees, jumped a little.

"Get a call out on the squadron net: fast-movers approaching from the south, low altitude. Tell everyone to look alive!" Johansen ordered.

As the radioman made the call, two more dark objects banked into the valley behind the first pair, and Johansen thought he could see a third flight descending into valley from the southeast. The roar of the jet engines returned until it was a scream as the first two Soviet jets shot past, almost directly over Erik and his two soldiers, dark arrowheads against the white-blue sky. Johansen's reconnaissance training paid off as he identified the Soviet aircraft in a moment. *Cigar-shaped fuselage, front air intake with shock cone, variable geometry wings, Su-17 "Fitter" fighter-bombers*, the *rittmester* knew, turning to follow the mottled green- and brown-painted jets as they flashed north towards the airfield.

The Soviet fighter-bombers were just nosing up to bomb-release altitude when Johansen heard the first staccato burst of machinegun fire from the direction of the airfield. He knew that the gunners would only have moments to aim at the old but blazingly fast and rugged Su-17s. The machinegun burst had no effect, and Erik watched as several objects detached from the Fitters and fell towards the airfield, then at the last moment seemed to split open, dozens of small bomblets scattered downward.

"Get down!" Erik yelled, pushing his signalman and driver towards the snow as the bomblets struck. The three men hit the ground as the first sub-munitions detonated, followed by dozens more in a firecracker string of blasts.

Looking up, Erik could see the taxiway and snowfields on the west side of the runway disappear beneath a blanket of sparking explosions and gray smoke. From his position Erik had a clear view straight up the runway, with the civilian passenger terminal and hangars on the right and the small collection of military buildings on the left. Both sticks of cluster bombs fell on the west side of the runway, between the tarmac and the small Coast Guard complex, but the military buildings themselves seemed to be intact amid the smoke and shrapnel. One of the Coast Guard helicopters was not so lucky, however. A yellow eruption of aviation fuel announced the machine's demise.

As the reverberations of the explosions receded, Johansen became aware of other sounds. The deep *pom-pom-pom* of the Bofors guns as they opened from their hidden positions around the airfield. He could see the tracers of the forty-millimeter rounds arcing upwards, chasing the two aircraft as they dove for the treetops once again and banked away to the east. A tearing scream announced the launch of an RBS-70 missile from west of the runway. Erik watched the thin white smoke trail of the weapon. The laser-guided missile sped after one of the Soviet fighter-bombers. Johansen willed it on, but instead saw the missile fall into the fjord as its rocket motor burned out.

The next pair roared overhead. This time the Norwegian defenders, anticipating the direction of the attack, responded with greater alacrity. Bofors rounds flashed between the Soviet jets as they climbed, and one shell passed through the left wing of the lead aircraft, leaving a softball-sized hole but failing to down the bird. The two Soviet fighter-bombers angled slightly to the right of the first two, and their high-explosive bombs straddled the hangar in which the civilian evacuees had assembled less than an hour before. One bomb crashed through the thin roof of the hangar, and a moment later the structure's wide doors blew outward with the blast. The *pom-pom-pom* of the Skyguard radar-directed Bofors guns continued to hammer into Erik's consciousness amid the larger explosions.

To his amazement, Johansen could see the two F-16s, unharmed, taxiing to the southern end of the runway, the end nearest to him. As the third pair of Su-17s roared overhead targeting the middle of the runway, the first F-16 began its takeoff roll northward, directly away from Erik's location. The Soviet fighter-bombers roared over the airfield and released their ordnance just as the first Norwegian Falcon was rotating off the tarmac. Erik watched in horror as one of the cluster bombs burst open directly above the ascending F-16. Three submunitions struck the fighter and exploded in miniature flashes. A moment later a yellow jet of flame shot out from the Falcon's fuselage. The jet's nose dipped, and it dove into the fjord, crashing through the sea ice along the shore and sending blue and white chunks flying. Incredibly, the second Falcon passed unharmed through the cones of smoke and shrapnel thrown up by the cluster bomblets. The pilot pulled back on his stick, at the same time punching his afterburners, and the nimble jet shot into the sky, banking west.

At this point the airfield's defenders finally managed to gain some measure of revenge. Another RBS-70 missile tore skyward from the northwest end of the runway just as the Fitters were banking east. Johansen saw the missile fly straight into an Su-17s left wing root and explode, sending the jet spiraling into the water.

A fourth pair of Soviet raiders was nearing the airfield, and the Norwegian Bofors gunners were now finding the range. The lead jet's nose disintegrated as it took a burst of forty-millimeter shells straight through its conical air intake. The Su-17 banked right and rolled over onto its back as its already-dead pilot slumped against his joystick. Johansen cringed as he watched the stricken jet disappear into the buildings of Lakselv. A red and black fireball rose from within the town to accompany the rumbling explosion. The pilot of the second of these two Su-17s forged on, however. This flight of raiders had been armed with rockets instead of gravity bombs, and now the pilot aimed his aircraft's nose at the gun position that had downed his wingman.

Erik heard a tearing roar above him and looked up to see streaks of gray smoke shoot out from two pods underneath the wings of the surviving Fitter, now passing directly overhead. Seconds later he saw and heard a string of explosions straddle the location of one of his Bofors guns in the trees on the east side of the runway. The gun fell silent, though another sent tracers up to chase the lone bomber as it banked east heading for home.

The air raid seemed to go on forever. A fifth pair of Fitters screamed overhead, then a sixth. These carried incendiary bombs, which they dropped into the tree line on either side of the runway. A third Su-17 fell to the defenders, struck by several rounds from a surviving Bofors gun. The fighter-bomber continued on for several moments, then nosed down and crashed with a tremendous white splash into the dark open water, near where the 332 Squadron Falcon had gone in.

Then, suddenly, the valley was quiet. Or at least relatively so, Johansen realized as the sounds from the Soviet jets' engines receded to the northeast. The roar of explosions and of military aircraft engines gave way to fire crackling from beneath dark pillars of smoke rising from the crash sites in Lakselv and east of the airfield, as well as from the eviscerated hangar. The scene around him was smudged with thick black smoke, sprays of dirt and concrete, and raging yellow fires contrasting dizzyingly with the whites and blues that had characterized their world just minutes before.

The raid apparently over, Erik climbed to his feet, grabbed the radio hand-mic from his signalman, and called his number two. *Løytnant* Berg was back at the airfield.

"*Dragon* Five, *Dragon* Five, this is *Dragon* Six, over." Johansen waited, but there was no response. "*Dragon* Five, this is Six," he repeated, "Respond, Five!"

Erik waited for several more moments, beginning to lose hope. Then his radio crackled with, "Six, this is Five, over." *Thank God*, the *rittmester* sighed.

"Five, give me a situation report. What are your losses back there, over?" Johansen demanded.

Another moment of silence, then, "Six, we have some casualties here, still getting a handle on it. Looks like one of the Bofors got hit. The whole crew is dead. Incendiary bombs fell in the area where one of the RBS-70 posts was, but the sergeant major hasn't gotten over there yet. One of the TOW carriers took some damage from a cluster bomb. Two of the crew are wounded. I'll let you know when we have a better idea of what's going on, over."

Johansen nodded. Did he need to return to the airfield? No, he decided, Berg had things under control. He'd always been impressed with the competence of his lanky deputy. Now he was really beginning to shine. The XO would be very busy indeed in the coming hours.

"Roger that, Five," Erik responded. "You handle things back there. I'm continuing on to 1st Troop's position. Six, out."

The *rittmester* climbed back into the G-Wagen. He'd heard nothing from Battalion for more than an hour. The silence was due, no doubt, to the increasingly effective Soviet jamming, but the lack of contact left him feeling alone. Were it not for his conviction that his countrymen wouldn't willingly abandon them, Erik might have thought that Banak and his men were being written off as a lost cause. Such a large strike could have been intended to prevent the airfield's use by the Norwegians but, Erik's stomach sunk with realization: *the Sovs had used only munitions that could not crater the runway.* That left the airstrip open for use. By anyone. Erik didn't like where this war was headed, and it wasn't even ninety minutes old yet!

Erik pushed aside his feelings and began to look at his squadron's situation as rationally as he could. His thoughts turned to the grandfather who had remained behind at the Lufthavn. *That man is taking his "Poster on the Wall" duty to heart,* thought Johansen. A plan began to form in his mind. It wasn't a plan that he ever wanted to implement, but if worse came to worst and his squadron did turn into the trip wire it was starting to look like, he and his soldiers could still cause many problems for the Soviets.

CHAPTER 73

1500 CET, Sunday 13 February 1994
1400 Zulu
Over Kirkenes Lufthavn, Finnmark, Norway

GUARDS COLONELS ROMANOV and Sokolov had retraced their course after observing the naval infantry assault on Vardø and were now approaching Kirkenes again after re-crossing the Varangerfjord. Sokolov tapped Ilya on the shoulder and pointed down, through the porthole window of the Il-22 command aircraft, "My first wave is approaching now."

Ilya could make out a dozen whirling rotors spinning against the bluish-white canvas of the snowy tundra. Helicopters laden with Sokolov's *desantniki* hugged the folds of the ground as they approached from the southeast. The radio operator flicked to the appropriate frequency, allowing Romanov to hear the radio chatter as the assault went in.

◆—

Anna Hagen shivered against the cold seeping into the attic of the Lufhavn's passenger terminal. She'd been hiding in this crawl space for just over an hour, but it seemed a frozen eternity. She sat huddling for warmth, absent mindedly watching through louvers in an air vent as men, wearing civilian attire like the one she had eluded earlier and armed with stubby assault weapons, moved about the airfield. The peaceful world Anna had woken up to this morning seemed like a distant memory now, and she wondered if she would live to see another day. Her cheeks were bright red from rubbing away frozen tears, tears of mourning for her co-workers, tears of anguish for the things she had not yet accomplished in her short life, and tears of terror for her current situation and the things that might happen in the next few hours.

The distant *crump crump* of artillery from the east continued unabated, but the sound had gradually changed, growing closer until it became thunderous *booms* that shook the entire building. Anna hugged her knees and rocked back and forth as *boom* after *boom* assaulted her senses. Suddenly a different sound startled her into heightened awareness. The sharp *popping* of gunfire. At first, just one or two shots, but it quickly exploded into an all-out firefight lasting about thirty seconds, somewhere behind her building, then it died down. *What could that mean?* she thought to herself.

Anna's hope that maybe the Home Guard soldiers would regain control of the airfield and rescue her was bolstered. The few Russians she'd seen couldn't possibly keep control of this airfield against the battalion of Norwegian border guards and soldiers garrisoned just to the south, could they? She renewed her vigil, watching the wind- and snow-swept tarmac before her for any sign of deliverance, and she shivered. *If I stay up here much longer, I'll freeze,* she thought, trying to shrink further into her winter coat.

At that moment a deep, rhythmic thrum or throbbing noise crept its way into Anna's consciousness. *An engine? No, multiple engines*, she decided quickly. *Helicopters.* The sound grew steadily louder, and Anna realized that the sounds of artillery had receded once again to the quieter, distant *crumps.* Now the thrum grew to a roar directly overhead that caused the whole building to reverberate. Anna, looking out desperately to see if the approaching aircraft could possibly be Norwegian, saw the dark shapes appear from behind the roof against the white-blue sky. She could feel the downdraft from the rotors blasting into her crawl space as the huge, bug-like machines moved slowly toward the runway. Amid a blizzard of swirling snow, Anna saw four helicopters flare and settle onto the runway between the yellow snow plows that still sat, parked, facing both directions.

Side doors banged open and Anna saw white-clad figures jump from the aircraft and run, hunched over beneath the spinning rotor blades towards the margins of the airfield burdened by weapons and large backpacks. The blowing snow cleared enough that she could see the red star of the Soviet military painted prominently on the side of the nearest helicopter. *More Russians!*

The helicopters remained on the ground only long enough to disgorge their passengers before lifting off ponderously, engines screaming, pivoting in sequence and accelerating towards the northeast. The first four helicopters were immediately replaced by more, bringing no relief from the noise or from the blowing snow, and unloading yet more soldiers. Her hope for salvation or escape was being trampled beneath the boots of each new soldier hitting the icy Kirkenes pavement.

Anna, her hands growing painfully cold, was now forced to reevaluate her predicament. If no one was coming to get her, she would just need to find a way to save herself and get back to her home in Kirkenes, or freeze to death, or get shot. Or worse. Her thoughts and emotions brought her back to a night, several years ago, when she'd been out snowmobiling in the wilds south of town. Being an independent teenager at the time, she had neglected to tell anyone where she was going. She'd driven out too far onto the tundra and her snowmobile broke down nearly ten kilometers from town. In the gathering darkness, Anna had been faced with the choice of waiting through the arctic night for help to come find her, or saving herself by walking the ten snowy kilometers back to town. She arrived at home several hours later to proudly face parents nearly beside themselves with worry. Her sister Kristen had alternated between hugging her and admonishing her for being so foolish. Now she faced a similar dilemma, one she would need to solve herself.

Hundreds of Soviet soldiers swarming over the airport couldn't fail to see her if she slipped out, but perhaps...perhaps she could blend in with them? Anna remembered that the drapes in the office beneath her were off-white. She could wrap herself in those, wait for another flight of helicopters to land, then make a break for it in the blowing snow...It was a long shot she knew, but... her mind kept returning to the image of the predatory Russian beast cleaning his knife, standing over the body of her friend, and she decided she had to try.

With the roar of helicopter engines filling her ears, Anna crawled back to the ceiling panel that gave her access to the maintenance closet and let herself down onto the wrought iron sink. She poked her head out of the closet into the office. No one was there. Wind blew through the office from the window she had left open. Anna dashed over and grasped the room-darkening drapes. Two violent tugs on the heavy fabric tore the curtain rod out of the wall, bringing it clattering down with a sound that Anna was sure every Russian on the whole Lufthavn must have heard. She stood stock still, listening for footsteps from the hallway that would signal her doom, her heart pounded.

Anna waited. Her warm winter boots, the same ones in fact that she had worn on her snowmobile escapade several years earlier, felt frozen to the floor. Finally, she gathered up the courage to bend down and slide one of the drapes off the curtain rod. Wrapping herself, she crouched down, waiting, willing her heart to stop beating so loudly in her ears, determined to make a break for it when the next wave landed.

— • —

Three thousand meters overhead, Romanov and Sokolov watched the helicopter assault go in. Another wave of four transports descended through a thin cloud of blowing snow onto the dark runway, landing between the yellow snow plows that stood out prominently, even from this altitude. Two platoons of *desantniki* were on the ground already, encountering no resistance. The *Spetsnaz*, Romanov thought, had done their job well.

Now the next wave was approaching. The first two had been composed of Mi-8 troop transports. Now it was time for the huge Mi-6s, carrying BMD armored vehicles in their spacious holds, to descend.

Sokolov called over to him, "Once those heavies are on the ground they will start advancing to seize the fjord bridges to the south."

Ilya nodded. The attack was going like clockwork. He noted that Sokolov had opted to put the entire assault battalion into the airport, rather than landing individual companies at the bridges, the unit's real objectives, as Romanov would have done. Bridges, in rough terrain such as this, were absolutely vital pieces of infrastructure, and Romanov would have elected instead to land right on them. Sokolov's tactic was a risk, giving the Norwegians time to blow the bridges as the Soviet paratroopers traveled from the airfield, though it also allowed Sokolov to keep tighter control of the battalion. Ilya was more inclined to trust his well-trained subordinates to achieve their objectives without him looking over their shoulder.

— —

Draped in her white curtain, Anna crouched below the window sill, peering over the ledge as more helicopters thundered overhead. She was working up the courage to make a break for the airport exit and then...*And then what?* She suddenly wondered. *Do I just jump in my car and drive home?* The idea seemed ridiculous, but what else could she do? If she stayed here there was no hope. The image of the Russian, blood on his long knife reappeared. She took in a long slow breath and steeled her resolve.

Out on the runway different helicopters arrived, massive ones. They had rear ramps that lowered to the tarmac, and Anna heard the throaty roar of diesel engines. To her amazement, she saw what looked like a tank, *Maybe a miniature tank?* She thought. It emerged from the nearest helicopter, nosing gingerly down the ramp. The olive drab vehicle rolled on thin tracks bracketing a boat-like bow. Its low, round turret sat far forward on the hull, sporting a stubby cannon. Anna could see a soldier standing tall in the turret, leaning forward at the waist to ensure his vehicle cleared the helicopter's fuselage. The vehicle was so small that the crewman was probably standing on the vehicle's floor. She could also see the padded helmet of the driver poking up from the hatch beneath the short cannon.

The little tank carefully inched onto the tarmac, then rotated until it seemed to be pointed directly towards her hiding place. Elsewhere along the runway, other little tanks were emerging from the other helicopters, the coughing of the engines punctuating the roar of the spinning rotors. Almost in unison, the Russian vehicles pivoted and drove forward to the edge of the runway, allowing the pilots of the monstrous helicopters to increase power and ponderously lift into the sky, driving snow through the open window of Anna's office and stinging her eyes.

The four armored vehicles formed into a column and drove towards Anna as the whirling roar receded. The little tanks rumbled past her window, rounding the corner of the building towards the parking lot, where her car offered her a chance at escape. As they crunched and squealed past the window, Anna saw her chance. Heart pounding in her ears despite earlier efforts to calm it, she crawled out of the window, clutching the white curtain over her head and around her shoulders like a shawl.

Once outside, Anna began to jog along behind the rearmost vehicle, the smell of exhaust reminding her of heavy mining trucks that came and went on Kirkenes' streets, while the purr of the engine made her think, oddly, of snowmobiling trips with her father and Kristen into the new Pasvik Nature Reserve south of Kirkenes. She was amazed by how normal it felt to trot along behind the Russian vehicle. Looking up, she saw that the soldier in the turret had dropped down so only his head was showing. The little column slowed to a walking pace as they rumbled onto the icy concrete of the parking lot. Looking beyond the vehicles, Anna could see her green Volvo in the mostly empty lot. If she could just get to it, then—*Then I'll think about what to do next*, she decided. *One step at a time.* Maybe she'd be able to hide in her car until the Soviet soldiers left. It was a hopeful thought, so she clutched at it. *One step at a time, get to the car.*

The little tanks were now heading towards the E6 highway, connecting the airport via two bridges to the town. Anna saw with rising hope that they would pass within feet of her car. Another flight of helicopters pounded the air overhead. With the distraction she might just slip out from behind the vehicle column and open her car's door—

"*Stoi!*"

The shouted command nearly caused Anna's knees to buckle. She froze in her tracks, looking around desperately. Her wild eyes quickly found the source of the command, and her hope of survival evaporated instantly.

Two soldiers, dressed in white parkas under their broad, drab helmets, were advancing towards her quickly, their weapons pointed directly at her. "*Stoi!*" the nearest one shouted again, "*Ruki vverch!*"

Not knowing what to do, Anna threw her hands into the air to show that she was unarmed. The white curtain fell to the pavement.

The soldiers pulled up short. *Perhaps they hadn't expected the intruder to be a woman,* Anna thought. The muzzles of both rifles lowered slightly. Beyond them, Anna noticed a knot of soldiers, several carrying radios, kneeling under a streetlight in the parking lot. With them were two men in civilian clothes, and all were looking in her direction. A soldier stood and started to walk towards the confrontation. Then one of the civilians rose and followed.

Anna stood still, her body unresponsive to her urge to flee. As the two men approached from behind the two soldiers, Anna realized with horror that the one in civilian clothes was the same man who had tried to kill her earlier. Even from ten meters away she could see murder in his eyes. She was a rat in a trap.

The uniformed man was obviously in charge, though, and he stopped near the two soldiers, looking Anna up and down quickly before issuing a rapid-fire series of curt commands. The soldiers quickly advanced and, grasping Anna by her upper arms, hustled her back towards the passenger terminal. She caught a last glance at the murderer's face, and the look of rage chilled her far more deeply than the wind whipping across the pavement.

The soldiers half pulled, half dragged Anna, whose legs felt like jelly, through the front doors of the passenger terminal. They stopped suddenly when she let out a scream. There, in front of them, were the two ticketing agents. The man and woman were lying in a pool of dark blood. Anna collapsed to the floor, sobbing at the sight of her dead coworkers. In such a small community, everyone knew each other to some degree, but these two had been her friends.

The soldiers pulled her back up, their actions less violent now, guiding her, still crying, towards one of the side rooms. Between her cries, Anna noticed one of the soldiers looking towards the bodies with apparent disgust as they pulled her into a room where she could no longer see the carnage in the ticketing area, shoving her towards a seat. They stepped back, not knowing what to do next with their unexpected prisoner. Anna, in shock from the sight of her friends and with her hopes for escape and survival dashed, collapsed into the chair and covered her face.

—▪—

"We have secured the airport perimeter," Romanov heard the radio crackle in his headset. "The first column of BMDs will move to secure Bridge Number One soon."

"Very good, *Yastreb* One-Two-One," Sokolov, sitting next to Ilya, responded into his radio. "Send the codeword on the command frequency once both objectives are secure. End."

Sokolov set down the hand-mic and looked over at his friend. "Things are going well, Ilya Georgiyevich," he said over the drone of the engines. He went on, "I was doubtful of the decision not to strike the airport itself with artillery before our assault went in, but those *Spetsnaz* boys seem to have done their job for once!"

Ilya nodded as he watched more helicopters go into Kirkenes. Things certainly were going smoothly here. More than an entire company, with armor, was already on the ground at Kirkenes Lufthavn. By confiscating civilian vehicles, these elite paratroopers would turn themselves into a rapid strike force, able to move quickly to their objectives. Moreover, capturing the airport intact allowed reinforcement and supplies to land by fixed-wing transport aircraft before nightfall.

Though the Norwegian border troops could do little to defeat the massed Soviet combat power coming towards them, they could, given some time, make things very difficult for the Russians by destroying the two bridges that crossed frozen, narrow branches of the Bøkfjord. The mission of Sokolov's paratroopers was to race south and east from the town to seize these two key pieces of infrastructure from the rear. This operation would allow the tanks and personnel carriers of the 69th Motor Rifle Division and the rest of the Archangel Corps to advance rapidly into Northern Norway. Ilya had to admit it was an elegant plan, and thus far, elegantly executed. He would have to reassess whether any existing infrastructure in his own objectives would be this useful, worth seizing early, given how little resistance he was told to expect.

The decisive battle for Norway would not be fought here in the north, however. The Norwegian strategy for defeating a Soviet invasion rested on defending successive chokepoints to the west and south, such as Kirkenes and the area around Lakselv. The most formidable bottleneck was the imposing Lyngen position southeast of Tromsø, where the Lyngenfjord and the Swedish frontier narrowed the width of Norway to a mere thirty kilometers of mountainous terrain. Romanov knew that other measures would be taken to nullify this position, but for now the Red Army's chances of penetrating down to central Norway depended on how quickly they could defeat the Norwegian forces *east* of Lyngen. If NATO was given time to reinforce and fortify the Lyngen Line, then it would be a stalemate. Romanov did not want to consider what the consequences of that would be for his country.

"It is time for us to move on to the main objective, Ilya Georgeivich," Sokolov said. Then, speaking into the aircraft's intercom he said, "Pilot, take us west to Banak. My pathfinders will be hitting the ground there soon."

 **CHAPTER 74**

US Coast Guard Sandy Hook Station, Ft. Hancock, New Jersey

C OMMANDER JIM INGALLS presided over the organized chaos in the Coast Guard watch center. Around him, officers spoke urgently into radios or telephones, others updated the status of sinking ships and underway rescue operations on dry erase boards around the room. More men and women moved magnets around the wall map to show the locations of the various wrecks as well as the rescue assets that were responding to the crisis. At the center of it all, Ingalls struggled to maintain awareness of where all the pieces were moving. His eyes focused in on the magnet representing *Adak* escorting the trawler-turned-minelayer *Trogg* back to port. That crisis was resolved at least, except for the mines blocking the harbor entrance. Beyond the Verrazano Narrow, things were much more complicated.

In total, at least eleven ships were sinking or had already sunk outside the harbor. Included in this number was the massive liner *Queen Elizabeth 2*, as well as the Coast Guard cutters *Dallas* and *Tahoma*, and the Soviet intelligence trawler *Kursagraf.* C-130 Hercules rescue aircraft from 102 Rescue Squadron at Gabreski had conducted flyovers of each of the wreck sites to evaluate the situation. One had flown over the dual wrecks of the *Dallas* and *Kursagraf,* where American Coast Guards and Russian crewmen were in the water together, sharing life rafts. A second C-130 had overflown the last reported location of the *Tahoma*, which had been obliterated by the Soviet missile. That pilot reported about thirty people in the water, and his crew dropped supplies and rafts to the survivors and radioed their position back to Sandy Hook.

Word of the *Tahoma* survivors had been welcome news in the watch center, but yet another rescue mission was impossible amid the overwhelming disaster confronting the Coast Guard. Indeed, the loss of the two cutters had gutted their ability to respond at all. To make up for the lost capacity, Ingalls had officers on the phone to local police departments, airports, hospitals, begging for whatever boats or helicopters they could provide to assist with the rescues. Most had responded enthusiastically, though much of the NYPD and FDNY fleets were engaged in rescuing people at the bombed bridges in Manhattan. In total, the task at hand was a daunting one. *We have thousands of people in the water over at the* Queen Elizabeth 2 *wreck alone,* Ingalls knew. *How on earth are we going to get to all of them before they die of exposure?* He knew for a fact they would *not* get to all of them, and he shuddered.

Through the buzzing activity, Ingalls saw four men in tan of US Navy duty uniforms enter the watch center. Three were carrying messenger type boxes filled with what looked like radios and, *Are those laptop computers?* Ingalls had only ever seen one or two of the new compact machines. The fourth Navy man, who wore the silver "railroad tracks" rank insignia of a lieutenant on his collar, spotted the watch commander through the commotion and made his way directly to him.

"Sir," the man announced, "I'm Lieutenant Shin from Naval Weapons Station Earle just up the road. I've been sent over to be your naval liaison officer until something more permanent can be worked out."

Ingalls nodded and beckoned the younger officer into his make-shift office. It was actually the station chief's office, but the man still hadn't arrived. The hive-like commotion of the watch center was somewhat less intense in the small, somewhat dank room.

Leaving the door open in case more news broke, Ingalls turned to the newcomer, "So what can you tell me? I know you all have that destroyer, the *Mahan*, out there off Jersey. That ship would be a big help to our rescue effort, especially if she's got a helo. I'm short two cutters that just got blown away and I've got probably two thousand people in the water who are going to die if we don't get to them fast enough, so please explain to me what you can do to help."

Shin nodded and said, "Sir, I understand your concern, and just so you know my real job is ammunition accounting, so bear with me. I don't know anything about that destroyer, the *Mahan*, you said, sir? But once I get the commo gear I brought set up I'm sure I can get you in touch with her captain."

"Ok," Ingalls nodded, "as quick as you can, Lieutenant. People are dying out there."

Shin went on, brightening somewhat, "Yes sir! I *can* tell you that we've got some assets en route to assist, sir. The ready ships down at Norfolk, a destroyer and a frigate," he took a notebook from his pocket and flipped it open, "Ah… the USS *Hayler* and USS *Sides*. They should be on their way. The news when I left Earle was that they would sortie within minutes and have helos inbound to start ASW ops."

Anti-submarine warfare. Ingalls let out a long steadying breath. *Warfare.*

Still reading his notebook, Shin scanned the next few pages while Ingalls watched impatiently, and then asked, "Along those lines sir, do you all have any idea where those Russian subs could be? To assist in the ASW effort, I mean."

"ASW?" Ingalls almost exploded in frustration. "What I need is rescue assets. How can the Navy help me with *that*, Lieutenant?"

The younger man nodded again, his enthusiasm dampened somewhat, then said, "Uh, yes sir, I was getting to that. At Earle I got word that NAS Norfolk is sending us four Sea King helicopters from the 'Fleet Angels.' Apparently, those guys are real pros at the rescue business. They should be taking off any minute. They'll refuel at McGuire and then," Shin's finger continued to run along his scrawled notebook, "then the flight lead would like to land here to discuss the situation with you while the other three head straight out to the wrecks."

Finally. That's what I wanted to hear, Ingalls thought. The "Fleet Angels" were experts in SAR—search and rescue—operations and had earned an excellent reputation responding to hurricanes along the US east coast in the past few years. The watch commander was glad to have them.

"As soon as I set my commo equipment up," Shin was saying as he shut his notebook, "I can get you talking to the ships and to the helos, sir. Should just take a few minutes."

"All right," Ingalls responded quickly, "get to it. We don't have the luxury of wasting time right now."

Both men stepped back out into the bustle of the watch center. Two of Ingalls' officers were waiting to talk to him as Shin scurried past. Ingalls turned to his surface ops officer first, saying, "What have you got for me, Bob?"

"Update from *Adak*," he answered. "They just delivered *Trogg* to the Army terminal. Lieutenant Jackson called to say that there was a bum rush of FBI agents and NYPD officers at the pier. They barely waited for it to dock before they were swarming all over that trawler."

"Okay," Ingalls said, "Call *Adak* and get them out assisting with rescues as fast as possible."

The officer looked uncomfortable. "Sir," he said, "we've still got those mines at the harbor mouth."

Ingalls swore to himself silently. *Problems inside problems. How are we supposed to get anything done?*

"Uh, sir?" Lieutenant Shin said excitedly, Ingalls noticed that the infernal notebook was out again, "I'm sorry, but I forgot to tell you. We can help with that! The Navy's planning to chop a detachment of MH-53 helicopters, mine-clearers from Norfolk to you. They could be here tomorrow, probably, maybe the next day."

Tomorrow? thought Ingalls, really realizing for the first time that one of the busiest ports in the world was going to be closed for business for a least two days, and probably longer.

"I'll get you comms with them as soon as the Navy gets me their freqs, sir," Shin said before hustling over to where his sailors were setting up their equipment.

Surface Ops went on, "The *QE 2* is our biggest problem right now. The Montauk Fire Department—I didn't know they had one, but whatever—called to let us know that they have a boat they can send out to the wreck. Also, they're closing off the beach and the highway there in eastern Long Island for use as a rescue center. We can start bringing the survivors to the beach and then ambulances will carry them to the hospitals."

Ingalls nodded, then asked, "Okay, what else?"

Surface ops continued, "We got a call from NYPD a few minutes ago, warning us to beef up our security around here. You saw the TV reports of the bomb attacks in the city. Apparently there's been at least twenty different incidents up there. The governors of both New York and New Jersey are going to declare a state of emergency, and they've already called up the National Guard. I got a call from the New Jersey Guard armory down in Freehold. They said they're sending some people our way to help with that."

That was something Ingalls hadn't even considered, that his own watch station might be the target of an attack. It seemed incredible, but it was certainly better to be safe than sorry. In any case, he was glad someone had brought it to his attention.

Ingalls nodded and said, "Thanks," then turned to the next man, his air operations officer, who looked ashen-faced. "What is it, Air?"

The officer handed over a printout, saying, "This just came in from the FAA."

Ingalls scanned the message, then stopped and went back to the beginning, reading more carefully. *Is this for real?* he wondered.

The message was a NOTAM, a "notice to airmen," transmitted from the Federal Aviation Administration in Washington. It read:

FDC 1/6565 FDC SPECIAL NOTICE - EFFECTIVE IMMEDIATELY UNTIL FURTHER NOTICE. FLIGHT OPERATIONS IN THE NATIONAL AIRSPACE SYSTEM BY UNITED STATES CIVIL AIRCRAFT AND FOREIGN CIVIL AND MILITARY AIRCRAFT ARE PROHIBITED, EXCEPT IN ACCORDANCE WITH ADVZY 043 OR AS AMENDED OR REVISED.

DUE TO EXTRAORDINARY CIRCUMSTANCES AND FOR REASONS OF SAFETY: ATTENTION ALL AIRCRAFT OPERATORS, BY ORDER OF THE FEDERAL AVIATION COMMAND CENTER, ALL AIRPORTS/AERODROMES ARE NOT AUTHORIZED FOR LANDING AND TAKEOFF. ALL TRAFFIC INCLUDING AIRBORNE AIRCRAFT ARE REQUIRED TO LAND IMMEDIATELY. ONCE ALL LOCAL OR SCHEDULED TRAFFIC

HAD LANDED ALL FURTHER ATTEMPTS TO LAND SHOULD BE REPORTED IMMEDIATELY TO THE FAA.
ALL IFR AND VFR GENERAL AVIATION FLIGHTS ARE PROHIBITED WITHIN THE NATIONAL AIRSPACE SYSTEM UNTIL FURTHER NOTICE.

Ingalls stopped to read the message a third time. This had never happened before. The US Government was closing American airspace to *all* non-military aircraft, ordering those aircraft already airborne to land at the nearest possible runway. His mind immediately went to the airspace over the wrecks, and the hundreds of flights currently outbound and inbound for just the three major New York City airports to the north, hundreds, maybe thousands more all over the US or inbound over Canada or one of the two oceans. The airspace would be a mess to deconflict. *But*, Ingalls thought, *If we can get our hands on some civilian helicopters to assist in the rescue…I wonder what authority I have to start federalizing helicopters and boats?* The Coast Guard officer honestly didn't know, had never considered that question before.

"Any idea what this is about?" Ingalls managed to ask the air officer.

The other man nodded, "That AWACS we've been talking to south of Long Island called a few minutes ago to say that they'd been picking up weird radar emissions from some of the private planes that are up over the water. The implication I think is that those may have been snoopers for the missile attack. I'm guessing NORAD wants to clear the air space in case they need to start shooting down intruders."

"Or more missiles…" Ingalls agreed. This was big. Thousands, no, tens of thousands of air passengers were going to be stranded all over the US. Air travel, and with it air commerce, were going to come to a screeching halt in the next few hours. *So*, the Coast Guard realized the word coming back to him again, *warfare. Right here at home.* His eyes swept his control room, *Every American is about to wake up to a world at war and the fallout effects of that.*

 **CHAPTER 75**

1035 EST, Sunday 13 February 1994
1435 Zulu
Brooklyn, New York, USA

T HE POLICE CRUISER slowed to a stop on the narrow street in front of Jack Young's row house. At most times, at least a few people would have been outside in this diverse neighborhood; kids playing street ball or sitting on the steps leading up to their front doors listening to boomboxes; women sharing gossip; or men talking politics in nasally Brooklyn accents. No one was in sight today. The only sign of life on the street was the muffled sound of a newsman on the radio coming through an open window across the street. Jack opened the passenger door of the cruiser and stepped out onto the pavement.

He turned and placed his hand on top of the cruiser, bending down to say to the police officer inside, "Thanks for the ride officer. I realize there are about a thousand places you'd rather be today than chauffeuring a reporter back home."

The officer only nodded. The police car's radio had been alive with reports from all over the city with details of bombs and ambushes the entire drive from the wreckage on the Brooklyn Bridge. Jack had seen the police officer tense with each new call of an "officer down" or, even worse, "multiple officers down." Most of the attacks seemed to be concentrated in Manhattan. Brooklyn was eerily quiet, as if the citizens of the city were burrowing in for a siege.

Jack waited an uncomfortable moment for the officer to say something in response. The police officer, clearly eager to get on with his job, remained silent, pensive, looking at his steering wheel. Finally, he said, "Well, keep your head down."

Taking the hint, Jack half turned towards the steps of his row house, but a screeching warble from the car radio stopped him in his tracks. For a moment Jack didn't realize that the same screeching was coming from the muffled radio from across the street. He turned back, eyes locking with the officer as they both listened. The sound was so familiar, and yet so terrifying under the circumstances, that for a moment Jack didn't want to admit to himself what it was.

C'mon, c'mon, say it's just a drill, Jack silently urged the radio as the distinctive warble of the Emergency Broadcast System screeched on and on. *Don't let this be the end of the world. Don't let this be the warning that tells us the nukes are fifteen minutes out.*

No voice broke in to give any such assurance, and after about a minute the police officer reached over and switched off the radio, silencing the ambiguous warning from his car but not the radio across the street.

"If ya don't mind, buddy, I've got places to go," the officer said.

Jack nodded, mumbled another "Thanks," and shut the door. The cruiser tore off down the street and Jack climbed the chipped steps to his home, which suddenly felt like a very lonely place. The radio from across the street continued to screech its warning, making Jack feel intensely vulnerable.

Once inside, Jack went to his narrow kitchen and sat down. He fought the urge to turn on the small TV in the corner, instead he sat, just processing what had happened over the past few hours. The carnage at the bridge. The ride home with the police officer's radio drumming out news of attacks all over the city. The start of World War III, and now the screeching broadcast that the government used to warn its citizens of tornados, or nuclear war. After several minutes of silence, the ringing of his phone nearly startled him out of his skin.

Jack recovered and grabbed the receiver. "Hello?"

"Jack? Where are you?" The question was asked in the normal, accusing tone used by Bill, his editor.

Uh, where do you think I am? Jack wanted to answer the self-evident question. Instead he said, "At home, Bill. What's up?"

"What's up? I've been trying to get ahold of you for an hour now. The phone lines are crammed and I need you to answer when World War III is breaking out. This is a big news day!" Bill's voice was almost whiny.

"I was at the bridge, the Brooklyn, when the bomb went off there. Just got home. I've got some notes and—"

Bill cut him off. "I've got four reporters at the Bridge right now, on the Manhattan side. We're covered there. Right now, though, you're the only reporter I can get hold of who's on the Brooklyn side of the East River, and it doesn't look like anyone else is going to be getting across any time soon."

Jack absorbed the information. *No bridges, no trains. The city's at a standstill.*

"Jack," Bill cut into his thoughts, "I've got a source telling us that there's been some sort of shipping disaster off the coast, says the Coast Guard is setting up rescue operations out at Montauk for some big disaster. I need you to get out there and see what it is. I smell a big story."

Montauk? Jack thought. *That's all the way at the eastern end of Long Island. That's more than*, he did some quick mental math, *more than ninety miles from here.*

"Bill," he answered lamely, "I was driving over the Brooklyn Bridge when the bomb went off. My car's still there."

"Well, call a cab then," Bill said, as if the Jack was a somewhat slow child for not thinking of this himself.

"That's going to be some cab fare," Jack commented.

"Trust me," Bill said, his tone softening, "if my gut's right, it'll be worth it."

1045 EST, Sunday 13 February 1994
144 Zulu
Dwyer Hill, Ontario, Canada

"Now they're saying someone blew up the Welland Canal. I'm telling you, Bear, the county's under attack and we're headed to Ottawa to guard the PM, and I'll tell you what's more," Corporal Tenny was saying as Sergeant Strong strode into their team's ready room, "I'm going to make it with one of those pretty staffers that are always working around those political types, eh? With us at war all of a sudden and the Reds around every corner, there's going to be plenty of ladies up there ready to throw themselves into the arms of a burly man in uniform." He ended the sentence with a thumb pointed at his chest.

Aclark "Bear" Brown smirked, but across the room Strong saw that Master Corporal Roy was paying no mind to the banter, instead re-checking the team's gear, weapons stored in hard cases, and all other equipment in drab duffels.

"Mouse," Strong said, addressing his hulking medic, "what say you? Where's the Queen going to send us? West to the Rockies to hunt *Spetz*? North to Ottawa to defend the PM? Or East to Halifax, like we always planned?" Ever since they'd been recalled early this morning, the rumors about where their team would in fact deploy had been wild and varied, especially with word coming in about attacks at key choke points around the country and down south in the US.

Looking up, Roy said, "Doesn't really matter. We're ready for anything. But by your tone I suspect you know."

Strong nodded as Tenny and Brown looked up at him, expectantly.

"It's Halifax. North Atlantic duty for us."

CHAPTER 76

1050 EST, Sunday 13 February 1994
1450 Zulu
Naval Air Station Norfolk, Virginia, USA

LIEUTENANT ABBY SAVAGE went through her pre-flight checklist rapidly while Buck went through the procedures of warming up the helicopter's engines. The aircraft's five-blade rotor was beginning to rotate as Savage, who looked and felt like the perfect size for the cramped cockpit, finished her checks and said, "Alright, let's stop wasting time. We get confirmation that our flight plan was approved?"

Looking over, Buck nodded with a, "Roger. Good to go," in his slow Texas twang.

"Angel Flight, this is Angel Lead," Abby called over the radio to the other three Sea King crews, "taking off now. Follow me out." As the pitch of the Sea King's engines increased to a roar, Abby said to Buck, "Okay, let's get going. There's people in the water who need our help."

Savage's helicopter dipped its nose as it rose, then pivoted over the landing pad and gained speed, flying northeast, toward New York. Behind, the three other birds lifted off one at a time under the leaden gray skies blanketing Chesapeake Bay. As the flight followed the ribbon of the Chesapeake Bay

Bridge, Abby saw two white vees that ended at a pair of gray Navy ships just transiting the point where the bridge dipped down into the sub-channel tunnels.

"Those are the ready ships from Norfolk," Savage heard Buck say. "*Hayler* and *Sides*. They're headed north too."

None of them had planned to fly today. Abby and her husband, a Marine captain who commanded a rifle company in 6th Marines at Camp Lejeune, had been sleeping in late, finally enjoying a precious weekend together while the Navy had them posted to different duty stations. Then the phone rang. Abby took the call on her apartment's landline while her husband, Will, received the alert on his pager a few minutes later: DEFCON One, all hands recalled to duty immediately. They had dressed and parted with a hurried kiss, neither of them knowing what crisis had ruined their weekend.

Abby found out soon enough. The mission briefing she and her fellow pilots received had been "abbreviated," to say the least. Rushed might have been a better description, but under the circumstances the helicopter pilots understood. The squadron commander hadn't known much, other than that World War Three had apparently kicked off in Europe and there were burning and sinking ships all up and down both US coasts. There was a question about whether Abby's flight would go north to assist with the wrecks outside New York, or south, where several ships were sinking outside Savannah and Charleston. The news of the stricken cruise ship off Long Island had settled that detail quickly.

Interestingly, there had as yet been no attacks around the mouth of the Chesapeake Bay, either towards the huge US naval base at Norfolk, nor further up the bay near the Capital. That, at least, was good news, Abby thought, though it did mean she and the rest of her squadron was out of position to respond quickly to any of the disasters. Haste was essential if they were going to do any good. The Navy pilot pushed her bird to its limits as they flew through skies busy with civilian aircraft heading to any airport with space, and with military aircraft headed out to clean up the first hours of war.

 **CHAPTER 77**

1055 EST, Sunday 13 February 1994
1455 Zulu
Piper Cherokee 213R, over the Jersey Shore
near Asbury Park, New Jersey

YURI WAS FRETTING, the cramped and drafty cabin making him feel more and more claustrophobic. He didn't want to die in this aluminum and plexiglass tube. The magnitude of what he'd done was starting to dawn on him. A few minutes after they transmitted his contact report, a bright flash on the gray water caught his attention. Looking down, he saw a dark column of oily smoke rising from a container ship heading north towards New York.

Other smoke columns began to mar the gloomy horizon around them. Instantly he realized he'd played a critical role in something far more serious than a non-standard intelligence-gathering exercise. His blood ran cold. *How can the Americans fail to find us and shoot us down?* The question assaulted his mind, pushing out thoughts of anything else. Yuri both envied and despised the *Spetsnaz* pilot up front who continued to fly the aircraft, seemingly oblivious to the danger they were in.

A few minutes ago, their commercial radio crackled to life. Yuri's English skills were poor, but the pilot translated that the American authorities were ordering all aircraft to land, and that he thought it best they put down as well. Silently Yuri wondered why they hadn't landed an hour ago. What happened next justified his trepidation.

They were descending and had just gone feet dry over the Jersey Shore, en route back to the abandoned airfield. Yuri was distracting himself with powering off the radar and erasing the radio's special digital communication codes when their Piper Cherokee buffeted violently, as if struck by a powerful downdraft. He looked up through the plane's front windscreen just in time to see the glowing tailpipe of an F-16 fighter roar directly overhead, so close that he felt he could have reached out the window and run his fingers along the jet's underbelly.

The *Spetsnaz* pilot pulled at the stick to regain control of the Piper, but Yuri's attention was squarely on the American fighter as it circled around to get back on the smaller plane's tail. *They know who we are!* Yuri panicked. *They know what we've done!* His insides clenched. This was not the excitement he'd been expecting when he volunteered for this assignment. All he'd wanted was to get away from the monotony of his naval bomber regiment in dull, frozen Murmansk, not end up dead on some American beach.

"Get us down! Get us down! They are going to shoot us!" he yelled forward to the pilot.

"Calm down," the *Spetsnaz* man said, his voice taught. "We're almost there."

Yuri watched the fighter until the Piper's fuselage blocked his view, but he imagined the lethal jet still circling, leveling out behind their tail. At that moment he was sure his life had reached its end. Closing his eyes, he waiting for the missile or the cannon shells to rip him and this flimsy airplane apart.

A cry almost escaped from Yuri's throat as his seat bumped violently. He opened his eyes, and nearly laughed with relief as they decelerated down the damp, grassy runway. Reaching the end of the landing field, the pilot turned the plane like a race car, veering off towards the old abandoned hangar. Yuri heard the American fighter jet thunder impotently overhead. *I might actually live through this*, he thought.

— • —

"Darkstar, this is Jackpot Two-Four, I lost them," the F-16's pilot reported, clearly frustrated. "He landed on a grass strip a few miles inland." Master

Sergeant Troy Funk noted that Jackpot Two-Four was circling over Asbury Park at a thousand feet altitude. The pilot went on, "Two guys jumped out of the Piper at a run. There's a second plane on the ground, also a barn and a couple cars. Can you get a call into the Jersey State Police or something? These guys are getting away."

"We'll see what we can do, Two-Four," answered Funk, "but for now come around to bearing zero-five-zero, angels five. We've got another one of those suspicious contacts, not responding to our calls. Looks like he's heading your way, over."

Jackpot Two-Four flew back out over the water and banked to get onto the suspicious aircraft's tail. At the same time, the fighter's pilot keyed his radio on the commercial emergency frequency and called, "Unidentified Beechcraft, this is the Air National Guard fighter that just did a close pass on you. You are instructed to alter course twenty degrees to the left and land at Lakewood County Airport. Respond, over."

Silence. The Beechcraft maintained its slow course towards the improvised airstrip where the other two suspicious contacts had landed.

Two-Four's pilot called, "Darkstar, this guy's not responding. What are your instructions, over?"

Funk replied: "Two-Four, we have just received authority to prosecute. You are authorized and instructed to shoot down that contact."

"Roger that, Darkstar," acknowledged the pilot. "Engaging with guns."

Yuri tossed his duffle bag into the back of their rented Ford Bronco when a tearing sound like some angry god ripping his table cloth caused the Russian's head to jerk upward. The sight that accompanied the sound horrified him.

He saw brilliant white puffs appeared like magic from wingtip to wingtip of the Beechcraft, the third radar snooper of their team. Yuri stared, transfixed as the small airplane slowly flipped onto its back and plowed nose-first into a copse of trees at the edge of the clearing. Pieces of metal flew off and cartwheeled in several directions. Then a growing, throaty roar forced his eyes upward once again just in time to see the dagger-like shape of the American fighter jet streak overhead, waggling its wings in victory.

"Let's go Yuri!" his *Spetsnaz* crewmate was saying, giving his shoulder a shove to encourage him into the Bronco. "We need to clear the area, NOW!"

Yuri needed no further encouragement. As the Bronco's engine revved to life, he prayed to a God he hadn't believed in a few hours ago, begging to be spared the fate that had befallen the other crew.

 **CHAPTER 78**

1100 EST, Sunday 13 February 1994
1500 Zulu
US Coast Guard Sandy Hook Station, Ft. Hancock, New Jersey

A T THE SANDY Hook Watch Center, Commander Ingalls and his staff were more or less oblivious to the drama going on in the skies above. Their interest remained fixed on the sea, and those in peril on it. *I need more assets if I'm going to rescue the people out there,* Ingalls thought for the hundredth time that hour. His eyes narrowed at the marker indicating the Navy destroyer smack in the middle of the disaster that, so far, was doing nothing to help. The Coast Guard officer intended to change that.

"Your radios up yet, Lieutenant Shin?" Ingalls asked his Navy liaison. The younger man and his three sailors had been laboring over the past few minutes to set up a bank of radios and computers, wiring them to antennae that one of the sailors had erected outside the watch center's windows.

"Just loading the frequency now sir," Shin answered and after a few moments. "Okay, ready for a radio check."

The Navy officer took a hand-mic from one of his sailors and, depressing the talk button, said, "Destroyer *Mahan*, destroyer *Mahan*, this is," he looked up questioningly at Ingalls. The Coast Guard officer mouthed "Sandy Hook," and Shin, nodding, went on, "this is Coast Guard Station Sandy Hook. Radio check, over."

Both men waited through several seconds of silence, then the radio crackled, "Sandy Hook, this is *Mahan*. We read you five by five, over."

Shin nodded, then handed the mic to Ingalls and asked, "You wanted to talk to them, sir?"

Ingalls grabbed the hand-mic and called, "*Mahan*, Sandy Hook. We've got a lot of people in the water and we were hoping you can assist at some of the wreck sites. There's a sinking container ship about eight miles to your northeast. Think you could help them out, over?"

Ingalls waited for a response, which took longer in coming than he thought it would. Finally, the speaker crackled, a different voice: "Sandy Hook, this is *Mahan* Actual. Negative on your request. I apologize, but the area here is not yet safe. We just barely dodged a few missiles ourselves, and we need to get the shooters before we can worry about rescue operations. We're currently prosecuting a contact, one of the subs that launched those missiles. Once we've killed him, we'll see what we can do."

Ingalls was both surprised and frustrated. At once he knew that the captain of the *Mahan* was doing the right thing, hunting the enemy, but at the same time he was leaving people, civilians, in the water.

"I've got a P-3 patrol bird that just arrived on station to support us," *Mahan*'s captain went on apologetically, referring to the four-engine sub-hunting aircraft that were the mainstay of the US Navy's aerial ASW force. "That should speed things up considerably. Over."

Commander Ingalls nodded, though it pained his conscience as a professional rescue-man for a big capable ship like the *Mahan* to be so close to sailors in need and not help. He pushed that aside. *So this is what war is like*, he thought, frustration turning into angry determination.

Pressing the transmit button again he said, "Understood, *Mahan*. Good hunting. Get those bastards for us!"

 **CHAPTER 79**

1105 CST, Sunday 13 February 1994
1505 Zulu
B Company 1-114 Infantry National Guard Armory,
Freehold Township, New Jersey, USA

T HE MOOD IN the motor pool was grim as the guardsmen tossed equipment into the boxy M113 armored personnel carriers. Sergeant First Class Bert Martinez watched as his charges made the transition from citizen to soldier. The men loading the vehicles were dressed in the mottled green, brown, and black battle dress uniforms of the US Army, but in their civilian lives they were plumbers, teachers, construction workers, grocers, and any number of other everyday professions. Martinez was a local police officer, having retired from the regular army two years ago. Today, though, they were soldiers.

New Jersey's governor, in office less than a month, had called up her state's entire contingent of National Guard units immediately after receiving word of the attacks in New York City and off the coast. Martinez understood the angry looks he saw on the faces of the men of his platoon. Many of them had friends, even family, in the city, and all had seen the dramatic news footage of the carnage on the bridges and tunnels in Manhattan. More troubling to Martinez, an infantryman for twenty years, were the ambushes outside several police precincts. The NYPD wasn't releasing information about how many officers they'd lost, but the Guardsman knew that a few of the resulting firefights had been ugly.

Seeing something he didn't like, Martinez called a guardsman atop one of the armored personnel carriers. "Hey Bill, stow that fifty inside the track. We'll mount the M60s instead. Wherever we're going, I don't see us rock'n the Ma Deuce."

The other man nodded and lowered the big .50 caliber M2 machinegun back down into the belly of the M113, while another soldier heaved the smaller M60 machinegun onto the vehicle's roof where it could be mounted on the track's pintle mount. Other soldiers were carrying green ammunition cans out of the armory and stowing them in the vehicles. *That* was how Martinez knew that this was serious. B Company's CO was notoriously skittish about issuing ammunition to his weekend warriors. *Drawing live ammunition and getting to roll out of the motor pool into suburban New Jersey*, Martinez mused. *The world has really gone mad in the past few hours!* Which made the NCO wonder where they'd be taking that ammunition.

The answer arrived with an overly loud, "Hey Sarge!" and a slap on the back as Martinez's lieutenant arrived from the company CP. The old soldier struggled not to cringe. "Sarge" was not an acceptable way to refer to a sergeant in the US Army, but no matter how many times Martinez quietly corrected Second Lieutenant Kirby, the young extrovert never seemed to get it. Despite that, Martinez couldn't bring himself to dislike the officer. Kirby was green but eager, having just completed the Infantry Officer Basic Course at Ft. Benning a couple months ago. Martinez, a Gulf War veteran who'd seen his share of both good and bad lieutenants over the years, could always work with someone who showed motivation, and Kirby showed plenty of that.

"Any news, sir?" Martinez asked as the younger man looked towards the men loading their platoon's four M113s.

"Yep!" Kirby said, too enthusiastically. "The whole company is getting sent to important spots around the local area. Third Platoon is staying here as the reserve, First Platoon is heading over to the ammo supply point at Ft. Dix, and we're going to the Coast Guard Station at Sandy Hook."

"Sandy Hook?" Martinez wondered. "That's almost thirty miles away."

"Yeah," Kirby responded, "the CO wants us to get on the road quick. Do we have everyone?"

"Watts, Silva, and Handler still haven't showed up," Martinez reported, "but at this point, sir, I recommend we roll without them. They can catch up later."

"Sounds good Sarge!" Kirby said. "Let's get this show on the road."

"Roger, sir," Martinez said, again working not to cringe. Then he yelled, "Second Platoon! Pack it up! Convoy brief in five minutes!"

Taking a column of tracked APCs thirty miles along suburban New Jersey roads was going to be interesting, to say the least. He would have said exciting, but the news footage from New York City had everyone worrying about their loved ones. No one was safe anywhere anymore.

— • —

Eighteen miles to the north, the van carrying Volkhov and his assault team was creeping across the Edison Bridge from Perth Amboy to South Amboy amid unusually heavy traffic. Sitting in the front passenger seat, the *Spetsnaz* officer's face remained coldly impassive. Behind this mask, however, his emotions were a violent mix of rage and elation. The elation stemmed from the news bulletins he was hearing over their van's radio. It was clear from the panicky American newsmen that the other teams around the city had achieved almost complete success. True, the American police had somehow thwarted the attack on the George Washington Bridge, but otherwise it appeared that nearly every attack had achieved its aim. Indeed, from what the radio newsman was saying about the Manhattan Bridge, *that* attack had far exceeded expectations. *All successful, except my own, that is*, he raged in frustration.

Volkhov had given himself and his team what he had judged to be the most difficult mission, *And I botched it*. Here they were, stuck in the panicked traffic streaming away from the embattled city, while their target, the rescue command center at Sandy Hook, continued its operations unmolested.

They were supposed to hit their target at the same time as the other attacks started on Manhattan. The stolen battery had laid waste to that idea, and they'd been lucky to get off Manhattan Island before the other teams' attacks began to close off access to the City. Now they were over three hours late and still far from the objective.

The erstwhile Mr. Taylor clenched his fist against his knee and allowed the frustration to burn in his mind for a moment. Then he closed his eyes, took a breath, and calmed himself. They might be late, he thought, but that might work to their advantage if the Americans' focus was distracted from security. He promised himself that when he and his team went into the attack, the Americans would not know what hit them. He intended to leave that command post a smoking ruin.

 **CHAPTER 80**

1615 CET, Sunday 13 February 1994
1515 Zulu
Ministry of Defense Building, Akershus Fortress, Oslo, Norway

"MISS HAGEN, THIS way, if you please," said Nils Dokken, one of the defense minister's senior civilian aides. He beckoned Kristen into the map room deep within the nineteenth-century masonry structure. This section of Akershus Fortress was the nexus for coordinating the defense of Norway. Dokken was a well-built, dark-haired, square-jawed man about Kristen's age. As she followed him into the room, he asked, "What made you take the walk over here from the Foreign Ministry? Ah, don't tell me. Now that the war has started there's not much left for you diplomats to do, yes?"

Kristen's blue eyes flashed. She let the tone of her response communicate her displeasure at the brash attempt at humor. "There's plenty for us *all* to do, Mr. Dokken. The foreign minister will have landed in Brussels by now. He'll be asking the North Atlantic Council for the reinforcements we need to safeguard our nation," she said. "The reinforcements that *your* ministry will need to win this war, I imagine."

That the foreign minister had seemed shell-shocked as he departed for the airport, Kristen didn't say. She'd expected to accompany him to Belgium in her role as his chief of staff, but at the last minute the man had asked in his usual soft-spoken, educated way, "Miss Hagen, would you please go to the Defense Ministry and work to keep me apprised of events in the North? I fear with the great struggle developing in Germany that," he'd paused and looked down then, "that our little country may be forgotten when it comes time to apportion reinforcements. Any information you can pass along will help me to argue our case."

Kristen agreed immediately and made the short trek from her normal post in the Foreign Ministry to the Akershus after her chief departed for Oslo Lufthavn at Gardermoen. The subject of the emergency session was obvious; they would be discussing the Alliance's response to the Soviet storm sweeping into three NATO member states on this day: the recently reunited Federal Republic of Germany, the Republic of Turkey, and Kirsten's own beloved Kingdom of Norway.

Kristen spent the entire walk to the thirteenth century Citadel tamping down a growing anxiety for her family in Kirkenes. She wasn't the only one fretting about the war. As she walked she noticed fellow citizens looking up at the sky as if it was about to fall on them. She desperately hoped that what she learned here at the Defense Ministry would assure her that the sky was not, indeed, falling. *Don't let yourself draw any conclusions until someone here gives you some real, hard facts about what's going on*, Kristen reminded herself. Now, after having waited for Dokken for over forty-five minutes, she could see that the state of affairs in this ministry was just as anxious.

Dokken, apparently unfazed by Kristen's riposte, led her to a large wall map hanging on the rough masonry. A nearby computer screen showed a hash of nearly indecipherable red, blue, and black symbols slowly meandering across a white map background. Kristen's eyes shot immediately to the top of the map, to the area around Norway's short frontier with the USSR where her home town also stood, but she could glean nothing useful from the symbols there.

Kristen was less pessimistic than her minister about their country's place in the priorities of the Alliance. On the other hand, she was keenly aware that her country was in desperate need of reinforcements, and that those reinforcements would be painfully slow in coming. Here amongst the harried staff officers in the map room she was convinced that the Soviet attacks in Northern Norway had already upset decades' worth of war plans drawn up in this very building.

She reigned in her fear for her family and annoyance at Dokken and waited for him to enlighten her about what all the symbols on the wall map and the computer screen actually meant. Once again, he made her wait.

"So, what's going on here?" Kristen finally prompted, gesturing towards the map and hoping that fear hadn't crept into her voice. After Dokken's earlier comment, she wanted to put up a completely professional front.

"Bad news, mostly," Dokken said, pointing with a wooden stick, his tone arrogant and oddly upbeat. "The Soviets started the war here with an aerial blitz across Northern Norway. They shot down the AWACS control plane that was supporting our pilots and destroyed nearly all of our ground-based radars in the first few minutes. Our pilots are claiming that they inflicted heavy losses against the first waves of Soviet jets, but who knows? You know how those fighter pilots can be." Dokken gave Kristen a significant look, as if to emphasize that *he* certainly knew what fighter pilots were like, and that he expected her to share his amused disdain.

She ignored the look and asked, "What about on the ground?"

Turning back towards the map, Dokken pointed to the towns that dotted Norway's northern coast. "Soviet marines and heliborne assault troops have seized several important coastal towns between Banak and the frontier. The Home Guard fought hard in a few places, but it was pretty hopeless. We really can't expect to stop the Reds anywhere east of Banak. We managed to get evacuation flights out of most of the *lufthavns* before the Russians got them, though."

"And Kirkenes?" Kristen asked, her hopes soaring.

Dokken shook his head. "Kirkenes Lufthavn went quiet exactly at noon. We've heard nothing from them, and no flights have come out of there. There never really was a chance for that place anyway, being so close to the border. The town isn't even a speed bump for the Russians."

Kristen was unable to stop a hand from flying up to her mouth as she thought of her sister, who worked at the *lufthavn* most Sundays. She fought back tears, but felt her vision blur anyway.

Either not noticing Kristen's discomfiture or not caring, Dokken went on, "Things aren't much better at sea. Our missile boats up there have traded some deadly shots with the Soviets' coastal fleet, but not enough to prevent their marines from getting through to our coast, and we've taken heavy losses ourselves." He tapped a section of the map further south along Norway's jagged coast and went on, "*Bergen* and *Stavenger*, two of our frigates, were hurrying north from Tromsø to support the missile boats, but they apparently ran into a Soviet diesel submarine. *Bergen* was sunk and *Stavenger* is limping back south with a five-meter hole in her bow. She'll be out of the fight for several weeks at least," Dokken concluded, and then paused as if expecting some sort of response from Kristen.

He thinks he's an expert here, Kristen could barely hold back her emotions, her mind's focus was scattered from Kirkenes to the Norwegian losses on all fronts, to her own powerless position and then back to Kirkenes again, and her sister in the *lufthavn*.

When Kristen didn't say anything, Dokken continued, "Ah, I almost forgot one of the worst bits." He pointed towards a spot on the map towards the northern end of the Porsangerfjord and said, "The Coast Guard cutter *Nordkapp* was evacuating civilians from Lakselv. She was caught in a Soviet air attack and crippled. The captain ran her aground to prevent sinking, but for now the crew and a couple of hundred civilians are trapped onboard. I'm not sure how we're going to get to them, either. Our navy is taking losses we can't sustain."

Kristen steeled herself enough to ask, "So we're losing, then?"

Dokken smiled in a way that made Kristen realize that the man was enjoying playing the expert on military affairs. *If you like all this so much, why aren't you in uniform?* The question flashed across Kristen's mind before Dokken answered: "Hardly. The Home Guard is mobilizing smoothly across the country, aided by the Directive. You know what the Directive is, don't you?" He gestured at a framed document hanging on the opposite wall. "It applies to all—"

"Yes, I know about the Directive," Kristen cut him off, getting her senses back. Her father had spoken approvingly of the fabled "poster on the wall" often when conversation turned to the possibility of a Soviet invasion. "Please continue."

Dokken nodded and said, "Some reinforcements are already arriving. The first American F-15s landed at Bardufoss from England," he paused to look at his watch, "a few minutes ago."

Kristen looked over to see that a tight grin had appeared on Dokken's face with that last statement. The Americans had always been the senior partner in the NATO Alliance, she knew, possessing more military resources than any other member state. Since the Gulf War, three years ago, expectations of what American air power could achieve had taken on mythical proportions. Kristen got the impression that Dokken thought the mere appearance of American fighter jets in the far North was going to be enough to turn the tide. His optimism had her questioning whether encouragement was really due. What could a few American fighter jets do against the might of Soviet aviation bearing down on her country?

"We've planned a counterattack in the air that's going to start," Dokken looked at his watch again, "just a few minutes from now." He guided Kristen over to the computer display and explained, "This is the data feed from our AWACS aircraft, just arriving from Orland and controlling the air battle up there. These," he pointed to several groups of blue symbols circling near Bardufoss, "are the jets that are going to sweep eastward in a few minutes to clear the skies over Finnmark. The Swedes and the Finns have closed their airspace to us and the Soviets, so the plan is to use their frontiers to anchor the right flank of the sweep. I'll admit," Dokken raised a hand as if he'd been the one to plan the operation, "this whole thing is being thrown together on the quick. We'll have F-16s from four squadrons involved, backed up by four of the American F-15s. You know what that means, of course."

Kristen did *not* know what that meant, and wasn't too proud to shake her head to indicate as much.

"Ah, of course," Dokken said with a smirk. He explained, "The American F-15Cs carry the new AMRAAM. Those are long-range missiles that have what we call 'fire-and-forget' capability. Most long-range missiles, certainly the ones the Soviets are using, require the firing aircraft to keep its radar pointed towards the target to guide the missile all the way to intercept. The drawback is that the pilot must keep his aircraft pointed a certain way and therefore he cannot evade incoming missiles. The AMRAAMs will allow our side to shoot at the enemy and still evade. So the plan here is for our F-16s to sweep ahead in a line from the Finnish border to the coast while the Americans and some of the AMRAAM-capable F-16s from our 338 "Tiger" Squadron hang back slightly. The AMRAAM shooters will distract the Soviets enough for our nimble F-16s to get close in for dogfighting. We showed in the first engagements that we are better at that sort of combat than they are," Dokken concluded, apparently forgetting his earlier disdain of the fighter pilots' claims. "We're putting more than thirty jets into the air for this sweep."

"This counterattack will stop the Soviets before they can get to—" *where was it that Dokken had mentioned as the first place the enemy could be stopped?* Kristen looked back at the map. *Ah, yes,* "—Banak?"

"Yes," Dokken said, in the tone of a surprised school teacher proud of a particularly dull student. "When we regain control of the air we'll be able to put a stop to these heliborne and seaborne landings the Soviets are using to push into our country. The whole thing hinges on one detail I haven't mentioned yet, of course."

"What's that?" Kristen asked, she was seething, but her anger wasn't her priority, she needed information and so was unable to resist the bait.

Pointing back at the computer display, he said, "The Soviets destroyed most of our ground-based radars in Finnmark and their electronic jamming has been surprisingly effective. That means our AWACS planes are having trouble seeing very far into the battle zone. But! This radar site right here," Dokken tapped a symbol on the screen in central Finnmark that bore the label "Backstop," "survived and has been feeding us valuable data all day. Our fighters have broken up two Soviet attacks on the site since then. If we lose Backstop, we could lose the ability to control our aircraft over the entire far north."

Kristen nodded. *So, this coming counterattack by our air force and the Americans will both stop the Russians from advancing further and protect our ability to see what's going on in the sky over Northern Norway,* she reasoned. That was all she had time to think before visions of her mother, father, and sister came flooding back; smiling in their Christmas photo; chatting on the phone about life, boys; waving goodbye to her from the window of the small Kirkenes airport as she boarded her plane. She quickly asked Dokken where the ladies' room was. He gave her brief directions, and she walked quickly out of the buzzing map room.

Once in the quiet solitude, Kristen leaned on her hands against a sink, her moist eyes looking back at her from the mirror. Were her parents all right?

Was Kirkenes even there anymore? Kristen had no idea what a modern war would actually look like. Would there be prisoners? The person she was most worried about was Anna. *The airport must have been a target for the Soviets.* Kristen shook her head, trying to shake off the fear gripping her, and the sinking despair that followed. She couldn't allow herself to think the worst. *If there's one girl who can make it through all this, it's Anna*, she told herself. *Anna can do it.*

CHAPTER 81

1620 CET, Sunday 13 February 1994
1520 Zulu
Tromsø Lufthavn, Tromsø, Norway

T HE WHEELS OF Jan Olsen's rearmed and refueled F-16 left the ice-swept pavement of Tromsø's civilian airport in a roar of hot jet exhaust. The fighter pilot could see the sun sinking low into the south-west horizon. The short Arctic day would end soon, though the sky would remain light for several hours more. Two more F-16s followed him into the sky. One member of Olsen's new, improvised flight was a squadron-mate from Olsen's own 332 Eagle Squadron, Willi, who had also diverted to Tromsø rather than landing at Bardufoss. The other jet, a two-seater "B" model F-16 from Rygge, had arrived at Tromsø an hour ago piloted by an old friend of Jan's, Sven Hokensen, who was serving his second year as an instructor pilot in the training squadron. Both of the other pilots pulled up until they were flying in an echelon formation off Olsen's wing tip.

Jan banked left to lead his improvised flight east. He should have been leading four ships, but the flight returning from Backstop had been delayed and only one had shown up, damaged, with no word on what had happened to his wingman. *Undoubtedly another name on a growing list of casualties.* Jan shook his head, *Time to focus.*

After desperately parrying the massed blows of the Soviet *VVS* all afternoon, they were finally going on the offensive. The three jets gained altitude as they flew east towards Bardufoss, eager to strike back. Nearly thirty NATO fighters were massing in circular holding patterns, preparing to sweep north and east against the Soviet fighters and fighter-bombers that were methodically attacking troops and infrastructure across Northern Norway.

The plan for their sweep was the very definition of improvisation, but Olsen felt confident nonetheless. Allied Forces North Norway, AFNN, the NATO command responsible for directing the war in this part of the world, had managed to mass an impressive aerial force for this first offensive sweep by pulling together aircraft from half a dozen bases scattered across the northern half of Norway, from one American and five different Norwegian squadrons. Few of the pilots had been able to sit in ready rooms together to discuss the plan, and many, like Jan, were already flying their second combat mission of the war. A replacement AWACS, bearing the standard callsign of "Magic," was aloft to help control the action and electronic jamming support would come from two Norwegian aircraft that would follow the sweep, Tasman One and Two.

Arriving over Bardufoss, Olsen led his small flight into a racetrack holding pattern east of the base at twenty thousand feet altitude. Above, below, and all around, Jan could see more F-16s and bigger, twin tailed F-15s circling, waiting for the command from Magic to turn northeast. A final group of four fighters, these ones the Norwegian 338 Squadron F-16s with the MLU upgrade able to fire the new AMRAAM missiles, joined the flock, making the mission package as complete as it would get. Through his helmet speakers, Olsen heard Magic call one final update:

"All flights, all flights," the controller's deadpan voice crackled in German-accented English, "be advised, it appears the Sovs have pushed one of their own AWACS forward across the border. They will have aerial radar coverage over most of the north. We are starting to pick up indications that they may be gearing up for another major push."

The news about the Soviet AWACS was unsurprising, but still troubling; it meant the enemy pilots would have the same advantages in situational awareness enjoyed by the NATO fliers. Despite that, Jan and his comrades were eager to get at the people who were invading and bombing their country.

Olsen rehearsed the coming engagement in his mind as the fleet of NATO jets flew northeast and rounded the "hump" of territory formed by Swedish and Finnish Lapland. Both Nordic countries had declared their airspace closed to the belligerents and were flying patrols of fighters over their territory to enforce the exclusion, though the Finns were not contesting the sky over the far northeast of their territory, where Soviet jets were transiting at will. Closer to where the boundaries of the three countries met, however, a flight of jets were squawking the radio identification codes of the Finnish Air Force, apparently a buffer against deeper Soviet penetrations.

The biggest disadvantage for the NATO pilots was intermittent radar coverage. The threat of losing another AWACS meant that Magic would be deployed further west and would be operating at the edge of the airborne radar's ability to see and coordinate them. In combination with powerful Soviet jamming it was very likely that Jan and his compatriots would need to use their own, much shorter ranged radars and expose themselves to detection.

The Backstop radar site was still radiating, which mitigated the handicap somewhat, being able to detect intruders through the electronic haze, and feed that information to Magic via digital data-link. As long as Backstop remained intact, Olsen and his compatriots would enjoy the advantages of radar-direction without having to energize their own on-board sensors.

Of course, Olsen thought briefly, *no plan survives first contact with the enemy, and we're approaching second contact now.* He put that thought out of his mind. He was going to kill some Russians to avenge Bjorn and the others, and he felt confident that now, several hours into the war, he was finally facing his enemy on equal footing.

— • —

A hundred miles to the northeast, the command Il-22 with the two *desantnik* colonels was circling over Banak. They flew high enough to disregard the ground defenses that had managed to knock down several fighter bombers, but still low enough that the embattled positions could be seen through the broken clouds below. The white of the snowy tundra and low, snow-covered forest around the airfield was already marred here and there by oily black smoke columns marking the carnage of war.

Sokolov was on the radio, describing his observations to the command post at Luostari. Pathfinders would be arriving soon to mark the drop zones for the *desant* battalion, and Sokolov wanted them to have the fullest advantage when they landed. Romanov watched his friend, appreciating his calm command of the situation.

The Il-22 was banking gently to make another lazy circle above Banak when Romanov heard his own radio headset crackle, "All fighters, this is Control Two," that was the callsign for the A-50 orbiting just to the east over Northern Norway, "a large aircraft formation is approaching from the southwest, sector three. This is the attack we've been waiting for. Execute Plan *Margaritka*, repeat, execute Plan *Margaritka*! Non-combat aircraft, withdraw to Line Yellow. Crane Flight, remain where you are until my signal. Respond."

Romanov did not completely understand what the commands meant, but as the various squadrons responded in the affirmative, he perceived that they were executing some pre-arranged contingency plan. This was confirmed when he looked out the Ilyushin's window to see their escorting MiG-29s, which had been on their wing since Vadsø, peel away to the southwest. At the same time Ilya felt his own aircraft continue to bank around to the east as the four turboprops buzzed to full power.

In the other seat, Ilya could see a worried look on Sokolov's face. The other man looked at him and said, "The helicopters carrying my pathfinder company are fifteen minutes from their landing zones. I cannot recall them."

Romanov understood his friend's sudden anxiety. Up to this point Sokolov had been in control of the battle. Now the safety of his men rested on the shoulders of others, and there was nothing Sokolov could do to change the outcome. It would be an unwelcome defeat indeed if even one enemy fighter got in among those slow-moving helicopters.

— • —

The NATO fighters spread out as they neared the Backstop radar site, diverged to sweep eastward in a long line with the American F-15s and Norwegian MLU F-16s hanging back.

Each pilot heard Magic's radio call reporting, "Be advised, we're picking up heavy activity to your east and northeast. ELINT says the bandits are multiple MiG-23s and MiG-29s. The Fins are holding firm to your south. Looks like the Sovs are coming out to play, over."

Good, though Olsen as his breathing quickened, *let the bastards come.* Keying the radio on his flight's frequency he called, "Willi, Sven, this is Lead. If it's Flankers, come in low and fast and get out quick. Floggers and Fulcrums we'll take head-on. Follow me." Two clicks from each wingman acknowledged his reminder.

Olsen took in the view ahead. The sky to the east was darkening to the deep blue of night, while behind and to the south was still the ice blue of arctic day. Far below, the blanket of broken clouds over Finnmark looked like clean balls of cotton, obscuring the view of the rocky forest below, slumbering under a thick blanket of white snow. For a moment, the whole scene seemed oddly peaceful, a singular moment of quiet in the chaos engulfing his world.

Then the moment ended. Chaos returned. "Viper Two-One," Olsen's flight, "Backstop shows four bogeys to your one o'clock, angels ten. Looks like they're making an attack run at Backstop. Come to heading zero-nine-five to intercept."

Jan edged his sidestick right as the controllers aboard Magic began to issue rapid-fire commands to other flights, maneuvering formations to attack the Soviet intruders.

"Eagle One-One, two MiG-29s approaching from your ten o'clock, angels twenty. Come to..."

"Cola Lead, bandits low to your front..."

"Lion Three-Three, come left ten degrees to new heading zero-seven-five for intercept..."

The leading twenty-three Norwegian F-16s diverged further, several flights turning northeast to meet a group of MiG-29 "Fulcrums" approaching from the direction of Banak. The rest continued east to intercept a growing number of older MiG-23 "Floggers" who looked to be running interference for a low-level formation of fighter-bombers making a run at Backstop.

Olsen heard a controller aboard Magic call dispassionately to the AMRAAM-armed jets further back, "Reaper Lead, Tiger Lead, this is Magic. Switches hot. Reaper, you take the targets to the east, Tiger gets the MiGs to the northeast."

Jan willed the American and Norwegian pilots behind him to start launching their missiles. Frequent chirps from his helmet told him that he was being "painted" by an enemy radar. It was only a matter of time before the tone would change to the all-too-familiar warbling scream of the missile lock-on warning.

Olsen's radio crackled again, "Roger Magic. This is Reaper Lead," the callsign for the senior American F-15 pilot, "Contact on a Flogger. Fox Three!" Jan listened as the three other Eagles also launched missiles in quick succession towards the nearly two dozen MiG-23s to the east. Seconds later, the pilots of the MLU Falcons, engaging the Fulcrums approaching from Banak, began to launch their own AMRAAMs. Looking straight upwards Olsen could see thin smoke trails of the four American missiles abruptly end as their rocket motors burned out. The missiles, now invisible to Jan's eyes, dove towards their targets ahead, relying only upon kinetic energy to intercept the Soviet jets.

Olsen heard Reaper Lead announce a second "Fox Three," the second of his four AMRAAMs streaking towards another MiG. To Olsen, it seemed that the entire engagement was unfolding according to the hasty plan they'd been briefed before takeoff. Then things began to change.

First, the tone in his helmet began blaring; an enemy targeting radar was painting his Falcon. Jan's eyes snapped forward, searching for the missile that was surely headed his way. *There!* A flash against the darkening sky announced where a MiG pilot had launched an Alamo missile.

"Evading right!" Olsen announced to his flight as he flipped his sidestick over and banked towards the Finnish border. He had already evaded these missiles twice on his first sortie of the day, giving him confidence that he could do it again. *This is almost becoming old hat*, he thought. Then the news took a turn for the worse.

"All flights, this is Tasman," called the technician aboard the Norwegian electronic warfare bird flying behind the trailing F-15, "I'm picking up emissions from multiple *Zaslon* radars to the east. My count is six...no, eight emission sources."

Dritt! Olsen swore to himself. He knew that the powerful *Zaslon* radars meant MiG-31 "Foxhound" interceptors. The MiG-31 was not a nimble dogfighter like the more maneuverable Su-27s and MiG-29s, but the big twin-tail, twin-engine Foxhounds carried the long-range AA-9 "Amos" missile which could hit targets at ranges up to a hundred and twenty kilometers, meaning they could hit any NATO plane in the sweep right now.

Olsen's grip tightened as he continued to evade the incoming AA-10. The Sovs would surely press their range advantage while remaining well out of NATO radar view. The urgent calls from Olsen's fellow Falcon drivers began to fill the radio waves, reporting that they were being targeted. The MiG-31 like the US Navy F-14 Tomcat, could use their aircraft's radar to target and launch multiple missiles at once. This they did, and more AA-9s arced into the air towards the NATO jets joining an increasing number of AA-10s fired by the nearer MiGs. The formations of NATO fighters began to fall apart as they evaded this two-pronged, multi-headed threat.

Jan flipped his stick over to the left, continuing to turn so as to bleed off the incoming missile's velocity until it no longer possessed the speed to make its intercept. At the same time, the turn allowed Olsen to dive towards his assigned targets at ten thousand feet, punching out packets of metallic chaff as he did so. A few more seconds and the AA-10 detonated into a cloud of foil far behind Olsen's bird. He had dodged death yet again. He barely noticed the victory though, as he listened to the tide turn. He had a gut feeling that if the Sovs had thought far enough ahead to bring in the MiG-31s, then there might be more to the plot than the NATO forces had anticipated. *They planned for this, for us,* Jan gritted his teeth and tried to keep his head in the fight.

Out of immediate danger, Olsen twisted his head around, looking for his two wingmen. Wili was gone, to where, Jan didn't know, but he could still see Sven Hokenson's F-16B tight on his right-wing tip. The other jet's elongated two-person canopy made picking Sven's bird out of the formation an easy task. Through his headphones, Jan could hear the entire NATO plan coming apart at the seams as pilots evaded wildly, all the while trying to bring their Sidewinders to within range of their Soviet adversaries. Then the other jaw of the Soviet ambush began to close.

"All flights, all flights, this is Magic." While he leveled out and switched his radar on to search for the fighter-bombers, Jan registered in the back of his mind that the controller's voice no longer possessed the almost-bored tone that was present only moments before. "All flights, the four bogeys over Finland just turned north and increased speed." There was a brief pause, and Olsen could feel the radar-man racing to get a grip on the situation, "Radars are coming on." Now the controller's tone changed from concerned to grave, "We identify those bogeys as Flankers! I repeat, four Su-27s bearing one-seven-zero. Contacts should be considered hostile and—fire control radars just came on! We have a fire control radar from Flanker's One and Three! Missiles inbound!"

Dritt! Olsen swore again. With Foxhounds to the east and now Flankers to south, the NATO fighters were being pressed into a vice where the Soviet advantage in numbers, not to mention range, could be decisive.

— • —

Major Sasha Mitroshenko grinned savagely into his oxygen mask as he watched his R-27 missile streak away northward towards the NATO jets. Things were going exactly according to plan. Earlier in the day, the Soviet ambassador had submitted a list of demands, instructions really, to the Finnish government. One of those demands had been that the Finnish Air Force not interfere, not even be present, in the far north on the first day of the war. The Finns had little choice, and had reluctantly submitted. For Mitroshenko, this meant that he and his flight of Su-27s had been free to circle over Finnish Lapland for the last hour, their transponders squawking Finnish Air Force identification-friend-or-foe codes, called IFF, that made the Soviet Flankers look like a flight of patrolling Finnish jets on any radar receiver, a classic deception.

Mitroshenko led his interceptors on afterburner north towards the gap between the leading line of NATO fighters and the trailing group of long-range shooters. Another four Su-27s were following him up from the south, and eight more were inbound from the southeast. With surprise and numbers on his side, the Soviet pilot was eager to avenge the losses and embarrassment he and his 265th Fighter Regiment had suffered in the opening moments of the war.

The tables were turning further against the NATO pilots. The Soviet AWACS reported that the American F-15Cs were turning south to meet the new threat from Mitroshenko's Flankers. The timing was perfect. Mitroshenko knew that the maneuver by the American interceptors would rob the AMRAAMs fired earlier of their mid-course guidance from the Eagle's radar and data-link. He listened over his radio, still burning northwards, as the American missiles streaked down among the MiG-23s with abysmal accuracy. Half of the advanced missiles missed their targets when the weapons' own short-range terminal guidance radars failed to detect that the Soviet aircraft that had maneuvered out of their engagement box. One of the Floggers exploded in midair while another turned for home with a shredded left wing and a leaking fuel tank, manfully informing the controllers that he intended to bring his jet home. The three other AMRAAMs missed.

Simultaneously, the Soviet AWACS announced hits against the American and Norwegian fighters from the AA-9s fired by the distant MiG-31s, along with more hits from the AA-10s arcing away from the surviving MiG-23s. Mitroshenko could see on his radar scope that the flurry of Soviet missiles was forcing the NATO pilots to evade wildly. First one F-16, then another winked off of his screen. Mitroshenko's hungry grin widened.

More clipped chatter from the MiG-29 pilots bearing down from Banak cluttered the radio waves as those dozen jets passed through a cauldron of Norwegian AMRAAMs. Then the jaws of the trap closed firmly as the Fulcrums came to grips with the northern F-16s, and Mitroshenko watched the tide turn decisively against NATO.

Then the Soviet fighter pilot's radar warning receiver began to blare in his ears as two of the American F-15s launched AMRAAMs at his oncoming Flankers just before his own flight's R-27 missiles lanced into the southern flank of the faltering NATO formation. Mitroshenko saw two of the missiles miss due to evasive maneuvers by the American and Norwegian pilots, but one of the Soviet weapons exploded mere meters from the cockpit of an F-16, blasting it into pieces, while Mitroshenko's own missile blew the left vertical stabilizer off an F-15, sending the American jet spinning uncontrollably downward. He didn't have time to savor his victory over the vaunted American jet, however, as he was already banking into a high-G turn to evade one of the dangerous AMRAAMs. This he managed to do, though one of his wingmen was not as lucky.

After evading the American weapons, Mitroshenko and the two surviving wingmen banked back northwards and plunged into the southern end of the hundred-kilometer-wide "furball," the churning, confused dogfight that was developing over Northern Norway.

— ▬

"All flights, this is Magic," Olsen heard the staticky voice through his helmet phones, "bug out! I say again, bug out! Vector west or north-west to disengage. Withdraw to west of the twenty-one easting, over!"

The command was delivered with a note of desperation, Jan thought as he and Sven continued to dive towards the flight of four fighter-bombers heading at low-level for the Backstop site. The controllers aboard the AWACS were ordering all the NATO jets to withdraw a full hundred-and-fifty-kilometers eastwards, to the skies over the vital Lyngen position, the eventual main line of resistance for the defense of Northern Norway. Lyngen was a mere hundred kilometers *east* of Bardufoss, the most important Norwegian air base in the north. Things were going from bad to worse, and fast, but there was barely time to be truly angry as F-16s, F-15s, MiGs, and Sukhois twisted and turned through the sky over his head.

"Viper Two-One, Magic...bandits from your one o'clock, angels..." Jamming interference muddled some of the controller's warning, but Olsen got enough from the transmission to pull his jet up and to the left, just in time to see two MiG-23s bearing down upon them.

Quickly Jan radioed Sven, "Two-Three, sort side-side," Ordering him to take the left-hand MiG while Jan dealt with the right-hand one. Two bursts of static signaled Sven's agreement.

Now that the opposing aircraft were so heavily intermixed in the furball, neither side could use their long-armed radar-guided missiles at anything close to their maximum range. Thus, as the two MiGs and two Falcons closed with each other at a combined thousand miles per hour, both Olsen and Sven were able to lock their Sidewinders' infrared seeker heads onto the oncoming Floggers and fire the missiles first, each announcing a hurried "Fox Two!"

Both Soviet pilots turned hard to evade, popping white hot flares out the back of their aircraft to confuse the missiles, but to no avail. Both AIM-9s bore in, and two black puffs in Jan's field of view marked where the missiles' warheads shredded the incoming Soviet fighters, sending them tumbling from the sky.

"Splash Two!" Jan announced, but he was already banking back down and to his left, searching for the bombers the MiGs had been escorting. Focusing, he saw them. Four Su-24 "Fencer" fighter-bombers flying westward in tight formation, their green and tan camouflage paint standing out darkly against the snow-covered forest two thousand feet below.

"Follow me around," Olsen ordered Sven. "We'll get on their tail." He barely registered the click response.

The two F-16s completed a tight one hundred eighty degrees turn and leveled out four miles behind the Fencers. Increasing power to close the gap, Jan heard unintelligible snippets from his AWACS controller, but all he could make out was a broken "...angels six..." amid the strained calls from the other pilots in the furball. He and Sven continued their chase.

After a few seconds, Jan settled the Sidewinder's seeker box on his heads up display onto the left-most Fencer until he heard the growl of a good lock. Squeezing the trigger, he announced "Fox Two!"

The Sidewinder shot off its rail under Jan's right wing. In the same instant, Sven's Falcon, off Olsen's right wing, exploded as a missile plowed into the top middle of the F-16B. Instinctively Jan yanked his stick to the right and punched flares. A white flash out of the corner of his eye and the violent buffet from an explosion told him that his abrupt maneuver had saved him from a second enemy weapon. Jan desperately scanned the sky above and to his front for the enemy aircraft that had just shot down his second wingman of the day.

— ▪ —

Mitroshenko banked his Su-27 to keep the maneuvering F-16 in his sights. After lancing into the flank of the NATO fighters, he had managed to use one of his heat-seeking R-73 missiles to shoot down another Norwegian fighter before his controller aboard the A-50 vectored him and his wingman northeast to protect a flight of fighter-bombers sent to strike the one remaining NATO ground radar. They went to afterburner, avoiding several aerial duels along the way. They arrived too late to save the two escorting MiG-23s, but when the enemy fighters turned to follow the bombers, he saw his chance.

The Soviets launched their missiles from above and ahead of the Norwegians, and Mitroshenko had watched his wingman's R-73 detonate into the back of one of the pursuing Falcons, sending it spinning immediately downward. To his dismay his own missile flew harmlessly into a flare dropped by the lead F-16. Worse, one of the Norwegians had managed to fire a missile, which streaked through clouds of defensive flares until it exploded into the tail of an Su-24. For a moment the bomber continued onward, but then yellow flames shot out from behind as its engines failed and it rolled over to the left. Both crew ejected just before their aircraft tipped onto its back and plunged into the snow-covered trees.

Mitroshenko followed the F-16 as it executed a tight, climbing turn. The nimble, single-engine Falcon was turning so fast that he struggled to lock a second R-73 onto it. Mitroshenko's wingman broke in the opposite direction intending to intercept the Norwegian as he reversed his course, but this was a mistake. The major grunted through his high-G turn, only to see the white smoke trail of a Sidewinder leave the other jet and streak into his wingman's left air intake a half mile away. The Sukoi exploded as shrapnel tore through its left engine and fuel tanks.

Still banking behind the Norwegian, Mitroshenko swore violently as he finally heard the tone in his ears telling him that his R-73 had locked on. Quickly, he squeezed the trigger, and the missile shot outward.

— • —

Olsen was amazed he'd been able to lock a Sidewinder onto the Flanker so quickly. Fleeing from the Su-27 on his tail, he'd been almost certain that the second jet looping around would be his doom. Instead, he'd added another of the dangerous Sukhois to his growing list of kills, though there was no time to tally them as he craned his neck to keep tabs on his pursuer. His Falcon continued to bleed off speed through a tight climbing. Then he saw the missile streak out from under the wing of the Flanker and barely had time to punch his flare dispenser before the AA-11's warhead exploded, riddling the left side of his jet with shrapnel.

The force of the explosion knocked Jan's F-16 over onto its back, sending it hurtling down to the clouds and snow below.

— • —

Mitroshenko clenched his fist in triumph as he saw his missile exploded just off the Falcon's left horizontal stabilizer. The *Norge* immediately winged over onto its back and dove, trailing smoke. He lost sight of his prey as the stricken jet plunged into one of the scattered clouds below.

He was about to follow the F-16 down to make sure of his kill, but a screaming tone in his headphones told him that he was being targeted by one of those blasted American AMRAAMs. Mitroshenko threw his jet into evasive maneuvers as he turned back west towards the threat.

Ahead through the broken clouds, the three surviving fighter-bombers released their ordnance. The Su-24s overflew the large, white globe housing the Backstop radar, leaving in their wake a series of massive explosions that sent translucent shock waves outward through the surrounding forest. One of the bombs crashed through the white plexiglass of the protective globe and exploded inside, ripping the structure apart. The data feed from Backstop to the NATO AWACS ceased abruptly, leaving the controllers aboard the NATO radar planes all but blind as to what was going on in the skies between Banak and the Finnish border.

— ◼ —

The remnants of the NATO sweep over Finnmark were extracting themselves with difficulty from the furball. Aided by American F-15s and Norwegian MLU Falcons, the surviving F-16 pilots fled westward on afterburner, chased by flocks of MiGs and Sukhois snapping at their heels. Once they'd expended all of their long-range missiles, the AMRAAM-carriers also turned and fled. To the rear, the MiG-31s, unable to safely target the Americans due to the proximity of their comrades, held their fire.

Aircraft on both sides were low on fuel after minutes of high-speed maneuvering on afterburner, and many were low on missiles. When a fresh flight of two American F-15s out of Bodø activated their radars, joined by a pair of Dutch F-16s from the newly-arriving 322 "Polly Parrots" fighter squadron, the Soviet controllers aboard the A-50 ordered the pursuers to break off the chase. The Soviets turned back, content to have won air superiority in the skies over Northern Norway from the Soviet border to the Lyngen position, two hundred miles to the west.

As the massive battle involving more than eighty aircraft subsided, each side tallied the results, and both came to the same conclusions. The Soviets had suffered the greater number of losses in the confused engagement, including a pair of Su-27s, four MiG-29s, and seven of the older MiG-23s, in addition to one Su-24 fighter-bomber. On the NATO side, the butcher's bill stood at eight F-16s and a pair of the vaunted American F-15s. But despite the nominally favorable kill ratio, the battle had been a disaster for NATO. To have any hope of weathering the Soviets' crushing numerical superiority, NATO needed to maintain a kill ratio of at least three Soviet aircraft for every NATO jet lost. In this engagement, the exchange rate had been less than half that, fourteen aircraft to ten. Worse, the Norwegian and American squadrons on this front would not again in the foreseeable future be able to put thirty jets into the air at once. The Soviets had brilliantly seized the initiative in the skies over Northern Norway. Both sides knew it, and now the Soviets began to exploit their success.

From the Soviet border to the east, flights of fighter-bombers, which had been circling over their Kola bases, turned west, fanning out towards targets west of Banak that had, up to now, been too dangerous to strike.

— —

Jan Olsen struggled to keep his damaged F-16 level and above the treetops as he flew northwest towards the coast. He had tumbled through the broken clouds in an uncontrolled, twisting dive as he fought to regain control of the aircraft. For an instant he'd reached up to yank the handles of his ejection seat, but then thought better of it. Instead, he used everything he had ever learned about flying to pull his Falcon out of its spin a mere two hundred meters from the ground.

Looking around, Jan was surprised to see that none of his adversaries had followed him down. He decided that his best chance of getting home with his crippled bird was to avoid any engagement and head to the coast. He could see that his oil pressure was dropping quickly. A look to the left revealed a dozen large gashes in his wing. In fact, one of the flaps was barely hanging on by its smashed hinges. He doubted that his barely airworthy airplane could perform even the gentlest maneuvers if he was faced with the necessity of fighting his way out. So Jan stayed low, his wounded bird fighting him the whole way. He just hoped his engine would hold out long enough for him to reach a safe landing field. *Preferably one where I can get into another jet*, he thought bleakly.

CHAPTER 82

1645 CET, Sunday 13 February 1994
1545 Zulu
Banak Airbase, Lakselv, Troms, Norway

R *ITTMESTER* ERIK JOHANSEN pulled his knit cap down over his ears as he walked out of the makeshift command post and into the biting Arctic evening. The tall and lanky *Løytnant* Sigurd Berg, his number two, followed. Neither man was aware of the epic aerial battles raging to their south over the past half hour, but they both noted troubling signs that things were not going well above their heads. The most obvious indicator was the four-engine turboprop that was orbiting above the airfield, just beyond the range of the Norwegian defenders' anti-air weapons.

At first the plane had lifted Johansen's spirits, as it looked for all the world like one of the P-3 sub-hunting aircraft flown by the Royal Norwegian Air Force, with its four engines mounted atop rather than slung beneath the wings. The soldiers manning the optical sights on the surviving RBS-70 posts and Bofors guns soon reported that the aircraft was actually a Soviet Il-18, or perhaps an Il-22 command variant. If the pilot of this slow-moving bird felt so safe as to loiter over Banak, it did not bode well for NATO's control of the air.

A half hour after the first bombing raid, another troubling sign: a lone jet, another Su-17 Fitter, roared across the airfield at extremely low altitude from the west. By the time the anti-air troops responded, the Soviet fighter-bomber was gone, leaving only the echoes of its engine to reverberate off the surrounding valley walls. Erik was certain that the lone Fitter was on a reconnaissance mission to judge the effectiveness of the earlier attack. If he was right, this meant that the Soviets really cared about this piece of real estate. *More will come*, he thought grimly.

Johansen saw several *dragons* from his headquarters section completing an "icecrete" fighting position in the wood line overlooking the access road leading to the Coast Guard hangars. Since the ground here in the Far North was frozen for much of the year, and thus unsuitable for digging foxholes, soldiers learned to improvise fortifications from the one thing which they possessed in abundance: frozen water. To create an icecrete fortification, they simply combined water with some reinforcing substance like sawdust, wood chips, or gravel, and then froze the mixture. The resulting composite material was much stronger than ice and, if thick enough, could serve nicely as protection from small arms fire and shrapnel. Sergeant Pedersen, the pioneer leader, had secured several bags of sawdust when he'd gone into Lakselv to check on the fire started by one of the downed Soviet bombers. Since returning he'd been busily supervising the construction of the small ice bunker.

Johansen nodded approvingly, then turned to Berg and said, "We can expect another attack at any time. I'm taking one of the snowmobiles around the airfield to check on the missile and gun teams."

Berg alert and ready, said, "Yes sir."

"Have we heard anything from Battalion?" Johansen asked. Contact with Major Laub or anyone else from the rest of 2nd Mechanized Battalion had been all but nonexistent since the fighting had started nearly four hours ago.

"Not since the last report that they were starting out from Skjöld," answered the executive officer. "Jamming has been the worst on the HF net, but I'll keep monitoring and let you know as soon as I hear something."

Johansen nodded again. His command was positioned as well as it could be given their limited resources. He looked up to the sky again, *It won't matter if the rest of the battalion doesn't get here to reinforce us.*

Erik mounted one of the Coast Guards' snowmobiles. The engine roared to life and he opened the throttle, driving northward through the low, snow-laden trees that lined the west side of the runway. After a hundred meters he passed through a stretch of forest where the incendiaries dropped by the Su-17s had melted the snow and blackened the ground and the trees. Two hundred meters more and he arrived at the first Bofors gun position.

Despite the recent Russian attack and decimation of the gun crew on the opposite side of the runway, Johansen found these men in decent spirits. The wounded from the crew had been rushed to the hospital in Lakselv, while the dead were under sheets, the bodies growing cold outside the bombed-out civilian terminal. It was gratifying to see the men's eagerness to bring their gun into action against another Soviet aircraft. "You watch, sir," the gun sergeant promised as Johansen remounted his snowmobile, "next time we're going to put a burst straight through the cockpit of one of those bastards!"

Johansen nodded back and drove on. Another hundred meters, and he came upon one of the RBS-70 posts. The two soldiers there were shivering and stomping their feet. Their launcher sat atop its tripod-mounted pedestal, the "post," while a missile reload lay on a tarp at their feet. Johansen asked the two men how they were doing.

"Cold, sir," one of the men answered, "and we only have two missiles left."

"I'll make sure your relief is out here soon," Johansen told them. "But we won't have any more missiles until the rest of the battalion arrives."

The soldiers nodded and mumbled, "Yes sir," through frozen lips.

The *rittmester* was just remounting his snowmobile when he saw the two men cock their heads to one side and stand still. Then he heard it as well. Above the constant droning of the four-engine aircraft circling overhead came the deeper rumble of jet engines, reverberating against the walls of the fjord valley.

— • —

From their perch aboard the command Il-22 three thousand meters up, the two colonels strained their eyes to watch the strike go in. Sokolov explained to his friend that the first strike by a squadron of Su-17s had been intended to close the Banak airfield to NATO use without actually damaging the runway and key facilities. It had been a costly attack, with three of the fighter-bombers going down to the Norwegian defenses. That was why another attack was now necessary to suppress those defenses before the arrival of the helicopters bearing the pathfinders for Sokolov's assault battalion.

Through his headset, Romanov heard the radio call, "Control Two, this is *Kondor* Lead, First pair are on their final approach to the target. Beginning attack run now."

Ilya saw a pair of low-flying MiG-27 fighter-bombers crest the ridge west of Banak and dive for the airfield, their swing wings swept back for added speed.

— —

Johansen decided to remain with the missile troopers. He didn't want to expose himself by tearing about on a snowmobile while attack jets roared overhead looking for targets. Instead, he buckled on his helmet and was now kneeling next to the two soldiers, one of whom was seated behind the launcher, his eyes pressed to the targeting unit with the green cylinder of the missile tube over his right shoulder.

From the air defense radio Erik heard the terse warning, "Air action west! Two contacts coming in low and fast!"

A few seconds later the loud *pom-pom-pom* of the Bofors gun across the runway from them began again, sending forty-millimeter shells over Johansen's head towards the approaching MiGs.

— —

From above, the two fighter-bombers looked like green and brown arrowheads flashing across the airfield's runway. Romanov saw flashes in the tree line as an anti-aircraft gun opened up against the raiders. Then a missile shot up from the northeast corner of the runway, streaking towards the left-hand MiG. Bright white flares appeared out the back of the aircraft, but the missile flew true and exploded, riddling the jet's tail with shrapnel. The jet shuddered but continued on, the pilot and his wingman releasing their fragmentation bombs into the already-gutted passenger terminal on the east side of the airstrip.

Over the radio Romanov heard a dispassionate voice call, "*Kondor* One-One-Three, this is Lead. I confirm a gun position three hundred meters from the northern end of the runway on the east side, and a missile launch point at the south end of the runway. Engage. Respond."

"*Da*, Lead," came the response. "Engaging now."

Out of the corner of his eye Romanov saw another pair of MiG-27s approaching from the southwest. These, unlike the pair that had just streaked across the airfield, were flying not much below the altitude of the loitering Il-22, and their swing-wings were extended for maximum control at low speed.

"This is One-One-Three," Ilya heard in his headset, "*Grom* away!"

At the same instant he saw a streak of fire and a stubby, white-painted missile shot out from under the fighter-bomber's wing. Seconds later the other MiG launched its missile. *Grom*, the Russian word for "thunder," was also the Soviet designation for the Kh-23M air-to-ground missile. These were laser-guided weapons that rode a beam, emitted by a laser designator in the nose of the launching aircraft. Two of these precision weapons were now diving towards Banak.

—— ——

Johansen pumped his fist and shouted "Yes!" as he saw the missile from the team across the runway explode onto the tail of the jet, just before the bombs tore into the smoldering shell of the passenger terminal. The two raiders, he thought, had done nothing more than pound the rubble left by the previous strike, and one of their aircraft had taken a hit doing so. He would happily take that exchange.

Then Johansen's feeling of triumph evaporated as the Bofors gun across the runway from them disappeared in an earsplitting explosion of fire, tree limbs, and gray smoke. Seconds later, the second Kh-23M slammed into the spot where the RBS-70 team had engaged the low-level raider. The one-hundred-kilogram warhead exploded as it burrowed into the snow, killing both men and obliterating the launcher they were busily reloading. Johansen looked on helplessly at the destruction of a third of his command's remaining anti-air strength.

As the reverberations from the missile strikes died away, Johansen heard the rumble of jet engines pass overhead. Looking up, he could see the silhouettes of two Soviet fighter-bombers banking over the airfield at about two thousand meters altitude. Suddenly, the *rittmester* realized what was happening. *The first two MiGs were bait!* he now understood. *Bait to get us to reveal the locations of our anti-air weapons!*

Johansen turned to warn the missile crew next to him, and to his horror saw the soldier training the launcher's sighting unit on the pair of jets far above.

"STOP!" Johansen shouted, just as the man depressed the firing trigger. The missile's rocket engine ignited in a flash and the projectile shot skyward, corkscrewing as it arced after the receding jet.

Erik didn't wait to see if the RBS-70 hit its target. He lunged the few steps towards the two soldiers and shouted, "Move move MOVE!" as he grabbed and dragged them away from the launch point, forcing them to abandon the launcher and its laser designator that was guiding the missile towards the enemy jet. The two anti-air soldiers were confused, but after a moment they complied with their commander's frantic order. The three men struggled through knee-deep snow between low, snow-covered trees until Johansen heard the ripping scream of another missile launch.

"DOWN!" Johansen screamed as he dove into the snow. The explosion shook the ground behind them. Erik felt something strike his left shoulder blade like a blow from a steel pipe, but there was no pain. Bits of ice and frozen sod rained down all around as the three men buried their faces in the snow.

— • —

Sokolov jotted marks in a notebook as he and Romanov observed the squadron of MiG-27s work over the airfield. The squadron commander, *Kondor* Lead, was loitering off the Ilyushin's wing tip, directing the fighter-bombers of his squadron against the Norwegian defenses that still dared show themselves. The initial salvos of Kh-23Ms had effectively suppressed the enemy fire. Romanov noted that no return fire had come up from the airfield since the third missile had struck the west side of the runway.

With no more missiles or gun bursts rising from around the airfield, Ilya listened as *Kondor* Lead directed his other bombers to methodically destroy the remaining targets around the enemy aerodrome. One pair of MiGs streaked up from the south and loosed a pair of *Grom* missiles into the small control tower next to the passenger terminal. Another Kh-23M blew apart the surviving Coast Guard helicopter, which had been sitting, unused due to a maintenance fault, on the tarmac in front of the military hangars. Romanov was impressed with the bombers' precision, which was so unlike what he had seen in Afghanistan.

The pilots, he noted with a trained eye, were being careful not to damage the runway, or the aviation gas storage area.

Sokolov tapped Ilya on the shoulder and indicated the tally in his notebook. He said over the drone of the engines, "I'm not sure we destroyed them all," he meant the enemy defenses around the airfield, "but we can't wait any longer. The pathfinders are here."

He pointed downward to the south. Ilya, following his indication, saw a dozen helicopters flying up the valley at treetop level. He watched as a quartet put down on the flat, white expanse of a frozen lake two kilometers south of Lakselv in a flurry of downdraft-blown snow. The other eight were continuing up the west side of the valley when Romanov lost sight of them as the Ilyushin continued to circle lazily. He caught a glimpse of another four helicopters putting down in what looked to be some snow-covered farm fields three kilometers east of the town, but his gaze continued to be drawn to the smoke rising from around the airfield, where the MiGs were completing their attack runs.

— • —

Løytnant Sigurd Berg knelt with Sergeant Pedersen and a radioman next to the icecrete bunker as they both listened to the ominous *thwack-thwack-thwack* of helicopter rotors reverberate from the south, west, and east. The MiGs' attacks against Banak had been savage, and Berg had thought it wise to take the commander's radioman and get out of the Coast Guard building before some Soviet pilot decided to put a missile into it.

The radioman knelt behind Berg and Pedersen, listening as the troop screening south of Lakselv called in a sighting report.

"Roger, Two," the radioman said into his handset, attached by a coiled black telephone-like cable to the radio on his back, "we don't know where *Rittmester* Johansen is right now, but I'll tell the XO, over."

He moved the handset from his ear to his shoulder and clapped Berg on the arm. "Sir," he reported, "2nd Troop says they just saw helicopters land south of town, just to the east of the E6!"

"Can they engage?" asked Berg quickly.

The other man shook his head. "No sir, it's too far for their machineguns. The troop commander wants to know if he can call for the artillery?"

Now it was Berg's turn to shake his head. He and Johansen had discussed their intentions for how to use the artillery battery. The time was not yet right.

"No," he said, "tell them—"

Pedersen slapped Berg's white parka and then pointed wordlessly to the western hills. The XO looked that way. His eyes adjusted quickly to the darker blues and grays of the shaded face of the valley wall. Motion caught his eye, and then he could make out the several green and brown-painted helicopters beneath the western cliff face. One by one they crested the top of the cliff, their silhouettes dark against the muted light of the sun setting in the southwest. Then they disappeared over the far side of the hill.

— • —

A pair of Mi-24 gunships set down in a cloud of blowing snow just back from the cliff face. From his vantage point high above, Romanov saw several figures emerge from the snow cloud, struggling away from the helicopters through the deep snow.

"Those are the forward air controllers," Sokolov told him, indicating the soldiers just dropped off by the gunships.

"A good place for them," Romanov responded approvingly. It was true. Once the specially trained Soviet forward air controllers—FACs—reached their observation points atop the cliff, they would have eyes on the entire valley and would be able to call down air attacks more accurately on the Norwegian defenders around the town and airfield. After depositing their human cargo, the gunships dipped their noses and took off again amid a blizzard of blowing snow.

Passing nearby, another pair of Mi-24s escorted a quartet of Mi-8 transports northward to deposit the last group of pathfinders at their designated landing zone up the fjord. Then, due west of Lakselv, the gunships peeled off and turned east. Gaining altitude, the pilots lined up their aircraft to execute a "form a circle" attack on the airfield.

"Now we'll see how well those bombers did at finishing off the air defenses," Sokolov noted, slapping his notebook closed.

The first Hind dove from above the cliff face down towards the airfield. After a few seconds Romanov saw dirty gray streaks of smoke flash out from under the gunship's stubby wings. The rockets shot down toward Banak and slammed into the hangars near the southwest corner of the runway. Suddenly Ilya saw a smoke trail corkscrew back up from the eastern treeline. A missile rode its launcher's laser beam straight into the Mi-24's air intakes above the helicopter's bulbous canopy, where it exploded. The helicopter fell like a stone.

"Apparently not well enough," Sokolov said dryly as the second gunship began its dive.

The gunner of the second Mi-24 loosed a salvo of rockets at the area from which the missile had been fired, then followed up with cannon fire that announced itself through dirty gray smoke. The final two Hinds made similar runs, shooting cannon and rocket fire into anything that looked like a viable target. Then, low on fuel after their long flight from the Soviet Union, the four gunships turned southeast and departed for a remote area along the Finnish border. There a flight of Mi-6 transport helicopters had landed to deposit fuel bowsers, armaments, and ground crews to set up a forward rearming and refueling point.

———

Berg ducked his helmeted head behind the shelter of the icecrete wall as the last Hind gunship thundered overhead, spitting rockets and cannon rounds into some Coast Guard maintenance sheds two hundred meters away. He tried to make himself small, regretting perhaps for the first time his tall, one-point-eight-meter frame. Next to him Pedersen and the commander's radioman crouched against the icy wall as well.

The reverberations of the rockets' explosions and the sound of the pounding Soviet helicopter's rotors faded. *Is it over?* After a moment he heard the familiar sound of a snowmobile engine. The *løytnant* slithered out of the bunker and stood up to see Johansen, riding a shrapnel-scarred machine, pull up to the makeshift fortification and dismount. Johansen moved stiffly, and Berg noticed that the *rittmester*'s face was pale, lips pinched.

"Sir," Johansen called to him, concerned, "are you alright?"

Johansen waved the question away. "Situation report," he demanded through gritted teeth as he walked up and leaned his rifle against the icecrete wall.

"Our air defenses were hit hard in this last attack, sir," Berg answered quickly. His commander was clearly in pain, but also still in command. "None of the RBS-70 posts are answering on the radio—"

"I just left Post Three," Johansen interjected, wincing. "They're alive but… launcher and missiles all destroyed."

Berg nodded. *That means that none of our RBS-70 posts are still in operation.* He went on, "Only one of the Bofors guns is responding, Gun Four, and the Skyguard radar took a hit as well when those jets came over."

Johansen shifted his weight and said, "I passed Gun Four on my way back. Told them to hold fire and save their rounds for the ground fight."

The "ground fight" was looking more likely every minute, Berg thought. He went on, "2nd Troop reported enemy transport helicopters disembarking troops two kilometers south of town. I think those Hinds also put some people up in the hills west of here. 1st Troop reported that they heard several helicopters east of town, but no visual. 2nd Troops asked for artillery against the landing zone south of town."

"No!" Johansen said firmly. "No. We need to keep our artillery…for when the enemy main force arrives. Those landings are just…the pathfinders." He was breathing heavily, needing to pause mid-speech to catch himself, but it didn't seem like he noticed this himself.

"That's what I told him, sir," Berg assured his commander. "2nd Troop is continuing to observe. They reported a few minutes ago that the enemy are south of town. They're probably setting up a drop zone for parachutists."

Johansen grimaced, then nodded his understanding. "You stay here, Berg," he instructed. "I'm going down to 2nd Troop to get eyes on that drop zone. Is there any word from Battalion?"

Berg shook his head no.

"Well, keep trying," Johansen ordered, grabbing his rifle and turning to walk back towards his snowmobile.

Then Berg saw his boss's wound. A piece of wood, clearly a shard of a tree, stuck several centimeters out through the left shoulder of the man's parka. The white material around the wound was dark with blood.

"Sir, you're wounded," Berg called. "Let me get you a medic."

Johansen paused, then nodded and slumped against a tree. Berg summoned the Squadron medic, who clucked his tongue as he peeled the parka off Johansen's shoulders. The *rittmester* winced as the aid man gingerly extracted the piece of lumber from his back and wrapped the wound with a bandage.

"This really needs stitches, sir," the medic said. "At the very least you need to rest."

Johansen waved the man's concern away. Instead, he grabbed his parka, picked up his rifle and walked to the snowmobile. "Just get us in touch with Battalion," Johansen ordered over his shoulder as he mounted the snowmobile. "We're going to have a serious fight on our hands soon. Tell them that we can't hold here without them. Tell them to hurry."

CHAPTER 83

1705 CET, Sunday 13 February 1994
1605 Zulu
Halselva Dam, fourteen kilometers northwest
of Alta, Finnmark, Norway

A HUNDRED KILOMETERS TO the west under a slowly darkening sky, the bulk of the Norwegian Army's 2nd Mechanized Battalion, the armored weight of the Norwegian Army in the far north, was stalled where the E6 highway bridged the frozen Halseva stream. The column of over a hundred dark green vehicles covered with mottled white camouflage paint stretched several kilometers north from the small dam. Leopard tanks, M113 armored personnel carriers, M109 self-propelled howitzers, trucks towing Bofors guns, and smaller G-Wagens were all interspersed on the snowy, windswept road, engines idling. The ribbon of E6 highway that clung to the western side of the Altafjord already lay in the shadows of mountains rising from the dark water. An icy wind blew under a blanket of high, scattered clouds turning a faint evening pink.

Major Laub clenched his jaw, trying not to shiver as the cold, damp wind seeped through his parka like it was nothing more than a wet blanket. He stood with the battalion commander and a knot of helmeted officers, gazing at the roadblock barring their way towards Alta, and Banak beyond. An abatis of more than a dozen trees lay interlocked in a tangled mess across the road a dozen meters beyond the dam. The tops of the tall Norwegian spruce now drooped into the waters lapping at the downhill side of the road to the left.

"This has to be the work of the same people that slowed *Løytnant* Berg's progress this morning," the battalion commander was grumbling as he bowed his head, studying a folded tactical map against the side of his command vehicle.

Laub, nodded sourly. Not known for his cheery disposition even during good times—which these decidedly were *not*—the major looked back at the motionless vehicles of his battalion with a look of pure vehemence. The soldiers in the lead vehicle, exhausted after a full night of preparing to move and then a full day of driving over icy roads, had been slow to radio back a report of the obstacle. As a result, the following vehicles had accordioned forward before stopping, compressing the previously disciplined spacing between the vehicles until many were nearly fender to fender. *If the Soviets catch us like this* we're in serious trouble, Laub fumed.

"Alright," the commander said, looking up from his map, "Laub, call C Company. I want a rear guard behind us until we get moving again, and tell B Company to throw a platoon forward across the obstacle. Whoever did this is still out there, and I won't have us surprised again. Where are the pioneers to clear this? We have to get moving!"

Laub snatched the hand mic from the radioman. He had called the support platoon five minutes ago and ordered their pioneers to come forward. The major pushed the talk button and hissed into it, "This is Griffin Three, *where are those pioneers, over?*"

Then he saw them, jogging forward past the stalled vehicles with their satchels of explosives.

"They're en route, sir," Laub reported to the commander, pointing.

The wind gusted again. This time Laub did shiver, but it was only partly due to the cold. The major couldn't shake the feeling of unease, of being watched.

—◂ ▸—

The dam formed part of the highway where the Halselva stream flowed into the fjord. Four hundred meters up the valley, *Spetsnaz* Captain Cyril Okhotnik, the erstwhile leader of the USSR's Olympic Biathlon team, lay prone atop a small tarp laid over the snow. They'd arrived at this destination on skis meant for competing against the world's best, though this was a much more *practical* use, if you asked him.

The athlete observed the milling knot of Norwegian officers on the road below him through the scope of his Dragunov SVD sniper rifle. To his right, another member of his team did the same. Behind them, a third ski soldier whispered into a high frequency radio. Today they were competing for far more than gold.

After slipping out of Lillehammer the previous morning, the Soviet biathletes had driven north on the E6 for twenty hours, stopping only for fuel and to steal what equipment they needed. In their wake they had left a small trail of bodies, including a security guard at a construction company who had come across the team as they raided the firm's explosives shed, and the driver of a truck carrying a load of pipes. After dumping the driver's body in a nearby stream, they'd overturned the trailer at a convenient bridge. Next, they had raided a local lumber yard for chainsaws and other equipment, then driven several dozen kilometers further to cut their first abatis. Their objective was the farthest north of any of their supposed Olympic companions, and there had been no time to lose on the trek north.

Okhotnik was disappointed a couple of hours later when a column of Norwegian Army vehicles rumbled through a village where the Soviets were devouring a quick breakfast. Apparently, the obstacles hadn't slowed the enemy as much as intended. The team leader almost despaired that his mission was a failure, but the column had been a small one and the biathletes resolved to redouble their efforts. They selected this site along the fjord north of Alta, and spent the morning and afternoon felling trees and preparing. Now with satisfaction the *Spetsnaz* looked down upon the fruits of their labor.

"*Sabra* reports they're on final approach," reported the radioman in a low voice. Okhotnik did not respond but continued to observe the knot of enemy officers through his scope, fixing his sights on the one with the map. *That's the commander*, he thought. His index finger remained outside the trigger guard, but he knew it would not be long now.

Laub froze and cocked his head at the sound. He wasn't sure he had heard it at first, but then it grew, the low grumble of jet engines from up the fjord. All the officers were looking that way now, shifting uneasily on their feet like a herd of antelope that smelled a wolf. They all squinted north.

Suddenly one man shouted, "I see them! Four aircraft, due north, coming in low!" From the rear of the column, vehicle horns, the warning for air raid, began to sound.

The battalion commander folded his map quickly and stuffed it into his parka, ordering, "To your posts! Get those Bofors guns into action now! I want—"

———

Captain Okhotnik watched as the man he guessed was the commander stuffed the map into his jacket and began issuing orders. It was time. He could hear the jets as well. "On me," he said in a low voice to the other sniper a few meters to his right. The other man did not move, except to join his leader in slipping his finger inside the trigger guard of his rifle.

The *Spetsnaz* officer applied slow pressure to the rifle's trigger mechanism, feeling the weight of the pull give way just so, just the way he had practiced it thousands of times over the years, just the way he had done when he had hunted Mujahedeen in Afghanistan and protesters in Kiev. He took in a breath, let it out, then allowed his finger to squeeze the trigger.

The round exploded out of the rifle's barrel. Before it had traveled halfway toward its target, it was followed by a second bullet from the other sniper, and already Okhotnik's semi-automatic rifle had chambered a second round, ready for a third target.

———

The commander was just turning away when Laub saw him spin backwards and crumple to the ground. Confused, Laub ducked as the report of the rifle shot washed over them. Then another officer dropped. As a second *crack* echoed in the cold, Laub knew instantly and screamed out, "SNIPER!"

It was too late. Laub never heard the third shot. The bullet slammed into his temple just below the helmet rim, and all went dark.

Okhotnik watched as four Su-24 bombers swept over the hapless column from north to south. Dozens of armored vehicles were trapped and in the open, packed together and waiting to be destroyed along the confining ribbon of the E6. He smirked, more than satisfied with his work.

The bombers began releasing their RBK-500 cluster bombs, first over the rear of the convoy, spacing them out so as to hit as many of the close-packed vehicles as they could. Through his scope Okhotnik saw the bombs work as, at a certain altitude, the outer panels of the weapons spun off and showered hundreds of anti-armor bomblets onto the vehicles below, detonating in fire-cracker strings of sparking explosions that sent shards of jagged, white hot metal through the thin top armor of Leopard tanks and M109 howitzers as easily as through the canvas tops of trucks.

Along the embattled column, fuel tanks exploded, ammunition cooked off, and the surviving Norwegian soldiers attempted to escape. Some tried to scramble up the icy cliff face on one side of the road while others slid, fell really, down to the small coves at the fjord's edge. A Norwegian shoulder launched missile shot up to harass the bombers, but a bomblet had exploded next to its launcher just as the soldier had squeezed the trigger, and the weapon went wild, missing badly. It was tragically impressive to Okhotnik as he watched the crew of a Bofors gun bring their piece into action on the crowded roadway, only to see them disappear in a hail of sparking cluster bomblets as the Fencers released bomb after bomb down the entire length of the column.

In a few moments the bombers were gone, winging south over Alta. The effect of their attack was devastating. They left in their wake dozens of disabled and burning vehicles. Minutes later, a flight of smaller MiG-27 fighter-bombers appeared overhead to work over what was left of the column with rockets. When these finished, less than a quarter of the battalion's vehicles remained operable and, working or not, they were still trapped on the E6 between cliffs, water, and fire. The men of the battalion had fared little better, with hundreds of soldiers lying dead or dying among the wrecks. Okhotnik and his men were packed up now, quickly and silently moving away from the columns of thin black smoke wafting into the frigid sky. The armored might of the Norwegian Army in the Far North was left in smoldering ruins. There would be no relief for any Norwegians farther north than this, the Olympian *Spetsnaz* team had seen to that.

 **CHAPTER 84**

1215 EST, Sunday 13 February 1994
1615 Zulu
US Coast Guard Sandy Hook Station, Ft. Hancock, New Jersey

A BBY SAVAGE APPLIED gentle downward pressure to the collective and descended towards the small patch of grass behind the Sandy Hook Coast Guard Station, nudging left to avoid the blue-painted water tower that loomed over the improvised landing zone. The area where she had elected to put down was small, tiny by most standards, but Abby knew her abilities. She also knew the value of face-to-face coordination in confused situations like this.

The Sea King's wheels settled down onto the grass, its rotors spinning mere yards from the water tower on one side and the watch center's parking lot on the other. Savage could see a Coast Guard officer standing on the pavement, ducking his bare head away from the downdraft of the aircraft's big rotor.

"I'm getting out to talk to him," Abby said into her intercom. Then she unplugged her helmet's umbilical, stood, and worked her way out of the cockpit between her own seat and Buck's. Abby's crew chief, waiting in the cargo compartment, opened the side door and she hopped down onto the ground.

She jogged across the grass towards the Coastie, awkward in her bulky anti-exposure flight suit and helmet. The man jogged towards her and they met at the edge of the parking lot.

"Lieutenant Savage, Fleet Angels," Abby introduced herself over the noise of her aircraft's rotors.

"Commander Ingalls," the other man returned the greeting. Abby was pleased to note that the Coastie recovered quickly from the realization that she was female and said simply: "Am I glad to see you!"

The man was obviously weighed down by concern. Ingalls' dark eyebrows were pinched in a frown, and his regulation mustache twitched as he spoke. Abby got right down to business, "Sir," she shouted through the swirling downdraft, "I've got four Sea Kings to put at your disposal. The other three are already heading out over the harbor. We topped off fuel at McGuire, so we're ready to do what you need us to. Just tell me where you want us."

Ingalls nodded. "I want you all working the *Queen Elizabeth 2* wreck. It's our biggest problem," he explained. "With you there I can use our local helicopters on some of the nearer rescue sites. FEMA has set up a frequency for air traffic control. The cruise ship is pretty far offshore, and there are hundreds of people in the water and in rafts, over a thousand actually." He handed her a piece of paper. "Coordinates to the wreck, and the air traffic control frequency."

Abby winced inside her helmet. *That many people in the North Atlantic in February? This isn't going to end well for a lot of them.*

"Roger sir," Abby answered, "My Sea Kings can fit two dozen rescues per trip. Where do you want us to take them?"

"We've got a rescue center set up at Montauk Beach," Ingalls shouted over the engines. "You can deliver them there. Ambulances will be standing by to take them to local hospitals. You can refuel at Gabreski as necessary. They're expecting you."

"Okay," Abby nodded, "anything else?"

Ingalls shook his head, then stuck out his hand. Abby took it, and the Coast Guard officer said, "Good luck, and thanks!"

"We'll get as many as we can for you, sir!" Abby assured him. She released his hand, turned, and jogged back to her bird. It would be a forty-minute flight from here out to the disaster off the southeast tip of Long Island.

— ◆ —

Volkhov studied the police cruiser parked lengthwise across the two-lane road leading to the Coast Guard station with disgust. The cruiser, along with its officer and a pair of Coast Guardsmen, sat two hundred meters ahead, directly astride his team's route to their target.

His casual reconnaissance of the site several days earlier, posing as a lost tourist trying to find the nearby World War One-era coastal artillery forts, had amazed him with how lax the security of this site actually was. He'd been able to drive right past the front of the enemy command center without being challenged by a single soul.

Now, things didn't look so easy. Volkhov sat in the front passenger seat of the cursed van, hours late to attack his target. A few minutes ago, a large helicopter had flown overhead in the direction of the command center, and Volkhov was sure that boded nothing good for his mission. Still, his professional pride mandated that he not be the weak link in the plan he had such an integral part in coordinating.

Volkhov decided that the task would not be that much more difficult. He saw only one police officer with the cruiser, his gray uniform and peaked cap distinct from the two Coast Guardsmen in blue dungarees and baseball caps. Only one of the three men even held a rifle. Volkhov made his decision.

"*Slushat menya,*" he ordered the other men in the van. *Listen to me.* He proceeded to outline the adjusted plan to his team.

The others nodded, and in moments his men were moving. The van backed up until it was out of sight of the American guards. Then the team's sniper slipped out with his American .303 deer rifle and disappeared to the left into the coastal scrub that lined the western side of the Sandy Hook peninsula. Volkhov waited five minutes, then nodded to the driver. It was time.

Slowly, the van rolled forward towards the roadblock. As it drew closer, the three Americans looked up at the approaching vehicle, though none of them seemed particularly concerned. When the van was within fifty meters, Volkhov gave the order, "Go!"

The van stopped. The side door slid open and one of the *Spetsnaz* soldiers stepped out, a small tube slung over his shoulder. Almost casually he snapped out the telescopic extension of the weapon and lifted the tube to his shoulder, aiming it at the police cruiser. Only then did the three men at the roadblock begin to react, but it was too late.

The M72 anti-armor rocket exploded out of its launcher and streaked into the cruiser with a loud *WHUMP*. The destruction the rocket caused to the police vehicle was actually quite underwhelming. The molten slug formed by the high explosive warhead, designed to pierce the armor of main battle tanks, went straight into one side of the car and splattered the interior with white hot beads of liquid metal. The force of the impact blew out the cruiser's windows and set some of the interior of the car on fire, but it was no Hollywood car-flipping fireball like Volkhov had seen on those ridiculous American action movies.

More importantly, the impact of the rocket caused the three Americans, who were slow to respond, to duck away. Their delay was fatal. Volkhov was already out of the van. He and the man who'd fired the rocket advanced, stubby assault rifles at their shoulders firing controlled bursts towards the roadblock, and dropped the three Americans in quick succession.

The driver pressed the accelerator to the floor, and the van roared forward. With fifty meters to build up speed, the vehicle rammed the police cruiser out of the way before hanging a left towards the command center. Volkhov and his counterpart sprinted in its wake. After several dozen meters they broke off to the right and crossed some tennis courts towards the parking lot at the rear of the Coast Guard building. Volkhov's subconscious again registered but ignored an input, this time the rumbling sound of vehicle engines from somewhere behind him. They needed to move fast.

The three remaining men of the team tumbled out of the van, now only two dozen meters from the front entrance of the command center, assault carbines at their shoulders and satchels of grenades slung at their sides. These three would assault the front door of the building, killing anyone they found and tossing grenades into each room for good measure. Volkhov and his compatriot would cover the rear entrance to the watch center, dealing with anyone who tried to escape out the back. Eliminating this command post and, more importantly, the people who manned it, would add one more obstacle for the Americans to overcome in their efforts to reopen their most important harbor.

The front door of the command center opened and another police officer emerged, his sidearm in hand. He was raising it towards the assault group when a shot from the sniper, crumpled him in the doorway. From behind the police officer, a blue uniformed Coast Guardsman fired two shots from his pistol, forcing one of the assaulters to take cover. Another shot from the sniper splintered the door frame next to the American's head, and he ducked. The police officer's legs disappeared as he was dragged inside.

By now Volkhov and his partner were in position, training their weapons at the rear entrance over the hood and trunk of a parked car. That was the moment when he could no longer ignore the rumble of engines behind him, and when his improvised plan began to fall apart.

——

Sergeant First Class Bert Martinez yanked back the charging handle on his M60 machinegun as the four M113 personnel carriers of 2nd Platoon, Bravo Company, 1-114 Infantry Regiment, New Jersey National Guard, careened left past the burning police cruiser onto the access road for Sandy Hook Coast Guard watch center, their mission: to protect it. Martinez swayed in his hatch as his vehicle, fourth in the order of march, clanked on its treads at full speed around the turn.

Martinez hadn't been happy about their mission up to this point. Taking his platoon's four boxy APCs over miles of suburban New Jersey roads and highways was never fun, and he did not enjoy the surprised and fearful looks of his fellow citizens, looking up at him and his loaded machinegun as the convoy clanked past. Now, though, he was glad they had the guns mounted and ready when they were needed.

Rolling up the road traversing the spine of Sandy Hook, expecting a quiet stretch at the end of the long drive, Martinez's experienced ears had registered the distinctive *wump* of an anti-tank rocket, something he'd heard many times before, but only once in combat. He immediately grabbed the hand mic for his vehicle's radio and called Lieutenant Kirby in the lead track, urging the young officer to pick up the pace. The lieutenant had complied immediately, and the four armored vehicles surged north up the road.

Martinez's eyes scanned the three bodies next to the burning police cruiser as the team blazed past. Holding onto the pistol grip of his machinegun, he reached down into the vehicle and grabbed the hand mic again. "Bravo Two-Six, this is Two-Five," he called to his platoon leader, "we may want to slow down, get our dismounts out, over."

There was no answer. Craning his neck, Martinez could see up to the front of the column, where Lieutenant Kirby was standing up in the hatch of own his track, riding towards the watch station at full speed, like an old-fashioned cavalry charge or something. He was about to depress the talk button on his hand mic again when he heard Kirby's young, excited voice yell over the radio, "This is Two-Six, follow me!"

The platoon sergeant heard a pop off to his left over the roar of the engines and looked that way. When he looked back, the hatch of the platoon leader's track was empty and the lead M113 was rolling to a stop.

Martinez didn't know what had happened to the LT, but he did know that someone needed to take charge of this mess.

"All stations, this is Two-Five," he ordered into his radio, "fan out! Two-One, swing around to the right through those tennis courts and secure the back of the building. Everyone else, drop ramps and set up three-sixty security. I think we have a sniper out there."

Immediately the two M113s ahead of Martinez turned off the road, the second one pulling to the left of the platoon leader's track, and the third tearing across the green tennis courts to the right. Martinez directed his own driver to pull up to the right of the LT's vehicle. Ahead, he saw a beat-up white van about twenty yards from the front of the Coast Guard station. He didn't see anyone near it at first, but then a man in civilian clothes stepped out from behind the vehicle.

Martinez saw immediately that the man held an assault weapon. The old NCO dropped down behind his machinegun as the gunman brought his own weapon up to his shoulder. Both men fired at the same time. Martinez heard rounds slam into the sloped frontal armor of his APC, splintering the wooden "trim vane" at the same time that he saw his own five-round burst stitch up the other man's torso, dropping him where he stood.

The sergeant didn't waste time with pleasantries. Keeping his eyes behind the gun, he shifted his aim slightly towards the white van. The M60 thundered again as Martinez pumped three long, ten-round bursts into the other vehicle, riddling it with seven-point-six-two millimeter slugs. By the time Martinez ceased fire, the rear ramps of all four of the APCs were down and the citizen soldiers of the platoon were pouring out, their M16 rifles at the ready.

"Behind the van!" Martinez shouted to the nearest squad leader, a man who owned a plumbing business when he wasn't playing soldier. The man nodded and, without hesitating, advanced slowly towards the van at the head of a wedge formed by the other members of his squad.

Then Martinez heard another *pop*, followed by a scream from his left. Looking that way, he saw another one of his soldiers writhing on the ground, grasping at his knee.

"AHHH!" the man kept yelling, then, "He got me! I saw him, over there in the brush! He got me!" The man took his hand away from the bloody mess of his knee long enough to point southward, towards the coastal shrub on the landward side of the peninsula.

Martinez didn't see what the wounded man did, but he quickly rotated the ring-mounted machinegun until it was pointing over the left side of the track, then let loose a long burst from the M60, spraying the brush from one end to another while two soldiers dragged the wounded man hissing and cursing back to the cover of an M113.

"Third Squad," Martinez shouted, "get over into that brush and flush that sniper out!"

The platoon sergeant turned his attention back towards the van, where the plumber's squad was converging. Another gunman darted out from the far side of the vehicle, trying to bring his weapon around. He died in a fusillade from half a dozen M16s. A few seconds later the plumber squad leader gave a thumbs up signal back towards his sergeant.

Martinez, continuing to cover the squad moving towards the sniper, heard firing erupt behind him, from the back side of the watch center. He snatched up his radio with his non-firing hand. "Two-One, this is Two-Five, what's going on, over?"

After a few moments the First Squad leader, a middle school history teacher, called back, "We've got a leaker to the north, boss. There were two of them. We got one, but the other scooted. Two of my people are wounded," there was a pause, then the squad leader came back, "Not bad, though. Both of them are good. Want me to chase, over?"

Martinez looked around. Where was the LT? The platoon was getting scattered to the four winds, what with one squad moving south to flush out the sniper, another clearing around the van, and now his Third Squad asking to go off in chase of one man. The decision was quick, "Negative, Two-One, do not pursue," Martinez ordered. "I want you to secure the building. Park your track to cover the back entrance. I'm going in to see if everyone inside is all right. Out."

Martinez ordered his track's driver to replace him behind the gun, then slipped down and exited out the back ramp of the M113, grabbing his M16 as he went. He was just starting forward when the platoon's weapons squad leader, a friend, called to him, "Bert!"

The platoon sergeant didn't like the resigned tone in the man's voice. He stopped cold, then turned and walked to where the squad leader was standing, beside their LT's track. The squad leader nodded his head toward the open ramp, a grim look on his face.

Ducking inside the M113, the first thing Martinez saw was the body of Lieutenant Kirby, stretched out between the benches that lined both sides of the vehicle's interior. The platoon's medic, an EMT by trade, was applying pressure to the officer's chest through Kirby's open flak vest, but Martinez could see that the floor of the APC was awash in blood. The medic looked up at Martinez and gave a slow, sad shake of the head.

Martinez knelt next to his platoon leader. The young man's mouth was opening and closing like a fish out of water. Then his eyes caught sight of Martinez, and he focused long enough to croak, "Did, did we get, get 'em, Sarge?"

Martinez's answer caught in his throat as he took his lieutenant's hand in his own. He composed himself, not caring anymore about the young man's misuse of his title. "Yes," the sergeant said, trying not to let his voice break, "we got 'em. You did good, sir, real good."

He thought he saw Kirby's chin try to nod once. Then the lieutenant's eyes lost their focus, and Martinez felt his hand go limp. He looked up at the platoon medic, who felt the LT's neck for a pulse. There was none. The medic withdrew his bloody hands, then threw the bandage he had been working with down in disgust before letting his head fall into his hands.

Martinez laid Kirby's hand across his still and bloody chest. After laying a gentle hand on the medic's shoulder, he told him, "Ryan, we've got wounded guys out there. Go see to them."

The medic nodded, and they both exited the vehicle into the gray light of afternoon. For the first time since the firefight began, the platoon sergeant let himself slow down. Somewhere in the distance he could hear sirens approaching. His hands began to shake, but he stopped that before anyone saw it by clenching them into fists. *That*, at least, wasn't hard to do. Anger was welling up inside him and it wasn't just about Kirby or Sandy Hook, it was an anger for the entire New York area. It wasn't supposed to be like this, he raged. Wars were supposed to be fought "over there," not here at home. Yet, here they were, duking it out at a Coast Guard station.

He felt that he'd failed in his most basic task of keeping his LT alive, of mentoring him and helping him to learn the profession of arms. Kirby had been a good kid, eager, aggressive, the kind of platoon leader that any platoon sergeant worth his salt loved, and he was dead because Martinez hadn't spent the time to teach him about tactical patience. He clenched his fists tighter. *No*, he told himself, *Kirby is dead because some Russian came over here and shot him. Came over here to our home, unprovoked, to kill our countrymen.*

Martinez looked up as a blue uniformed Coast Guard officer came around the side of the M113, led by the plumber. The officer wore silver oak leaves on his collar. Martinez straightened and saluted. The officer returned the gesture quickly, then offered his hand to Martinez. The platoon sergeant noticed the name "Ingalls" stenciled on the officer's name tape.

"I can't thank you boys enough," Ingalls was saying. "We thought we were goners there for a second until you rolled up. You got here just in the nick of time."

The National Guard sergeant released the Coast Guard officer's hand and said, "Don't thank me, sir. Thank him." His head inclined towards the M113 where Kirby's body lay. "He's the one who led us here."

Ingalls nodded, understanding.

Martinez gave the Coast Guard officer another salute and walked away to see to his platoon's positions. *He* was the platoon leader now, and he had a command center to secure. He wasn't about to let his LT's sacrifice be in vain.

— —

Volkhov drove the car south on the trunk road that led off the peninsula. After barely escaping from that blasted American armored vehicle, crashing like an angry bull into the parking lot between himself and his target, Volkhov and his partner had tried to sneak away from the soldiers spilling out of the boxy track. They were seen crossing the grassy field between the lot and a water tower. They sprayed rounds from their assault carbines back towards the Americans, then made a run for it, but somewhere along the way the other man had gone down.

Volkhov kept running, eventually making it to a tourist area at an old artillery casemate on the east side of the peninsula. There was only one car in that lot, its owner taking pictures of dark pillars of smoke rising out to sea. Volkhov killed him, after ensuring that he had the man's keys.

A line of police cars, lights flashing and sirens blaring, roared past headed towards the Coast Guard Station. The *Spetsnaz* officer was filled with rage at the failure of his mission, but for now he held it down. It had all become impossible when the soldiers had arrived. If Volkhov and his team had been just a few minutes earlier, they'd have wiped out every person in that building. Instead, here he was, evading to save himself.

Half a mile down the road, Volkhov pulled off onto the shoulder and waited, engine idling. He looked west towards the coastal scrub. After a moment, a figure stood up and jogged towards him. It was his sniper, sans the hunting rifle and gripping his forearm, blood oozing from between tightly clenched fingers.

As his wounded man climbed into the car, Volkhov counted his losses. Of the six members of his team, four were dead. Or captured, Volkhov allowed.

He couldn't be sure. Probably dead. The one next to him was wounded. That left only himself. *Well*, he thought as he pulled back onto the road bearing south, *that will have to be enough.*

 **CHAPTER 85**

1730 CET, Sunday 13 February 1994
1630 Zulu
Tromsø Lufthavn, Tromsø, Norway

OLSEN WRESTLED TO keep his wounded jet level as he descended towards the Tromsø airstrip. He refused to let himself even glance left, where he knew the wing was streaked dark from multiple jagged punctures. The vertical stabilizer was in similar shape, compliments of the shrapnel from the missile that had nearly killed him. The port flaps were non-functional. He could still use his tail rudder, though he didn't trust the damaged control surfaces to hold on through anything but the gentlest of maneuvers.

Looking down, Olsen saw the deep blue of the Tromsøysundet Strait give way to icy white surf breaking against the jagged islets and rocks sticking up from Tromsøya Island. *Almost there*, he urged his wounded machine, descending towards the black strip of asphalt ahead. A crosswind gusted from the east, and it took all of Jan's concentration to nudge his normally nimble Falcon back into a good landing glide. The rocky coastline gave way to the colorful, snow-covered homes to his left. Then he was flying over the tarmac, painted white lines and black skid marks streaked backwards past his cockpit on both sides.

Just before his wheels touched down, Olsen remembered to question whether his landing gear had been damaged. If so, if even one of the tires on his tricycle landing gear was flat, then this would be a very interesting landing indeed.

It had already been an interesting flight south. After escaping from the Soviet aerial ambush around the Backstop radar, Olsen had limped north-westwards at low altitude, trying to avoid any subsequent dogfights. The acrid smell of burning oil permeated the cockpit, and unexpected *thunks* told him when another piece of his aircraft had broken off and fallen away. He had even avoided calling on his radio for fear that the sensors on the Soviet electronic warfare aircraft lurking to the east would sniff him out and vector a pair of fighters to finish him off. Despite his precautions, he narrowly avoided a flight of four MiG-27s as the Russian jets dove to bomb the Norwegian Coast Guard frigate *Nordkapp*. The Soviet pilots, apparently intent upon their assigned target, hadn't noticed Jan in his crippled Falcon beneath them, and Olsen wasn't about to attract their attention.

Not until he was further northwest did Jan breathe a sigh of relief. The likelihood of Soviet fighters patrolling up here, far from their EW and radar support, was much less. Olsen had coaxed his F-16 around to a southwesterly heading over his country's jagged fjord lands. That was when he became aware of his true peril. Deciding that the time was right to break emissions silence, he had keyed his radio to call Magic, letting the controllers on the AWACS know that he was alive, but there had been no answer. He realized the radio had been silent since the missile had exploded, damaged in the blast, no doubt. Jan had no way of knowing if anyone was receiving his transmissions. He was alone.

He had considered his options. The flight of MiG-27s were troublingly far to the west. That meant Tromsø, where he had launched from and where he was attempting to land, was also in danger, and maybe even the main base at Bardufoss as well.

The rear wheels of Jan's jet touched down in puffs of burning rubber on the icy, windswept runway. Jan cringed, waiting for a tire to blow, or a landing strut to collapse, but nothing happened. The Falcon's front wheel touched down with a *thump*. All three wheels were down and he was rolling safely. Now Jan dispensed with all pretensions of being gentle. He threw his engine into full reverse, deployed what flaps still worked in his wings, and stood on his brakes. His trusty fighter shuddered to a stop half-way down the runway. Only then did he allow a ragged breath to escape from his lips.

A guide vehicle approached, orange lights flashing. The driver signaled Jan to follow, and he taxied off to the right. In a minute they were in among the hangars north of the small airport's passenger terminal. Olsen saw that the large doors of one of the hangars was open, revealing a ground crew swarming over a pair of F-16s, one of them a two-seater that reminded him of Sven. He was sure he'd seen Sven Hokensen, in his "B" model F-16, eat a missile before Jan's jet had experienced its own mid-air interaction with a Soviet weapon. He had to assume that Sven was dead. Just like Bjorn. Just like three of the other pilots that had flown north to Banak with him this morning.

Jan, following directions, brought his beleaguered Falcon to a stop on the far side of the hanger next to a C-130 transport. Ground crew hooked a ladder over the edge of the cockpit, but Olsen sat for a moment, remembering. What could he have done differently to keep his fellow pilots alive? He replayed each engagement in his head: the one Flanker shot down in the opening seconds of the war and another possible, the two MiG-23s over the North Cape. That was when he'd lost Bjorn. Should they have stayed together? Then on this second ill-fated sortie he had bagged another MiG-23 and a Fencer with Sven tight on his wing, before his friend's F-16B had disappeared. Should they have split up for the engagement? Finally, there was that last Flanker in its scissor turn...The realization hit Jan: *two Flankers, three Floggers, a Fencer, and another Flanker possible, that was at least six kills, maybe seven. I'm an ace!* Somehow the elation he had always imagined he would feel at this, the pinnacle of any fighter pilot's career, did not come. He just wanted to kill more of them.

Jan pulled the canopy release, allowing the perspex dome to raise, exposing him to the icy wind blowing in from the east. He was suddenly very tired. An overwhelming urge to close his eyes right here in the cockpit and go to sleep forced aside all other emotion. Then another icy blast struck him and he forced himself to get out of his seat and down the ladder.

A group of half a dozen pilots, all wearing exposure suits and carrying their helmets, emerged from the terminal walking towards the hangar just as Jan's feet touched solid ground. One of them peeled off in Olsen's direction, and Jan recognized yet another old comrade. Lieutenant Colonel Arne Anders, he'd been one of Jan's flight instructors years ago, someone he looked up to as a mentor.

"Jan!" Anders called through the icy wind, "Good to see you alive! We've heard things have been rough up there." He took Olsen's hand, looking onto the younger man's eyes.

"Yes, well," Olsen answered, releasing the older officer's hand, "I got…I got a few of them. Six, maybe seven, but I need a new plane." He swept his hand back towards the pockmarked Falcon.

Anders nodded. "I can see that," he said, surveying the shredded wing and tail. Then he bit his lip. Jan had spent enough time with this man in flight school to know that Anders only did this when he was deciding whether one of his trainees was ready for the next step.

After a moment Anders looked back into Olsen's eyes and said seriously, "Jan, I've got a plane for you, a two-seater. If you feel up to it." He indicated the F-16B Jan had seen.

Jan hadn't flown a "B" model Falcon since flight school. The aircraft handled somewhat differently than the single-seat F-16A he had just landed, but it didn't matter. He would have said anything, *anything* in that moment to get back into the sky, back to where he could kill more invaders. "Of course," he answered quickly.

"Very good," Anders said as another gust of wind caused both men to shiver. "One of my pilots, very junior, just froze up during the mission brief. I grounded him. I'm going up with two flights, seven ships in all. You would make eight. You can fly with me, since I was only going to have three in my flight anyway. I have a jet armed, fueled, and waiting for a pilot. But I have to warn you, Jan, we've got a tough mission."

"What's the mission, sir?" Olsen asked.

"It looks like the Soviets are about to make a drop on Banak," Anders said, "an ad-hoc force including 340 Squadron is going to support us in trying to stop it." In that moment Olsen knew the situation was bad. The Soviets had just driven him and thirty other pilots in state-of-the-art air superiority fighters more than two hundred kilometers *west* of Banak. Now Anders and his fellow pilots were going back to the airbase with a scratch force of whatever could be thrown together? What had happened during his half-hour of radio blackout? 340 Squadron flew the F-5A Freedom Fighter. It was a good jet, small and maneuverable, but it was no match for the modern Flankers and Fulcrums that were swarming over Northern Norway at this moment. The plane didn't even have a radar! If this squadron, which specialized in ground attack, was being committed to the fray under those circumstances, *Things must be as desperate as they feel*, Olsen thought.

"...we're going to loop up around the Cape and come at Banak from the north," Anders was saying. "We'll take our F-16s in at low altitude up the Porsangerfjord and try to get in among the transports before they drop. 340 Squadron and some American and Dutch fighters are going to try to draw the Russian CAP off to the south long enough for us to get in, hit the wide-bodies, and get out."

"Wait," Olsen stopped the older man, "340 Squadron is being used as air-to-air, not air-to-ground?" He had assumed the F-5As would be conducting ground support.

The other man nodded gravely. "Us and them are all that's left to feed into the fight for now," Anders said slowly. "As I said, the plan is for 340 Squadron and the Americans to draw the escorts away so that *we* only have to deal with defenseless transports. With luck, we'll never see a Russian fighter. Do you still want in? You know better than us that it won't be easy, and I won't order you."

Jan swallowed once as he considered. He wanted desperately to get another shot at the Russians, but, *I'm not suicidal. Is that what this is? A suicide mission?* Again the fatigue hit him. He was exhausted after two hard sorties. He needed to rest, to process what had happened. But could he really do that when Johansen, now isolated with his command up at Banak, was counting on him? *I promised him*, Olsen remembered. *I promised him we wouldn't leave him on his own to die.*

Jan made his decision. "Where's my plane, sir?" he asked.

Anders nodded, unsmiling. "Follow me."

CHAPTER 86

1750 CET, Sunday 13 February 1994
1650 Zulu
Two kilometers south of Banak Airbase, Lakselv, Troms, Norway

JOHANSEN WINCED IN pain with each step as he climbed the stairs. His wounded shoulder had been numb in the minutes after the shard of wood embedded itself in his flesh, but now his entire back felt as if it was on fire. It was all Erik could do to keep climbing instead of sitting down, right here in the stairway. If he could just be still for a few moments, but there was no time. Sweat beaded on his forehead beneath his white cloth-covered helmet despite the chill air flowing down the stairway. The *rittmester* kept climbing.

The stairway led to the second floor of a small house south of the town of Lakselv. No lights were on in the home, and the insides of the rooms and hallways were dark with the fading light of evening. Johansen emerged into an upstairs bedroom with a south-facing window, open to a frigid breeze. Two soldiers huddled at the window, stamping their feet. One of them held a set of binoculars in his gloved hands and peered south, while the other held the hand-mic of a radio set that leaned against the wall beneath the window sill. A cable snaked out the window to an improvised wire antenna draped back over the house's roof in the direction of the gun battery at Banak. Three rifles leaned against the pastel blue-painted wall, creating a jarring contrast in what was clearly a child's room. The third member of the team, a *kaptein* of artillery, was in the back of the room, examining a map spread over a bed under the red-filtered beam of an L-shaped flashlight.

They were one of the two artillery forward observer teams that had accompanied Erik on the flight from Bardufoss this morning, and this was the best vantage point covering the southern approaches to the town. A hundred meters to the south, a section of Johansen's B Troop was deployed in concealed positions among the brush and low trees on either side of the E6. One disadvantage of the reconnaissance squadron's organization was that Johansen only possessed two Troops with which to maneuver, and these were stretched very thin to defend Banak. Another was the size of the defense in general. *It doesn't feel like any number would be enough.*

The *kaptein* looked up from his map. Erik knew Hans, he was a good man, great at his job, and a talented alpine skier. There was no time for ski-talk. "Any changes?" Johansen asked, trying not to let the pain affect his voice.

The artillery officer shook his head. "Well," he answered, "they've got a smoke pot burning here now." He indicated a series of small, irregularly-shaped lakes just to the east of the E6 two kilometers south of town. "That's the best spot for an airdrop if that's what the Sov's are planning."

"I think that's what they have in mind," said Johansen, trying to excise the tone of dark foreboding from his voice.

A gust of icy wind whipped in through the open window, and both men tensed against the cold. Then the artilleryman asked quietly, "Any word from Battalion?"

Erik didn't answer. He'd heard nothing from Laub for hours. *Nothing.* The last time he saw a friendly aircraft overhead was, well, when he had watched one of the F-16s taking off from the airfield eat a cluster bomb. *We really are being left out here on a limb,* he thought. *Where are Olsen and the rest of his pilots? Where is the rest of the army?* He decided no answer was the best answer at this point. Again, his mind went to the "Poster on the Wall." *All available forces must be committed to the defense, resistance will continue even if the situation is hopeless. Hopeless,* Johansen thought grimly, *is where we might be.*

Framed by the window's rectangle, Erik could see a thick column of purple smoke rising over the bare branches of the stunted deciduous trees that covered the valley floor. The Soviets who landed an hour ago would only have one reason for setting up such a smoke pot: a signal. *Undoubtedly to mark a drop zone for aircraft bringing parachutists.* The thought made him shudder, the movement inflamed the pain in his shoulder, which sent further un-asked for shudders through his body.

Working not to flinch, he turned his attention to the map, asking the artillery *kaptein*, "You've plotted targets for the guns?"

"Yes," the other man brought a finger down on the map, indicating a spot about a kilometer south of their current position. "The best place to hit them will be here. If they drop on the lakes like we expect, this gravel road will be their best route off the drop zone, and the river here will funnel them onto the E6." The man continued in a relentless kind of way, "I have three pre-planned targets plotted, here, here, and here," his finger pointed out each target, but Johansen barely registered them. "And one more on each of the lakes. It would be better if we could have registered the guns but—"

Erik shook his head. "No, we have to keep them hidden for as long as possible, until we can use them to best effect. I think those helicopters put some observers up there," he jabbed at the map where sheer cliffs bounded the valley in which they found themselves, "and they'll be able to see the guns as soon as they fire. You'll have to adjust as best you can."

The artilleryman acknowledged his responsibility. "Registering" the guns was a process where observers would call in single rounds of artillery to ensure that the howitzers were laid correctly and that their fire would land accurately. Not doing this in advance—firing on a map plot only—was a risk, but under the circumstances, Erik judged, not a large one. Remembering how he had received his wound, Johansen thought it better to keep this trump card hidden for now.

Suddenly both he and the artillery *kaptein* were standing stock still, cocking their heads to one side and listening to a sound growing loud enough to identify. The maddening buzz of the Soviet control plane, circling overhead, had long since faded into their subconscious. This sound was new. It wasn't the low, screaming roar of attack jets, which were by now all too familiar. No, this sound was more like the droning propellers on the control plane, Johansen decided, only there were more. *Many more.* Johansen tensed and pain shot down his back again. The sound was growing with each passing second. "That's it," Johansen said quickly, the burning pain in his back pushed away for later, "They're coming."

— • —

Romanov looked west towards the gathering dusk where three columns of Antonov An-12 transports were descending towards drop altitude in vees of three.

In the long-shadowed panorama of snow, rock, and forest surrounding the town, Romanov could also see their drop zones, where three thick columns of colored smoke billowed. South of Lakselv, up the valley from the town, purple smoke contrasted sharply with the whites, blues, and browns of the small frozen lakes that dotted a sparsely treed plateau just east of the E6. This was where the main assault would drop. Snow-covered farm fields east of the town sprouted a similarly obvious red smoke column, while a yellow column rose from a large sandbar that sat aside the E6 north along the west bank of the Porsangerfjord. These drop zones would receive supporting assault elements, isolating whatever Norwegian defenders were present at Banak.

Sokolov was busy nearby, giving final updates and orders via radio to the commander of his assault battalion, who even now were standing up inside the crowded transports, preparing to jump. Romanov listened on his own headset as the assault pattern unfurled. Had he been in Sokolov's place, Romanov would have preferred to be one of the jumpers at this moment, but he knew his friend was right to be where he was. An officer's place was where he could best direct the operation, and not necessarily forward with his troops. Soviet officers often forgot this principle, leading too far to the front and becoming casualties, leaving their formations leaderless as a result. Despite his friend's characteristic bluster, he was a cool professional in situations like this, which was how he had risen to command one of the Red Army's elite *desant* regiments in the first place, just like Ilya.

Ilya's headset crackled to life again, "All units, this is Control Two," called the officer aboard the A-50 AWACS, orbiting now fifty miles to the east. "Enemy aircraft approaching high from the southwest and low from the northwest. *Rapira* Three, take the northern group. Vector three-three-zero to intercept. *Grif* and *Sushka* flights, vector two-five-five to engage."

Romanov hadn't noticed the escorting fighters around the transports before this moment. Now he saw the setting sun glint off cockpits and wings as the smaller MiGs and Sukhois banked from their positions abeam and above the columns of An-12s and accelerated on their intercept courses towards the approaching NATO jets.

Sokolov turned to Ilya and said over the drone of the engines, "I expected this. Those NATO dogs can't let us land unopposed. The *VVS* has promised me the 'strongest support' for the landing." His tone and body language betrayed his anxiety, openly showing what Sokolov really thought of his nation's air service and their promises. "We shall see."

— —

Flying just off the wingtip of Lieutenant Colonel Anders' F-16A, Jan Olsen concentrated on maintaining his station in the four-ship formation as the nimble F-16s crested the snow-covered western wall of the Porsangerfjord and nosed down to skim above the gray waters below. Overhead the sky reflected the orange of the setting sun. In the shadow of the high rock walls night had already fallen. Jan kept his jet just behind and to the left of Anders, trusting his erstwhile flight instructor to not fly them all into the sea. It was a relief not to have the lead for a change.

Behind Anders' flight of four followed a section of two F-16As, and another pair was just cresting the fjord wall further north. They were trusting in the rugged, snow-covered granite hills and cliffs to keep them hidden until they were in and among the Soviet transports. Magic had been giving them updates on the approaching heavies, but Russian jamming was interfering with their radios more and more as they drew near to Banak. Jan only caught snippets of the AWACS's instructions through the electronic fog. *Doesn't matter anyhow,* Jan thought, *we are all, Norwegians and Soviets, making for the same patch of air.* For what seemed like the hundredth time since he'd taken off from Tromsø, Jan reviewed in his mind the scratch plan that they would be executing in the coming minutes.

If everything was on schedule, the first arm of the NATO thrust would be developing from the south any moment now. Four Dutch pilots would be streaking in at high altitude from the southwest in their F-16As. Supporting them was a pair of AMRAAM-wielding American F-15s and a single Norwegian MLU F-16. Finally, four of the hopelessly outmatched F-5As from 340 Squadron would try to make themselves look as much like F-16s as possible. This ad-hoc force's mission was to press in on the southernmost transport column as it approached its drop zone. Two more Norwegian F-5As, rocketing east from Andøya on afterburner, would join the fray as backup. Short bursts of choppy radio conversations told Olsen that the southern thrust was unfolding on time. It appeared that the Dutch, American, and Norwegian pilots were being met by Su-27s and MiG-23s.

As Olsen and his comrades sped south towards Banak at wave top level a twisting furball developed at high altitude to the southwest. Over the radio Olsen managed to cobble together the story: An initial salvo of AMRAAMs from the F-15s knocked down two MiG-23s and sent an Su-27 turning for home on only one engine, and the Americans held back as planned, cautious of the lurking MiG-31s which had proven so dangerous earlier in the day. Their Dutch comrades bore in to press the advantage.

Soviet radars began to burn through the NATO jamming and missiles shot out towards the oncoming Dutchmen. Olsen could hear snippets of radio calls as Dutch pilots turned and released chaff in well-rehearsed defensive maneuvers to confuse the oncoming missiles. One missile sent several pieces of shrapnel through the tail of an F-16, disabling its rudder. The Dutch pilot broke off, leaving his three comrades with the Norwegian MLU F-16 and F-5As to press the assault.

The transmissions became clearer as these badly outnumbered aircraft, decoys really, put the maneuverability of their nimble Falcons and Freedom Fighters to good use. "Splash one!" came a Dutch voice over the net followed by frantic calls for evasion. Jan imagined the two sides intermixed, twisting and turning, the pilots trying to get onto their opponents' tail for a gun or missile shot. The Norwegian F-5As joined the fray as he heard "Splash Two" in a voice he thought was familiar.

Olsen hoped that surprise would be enough to make up for what they lacked in strength. He knew the nineteen NATO aircraft pressing in towards the three streams of Soviet transports weren't nearly as powerful as the force in his earlier flight, particularly since the F-5As were inferior as air superiority fighters. *This is what we have though, so we'll have to work with it,* Olsen thought.

Olsen's element was now close enough that he could clearly hear all the radio calls of the Dutch and Norwegian pilots burning through the Soviet jamming. Their voices were curt and disciplined, spoken in tones that communicated the intense stress of the combat in which they were engaged.

"Eagle Five, this is Three, you've got a Flanker on your tail!" called one. "Break right, now!"

"Four, two MiGs to your two o'clock high, diving. Watch out!"

"This is Three, Fox Two!" Then a few seconds later, "Splash! Splash a MiG!"

The decoy group did their best to threaten the transports, evading to the northeast whenever they could, but the confusion of the furball and the Soviet numbers prevented them from drawing within range of the lumbering heavies still more than thirty miles away. Neither could the F-15s get in range to fire their remaining AMRAAMs at the paratrooper-laden planes. However, the goal of this thrust wasn't to strike the transports but to draw the Soviet escorts away long enough for the eight F-16s, approaching from the north so low that sucking seawater into their engines was a real concern, to get in among the An-12s and do the real damage.

Looking ahead over the foaming white tipped wavetops, Olsen could just now make out the glow from the fires around Banak at the head of the fjord. High and to the left he could see the dark silhouettes of the lead transports, a line of black dots against the orange sky, flying west. *Almost.* Olsen tightened his jaw in anticipation, all thoughts of weariness behind him.

— —

The high-G maneuver forced Major Sasha Mitroshenko down in his seat. He grunted through the turn, bringing the nose of his fighter down towards the floor of the fjord. Glancing at his controls confirmed that he still possessed four of his original six R-27 radar-homing missiles and one of his two short-range R-73 heat-seekers after his earlier engagement over southern Finnmark.

Fuel was Mitroshenko's cause for concern at this point. The Soviet major's mouth twitched into a steely grin. He only had fuel enough for one quick dogfight on afterburner. *Let's see if I can't make ace in one day.*

Control Two in the Beriev A-50 was giving Mitroshenko and his wingman their directions, reporting numerous unidentified contacts entering the fjord from the north, but could not get a good count due to radar shadow. One thing was certain: the contacts were not Soviet and must therefore be engaged *before* they could reach the transports. Behind Mitroshenko's two Su-27s came four smaller MiG-29s, who'd been screening the northern flank of the transports.

The Flanker bottomed out of its turn a thousand meters above the dark waters, heading south towards the airbase. His sharp eyes scanned below for any sign of the contacts. He didn't want to use his radar yet, preferring to maintain the element of surprise for as long as possible.

There! A pair of dark shapes flitted above the wavetops. Adjusting his eyes, he saw four more two kilometers ahead. Keying his radio he ordered curtly, "Two, this is Crane Lead. I see two enemy jets directly below. You engage. I will take the four farther ahead. Don't activate your radar until the last moment, and don't engage until I tell you!"

"*Da*, Lead," answered his wingman, and they dipped their noses to dive on the intruders from behind.

Mitroshenko pushed his throttles forward to their stops, remaining high for the few moments it took to close the distance with the lead group of NATO jets. He could now identify them as F-16s in the fading light. Reversing roles with the nimble fighters who had ambushed his flight in the opening moments of the war, he intended to press every advantage to gain sweet revenge. He locked the seeker of his one remaining infrared-guided R-73 onto the rear-most enemy aircraft. When the indicator buzzed in his ear that the missile had gained a good lock, he squeezed the trigger on his joystick.

As his missile left its rail, Mitroshenko ordered, "Engage NOW!"

The flash of his missile's rocket motor briefly dazzled him in the fading light and shadows. The weapon shot forward, but Mitroshenko didn't watch it. Instead, he reached down and energized his radar, quickly acquiring the contacts ahead. He locked onto the Falcon furthest to the right and squeezed his trigger a second time, this time sending a radar-guided R-27 streaking forward.

———

Olsen was skimming across the water at full military power. They were close. Anders had just given a clipped order to ascend towards the transports, only fifteen miles away. Suddenly, Olsen heard the flight leader of the trailing section call frantically, "Bobcat Lead, this is Five, you've got—"

A yellow flash lit up the darkening valley. Olsen felt an explosion buffet his jet. Looking around quickly he saw the fourth jet in their flight, the one on the far left, disintegrating in a fiery explosion. He was about to key his radio to warn Anders when another flash lit his cockpit from the right. He twisted his head to see that the third member of their flight spiral into the sea. Then Jan's mind registered that his radar warning receiver was blaring.

Olsen tensed. The radio net was alive with frantic calls from the formations to their rear.

"This is Bobcat Five, I'm hit! Ejecting!"

"Six, they're behind you! Break left, NOW, NOW, NOW!"

Anders' voice cut through the panic, calm and collected. "Bobcat Flight, this is lead. Abort! I say again, abort! Jan, break right and get out of here."

Olsen complied immediately with the abort order, banking sharply up and to the right, but immediately realized that Anders hadn't followed. Craning his neck over to look back, he saw his one-time instructor continuing to ascend towards the transports.

"Lead, what are you doing?" Olsen shouted desperately.

"Get out of here, Jan," Anders repeated. "That's an order. I'm going for the transports."

Olsen, his heart pounding, continued his hard, climbing bank towards the lip of the western fjord wall looking back desperately for their assailants. Back up the valley, the surviving F-16s of the squadron were scattering as the Flankers tore into their formation with missiles.

———

Mitroshenko who had just locked another R-27 onto one of the two surviving Norwegian F-16s saw, his target suddenly bank to the west and climb. He needed to make a split-second decision; did he stay with the evading jet? Or target the one still making a beeline for the transports. The choice was an obvious one.

Behind him his wingman announced two victories as he annihilated the second pair of enemy jets, but Mitroshenko intended to take the lead in this turkey shoot. Locking his radar onto the Norwegian jet ascending directly ahead, just ten miles from the stream of transports, he squeezed his trigger once more.

— —

Olsen caught the white streak of an igniting rocket motor in the corner of his eye, showing him the location of their assailant. There was nothing he could do. He didn't even have time to shout a warning to Anders as he watched the Soviet missile shoot forward and explode. Anders' jet shuddered, then began to come apart. Olsen saw it slam into the waves in a massive white spray. There was no chute.

Jan didn't have time to grieve. Twisting to face forward he saw an outcrop of rock approaching fast. He yanked his stick backwards, and the nimble F-16 cleared the rocks with just feet to spare. The third section of Norwegian jets, forewarned by the carnage ahead, was breaking off to the west, pursued by two MiG-29s, screaming for help.

Olsen's rage returned now. He wasn't going to lose more friends to these damned Russians tonight, not when there was any ounce of fight left in him and his aircraft. Continuing to bank around to the northwest, he picked up an intercept course with the surviving members of his adopted squadron.

— —

Mitroshenko watched his target careen into the black waters, sending up a geyser of white spray. That made three of the four Norwegian's that he'd ambushed. *Ace!* He clenched his fist in triumph, but he still wasn't satisfied. He wanted the fourth. Pulling back to gain altitude, and also to allow his radar a better look, he was hunting again. In the gathering darkness he used the radar like an invisible flashlight, searching to the west. After a few moments he saw it on his scope: a lone contact fleeing northwest at treetop altitude.

As he was about to push his throttles forward to give chase, Mitroshenko remembered his fuel, which was perilously low.

In frustration Mitroshenko called his wingman. "Two, this is Lead. I have a contact fleeing northwest at low altitude, twenty kilometers range. Do you have fuel to pursue?"

The responses came quickly. "This is Two. Negative, Lead, my fuel state is critical."

Mitroshenko swore into his mask in frustration, but there was nothing to be done. Banking back east he called the controller on the A-50, "Control Two, this is Crane Lead. Fuel is critical. I am returning to base."

— —

Olsen was not fleeing. Quite the contrary, he was seeking an engagement. His instructor, mentor, and friend, Arne Anders, had just sacrificed himself so Jan could get away and he didn't intend for the man's heroism to go to waste. He would exact a price from the Russians for Anders, and Sven, and Bjorn, and all the others, and he would start by saving the remnants of this raid from their pursuers.

The two other F-16s *were* fleeing. They were tearing west at scrub-top altitude over the rocky, snow-blanketed tundra, their pilots trying to open the range from the pair of dangerous MiG-29s pursuing them. Jan didn't know exactly where they were, either his compatriots or their pursuers, but he put the pieces together based on their radio chatter.

Olsen's plan was to cut the corner and come up from below the pursuers, blasting them out of the sky before they knew he was there. At least he could put the Sidewinders under his wings to some use, if he couldn't use them to send planeloads of Soviet paratroopers to their deaths. His eyes scanned the northwest sky ahead and above, where the stars were beginning to wink from a deepening blue.

After a few moments his trained eyes fixed on two small, dark silhouettes. Seconds of squinting confirmed that they possessed twin vertical stabilizers, and now he could see the blue glow of their twin engines. *MiGs.*

Jan remained at low altitude, maneuvering into the wake of the Fulcrums and kicked on his afterburners to close the range. In short order the seeker of his first missile locked onto the exhaust of the rearmost MiG, the growl feeding his predatory smile.

When Jan assessed the range short enough, he squeezed the triggers twice, sending two AIM-9s shooting out towards the first MiG. Quickly shifting his attention to the other, he locking onto the second Soviet fighter. In seconds two more Sidewinders were darting towards that target as well.

The Soviet pilots never even knew the tables had been turned. Their first warning was when the flight leader's Fulcrum shuddered, then disintegrated in the twin explosions of Jan's missiles. The wingman fared little better. In seconds both MiGs, along with their pilots, were oily pyres of red and orange smoke billowing up from the snowy tundra.

Jan caught up with his shaken compatriots, and the three jets turned south for Tromsø. Five, out of the eight that had left to ambush the Soviet transports had been lost, and now those transports were disgorging their cargo of paratroopers into the skies around Banak.

 **CHAPTER 87**

1800 CET, Sunday 13 February 1994
1700 Zulu
Over Banak Airbase, Lakselv, Troms, Norway

S OUTH OF LAKSELV, Ilya Romanov watched parachutes blossom out of Antonov transports and descend over the frozen lakes. He'd long since estimated how small these drop zones were. Each of the four lakes measured just five hundred meters by two hundred meters, and they were separated by necks of rocky ground bristling with low trees and brush. *Even if the pilots are perfect in their navigation, Sokolov's* desantniki *will suffer casualties just from the landing.* He cringed as he watched round, white canopies fall towards the snow and trees among the huge parachutes that were conveying armored vehicles to the ground. He took a notebook from his breast pocket and began jotting notes. If anything, the drop zone that his first battalion would jump into tomorrow was *more* constrained, and far more dangerous, than the ones he was currently observing.

Retro-rockets on the vehicle platforms began to fire in flashes of yellow flame that were quickly obscured by dirty brown smoke and white clouds of snow and ice. One of the vehicles came down on the steep bank of a lake. Its rockets fired properly, but they were insufficient to prevent the BMD from rolling onto its side as it landed on the slope. Romanov reached into his tunic to finger a pendant of St. Michael and said a quick prayer for the safety of the crewmen inside.

"We expect at least ten percent casualties just from the drop," Sokolov said, echoing Romanov's thoughts. Ilya nodded, it was simply the nature of parachute assaults under these conditions.

The first three vees of transports carried armored vehicles and the lead jumpers for the lake drop zone. These aircraft were now banking away to the southeast. The following groups were loaded entirely with *desantniki*. As the BMDs and mortar carriers on the drop zone rumbled to life and clanked off of their drop platforms, they did so under a blanket of descending parachutes, each one conveying a paratrooper to earth. Several parachutes drifted down among the trees, slamming their human cargo into rocks and tree boughs, though the blows were at least softened by the deep snow. In minutes the drop was complete, and Ilya could see the long shadows of *desantniki* shrugging out of their parachute harnesses, most donning snow shoes but others struggling through knee-deep snow towards their assembly points.

Then the command plane banked away, and Ilya was treated to a view of the last parachutes descending onto the northern drop zone, where a company was jumping onto a large spit that jutted out into the dark water. This was the landing zone that made his skin crawl. On the frozen lakes, if the transport pilots misjudged, the jumpers would land in the trees, perhaps breaking bones or suffering concussions. If the pilots misjudged the drop over the icy waters of the fjord...*I must speak with the pilots before tomorrow's drop*, he decided, thinking of the coming mission. Ilya's ears perked up as the radio calls began to crackle over the net from the soldiers assembling below.

"*Yastreb* Command, this is *Lev* One-One-One, we are thirty percent assembled," reported the commander of the company on the lake. "I'm moving my vehicles to the western tree line. Mortars are establishing their firing positions, end."

"This is *Yastreb* Command, I acknowledge," responded Sokolov from his seat beside Ilya. "Have the mortars made radio contact with the spotter element?"

"*Nyet*," responded the on-ground commander, "but they are setting up now. It shouldn't be too much longer."

"Quickly," urged Sokolov. Ilya knew that his friend didn't have to outline the consequences of spending extra minutes getting into position.

"*Da*, Command. I'm moving to them now to see what is taking so long."

Sokolov looked at Ilya and said, "I hate to rely on the flyboys so much for our fire support. Better to do such things on the ground, in our own hands, *da?*" Sokolov had lifted his hands as if he were grasping the whole world in them.

Ilya smiled. Sokolov's bravado was showing through once more, indicating that he was beginning to feel confident about the outcome on the ground.

"Of course," Sokolov was saying with a smirk, "it is nice to have air support, when they can manage to drop their bombs on target and on time." Sokolov checked the time, "Speaking of which." He turned and keyed the transmit button on his radio headset and called, "Control Two, this *Yastreb* Command. What is the status of *Grach* Flight?"

The controller on the A-50 responded quickly, "*Yastreb*, Control. The lead element is five minutes out from Banak. Twelve aircraft total."

"Very good," Sokolov acknowledged with satisfaction. His dark hair and dark mustache were making him look ever more the Cossack raider that his forefathers had been.

— • —

Johansen could hear the clanking coughs of BMD engines and treads from the lakes to his south. The *rittmester* had counted a dozen transport aircraft, at least six of which dropped large platforms bearing armored assault vehicles. Now, Erik knew, the paratroopers were assembling to begin their assault on his post. He leaned against the wall and pulled his canteen out from inside his parka, where his body heat kept the water from freezing. He took a swig, returned the canteen, and then checked to make sure the magazine in his long barreled G3 rifle was seated properly. *Patience*, he told himself, *wait until the guns can have their full effect*. Minutes passed.

Judging the time right, Erik clapped the artillery *kaptein* on the shoulder, "Alright, Hans. It's time. Let them have it."

The man nodded grimly, then lifted his radio handset to his mouth and spoke, "One, this is One-Two Alpha. Fire mission: battery. Target: Zulu Tango Three-Four-Zero-Seven. Variable time, three rounds. Fire for effect, OVER!"

The command initiated a dance that the *rittmester* knew but that Hans, the artilleryman standing still beside him could have recounted in his sleep.

Five kilometers away, in the wood line to the northwest of the air strip, Erik could practically picture the muzzles of the six howitzers elevate and traverse in unison. Each of the well-trained gun crews performed the same identical drill around their piece, setting the fuse, slamming the high explosive shell coupled with its brass cartridge into the breech. In seconds, each gun was loaded and properly laid to lob its shell towards the Soviet paratroopers struggling through the deep snow of their drop zone seven kilometers away. Beside each howitzer stood a soldier holding the lanyard, a steady pull on which would send the dangerous projectile on its parabolic arc southward.

A metallic voice barked "FIRE" over speakers at each of the guns. Six gun detachment commanders echoed the command. Six hands pulled six lanyards and almost in unison six barrels belched flame and recoiled backwards. Six shells arced southward, unstoppable now with the force of their propellant behind them.

The gun crews would not wait to reload their pieces. The call for fire from the observer meant that each gun would fire three rounds in rapid succession, delivering eighteen high-explosive, air-bursting shells into the target area in a matter of seconds. Erik listened as, within seconds, each gun fired again as it was ready. Not quite in unison now, the muzzles bucked backwards in recoil to send a second salvo southward before the first even landed. Erik watched the drop zone ahead in grim anticipation of the destruction about to be unleashed on the struggling Soviet paratroopers. Nineteen seconds after the guns had first spoken, the first six high explosive rounds reached a point seven meters above the snow-covered lake and blasted a small hell of shrapnel on the Soviet soldiers below.

Romanov cringed as black puffs appeared in the air over the southern drop zone. Beneath the small, ugly clouds, puffs of snow rose from the flat blanket of the frozen lake as shrapnel streaked downward. Ilya saw several *desantniki* stagger and fall as razor-sharp shards of metal tore into their bodies. At the southern end of the lake, more shrapnel ripped the radio antennae off one of the BMDs, leaving its crew unable to communicate, though the metal shards failed to penetrate the armor of the assault vehicle.

As the second salvo of dirty black puffs appeared above the drop zone, Sokolov was already speaking with renewed urgency into his radio, "Spotter One, get me a fix on those guns! Where are they?"

———

Atop the cliffs west of Lakselv, Spotter One was well settled. The four-man observer team perched overlooking the town and airfield. Since alighting from the Mi-24s, the team had struggled the few hundred meters through the treeless tundra atop the ridgeline to arrive at their current position, where they were now hunkered down facing the north wind sweeping down the valley as night fell. Below them the broad sweep of the glacial valley formed a darkening panorama for the unfolding Battle of Banak; from the frozen lake drop zones nestled in stunted brush forests to the south, through the grid-like town of Lakselv directly below, to the single runway of the airstrip jutting northward into the waters of the fjord. From the trees at the northwest end of that airfield, the Red Army major of artillery had just observed the telltale flashes of howitzers firing into the deepening darkness.

"Give me the air support radio, now!" the senior observer, a major, ordered.

A junior man complied immediately, handing the major the hand mic and saying, "Command asks where the enemy guns are."

"*Yastreb* Command, Spotter One," the major said quickly, "I see the guns just to the northwest of the airfield, sector B-One-Five. Do you have something for me to hit them with?"

"Call *Grach* Lead on this frequency," Sokolov responded from aboard the command plane. "They are two minutes out."

"*Da*," acknowledged the major, then, "*Grach* Lead, *Grach* Lead, this is Spotter One, I have a target for you."

———

Grach, meaning "Rook" in Russian, was the Soviet nickname for the Su-25 ground attack jet. Another nickname bestowed by Soviet ground troops in Afghanistan was the *Rascheska*, or "Comb," a nickname it had earned because its underside bristled with hard-points for ordnance. It was heavily armored with two widely-spaced jet engines that ran the length of either side of the aircraft's fuselage and packed a thirty-millimeter cannon, making the "Frogfoot," as NATO had dubbed it, comparable to the American A-10 "Warthog."

Romanov could now see the first four Su-25s sweeping up the valley from the south, wings nearly sagging under the weight of the ordnance hanging off them. Silently Ilya urged them on to their target as more dirty puffs appeared over the frozen lakes, the howitzers' third salvo.

The pilots bore their deadly cargo northward and, under the direction of Spotter One, veered left. The guns were well camouflaged, but luminescent clouds of ice crystals caused by the expended propellant hung in the freezing air around each firing position, forming halos that provided easy aimpoints for the oncoming Soviet airmen. The four Rooks dove into the attack.

At the window, Johansen was ordering Hans to shift fire to the next target. The Norwegian fire plan would blanket each lake in succession with variable-time rounds: artillery shells that contained a small radio transmitter and receiver that detonated each round exactly seven meters above the snow-covered lake ice. Then the guns would shift to point-detonation rounds targeted at the narrow path that led from the lakes to the E6. These latter rounds would strike the ground before exploding. Although they would be muffled by the deep snow, they were also the best tool for destroying Soviet armor. The *kaptein* was just completing his second call-for-fire when the tearing roar of jet engines directly overhead drowned out his words. Johansen knew immediately what the sound portended.

Erik grabbed the other man's shoulder and shouted, "Tell those guns to move, now! They've got an air raid incoming!"

The artillery officer swallowed quickly and complied. A moment later he reported, "They're already displacing. The battery reports they should be repositioned for their next fire mission in ten to fifteen minutes."

The crackle of gunfire rattled from the south. The Soviet paratroopers were apparently pushing off their drop zone, encountering the outposts of the troop guarding the approach up the E6. Johansen heard the distinctive, deep rhythmic booming of one of the M2 heavy machineguns, followed quickly by the crackle of smaller caliber rifles. Silently Erik urged the gun crews to work faster to reposition their pieces. He and his soldiers could not afford their loss.

Four of the six gun crews had managed to hitch up their guns to their tracked, snowcat-like Bv-206 prime movers when the Su-25s struck. Aiming for the dissipating white clouds in the dark blue evening light, the pilots swept past the west side of the airfield in a line abreast and released a mixed strike of cluster munitions and incendiary bombs towards the struggling artillerymen. The ordnance slammed into trees amid the battery and exploded in firecracker flashes of white shrapnel and billowing plumes of yellow flame.

The guns of the Norwegian battery had been widely spaced to prevent any one strike from destroying the entire unit, but Erik knew the Frogfoot carried enough ordinance to blanket a large swath of woods with explosives and fire.

Two of the howitzers were smothered by cluster bomblets that wrecked sights, damaged equipment, detonated ammunition, tore through vehicles, and killed soldiers. A third gun vanished in the billowing yellow flame as an incendiary bomb ignited the propellant of the ready ammunition, engulfed it and its crew. Two of the remaining three gun crews took casualties from flying shrapnel. In seconds the battery had been reduced in strength by fifty percent. And four more Rooks were already starting their attack run.

"I have no contact with Gun Three! Gun Two is gone—" the crackle of the fire support radio went in and out. Hans was looking at his handset, blank faced, stunned. Johansen felt the same sinking feeling as the report continued. If they couldn't use their artillery, his key force multiplier, then… the realization staggered Erik: *We're going to be overrun.*

— ◆ —

The plight of the embattled artillery battery worsened. Unseen by the defenders, an Su-24 bomber, specially configured to sniff out and localize the electronic emission of enemy command posts, was turning in a lazy racetrack pattern high and to the east. The sensitive antennae on this electronic intelligence-gathering platform picked up the strong radio transmissions from the artillery battery's fire direction center, and had finally triangulated their source. A second Su-24, this one a bomber, turned west and released a single Kh-59M missile, aimed at the deduced coordinates.

Designated the AS-18 "Kazoo" by NATO, the Kh-59M was a medium-range ground attack missile that flew the first leg of its flight under inertial guidance, then performed its terminal dive under televised control from the launching aircraft. In this case, the missile did not have far to fly. The weapons officer aboard the Soviet bomber guided the big projectile downward, now able to see the small forest of antennae and white camouflage netting of the battery's fire direction center through the weapons camera. He watched until the feed on his small television guidance screen flashed to fuzzy static as three hundred kilograms of high explosive detonated. The blast wave sent shrapnel through tents, radios, vehicles, and men. Radio transmissions from the artillery command post ceased.

— —

Gunfire continued to crackle to the south. The troop *løytnant* called over the squadron net to report that Soviet soldiers were maneuvering off the lake. He had already lost one of his four M113s to a shot from a BMD, and wanted permission to begin a fighting withdrawal north. Johansen assented. The troop was deployed just a few hundred meters south of his current position and wouldn't be able to resist the weight of an attack by a full company of Soviet paratroopers supported by light armor.

With barely a moment to take in that news, more came over the radio when Berg, back at the airfield, called to report that Soviet paratroopers were advancing on the town from the east. The troop there had knocked out a BMD on the bridge over Brennelvo Stream, but infantry was working their way around their flanks. The *løytnant* there was also asking permission to pull back towards the airfield. Even worse, Berg went on, at least a company of Soviet paratroopers had landed north of town, on a spit that jutted into the fjord next to the highway. These were now approaching from the northwest, into the squadron's rear.

Johansen felt trapped. He *was* trapped. Where was Laub and the Battalion? Where was Jan and the air force? His command was a reconnaissance squadron, designed to find the enemy for the larger forces to deal with. He didn't have the firepower to stop a determined assault by a full battalion of Soviet airborne troops.

The second flight of Su-25s roared overhead. Erik closed his eyes. They would be headed for the remaining howitzers. Erik grabbed the HF radio and switched it to the Coast Guard emergency frequency. He'd heard nothing but static over his unit net for hours due to Soviet jamming, so this was his only remaining link to the rest of the world. It was all the hope he had left for the survival of his squadron.

Johansen depressed the talk button, "Anyone on this net, anyone on this net, this is Banak. If you can hear us, we have Soviet infantry and armor advancing on us from every direction. We need support, *any* support! We can't hold out much longer. If you can hear me, please respond!"

━ ━

"—please respond!" crackled through the radio in Olsen's F-16B.

A hundred kilometers to the west, Jan had just ascended to cruising altitude with the remnants of the failed attack on the incoming Soviet transports.

Electronic noise from the Soviet EW aircraft circling east of Banak was filling the airwaves, but now as Jan and his fellow pilots opened the range, Erik's transmissions suddenly crackled clearly across the emergency net. Jan recognized his friend's voice immediately.

Olsen keyed his own radio and responded, "Banak, this is Bobcat Flight. Can you hear me?"

Johansen's pleas continued, oblivious of the calls traveling back to him from Jan's radio. Olsen's responses could not penetrate the electronic haze bombarding the receivers to the north.

"If anyone can hear this," Erik was saying, "I am pulling my unit back to the airbase. Tell 2nd Mechanized Battalion to hurry. We can't hold out long…heavy air attack…artillery destroyed…enemy are advancing on our rear and…"

A burst of static flared out the HF radio feed in Jan's helmet. After that Johansen's voice was gone. All Olsen could do was continue to withdraw west, away from Soviets, away from his friend. He reached up quickly to wipe away tears of rage. *Anders, and now Erik too?* he thought. *How many more?*

Jan took a deep breath and refocused on the task of bringing his jet, and the two other survivors, home through the quickly deepening blue of night. He needed to live if he wanted to fly another day, to even the score.

— • —

Johansen and the forward observer team barely escaped the observation post before Soviet paratroopers swept over their position in the house south of town. Hans was trying to reestablish communications to direct fire onto the Soviets advancing up the E6 when a squad of paratroopers emerged from the woods to the southeast. Johansen dropped an advancing paratrooper with the first shot from his G3, but the recoil sent shooting pain from his wound through his back. Hans gave up his attempts to communicate with the battery and grabbed his equipment.

They and the rest of the forward observer team escaped down the staircase as a long burst of machinegun fire poured through the window, shattering the toys and decorations in the child's room that constituted their observation post. With the house as a shield, Erik mounted his snowmobile but a BMD fired a high explosive round into the spotter team's G-Wagen, blowing the vehicle apart and killing the two enlisted men. Hans slumped against Erik, groaning, shrapnel peppering both his legs. Johansen draped Han's arms over his back and accelerated his snowmobile away through a hail of bullets.

Johansen's squadron folded their perimeter back towards the airfield, fighting the Soviet *desantniki* through the dark streets of Lakselv, both sides taking and inflicting casualties. *The only difference is that* we *don't have men to spare,* Erik thought darkly. The fight moved through the stench of acrid smoke, past the crash site of a Soviet Su-17, and numerous other fires now smoldering against the frigid night. Here and there frightened civilians scurried across roads, trying to remain out of the crossfire. The single remaining TOW missile-equipped M113 fired at a BMD but missed when its control wires tangled and snapped in the underlying brush, sending the weapon corkscrewing harmlessly upwards. It quickly died from a seventy-three-millimeter shell to the front glacis from that very BMD.

Johansen arrived at the icecrete bunker where Berg was coolly organizing their last stand with the remnants of the squadron. The two reconnaissance troops had acquitted themselves better than the anti-tank section and the observer team, knocking out two of the thinly-armored BMDs with Carl Gustav shoulder-fired anti-tank rounds. In exchange, the Soviets had exacted a heavy toll, reducing Erik's force to half strength. All were now joined up under Johansen's direction at the airfield. One of his *løytnantar* was dead, the other had taken a ricochet to the foot and hobbled from one fighting position to another using his rifle as a crutch. Altogether, the squadron had less than thirty *dragons* still effective as the *desantniki* closed in on their final position, centered on the icecrete bunker.

Clouds obscured the moonlight, and snow began to fall on the small perimeter as Berg and Pedersen helped Erik carry Hans into the bunker. The *rittmester* sighted down his rifle over the ice parapet as they all heard the treads of Soviet BMDs clank and squeal, signaling that the final assault was closing in.

Erik looked around at the wreckage of his command. A few men occupied the bunker. Others lay behind trees or huddled against the bombed-out hangar, rifles and machineguns trained outward. Many were clearly wounded, and many more wounded men filled the squadron's casualty collection station behind the hanger. A pair of the boxy M-113s sat back deeper in the trees, soldiers manning the M2 machineguns in their hatches. Snowmobiles and G-Wagens littered the surrounding woods like toys in a messy child's room. The circling Su-25s had long before put the one surviving howitzer out of action with cannon fire. Erik could count only one Carl Gustav recoilless rocket launcher among the defenders, his only remaining anti-armor weapon. The sound of Soviet vehicles grew louder from the direction of Lakselv.

Johansen's thoughts turned once more to the Poster on the Wall. One of its provisions read, "If retreat is the only option, resistance shall continue on other fronts…" Retreat was no longer an option for Johansen. In reality, it never had been. His back burned from the wound and he could barely move from his spot within the bunker. Nor was retreat an option for most of the survivors of his squadron, with Soviet paratroopers closing in from three directions.

Erik looked out and saw his lanky executive officer moving coolly from soldier to soldier, giving words of encouragement and redistributing ammunition. *Perhaps*, thought Johansen, *a smaller contingent might have a chance.* Elsewhere, the pioneer sergeant, Pedersen, was doing the same. A plan solidified in the *rittmester*'s mind, a plan that had been forming in his subconscious for much of the day, since he had seen that old man at the passenger terminal.

"Berg, Pedersen, on me!" Johansen croaked as loudly as he could. The two leaders trotted back to the bunker, their white parkas ghostly amid the snow that had begun to fall.

The *løytnant* and the sergeant looked at their commander, exhausted but attentive. Gritting his teeth against the shooting pain that sprang through his shoulder with every word, Johansen rattled off his instructions. "Gentlemen, our situation here is hopeless. 2nd Battalion is not coming, and neither is the air force. It's only a matter of time before we're overrun."

Both men looked uncomfortable, but neither objected to their commander's bleak analysis. Johansen went on, "The Directive orders us to continue the resistance on other fronts if retreat is the only option. That is now the situation we face. I am ordering you two to gather up as many of the men as can still ride a snowmobile," he let that hang, doing the math just like Pedersen and Berg were—maybe ten men?—Johansen swallowed and continued, "You will break out from here. I would suggest an escape to the southeast, but I leave that decision to you. The rest of us will cover your departure."

Berg opened his mouth to object, but Johansen cut him off. "I am *ordering* you, *Løytnant* Berg! Break out from here and link up with the Telemark Battalion to our south. They will need all the help they can get. I count five snowmobiles that you could use to get away, so…ten men? Yes, start choosing them now. There's not much time."

Berg and Pedersen remained crouched, grimly silent for a moment. Then the sergeant said, "I'll grab some explosives. Should be useful."

Berg nodded, saying, "I'll get the men and snowmobiles."

Johansen only nodded through clenched teeth, uttering an unnecessary, "Hurry." *The Russians will be coming any minute now.* They all knew that every second counted.

Pedersen jogged to his section's M113 where he began stuffing blocks of C4 and det-cord into satchels that he loaded onto an arctic toboggan hitched to one of the snowmobiles.

Berg moved quickly from fighting position to fighting position, tapping unwounded men on the shoulder with a quiet, "Follow me."

In five minutes, both men were back with their small force. The sounds of approaching armored vehicles were growing louder, even muffled by the now steadily-falling snow.

"You know what to do?" Johansen asked, eyes locking with Berg.

Berg nodded, but it was a stiff, reluctant movement. His blue eyes were pained.

"Sigurd," Johansen addressed the *løytnant*, and then he looked past the officer to the other men gathered behind him, "All of you. Continue the fight. You can make things difficult for these monsters. Remember the Directive! Go!"

They scattered to the snowmobiles and were roaring away into the snowy darkness seconds later.

The buzz of their departure was still fading when ghostly figures emerged through the softly falling snow, bounding from tree to tree. The remaining defenders held their fire until the Russians were close. Then, with his remaining strength, Johansen heaved himself up onto the parapet and shouted, "FIRE! Let them have it!"

Every rifle and machinegun in the perimeter blazed. The enemy dropped, some with wounds, others for cover. Return fire winked out of the darkness, and mortar rounds began to fall and explode around the small icecrete bunker. The defenders fell silent, one by one. A Soviet BMD clanked forward through the trees and swirling snow. Just outside the bunker, the Carl Gustav team rose out of hiding and knelt, training their launcher, but before the gunner could depress his firing trigger a burst of fire from deeper in the forest tore into them, felling both men.

Enraged at the death of his men, at the whole situation, Johansen rose up and blazed away at the Soviet vehicle with his rifle. To his right within the parapet of the bunker, a rifleman did the same, though with single, aimed shots. To Erik's left, a man wielding a belt-fed MG3 machinegun rattled off bursts into the snowy darkness.

The BMD continued to rattle towards them, a monster oblivious to the rounds sparking off its armor, treads grinding through the snow. Johansen kept firing until his bolt locked backwards on an empty magazine. The Soviet vehicle stopped. The turret rotated towards the icecrete bunker. Time seemed to slow until Johansen felt he was looking directly down the muzzle of the vehicle's stubby gun. Still staring down the Soviet barrel, Erik reached for a full magazine in his webbing. There was a flash that reflected off the falling snowflakes like a thousand points of light, and Erik Johansen's world went dark.

— —

"The airfield is secure, I repeat, the airfield is secure. We've captured all of our objectives, *Yastreb* Command," crackled the radio in the circling Il-22.

"Well done, *Lev*," Sokolov complimented his assault battalion commander. "What of your casualties?"

"Heavy," came the response. "Heavier than expected. The defenders around the airfield fought hard. We have only a few prisoners. Some may have escaped before our final assault, but we couldn't pursue."

"Very well, *Lev*. Organize a defense. The motor-rifle troops should be passing through your position by daybreak."

"*Da,* Command," responded the assault battalion commander.

The gathering dark and a snow squall blowing in off the fjord had obscured the end of the battle for the two colonels, forcing them to listen much like two men listening to a football match with money in the game, only it was lives and the fate of nations that was at stake here. Romanov said a quick prayer for the soldiers down below, both the Russians and now for the Norwegians who had resisted them so valiantly.

Sokolov removed the radio headset and looked at Romanov. He said, "Our air force cousins will have interceptors operating from the airfield within hours. The first MiGs are scheduled to arrive in," he looked at his watch, "ninety minutes from now. They will likely be slightly delayed while we clear the runway, but overall we are on schedule. For now, we should get you back to your own unit. Tomorrow, it's your turn."

Romanov nodded. His regiment's part in the plan did indeed begin the next day, but in a setting more desolate, cold, and far lonelier than this battlefield.

 **CHAPTER 88**

1415 EST, Sunday 13 February 1994
1815 Zulu
Over the *Queen Elizabeth 2* wreck site

A BBY LOOKED DOWN with horror at the hundreds of colored dots that sprinkled the dark gray surface of the water below. Bodies, like soggy confetti scattered on pavement after a long-departed parade, paper disintegrating in the elements. Each body had been a person, a person whose life had been slowly sucked away by the cold waters in which they were trapped. No more lifeboats plied the patch of ocean where the *Queen Elizabeth II* had gone down. The boats that survived the missile strikes had already departed, motoring north towards Montauk, crammed to the gunwales with as many of the survivors as they could possibly fit.

Abby and Buck had already rescued one load of stunned, half-frozen survivors, taking them at maximum speed to the evacuation center at Gabreski Field, Long Island, where ambulances were lining up to rush the hypothermic victims to local hospitals. Now they were back, but looking out over the disaster area she felt a moment of hopelessness wash over her. There were so many.

Still, she saw some reasons for optimism. On the flight back to the wreck site, they'd seen more than a dozen boats churning south through the Atlantic swell, including local police and fire boats, but also several commercial fishing trawlers and even a few yachts from the marinas that dotted Long Island's south coast. The ever-present Coast Guard Dolphin helicopters were dangling rescue swimmers at the end of lines to pull in survivors, and now some small civilian choppers were flitting around trying to help as well. Thanks to the amphibious design of the Sea King, she and other members of her flight were landing directly on the water so the crews could drag survivors up through their open doors several at a time.

As she nudged her helicopter downward to do their part and scoop up another load of survivors, Abby's heart skipped a beat when a local Bell 212 dipped its nose to fly north and almost collided with a Coast Guard Dolphin, whose rescue swimmer was just reaching the waves. The civilian helicopter pilot, belatedly realizing his mistake, pitched to the side, the two aircraft's whirling rotors missing each other by mere feet.

"Holy crap!" Abby heard one of the pilots key over the rescue frequency, then, "Hey asshole, watch where you're flying or stay out of this area!"

"Hey, how about you don't set down right in my blind spot, Coast Guard," came the angry response.

This is a recipe for disaster, and we don't need any more of that today, she thought. *Someone needs to take charge.* In an instant she realized that the "some-one" should be her. "Buck, take over the controls," Abby ordered. "Take us up. I need to see the airspace so we can get some organization going on here."

"You got it, Abbs," said Buck, gunning power to the engines to arrest their descent and get the helicopter climbing again.

Abby let go of the controls once she was sure Buck had them. Pulling a pen out of one of her flight suit pockets she began jotting notes on the notepad velcroed to her knee. Then she keyed her HF radio.

"Sandy Hook, this is Angel Lead, over."

The answer took longer than she thought it should have. She was about to call again when she heard, "Angel Lead, Sandy Hook. Go ahead, over."

"Sandy Hook, who's managing the airspace over here at the *QE 2* rescue site, over?"

Another long pause, then, "Uh, Angel Lead, there was supposed to be a C-130 quarterbacking things out there. We're still pulling ourselves back together here. We just had a gun battle outside the center."

Gunbattle? Abby wondered. *I was just there not two hours ago.*

She pressed past her questions to what was important in the here and now, important to the people slowly dying in the water below. "Sandy Hook, give me a control frequency. I can act as air traffic control until you guys get your own bird out here, over."

The voice from Sandy Hood agreed, and in moments Abby was issuing orders to the other fliers. "Okay, everyone working the cruise ship wreck, this is Angel Lead. Listen up. I'm going to organize the airspace here so we don't have any more close calls." Without pausing for anyone to object she went on, "we're going to set up a holding area two miles to the north. Everyone comes there and circles, okay? When I call you forward, you leave the holding pattern and I'll guide you in to where the most survivors are. Any problems?" Now she did pause. "Okay then, unless you have a swimmer in the water, everyone back off to the holding area."

Abby resolved to remain as the airspace controller until one of the rescue C-130s arrived to take over the job, but seeing people down there in the water while her big helicopter's cargo compartment remained empty pained her. Switching to her HF set, she radioed back to Sandy Hook to see when more help would come on station so she could get back to the work of saving lives.

 **CHAPTER 89**

1925 CET, Sunday 13 February 1994
1825 Zulu
Ministry of Defense Building, Akershus Fortress, Oslo, Norway

T HE MOOD WAS grim among the staffers of the Norwegian Defense
Ministry, both uniformed and civilian, as they gathered around the
television at one end of the large, masonry-walled room, their low
murmurs giving the place the feel of a funeral parlor. Large maps of Norway
and the far north adorned the walls of the expansive room. Kristen Hagen
had watched as one bleak message after another from the Far North battered
down their morale. Now, they gathered around the television, each hoping to
hear a word of comfort, a word of strength, some assurance that their world
was not descending into some new dark age of history. They were waiting for
a word from their King.

The men and women inside the walls of the fortress were dealing with the
same emotional whiplash as their fellow citizens outside the ministry. Just yesterday, they had all been anticipating the happy and historic moment when their
country would host its first Olympic Games, when Norway's winter sports com-
petitors were sure to achieve excellence, when all had been right with their world.

Then came that jarring series of events: the disappearance of the Soviet
athletes, the cancellation of the games; the realization that war, so unthinkable

just days before, was imminent; and then, just six hours ago, the stunning news that their country was being invaded for the second time in half a century. The confidence that Kristen had seen on Nils Dokken's face over the intervention of the US Air Force made the subsequent aerial defeats over Finnmark all the more jarring as Kristen saw that confidence turn to disappointment and then despair on faces throughout the map room.

The latest blow arrived only minutes ago. An urgent message from AFNN confirmed what the staff officers in the operations center already suspected: Banak had fallen. The news was not unexpected. Even the most optimistic staffer had known the position was lost when an RF-5 reconnaissance jet over-flew the wreckage of 2nd Mechanized Battalion north of Alta. The smoking devastation along the Altafjord meant that any hope of meaningfully slowing the Soviet onslaught east of the Lyngen position was pure fantasy.

"I thought," Kristen started to ask Dokken, who had just explained all this to Kristen, "I thought our war plans always envisioned us ceding Finnmark to the Soviets and stopping them at the Lyngenfjord?" This strategy had been the hallmark of Norwegian defense planning since at least the 1960s, to trade space for time in the rugged Far North.

Dokken nodded his head, "Yes, but we always planned to execute a fighting withdrawal, slowing and bleeding the Soviets and giving our own forces time to mobilize and move north. *None* of our plans anticipated the Soviets penetrating all the way to Banak in just *six hours*. At that rate, the Russians will be *here* soon." Dokken's eyes looked far away, like that fact had just dawned on him as he said it.

Kristen didn't like that the man's earlier optimism had shifted so quickly to pessimism, but she understood it.

"We haven't even fought the heavy Soviet armored forces yet," Dokken continued, his head shaking. Kristen thought that if he kept it up he'd get dizzy. The man continued, "Compared to what's going on in Germany right now this is…And when—" he cut off, unable to say the words, which was fine as a hush fell over the map room.

"Shh!" people around them shushed, hissing and calling, "Quiet! The King! Listen."

The live feed from the Norwegian news agency was broadcasting a view of the interior of the Storting. The red carpet of the legislative chamber offset the room's ornate wooden walls to create an effect that was warm and Nordic. The members of Norway's government sat, packed close together in leather chairs behind standing desks that formed a U around the Speaker's podium. Elsewhere around the operations center, two other televisions were broadcasting feeds from CNN and BBC, both showed the same picture from a slightly different angle. The prime minister had just finished his brief remarks introducing the monarch, and now the King was striding towards the dais.

The assembled staffers maintained quiet respect as their Sovereign, tall and dignified in his business suit and tie, strode to the podium and looked around the room at the elected representatives of his people. Kristen, like nearly every other Norwegian, was a firm supporter of the monarchy. Now, she and her companions waited with quiet respect for their King to step into his role of leadership in the hour of crisis. She hadn't realized until that moment how much she *needed* to hear from the King, how much she craved words of reassurance from the man who embodied her nation's soul. Prime ministers and legislators came and went, and Kristen knew how fickle and inconsistent politicians could be, but the monarchy was an anchor for the political life of their country.

The King looked around the legislative chamber from one end to another, making eye contact with as many of the representatives as he could in a brief moment, then bowed his head. He opened a folder on the dais and paused to add gravitas to the words he was about to speak. After a moment he looked up and began in a voice that was low, dignified, and reassuring to the people around her, and also to millions of Norwegians watching in their homes, in Home Guard arsenals, in flight ready rooms, and anywhere else a television could be found.

2133 MSK, Sunday 13 February 1994
1833 Zulu
Main Ministry of Defense Building, Arbatskaya Square,
Moscow, Russian Soviet Federative Socialist Republic

Ivan Ivanovich Khitrov sat in his cramped office, watching the CNN feed broadcasting from Oslo. He blew a satisfied stream of cigarette smoke out of his mouth and leaned back, listening as the Norwegian King delivered his address. In his hand he casually twirled the king piece from his small chess set. The symbolism of his actions was not lost on him. The speech was in Norwegian, but a woman's voice was translating in a hushed, respectful tone, and Khitrov was fluent in English. It was a fine speech, he admitted to himself after a few moments, a damned fine speech. The Nordic monarch was displaying just the right balance of strength, concern, defiance. *It's just the sort of thing to rouse a people to defend their land from a brutal invader*, Khitrov thought. *Absolutely perfect*. He took a long drag from the stub between his lips, then delicately crushed it into the steel wastebasket by his desk.

Everything had gone well to this point, Khitrov reflected, better than he had even hoped, in fact. The attacks in North America, the chaos now engulfing the Turkish government in Ankara, even rumblings of the shipping losses outside the American ports, all his handiwork, had been brought to him right here in his office, and to tens of millions of households around the world, courtesy of the west's voracious appetite for entertainment in the form of news. Watching his plans unfold had been supremely satisfying, in the way that a chess master enjoyed executing an artful opening. Or, more accurately, the way a hunter enjoyed stalking a particularly rare trophy. On that thought, Khitrov decided to replace nicotine with some of the celebratory vodka stashed in his desk for just this moment. He poured a finger of the clear liquid into a tumbler, swilled it around, and waited.

The King's speech was rising now in cadence and defiance. Legislators around the hall were nodding in approval, and Khitrov could almost feel the pride growing in the hearts of Norwegians everywhere, their commitment to defend their homeland hardening with each word. *Perfect*. He saluted his glass to the television. *Absolutely perfect*.

1935 CET, Sunday 13 February 1994
1835 Zulu
Töcksfors, Sweden, six kilometers from the Norwegian frontier

In a restaurant on the Swedish side of the border with Norway, Anatoli Skorniak had just signed the check for his dinner using the Finnish name of Kinnunen.

He was watching the television along with the other patrons as the Norwegian King's speech built to its climax. After poisoning the delivery truck driver this morning, the KGB agent had driven straight to the Swedish frontier, crossed over, and checked into a small hotel here in the sleepy village of Töcksfors. The rest of his day had been quiet as he waited to play his next part in the drama.

Deciding the time was right, he stood and wandered out into the cold night, unnoticed by the other patrons, enthralled as they were by the spectacle of a monarch calling his people to arms. Skorniak turned left and walked the twenty meters to a phone booth outside a local bank. Entering the booth and shutting the door behind him, he removed a slip of paper from his breast pocket. He had of course memorized the number, but, being a professional he was taking no chances with the accomplishment of his mission. Skorniak dropped exact change into the machine for a call to Oslo before carefully dialing the number as he read it off the paper.

As the Soviet agent entered the last digit of the call, a chain reaction began. Skorniak pictured it like the sparking tail of TNT, lazily racing toward it's inevitable conclusion. The electrical signal from the phone booth's telephone traveled east to the major telephone exchange in Karlstad. There, the automated system recognized the signal as an international call and connected it to cables that carried the electrical impulse back westward, to Oslo. Once the call arrived at the main Oslo exchange, the machines sent it racing at light speed along its way to one of the new towers that were giving downtown Oslo's residents the novel ability to take advantage of an emerging technology: cellular telephones. One of these towers connected the signal with its final destination, a boxy mobile phone. This cellular phone had been waiting patiently inside the cargo compartment of Sven Sorensen's delivery truck, parked flush against the south wall of the Storting, where the King of Norway was now making his impassioned call to arms to his country, and to the free world.

The signal arrived and a circuit closed. The device began to ring, unheard in the darkness of the truck's cargo compartment. The same closed circuit that activated the phone's ringer also sent electrical shocks down three wires leading to three improvised explosive detonators. These small, firecracker-like devices were initiators for a much larger, specially-designed bomb that occupied nearly the entire cargo area of the delivery truck. The explosives were shaped in such a way that much of the force of their detonation would be directed through the left side of the truck, the side that was currently parked inches away from the masonry of the nineteenth century south wall of the Storting.

1936 CET, Sunday 13 February 1994
1836 Zulu
Ministry of Defense Building, Akershus Fortress, Oslo, Norway

The King's address was reaching a dignified but defiant crescendo. Many legislators were nodding vigorously, others began to clap. Kristen, along with all the other occupants of the operations center huddled around the television, nodded in steely determination at their monarch's compelling show of defiance.

A white flash, like lightning, briefly strobed into the room from north facing windows in the operations center. Kristen looked that way quickly, then back to the television in confusion. The screen now showed only the colorful bars of a lost signal. She was just opening her mouth to ask what the matter was when the windows of the room rattled loudly with the sharp *boom* of the passing blast wave, the effect of more than a ton of military-grade high-explosives. Kristen flinched, startled by the sound and shock. She looked back out the window in horror as a massive yellow plume of fire rose into the black sky over downtown Oslo. It was rising, exactly, from the direction of the Storting. Kristen's hand flew to her mouth as she watched the flames dissipate into orange and yellow billowing clouds, then smoke. Around the room, dozens of others stood looking as well, all of them in stunned silence.

2137 MSK, Sunday 13 February 1994
1837 Zulu
Main Ministry of Defense Building, Arbatskaya Square,
Moscow, Russian Soviet Federative Socialist Republic

Khitrov raised his glass of vodka to the CNN commentator in Atlanta who was confusedly trying to explain to his viewers that they had lost their feed from Oslo but were working diligently to get it back as quickly as possible. *Good luck with that,* Khitrov thought with a comfortable smugness as he tipped the glass back and allowed the fiery liquid to travel down his throat. *Perfect*, he thought, and he reached forward to set the king piece back on the chessboard then knocked it over with a flick of his finger. *Absolutely perfect.*

PART VIII: COMPASS ROSE

"The quickest way of ending a war is to lose it."
—George Orwell

 **CHAPTER 90**

2025 EST, Sunday 13 February 1994
0125 Zulu, 14 February
Montauk, Long Island, New York, USA

THE LAND BREEZE had blown some of the sheets off corpses lying on the sand. Moonlight reflected here and there off shocks of silver hair matted by seawater. The rows of bodies stretched down the beach and into the darkness, seeming to go on forever. Jack Young hadn't wanted to see this. Death was an integral part of the stories he'd covered. An image of those terrible shallow graves in Ossòwka, Poland, flashed into his mind. For Jack, the sight of bodies had never grown familiar to him, and he had certainly never expected to see a sight like this so close to home.

The sleepy village of Montauk on the eastern tip of Long Island was the closest and most convenient place for rescue craft to deposit the *Queen Elizabeth 2* survivors and victims before heading back out to sea to pluck more out of the cold waters. A steady stream of ambulances, police cruisers, rescue vehicles, and private automobiles took the more fortunate to local hospitals across Long Island to be treated.

By the time Jack arrived, the flow of rescue vehicles was ebbing. The only victims remaining were destined for a morgue, not a hospital, and their transfer there was obviously a matter of far less urgency. He shook his head, forcing himself to take in the whole moonlit scene. There was a story here that needed to be told. The passengers of the luxury liner had, largely, been elderly, some on second or third honeymoons, many enjoying the fruits of retirement, others seeking the nostalgia of the days when ships rather than airplanes carried people across the Atlantic. All were ill-prepared when fate dumped them into the waters of the North Atlantic, and the death toll showed it.

Jack took out his small reporter's notepad and flipped it open, scanning his observations from earlier in the day. He'd stopped at Gabreski Airport, thirty miles back along Route 27, to investigate what had become the hub of the air rescue effort for the offshore disaster. There, stunned and confused victims told him that the cruise ship had been struck by a missile, two missiles, three missiles, a torpedo, a terrorist bomb. Even the rescue crews he spoke to were unsure about what had actually happened.

Jack was already formulating the piece he planned to write for the morning edition. At Gabreski he'd found one of the rescuers more compelling than most. While walking among the shivering, blanket-clad victims inside a hangar, he spied a blond-haired woman wearing a flight suit, sitting on a bench with her head in her hands. Approaching and using his best reporter's tone, he introduced himself, "Excuse me, Miss, I'm with the *New York Times*. May I ask you a few questions about what happened here?"

The woman looked up, eyes red from exhaustion. The name tape of her flight suit read "Savage," and he could see by her rank insignia that she was an officer. She nodded raggedly, and Jack began the interview. The flood of words that followed almost overwhelmed his ability to jot notes. She'd clearly needed to process what she'd seen.

"There was no way we could save them all," her voice cracked. "The water was just full of people floating in their orange vests, you know? My helicopter's big, but...but we can only fit so many in one trip. We'd pull as many as we could but there were always more. More faces looking up at us, begging us to take them too. And every time we came back fewer of them were alive. On my last flight," Savage swallowed, trying to maintain her composure, "on my last flight, most of the people we picked up were already gone. Two died mid-flight." Her voice trailed off, then she shook her head.

Jack was about to put his notebook away and let her be, when she looked back up at him and said, with steel in her voice, "I don't care what it takes. I'm getting a job hunting the bastards who did this. I don't care if the Navy says I can't do it because I'm a woman. I can fly a helicopter and hunt submarines as well as any man, and that's what I'm going to do. You'll see."

Jack had no doubt that he *would* see. The flint he saw in this petite woman's icy blue eyes at that moment was enough to send chills up his spine. As an American, with his country now unexpectedly at war and under attack, he wished that their president had shown as much determination in his underwhelming, politically safe speech earlier in the day.

After interviewing Savage, Jack had gathered with the exhausted rescue teams around a small television set up at one corner of the hangar. CNN was previewing the president's much-anticipated address to the nation since the early afternoon, but world developments had continued to delay the speech. The most dramatic of these, in a day that had featured a continuous litany of dramatic news, was the attack on the Norwegian parliament. Jack didn't know for sure, but he imagined that the bomb that destroyed the Storting had convinced the president to stay away from the Oval Office when he addressed the country an hour ago.

Jack remembered his heart sinking as the president spoke.

"My...my fellow Americans—" Right off the bat the man's voice had faltered, as if he were unsure of even this, the most basic salutation American presidents gave to their people. "My fellow Americans," the president repeated in a stronger voice. *The words were all right*, Jack thought as the speech went on. *Soaring rhetoric worthy of Roosevelt or Churchill, but...but he comes across more as if he's been insulted personally rather than as the standard bearer for the cause of freedom under siege in the world.* He had looked around the hushed room to see if his fellow viewers betrayed any of the same thoughts, and the worried looks on the rescuers' faces had told him that they did. As he looked around the shore and saw sea-encrusted bodies, he remembered the shaken rescue workers, all he could think was that the president owed them, at the very least, courage.

The middle part of the president's speech had been the best, limited to a simple cataloging of Soviet attacks around the world. "As I speak, our brave men and women in uniform are fighting desperately against this new onslaught of darkness in the world." For some reason, the cynical side of Jack's brain had rebelled against accepting this particular bit of melodrama. *New onslaught of darkness?* "In Germany," the chief executive continued, "they stand alongside our NATO allies to defend the freedom of that reunited country, where a massive Red Army is moving to threaten the great city of Berlin. Turkey and Norway have been invaded, and our naval and air forces stand ready to assist these two nations as they defend their sovereignty against this naked aggression. In Asia, our friends the Japanese are under threat, and in the Caribbean and Central America, Soviet vassals have struck at the very heart of world commerce, closing the Panama Canal to shipping. Here, on the very shores of our great country, American men and women have died by the thousands in what can only be described as a campaign of terrorism, the likes of which the world has never seen."

Again with the melodrama, Jack had thought. *I wonder if Londoners who lived through the Blitz would agree that this is something new under the sun.* Still, he wanted to believe in the truth of what his president was telling him.

The end of the speech was the weakest part. Once again, the substance was right, Jack remembered, with words about winning through to the end, the triumph of light over darkness, of freedom over tyranny, and how the strength of the free world was now gathering, but they had been delivered in such a faltering style, and so rushed, that they lacked the necessary conviction.

For some reason the whole speech had just felt hollow to Jack. The calming effect that citizens of the country needed right now was nowhere to be found. Millions of American families were sitting in their homes, and they were scared. The terrorist attacks here in New York, San Francisco, and Los Angeles, and the missile attacks all up and down both coasts, had brought this unexpected war home to the average American with a terrible swiftness that forced everyone to remember that, at any moment, they were only thirty minutes away from nuclear annihilation. They needed to hear and see strength from the leader of their country. His delivery communicated something else entirely. Several times the president stumbled over phrases, allowed his voice to quaver, he'd even wiped sweat from his brow. *The man must really be rattled,* Jack thought, knowing that the president was a seasoned politician, adept at using the camera to best effect. The contrast between the president and Lieutenant Savage, the Navy pilot with flint in her eyes was painful to behold.

Not that Jack could blame the man for feeling shaken. CNN had been broadcasting footage all day, for all the world to see, of the chief executive and his family being hustled half-dressed out of the White House. In the video, black-suited Secret Service agents, guns drawn, dragged the First Family through the Rose Garden to a waiting Marine One, while the helicopter's rotors whirled at full power, blowing leaves and agents' ties every which way under low, gray skies. Later footage showed Air Force One hurtling down the runway at Andrews Air Force Base before lifting off and disappearing into the clouds. It was all very dramatic, very frightening, *And very counterproductive*, Jack thought.

Jack did some quick math with the timestamp on the video. One of the rescue crews told him earlier that the *QE 2* wasn't the only shipwreck off Long Island, that several ships had been hit at around the same time, just after nine in the morning. If his information about the missile strikes offshore was correct, and if the timestamp on the video was correct, that meant that the president was boarding Marine One several minutes *after* the Soviet strike. The implication was clear. If they so intended, the Soviets could have easily conducted a decapitating nuclear strike on Washington D.C.

Jack shivered at the thought, a reaction that probably mirrored the president's. The man was only human, after all.

Worse than the fumbled speech itself, a broadcasting glitch showed the nation and the global audience that the address was from Air Force One and not the Oval Office. The President of the United States didn't even feel safe enough to broadcast a live address to his nation from the White House. *If the president doesn't feel safe, why should anyone?* Jack wondered.

The evidence to the fact that no one, *no one*, could feel safe was lying in cold, grisly rows in front of him on the sand. Jack had seen enough, or at least enough for the story he was formulating for tomorrow's paper. He jotted some final notes on his pad, then stuffed pencil and paper into his sport coat and turned to walk back up the beach.

In the yellow light of the makeshift command center in the lobby of a beach front resort, exhausted police officers, firefighters, paramedics, and volunteers sat on the lobby's couches and on the floor lining the walls. Many eyes were closed after a physically and emotionally draining day. The Coast Guard had called off the rescue operation an hour ago. Jack overheard two Coasties talking about an attack at their HQ over in New Jersey, but he didn't know quite what to believe anymore. The tinny voice of a portable AM radio was broadcasting the latest war news from around the world into the now-quiet lobby. Jack wasn't sure he recognized the world that the newsman on the radio was describing.

Spying a telephone at the hotel desk, Jack walked over and dialed his editor's desk from memory. The lines were now open, surprisingly. They'd been jammed all day, overwhelmed by loved ones desperate for news from the city.

He dialed Bill's desk at Times Tower.

"Yeah?" Bill answered.

"Bill? Jack," the reporter answered. "I've got a story for you. A big one. The cruise ship you heard about? It was the *Queen Elizabeth 2*. Two thousand people on board, or more. The death toll is going to be big for this one" Jack went on a few minutes more.

"Phew!" Bill whistled, not unhappily. "Modern-day *Lusitania* on our hands! This is just what we need for the front page under the fold for tomorrow. I'll pass you off to Jeannie. You can dictate your copy to her."

Jack didn't appreciate his editor's glib response, but that was the news business. High death tolls meant good payrolls, which was one of the less savory parts of journalism. War was big business for newspapers and TV news ratings, but for Jack, these stories were too short-sighted. He wanted to tell the important stories, the stories of how people overcame the horrible situation they found themselves in. A corpse didn't let him do that.

Bill came back on the line after Jack finished dictating his story.

"Say Jack," Bill said, "I've got another assignment for you. Should be right up your alley. Defense Department called and they want our list of reporters for the combat press pool. Some sort of new idea, 'embedded reporters,' or something like that, like we were doing in Bosnia last year. Probably a military idea to keep us from squawking too much."

Jack felt his heart begin to race, "Where am I going?" It went without saying that he would accept the assignment.

"Jack, my boy, we're sending you off to war again!" Bill said in a teasing tone. "You know the Pentagon likes to keep their cards close. Could be anywhere, Germany, Turkey, Norway," Bill trailed off and Jack could picture the old guy waving his hand in the air. "Wherever Uncle Sam decides to send you," Bill was saying, "you'll be leaving from Norfolk."

The reporter let out an annoyed breath. After everything he'd seen in the past several hours, he wasn't in the mood for Bill's uncharacteristic and unfunny joshing.

CHAPTER 91

2105 EST, Sunday 13 February 1994
0205 Zulu, 14 February
US Coast Guard Sandy Hook Station, Ft. Hancock, New Jersey

JIM INGALLS LET out an exhausted breath as he pushed open the front door of the watch center and walked outside into the chill darkness of the New Jersey night. The door didn't shut completely behind him, compliments of a Russian bullet that had shattered the door frame, but he hardly noticed. The gun battle felt like a lifetime ago. With so much happening, Ingalls couldn't quite make sense of it all. He paused in the darkness, savoring the cool air and the quiet after a full day of chaos.

His shift had lasted only three hours longer than it would have in peacetime. Of course, that didn't mean that he could go home. Members of his shift were setting up cots in one of the conference rooms, preparing for the long haul. Ingalls had just briefed his counterpart on the incoming shift, the station chief, about the current situation. He was starting to feel the illusion that they were getting things under control. Lieutenant Shin reported that the Navy was flying some people up with a plan to outfit one of the harbor tugs as a minesweeper to proof the channel. Until that happened, nothing would be entering or leaving New York Harbor.

Of course his fleeting feeling of control vanished when the shift change brief moved on to the rescue operations. The entire afternoon made him feel like one of those performers keeping plates spinning at the top of long poles. Except when the plates fell in this line of work, people died, and a lot of people had died on his watch today.

"Everything all right, sir?" Ingalls heard from the darkness to his left.

He turned and saw the dark silhouette of the National Guard platoon sergeant; *Martinez*, remembered Ingalls.

"Not really," Ingalls answered the man. He didn't want to have a conversation right now, but felt obligated to ask, "Everything alright with you, Sergeant?"

He heard Martinez grunt, then parrot, "Not really," in response.

Ingalls smiled at that. "We've had a hell of a day, haven't we, Sergeant Martinez?" he asked, breaking the ice.

"We have at that, sir," Martinez said wearily.

Ingalls saw the other man reach into the breast pocket and take out a white paper package. A second later a small flame illuminated Martinez's face with yellow light as the soldier lit up a cigarette. Ingalls watched him take a drag. Then Martinez gestured towards him with the pack.

"Smoke?" he offered.

"You know these things will kill you, don't you?" Ingalls asked as he accepted. Using the tired old joke seemed appropriate under the circumstances.

"These and a few billion other things," Martinez said as he handed his lighter over, using the tired old response with ease. Both men lapsed into silence, reflecting grimly on their own mortality in this new, very frightening world.

"Sergeant Martinez, can I ask you a question?" Ingalls said.

"Shoot, sir," the NCO answered, drawing in another lungful of tobacco smoke.

"You lost a man today protecting us. We're grateful, by the way, but," he paused, picturing the back of the ambulance taking Lieutenant Kirby's body away. He'd seen the tears in Martinez's eyes that the old sergeant had tried to hide. "How do you move on, keep going?"

"What do you mean, sir?" Martinez asked, almost sounding annoyed. "You just *do*. Not like you've really got a choice."

"I mean," Ingalls went on, feeling a little sheepish now, "that I just got done spending fourteen hours trying to save probably twenty-five-hundred people that the Russians managed to dump into the drink today. I poured everything that I am into it, and at the end of the day I still let more than half of them die." Now Ingalls' voice turned heated. "I couldn't get any help from the damned Navy, either. When those two ships from Norfolk got here, the *Hayler* and the *Sides*, did they start pulling people out of the water? No! They went tearing off east with *Mahan* on some wild goose chase for those submarines. Still haven't found any of 'em, either. They sure let a lot of people die of exposure while they pissed around, though," he concluded bitterly.

Looking over at Martinez he knew he'd said too much. The NCO was shifting uncomfortably on his feet, but Ingalls needed to get this off his chest. He needed to talk to someone about his guilt.

"How do you move on, sir," Martinez answered after a minute, sidestepping Ingalls' frustration with the Navy, "Well, you gotta remember it was the enemy that killed all those people. Not you. Not the sailors on those ships out there. *You* all are working to *save* them. Just like my Lieutenant was working to save you." With that Martinez fell silent.

"So," Ingalls prodded, "does remembering that the Russians killed your people and not you make you feel any better?"

"Nope."

"Then how do we move forward from here?" Ingalls asked again.

"You wake up tomorrow," Martinez answered, "and you keep trying to save people. You can bet the Russians aren't done trying to kill them."

Ingalls nodded again, accepting the mild rebuke.

"A lot more people are going to die before this is all done, aren't they, Sergeant?" he asked the other man.

"Yep," answered Martinez.

They both fell silent again, puffing on their cigarettes. The men smoked together in silence until they only had nubs left. Then Ingalls dropped his butt on the pavement, ground it with his heel and said, "Well, Sergeant, in that case I better get some rest. It's going to be another long day tomorrow."

 **CHAPTER 92**

0810 MSK, Monday 14 February 1994
0510 Zulu
Main Ministry of Defense Building, Arbatskaya Square,
Moscow, Russian Soviet Federative Socialist Republic

"—AND THAT WILL conclude my assessment of the German front, *tovarich* President," Marshal Rosla said as he and Medvedev leaned over the huge map of Europe. Other members of the Red Army's High Command—*Stavka* in both Russian and American parlance— clustered around their president and defense minister, though the constellation of generals and admirals made sure not to crowd their chiefs too closely.

"To summarize," Rosla continued, "our attacks are proceeding as planned. We have made slow progress against the American V Corps in central Germany. Their counterattacks have been very sharp, as expected, and I do not anticipate any great successes in that sector. In the north, however, in the former East Germany, initial indications show that the British I Corps and the German III Corps are moving forward to meet our northward thrust from Czechoslovakia to Berlin. We should know for certain in the coming days if they have fallen into the sack we are opening for them, but as I say, conditions look promising."

Rosla paused, allowing his president to study the situation for a few moments. Medvedev's eyes wandered over the dozens of red and blue markers that adorned the room-sized chart. The strategic geometry of the war in Central Europe had changed radically since the reunification of Germany, and not at all in the USSR's favor. Medvedev's goal was to modify it again, creating conditions that would assure the safety of his country from the German threat for at least another generation. Soviet-controlled territory in Central Europe consisted of the knife-like westward protrusion that was the unhappily Socialist state of Czechoslovakia. That country had served for three years now as a staging ground for the combined weight of Red Army forces that used to occupy both East Germany *and* Czechoslovakia.

One cluster of red markers, each representing a division consisting of thousands of troops and hundreds of armored vehicles, showed a shallow advance by Soviet forces westward into the Fulda Gap area of central Germany. A larger cluster of icons occupied a deeper salient that pointed north from the Czechoslovak border towards Berlin, via Leipzig. The largest cluster of red markers, however, remained still on the Czech side of the international boundary, waiting.

Medvedev nodded and asked, "Is NATO respecting the neutrality of our Czechoslovakian friends?"

The issue of Czechoslovakian belligerence in the unfolding conflict was an interesting one. At the same hour that the war began, the Soviet ambassador to the Czechoslovakian government presented the country's premier with a note containing two demands, one of them surprising, the other less so. The unexpected demand was the brainchild of Georgy Garin, Medvedev's foreign minister. It ordered the Czechs to immediately and publicly declare their neutrality in the unfolding war, and to loudly request that all of the belligerents respect the territorial integrity of Czechoslovakia.

The Soviets, of course, had no intention of honoring this request, what with the weight of their army already stirring in that country's woods and hills. Nevertheless, the Soviet foreign minister *had* pledged in the note that Red Army forces would vacate the now neutral territory of Czechoslovakia, "As soon as the conditions of the war situation against the imperialists allowed."

For now, though, the Czechs would have to settle for the USSR's public declaration of support for their neutrality, while at the same time the Red Army used the country as their staging base for the largest military operation in Europe since the last World War. Regardless, the declaration forced upon NATO the odious political decision of whether or not to willfully violate a nominally neutral country's airspace and territory, which was a step that the Alliance seemed as yet unwilling to take.

"*Da*," Rosla responded, shaking his head ruefully. "I do not understand it myself, my President, but other than a few minor incidents, no NATO forces have crossed into Czech territory, not even air forces. Our air bases and staging areas are operating without interference."

Medvedev clapped the big man on the shoulder and said, "You see, Aleksandr Ivanovich, we politicians can be good for something, eh?" Then his countenance turned more serious. "It will not last, of course. NATO cannot allow us secure lines of communication for long."

"We only need a few days," offered Rosla, "only until we can reopen a path through Poland. Resistance there has been almost non-existent. Warsaw is firmly in our hands and our forces from the Belorussian Military District will be closing on the German border by the end of the week. As we initiated hostilities from a 'standing start,' as the Americans like to say, our reserves are only now mobilizing, except for those we activated for the Poland operation. We will be able to feed our Category B and C divisions into the front over the coming weeks. Our reserves are, of course, of lower quality, but so are NATO reserve forces, and we have more depth. Add to that the forces we are transferring from Siberia," Rosla ended on a shrug.

Medvedev dove coldly from one subject to another. "The Chinese understand the consequences for their existence as a people if they try to take advantage of our temporary weakness in the east?"

"*Da*," answered Rosla, looking Medvedev in the eye. "They have been informed in very clear terms. We should have no trouble from them. Their army is mostly a police force, anyway," he added dismissively. "We demonstrated that during our little spat with them back in the sixties."

Medvedev nodded again. "Very well," he said, "what of the other fronts."

Rosla allowed the commander of the Southwestern Military Front to update the president about the progress of Plan *Boyar*'s southern arm.

"Things in the south are still confused, *tovarich* President," the colonel general reported. "Our attack on the Straits is still in progress. We are doing what we can to support the progressive elements who are friendly to us in Ankara, but," the man hesitated and that allowed Medvedev to see why Rosla had deferred to his subordinate to brief this front. The general was hedging his bets. The operation in Turkey, the Soviet play to topple the Ankara government and seize the Dardanelles, must be in jeopardy. *How disappointing*, thought Medvedev.

Medvedev didn't wait for the excuses to continue. He cut in, "What do you estimate are our chances of success in the Dardanelles operation?"

The man swallowed, looking to Rosla for help. Rosla returned the look, stony-faced, but offered him a slight nod.

The officer swallowed again, then said, "Less than fifty percent, *tovarich* President."

Medvedev openly considered the man. The room was silent as he did so, the other commanders watching, waiting to see what potential failure would bring to them. At the very least it had taken guts for the commander to admit that his assigned part in the grand plan was not going well.

"General," Medvedev said coldly, "were you not given sufficient resources to accomplish your mission? How can you say that your chances of success are so low? Are you not fighting those pathetic Turks?"

The officer licked his lips but stood his ground. "My President, the Americans and their allies are strong in the Mediterranean right now. I know they are weak in the main sector, in the north, and this was our intent, but they must be strong *somewhere*. That somewhere is my front. I must report, just an hour ago we experienced an American cruise missile attack against our bases in the Crimea—"

"What?" Medvedev blurted, interrupting the commander and at the same time fixing him with a fiery look.

Rosla cut in quickly, "Our air defenses shot down every one of the American missiles. We suffered no damage. My President, I think we may consider this attack as retaliation for our own, *infrastructure* attacks in North America."

"Were any of their missiles carrying atomic warheads?" the president asked.

"That we cannot know," the southern front commander responded, recovering. "Since all the missiles were destroyed."

"Unlikely then," Rosla cut in. "Such an isolated attack so early in the war, no, no atomic weapons."

Medvedev relaxed somewhat. He trusted these men, trusted Rosla, to fight the war for him. His role, he knew, was managing the strategic situation so that NATO never felt so threatened that they would resort to the expedient of atomic weapons. His role was to ensure the ultimate *political* success of the war he had launched, and that the conflict did not spin out of control and into nuclear fire.

The Soviet missile attacks against the shipping along the American eastern seaboard had been carefully choreographed months in advance so as *not* to directly threaten the American government in Washington. So far, the American atomic forces had remained dormant, as did the Soviets', but Medvedev could feel that the world was on a knife's edge now at the start of this, his war. An irrational act by the President of the United States could bring about catastrophe. Medvedev pushed the thought from his mind. He wouldn't let that happen.

"Very well," the president allowed. Looking again at the southern front commander, he asked, "Do you have a plan for the failure of your assault on the Straits?"

The colonel general looked surprised for a moment, but recovered quickly. Over the next few moments he outlined his contingencies. Satisfied, Medvedev nodded. The man was right, after all. The Americans could not be weak everywhere, and he did not seem incompetent, at least. Things were going according to plan in the Pacific and in Europe, and in truth, Medvedev required only the European theater to be ultimately successful in order to meet the war aims for the Soviet Union.

"Very well, Defense Minister," Medvedev said, nodding to Rosla, "please continue."

"*Da*, my President," said Rosla, beckoning Medvedev to follow him up to the top of the map, the part that spanned from western Greenland to the Kola Peninsula. "We can discuss the goings on in the Pacific later. For now, let me brief you on the main front here in the north, where we hope to secure political, if not military, victory for our country."

 **CHAPTER 93**

0025 EST, Monday 14 February 1994
0525 Zulu
Pier 11, Naval Station Norfolk, Virginia, USA

A COLD, MISTING RAIN was falling on the piers at Naval Station Norfolk, and on the gray leviathans tied up to them. Water beaded on Admiral Falkner's belted all-weather trench coat and service cap, neither of which revealed any indication of rank to the bustling sailors and dockyard workers swarming over the ships that towered on both sides. Not that they had time to take notice of their unassuming commander anyway. The white beams of arc lights lit up the black night as thousands of workers, uniformed and not, feverishly readied the ships. To Falkner's left, sailors practically tripped over each other hauling stores up multiple gangways into the carrier *Carl Vinson*. To the right, workers threw cables and sparked arc welders through the glistening rain to make the *Theodore Roosevelt*, in the midst of a four-month refit, ready for sea. At other piers along the waterfront the scene repeated itself as cruisers, destroyers, frigates, submarines, and auxiliaries made ready for war.

Falkner knew that this collection of warships represented perhaps the greatest combination of naval might in the world, perhaps in all of history. He also knew that despite its power, and despite the urgency with which the thousands of sailors and dockworkers were laboring, the bulk of it would not be going anywhere soon, or at least as soon as its commander would like. Even so, the admiral remained calm, watching it all, feeling his fleet gaining strength from the human beings who served it.

He sensed rather than saw his tall N2, Ed Franklin, stride up and stand beside him. The Admiral's staff knew he liked to be out among his sailors, and knew they could catch him at these times if they had something important to discuss.

"Any updates, Ed?" Falkner asked without turning.

"Yes sir, a serious one."

That made Falkner turn. Franklin always chose his words carefully, and he didn't call something "serious" unless it was.

"Go on," Falkner ordered.

"The situation in the Eastern Med is still up in the air. The Turks are fighting, but we just don't know what's going on in Ankara. CNN is showing people and troops in the streets, but no one seems to have a firm grasp on who's actually in charge, not even our embassy."

"And?" Falkner prompted. Nothing Franklin had said was news, or more "serious" than anything else that had happened in the past twenty-four hours.

Franklin visibly drew in a breath, then said, "Sir, one of the *Eisenhower*'s escorting destroyers, the *David L. Ray*, emptied a full load of Tomahawks at Soviet bases in the Crimea early last night."

The light rain *tap-tapped* on both officers' service caps for several heart-beats before Falkner cut through the tension with a long, low whistle. Leaning towards Franklin he said, "That was a ballsy move, Ed. What was 6th Fleet hoping to achieve with that one?" Cruise missile attacks against the USSR itself marked a major strategic escalation

Looking his chief square in the face, the N2 answered, "It wasn't 6th Fleet's call, sir. Apparently, the orders came down straight from the National Command Authority."

Falkner nodded his understanding. The admiral was too professional to voice his doubts about what Franklin had just revealed, but he and his N2 understood each other. Slinging nuclear-capable cruise missiles at the Soviet heartland was a dangerous escalation, and one that Falkner was not sure the president and his staff had fully thought through. "Okay, Ed. That *is* 'serious.' What's it all mean for us getting Ike out of the Med?"

"Realistically, not much, other than that the *Ray* is now short a bunch of missiles that need to be reloaded. There's other rumblings out of Libya that might slow the *Eisenhower* down more."

Just then the tall, dark figure of Rear Admiral Johnson loomed out of the flood lights, his dark face streaked from the misting rain. Droplets tumbled off his service cap as he nodded a greeting to his two compatriots.

"Evening, Xavier. Or morning, I should say." Falkner greeted. Indicating an awning on one side of the pier, he led the group there for a little shelter from the rain, then resumed, "What sort of 'rumblings?'"

"The Libyans don't bring anything to the fight that Ike can't deal with, sir, but there's a Soviet task force built around the *Moskva* in Tripoli harbor. We don't know what they're doing there, but those ships *plus* the Libyan air force and navy could pose a problem."

"*The Eisenhower* can handle them fine, if it comes to that," rumbled Johnson. "The biggest issue with handling the Libyans will be logistics. The battle group will need to replenish before they move north to join us."

"What about 6th Fleet? Can they manage without Ike?" Falkner asked. He was pleased at another flattop in his fleet, but sure his counterpart in Naples was grating at losing such a powerful force.

"They're being backfilled by the *Nimitz* out of the Indian Ocean," Johnson explained, "now that we know the Suez Canal is still open, that is. Close call, that one was."

"You can say that again, sir," Franklin opined. "That'll make quite a sea story when this is all over. Apparently, a container ship 'just exploded' right in the middle of the canal yesterday." A raised eyebrow showed who Franklin thought the author of *that* mishap surely was. "Anyway, some quick-witted Egyptian tugboat captain saw what was going down and managed to push the hulk, still burning, right out of the channel."

Falkner loved a good sea story, and this sounded like it had the makings of one, but right now he was focused on getting his fleet ready for war, and that meant focusing on the things that could slow the process down.

"Tell me what we know about the attacks here at home, Ed," Falkner ordered.

Switching gears, Franklin pulled a notebook out of his trench coat and used the light of the flood beams to read, droplets smeared his orderly handwriting. "Let's see," the N2 said. "Sir, you already know the highlights; a little after zero-nine-hundred yesterday morning, just as Soviet forces were crossing into Germany and Norway, they hit shipping and infrastructure targets here in the US and in Canada. Submarine-launched cruise missiles struck shipping off Miami, Savannah, Charleston, and New York on the east coast, as well as Long Beach and Seattle out west." He paused, scanning his notes, then said, "Ah…here's something new: there's a report that a Soviet sub penetrated into San Francisco Bay, but that's so far unconfirmed. We're still tallying the butcher's bill, but for now I count forty ships of various types sunk on both coasts, with at least four more damaged. Looks like there'll be more than a thousand dead from the *Queen Elizabeth 2* alone."

"Any indication they were deliberately targeting the cruise ship?" asked Falkner. "Doesn't really seem to fit the pattern. Might end up being counterproductive for them, really."

Franklin shook his head. "Sir, I'd assess that the shipping attacks were largely opportunistic. We think the Soviets were using small, independently operated airplanes to run targeting for the missile subs. They wouldn't have been able to distinguish between a container ship and a cruise ship."

"And," Johnson's baritone interjected, "they emptied a lot of their subs' missile tubes in those attacks. That'll make it easier for us to push north, especially if we can catch some of those boats as they withdraw."

Franklin nodded agreement and continued. "Yes sir, but right now we haven't caught a sniff of a single one of the subs that launched the attacks."

Taking in the words, Admiral Falkner could visualize the dozens of P-3C Orion sub-hunting aircraft that were now scouring the waters off both coasts of the United States, their crews searching angrily for the Soviet missile submarines that had been so brash as to approach within striking range of the American homeland. He could even feel the presence of the French and British patrol aircraft taking off on the far side of the ocean to sanitize the convoy routes across which the might of American military power would have to flow.

"Ingenious, really," said Franklin, bringing Falkner's thoughts back to the issue of the shipping attacks. "Sink the cargo ships before we ever have a chance to get them into convoys. Doesn't matter if they're carrying war materials or not. They probably did more damage in those first few minutes than they could have hoped to in weeks of trying to get at our lines of communication to Europe. That's not even mentioning the mining of the New York Harbor. It was all done on the cheap to boot."

"Agreed," Falkner said. "What about the terrorist attacks onshore?"

Franklin continued, "A lot of targets were key infrastructure and law enforcement facilities, mostly bombs and some commando assaults. New York is definitely the hardest hit. Nearly every bridge and tunnel leading into Manhattan was attacked at about the same time with massive truck bombs. Some crazy NYPD cop managed to defuse the bomb on the George Washington Bridge, but the Manhattan Bridge is a total write-off, and that's closed off access to the East River and the Brooklyn Naval Yard until the Port Authority and the Army Corps of Engineers can clear the wreckage.

"Similar story out in San Fran," Franklin went on, referencing his notes. "A truck bomb went off mid-span of the Golden Gate. The bridge is still standing, but it's closed to traffic while the engineers assess the damage. Besides the bridges and tunnels, targets included," the N2 flipped a page in his notebook, "at least five different subway stations, Penn Station, the World Trade Center, the Stock Exchange, City Hall, three police stations, two fire stations, the Hillview Reservoir water distribution station and the Croton Filtration plant, along with two power plants: East River and Brooklyn. A lucky break prevented a bomb attack at Grand Central Station. Casualties are in the hundreds, at least."

Franklin paused to let the extent of what he had just said sink in before going on. "The governors of both New York and New Jersey have declared states of emergency, and National Guard troops are on the streets in the city. The NYPD took some pretty heavy casualties. Right now," Franklin again referred to his notes, "they're main concern is assessing whether they need to ship drinking water to Manhattan. Our news services are reporting more on the terrorist attacks than on the war, right now."

Might be better that way, thought Falkner wryly, thinking of the media and their understandable obsession with their audience. *Only gives the average American one thing to panic about at a time.*

"It's not just here in the US, either." Franklin went on. "Bombs also targeted the Welland Canal locks up in Canada, near Niagara, and the Rogers Pass railroad tunnels through the Rockies. We're not sure how bad the damage to the Panama Canal is right now, but initial reports don't look good. The Soviets are clearly targeting our strategic mobility."

"Any idea who these guys are?" Falkner asked. "How they got here?"

"The few attackers taken alive aren't talking, sir," Franklin answered his chief. "The best lead the FBI actually has is a survivor from the trawler that was dropping mines at the entrance to New York Harbor. The guy apparently lost his arm and is pretty drugged up and delirious. He at least is talking, and he's talking in Russian, which is surprising to no one. What's troubling is that the Soviets were apparently able to infiltrate what I estimate were dozens, if not hundreds, of *Spetsnaz*, GRU, and KGB operators into the US without anyone getting even a sniff."

"Alright, Ed, let's talk our own theater. What's going on in the North Atlantic?"

Franklin flipped to another part of his notebook and said, "Okay, here goes sir. Big units first. As you know, nearly the entire Red Banner Northern Fleet has sortied from their bases in the Kola over the past twenty-four hours. What perhaps none of us anticipated, however, is that the Reds put to sea with *two* large carriers, not one. *Connecticut* up on X-Ray Station reported that *Admiral Kuznetsov*, with a strong escort, sortied from the Kola Inlet just a few minutes before the Soviets kicked off their attacks around the world. Later, she reported a *second* carrier, also *Kuznetsov*-class, putting to sea with an equally powerful force of escorts. This has to be the *Varyag*, which we thought was still about a year from joining their fleet."

"Any chance *Connecticut* mistook one of the *Kiev*-class for a second big-deck?" rumbled Johnson.

Franklin shook his head. "No sir, not a chance. The *Kiev* was already at sea to the north when the balloon went up, and one of our other subs got a positive ID on the *Baku* outside the Kola Inlet a couple of hours *before* the *Varyag* sighting. The Soviets definitely have four flattops at sea, two big ones and two little ones."

Johnson fell silent, satisfied but not happy with the news.

Franklin continued, "Also, the Brits report that one of their subs, *Trafalgar*, is shadowing a large force of amphibious transports heading due west about a hundred miles north of the North Cape. Based on the report, it's enough transport to lift an entire brigade of Soviet naval infantry."

"Any better indications where they're going, Ed?" asked Falkner.

"Negative, sir," Franklin shook his head again. "Right now they're positioned to make a play anywhere from Greenland to Norway. I think the most likely targets for that brigade are Iceland or somewhere south along the Norwegian coast. A massive missile attack shut down the runway at Keflavik yesterday, so we haven't been able to fly in any reinforcements. That might indicate that Iceland is the target. On the other hand, the Soviets' push into Norway is much more powerful and is proceeding much more rapidly than we anticipated, and a brigade of marines in the *Norges*' rear could really pose some serious problems for their defenses. We can't rule out a thrust towards Scotland, either. The Shetlands and Faroes are vulnerable."

Falkner grunted, thinking of Rob Buckner now in Portsmouth, getting ready to put to sea with Admiral Reeves with his flag aboard HMS *Invincible*. Giving voice to his concerns he muttered, "One baby British flattop against the whole Red Banner Northern Fleet."

He'd spoken with Reeves earlier in the night, with the British Admiral assuring him, "Don't worry about us, old boy. We can look after ourselves 'til your chaps arrive. We've done it before, y'know. More than once, I believe."

Falkner grinned at the phone and said back in his best Midwestern lilt, "Of that I have no doubt, Sir Peter, but we'll try not to be too late to *this* war. How soon do you expect to be 'looking after yourselves' up there?"

"Not for another day at least, Art," responded Reeves, the humor gone from his tone. "Seems the Sovs have caught us all napping a bit, this time. *Gloucester* will sortie within the hour. She has some history protecting you chaps, I think. The entire task force won't be able to move much sooner than tomorrow, I'm afraid."

The Royal Navy destroyer HMS *Gloucester* had made history three years before during the Persian Gulf War when her Sea Wolf missiles shot down an Iraqi Silkworm anti-ship missile heading for the American battleship *Missouri*. This feat had made the British warship the first in history to destroy a modern anti-ship missile in combat. Falkner expected many more ships would be required to match *Gloucester*'s exploit in the coming days and weeks.

"Okay, you all hold on up there. We'll have Big E up to support just as quick as we can," Falkner assured him before hanging up.

Now, standing in the rain, he needed to make sure of his promise. Speaking directly to Johnson, he asked, "How long until *Enterprise* is within range to support the Brits?"

"Several days, still," answered Johnson. "They're making best speed north from Puerto Rico, but remember, they were on a training cruise. They'll need to stock up on war shots and cold weather equipment en route."

"STANAVFORLANT?" Falkner queried.

The only other ships standing in the Soviets' way were NATO's Standing Naval Force Atlantic—STANAVFORLANT—a collection of destroyers and frigates from several Alliance member states. The idea behind this polyglot task group was to have a respectable force of warships always at sea, always ready to respond to a crisis. The crisis had now arisen, but STANAVFORLANT, racing north from Amsterdam, was looking decidedly vulnerable in the face of four Soviet carriers.

Johnson shook his head. "At least two days before they can rendezvous with *Invincible*."

Again, Falkner grunted. Then, addressing both of his key staff officers he said, "Well, if we expected the Russians to fight stupid, they've certainly disabused us of *that* idea. They've hit us in ways that we didn't expect and in places where we weren't prepared. They've got us dancing to their tune right now, and they're going to do their best to keep us dancing. Is that about right, Ed?"

Franklin nodded. "That about sums it up, sir."

"What assets do we have to track the Soviet task forces, Ed?" Falkner asked next.

"Not much sir," responded the N2, "especially after the Reds took out both of our Lacrosse satellites earlier in the day."

"Any word on when the National Reconnaissance Office plans to get replacements up?" asked Johnson.

Franklin shook his head, "Negative. It's a good bet that the Soviets have more ASATs than we have new satellites sitting on the launch pad. The NRO doesn't have many replacements, and they're husbanding them until there's a specific, timely need. Those birds will probably have a short, exciting life once they're in orbit."

"What about the Soviet RORSATs?" Falkner asked next, referring to the Soviet Union's Radar Ocean Reconnaissance Satellites, the USSR's answer to the Lacrosse program.

Johnson spoke up again. "Sir, NORAD plans to start knocking the Russian recon satellites down starting tomorrow morning. They would have done it sooner, but those Soviet birds have nuclear reactors aboard and they want to make sure we're not raining radioactive debris down from space on friendly heads."

Falkner and Franklin absorbed *that* idea for a moment. Then 2nd Fleet's commander re-centered them on the problem at hand.

"Assuming we can track them, what indication will the Soviets give us about which way they plan to thrust with those amphibs, Ed?" Falkner asked.

Franklin pulled a small map of the North Atlantic out of his notebook and unfolded it. Tapping a speck of an island in the Greenland Sea, he said, "Jan Mayen Island, sir. That's our indicator. If the Russians make a play for Jan Mayen, it's a good bet they're planning on using it as a stepping-stone to Iceland. If they ignore it, then best bets are that they're going to focus on Norway."

"Thanks, Ed." Looking at Johnson, Falkner said firmly, "I want plans for two contingencies, and I want you to find ways to get the Reds reacting to us, rather than the other way around. First," he raised a finger, "I want a good plan for counterattacking against Iceland and preventing the Soviets from breaking out against our lines of communication to Europe. Second," he raised a second finger, "a plan to hit the Soviets in their seaward flank if they're making a hard push against central and southern Norway. Understood?"

Johnson nodded.

Falkner paused. Light rain continued to dribble onto the three officers, the men coming and going around them, and the hulking, powerful carriers to their left and right. Then the Admiral said slowly, "I also want a third plan."

"What plan is that, sir?" asked Johnson, leaning in.

"I want a plan in case the Russians try to go for both Iceland and Norway at once."

 **CHAPTER 94**

Eidsvoll Square, in front of the Storting Building, Oslo, Norway

S OFT, COLD FLURRIES fell mingling with ash around the brightly clad emergency workers crawling over the jumbled masonry wreckage of the Norwegian parliament building. Cranes and construction vehicles moved in slow motion, like mournful dinosaurs grazing on what had been a cornerstone building in the Norwegian national identity. Kristen Hagen, standing in a small but growing crowd of onlookers, fought back tears as she watched the rescuers crabbing over the jumbled blocks. Flashing blue emergency lights pierced the gray pre-dawn darkness. Rescue vehicles stretched away from the disaster in every direction, filling the beautiful nineteenth century boulevards of Oslo's downtown area. The windows all around the plaza were shattered, giving the surrounding square an aura of abandonment and death. The rescuers were no longer moving with the same sense of urgency as had marked their efforts through the night. For the past two hours they'd pulled nothing but corpses from the wreckage.

Kristen could only watch in a state of slow shock that refused to go away. The powerful blast had rattled the windows even at the Ministry of Defense, one kilometer away. It felt, Kristen thought, exactly as it was meant to feel: terrifying.

The directional blast of the massive shaped charge had almost completely demolished the building, leaving only a shell of the north wing still standing. The rest lay collapsed in on itself, and upon the gathered representatives of the government of Norway. Kristen cringed as she remembered the last moment she'd seen her King on television, addressing the nation. She watched the rescuers and waited for the blow to her soul that she knew must come out of the wreckage. Then it fell.

A knot of neon yellow-clad workers congregating near the center of what had been the building's parliamentary chamber drew Kristen's attention. A crane was just pulling up a section of the circular roof of the legislative space. Kristen saw a man wearing an orange reflector jacket dart down into the wreckage as the crane pulled it away. Then, from a hundred meters away, she heard the call.

"The King, it's the King!" The softly falling snow muffled the call. For a moment Kristen's hopes soared as more rescuers scrambled across the jumbled masonry blocks, converging on the source of the call, but their body language quickly dispelled any misconceptions that the monarch had survived. As the crane finished rotating the piece of roof away, shoulders slumped and heads bowed.

A call went out. Kristen saw someone scramble up into the wreckage, a scarlet object in his hands. The man arrived at the hole, then descended into it with several others. Kristen held her breath, dreading what would come next.

Gingerly, the men lifted their King out of the hole, using a splintered door as a litter. They'd draped the body in a Norwegian flag, the banner's scarlet field and blue and white cross standing out starkly against the grays and whites of the rubble. All work stopped. Everyone turned, watching as hands gently pulled the flag-draped body out of the hole, then lifted it until it rested atop the shoulders of six waiting men, who carried their burden. *Pallbearers*, Kristen thought.

Kristen struggled to keep her composure as they carefully picked their way down and out of the wreckage. She swallowed the lump in her throat as they emerged onto the pavement between the ruined Storting and Eidsvoll

Square, where they transferred their burden to six uniformed soldiers from the *Hans Majestet Kongens Garde* Battalion, the Royal Guards of the Norwegian Army. The soldiers took custody of the body, one whom they had been sworn to protect, and carried it respectfully the last few meters to the open back door of a waiting ambulance. After the body was placed inside, still draped in the flag, the ambulance slowly drove away, escorted by several HMKG and Oslo police vehicles.

"They will find the prime minister's body next," said Nils Dokken, standing next to Kristen. She nodded, not trusting herself to speak just yet. "When will the new prime minister be back in Oslo?" he asked, quietly.

The question startled Kristen. For a moment she didn't comprehend what her colleague was asking. Then it dawned on her. Her own chief, the foreign minister, was the most senior surviving official in the government. He was in Brussels. He'd asked her to stay and feed him information so that he could represent Norway at the emergency meeting of the North Atlantic Council. "He," she swallowed again, regaining her composure, "his plane should leave Brussels within the hour." She wiped her eyes with gloved hands and pushed a loose lock of hair behind her ear before continuing, "There was some delay when the Russians threatened an air raid over the Baltic."

"Do you think he's up to this?" Dokken asked with a sweep of his hand towards the floodlit ruins.

Kristen considered the question for a moment, and its context. Nearly every member of the Norwegian parliament lay buried under the rubble in front of her. A few had been pulled out alive during the night, battered and dazed, but in nearly every meaningful sense Norway's elected government had ceased to exist. That left the foreign minister as the legal head until a new government could be formed. Kristen thought about her chief's character. He was a brilliant diplomat and an able administrator, but Kristen knew how shaken he'd been by the impending war, how unwilling he was to accept the reality that their country was in real danger. Was he up to the task of leading their country through its greatest challenge since the German invasion? She didn't know the answer to that question, giving rise to a darker thought. Why was the man next to her even asking?

Kristen sensed out of the corner of her eye that Dokken was looking at her. The defense minister was still alive as well, having remained at the Akershus fortress. Did *he* intend to try to lead the government? Suddenly she wondered if a crisis was brewing in the succession of leadership for her nation.

She decided to change the subject. "Where is the Crown Prince?"

"The Crown Prince," the Dokken paused in realization, "Excuse me, the *King*, is safely under guard and being escorted back to Oslo from Bergen. Apparently it took a lot of convincing by the *Kongens Garde* to get him off his missile boat. The Prince's commanding officer almost ordered him to perform his duty as monarch."

Kristen breathed an invisible sigh of relief to hear that the man was safe. A living monarch could at least arbitrate disputes of succession for the government. *That* was a fight that Kristen wanted no part of, and one she hoped would never actually occur, despite her reservations about the foreign minister's abilities as a national leader.

"So what are your plans?" Dokken was asking, returning the conversation obliquely to the subject of the succession of Norway's government. "Will you remain at the Foreign Ministry?"

At that moment, tired and grieving, Kristen Hagen realized that she wanted nothing to do with the goings on in Oslo anymore. She'd come to the capital in a different context than the one that now existed. The job had been rewarding, even exhilarating at times, as her boss worked to fulfill Norway's traditional role as global peacemaker. But now that diplomacy had failed utterly, it all seemed so meaningless. Being at the Defense Ministry through the previous night, seeing officers making minute-to-minute decisions with direct and immediate effects on the defense of their nation, Kristen had started to lose the taste for the slower, softer workings of diplomacy.

"I don't know," she answered truthfully, seeing the scene of destruction in front of her. "I want to do something more to resist the Soviets," she paused, trying to think of the word, "More directly. Do you know of any such jobs that a Foreign Ministry staffer might be able to fill?" Kristen finally looked over at the Defense Ministry man.

Dokken nodded. "Don't you have family in the North?"

The emotion returned to Kristen's throat. She had worked hard to push those thoughts from her mind. She once more could only manage a nod.

"Yes, I think we can find a job for you," Dokken said with that annoying, knowing smile.

 # CHAPTER 95

0110 AST, Monday 14 Feb 1994
0610 Zulu
Over the Bay of Fundy, between Maine and Nova Scotia

S TARS BLINKED IN a black night sky as Sergeant David Strong stared out the window of the chartered airliner, flying east above a thick layer of clouds towards the port of Halifax. The sky felt large and strange, so different from any other time the Canadian commando had flown. David hadn't been able to put his finger on why he felt so uneasy until well after they'd departed Ottawa. Then it hit him; theirs was the only plane in the sky, so far as he could tell. He could see no evidence of other aircraft carrying on the commerce of North America, no red and green blinking anti-collision lights, no bright landing lights, not even the soft glow of cabin lights through rows of airplane windows. When David's jet had rotated off the runway he'd seen the tarmac at Ottawa packed wingtip to wingtip and nose to tail with passenger jets that suddenly had nowhere to go, the terminals full of stranded travelers.

The previous day had been tense for the Canadian elite warriors of JTF 2, sitting around on high alert since the early morning. Then the news of bombs, missiles, and small arms attacks in New York City and elsewhere in North America shocked everyone. For several hours David half expected to be ordered south towards the St. Lawrence Seaway or even west to the Rockies to hunt

Spetsnaz. Instead, the teams spent an awkward afternoon unsure about what to prepare for. The prime minister almost immediately issued a statement that Canada would honor her commitments to her NATO allies, being one of the first governments to do so. The question wasn't if David and his comrades would fight the Russians, but where, and when.

Finally, orders came for David's entire troop to deploy to their planned war station in Halifax in preparation for missions in the North Atlantic. The news broke some of the tension, at least for Strong and his team, who'd spent the last year training to conduct special reconnaissance missions from there. At least *that* was going as expected. Busses arrived at the secretive Dwyer Hill base, and the men of JTF 2 loaded their packs, equipment, and weapons before grabbing seats for the drive to Ottawa, escorted by a phalanx of armed Mounties in marked vehicles.

A chartered airliner waited for them, and after they boarded, most of the seats were still empty. In the next row, the hulking Felix "Mouse" Roy stretched his big frame out across three parallel seats and snored peacefully. Felix was always encouraging his sergeant to rest whenever he could, and the team medic usually followed his own advice, seemingly able to sleep anywhere, any time. David suspected that Felix actually saw their deployments as chances to catch up on the sleep that his pack of rambunctious children usually denied him.

Tonight David found that he couldn't follow his friend's advice. He was too amped up for the chance to prove himself on the greatest stage any warrior of his generation could hope for: World War Three. He didn't particularly care where they were going, other than for curiosity's sake, or what they would be asked to do, or even who exactly they would be asked to fight. If he was honest with himself, David was actually excited that he had a war to fight, that he would not grow old wondering if he had what it took to fight and win. He was excited for the chance to prove that he was ready.

Two rows back, the other members of Strong's team, Corporals Brown and Tenny, were engaged in a quiet game of cards to pass the time and distract each other from their own anxiety. David envied them the diversion, the comradery that he had always struggled to find in his position of leadership. He was in charge, and he had never been able to delegate his responsibility easily. Not that he actually wanted to. So he turned back towards his window, his eyes watching the dark, empty skies while his mind worked overtime, questioning every deficiency in training and equipment in his team, questioning his own abilities, hoping to play a vital role in the coming drama. Whatever lay ahead for Strong and his team, it would start once they touched down in Halifax, on the cold, western shore of the North Atlantic.

CHAPTER 96

0920 MSK, Monday 14 Feb 1994
0620 Zulu
Olenya Airbase, Murmansk Oblast, Russian
Soviet Federative Socialist Republic

G UARDS COLONEL ILYA Romanov's right hand ached from the cold as he stood in the predawn darkness, watching his white-clad, leather jump-helmeted *desantniki* file past, bent under the weight of their weapons, packs, and parachutes. He refused to pull his glove back on against the icy wind blowing off the airfield's tarmac. The responsibility he was now fulfilling was too important to allow a little discomfort to interfere.

As each man trudged out of the relative warmth of the hangar, in which they had assembled and rigged their parachutes, and into the biting cold of the pre-dawn darkness, Romanov grasped his hand in his own and gave each a single, firm, Russian shake, accompanied by the words *"Bozhestvennaya skorost."* *Godspeed.*

The normal breed of political officers would have been appalled at the spoken blessing and the accompanying inward prayer, but Major Ivan Sviashenik, didn't object in the least. The political officer stood beside Ilya and offered each man a simple *"Udachi."* *Good luck.*

This was Romanov's normal pre-jump ritual, one he had practiced before every jump he had ever commanded. He found that rituals like this calmed the men's nerves, and his own. More importantly, it told the younger soldiers and officers that their commander valued them, acknowledged the risk they were taking for their country in jumping out of airplanes with nothing to save them from certain death except good planning and a dome of silk. Ilya wanted to look them in the eye one last time before they went. The ritual was even more important now. Today these *desantniki* would be making their first combat jump, and Romanov was keenly aware of the danger that accompanied this particular assault.

After returning from observing the 36th Air Landing Brigade's assault into Norway, Romanov spent ensuing hours debriefing his subordinate battalion commanders on what he had learned. These lessons were important. The drop zones for today's assault were far more dangerous than the ones Romanov had seen yesterday, and that was *before* one factored in the possibility of armed resistance.

Ilya had already shaken nearly three hundred hands, two thirds of the departing formation, the 1st Battalion of Romanov's 234th Guards Airborne Regiment. The third and final company was now filing past, troopers humping their loads in snaking lines towards the Antonov An-12 and huge An-22 transports that would convey them to their desolate objective. The twenty aircraft required to carry the assault battalion and its vehicles positively crowded both sides of the Olenya Airbase's apron.

Finally, the battalion commander, Lieutenant Colonel Filipov, and his political officer exited the hangar. Filipov took Ilya's proffered hand, but this time Romanov did not let go. The battalion commander looked up into his chief's eyes, and Romanov said with feeling, "Take care of your men, Colonel. I send you because you're my best. Have you spoken to the pilots?"

"*Da*, Ilya Georgiyevich," answered Filipov. "I gathered them together an hour ago and reminded them how small our drop zone is, and how important it is that they stick *exactly* to the flight plan." He then paused before saying wryly, "I told them that if they drop me in the drink, they could expect me to hunt them down, either in this life or the next. The younger ones I think bought it," he concluded with a barked laugh.

Romanov smiled appreciatively and released his subordinate's hand. He appreciated Filipov's gallows humor. Such jokes were common among paratroopers of any army, but particularly here in the Soviet Union where cynicism was something of a national pastime. Both officers understood that if Filipov were to haunt any of the transport pilots, it would be from beyond the grave. None of the assembled paratroopers could expect to survive being dropped into the icy waters of the Arctic Ocean. Romanov prayed that none of them would find need to discover this fact.

As Filipov moved on, following his men to their planes, one last officer emerged from the hangar.

"Ah, Major Medvedev," Romanov grasped his young staff officer's hand, "I thought I might have missed you."

"*Nyet, tovarich* Colonel, I'm the last one out," said Medvedev.

Romanov smiled and released the younger man's hand, finally returning his own achingly cold hand to the warmth of its glove.

"The good Colonel Filipov has no objections to you accompanying him?" Romanov asked. Filipov was a good officer, but he could be touchy about people looking over his shoulder. Of course, looking over Filipov's shoulder was not the reason Romanov was sending one of his staff along on this jump. Rather, he wanted at least one officer in his headquarters to see the conditions at the vital preliminary objective that Filipov's battalion was to seize today, to really understand the vital supply line to their ultimate objective: Iceland.

"To be honest, I believe he's thinking too much about the water to even notice me, my Colonel," answered Medvedev with a half-smile. "He really does fear being dropped in the drink, and he doesn't care who knows it."

"Yes," Romanov said, "as he should. You take care of yourself, Major. I do not wish to have to explain to your father how I managed to get you killed on the second day of the war."

"No, he can be a difficult man to explain such things to," smiled Medvedev. He knew that Colonel Romanov was one of the few people to whom his big name did not mean a whit. Romanov consistently showed the same individual concern for *all* of his men.

Medvedev moved off, hobbling to catch up to Filipov and his file as quickly as his heavy load would allow. Romanov and Sviashenik turned to watch them go. The turboprop engines of the transports on the airfield were starting to cough, filling the air with the drone of propellers and smell of aviation fuel.

Romanov hated that he was not accompanying his men on this dangerous mission, hated that they would be going into harm's way while he was still safe here in Russia. He knew that it had to be this way. Filipov's mission was only a preliminary one. The big show for Romanov's regiment would not occur until a day from now, and Ilya was experienced enough, and professional enough to know that his place would be with the other two-thirds of his command.

Watching the last few *desantniki* file up the ramps onto their planes, Romanov said to Sviashenik, "They are good men, Ivan Avramovich. I only hope that the cause we are sending them to fight for is worthy of them."

"It's not," the political officer said with his usual irreverence. "It never is."

A NOTE FROM THE AUTHORS

Northern Fury: H-Hour is the first in a series of books that tell the story of the northern front of World War III. To hear about upcoming releases and progress in this series, as well as the book series that will cover other theaters of the war, you can sign up to our mailing list here: http://eepurl.com/gkyzaX.

If you have an interest in more detailed subjects linked to the *Northern Fury* series, you can go to our companion website here: www.northernfury.us and find a treasure trove of information on units, equipment capabilities and tactics.

Are you a wargamer? Interested in how we created some of the action scenes? Curious about how modern technologies are employed? You may want to try out the game: *Command: Modern Air/Naval Operations* from WarfareSims. com available from Matrix Games or on Steam.

Finally, if you enjoyed the book and would like to share your thoughts with others, you could rate the book and leave a review on Amazon. We would very much appreciate your feedback.

ABOUT THE AUTHORS

 **Bart Gauvin** is a veteran of more than thirty-years of service as an artillery officer in the Canadian Army. In his free time, he builds exciting scenarios set in the *Northern Fury* universe for the war game *Command: Modern Air/Naval Operations*. He resides with his wife, Tammy, and two distracting pugs in Ontario, Canada.

 **Joel Radunzel** is a veteran of more than ten years' service in the US Army. As a kid, he occasionally provided cover for his missionary parents to smuggle Bibles through the Iron Curtain into Eastern Europe. He resides wherever the US Army sends him, along with his wife Jill and growing passel of kids.

Made in the USA
Las Vegas, NV
23 May 2023

72419355R00364